H A B I T U S

'Flint's observation is entrancingly spot on, but it is in his ambitious meld of mathematical philosophy, laid against a backdrop of gambling and the development of the computer (there's enough info here to bore your friends at parties) that *Habitus* succeeds. Alongside perhaps only Richard Powers, Flint has managed to find an enthralling fictional world in the contemporary technological maze.'
Time Out

'A slick, often funny sideswipe at the digital revolution. Half novel, half philosophical discourse – a load of fun.' *Big Issue*

'Hugely ambitious – a highly original début.' Tibor Fischer

'It is to Flint's credit that the ineffability of his ambitions never infects the precision of his highly charged prose.' *Independent*

'I applaud the innovative approach to literary form. Flint almost succeeds in stitching literature and science together, and he has a sure sense of structure.' *Daily Telegraph*

'Here comes one astoundingly good storyteller.' Douglas Rushkoff

'*Habitus* is an extraordinarily impressive first novel . . . For a novel so dense with science, it is surprisingly romantic. The stale whiff of the student computer room is entirely absent, and Flint manages to make even quantum theory seem sexy. *Habitus* provides the perfect tonic for anyone who still believes the English novel is suffering from a dearth of ideas.' Matt Thorne

'Flint's inspired début is a looping, proliferating, thought-provoking novel.' *Sunday Times*

HABITUS

Habitus is James Flint's first novel. Born in Stratford-upon-Avon in 1968, he now lives in London.

HABITUS

James Flint

FOURTH ESTATE • *London*

This paperback edition published in 1999
First published in Great Britain in 1998 by
Fourth Estate Limited
6 Salem Road
London W2 4BU

1 3 5 7 9 10 8 6 4 2

A catalogue record for this book is available from the
British Library.

ISBN 1-85702-832-5

The first two part-title illustrations
are reproduced from
The Arrow of Time by Peter Coveney and Roger
Highfield, published by WH Allen.
The third part-title illustration is reproduced from
Chaos by James Gleick, published by William
Heinemann Ltd.

Typeset by Rowland Phototypesetting Limited,
Bury St Edmunds, Suffolk
Printed in Great Britain by Clays Ltd, St Ives plc

To Elaine

In essence, habit is contraction. . . . What we call wheat is a contraction of the earth and humidity, and this contraction is both a contemplation and the auto-satisfaction of that contemplation. By its existence alone, the lily of the field sings the glory of the heavens, the goddesses and gods that it contemplates in contracting. What organism is not made of elements and cases of repetition, of contemplated and contracted water, nitrogen, carbon, chlorides and sulphates, thereby intertwining all the habits of which it is composed? . . . We are made of contracted water, earth, light and air. . . . An animal forms an eye for itself by causing scattered and diffuse luminous excitations to be reproduced on a privileged surface of its body. The eye binds light, it is itself a bound light. . . . This binding is a reproductive synthesis, a Habitus.

Gilles Deleuze, *Difference & Repetition*

CONTENTS

PREAMBLE

001

0 1 0

011

PREAMBLE

Alfalfa & O Mother!

30 January 1950, North-west of Montreal, Canada

The ringdingding and the rend. It all starts somewhere in the middle, just below the glans, where the life-blood quivers then withdraws then courses again through the corpus spongiosum of young Joel's tiny manhood as the cold fingers of the mohel firmly grip it in the mechanism of their arthritic knots and folds. The amulet of Adam Ba'al Shem Tov, man of good repute, Master of the Name, flickers in the menorah light and fills the boy's dark and massive eye. Moshe Kluge, proud father, places his hand upon the forehead of his son and holds him steady. The mohel gathers the tiny prepuce between the hard old whorls and ulnar loops of his desiccated pads, then with the other hand brings the scalpel down and quickly round. It's a fluid movement, the movement of a piston joint, of a matador who ducks the prize bull's curling horns and weaves quickly up behind the head, slices down with steel, steps nimbly to one side so the blood shan't stain his silky pants.

The circumcision complete, Moshe breathes out. Joel trembles with the throb between his thighs and begins to wail for his mother, who is not there. The purse of flesh is already dealt with, disappeared – the snake has shed its skin. The Ba'al Shem gathers the blood in a small china bowl and swabs the wound, whispering to himself Joel's other name, Balaam. There is urgency in his voice; Moshe pats his pockets.

'Master . . .' he begins, his voice soft with the rising doughs of the years spent in his bakery. But transfixed by the name, the mohel is already staring into space. Moshe clears his throat, repeats: 'Master?'

Outside it's January. Montreal is away there to the south. The winds come off the Cabonga Reservoir, its surface a massive sheet of six-inch ice, cracked and fissured into giant hieroglyphs. The Ba'al Shem is above it, he is below it; the cries of the boy have triggered something – a state change, a reconfiguration – and the mohel is no longer in the room. He is where the moon shines through the ribbon patterns of the ice and lays a silver meniscus across the chilled and silent depths. Away to the north, squalls storm their way across the Hudson Bay, the cabin fevers of the minor gods. His eyes shine with cataracts of frozen water, the fissures and patterns slowly glisten brighter. Slowly they turn from crystal to blue to a thin sodium fire which travels and webs across the surfaces before him. The mohel is an initiate, one who has studied the writings of Eleazar of Worms and Isaac the Blind, one who can decipher the alphabet of Metatron.

Now he is back in the room and gazing at the boy, who is bathed in a palpitating iridescent glow. The hieroglyphs from the fractal cracks of the ice splinter the haunting light above Joel's head. Adam sucks in air and begins to enunciate the letters of the Tetragrammaton as they unveil themselves before him. The words twist out into the candlelight like strands of bronchial sputum and Moshe falls to his knees at the strange and guttural sounds. The child no longer cries but looks on with soft, unblinking eyes, calculating distances and counting syllables. The figures disappear and the voice stops; now the mohel sees a room, faded plasterwork, metal that breathes and buzzes, metal that thinks, the child grown, the child gone, a nose, a woman. Then nothing. The moon, the lake, the ice, the room . . . all gone. The dark-brown walls of his house close in, he breathes and gibbers for a moment. Looking down, he spies Moshe, grabs the man's hands and pulls him to his feet. He pulls him so close that Moshe can hear the Ba'al Shem's breath congealing on his teeth.

There is silence for a moment, then he begins to talk: 'This is not a dream. This is not a dream. Do you understand? There is no dream here. There is no sleep here.' There is a pause. Moshe nods nervously, not knowing what else to do. The mohel has gone further than he has ever gone before. 'Everything flows through this space. It belongs neither to me nor to the night. Everything flows through. You do not know this space, Moshe Kluge. Your child is dead and dead again. The air is of hot streets. The wasps blow to and fro. Time will work itself out. It grows and evolves, like a yeast, or a mould. It feeds. There are three kinds of time to make this possible.'

'Yes, Master, three kinds. M-Most interesting.' Moshe tries to remove the man's hands from his lapels but the mohel's grip is remorseless. He trembles to think of his son's penis in the thrall of these manipulators. The mohel draws him closer. 'Repeat: *zimzum, shevirah, tikkun. Zimzum, shevirah, tikkun.* Repeat it!'

Terrified now, Moshe says the words, his voice barely quavering up from his throat. 'Zimzum, shevirah, tikkun.' He has heard them before, they are part of Kabbalistic doctrine, but as to what they mean he has no idea. He is just a baker and a dabbler, and cannot be expected to know of such things. Perhaps, then, this is an important lesson. He repeats the words again, more slowly and more seriously now, swallowing his fear and finishing with: 'The three kinds of time. Yes.'

'Zimzum, shevirah, tikkun,' mutters the mohel one last time and lets go of Moshe's lapels.

Immediately the baker turns to Joel – who is screaming in his crib, desperate for attention, still flushed with throbbing pain from the unexpected amputation – intending to gather up the boy and make good his exit. But with a roar that seems to shake the very foundations of the house the mohel spins the baker back to face him and seizes him in a bear hug. 'Do you not understand?' he spits from lip to lip, the words bubbling up from deep in the flux of his visions. 'Do you not understand that your son is only a third, only a third of something that will be larger than us all? It's coming. The lizards know it, they watch it with their cold eyes and taste it with tongues that dash faster than the angels. The three-in-one draws near. Look to the river! Look! Look! Look to

3

the river, oh, how it lies! Which is your son, which one is he? He knows, he knows, look in his eyes and you know that he knows.' The mohel directs a look at Joel so piercing it makes the infant redouble his bawling. 'Yes, Balaam, you! Which one are you?'

Frightened for his son, Moshe acts at last, shoves the mohel in the chest. At the instant of contact the man goes limp and crashes to the floor, knocking over an iron scuttle as he falls. Black coals roll across the hearth and particles of coal dust are sucked up the chimney by the roaring wind. The fire cackles grimly and tries to send up flames in pursuit. Joel falls silent and Moshe strains his ears in case there should be voices on the wind. When he is sure that there are none he turns his attention to the fire, searching for faces in its dance. But there is only the turquoise flicker of the flame. Joel begins to whimper once again and Moshe takes him in his arms and holds him for a while, then attends to the Ba'al Shem, who is still stretched out on the hearth. His breathing is weak; Moshe squats down behind him and putting his hands beneath his armpits drags him up into a chair. He fetches a glass, fills it with water from a metal jug and holds it to the man's lips. The liquid tumbles down his chin and drums upon the starched fabric of his shirt, but some of it must have found its way inside for the mohel coughs and turns away into the wing of the chair, pulling his feet up into a foetal position. Then he falls asleep.

Keen to make good his exit, Moshe scoops the coals back into the scuttle, drops a couple into the grate to replenish the fire and leaves a sum of money on the sideboard. Then he carefully swaddles Joel against the cold and holding him firmly to his chest steps out into the street. Outside the wind is blowing up terrific flurries of snow that stencil in the air the vortices virtual in the geometry of the rude buildings. It is hardly even a hamlet, this settlement: the mohel's dwelling makes three in all and there are two wooden barns besides. Moshe turns up his collar, pulls down his hat and sets out against the night. The lantern swings freely in his hand, its feeble light guttering continually. He makes his way along the track that leads back to his uncle's farm, some two miles distant, where his wife lies sick but still awake, worrying for the safety of her child. Out in the open, Moshe struggles against the unchecked wind. He is bracketed by fields: all around him, under their mantle of snow, the seed oceans of alfalfa groan creak swell with the rhythms of sleep.

Far away to the south, in Washington DC, President Truman announces his decision to go ahead with the hydrogen bomb development program. That month's issue of *Time* magazine carries on its cover a picture of something most people have never seen before: a computer. Dressed up in a jaunty sailor's cap.

May 1973, Somewhere near Stratford-upon-Avon, England
A brittle plastic twelve-inch ruler, sheared off at the baseline, just at the point where the inch scale should say 'o'. Half of the number is still visible, like a weak 'c', or half an egg, or a shallow cup. Judd reaches into his satchel and fetches out the ruler. Through the window comes the soft rattle of the tractor-mower passing to and fro, ruling the playing fields like a page. Grass clippings and daisy heads fly up behind the machine in a patterned spray damp with the scent of clover and dog turd. Inside in the classroom the rows of boys transform the teacher's words into inky lines, little farmers cultivating blank white plots.

Judd is not writing. He is listening to the drone of the tractor, his favourite sound in all of England. The fresh-cut fields with their mulch musk hovering on the limp air bring him something new. In Los Angeles cut grass is dry and harsh: there, lawn-mowers throw up wafting rinds of dust which are tacky on the back of the throat. This is the only thing which is bad about home, the only thing. Everything else is better there.

The pitch of the sound changes as the mower head is disengaged and lifted; the tractor has reached one end of the fields and is turning to retrace the shallow path it has cut. The rattling fills the air like the hollow gasps of a sick dog. The blades descend and their cough is damped by the green expectorant of the grass. His hands hidden by his desk, Judd works at the manufacture of a small projectile.

Doreen Buerk, geography teacher and Tory wife, turns her back on the class for the briefest of instants in order to draw an oxbow lake on the blackboard. Back in America – land of dreams, of memories, of clipped blue sky and vapour trails – something is happening on Pad B, Launch Complex 39 of the Kennedy Space Center, Florida. The liquid oxygen in the F1 boosters has ignited and the Saturn V rocket carrying the first unmanned sections of the Skylab space station is lumbering into the air. As the gantry falls away and early morning desert ice showers magnificently from the three-million-kilo hulk, Judd's ruler twangs. Seconds later the Saturn V has sliced the sky's blue dome in two and Judd's projectile has arced across the great divide of several desks; this boy's amazing, quite a prodigy it seems; in World War Two they needed firing tables to do this stuff; hell, they even invented computers to help 'em work those tables out and here he is, this small black boy, doing it by feel and intuition. This boy's got soul.

But wait, hold fire, so to speak. An error has been made. The meteoroid shield has deployed inadvertently and been ripped off by atmospheric drag. Similarly, a stray fold of paper has come apart from Judd's pellet and the extra drag is pulling the projectile off target. Instead of connecting with the pearly pink epidermis of Jacob Hethlethwaite's neck the missile veers to the left, misses Jacob by millimetres and strikes instead the acne scars of Lewis, oldest boy in the class and hardest too.

Lewis gasps and squirms; at his outburst Doreen Buerk spins on one heel; with no compunction Lewis points: 'It was him, miss, he flicked summat at me!'

The Buerk stares at the small American down the length of her nose, fixing him like a doomed field-mouse with the ball-bearing pupils of her grim stoat eyes. For a few dark seconds she just lets the silence gather. It works: the class is in her thrall (for the first time that afternoon – violence appeals more than river action). Then the tension is released: 'That's it! Out! Out you go! I've told you and I've told you I won't put up with this kind of behaviour. You will be penalised after school. Outside the door! Go! Now! I'll deal with you after class. It may come as a surprise to you to learn that some of us . . .' (who, they all think, who could that be?) '. . . would like to continue the lesson without interruption.'

6

Judd opens his mouth to protest. 'I don't want to hear it. Do you understand me? One more disobedience and you'll go to the Head. Now get out!'

Pouting slightly (and blushing too, though it's difficult for these white folks to tell) Judd slouches out between the rows of boys. They snigger as he passes and surreptitiously kick at him from under their tables with the scuffed toes of their battered black shoes.

12 August 1960, Hatton Central Hospital, England
Nadine Several lies screaming, arms and ankles strapped to a hastily adapted gynaecologist's chair. Her short, badly cropped hair is thick with sweat and her eyes claw wildly at the room. At intervals a nurse applies a damp flannel to the woman's forehead and wipes away the spittle that foams up from between her purple lips. But her main job is to keep Nadine from swallowing her tongue and she has a wooden spatula at the ready for just that purpose.

Down below, somewhere beneath the sodden hospital gown that rucks up around the patient's waist, a midwife waits patiently for a glimpse of the baby's head to appear from between the heaving thighs drenched in fluid. Slightly bored, she threads her fat fingers in and out of the handles of the birthing forceps she has with her. She's long ago lost any sense of either the beauty or the horror of this process, of this turmoil of the flesh. But what she most definitely hates is having to deliver babies in this Unit. It happens far too often; do they have no control over the patients here? It's disgusting, that's what it is. If she were running things they wouldn't come to such a pass and that's a fact. Look at this poor woman. Sweat pouring off her, lamb, she doesn't even know what's happening. How could they let them do this to her? Just goes to show that they're not like the rest of us, not at all, and you can't let them wander around on their own. It's just not on! They should be kept apart and under constant supervision. But these days you just can't get the staff.

Nadine was four months pregnant before someone noticed. When her periods ceased they just forgot to bring her sanitary towels and it wasn't till her belly was obvious that a houseman figured it out. He remembered the day because it was the same day Princess Margaret sent a command to the probe Pioneer V, which was then exactly one million miles from earth. The probe's response came back just twenty-five seconds later. It was in all the papers. They tried to talk to Nadine about it, ask her who it was, but she just kept saying how she was growing, growing, how her tree had a new branch. She hadn't made sense for years; it was no surprise she couldn't manage to be coherent now.

Explaining the situation to her husband, Henry, was extremely difficult. He didn't take it well; in fact, he sued the hospital for negligence and notified the police (who didn't manage to find the culprit and who suspected, privately as it were, that Henry himself was responsible). As for Nadine, she seemed cheerier than ever. She wandered around the wards with a beatific smile slanted across her face, munching on the apples that Henry brought her. The only problems she seemed to have with the pregnancy was the jealous reactions her distended shape provoked among some of the other female patients.

Jennifer Several, our missing link, was born to Nadine on 12 August 1960, at the same moment that NASA's ECHO I successfully reflected a radio message from President Eisenhower down across a footprint that included most of the United States, thus demonstrating for the first time the feasibility of global satellite communications. Bizarrely, the view the midwife has of Jennifer's head emerging from Nadine's vagina (a small sliver of white in the darkness that grows quickly to a full white round) is not dissimilar to that she'd had, if she'd have been orbiting the earth, of ECHO I itself as its one hundred-foot diameter aluminised Mylar-plastic sphere rose up slowly from the shadow of the planet and caught the sun.

The birth of a new age? Perhaps. Or perhaps the continuation of an old one, for via her mitochondria – the tiny energy factories to be found in every one of her body's cells, the DNA for which is passed exclusively down the female line – Jennifer is linked to the eukaryotic cell from which all plants, fungi and animals are descended and, beyond this, to the prokaryotes, the bacteria and cyanobacteria, the earliest forms of life and after three billion years still the most dominant.

Ignoring the fact that he is not the natural father, unc̲ɔ̲.
with the intricacies of Jennifer's cellular pedigree and blind to ʋ̲
issue of whether or not, as a man, he could ever be more than a
mere adjunct to this spectacular lineage, Henry shouldered his
responsibilities and took the child on as his own. He won his suit
against the hospital, too, and placed the compensation money in
trust. It wasn't much, but it was something.

3rd November 1957, Baikonur, Kazakstan
On the day of Joel's circumcision (and the day of President
Truman's announcement) Soviet troops rolled into a stretch of
countryside which lies to the north of the town of Leninsk, which
sits on the banks of the Syr Dar'ya river, which runs from the
Kazakstan plain into the lowlands of the Caspian depression. They
were there to break up any settlements in the area and relocate
their stone-skinned occupants either to the collective farms in the
north or, if any of them choose to argue, to oblivion. Some time
later huge earth movers arrived by rail, constructivist visions realised
in poor quality steel, and began to level a vast tract of land which
over the next few years would slowly, as concrete scabbed its way
across the countryside, become the Baikonur Kosmodrome. From
here, on 4 October 1957, carried by an R7 ICBM test vehicle, the
first man-made satellite would be launched into space.

Laika was born and bred at Baikonur. Not much of a home for
a dog, she shared it with sixteen other pups of various breeds,
some thoroughbred, some indeterminate. They lived in a com-
pound behind the MIK assembly building in a collection of concrete kennels on stilts and their programme was supervised by one
Pavel Renko. Renko was a jack of all trades, part rocket technician,
part veterinarian, part dialectician, a veteran of the intellectual
migrations set in motion throughout Stalin's United Soviet. It was
a biography which had embittered. Originally from Murmansk,
he resented his transfer to Baikonur on the grounds of the weather,
convincing himself that he missed the endless Arctic winters and
the sheer desolation of the Kola Peninsula.

In his training of the dogs he was somewhat over-enthusiastic,
killing three and crippling two of those in his charge. But he

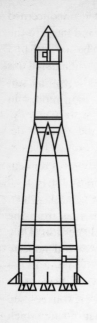

Launch Vehicle Characteristics – Sputnik 1
Family: R-7. Country: Russia. Status: Hardware.

Designations: Official: 8K71PS; OKB: R-7; Popular: Semyorka; US DoD: SL-1; US Library of Congress: A. Relatively unmodified R-7 ICBM test vehicles used to launch first two Sputniks.
Total Mass: 265,500 kg. Lift-off Thrust: 396,298 kgf. Core Diameter: 2.99 m. Total Length: 28.00 m. Total Cost: $33.00 million. Launches: 2. Failures: 0. Success Rate: 100 percent. First Launch: 10/4/57. Last Launch: 11/3/57.

● **Stage 1 : 1 × Sputnik 1–1. Gross Mass: 93,500 kg. Empty Mass: 7,495 kg. Thrust (vac): 93,000 kgf. Isp: 308 sec. Burn time: 300 sec. Isp(sl): 241 sec. Diameter: 2.99 m. Span: 2.99 m. Length: 28.00 m. Propellants: Lox/Kerosene. No Engines: 4. Engine: RD-108 8D75PS. Pc: 53 bar. Used as: Sputnik 1–1. Other Designations: R-7; 8K71PS; SL-1.**

● **Stage 0 : 4 × Sputnik 1–0. Gross Mass: 43,000 kg. Empty Mass: 3,400 kg. Thrust (vac): 99,000 kgf. Isp: 306 sec. Burn time: 120 sec. Isp(sl): 250 sec. Diameter: 2.68 m. Span: 2.68 m. Length: 19.00 m. Propellants: Lox/Kerosene. No Engines: 4. Engine: RD-107 8D74PS. Pc: 60 bar. Used as: Sputnik 1–0. Other Designations: R-7; 8K71PS; SL-1.**

got results and they were only dogs, so what did it matter? The important thing was that one of them should be ready for the launch. They needed to find out if it was possible to survive. They had started work on Vostok I and were already training Gagarin.

They chose Laika because of her name. Laika means 'barker' in Russia. She had yelped almost as soon as she'd slid out the womb, still hot from her mother and fragrant like freshly baked bread, and she'd expressed herself that way ever since. Renko's assistants, Alexei and Mickl, took a shine to her because of it; they had to exercise the dogs every day and the way Laika sat and cocked her head and woofed in response to anything they asked her made her seem that bit more intelligent, that little bit more human. And so they sent her into space, because she was more human, because it was an honour, because she'd be on postage stamps and she'd have streets and rock bands named after her.

As if any of that mattered to Laika. After all, she was only going to get seven days up there and then they'd pull the plug.

They trained her up, it took months, they trained others too, but they always knew it would be her. They got her used to the harness, shaved her, accustomed her to the electrodes, shaved her again. She was cold without her fur so they made her a coat, but it rubbed and so they trained her not to tear at it with her teeth. They taught her how to eat and how to shit. And what to do once she'd eaten and shat. They made her drink from a teat on the wall, it wasn't like lapping, certainly not. They taught her other stuff too, secrets, things we can't mention here for fear of the consequences, though the information is out there if you know where to look. It's most definitely out there. It is.

She didn't bark too much when, already sealed inside Sputnik II, they wheeled her out to the rocket. She sat there whimpering nervously, the acceleration harness making it impossible for her to move, her limp tail disturbed only by an occasional half-hearted wag, not sure whether to be excited or afraid. She licked at Mickl's fingers through the glass of the one small porthole and was confused by the sadness she saw in his eyes. And then she was in the air, hoisted aloft by a crane and lowered into position in the nose cone of the R-7. A group of jump-suited technicians had been waiting at the top of the gantry and now they went to work, attaching release bolts to the capsule and running several hours' worth of last-minute checks. Consoled by this human activity and no longer able to see that she was perched high above the ground, Laika calmed down a little, though not enough to doze as she generally liked to do of an afternoon.

And then the checks were complete and the nose cone was clipped shut, and suddenly it was all dark for the dog. The radio and monitor crackled awake: Renko's face flickered before her and his voice was there, too, though some way off to one side. He spoke a series of words into a microphone, not looking into the camera, just reeling them off, words to which she knew how to respond. She gave a bark at each one, as she'd been taught, and waited tensely for the yell or the biscuit, whichever would come. And then the earth cracked apart and she barked and she barked

11

at the figure of Renko; there was nothing else for it, she had to, she had to bark, and louder and louder because she couldn't hear herself, no matter how hard she barked she could hear nothing at all and then she was pushed down, down, a huge thing pushing her down, it had never been like this, she had done what they'd asked, it was never like this.

The forces rippled her skin as easily as if it were oil. As she shot into space she thought of her mother, of her smell, a good smell it was. Later, she took up a low orbit at a height of 298 kilometres above sea level and swung round the earth like a star.

0 0 1

And, if we want to write history, we have to pull together at least three kinds of time: the reversible time of clocks and mechanics, all to do with cogs and levers; then the irreversible time of thermodynamics, born of fire; and finally the time of what is called 'negative entropy', which is what gives rise to singularities. 'History no longer flows in the way we once thought.'
'A small world history of work in three acts, three times, three figures or actors, three states of matter, and three words which are in fact only one, by Pia, the flying doctor!'

Michel Serres, *Angels*

1

Dance and contagion

We took a step forward, met Jennifer, Judd and Joel – now we must take a step back. Nadine Rachel Several, née Flowers, wife to Henry and mother to Jennifer, had been born an Aquarian in 1924. Nadine's father owned and ran a successful business manufacturing tyres, a line that had suddenly become extremely profitable during the Great War. Her mother had studied mathematics at university and had, in a small way, been a suffragette. Both her parents considered themselves 'free thinkers' – it was that which had brought them together. They read Lawrence, Fitzgerald, Mann, owned a gramophone on which they listened to ragtime and Stravinsky, travelled to cocaine orgies in the Home Counties and swilled cocktails in London clubs. Indeed, before Nadine was born her mother had had a full-time job as a typist, part of the flood of women taking skilled office jobs at that time. The office environment was changing: all those in-trays, oak desks and efficiency drives took on a different taint, one that thrilled with differences and obscurities. The office was becoming a sexual environment and things would never be the same again. Although she stopped working for two years to look after her daughter, as soon as she could, Nadine's mother returned to work, this time as a computer in Leslie Comrie's department at the Nautical Almanac Office where, part of a mathematical production line, a successful attempt to compartmentalise mental labour, she helped to produce astronomical tables.

★

Nadine's parents had always felt very strongly that their daughter should express herself in whichever way she saw fit. Nadine had no difficulty in following her whims and from a very early age she dreamt of being a dancer. Whenever her parents threw a dinner party she dressed herself in silks and leapt about the house soaking up applause from the guests. She was intoxicated with music and flow. She charted the career of Isadora Duncan quite obsessively and collected pamplets that summarised the teachings of Mary Wigmore and Rudolph Laban.

Duncan had made the new dance fashionable and removed much of the social stigma that was attached to the profession. Dance schools became popular and Nadine's parents enrolled her in one in Blooms-bury. When her father expressed his one reservation – that such a career might be too physical for his delicate and possibly intellectual child – his wife rebutted the objection by quoting at him something from William James. 'Muscular contraction appears to be closely related to the genesis of all forms of psychic activity,' wrote her favourite psychologist. 'Not only do the vaso-motor and muscular systems express the thinking, feeling and willing of the individual, but the muscular apparatus itself appears to be a fundamental part of the apparatus of these psychical states.' And so the matter was settled.

'Spin! Spin, girls, spin! And waft left, and waft right . . . and still, and up, and breathe, and down, and sti-i-ill and up, and bre-a-the and down. And relax. And breathe. Breathe Lydia, breathe. From here, from your di-a-phragm. You look like a rabbit that's about to choke, my dear. Fill your lungs slowly, from the bottom. That's it, that's better. Good Rose, good. Watch Rose, Lydia, see how she does it? All right everyone? Breathe. And relax. Now, take your seats.' The girls clattered to their desks like starlings to a telephone line and installed themselves facing Miss Bryant, who flexed herself against the rail of the blackboard while waiting for them to settle.

'Does anyone know what today is?' she finally asked.

Immediately Deirdre's hand shot up. Deirdre was always most keen to participate: before being enrolled at the dance academy she had briefly attended a very exclusive finishing school, one of the few which still used restraining devices to control the girls. Several of the teachers had demanded that the children wear leather silencers throughout their classes, a practice that Deirdre found particularly hateful. Freed from that regime, she now compensated by attempting to answer all questions that were put to the class. 'The King's birthday, miss.'

'No Deirdre, it is most definitely not the King's birthday.' Miss Bryant was a republican and had once conducted a tempestuous affair with a Bolshevik who had for a brief period worked as a waiter in a restaurant off the Charing Cross Road. She was grimly aware that the King had not one but two birthdays. And that neither of them fell on that particular day. No other hands went up. Happily, Miss Bryant began to answer the question herself. 'Well girls, exactly thirty years ago today an American named Wilbur Wright took off from the ground in his biplane, flew it around in a circle and landed again. Has anyone ever been up in an aeroplane?' This time a few arms made their way skywards. 'Does anyone know why this fact is important to us?'

'So that we could win the war against the Kaiser, miss,' offered Deirdre.

'Well, perhaps Deirdre, but it wasn't quite the answer I was looking for. No, the reason that this is important to those of us who are gathered here today . . .' Miss Bryant paused for effect, 'is because of all the tremendous impacts that this event has had upon our modern world it may well be true to say that it impacted harder upon the world of dance than on any other.' Again she paused, but this time the children stared back at her with blank faces. Undeterred, she blustered on through her little speech. 'Wilbur Wright, you see, had outdone the ballet! I know that sounds strange, but it's true in a way. Ballet dancers had always prided themselves on defying gravity. They were better at it than anyone else, and its one of the things that made the ballet so wonderful to watch. But with the arrival of the aeroplane a machine now did this much better. It could take off and land better than any ballerina, and it could *circle around*, which no ballerina could. In that respect the ballet had been outdone. But what it meant was that since you didn't need any longer to judge dancers only by how beautifully they could leap, new styles of dance were free to develop. Which is where our patron Ms Duncan comes in. Does everyone understand?'

Deirdre's hand shot up again. 'But Miss Bryant, what about the boomerang, Miss Bryant. Doesn't that return to the place from where you threw it?'

'From *whence*, from *whence* you threw it, Deirdre,' replied Miss Bryant, effortlessly deploying a traditional teacher's parry. 'And it's not quite the same thing, is it?' Unfurling her wings on this slim updraft, Miss Bryant continued, 'Just as Wright had controlled his aeroplane from a central control stick which bent its wings this way or that, so Ms Duncan's new style of dancing had a centre too: the solar plexus. Placing the centre here leaves the spine free to channel energy between both the earth and the heavens, you see.' She illustrated the point with an exaggerated movement of her left arm. 'Ballet has always been built on straight lines. Only by running in a straight line could you get enough speed to leave the ground. But the new dance had no need to leave the ground – the aeroplane did that better than any person could. No, if you examine it you'll see that all the dancing we do here is based not around the straight line, but around the *spiral*.'

Spiral or no spiral, Nadine was not destined to make the grade as a dancer. She soon tired of 'the new dance', more a kinaesthetic than a craft, and transferred to a ballet school. But for ballet she had neither the application nor the talent. She was more than competent and was no disgrace to her teacher or peers, but after a year at the academy they all knew that she wasn't long for it. Nadine suspected this but could not understand it. What did she lack that the others, the golden pupils, supposedly had? Once she knew she had a poor reputation, Nadine practised and rehearsed harder than ever. Late into the night she'd go over her steps in her room, pirouetting around as quietly as she could. She stretched and exercised and hardly ate, arched her feet whenever she sat down, counted time and rehearsed moves in her head at every opportunity. But at the same time as she was working so hard, all this effort was killing something in her. Her desire to succeed became centreless, pointless. Deep down she had wanted to be a 'natural talent'. She felt that the skills should just come to her effortlessly. If she had to work so hard for them, then what was the point? She could never be relaxed, blasé, emotional about her art if she knew so intimately how it had been won. She could never be *creative*.

Then war broke out again and she was evacuated along with thousands of others to rural communities and village schools. In time she managed to forget about the slight clumsiness that she'd never managed to shake and which her dance teachers had known she never would, and also about her own waning drive. She cast herself instead in the role of talent passed by, beauty destroyed by the war, a precious and ever so slightly tragic figure.

Nadine did have a talent, though, one which she'd inherited from her mother and which began to blossom in the cold Midlands school-room where she took all her lessons. It was an affinity for numbers and she found, quite by accident, that she rather enjoyed solving numerical puzzles and writing out formulae and algebraic equations. She was eighteen in 1942, old enough to join the rows of women on the belching armament production lines or train to be a driver or a nurse. Although these options didn't appeal to her she was excited by the prospect of working and kept a look-out for something she wanted to do. When she saw some newsreel footage of comptometer operators in the local cinema she knew she'd found her niche. The machines shown were the first to have a keyboard for inputting numbers rather than an awkward set of levers or dials and the film was remarkable for the fact that the fingers of the women who oper- ated these keyboards moved so quickly that the twenty-four-frames- a-second could not keep up with them. Six feet tall, the digits blurred across the screen before her, so fast it seemed even sight could not contain them. It was as if they had escaped, as if they had achieved a physicality which had gone beyond the realm of the day-to-day, and the effect was heightened by the simple, efficient clothing the opera- tors wore and their obvious focus and determination. It was a dynamic, and Nadine recognised in it that which she had wanted from dancing. The discipline, the restrictions of the machine hyper- sensitised and titillated, while the virtuosity of the finger movements freed and expressed. She went for it.

There was a comptometer training centre in Birmingham, run by a woman who, as chance would have it, had worked as a computer with Nadine's mother under Leslie Comrie. She still had the clippings from *Illustrated* magazine pinned up in her office, from the time when Comrie had won a War Office contract for his own company, Scientific Computing Service Limited, to produce gunnery tables just three hours after Britain declared war on Germany. 'Comrie's girls do the world's hardest sums!' the thirty-six-point declared.

The woman agreed to take Nadine on, and Nadine learned fast and loved it. She made friends with the other girls, embarked on a new social life and dropped her tragic, narcissistic airs. She was good at the work, too, so good that she found a part-time job only a few months into the course – working on the accounts in one of those armaments factories she'd looked down her nose at. But at the same time she continued with her training and when the special operations centre at Bletchley Park put out a request for computers the woman who ran Nadine's course put forward Nadine's name and she was selected.

Bletchley, Alan Turing, Colossus – names the public wouldn't know until long after the war was over. This is where they helped the man who made the thing which cracked the codes that Jerry built. Nadine arrived just as Colossus became operative. One of the very first electronic digital computers, its 1500 vacuum tubes needed a room of their own. Nadine only saw the monster once: her security clearance didn't give her access; but while she was at Bletchley she had a number of more or less torrid affairs – it was the war, dear, what would you have done? – one of which was with an MP called Tom who had the keys and who snuck her in one night. With the panels of lights clicking away behind them and the fans filling the room with noise they made love in front of the thing, made it an offering though they didn't see it that way, no, it was just sexy, all that power, and Tom's thick cock dug away at her like a piston and he showered her he showered her with sparks.

After the war Nadine moved back to bombed-out Birmingham and found further work as a computer. She liked her independence, wasn't about to give it up, even when she agreed to marry Henry, a man she'd vaguely known at Bletchley. He'd been one of the mathematicians, slightly older, not bad-looking, though back then she'd preferred the soldiers. But he'd remembered her all right, they had a name for her in his set, something to do with her surname, Flowers, which it didn't bear repeating, and back in Birmingham, an accountant now, he looked her up and asked her out. They courted calmly amid the ruins – it was so romantic, citizens with a responsibility to rebuild their country and their world, it was something amazing – and in 1948 they married.

Apart from the fact that she liked him there'd been another factor favouring Henry as a husband: he was sterile. Nadine wasn't interested in children, never had been, she loved her job. She didn't want some man nagging her to give it up and sit at home and coo. So Henry was perfect – handsome, kind, with interests of his own and surprisingly fierce as a lover. They had three perfect years together, before Nadine lost her job and her career. Vacuum tube machines were moving into the business environment and her virtuosity was no longer required. Artificial intelligence was here! It was efficient! It was clean! There were plenty of other jobs for people to do! Women! Britain needs children! We have a country to build!

But Nadine didn't want to do anything else. She didn't want to work in a bank, serve as a secretary, teach nursery school. And she made a useless housewife, too – she hated washing and cooking. She was a computer; nothing else would do. But she couldn't find a position in the new industry; no training, apparently. What did they want her to do? A college degree? She typed out dozens of applications, but no letters came in reply. She went to the movies, again and again, hoping for another flash of image-induced inspiration like the six-foot fingers had brought on before. She became obsessed by the idea that she would find an answer here, but when it became apparent that no such inspiration would come she became obsessed by the movies themselves. The picture houses were a parallel world for those who could not deal with their memories of war or with the hardships and penury of peace. Nadine joined them, disappeared into the flicker of images, grew into her seat like some plant that thrived on the strobe effects of projected chiaroscuro. Many nights Henry would trawl the theatres in search of her, stumbling up and down aisles in the semi-dark, yelled at by addicts stirred from their wide-eyed narcosis by the blank of his form. But when he brought her home she continued to grow, the blank living-room wall or the log fire her silver screen. She was a dancer who had put down roots, she was the woman who had held her hands to the sky and branched out, she was the ornamental bush gone to seed. She'd grown above and apart, and she wanted to grow further still. Soon, strung out, no one could touch her reach her climb her. She wound her limbs through their house in Hagley Road, peeped her shoots through the letter-box and out between the tiles, ransacked all the dark corners lest something had slipped out of sight. She grew her bark thick to resist all attack, crowded out the weeds which pulled at her feet.

She became so entwined and entangled, such a thicket, that in order to breathe her trunk had to split. With a wrenching sound it opened like a follicle and unfurled. A pillar of chitin grew forth and fountained out the spores of self-pollination. She no longer needed letters to come, for now she had leaves of her own.

Captain Henry

A decade later Henry Several settled back against the chafed leather of one of the armchairs of the lounge bar of The Crown on Birmingham's Corporation Street and adjusted the three watches that he now wore on his wrists – two on the left and one on the right. The pub's clock said six o'clock and none of the watches agreed, so he reset them all and gave them a wind. Then he picked up the *Birmingham Post* and gazed at the business pages, trying to make out the articles through the haze of his third gin. Between headlines he glanced up, shifted in his seat and smiled at whoever caught his eye.

The pub was humming with the usual early evening crowd. Greasy articled clerks fresh out of Chambers were drinking Bass and throwing packets of crisps back to their pals over the heads of the other patrons. Portly solicitors drank to forget their liver troubles and sounded off on favourite subjects. Starched accountants wheezed away in the smoky corners. Dressed in dark suits that sagged at the elbows and seat, the youngest of them sporting pimples and bright ties, the oldest combining the two effects in the patches of broken blood vessels years of drinking had splashed across their cheeks, the men filled the room with their caws and guffaws. Henry knew most of the drinkers by sight but, unusually, there was no one present to whom he'd actually been introduced. It wasn't until Sneak Riley swaggered in through the door that he was saved from the sad bastard fate of drinking alone.

Riley made a beeline for him, and Henry got to his feet and greeted the new arrival with an affable grin. 'Mr Riley, sah, good evening to you. And what will you be having?' he asked, shaking Sneak's hand and guiding him in the direction of the bar. Riley was not one to stand on ceremony and rather than spar for the honour of buying the round he murmured, 'Very kind, very kind,' in his obscurely affected way and requested a gin and tonic.

'And make it a double,' Henry called to the barman, an Irishman name of Sean Finnegan who worked the bar a couple of nights a week and occupied the rest of his time buying black-market product for a Dublin-based condom-smuggling ring. It was the kind of business in which Sneak might have been involved had he known about it and knowing Sneak, it was probably not going to be too long before he did.

'Very kind,' Sneak murmured again, sizing up the curves of Sean's arse as the barman reached down for a fresh bottle of gin.

'And one for yourself, barman,' added Henry, on a roll now.

Finnegan turned round, and Sneak coughed and laid his neatly folded newspaper on the counter. 'Don't mind if I do, sir.'

The drinks came and the two men transported them across the room to Henry's table, Henry slopping his a little. They sat down and Sneak took a gulp of his and fetched out a fag. Henry pulled out his lighter and leant across to light Sneak's cigarette, the ash from his own falling into his drink as he did so. Sneak noticed; Henry did not. Sneak said nothing, preferring the small twinge of pleasure to be procured from watching Henry drink down the ash.

Ostensibly a barrister, Sneak Riley made his own living and that of several other people besides by noticing just these kinds of minutiae. He cared nothing for the law but knew it well – the many intricacies of tort and precedent were useful tools in the bigger game of getting people to do what he wanted them to do. 'Have you heard about Donald Buerk?' he said, out of the blue. Henry replied that he hadn't, that he didn't know Donald particularly well. 'Bought himself a television a while back. Much to the annoyance of Doreen. Have you met his wife?'

'Er, no, I don't think so. She's a teacher, isn't she?'

'That's right. She hated it, apparently. The television, that is – though I'm pretty sure she's not too partial to the other as well, if you know what I mean.' Henry smiled thinly, still enough of himself at this early stage in the evening to be unimpressed by Sneak's repartee. 'Well, to cut a long story short, it's twisted his head. So I'm told.'

'What?' said Henry, suddenly interested. 'Lack of . . . you know?'

'No, you fool. The television. Though you never know.'

'What, you mean he's gone . . .'

'Yes, quite loopy, apparently. Sits at home in front of it all day. Masturbating. So I'm told.'

'That's terrible.'

'Aye.'

'Good God.' Both men fell silent for a while and sipped at their drinks. Henry noticed that his cigarette had burnt its way down to the filter, so he dropped it in the ashtray and lit another. He offered one to Sneak, who declined. 'You were his best man weren't you?' asked Henry.

'That's right.' Another pause.

'You two go back a long way, then.'

''S'right.'

'You must be devastated, old man.'

Sneak raised up his palms and brought them back into his lap. 'Well, these things happen. Want another drink?'

'Oh, yes. Same again, I think.' Sneak sloped off to the bar and left Henry to ponder the news. It had set off cascades of alcohol-blurred associations across the surface of his mind and the lineages of thought fell into two broad families. On the one side there was a bloodline of debate over the question of whether or not he should get a television for his daughter, Jennifer, who was seven that year. On the other a tribe of memories of his wife's insanity trekked about his tilted mental plane like Scythians across the steppe.

Sneak returned with the two drinks.

'Do you know who my best man was,' Henry said, taking a slurp of his gin and suddenly eager to change the subject.

'No. Who?' said Sneak, always up for a new bit of information to process.

'Alan Turing.'

'Alan Turing? Don't think I know him. Should I?'

'The mathematician.'

'Don't know any mathematicians. Never was the academic type.'

'No. The famous one. Chap who did all the code-breaking during the war.'

'Oh, the Bletchley Park chappie. The one who topped himself. Woofter, wasn't he?'

'So they say,' said Henry coldly. 'Always seemed like a splendid fellow to me.'

'Obviously.'

'What?'

'Well, old chap, you did make him your best man.'

'Oh, yes. Of course. Yes.' There was a slightly embarrassed pause.

Sneak, delighted with the way things were turning out, broke it: 'So, er, when were you married?'

'Not long after the war, 1948. I'd spent a lot of time with Turing between 1940 and '45. Worked with him on the Enigma project. Always had a bit of a dodgy ticker and having a head for numbers I was more useful to them back here than over there.'

'So you were one of those code crackers, too, then, were you?'

'I suppose so. It wasn't a bad war for us, you know. Clever bunch of chaps. Never met their like. Good company, too.'

'Never interested me, personally. Bright, was he, this Turing?'

'Oh, yes,' said Henry, maintaining an esoteric air. 'Extremely bright. Outrageous what they did to him. Poor bastard.'

Sneak said nothing for a while. Then: 'She passed away a while back, didn't she?'

'Who?'

'Your wife.'

'That's right.' The booze sloshed around him; he was all at sea. It was the element in which he was most at home. 'He was a great man, you know!' The words fell from his mouth and paddled around the glasses on the table like two great blobs of mercury. His eyes clouded slightly and he rubbed at them with his left hand.

Sneak leaned back a little in his chair, intrigued. 'You all right old man?' he crooned. 'I say, don't you think you've had enough?'

On the train back to Stratford Henry fell asleep. If it weren't for the fact that the guard was used to him he would have missed his stop. He'd done it before – and spent the night in a park in Oxford, a fresh topic of conversation for the local drunks and tramps. As he walked home, the streets were full of Turing and Nadine. When he reached the bridge he stopped, as he always did, and gazed out at the theatre. Its lights raked the water into furrows; there was no breeze and the reflection on the river's surface resembled a row of ultraviolet striplights, arranged to bring out the secrets in the sky. Back home, he shut himself in his study and poured himself a whisky. He sat in his chair for a while, swivelling nervously and trying to refill his lighter with fluid. He missed the hole and the petrol squirted out on to the desktop and bloomed across the leather. The stains looked like flowers, then gunshot wounds. Henry began to cry. He heaved great sobs into the room and his tears turned the wounds into a mutilation.

When the sobbing stopped he pulled out his handkerchief and wiped his face, then took a key from his pocket and went over to a small chest in the corner of the room. He unlocked it and took out a bundle of letters.

He untied the ribbon that held them all together and let the envelopes tumble on to the desk. He chose one and removed the contents. He thought of Nadine, of how she'd become hard wood

26

and pale grey. When she could no longer speak there were buds blossoms twigs where her hands had been. Henry fingered the violet sheets, held one to his cheek. He glanced at the words.

Jaundice . . . Skin . . . Jade
Ether . . . Blaze . . . Leather
Weather . . . Grammar . . . Heather
Two Poles . . . Descent . . . Spin
Colossus . . . Vortex . . . C(l)ock
Lung . . . Lightning . . . Elastic
Connect . . . Flight . . . Fuck
Voice . . . Anchor . . . Shoal
Nadine . . . Inching . . . Turquoise
Cunt . . . Damp . . . Metal

When she'd no longer been able to speak, she used to write these letters to him, often while he was sitting there in the room with her, then seal them in envelopes and hide them for him to find around the house. Back then, whenever he'd found one under his pillow, inside the fridge, slipped in between the flowers in a vase, he would pore over it as if it were a rune or a glyph which held the key to her condition and, if deciphered correctly, would make sense of it. But an interpretation had always escaped him and now, even now, he couldn't read another word. Couldn't. Didn't.

On the bottom of the bundle was another letter, carbon on stiff white. He looked at that instead.

19 December

Dear Dr Supine,

I am writing to thank you for taking on my wife's case. I know how busy you must be, and I feel forever indebted to you for the interest you have taken in her. If there is any way that I can ever return the favour, please do not hesitate to call on me.

I am aware of the possibility that Nadine may never return to her former self. I am also aware, drawing my own conclusions from what you have said, as well as from comparable case histories that I have taken the liberty of looking into, that this possibility, grim and hard to come to terms with as it may be, is also the most likely one. Should the prefrontal leucotomy that you have recommended prove unsuccessful in effecting a cure then it will be incumbent upon me to organise the setting up of a fund for her provision throughout her remaining years. I therefore seek your advice upon selecting a suitable institution in which she might be housed and in which she would be surrounded with the usual comforts befitting a lady of her standing and reputation.

May I repeat that should you ever require my help concerning any matter, then I shall remain,

Your Obedient Servant,

Henry Several

The great gig in the sky

The hair is shaved away and the scalp disinfected. Above the hairline a transverse incision is made. The scalp flap and a flap of epicranium are reflected forward and large trephine circles are drawn to within one centimetre of the midline, as low down as possible. The dura is opened and a transverse incision two and a half centimetres wide is made in the cortex. A two-centimetre cleft is then opened in the white matter, which is divided using a fine suction tube. Simultaneously, spatula forceps are introduced; the incision is then deepened. Puncture with a ventricular needle ensures that the cut is kept one centimetre above the orbital roof and the incision is kept on this descending plane as it passes below the head of the caudate nucleus. The underlying cortical area (Area 13) lies behind and below the ascending thalamofrontal radiation, which passes between the caudate nucleus and the putamen. The posterior vertical incision crosses the corpus striatum before entering the posterior orbital region. Direct observation confirms that the inner tip of the spatula blade is kept one centimetre from the falx. Unless this point is checked the weight of the spatula handles may cause right lateral deviation with the result that the incision misses the objective and passes laterally to Area 13 – an event which will surely vitiate the result, as shown by the difference in effect between unilateral and bilateral stereotaxic implants.

Maximum benefit is derived from the posterior two centimetres of the incision. There appears to be a concentration of fibres in these last two centimetres, division of which produces adequate relief of symptoms. Whether these are descending fibres passing down from the frontal cortex through the substantia innominata towards the hypothalamus, or whether these are directly connected with the primitive agranular cortex of Area 13, cannot be stated, but we regard this area of the substantia innominata, lying beneath the head of the caudate nucleus and the overlying Area 13, as an important objective in treatment. Vertical incisions which enter this area, however, produce serious damage, as a result of which this area has for long periods been regarded as taboo.

Nadine had been committed in 1957, on 3 November, the day of the Sputnik II launch. Throughout the following year, as the North American Space Agency was inaugurated and the European Centre for Nuclear Research began operation, her condition deteriorated until finally the decision was taken, with Henry's approval, to operate. On 12 September 1959, at the very moment that Luna 2 impacted upon the surface of the moon and deposited there the Soviet Coat of Arms, Jennifer's mother became the last person in Britain to undergo a pre-frontal leucotomy. At that moment Nadine and Luna 2 both disappeared into their respective twilight worlds and shortly afterwards Nadine – though, as far as we know, not Luna 2 – became pregnant.

X and Y

'Nadine Several, Room 35. Nadine Several, Room 35.' He didn't bother to knock, just kicked the door open with his heel and stepped backwards into the private room, pirouetting as he went so that when he brought the tray down he was facing the patient. He had the face of a chisel and his clothes – regulation hospital garments – while clean, were well-worn from washing. Nadine registered his entrance and let her head roll away from him and towards the wall. 'Uh uh, oh no you don't. Sit up now. You've got to eat. Got to keep your strength up, haven't you, my sweet.' He set the tray down on the table and came up close to the bed, placing one mildewed hand on Nadine's shoulder. But she flinched away, so he seized her by the earlobe and brought her head back towards his chest. 'Sit up, I said. Didn't you hear me? Sit up!'

It wasn't really clear to Nadine what was happening. The sunlight was not moving across the wall and that creeping line, the cross of the window's shadow that deformed as the day came and went, was the only thing that was real to her now. Then there was pain, pain was real too, pain like the pain on her now that meant she had to go this way. She didn't want to go this way, there was something this way that she did not want, but the pain said go this way and so she went.

Davie Costain kept his fingers pinched upon her earlobe and reached his free hand around to her right armpit. By digging his index fingers into its joint he managed to force Nadine into a sitting position. Once she was upright he knew he could release her. Put her somewhere and she rarely moved, the doll. He slid his hand down the front of her starched blue smock and fingered her nipples and she stared right ahead as usual. Then he fed her, helped her to spoon the grim hospital food into her mouth, regaling her with compliments and obscenities as he did so. 'That's right, eat it up. That's right. You know that Davie loves you, don't you? That's right. You've got beautiful hair, you know. Are you my baby slut? Yeah, that's right. Must have been a lucky bloke to have had you. Did you let him take you up the shitter? I bet you did. Bet you two got up to all sorts. Pretty girl like you.'

Nadine finished, but not before Davie had spilt jelly down her chin and chest, and rubbed it in with a tissue. He piled up the tray and pocketed the chocolates that Henry had brought her the previous afternoon.

On his way back to the kitchens Smythe, another of the porters, caught up with him. 'You coming for a drink, Davie?'

'Nope, not me. I'm on duty tonight.'

'Well, don't get bored.'

'Me? Bored? Don't be daft.'

Davie delivered a few more trays, said good-night to the nurses, bagged up the laundry and mopped the lino in the ground-floor corridors. Then he went round all the rooms checking the windows were securely fastened and settling everyone into their beds. There was rarely any trouble on B wing at night. This was where they kept the dopes, the dociles, the zombies as Davie liked to call them. As a rule the duty nurse spent the whole of the graveyard shift on A ward, with the crazies. And it was a full moon tonight – she'd really have her work cut out.

Davie worked his way around the rooms in such a manner that his last call was Nadine. Nadine was by far the youngest woman in his care: most of them were over sixty and kept in a state of dumb fascination by the ever rising tide mark of senility. He let himself into her room and walked across to the bed. She was already asleep. He patted the blanket and drew it up to her neck as if tucking her in, then quickly slipped his arm beneath her chin and caught her in a head lock. She awoke immediately, of course, and opened her mouth to scream, allowing Davie to jam in a squash ball and fix it in place with a few turns of surgical tape. So she scratched at him, and he grabbed her hands and roped them together with a length of cord he'd pulled from his pocket, then tied them to the bed frame behind her. More calmly now he took out two more pieces of cord and tied them around her ankles then, utilising the bedstead once more, he tied her legs apart. Lastly he took out a pair of surgical scissors and cut her gown from her body, leaving her naked. Then he threw the covers back over her – not before first exploring her body to his own satisfaction – and strolled downstairs to the delivery bay where his friends were waiting with their money, whistling under his breath as he went.

2

The international front

The winds that blew in to Brooklyn's Williamsburg as December staggered on brought with them the razor cut of the Great Lakes' vast sheets of ice and the whittled odours of the billion trillion New England reject leaves whose dying flames they'd fanned upon their way. A clump of oxygen molecules, released by bacterial activity from the Lake Huron silts, bubbled their way to the surface just off Tobermory point to be thrown up in the foam of white horses and absorbed into air flows which flickered down to the great falls at Niagara. There the winds banked west and blustered over Geneva, Rome and Amsterdam, until they discovered Troy. Here they turned south along the line of the Hudson, clogged as it was with logs, oil sludge from the mills and plants that backed up its banks right into the Adirondacks. The molecules stayed aloft, their motions tracing out the giant tubes of turbulence, and only began to descend when they reached the Bronx. Whipping low between the tops of the buildings they described loops and vortices, and consorted with the sluggish petrocarbons and particles of filth coughed out by the vehicles and the people. By the time they made Williamsburg they were running close to the ground and at just the right height to be sucked into the welcoming lungs of Moshe Kluge as he stepped into the street outside his bakery and took the morning air. Down among his bronchioles, their freedom severely restricted, about half of the molecules were trapped by tar deposits and about half were bound by haemoglobin. For days they circled around Moshe's body, losing one another in the veins and capillaries, until each of them was married with one of the carbon atoms they had so long despised – some strange shotgun wedding deep down there in the flesh. A week later they were all farted out as the baker emptied his bowels the morning after the Sabbath. Their pit stop over, the molecules seeped out into the cold November air and with their high spirits severely dampened they slunk away from the drifting cloud of methane and looked for somewhere else to play.

Moshe Kluge, taciturn but loving father, massive, powerful and round. Moshe Kluge, sometime Kabbalist, kaposzta lover and king baker. Moshe Kluge, switching on the single light bulb hanging in the centre of his shop. The light illuminates oven, preparation tables, counter; in their racks the basted crusts of loaves shine from the shadows like the polished backs of skulking reptiles. The light bulb is caked with flour: it's the only area of the room that Moshe's wife Judith has not wiped clean (she loves the faint smell of burning it gives off once warmed up). It's a smell alien to the bagels and breads which come out of the oven hot, soft, delicious and perfectly glazed, the best in the district and perhaps in the city – a fact to which many a customer will testify. There is even an enclave of fans, way over on the Upper East Side, so devoted to Kluge's wares that they'll send daughters and lackeys right across town to pick up orders. They are the ones who have 'discovered' the little bakery, as if it were the source of some minor river, and have passed the word around at PTEs and coffee mornings. We are in the fifties now, remember, and both Jew and Gentile purchase Tupperware.

'Moshe,' Judith would nag every time one of the golden-haired girls came into the shop to collect an order, 'Moshe, when are we going to get this van? Every week I explain to you how much sense it makes, look at this poor young child, each week she has to come here on that dreadful IRT with the schvartzes looking her up and down every inch of the way. But what do you care? You are a heartless man, Moshe Kluge, a heartless man! Sometimes I think you think only of yourself. It's not so many years before

Joel will be old enough to drive, you might think about him for a minute, what's he going to do? Now if we had a van, of course, the answer would be simple . . .' But Moshe would only throw up his hands – releasing clouds of flour out into the room – and mutter into his beard that he was working on it, that they couldn't afford it, that he had better things to think about than pouring money down the drain. Then he'd turn back to his bagels, his knishes, his mandelbrot, pound the doughs out on the stained wooden kneading board, roll them in flour or sugar and slap them expertly on to large metal baking trays ready to be slid in and out of the oven with great sweeping movements.

Bagels were his speciality, he could make them perfectly: firm yet yielding, sour yet sweet, light yet moist. But the secret of their taste lay not just in the flour he used, nor in the heat of the oven, nor in the subtlety of the flavourings he kneaded into the dough, but in the very way he handled the dough itself, gently persuading it into long thick ropes without introducing the slightest tear or stress. When he cut the ropes he did not simply slice them into suitable lengths, as was common practice among many lesser bakers, but twisted and teased them apart at suitable points of weakness, the accurate identification of which was a skill he'd developed over decades. Once ready, the lengths of dough were grabbed by one end and whipped around into the familiar circular shape. The process appeared simple, elegant, rapid and effortless, but of course it had taken many years to perfect and Kluge's skill ensured that his shop was generally busy with intrigued onlookers, many of whom bought his bagels just in order to admire the production process.

But apart from their taste and consistency, Kluge's bagels had another unique feature. At the final stage of his production cycle, just before Moshe joined the ends of the dough, he would give each rope one half-twist at its centre. Thus, every bagel had its very own torso of torsion and each was, in fact – if inspected closely and imagined topologically – a little Möbius band, a hoop of bread with only one surface and therefore neither an inside nor an out. It was this, speculated many of the customers, that was responsible for their wonderful flavour.

34

It would not be right to attribute to this curious fact Joel's early fascination with mathematics. For Joel did not even like his father's bagels, even though he was quite possibly the only soul in Williamsburg (nay, in the whole of New York) who did not. Perhaps there was something Freudian going on here – perhaps. Or maybe Joel didn't feel comfortable eating an object with only one surface, maybe he felt there was something indigestible about the idea. This was certainly possible, for from the moment his brain had come online Joel had comprehended the world in mathematical terms. Logic and geometry came more naturally to him than walking or speech; he subordinated infinity beneath his scrawny childhood thumb as other boys subordinate insects. As an infant he didn't speak at all for three years, by which time Moshe and Judith had all but given up on him. But then, in January 1953, on the day that Moshe read in his censored copy of the *New York Times* (Judith, like all the wives in their community, bowdlerised it for him every day, cutting out or deleting with the thick marker pens she purchased from Zvi's stationary shop two blocks away anything that might tempt, co-opt, or be otherwise unsuitable for her husband) that a United States Airforce Advisory Panel concluded that unidentified flying objects or UFOs: (1) constituted no direct physical threat; (2) were not foreign developments; (3) were not unknown phenomena requiring revision of current scientific concepts; and (4) offered an opportunity for mischief by 'skilful hostile propagandists', Joel spoke his first word: *ein*. Oy vay, so it was not so much, but it was a start, and he quickly progressed on to the other numbers until Judith and Moshe would carry with them for the rest of their lives happy memories of Joel sitting up on the window-sill or on the table's edge counting away to himself, quietly, under his breath, for hours and hours. It wasn't until 18 May, the day that Jacqueline Cochrane climbed into the cockpit of an F–86 and became the first woman to fly faster than the speed of sound, that Joel managed a word that wasn't a number. It was his own name and it popped out at the dinner-table bundled in an expression of great surprise. The meal, a turgid, standard affair until that moment, came alive: everyone cheered and tried to encourage Joel to say something else (all secretly wanting their

35

own names to be the next to issue forth). But Joel was in no hurry and, happy with the technique he'd developed with numbers, he just repeated his name over and over for a week or two until he was thoroughly used to the sound of it. Other names and words slowly got added to the list until 12 August when, at the moment that the USSR exploded its first hydrogen bomb, Joel strung together something that had the right to be called a sentence as opposed to a mere list. So it was – halting, brittle, spavined with logic to be sure, but it was a sentence and it meant that the boy was a mensch.

Now that he could talk he could attend Yeshiva, and the following year he joined the other boys in the exhausting school schedule which began at seven every morning and continued until four in the afternoon for the younger boys and six or seven in the evening for the older ones. The next few years would be spent learning Hebrew in preparation for the rote learning of the religious texts – the Pentateuch, the Talmud – which would dominate their education.

Joel found Hebrew much easier to figure than Yiddish. Yiddish, it seemed, was about sounds alone, strange clouds of noise the meaning of which was nebulous at best, but when the boys started Hebrew they were taught about gematria and about how there were numerical values to this new alphabet and how this meant that every letter – and therefore every word – had a corresponding number. Joel didn't quite understand how this worked yet: making words into numbers was one thing but recombining them, making numbers into words, that he couldn't quite manage. Still, the fact of the numerical connection gave him the confidence he needed, it tied things down, and he had little trouble with the ancient language. And when it came to memorising he had a distinct advantage over the other boys, for he could remember entire passages by keying the words to planes of numbers that he found it easy to visualise in his head.

And while the other boys struggled with the rudimentary arith-metic that was studied in order that they might understand the stocktaking procedures of their fathers' businesses, Joel solved the problems casually and almost instantly, computing the solutions spatially in his imagination. In those lessons he kept himself from boredom by inventing and solving logical puzzles. After a while he learnt to do this in his head as well, because the rabbi hated doodling and fetched any boy he caught at it a hard smack across the open palm with the short thick flat bar of wood he always had about him. So Joel began to pretend instead that he was struggling over the problems like his peers. That way he was left alone, free to sit at the back of the class and speed about in the crystal spaces of his mind.

So, like a modern Euclid, Joel developed his talent in secret, though less out of fear – as a rule the Hasidim do not share the Christian taste for the tang of forbidden fruit – than because he remained completely oblivious to the possibility that anybody else might think with numbers as he did. The numerological possibilities of gematria were one thing, but the joys of pure mathematics, of geometry and algorithm, were something of which the rabbis never spoke.

His talent for numbers was eventually recognised, of course. Something of a schlemiel, thanks to his short sight and lanky limbs, he was too clumsy to help his mother with the household chores like the other children (*Oh, that Joel, he only has to look at something and it breaks!*). So Moshe found a use for him in the rear of the shop, got him to do the stock control and the bakery's balance sheets. It was a job that strictly should have been allotted to Joel's older brother Shimon, but Shimon wanted to be a rabbi and was far too ethereal to dirty his hands with money matters. Although the fifth child of nine, Joel was effectively the number-one son where the bakery was concerned (with the exception of Shimon, all of his elder siblings were girls – Rachel, Judith and Sarah). He had two younger brothers (Moshe and Abraham), and then there were the twins, one male, one female, who were still toddlers. As a family they had been lucky: only one child had died – a girl born the year after Joel, who had contracted tuberculosis at the age of five. On holy days the family would visit her grave out in the Jewish quarter of the cemetery in Queens, one tiny plaque among the hundreds of thousands of markers and gravestones which ate up the grass and even the trees until there was virtually nothing left on the gently rolling hills but crosses and plinths and tombs and slabs, an entire metropolis of death, bordered by expressways and echoed by the skyscrapers that shivered on the overcast horizon with its clouds like sheets of tin.

When he finished each week's accounts, Joel would lay a sheet of greaseproof paper across one of the metal baking sheets, take a pencil and plot the loci of theoretical objects moving through space. Then he'd integrate the curves of their trajectories in his own peculiar algebra. Absorbed and happy, he'd sit for hours among the bags of flour and the mounds of sour-dough, keeping out of harm's way while his father worked. Even though Joel wasn't helping, the baker liked to have him there, scribbling away. He would take the finished sheets from the boy and pin them on the wall in the front of the shop, the better to point them out to his customers with the cracked pride of a man who knows that his second son, like his first, was not quite as he would wish him to be. *Look, this is Joel's latest, not bad you think, yes!* And the men and women of the neighbourhood would smile and pat Joel's yarmulke and murmur: *Oy, Moshe, he'll make us a clever lad yet for one so quiet.*

In his quest to conquer words Joel tried to discover all meanings logically. When he first began his English lessons he was perplexed to find that the words of the new language could not be discovered by translating letter for letter the corresponding Yiddish term. And try as he might, the English teacher – an Italian who came in to teach the boys for the last hour of each day Monday through Thursday – never could convince Joel that language was not a code that only lacked a key. For hours each night Joel worked on algorithms and procedures that would translate one tongue into the other. But he met with not the slightest success and finally decided that a higher order was required. He knew there were books on mathematics – he had seen them in the windows of bookstores the few times he had been to Manhattan – and he thought that he might be able to find some of them in the school library. But the library was out of bounds to the pupils and to gain access to it he had to run favours for the rabbis for weeks. Eventually he was trusted enough to be sent in there alone on errands, fetching globes and textbooks for the lessons, but to his dismay though he looked through every book on the shelves (and there were not that many) there was nothing that was remotely useful to him. Were there no mathematics books then? Had they taught him everything? He immediately stopped volunteering to help and went back to his day-dreams, which greatly confused the teachers who had been convinced that he'd been making some progress. Still, he couldn't believe there was no more to it and so began to harass his father, eventually finagling him into taking him to the public library in Park Slope.

Neither of them had ever been in the building before, and both were awed by the great façade. Moshe was reminded of pictures of giant and ancient tombs that he had seen occasionally in the magazines. Egyptian figures and peculiar runes were embossed in gold on to the stone and at the base of the enormous doors stood two massive book depositories, one to each side, like the paws of some metallic sphinx. Imbued with the appropriate amount of respect, son and father climbed the steps and went on in. Once inside, the place seemed even bigger. The ceiling of the atrium was several storeys high, and the walls and floors were panelled with long strips of dark wood. Low steel pillars slung with velvet ropes led them towards a panel of security guards who nodded them through to the central area. To the left and right, elevators fed a mezzanine across which people walked, books in hand, looking intelligent and completely at home.

Father and son stood at the centre of the vault, not sure which way to turn. Both of them felt swamped. Moshe eyed the check-out line and considered joining it; at least then it would look as though he knew what he was doing. Joel ran his eyes along the rows of Kardex cabinets, wondering at all these tiny drawers. Finally, when nobody volunteered to help them, he decided to take matters into his own hands and approached an Ashkenazi boy who was flicking through a catalogue. The boy was helpful and explained the system to Joel and Moshe, then pointed them in the direction of Mathematics.

When Joel saw the shelves and shelves of books dealing with

his obsession he almost fainted. With breathless excitement he pulled down volumes at random and thumbed his way through them, not reading the words but just trying to follow the equations, not finishing one page before he started another. He had never come across standard algebra before and initially it completely threw him, but after he had seen a few things that were obvious he began to deduce the meaning of the more esoteric operators and functions without too much trouble. This done, he began to build himself a mental map of what was available on the shelves.

Moshe hung around him for a while but soon got bored. He had no interest in math at all. With Joel engrossed and unlikely to come to any harm, he wandered off along the rows of shelves past the students fidgeting at their desks and the sleeping bums who had come in out of the cold, until he found himself in the Geography section. Geography! It had always been his favourite subject during what little schooling he'd had. He hadn't looked at an atlas in years! Guiltily he lifted one down and opened it as furtively as if it were a women's magazine. He found North America and ran his finger to and fro between Brooklyn and Montreal, the locus of both his life and Joel's and as defining for him as the sequence of genes on his chromosomes.

He had forgotten how vast a country America was. He looked at it in comparison with Germany, with Poland. The maps weren't as he remembered and he found certain places difficult to locate. When he came across Israel he coughed with surprise. *So, yes, it is real after all.* He searched along the shelf for the 'I's and pulled out a book on the country. As ever when he was confronted with Zionism, he felt no anger, just a numbness, a sort of dulled realisation that there would always be those who failed to understand. Out of curiosity he pored over detailed maps of the new state and read as much of the text as his English would allow. At one point he stumbled into a chapter discussing the impact of the Holocaust. One double-page spread consisted of a single photograph of a great black board on to which names of European towns and villages had been pinned in their relative positions. No borders or coastlines were shown and each name was accompanied by a number. It was an arresting image.

Moshe searched for the town of Treblinka, where his brother Isaac had been sent along with his wife and four children. Isaac had returned to Poland before the war. It was a peculiar feeling, seeing in the anonymity of print the bare facts of what he lived with every day. It was always with him, not thanks to some conscious level of pain – the agony had subsided long ago – but in the way that a severed limb in some strange way remains, the nervous system never having quite adapted to its absence. As the agony had subsided so had his anger, which had become so generalised that it had tainted his whole world and in the process made itself ridiculous and untenable. But when it had gone, Moshe found that it had taken with it his faith: expansive and good-humoured before the war, the Holocaust had burnt it out and nothing had risen from the ashes, soaked and hindered as they were by the constant drizzle of the horrors unearthed by the media in the ensuing decades. For a period he had sought recourse in esoterica and ritual, turning to the Kabbalah. This led him, among other things, to take advantage of his wife's illness and have Joel's circumcision conducted by a Ba'al Shem in private rather than under the more public – and more traditional – gaze of the entire family. But the collapse of the old man during the ceremony had frightened him and it was to be the last time he dabbled in the mystic arts, deciding then and there that the only arts which it was his place to practise were culinary. Yeast and heat produced tangible results – they smelt good and they filled your stomach. Upon that, one could build. That was enough philosophy for Moshe Kluge.

He closed the book, his eyes dry, and wandered back to look for Joel. But the boy was still engrossed so he sat in a chair by the radiator and dozed, memories of Isaac buzzing behind his eyes, until Joel had decided on the books he wanted and it was time for them both to leave.

They stood in the line to register and the boy checked out his books. Then, on their way out of the building, which Moshe remained impressed by but which Joel had already assimilated as part of the scenery of his existence, a voice called out Moshe's name. One of the librarians was striding up to them, his hand stretched out in greeting. 'Mr Kluge, Mr Kluge, what brings you here?'

Moshe hadn't expected to see anyone he knew that day and it was a moment before he recognised Bernard Millstein, an Austrian Jew whose family had left Europe in the mid-thirties. He was a regular customer at Kluge's shop, but the older man knew little about him apart from the fact that he had attended Columbia University. 'Mr Millstein, is that right, Mr Millstein? So . . . yes.' Still groggy from his nap, Kluge couldn't think of anything to say. Eventually they both asked each other 'So what are you doing here?' at the very same moment.

It broke the ice and they laughed, but it was Joel who spoke up: 'I wanted some books,' he said, and he offered his string-tied bundle up to Millstein who did little more than glance at them, anonymous as they were in their hard brown covers.

It was some months before Millstein and Joel saw one another again. Millstein had moved to an apartment in a different part of Brooklyn and had not been into the bakery for some time, but his wife had grown so appalled with the standards of the local bread shops in their new area that one Friday she demanded that Bernard call in at Kluge's place on his way home and pick up some decent bagels for the weekend. It was dark and snowing lightly, the snow invisible except in the cones of light thrown out by the street lamps or car lights where it flecked the night like so many motes of gold. Millstein pulled up his Chevy across the street from the bakery and leaving it unlocked, ran across the road with his scarf flying out behind him and catching snowflakes in its tassels. As he went he tugged up the collar of the light mac he wore as high as it would go – only a week before the weather had been mild and it was still a shock that suddenly fall was over and that winter had arrived. When he entered the shop his glasses steamed up and he could perceive nothing but the gleam of the reflecting surfaces and the noise Kluge was making way back in the shop among the ovens. He removed the glasses and wiped off the condensation with his cuff.

Moshe spotted him from the back of the shop. 'Ah, Mr Millstein, no problem, I'll just be one minute only.'

'Hello, hello. Yes, that's all right,' Millstein called, 'I just want a dozen bagels.' He took off his spectacles and looked around the room while he dug in his pockets for a handkerchief. In the myopic blur he mistook Joel's graphs for some kind of abstract artworks and moved closer to get a better look, wondering at the incongruity of such pictures in the baker's shop.

As he was replacing his glasses, the baker strode up behind him. 'Do you like them? They are my son's.'

It was a few moments before he realised that he was looking neither at Kandinsky sketches nor at childhood scribbles but at a tangle of graphs, diagrams and matrices. 'I didn't know you had a son who studied math,' Millstein remarked, wondering at the peculiar syntax of the pieces. 'Which school does he attend?'

'Oh, just the UTA.'

'The UTA? But surely he's too old for that now? Do they take students over seventeen?'

'Oh, no. Joel's only thirteen. He was with me when we met in the library.'

'Wait a minute. You mean Joel did these? *That* Joel.'

'Oh, yes, he does them all the time. He seems to like it. You know how they are.' Millstein let this sink in for a while. Had they modernised the UTA? He could barely believe it; for all the sympathy he had for the Hasidim, he pitied them massively for having turned their backs on the twentieth century. It surely wasn't possible that they had begun to teach this stuff. And besides, it was at least undergraduate level, what he was looking at. 'Here he is now. Say hello to Mr Millstein, Joel.'

After a brief talk with Joel, Millstein left for home more elated than he had felt in years. All evening he rattled on to his wife about this prodigy he had discovered. It was extraordinary, he said it again and again, it was quite extraordinary. It was as if he had stumbled across the young Mozart. On his way to work the next day he stopped off at the bakery and offered Kluge his services as his son's personal tutor. Moshe was not sure at first, but he consulted his wife, who agreed – Joel was little help around the house and it would keep him out of her hair. Two days a week Joel was to come by the library after school; Millstein would drop him home after a couple of hours of tutorial. Before long he was trying to persuade Moshe that he should take the boy out of UTA and have him enrolled in a 'proper' school, but Joel's father would have none of it and, when he saw that it was threatening the little influence he did have over the child's development, Millstein dropped the subject.

Let's fold America

The same November night on which Millstein discovered his prodigy found Melinda Volitia (her stage name) pacing the living-room of the cantilevered cliffside Malibu property she co-owned with her husband, Moses Axelrod, and unable to sleep. Melinda was due any day now, and her belly was painful and (she thought) ugly. And she could not she could not get to sleep. Trixie and Donna, Donna Clearwater and Trixie Moxie (what sort of a name, no, really, just what sort of a name was Trixie Moxie? thought Melinda and felt thankful for her Englishness) would still be at Homer's party, the party that she hadn't been able to attend because of the tiresome infant ballooning below her breasts. That was her perspective on him–her–it; as the thing below her breasts, her monstrous third mammary.

She slumped down by the phone and dialled Homer's number. It rang over twenty times before a voice she didn't recognise screeched a hello into the receiver. She couldn't tell if it was male or female, which reminded her again of the child she was carrying.

'Can I speak to Homer please?' *Love Me Do* was blaring in the background, making it hard to hear anything. 'I SAID CAN I SPEAK TO HOMER!'

The voice at the other end giggled. 'Hey, sure, hey, like, who the fuck is Boner. Hey, come here, hey, everybody, there's someone on the line who wants to suck a boner! Check it out.'

'Look, will you cut it out. I need to speak to Homer . . .'

'Look, honey, I don't know anybody called Homer. I think you got a wrong number.' The record started into the chorus and Melinda heard a couple of voices in the background join in, then:

'Hello? Hello? Hey, who is this?'

'Oh, Homer, is that you? Oh, thank god. Who *was* that on the phone now . . . it's Melinda.'

'Oh, hi, Melinda, how ya doin'? Sorry you couldn't make it. Hey, I'm sorry about Ed there, he's drunk, you know how he is.'

'Oh, was that Ed? I didn't recognise him. Oh, oh, he's not . . . no, don't tell me, he's come in his dress, hasn't he? Jesus. Is Kathy with him?'

'Yeh, yeh, she's here.'

'Is she OK?'

'Yeh, she's fine, don't worry, you know she can cope.'

'Look Homer, is Trixie or Donna still there? Can you put one of them on?'

'Yeh, Trixie, Trixie's right here . . . Trixie! TRIX! Phone! Melinda!'

'Hi honey, you OK? Donna and me were just leaving.'

'Oh, Trix, no I'm fine, I'm just bored out of my mind! Look, if you're not too tired, would you guys mind stopping over here on your way home and bring me something to smoke, some grass or something? I can't sleep and I'm in agony, and I need some cheering up.'

'Yup, no problem, it'll be more fun than this party. A whole load of Homer's long-lost friends from college turned up like outta nowhere and it's turned into some kinda fratboy reunion. They already threw four girls in the pool and one of them's screaming blue murder 'cuz her outfit's ruined and she's threatening to sue. Look, honey, we'll see you in thirty. All right?'

'Uh, you saved my life.'

Melinda had met Trixie when she'd first arrived in LA back in 1960 to play a supporting role in a movie starring Sophia Loren – her first big break. They'd met at a party given by the film's producer, with whom Trixie was sleeping at the time, and they'd clicked and had been firm friends ever since. Donna she had met more recently. A languid beauty, she and Melinda had worked together for a few episodes of a television series in which Donna played a frontierswoman making her way in the West without the aid of a man. They had met the day that Melinda had conceived, which was also the day that the US military launched Operation Starfish over Johnson Island in the Pacific. Following the discovery of the ionosphere and the Van Allen belt, there had been much speculation as to the origin of the charged particles that flowed around the planet. Certain minds at the Pentagon had it that the entire phenomenon was due to atmospheric nuclear tests being carried out by the Russians, so a series of similar tests was commissioned. Codenamed Operation Starfish, several launches were scheduled for July 1962. Most failed (one blew up on the launch pad, causing radioactive contamination throughout the entire area), but one succeeded in exploding its warhead at the correct height. The electromagnetic storm that ensued put out all the lights in Hawaii, disabled Tiros I, the world's first weather satellite, and caused one of Melinda's ova to be released a day before she was due. And as Sputnik II was in the vicinity, the blast also woke Laika from one of her long sleeps.

Woke Laika? Yes, it's true. High above the earth, slowly orbiting at a height of 300 kilometres or thereabouts, was another egg of sorts – a metal egg with a Russian dog of indeterminate pedigree curled up inside like a hairy embryo. Fast asleep, she twirled around in the tiny space yelping to herself as from deep in her limbic system a dream emerged, which made her paws twitch to and fro. She dreamt of rabbits, of hundreds of rabbits in a great wide field, a field of clouds like the one she could see from her porthole, the one which wrapped itself around the world. She bounded among the bobbing creatures, almost as divine in their fluffiness as the water vapour they scampered upon. Laika ran and panted, and chased them down their burrows. She was in doggy heaven. Which for once was where she was supposed to be.

She was certainly not supposed to be having a one-dog party at the USSR's expense. As far as the world was aware, Laika was dead. Had she been given a lethal injection? Had she run out of air? Or had she just burnt up upon re-entry into the atmosphere?

Soviet ground control had neglected to say when they'd declared her officially dead some years before.

Their instruments had told them Laika was dead because Laika had disabled them all when, after a week in space, she had tired of being observed. She had been subjected to human scrutiny for her entire life and it had begun to offend her dignity. Once she had completed the requirements of her mission by managing to survive the launch and stay alive beyond the confines of the atmosphere, she'd decided that enough was enough. It was time to turn the tables on her tormentors. She was quite possibly the most highly trained dog in the world; decoupling the electrodes inserted in her brain and disabling the syringe designed to kill her did not present a notable challenge.

But that was only the start of it – Laika was soon able to do much, much more. One does not become the first living creature in space and remain unaffected. Laika had always been a clever dog, but the act of witnessing the earth in all its beauty, a polished turquoise ball rolling gently through the void, caused a phase transition in her mind. How so? How does self-consciousness begin? Of what does it consist? Is it a global process, coherent enough to ground an identity, or is it the epiphenomenal by-product of innumerable series of smaller operations? Did this vision of the world as a perfect sphere, a holistic unity, produce a corresponding organisational geometry across the space dog's brain? Certainly the great logicians of Western metaphysics – Plato, Descartes, Marvin Minsky – might well have argued for such a interpretation. Others, however – Heraclitus, the German Romantics, Paul and Patricia Churchland – might have wished to pursue a more complex interpretation. Had Laika, as the poet Hölderlin suggested, placed herself 'in harmonic opposition to an external sphere', thus allowing her idealism to act as a matrix for itself (as Schlegel described) and begin a process of infinite overturning (as Hegel insisted)? Or were the processes involved too intricate, the constant rippling and annealing of the vast, tiny and biologically complex networks that make up the brain too motlied to be described either by the broad strokes of poetry or the fine boxes of science, creating a consciousness that is never completely coherent, never complete, always over-layered and fractured and not in fact global at all?

And where is the illusion here? And why does such incoherence worry us?

It didn't worry Laika. For the first time, she knew who she was (or thought she did). The astronauts who followed her were not so lucky. Their imaginations already choked with paranoid structures as a result of decades of service in the military, the globe suspended magically in front of them had a less profound effect, merely resonating strongly with the concentric circles of their fear. Many of them sought refuge in the visions of universal harmoniousness offered by religion and set off to look for arks on their return to earth. Others took a more materialistic turn, playing psychedelic rock music in their capsules and becoming boundlessly enthusiastic consumers: *Hey! The earth's a planet! It's round and it's hanging right there! Wow! Hello mom! Look, it's your son Bud eating dehydrated ice-cream! I'm on TV!*

But Laika was not so frivolous. There's something about being first that injects seriousness into the situation. Once she'd achieved self-consciousness the first emotion she felt was a sense of guilt. She'd torn off her electrodes after all – something which she'd been told never to do. The thought that everyone at Baikonur would think she was dead saddened her because she'd made some good pals back there. She thought of Alexei and Mickl, who had taken her for walks and smuggled her bits of steak when she was supposed to be on a restricted diet. Perhaps they were down there right now, shedding a tear or two over her empty kennel. She remembered Mickl's face as he'd wheeled her to the gantry and suddenly a dose of nostalgia was added to the guilt as Laika remembered the good times they had spent together: the laughing, the woofing, the running round in circles, the rolling over and the scratching of the stomach.

And then a blast of hatred hit her as she recalled all the needles, the endless tests, the harsh training and Renko, the evil Renko, who would deny her food if she so much as failed to crap in exactly the right spot. How immediate was her memory of the man's malicious grin as he inserted another reinforced thermometer into her arse, or shoved another capsule up her nose? If she knew

Renko, there'd be a back-up system in here, some other way of monitoring her, some spy machine that could probe her private moments. . . . Inch by inch, she hunted through the tiny cabin until she found a tiny television camera hidden between two wiring ducts. With a doggy snigger she blocked the lens with a gobbet of the high nutrient porridge that they had provided as her only source of food. (Bastards. Not a dog biscuit in sight.)

Enough was enough. It was time for her to do some observing of her own. Fortunately the capsule was equipped with a television monitor and receiver as well as radio technology; the mission's technicians had thought it was wise, should Laika cease to respond to oral commands, to be able to instruct her visually. She watched now as Renko appeared on the screen, waving his arms and swearing and coaxing in an attempt to get her to re-establish contact. Laika sat back and enjoyed the show, laughing a doggy laugh. After a while, tired with all the excitement and on a little high of self-satisfaction (being self-conscious she now had an ego to massage) she fell asleep. When she awoke she would rewire the receiving equipment so that she could tune in to other signals. It would be too dull to have one channel as the sole entertainment for the rest of her stay up here.

There were various other problems to be considered too. Disposing of her waste products was already taken care of: there was a clever little toilet on board which ejected everything into the great vacuum outside and left her shit for ever circling the earth. But she was going to need oxygen and, of course, food, and then there was her deteriorating orbit to consider . . . she had a busy and difficult time ahead of her for sure. But Laika was the most highly trained dog in the world and she knew her stuff. They were only problems and she was sure that she'd figure out ways round them.

Trixie and Donna arrived as promised and settled down on Melinda's matching leather sofas.

'Oh darling, it'll soon be over, and then you can go back to being beautiful again,' Trixie consoled. 'And, like this is totally secret, and it's just between the three of us, but I heard at Homer's tonight that Roberto Merdo, who's been on the look-out for an English actress to star in his new thriller, has just seen *Two Girls, Two Guys* and guess what? He wants you for the part, darling!'

'You're joking!'

'Would I lie?'

But Melinda's interest was only feigned. Work was the furthest thing from her mind. What she really craved was cigarettes, cocaine and good sex, the first two of which she had given up to avoid the Hollywood life-style snipers and the last of which seemed to have given up on her. She wanted her body back and it was difficult to allow herself to be comforted by Trixie as she suspected her best friend – with a paranoia worthy of the initiators of Operation Starfish – of seeing to her frustrated husband behind her back. Suddenly she couldn't bear to keep up the pretence a moment longer. 'Yeh, well, Merdo, fuck that creep, I wouldn't work for him if he was making the last film on earth.'

'Oh, but he is, darling!' Trixie tittered her favourite titter and lit a cigarette. 'The film's going to be about a giant meteorite on a collision course with earth. Mankind's only hope lies with a team of scientists who are racing against time to build a spaceship that can fly up and attach a nuclear warhead to the thing and blow it apart. But meanwhile the change in the earth's gravitational field as the meteor approaches is causing earthquakes and hurricanes and riots, and everything is just going crazy.'

'It sounds fucking awful and I don't want anything to do with it,' moaned Melinda. 'I feel fat, I feel ugly, I can't do anything. I can't even sleep for chrissake! I want it all to be over!' And she rolled over into Trixie's lap and blubbered theatrically.

Donna came over. 'Calm calm calm calm calm, darling. Calm. C'mon now, don't cry. It's going to be over any day now.' While she talked she rolled up a joint and insisted that Melinda have some, telling her that at this stage it couldn't do any harm, that it would be good for her, calm her down, she was sooooo strung out, poor darling, and who was to know. They passed it round, the weed leaving an acrid film on their lips, and before it was finished Donna had one of her 'brainwaves' and suggested that they get out the Ouija board.

When no one objected outright she cleared off the wicker-and-glass coffee table, piled the cups, magazines and ashtray on top of a pouf, and slid it across the hardwood floor and out of the way. Then she pushed the sofas together, admonishing the others when they would not budge to help. She drew all the blinds and closed all the windows but one, and made a point of blocking the door ajar. 'Okay darl', where d'you keep the rest of the kit?'

'The board's in the games cupboard which is out on the patio by the hot-tub and there's candles in the kitchen drawer. The one to the left of the sink!' Melinda called as Donna disappeared into the other room. 'And I think we've lost the pointer so you'll have to use a glass!'

Donna fetched everything and arranged it all, while Melinda let Trixie feel her stomach because the baby was kicking. 'C'mon, c'mon, give me your hands, d'you wanna do this or not?' Trixie stopped prodding at Melinda's bulge and the two of them sat round and placed a forefinger on top of the glass.

Donna lit the candles and dimmed the lights, then put her finger along with the others'. 'Is there anybody there?' She paused, while Trixie swallowed one of her famous giggles. 'I said, is there anybody there?' The giggle exploded and Trixie tried to turn it into a cough, but Melinda shushed her. She was already digging it. 'If there's anybody there, we would like to invite you to join us.' Melinda loved it when Donna did this, put on her best *Sunset Boulevard* voice. It made her want to touch her. 'Please, is there anybody there?'

Abruptly, the glass shifted a fraction of an inch. 'It moved,' cried Trixie.

'Trixie, darling,' said Donna, still intoning like a fading screen siren, 'if you don't shut the fuck up right now I'm going to take you outside, tie you to a tree and pluck your pubics out one by one. And then I'm going to smear your naked pussy with raspberry jelly and leave you there as a present for the racoons, while Melinda and I continue the seance in peace. Understand?' Trixie straightened out her smile and tried to concentrate on the glass. Donna continued, 'Whoever you are, I apologise for the interruption. Please don't be afraid. Come back and tell us who you are.'

The three women sat in nervous silence for a while. Donna had her eyes half closed, only her whites showing beneath the lowered lids. Trixie's left leg was trembling, the knee jerking up and down in its own spastic rhythm, as if she were experiencing extreme cold. Melinda's mind seemed to have gone completely blank apart from one fact on which she focused with a sublime intensity: deep in her womb, the child was lying completely still and she could no longer tell whether or not it was there.

Then the candles guttered and the glass glided across the board until it reached the foot of the letter K and stopped. Trixie gasped and her leg stopped vibrating. Melinda barely noticed.

'K,' said Donna softly. 'Does your name begin with the letter K?' There was nothing for a moment, and then the glass moved again, in its uncanny, frictionless fashion, across to the letter J. 'KJ. Are they initials? Are they your initials?' The glass slid four letters to the left, paused at the F and looped back to the letter K. With great gentleness and patience (she should have been a nurse, Melinda thought) Donna asked for more specifics. But whatever it was did not seemed inclined to give them. The glass simply slid back to the letter J, went from there to the letter F, then moved across to K, and it traced this curious triangle in response to any question Donna happened to ask. 'I'm sorry, we don't understand. I'm sorry,' Donna kept saying, infected by the repetition, and after a while they all got bored and she broke the circle. Melinda stood up, raised the lights and extinguished all the candles.

'Kujuf. Krajif. Karjaf. Keejef,' offered Trixie. 'I tell you there's no such word with those letters like that in it. I think the whole thing's stupid. I thought in seances people were supposed to have fits and speak in tongues and all. I thought that we'd get that ecto-goo stuff all over the place, not get visited by some jive-ass spirit that can't spell.'

Donna tried to explain to her that you couldn't simply demand whatever you wished from the spirit world and maybe it was the dope, but Melinda suddenly felt a little cold and weird and her mood shifted accordingly. It was all nonsense anyway, she said abruptly; it was probably just Donna moving the glass. She was glad she hadn't done it for years and she wouldn't be bothering again. The board could go back in the games cupboard where it belonged, and at this she experienced a tiny shiver. Anyway, she was tired out now but thanks for coming over it was lovely to see you both.

Still arguing, Donna and Trixie backed their cars out of the driveway and left. As their headlights wound down the canyon road Melinda could hear them honking to one another across the hollow night. It was on nights like this when the air tasted of bark and cactus and gasoline that she thought a little of the wonder that was Los Angeles. Los Angeles, this sprawl, glass and desert, glitter and freeway, machine and boutique. Away around the massive bay it gleamed, its billion red eyes sullen, its white lights barking at the night, its buildings sulking beneath their cloaks of filth. Melinda turned inside and waddled through the house. Trixie had left her cigarettes on the coffee table and the night's glamour made her break her vow. She walked out on to the deck and lit one, gazing out at the moon where it glittered away above the Pacific, out there, between the banks of this gully that they called a valley. She tried to stretch the romance of the moment, to sink into the image like a character she might have played, might yet play, in a film. She tried to think of her husband, Moses, to wonder where he was now as he flew through the night to be with her, tried to conjure the love that had made her leave England behind and make her home on the edge of the Pacific. But the cigarette tasted foul, of chemicals, and she couldn't finish it. She stubbed it out on the rail and dropped it over the edge, then went back inside and cracked open a Dr Pepper that she took from her enormous fridge.

Moses came home at around 5 a.m. Melinda was lying on the sofa asleep, one of the many post-natal self-help volumes that she owned opened out on her belly, as if the child were supposed to absorb its wisdom by some kind of cellular osmosis. He bent down over her and tucked a loose curl away behind her ear, his huge hands almost as large as her face.

He had joined IBM in 1957, the same year that Laika had been launched into space. It was a good year for the company. Apart from the paranoia sparked in America by the fact that the Russians were launching satellites – which translated into orders for ever larger computer systems by the Pentagon – American Airlines contracted IBM to devise a solution to the problems they were having with their flight reservations system. The computer company's answer was SABRE, the Semi-Automatic Business Research Environment. SABRE was a peach of an idea, not least because IBM had most of the technology for it already available, thanks to a government-funded project called SAGE that it had been building for the best part of a decade, but which was completely obsolete by the time it was ready for use.

SAGE, the Semi-Automatic Ground Environment, had also been cultivated in a climate of paranoia, this time fostered as a reaction to the exploding of an atomic weapon by the USSR in 1949. Airforce minds panicked at the thought of hordes of Soviet bombers taking a short-cut across the Arctic Circle to bomb the United States, with nothing to stop them except a few old radar stations left from World War Two. The USAF needed more; it needed battlements and lines of sight; it needed the first large-scale real-time computer system which, as a first priority, had to be better than the one, code-named Nike, that the US army was developing.

When finally completed, SAGE consisted of twenty-three 'Direction Centers', each of which had at its heart a duplexed IBM vacuum tube computer covering an area the size of a football field. Each Direction Center was manned by around a hundred personnel and linked to around a hundred sources of radar information – plane-based, ship-based, ground-based, missile-based – as well as to the other Direction Centers. Each was also linked to anti-aircraft missile silos whose missiles could be launched remotely by SAGE operators in response to any threat. But SAGE would have been of little use in the event of an attack. To save money (the project ended up costing eight billion dollars) the computers and command centres had been placed above ground rather than below, and in areas which were already major targets (the air force having decided that their people wouldn't want to work out in remote locales). Not only that, but radar jamming and radar decoys, likely to be deployed by any invading force, would have confused the system

54

instantly and rendered the aircraft tracking systems useless. All of this was, however, irrelevant, for by the time SAGE went online the Intercontinental Ballistic Missile had been born and the Commies no longer needed bombers to blow up America.

Moses himself had got into computing through politics, in a roundabout kind of way. He was at college during the 1952 presidential elections and he'd never forgotten the night the results came in. CBS, the channel he had been watching, had organised a UNIVAC computer as a back-up for Walter Cronkite's election coverage. They were going to use it to predict the results – it was a PR stunt by Remington Rand, who'd built the machine. They had a program set up to monitor the returns in various key states and guess the outcome on the basis of that. Moses had been glued to the screen. He thought this machine was the coolest thing, that the huge cabinet filled with electronic arrays and flickering lights was just too sexy. He'd worked in all kinds of offices, getting himself through his college course, and he knew about the power structures in those places. He could *feel* the way they worked, all those self-important execs charging around, all those clerks getting uppity about their boring little jobs, all those typists and receptionists getting a kick out of their own efficiency. Offices were machines, wood and flesh and stone machines, and you could disguise it all you liked with gossip and internal politics but that's the way they were. And it was completely obvious to Moses that what they all cried out for was one of these things, one of these data processors, these electronic computers. He could see as clear as his own hand in front of him how this machine would fulfil the desires of all those white-collar workers with their fetish for getting the job done. For here was the perfect employee: give it some information, tell it what to do, get an answer. It was what everyone wanted, he had thought at the time and many times since, because from top to bottom in every organisation what drove these people was the twinge of pleasure they got from completing a task, from emptying their in-tray, from taking a shit. That's what this machine could do for them. It could help them take a shit. And that was when he realised there was money to be made here. Lots of money. After all, Americans loved to shit.

It was a bit of a disappointment, then, when UNIVAC predicted Eisenhower to win with odds of 8 to 7 and he went and won with a landslide, 442 electoral votes to Stevenson's 89. But then, and here was the miracle, Cronkite admitted that his team had *lied* about UNIVAC's prediction. Yes, it was true: at 8.30 that evening the computer had predicted a landslide for Eisenhower, 438 votes to 43. But all the opinion polls had said a close race and fearing PR disaster – a grim fate, not one you want to court – the operators had rejigged the machine, made UNIVAC say a close race as well. The computer was vindicated. How excited was Moses? Charles Collingdale, man on the spot at UNIVAC headquarters in Philly, patted the machine's monstrous cabinet and reassured the viewers. The age of the computer had begun, he said, or something like that, no more covering up for it now. Didn't need it.

Moses went out the next day and enrolled in sales school. He knew where he was going. He wanted to see those cabinets in every damn office in the country and the commissions in his pocket. It was five or six years before he found out that they'd faked the cabinet too, it was a dummy, the real machine was so unwieldy they couldn't set it up for the event. And it was too hot – it would have made Collingdale's make-up run. So they'd rigged up a fake, filled it with Christmas tree lights. It was funny, but though he'd have been bothered by that fact if he'd known it at the time, when he eventually did learn about it it didn't seem to matter. After all, he understood enough about computers by then to know that it was their logical identity which was important, not their physical realisation.

But Moses was working his way up the ranks by then and was in it up to his neck – so much so that he sometimes found himself wondering if humans were the same as computers in that respect: that it was their logical identity which was important and not their physical body. It was a comforting and consoling thought, this. It helped him to cut deals, it helped him to objectify women and, eventually, it would help him to deal with certain problems that would one day be posed by his son. He made his name on the old 1401s which sold so well because they came equipped with the new 1403 chain printer which at 600 words per minute was four times faster than its nearest competitor. For that they'd junked the old cabinets too, jettisoned the old grey boxes with their rounded corners and Queen Anne legs and gone for this light-blue, very square, modernist number – very cool, very slick. Moses had loved the new design and it showed – he was top salesman in the country two years running. He was cooking, he was in a different league. Suddenly he was mixing with the company execs, was blue chip, was at all the parties, mixing with the stars too, at those big industry benders out in Hollywood. That's where he met Melinda, at one of those, and she lapped him up. He was hot property. He knew it, he dug it.

By the time Judd was conceived Moses was closely involved with a top-secret new product line that would eventually be launched in 1964 under the name System 360 (for 360 degrees, like it was an all-rounder, like it could do anything). The thing had the biggest civilian budget of anything in history: IBM threw more funds at it than the government had at the Manhattan project. When they launched it they held press conferences in fifty-three US cities and fourteen other countries simultaneously. The market had dipped a bit when Mariner I was taken out by a bug four minutes after launch, a comma missing from the Fortran code. Flight path had gone crazy, they'd had to blow it up by remote, 22 July 1962 (Moses remembered the date because that same day he'd asked Melinda to marry him – better get that nailed down before things crashed and burned). That missing comma was big news; everyone had thought: what's the use of these machines; if they're no more robust than that, then what can they do for me? Suddenly computers weren't so perfect any more, they'd lost their cool, they'd lost their sex appeal. Moses knew that the 360 had to put it back. He said so, too, and that was enough to get him taken off direct sales and put on the 360 concept team as a consultant. Big time.

And now here he was, criss-crossing the country, an electron helping the vast transport network of America to process whatever arcane calculation it was bent upon, forever moving from airplane to hotel to meeting to airplane, not understanding till now the value of home. 'My little Desdemona,' he whispered, and Melinda rolled in her sleep and threw an arm around his neck. He picked her up and carried her through into the bedroom and laid her out on the bed, then took a quick shower. Having dried himself off, he climbed in beside her and spooned her. Their bodies threw each other into sharp relief as they lay there, cosy as piano keys.

The next morning she awoke before he did. And she awoke suddenly, with a start, straight into the bright day. She had dreamt of him and was only half surprised to find him there. She slipped out of the waterbed as gently as her stomach would allow and went into the kitchen to fix him some pancakes and eggs. It was when she turned on the small television that they kept in the kitchen and saw that John F. Kennedy had been shot dead in Dallas that her waters broke.

So Judd entered this world already mixed up with events out of his control and beyond his ken. It was a nice childhood for sure: house in the Malibu hills, Mum pretty famous, Dad pretty cool. Trips abroad: Hawaii, Europe, Japan one time, England now and then to see Grandpa and Grandma, weird times, those, because it was often just him and Mom on their own and everyone always argued such a lot. He went to a real nice school, mostly white kids, but he didn't actually think of himself as black. Well he did, but it wasn't, like, an issue for him. It didn't seem to make any difference to anyone, 'cept sometimes when he was at the mall with Mom and they'd get strange looks and someone would shout something or spit, or maybe they'd come outside and find their tyres slashed – that had happened once or twice – and Mom would get real upset. But mostly it was okay.

Judd wasn't so academic anyway. He liked sports a lot, baseball 'specially, and he liked building model aircraft, the kind you make from kits. The teachers said he was bright but wouldn't concentrate. He got into all sorts of trouble for this. Every term his report would say the same thing and it would mean the same thing, too: a vacation full of lectures from Moses who would tell him it was harder for him because of his colour, because everything was against him, because he had to be twice as good as everyone else to get half as far, because this was a white man's world and how the hell did he think that his own father had achieved what he had, a bigshot at I–B–M, yeh, that's right, Big Blue, the highest-up black man in the corporation, with this beautiful house and a beautiful wife like his mother and three cars to drive and more if he wanted, and holidays in Europe and all? Not by not concentrating, that's for sure. And Judd would say 'Sure Dad', and blink back the tears, but not really see why it was all such a big deal. Then he'd forget about it and his mind would wander somewhere else, and he'd be pretty happy again.

Because Judd suffered from a curious condition that was called picnolepsia. Many times each day, for periods that could last from a few seconds to an hour or more at the extreme, Judd dropped out of whatever happened to be going on around him and on to a plane where time itself was deformed, and no longer regulated by the clock, the chant, the TV, the conversation. His senses still operated, his eyes and his ears, but he received no data from them.

It was as if he fell in-between the frames of a film, expanding the gap between one stationary twenty-fourth of a second and the next into an entire universe, just as the universe itself had expanded from a minuscule tear in the field of some inconceivably tiny quantum force. And just as the frames of a film point to a reality that lies beyond the camera, so Judd's picnolepsia directed him towards an understanding that there was an aspect to time that escaped apprehension, that defied linearity and the quartz movement of his father's digital watch. He'd found free time, a time which was in some way his own.

When he returned to his senses he usually didn't even notice he'd been gone – his mind just picked up where it had left off, pulling the threaded loop of cotton closed, and that would be that. But often he'd come round to someone speaking loudly at him, repeating his name perhaps, and generally it was Moses. Disorientated, Judd would utter a 'huh?', for which he'd receive a clip round the ear from his father and a short lecture on the need to pay attention and get some common sense into his head.

Sometimes he'd wander off and do something, only to forget not only what it was he'd done but the very fact that he'd done anything at all. It was as if his memory of what took place during the dilated period was sluiced from his mind by his re-immersion in the everyday temporal ocean. Once, when he was very young, he'd wandered out of the house's backyard while his parents were sunbathing and taken a walk. When Moses and Melinda discovered that he'd gone they panicked and went crazy looking for him (at the time they were still receiving threats from white supremacist organisations). They called the police, only to find him playing naked in the stream at the bottom of the canyon at the end of it all, unabashed and unable to work out why he was in trouble. Moses gave him a whipping after that, one which neither of them would ever forget, and from then on whenever he caught Judd at his day-dreaming it would echo in the air about them, a spectre.

As a result Judd started to invent narratives that would dovetail with events on either side of the vanished periods of time, making up stories that smoothed over his absence, not just for the sake of others, but for his own sake, too, so that he could have some kind of coherent account of the past. The important thing was that the story, the image he invented, should be a catalyst, one that would react with patterns lying virtual in the possibilities created by his lapse, crystallising them into plausibility. He was often extremely successful and events that he knew never to have taken place (unless by some bizarre freak he'd reinvented that which had been forgotten) entered family folklore, to be related and misremembered in their turn.

He learned, then, to treasure his lost minutes, came to think of them as the moments when he was really at liberty, and in this perhaps they came to function as a tiny secret stand against his father – not just against Moses the man, whom Judd was too young to know properly yet, but against what he stood for. And what he stood for, in Judd's eyes, what, in fact, he was a relay for, was these machines, these computers, which he worked with and which Judd had been taken to see once or twice and which were, Moses said, accurate and logical and, always, faster, faster, faster than their predecessors. They awed him, these great collections of cabinets that seemed from the noises and heat they gave out to be roiling with beetles and insects. Judd's mind recoiled at the thought of them; the dry, coppery tang that they traced through the air was almost capable of turning his stomach. The result was that he was frightened of them, and he became determined that he was not going to become one of his father's machines. I'm not a computer, he thought under a spout of petulant anger whenever Moses disciplined him. I can't be programmed. You can't tell me what to do. I'm not a machine.

Once or twice Moses spoke with Melinda about sending the boy to see a doctor, but she wouldn't hear of it: he was normal, she said, and he'd be fine if his father would just stop pushing him so bloody hard. And then Melinda took this job in England and Judd met Jennifer and everything got rewired.

Sex and the media

Doreen Buerk, Judd's Geography teacher during the spring and summer of 1973, was a woman who had trimmed her sexuality down to the point where its knife-like edge could continually precede her like the prow of some diabolic snow-plough. Amazingly, she had managed to achieve this effect while remaining convinced that she was completely sexless. In fact, she had managed to achieve it *by* remaining convinced that she was completely sexless. Judd had never met anyone so . . . so *repressed* before.

She made him feel guilty just for existing. He couldn't enter the Geography classroom without feeling that he'd done something wrong. The way she looked at him, it was like those people in the mall, the ones who couldn't help but stare. For them, as for Doreen, just by being there he was already at fault.

There was no sense with her that they were humans together. The teachers back home were not always so great, but at least they spoke to you occasionally, not just *at* you, *at you at you at you* all the time. It made Judd's head spin in peculiar orbits, made him feel that his thoughts were being constructed by the Spirograph that he'd been given last year for Christmas and which he'd brought with him over to England to do pictures on, pictures that he pinned to the walls of his room. He didn't understand that he already thought a bit like this, that his mental processes were so many intersecting ellipses and multicoloured spirals on a flat plateau, and that it was merely Doreen's strange scrutiny that was making him become aware of it.

Can thoughts have colours? he wondered. He closed his eyes and thought of red. I guess they can. So what colour was the thought of Doreen Buerk? Kind of puke. With purple patches and green lumps. A strange colour, one from the covers of horror comics and fantasy paperbacks. A colour that was sort of scary but in a roundabout way, a way that meant you weren't sure. A colour that twisted your gut and pinched up your anus and made you want to misbehave.

Judd couldn't help it. Doreen Buerk gave him the evil eye and that gaze of hers did something to him. Made him squirm. Made him put all of those bits of himself in line. He wasn't allowed to let things drift off, to leave things lying around, to drop out of time to his dilated realm. She looked at him and he was *focused*. It made him want to do bad stuff. He didn't want to. He just had to.

Doreen Buerk had developed her peculiar colour in a darkroom of spite she had constructed as a child, outraged at her parents' permissive attitudes. Her folks had been swingers in the 1920s, well-to-do, fashionable parties and sojourns abroad, and they had little time for the austerities brought on by the war. But daughter Doreen had followed the government instructions for the populace with keen delight; to her, the ration book was a symbol of the divine order, a King James Bible for the twentieth century. Throughout her childhood she shrank from the dealings her mother and father had with assorted black-marketeers – whom she regarded as 'shady characters', even though they were mostly neighbours, uncles, cousins, people whom she had known all her life – and she despised them for preferring their decadent memories to the resurgent moralities of the 1950s. In her eyes they were sullied and Doreen hated them as only a child can hate.

She had grown up and gone to university and there she had met Donald. Donald was Mr Moral and Correct, Donald cut a fine dash in his tailored suits and gowns, Donald spoke with authority at the debating society and held fine get-togethers in the city's better restaurants. Having sized up his pedigree as she would that of a dog she wanted to breed, Doreen took the necessary steps to secure him in marriage. She played it well – in Doreen, Donald saw all of the qualities he thought necessary in a wife. Not only was she pristine, prissy and controllable, but these attributes seemed to him to stem not from a particularly pliable nature but from the elaborate framework of judgement with which, like some scholastic philosopher, she had surrounded herself. She lived a life of pure form, into which all experience was to be inserted.

With this insight Donald imagined that he had stolen a march over Doreen and when they married he had no doubts that he would prove to be the dominant partner. What he did not see, however, because it was in himself, was how much difficulty he would have in coping with that position of power. But Doreen *had* seen this and that is what gave her the edge. For her plans were long-term and she saw that ten years of submission would be more than compensated for by the thirty or forty of dominance that she was certain she would subsequently come to enjoy.

By the time they were in their mid-twenties Doreen and Donald were ensconced in a suitably large house in Edgbaston and Donald was 'doing things' in the city. They remained childless, which, though a problem for Donald – who saw offspring as a necessary career accessory – suited Doreen, who had no desire for children, nor even for physical intercourse (which she put up with on a minimal basis). She got her kicks in other ways and she rather hoped that her husband – like most of the men in the Conservative Club, who kept the street trade in Balsall Heath ticking over – would begin to go elsewhere for his. However, he did not and this, as she later came to realise, was the first sign of trouble.

She knew that something was amiss when Donald began to leave the office on time and come straight home from work. When confronted he always made out it was because he had a job to do in the house or, in the summer, in the garden, but she could tell from the glaze in his eyes and the way in which he continually hung about her as she did the housework or cooked the dinner that she was his chief object of interest. In the beginning he had enough restraint to keep his newly fanned desires on a Platonic level, but after about six months of this behaviour Doreen began to worry that the long resisted descent of his mind and intentions to the level of her body was now imminent and she took care to remind him in those little ways – such as replacing their divan with two single beds – that they had agreed when they'd been married to keep those activities to an absolute minimum. Thankfully, the increase in Donald's emotional intensity was accompanied by a proportional decrease in his prostate control, so Doreen never had to submit to him for very long.

The Balsall Heath thing had been a problem, because she had hoped to use as the first weapon in her domestic coup d'état any guilty feelings Donald had due to extra-marital activities. But as they became more emotionally and physically intertwined Donald began to develop guilt in far more complex and interesting ways. He had actually started to idealise Doreen, not abstractly as she might have expected, but sexually. He went on about how he loved the soft touch of her skin, the smell of her, the way she moved to the bathroom or talked on the phone, the quizzical expression that she occasionally wore, the dimples in her downy cheeks. He cooed to her that he loved her strength; he became aroused by the clack of her shoes in the hallway. And as he began to squirm with this lust for her he started to blame himself for her failure to conceive. 'But I do feel responsible,' he would whine in an agonised tone while he lay curled on the edge of his bed after they had made what passed for love. 'What if it's my fault? What if it's me who's somehow . . . somehow . . . deficient? You wouldn't leave me, would you, for another man? I mean, for one who could, you know . . . ?'

Glancing across at the pathetic figure of her husband, his muscles already turning to flab, Doreen would give out a little shiver and tell him not to be so ridiculous and to go to sleep. She hated these exchanges. They seemed so pointless. What, after all, did he want from her?

Once he realised that he was not going to get what he regarded as the appropriate reaction, Donald began visiting several specialists, all of whom told him he was fine in that department. But this made matters worse, for rather than berate himself he now began to berate his wife. Doreen, worried that the doctors might be able to solve her 'problem', absolutely refused to have tests and since she could not get Donald to drop the matter she began to criticise him for even suggesting that she might be somehow inadequate. And why, she demanded, did he want her to demean herself by exposing her secret parts to some greasy gynaecologist? Wasn't it enough that she had to do it for him? Finally Donald, who by now was living inside an elaborate filigree of bad faith and self-doubt, took her words at face value, chastised himself for ever having doubted her and revamped his image of her by moving it more than ever into the realm of the ideal. For the childlessness he began to seek out ontological causes and he started his quest by superimposing the paranoid complex which by now choked his mind on to the whole world of his experience, becoming in the process the perfect theologian to Doreen's philosophe.

Soon he began to splinter, the limit-cycles of his personality destabilising until they became chaotic. Donald had always been confident, conservative, persistent, balanced and arrogant; now he was excitable, obsessive and finicky. He decided that as a couple he and Doreen were too isolated, so in November of 1963 he purchased a television set, something that neither of them had owned before. The news broke that Kennedy had been assassinated and Donald went right out of the office and bought one with cash. The shop delivered it that evening and he had it set up in time for the nine o'clock news, much to Doreen's horror.

'I thought I told you I didn't want one of those unholy things in my house.'

'Darling, I'm telling you, we just can't go on without one. How am I supposed to keep abreast of events? It's a global village we live in now, everything's linking up and we can't afford to be left behind. You know, the medium is the message and all that. Think of the opportunities for business . . . and education . . . and so on. It's the human spirit you know, joining all together across the planet in one great consciousness.'

'The radio has always been quite enough human spirit for me.

If you must speak to fools, please do me the courtesy of not repeating their nonsense to your wife. Spending our money on that thing, that heathen object. Do you want to join all those horrible little people who sit down in front of it every night, their eyes going square and their brains turning to mush, worshipping it as if it were some kind of pagan orifice? My husband, my very own husband, a member of the common rabble!' She stormed out into the kitchen in tears and started on the washing up, and it took Donald several hours, a dinner out, one promise to keep the thing in his study and another not to touch her for a month, before she was finally appeased and allowed him to keep it.

Donald was delighted with his new toy. Whenever his thoughts drifted to the television he experienced a frisson of excitement that ran through his entire body. It was similar to the feeling he used to have as a boy when, shut away upstairs in his room at the top of his parents' firm old house, he would drag voices out of the ether with the aid of a cat's whisker radio set that he had built himself inside an old cigar box from a kit that his father had given him one Christmas. He could smell the cracked perfume of the splintery wood right now, as if he had the box in front of him. The radio had been as magical an object to his childish mind as a flying carpet – being able to pull storm warnings, snatches of police reports, strains of music from out of the background static was like being able to swoop around the sky. Afterwards, he would lie in bed awake, his ear sore from the small plastic speaker, and try to comprehend how all these sounds managed to be everywhere at once. How was it that all of them were there, in the air around him, not just when he was tuning his set but when he was walking down the street or sitting in a classroom at school or eating dinner in silence with his mother watching him carefully to make sure he ate his boiled and tasteless vegetables right up, or else there would be no custard and no bread-and-butter pudding for dessert?

Now it was not just sounds but pictures which were everywhere. And this time their reach was not just the city of his childhood, the meagre range of the old antennae, but the world itself: New York, San Francisco, Tokyo, Shanghai, Saigon, New Delhi, Moscow, Tel Aviv, Rome, Berlin, Cape Town, London England.

Sputnik I had been above them for six years, bouncing frequencies back through space, and Sputnik II was up there somewhere too now, with Laika on board – and many more satellites were soon to follow. And the world had been divided into two: capitalism and communism yes, but also the places the cameras went and the places that they didn't, with the second category rapidly dwindling relative to the first as, propelled from its dignified black-and-white chrysalis by events like the Kennedy assassination, the media began to unfold its creaking new body and stretch its iridescent wings out to dry around the globe.

'It's the news I need it for, primarily,' Donald explained to Doreen in a calmer mode as they crunched the lobsters they had ordered. 'Now I'm a councillor, it's vital that I know what's going on and the papers just aren't enough any more.' The squeaky meat was delicately flavoured with heavy metal trace elements and oestrogen. Doreen waited for the qualifier and Donald splashed more of the icy Chablis into their tall glasses. 'Although, of course, one still needs them for depth of comment and so on; that's something the box will never replace. For real reporting one just has to have *The Times*. But when you need only the facts, and on the button, well, that's why we have to have a set. With a piece of film you can see for yourself. Don't need to take some other fellow's word for it. These journalist Johnnies can't mess with a picture, can they? What you see is what you get, story of the eye and all that. Not like the papers, or the radio, when you can never be quite sure. Even with *The Times*, yes even with *The Times* I'm sorry to say, it has been known to happen. That's what the world's coming to, I'm afraid.' Doreen scraped a gooey clutch of orange eggs away from her lobster's belly and lifted one up on a prong of her fork for closer inspection. Then she nodded agreement and popped the tiny egg into her mouth, not because she saw the situation Donald's way (it was, unfortunately, painfully obvious to her that he didn't know what he was talking about) but because she had already worked out that now Donald had got the damn thing he would probably spend less time pestering her and more time gazing into its flickering kaleidoscopic screen like the fascinated child he was.

I scry with my little eye

The first time she found Donald sitting alone in an armchair, lights off, transfixed by the television, Doreen had just returned from her weekly Women's Institute meeting. High, high above, beyond the clouds, Laika slowly orbited, on her way to Hollywood where a young Judd – just four years old – sat beneath the sky and stared earnestly into his own TV, flicking from channel to channel in the hope that rapid juxtapositions of these images which moved so fast would capture them, slow them down, make some sense of them. Sometimes he found it as impossible to remember what he had just watched on TV as he did the events which took place during one of his picnoleptic lapses, and this confused him. There seemed to be a link between the two experiences: although they weren't the same, he got the same feeling in the pit of his stomach when he thought about either of them.

Jennifer, on the other hand, didn't have a TV set. Three years older than Judd, at that time her entertainment consisted of charging round the streets of her estate on her new bike and meeting up with her friends to talk about Incredibly Important Things. Like a droplet of mercury she scooted from house to house, calling up at bedroom windows, shouting at people in the street, slipping secretly into garden sheds and the spaces behind garages. That evening, in fact, she had been cycling along the main road when she had nearly been run down by Doreen Buerk herself, who had too much on her mind to pay attention to other road users.

Drugs was the topic which occupied Doreen so. Her WI meeting had been graced by the presence of the local police inspector, who had come to speak to the assembled ladies about the threat to society posed by that particular evil menace. Doreen knew the inspector vaguely from the Conservative Association. He seemed very capable and was certainly very popular: thanks to his rugged good looks and army manner, seats at meetings at which he was scheduled to appear were always at a premium. On this occasion he had brought with him a small amount of cannabis resin, which he'd held between a pair of tweezers and heated with a lighter before walking around the room so that all those present should get to know the smell and be able to report it should they encounter it. Elspeth Peterson, who had been sitting near the front, got quite giggly, and Doreen remarked quietly to her neighbour, Agnes Batts, that that was typical of her, and Agnes remarked back that she was sure she had smelt that smell on several occasions when she had had for some reason to walk through the local council estate, and Doreen nodded and said sagely that she wasn't surprised, she'd known from the start that estate would be trouble.

When Doreen got home and found her husband silent and motionless in his study chair (she still would not allow the set in the living-room) she thought at first that he was asleep. It was only after she had put a pan of milk on the stove and come in to wake him that she discovered his eyes were wide open, dilated and unblinking. He was staring straight at the screen and its blue-grey shut-down flicker was reflected in their tacky glaze. Her first thought was that he was on drugs.

She shook him by the shoulder. 'Donald. Donald!' Thinking of the television, it struck her that what she had heard about the pernicious effects of the device might after all be true. She made her voice shrill and hard as a diamond drill, the same voice she used to control the boys at school. 'Don-ald!!!' It worked: Donald started out of his trance and seemed to ripple from head to toe.

'Oh. Oh. Hello, darling. Is that the time? Just watching a spot of telly.'

Doreen's fears evaporated and left behind a little precipitate of disapproval. 'Yes, well, perhaps you've been watching a little too much. You don't know when to stop, Donald Buerk. Come to bed. I've made you some hot milk.' Donald shrugged and walked over to the telly to switch it off. Then he followed Doreen upstairs to the room which contained their respective beds.

Donald's descent into this trance-like state was by no means an isolated occurrence, despite its being new to Doreen. This was the fourth or fifth time that he had slipped into resonant harmony with his television set. The previous weekend Doreen had gone to visit her parents in Cheltenham and her husband had been left to his own devices. He had spent the entire two days watching a single channel and sleeping fitfully in his chair between viewing sessions. It had been a fantastically uncritical experience: it made no difference to him whether he was watching a scheduled programme, the test card, or white noise. On his wife's return he avoided the set for a few days, resisting the temptation to switch the thing on, until one lunch-time he became inveigled into another cathode fascination by a set in the window of an electrical shop. The news was playing and the launch of the first of the Soviet Venera probes was being reported, although Donald couldn't hear what was being said. But he was fixated none the less and he stood there, stock still, while other pedestrians hurried by him until Mandy Davies, the shop-girl, whose chief worry for several years had been that her name had no 'Rice' in it (if it had, she thought, her life might have been a whole lot more exciting), emerged to check if he was all right.

'Would you like some help, sir?' Pause. 'Excuse me, sir, are you all right?' Pause again. 'Eh luv, what's the bother?' Donald started, rippled, flashed her a psychotic glance and shot off down the street.

Doreen didn't begin to get really concerned until she awoke in the middle of the night a few weeks later to find the bed beside her empty. 'Donald! *Donald!*' she hissed, but there was no reply, so she stomped downstairs in search of him (she was never much of a one for creeping). Once again, she found her husband in his study, slumped in front of a screen full of static. He looked pale, his face was silvery with beads of sweat, his features had the metallic sheen of blood-starved skin. The test signal filled the room like the sound from a flat-lining ECG. Doreen left him there and went back to bed, where she made the decision that from that moment on she would start to distance herself from this man. She would begin with her closest friends and see where it led. She'd drop hints that all was not well between them; nothing too specific, nothing to suggest that there was something wrong with his mind. Vague references to a physical inadequacy would probably do the trick.

Donald developed an illness, something indeterminate, which

led to him missing days from work. He began to spend the time at home, his movements restricted to a series of vectors, of energised channels. He seemed only able to move between the television, which was constantly on, the refrigerator, which had also begun to interest him, and the downstairs toilet, where he voided himself repeatedly and scrubbed his hands until they were pink. This pattern of behaviour, providing as it did for all his needs, might have gone on indefinitely but for Doreen's generally successful attempts to short-circuit it by making sure that there was, for example, nothing readily edible in the fridge, or no toilet paper in the loo. Remonstrating with him was useless; he had gone into decline extremely rapidly and already barely spoke at all. If he did, it was only to murmur, 'I'm not well, dear, can't you see, please don't take the cheese away from me again,' or some such thing, and whatever he said was voiced in such a sorry tone that rather than evoking pity in his wife it almost moved her to slash his throat. Then he stopped going in to work at all. Doreen had the doctor pay a housecall – Donald did not feel up to going to the hospital – but the man could find nothing physically the matter and prescribed amphetamines to perk him up.

Doreen had been feeling increasingly agitated herself, but it was not until she discovered that Donald had been powdering his pills and mixing them in with the sugar (which she had been heaping liberally into her tea) that she finally came to the end of her tether. 'NO MORE NO MORE NO MORE!!!!' she screamed, her face right up against his, and with the strength that supposedly visits women in times of terrible danger (as when their child is trapped beneath a ten-ton truck) Doreen picked up the television and carried it up the stairs into the attic, trailing cables behind her as she went. If it hadn't been for the fact that the neighbours would talk she would have thrown it from the window and into the street.

When she returned, she found Donald stretched out on the floor in a hebephrenic state. He was barely breathing, his eyes were open and his body was all strange angles. The last thing he had seen on the screen was the head of a small brown-and-white mongrel dog. The newscaster had said that today was the tenth

71

anniversary of the 'muttnik' Laika's trip into space. For the first time in human history, he said, Soviet scientists had managed to put a live animal into orbit. But, he said, his brow furrowed with irony and his lips twitching at their edges in a patronising manner, they had neglected to work out how to get it back. The cause of Laika's death had never been made public by the Soviets, he continued cheerily. Was she terminated by lethal injection? Did she run out of air and suffocate? Did she simply burn up in the atmosphere? Perhaps we'll never know. Then he spoke for a while about other dogs that had been sent into space since: Belka and Strelka, for example, and Pchelka and Mushka. Pchelka and Mushka had burned up on re-entry, but Belka and Strelka had returned to earth in good health. Indeed, Strelka had had a litter of puppies on her return, one of which was given to President John F. Kennedy as a gesture of good will from the USSR. 'Unfortunately,' said the newscaster, 'it was discovered around the time of the Cuban missile crisis that the puppy had an electronic bug concealed in its skull. In politics, you should probably always look a gift horse – or gift dog – in the mouth,' he said. 'Laika means "barker" in Russian,' he said.

When Donald saw Laika on the screen he knew she was looking at him. There was something calm in those eyes, something incredibly knowing. In those eyes, Donald knew, he had seen God – or something similar. And then he collapsed and Doreen finally had the excuse that she needed. Immediately she telephoned Hatton Central for the doctors who would come and take her husband away.

3

Inferno

Was Joel born a mathematician, or did the seed of mathematics take root in his mind at an early age and flourish like a bramble in the sheltered woodland of the Williamsburg Hasidic community? Did he come into this world already prodigiously equipped, or was his ability engendered by some freak of circumstance, sunned and watered perhaps by the incessant rote learning of religious texts that was required of all the boys, the probe heads and radicles squirming through his mind until they compacted all of his experience into the infinite horizon of unforgiving compartments that is logic? Neither, of course, and yet both; there is no law of the excluded middle, no either–or, in biology. Rather a tendency existed, a string of singularities was followed, ability resulted just as pot-holes and caverns result from water eroding its way through the fault lines in some buckled hunk of limestone, just as a silver mine results from a group of dwarves following an unwinding skein of ore.

His encounter with the wider mathematical community came as something of a shock to Joel. Until that day in the Brooklyn library he had never even seen a conventional '+' sign. At the Yeshiva, the addition function had been represented by a horizontal line with one perpendicular vertical sprouting from the uppermost side alone. The boys were forbidden to write or even look at the sign of the cross (it was a punishable misdemeanour in the school to cross your 't's without first curling up the foot) and it had taken Joel a few moments to realise what the new symbol was.

73

Millstein had to replace the private systems of abstract signs Joel had developed with those more universally recognised, whether or not they conformed more fully to criteria such as logical consistency or ease of use. He had to teach him to use the Greek alphabet for algebra rather than the Hebrew, and he had to demonstrate to him that many of the spaces and phenomena he had explored had been thoroughly charted before, often from several different perspectives.

Once he had schooled Joel in the appropriate idioms and introduced him to the world at large, there was little Millstein could actually teach him. Like the young Stradivarius, the pupil outstripped the teacher by such lengths that at their weekly sessions Millstein felt more like a helmsman desperately trying to keep a wind-driven schooner on course than a teacher, although he consoled himself with the thought that this was probably the best kind of teaching of all. He set Joel problems, tasks, tests and calculations, maintaining as rigorous a programme as he thought fair, but still he had the suspicion that it was all little more than hack work for the boy and that Joel's real interest lay in material which he kept hidden from Millstein. His hunch was right: precocious Joel had decided that he had bigger fish to fry and had struck up a correspondence with the Cambridge-based editor of one of the academic journals that Millstein had introduced him to, a certain Professor Metric.

Millstein had spent a year at Cambridge himself, as part of an exchange programme, and often told Joel stories about the famous university. He loved stories even more than he loved mathematics and would slip freely between tales of his own student days and anecdotes of the great mathematical philosophers who had taught there. Men like Bertrand Russell and A. J. Ayer, both of whom Millstein had met on several occasions and whom he described in vivid detail, lauding their achievements, idolising them. He talked of Whitehead, Wittgenstein, Moore as if he had known them too, and he also pointed out for Joel's benefit similarities between the work of the logical positivists and some of the ideas of Jewish dogma. Joel absorbed it all but haphazardly, and the more confused the oddments of information became the more fascinated he was by them. He had never paid much heed to the world that existed beyond the crumbling confines of Brooklyn but now he began to weave for himself a thoroughly mystical picture of the town of Cambridge and its ancient university as a kind of intellectual promised land where mathematics was the preferred form of discourse and scholars wandered as freely among the branches of thought as they did beneath the arches and cloisters of the time-worn colleges.

So he sent this professor one of his proofs. Metric, receiving a letter from what he assumed to be an American post-graduate student, was initially tempted to dismiss it – he regarded himself as a very busy man – but something about the maths caught his attention. Although deeply faulted, the proof demonstrated a certain flair, an originality of approach. There was something quite beautiful about it, in a way. He corrected a couple of minor errors and sent the paper back, suggesting one or two possible new approaches. But he kept his best insight to himself and over the next few weeks picked away at Joel's central idea. Finally he perfected the proof, managing at the same time to retain something of the style and yet insert into it aspects of his own, and he sent it away for publication in a rival journal, a broadside in an academic battle in which he had been embroiled for several years.

Joel didn't see Metric's paper and, encouraged by the response, sent other work. Gradually a fairly regular correspondence developed, fuelled on the one hand by Joel's enthusiasm and on the other by Metric's increasing reliance upon the flow of these fresh and quirky ideas as a prop for his flagging career.

Around this time, Joel began to argue with his parents and teachers. Suddenly everyone in a position of authority seemed like a fool. Williamsburg became a ghetto, a holding bin, and the Sodom walls which surrounded him – those giant needles which had torn at the clouds of every sky of his life – began to lose their spiky inhospitality and beckon him. Less and less able to endure the rituals and garbs and stratifications of his home and his school, and of the community and culture with which they were so thoroughly interwoven, his thoughts turned towards Manhattan. Concomitantly he lost his taste for Yiddish and Hebrew (he conversed with both Millstein and Metric in English and algebra, and these were now the most important relationships in his life) and the long sessions of religious teaching became at first a pretence and then a complete charade. His hand played host too often to the short block of wood that the rotund duty rabbi carried with him as he patrolled the corridors of the school, sweating and wheezing and alternating between the roles of avuncular protector and strict disciplinarian. But despite the man's best efforts on both fronts, Joel took no notice and soon became the bane of both school and household. In the latter his mother overcame her reluctance to chastise him, secretly her favourite, and now her voice broke glasses vases mirrors as she shrieked and yelled: 'Chas vesholem my son should be like this, an apikoros!' Moshe would sit and nod: 'Respect your mother, Joel, respect, you must learn respect,' then he'd go back to nibbling on his latke and thinking of Joel's bris, his circumcision ceremony, remembering that night of fear and visions, wondering if it was right to chastise his own son, Joel Balaam Kluge, this son who seemed at once both chacham and dybbuk, both wise man and evil spirit. Perhaps Moshe was even a little afraid. Judith would go on and on, eventually diverting her anger with her son towards her husband, where it would combine with his fear and react into violence. Then Moshe would take his belt to the boy and try to beat the goyim nonsense out of him, though with little enthusiasm.

Joel's three elder sisters began to shun him and his brothers exploited their parents' anger and picked on him, even though they were both smaller and younger. Even the twins seemed to dislike him now. He began to feel that his dead sister, who would have been closer to him in age than anyone else in the family had she lived, was the only one who understood. He took to visiting her grave alone, tending it with flowers and talking to her. The vast graveyard was a special place for him; the endless and exact rows of pale headstones dissected the landscape into discrete chunks and reduced everything to similarity and repetition, and this he found comforting. They were miniatures, too, of the buildings on the ever present skyline, and Joel felt that this resonance was somehow important, that it gave a clue to the correlation between the world of the living and the world of the dead. But for all his talking and praying, his sister never answered and the only reply came from the city which lay suspended from the metal clouds, over there beyond the trees, and as he learnt the meaning of alienation and found it fitted well with the way he felt when he stepped inside his vaulted inner space he became more and more tempted to give in to the subliminal siren pulse of Manhattan. Eventually he did – one night he snuck out alone and let the subway carry him across the East River and on to the uncharted island beyond. And so he exchanged his trips to Queens for illicit forays to that great gobbet of phlegm poised behind the river's parted lips.

The air in the carriage is already stale when he boards, and by the time they get to York it's been gathered, recycled and shared again, and the smell of it makes him want to hold his nose. Then the train begins to rise and suddenly Joel's out above the river, held high up in the swampy shades of a dark winter afternoon, and at his elbow some old man gasps *Dis great Manhattoe it reveal itself at night*. Joel looks around: the lights pick out the city, those illuminated highways curling round, the hawsers dimly lit and pylons, rust-brown, strung lacy high, and a zorby glow from these thousand fires picks out the clouds. Battlements and towers pass in and out of view, blazing like braziers on cold street corners, deep and ozone orange the smog that lopes above them, char grey the silos, the cooling towers. Supertankers churn, feeding from the wretched water, next to vessels cracked upon the rim, awaiting condemnation . . . spires rend the heavy fog, poison seeps out through the slits . . . people swarm about the streets like flies on open wounds . . . apartment blocks sag like wasted muscles, warehouses bulge like blisters, gleaming Citicorp is a lancing needle, towers of Moloch . . . Joel looks far to the south, far to the north, across infested wetlands, iron plains, gulching plumes of flame . . . all the way to the compressed horizons the views are cluttered with industrial bric-à-brac and cranes and el lines hung with coloured lights.

At first he couldn't bear the thought of coming to the surface, breathing in the island's foetid air, so he stayed in the subway tunnels and crept beneath the skyscrapers, doing the D-train yo-yo. But little by little he found the courage to disembark, to stand around on the platform for a while, checking out commuters and feeling conspicuous in his long black coat, fiddling with a payot. Gingerly he made his way beneath the soul-reading stare of the attendant, then along the dank corridors and up the concrete stairway step by reeking step.

Finally, he pops up. Broadway splits and races to the north, trammelling the log flow traffic between steep and craggy banks. This is what he came for – Empire State pins down the place. No need for hillside watch fires here: his eyes carry the night, and the flotsam trees are torched with Christmas lights. And once he's done it, he has to do it again, has to stand for a few moments on Fifth Avenue, take a quick walk around Grand Central Station, wander down Wall Street or through the West Village, suck tentatively at the tawdry, quilted air, before disappearing back into his burrow.

Back on the platform he'd take the first train that came and repeat the process over. As his fear diminished and his nerve grew, he ventured further and higher. He took tourist trips up the Empire State and marvelled at its height. The view from the top was exhilarating and terrifying and utterly demonic. It was like daring G*d, it was like screaming an insane challenge to the skies, *I can see how it works, I can see what it looks like to you! The only difference between you and me is that you've got the equations!* For the first time he saw with his own eyes what he had always sensed to be true: that people were just like the ants and roaches which streamed through the apartment in the summer, trapped in patterns, exercises and regimes much larger than they could ever imagine. The sheer audacity of whoever had built these towers took his breath away. And it wasn't only the heavens they'd taken on, but the depths too – he thought of the skyscrapers now, reaching down and burrowing into Manhattan's meat for the human nutrients which would course as sap through the radicles of underground car-parks and up the nervures of elevators to push the brick and metal stalks leaves blooms higher ever higher. And the subways fed this Babel city, put wind into its pipes, stoked its fires, fuelled its engines, peopled its streets, crammed its nurseries, packed its apartments, tamped its office blocks, jammed its automobiles, nourished its greed, nurtured its contempt, pampered its criminals, barrelled its trash, incubated its pretension, guided its growth, constricted its vision, multiplied its tongues, publicised its disharmony, regurgitated its victuals, encouraged its poisons, drove it drove it drove it drove it on, drove it on till on its own air it would choke.

Thus Joel discovered the city. It was his first machine. He discovered the vast libraries and the bookshops, the halls of the universities, the nomad odours of the trayf food emporiums and fast-food joints. He discovered that the clothes he wore could make him either invisible or the centre of attention. Sometimes it was as though whatever he did he just wasn't there – he could bend down and touch his toes in the street or swing round a lamp-post or hop up and down the cathedral steps and no one would even react; other times, though, someone would mutter 'Fuckin' Yid!' right out of the blue, or a rich woman would yank her curious lapdog up and away from his trouser cuffs, or a workman idling against a building would spit on the hem of his coat without altering the middle-distance gaze of his eyes or breaking the rhythm with which he chewed his gum. But despite all this there was not the continual paranoia with which he had lived since birth, there was not the bubbling fear of the Crown Heights Blacks who were the Satmars' neighbours and supposed enemies, no matter that the number of 'incidents' between them were few. And one time on the elevated line that brings you back into Williamsburg it struck Joel, as he looked down on the rotting buildings and pot-holed streets that made up his neighbourhood, that the two communities which shared this desolate patch of real estate were pretty similarly shaped pieces of the jigsaw puzzle that was the city's social meshwork. How convenient it no doubt was for the people on the other side of the bridge that they should hate each other, and how much harder it made it for people like him ever to get out.

The women amazed him. Satmar boys are forbidden to look at any women other than their mothers and their sisters. Since even the sketchy pictures of little girls in the primers that were handed out in the English class by the one Gentile teacher in the school had all been heavily censored with the same black marker pen, the acres of flesh that were revealed in the streets now that it was

79

summer bemused and amazed him. His attention would be captured by long, thin, tan legs disappearing up miniskirts, by bare arms in the sun, by pale skin and fine features and rolls of startled flab peeping out into the daylight like grotesque tubers pushing back top soil. He would be fixated by bright eyes and white teeth and silk-screened expressions and buttocks sagging or pert, and by faces daubed with make-up – something garish and bewildering to Joel for whom its purpose was frightening and obscure.

It was all fun and fascination, until he wandered into Times Square one day and found it all for sale, men and women in doorways, so plastic, blank and bright they hurt his eyes. They beckoned him and he did not understand and wandered on until three whores standing in a group around a hydrant began to tease him. 'Aw, gee, it's a little schmuck. C'mon over here honey. Want some honey? Get some honey, we'll give you some honey.' Joel stood still and blinked before them.

They were bored. One of them sauntered over and took him by the hand, led him to meet the others. 'This is Lindy, this is Amy. Say hi, girls.'

'Hi.'

'Howdy.'

'And what's your name, young man?' She spoke with a soupy drawl and while Joel was thinking about her question she pushed the hand which she was still holding up inside her leather skirt. At the same time Amy reached over and grabbed Joel's balls. Then: a flood of blood to his virgin member, a soft forgiving warmth between her legs and tangled hairs, a cold pain as she squeezed, a strange mucus that stained his fingers with a smell that he could not remove no matter how much he later rubbed with his saliva-wetted handkerchief. And the lights and the buildings with their hoardings and the reflections and the dissonances in the soft drug faces leering all around swam together, a hot rush of sweat and nerves and lava as the city plugged itself into the negative terminal of his scrotum and the positive terminal of his hand.

And then he was running, running from the laughter of the women towards the subway entrance far off in the crepuscular night. And as if to confirm that he did not belong, a shadow stepped from a doorway and took him by the throat, shook him down, took all his money, what little of it there was, and knocked his head against the filthy wall. He did not cry or move until it was gone, but when he found his broken spectacles he began to blub in deep deep spasms, the tears running down his cheeks and through the nap of fluff that was his beard, then either off on to the sidewalk or down inside his collar, depending on their velocity and mass when they reached the angle of his jaw.

With his fare gone, Joel had to walk. All the way to Williamsburg, half blind and fully decided. It was time to get out.

It came from Outer Space

It's 18 March 1965 by the time Joel makes it back across the bridge. And if we spiral up above his head to where the sky gives way we'll find a spaceship there, Voskshod 2, circling the earth. It looks real still, but it's moving fast, shovelling shit round the planet like you wouldn't believe. Dangling from it, his arms and legs sticking out at strange angles, is Cosmonaut Vsevolod Leonov, who's been told 'it's time to leave the capsu-elle if you dair-air-air' (in Russian) and has taken up the challenge. It's the world's first space walk, though to be fair, 'walk' is not really the right word, 'float' would do better, but what the hell, this is space after all and the normal rules don't apply here.

Which is lucky for Laika, who's coming out of the sun towards the Soviet craft, trying to manipulate a large syringe and inject her leg full of Phenergan; yup, she's doing her own experiments now, trying to combat space sickness, beating back the boundaries of science. Our plucky little pooch is concentrating hard on staying alive and she's succeeding – her eighth year up here has just begun and that much weightlessness isn't too good for the system. Anaemia, falling blood pressure, reduced capacity of muscles to burn fat for energy, declining baroreflexes, cramp, increased levels of toxicity in the blood, and that's just the least of it – not much Laika can do. Stress is a killer too, remember, she mustn't get stressed now, got to keep calm, sit back and watch the world on TV, take some exercise whenever she can (increasingly hard, now that she's almost entirely filled the cabin with her bulk – unable to burn off fat she's kept it all, rolls and rolls of it).

So it is that on 18 March she's thinking of her health and not paying too much attention to what's going on outside, when suddenly through her little porthole she spies something glinting in the light ... it's a rocket, it is, and that, that's a man! She recognises the insignia on the helmet. Company at last! She drifts alongside, barking madly. Vsevolod doesn't see her at first, she's not quite what he expects, it's only when he waves to his pal back in the ship, creates a photo opportunity, that he figures something's wrong. Vladimir's mouth is open and his camera's floating in the air beside his head. What's he looking at? Vsevolod grips the umbilical hose and swings himself round ... stares straight into the face of muttnik, who's grinning ear to ear, hot dog fat dog, furry face in round porthole, zinc capsule. Woof woof.

Vsevolod freaks, scrambles for the hatch, Vladimir recovers his wits, tries to get off some snaps, but Sputnik II's already spinning to face the earth above and Laika's mug disappears from view. It's over. The satellite wanders off.

Vsevolod gets back inside. 'Did ... did you see what I saw?'

'I ... I think so comrade, but I can't be sure.'

'A dog, right, it was a fucking dog! That looked like Sputnik II to me.'

'No, couldn't have been. Sputnik II? Burnt up years ago. And yeh, it looked like a dog, but it couldn't have been one. Trick of the light.'

'D'you get pictures? Did you?'

'Er, no, it was happening too fast.'

'Too fast? Too fast! That thing was out there for a whole god-damn minute! Why the fuck didn't you get pictures ...'

'I, I ...'

Their argument goes on a while, which is just as well because they don't switch on the radio and so don't hear Laika's broadcast, a little soliloquy of yelps and howls that goes on till she's shielded from them by the earth.

Do they tell Ground Control? Do they hell. Some things are better left unsaid. The space walk went without a hitch, all right?

Family politics

After the incident with the three prostitutes Joel's trips to Manhattan tapered off, and Cambridge took its place as the centrepiece of his fantasies and dreams. But with the transition Joel's behaviour became worse and worse, so bad indeed that the UTA declared he was too disruptive to remain in the school. At his wit's end, Moshe called up his oldest brother, Gershom, for advice. Gershom owned three small restaurants in the area and told Moshe to meet him at his kosher pizza house after closing one night. The two men sat down among the vacant tables and up-ended chairs to talk until they had found a solution to the problem.

'We could send him up to Canada,' Gershom suggested. 'I remember how envious Joel was when Shimon came back last summer with all his tales. And he was born there, too. Maybe he belongs there. He could stay with Zevi and Elisabeth.'

'Chas vesholem! They are farmers, they would work him into the ground. He is not strong, it would kill him, everything with Joel is up here.' He tapped his head with his fingers.

'But Moshe, perhaps that is what he needs. The boy never takes any exercise, he is as thin as a rake. If it wasn't for Judith's cooking he would have wasted away years ago. The open air might do him good.'

'No, you forget that after everything he is my son, not some mamzer orphan we are trying to parcel away out of sight.'

'Yes, but you must do something. It has been going on too long. The school are going to expel him. I have spoken to the rebs and melameds myself, there is nothing they can do with him any more. He is making it impossible for all the other boys.'

'He can help me in the bakery. He can do the accounts.'

'Moshe, you are crazy! How long would that take him? One hour a week if that? And the rest of the time what will he do? There's no room in there for him to help you bake. Within a month he'll be driving you crazy and you'll want him out of your sight, and he'll be walking the streets again and nothing will have changed.'

Moshe lost his temper. 'Well, what do you want me to do then?'

'Relax, relax will you. We are all trying to help, Joel is very dear to us all. We only want the best for him.' Moshe sighed a heavy sigh, a sign of defeat. 'Okay, okay,' snapped Gershom, giving in to the idea he'd had all along, 'he can come and work for me here. How does that sound? I'll start him off out front, waiting tables. He can help with the accounts and I'll teach him the business at the same time. And if things work out maybe he could help me run a new place I want to open up.'

Moshe brightened, then quickly tried to look doubtful. 'That's . . . I don't know if . . .'

'This is the best I can do. But I'm telling you now Moshe if the boy doesn't shape up we're sending him to Canada – and that's the end of it.'

So in 1965, around the time that the PDP–8 – the first computer to use integrated circuits – went on sale, Joel left the Yeshiva to work in one of Gershom's restaurants, keeping the books and cleaning the floors and waiting on tables. Moshe had told him, perhaps unwisely, of the threat to send him away to work on the farm if he didn't behave and the threat was a real one: Joel knew full well that the isolation he felt in New York was nothing compared with the loneliness he'd feel up there. At least here he had Millstein and the libraries. So he knuckled under, learnt how to conceal his feelings, became a golden boy again, though it was harder now because everyone was on their guard against him. And at night, while he lay awake between his sleeping brothers, he no longer surfed his infinite mathematical vistas. Not at all. Now, using as raw data the potted biographies on the fly pages of his books and Millstein's stories and a few old photographs he had found in the library, he constructed an image of Cambridge behind the sparkling black lids of his eyes.

With a resignation devoid of melodrama this empty vessel was slowly being filled with dreams and wishes and hopes, this tabula rasa was being scribbled upon, and Joel began to mature. But it seemed that the tablet was cracked, the machine malfunctioning. His mind had always been a store-and-forward network: information was broken down on entry, routed around his brain and reassembled at its destination. Packet switching it was called (Donald Davies coined the term that year). But now the restaurant filled his time, kept him busy with menial tasks that weren't challenging enough to interest him and yet prevented him from indulging in the mental number play with which he'd filled his time at school. Furious at this and feeling threatened by the dread prospect of Canada and what he saw as a family plot against him, Joel had nothing to contemplate all day except his anger and, with no outlet for this, the information in his brain was put into endless circulation. The constant reiterations made him bitter. He learnt dissimulation and deceit, to despise his parents and his culture. He learnt how to twitch out glances when others were off-guard, how to sum them up in terms of their usefulness to him, how to use them or avoid them. Millstein was the only one really to chart this transformation, noting quietly to himself that his perfect pupil, his little Pinocchio, was growing up – although in Joel's case the nose remained the same while downcast eyes replaced the clear, absorbent man-child gaze, a rash of acne and seeping scars replaced the unblemished pre-pubescent skin and a rangy stoop replaced the old automaton glide as an increasingly beanpole body tried to convince itself and those around it that it was still short and perfectly proportioned.

Joel soon sensed that Millstein was the only one to see through him, and he initiated a series of pilpul – or hair-splitting arguments – in order to have an excuse to break off the lessons. He would niggle with his tutor over trivia such as the definition of terms and although he was to discover much later that these dogmatic rows were in fact the first tears in the hitherto seamless fabric of his mathematics, for the time being they served their purpose. But like tiny mouths, purple-lipped and silent, they would remain among the curtains of his mind until the time came for them to open and help Joel scream his final scream.

The disagreements, initially analytic, became increasingly personal until one winter's day, when the snow on the sidewalks had been crushed by passing feet into a single thick cake of crisp ice which filled the neighbourhood streets like a gridlocked glacier, Joel ended up yelling that Millstein was a blind fool, that he had nothing to teach him. Then he walked out of his tutor's apartment, never to return.

He had chosen a bad moment to leave because outside the wind was blowing with all the ferocity that a New York winter can muster. It had started to snow again, too, and blinded by the driven flakes, Joel slipped off an icy kerbstone into a deep puddle of slush that instantly soaked his shoes right through. His feet froze and trudging home he would have cried, except that the wind froze the tears in their ducts and he discovered then that sometimes you cannot piss your emotions away, however much you may want to. And this made him even more determined than ever.

All the while he had been repairing relations with his family and destroying those with Millstein, he had been communicating with Metric. With the increasing resourcefulness that characterised his growing alienation, Joel did not have Metric's letters sent directly to his home but to a mailbox address. In addition to what he was being paid by Gershom, most of which went straight into the family account, he was earning a little money on the side by doing the prize puzzles in the newspapers. The puzzle pages were not considered to be culturally dangerous and no one knew that he sent his answers away, or indeed that he scavenged puzzles from other newspapers which he found left on seats in the subway or stuffed into dustbins or bundled into piles by the vending machines and newsagents' shops. Once a week he would visit the mailbox and pick up any correspondence. Any cheques – from time to time he won quite substantial amounts – he would take to the bank and convert into cash, which he would then secrete inside his mattress.

As his funds grew, so did his plans. His regular exchanges with Metric impressed the professor so much that when Joel insisted that he be allowed to sit the Cambridge entrance exam by mail Metric was delighted, although he vacillated for the sake of good form and so as not to give the boy too many big ideas.

Joel broke the Sabbath in order to take the exam, a consciously symbolic action. He was at home with his family as usual; it was now the only day of the week when he was likely to see all of them at once. Feigning illness, he spent the day in his bedroom and while the family sat around at the other end of the apartment he had four or five uninterrupted hours in which to complete the papers.

But this was only the first hurdle; if Metric hadn't been so desperate to have him attend he would never have succeeded in getting to Cambridge. He also had to lie elaborately about his background, pretending that he was an orphan so that the university would not demand that his parents ratify his decisions. He also had to persuade the professor that he needed a full bursary; he had to organise a passport, to purchase a plane ticket and, most complicated of all, he had to work out a way to extricate himself from his family.

It was clear to Joel that his parents would only ever agree to him leaving the community if it was to go and live with Zevi and Elisabeth in Canada. To begin with he considered becoming a 'problem teenager' again, getting himself relocated to Montreal, then disappearing at the earliest opportunity. It shouldn't be too difficult to get on the wrong plane at the airport, something like that. But on no account did he want his family to know that he had betrayed them and this made the Canada plan problematic. Zevi would contact his father as soon as Joel failed to arrive, and they would worry and suspect and search for him. He didn't want to hurt them and the thought of his mother hysterical with anxiety did not appeal. Still, he looked into the possibility, just in case. So many airplane tickets were issued, he thought, that they couldn't keep track of them all. If there was a system, there'd be a way to fool it. Wouldn't there?

Unfortunately for Joel, by this time the airlines had figured this out themselves and, as we already know, had asked IBM to do something about it. The scale of the problem was enormous. By the early fifties the traffic scheduling of American Airlines flights was already reaching crisis point. The availability boards of the original manual reservations system had become so large and so crammed with information that the growing crowds of reservations clerks had to use binoculars to see the details displayed on them. The system needed to be updated and it was – using electromechanical technology, the boards were replaced with terminals. The new system was called the Reservisor.

But although the Reservisor could cope with two hundred extra flights a year, it was really just an automated relay sitting on top of what remained essentially a manual system. Passenger and reservation records still had to be updated by hand and so many flights were wrongly booked that at busy times businessmen would make double reservations to guarantee a ticket. By 1952 AA was planning a new 30,000-square-foot manual reservations office that could accommodate 362 clerks who between them would be able to take 45,000 telephone calls a day. But even this would not be enough, because the company was not just struggling to cope with rising demand – it was also trying to cope with the ever increasing speed of passenger aircraft. Boeing had just introduced the 707 model and AA had ordered thirty of them. These planes could fly across the nation in just six hours instead of ten – faster than the reservations system could transmit information about a flight. Information space was now less navigable than physical space. This was no way to run a business.

IBM's solution, SABRE, had the biggest storage capacity of any system ever assembled until that time. It ran on two IBM 7090s and had a price tag of forty million dollars. Networked to 1100 agents in fifty cities over 10,000 miles of telephone lines, it was a monster, a data behemoth. It could handle ten million reservations a year and turn each one over in three seconds, as well as integrate passenger details with flight scheduling, fuel management, in-flight catering, toilet cleaning, aircraft maintenance, sexual intrigues between members of the cabin crew and the official records of the Mile High Club. It went online in 1964.

SABRE was the final nail in the coffin for Joel's Canada plan. Although its predecessor, SAGE, was still top secret, there were plenty of newspaper articles about the commercial spin-off, and while SABRE's data integration capabilities scotched any ideas he might have had of changing planes at the airport, this was more than compensated for by the knowledge that when he did book his ticket to England, some time soon, his name would go into this giant system, *his* name, and would become electrons and fields and would whirl around the country like a particle, like a wave, would be everywhere at once. Clicking and triggering, disappearing and appearing, his name would be a harbinger of some new American dream. Just imagine, he thought, just imagine, and imagine he did, nights in his bed, his brothers gently snoring beside him, SABRE like a quilt of stars laid upon the nation, blinking and thinking – and Joel a part of it, like a comet and gravity both, his presence there unique and yet part of forces, statistics, habits and shapes. Unique and absorbed. The idea excited him like no other, it made his heart race and his belly flush, made him project lines of desire across the future, across the world; it brought aircraft and thought and flesh together, a jabbering mass, a squealing infiltration, a testicular growth. Many nights like this: the curtains apart, his hands on his groin, hot there, warm, softly sweating his own dear musk, the Milky Way a cosmic computer curved above his head.

After much consideration Joel came to the quite rational conclusion that it would be better and simpler for all concerned if he were dead. It was the first human problem he'd worked through to a solution and when the answer came to him he felt as though he'd finally come of age. Family honour would be retained, his parents' grief would be harsh but short. The plan was straightforward, elegant, beautiful. He had no place here in any case. His home was elsewhere. But there was an emotional element, too, though Joel didn't give it much weight. The notion of in some way joining his beloved dead sister tugged strongly at his heart.

So one September night, eight months after he had stormed out on Millstein, when the fall was coming on like a rash and the trees were scabbed with mildew and the clotted flakes of their leaves clogged the drains and culverts of the city, Joel crept past his sleeping brothers and inched his way out of the apartment. He was so numbed with fear and apprehension that it threw his perceptions out of joint, so much so that when he clicked back the latch of the front door and made his way down the creaking stairway and out into the street everything seemed utterly normal, as if to leave your whole world in the depths of the night and set out across the planet was the most ordinary thing in the world. With a small satchel of books slung from his right shoulder and a canvas bag clutched in his left hand he set off down the street in the direction of the Williamsburg bridge, a small figure drifting down the night city's stellar lanes of light.

The bridge led out into the dark like an axon. He made his way across it until he was nearly half-way and then stopped. He seemed to breathe only the air that rushed down from the north along the tarry waterway. The wind plucked at his hair and lodged particles among it, the low bytes of America that did not come with the settlers but which aeons ago descended with the earth's crust into the caesura that is the Great Lakes. The low bytes which lay there on some submerged shore bound fast to others like them, one tip of a horseshoe pattern, imprint of some ancient stress. The low bytes, loosened by a millennium's worth of freezings and thawings of the great ice sheets that lie virtual across the surface of the waters, drifting upwards in suspended solution, carried by the convection currents set up by the action of the sun upon the lakes and later picked up by the wind.

Joel, himself not much more than an upright puddle of Hudson brew, looked down at the yarmulke in his hand. Inside the crown his name had been sewn with tiny white tacking stitches, *Joel Balaam Kluge*, his mother's work. He placed the cap on the metal grid on which he stood, a smudge on the perfect segments the bars made of the void below. Then he leant out over the rail and gazed at the night which filled the space between the safety lights and the glinting surfaces of the water, remembering his forays on the train. Removing his scarf, he threw it back beneath him so that it caught upon a girder and hung there, limpid and vain. Then he emptied out the canvas bag, selected from its contents two exercise books, a shirt, a pair of worn shoes and a puzzle game that his father had given him two years previously for winning a school prize, and one by one flung all these things out into space, waiting after each for the splash that never came. Far below, they floated on the surface of the river, revolving round each other in a strange and plastic configuration, feeding off the velocity of the water and odd ribbons of breeze. So powered, these elements hung together in a habitus which bound the heterogeneous possibilities that would be put into play by Joel's disappearance and channelled them into a synthesis, a coherence, an explanation. For these objects that spiralled down the East River formed an engine, an engine with a double task: both that of giving impetus to the story of Joel's suicide and that of propelling Joel himself into the new life that he so longed for. Well designed, the pattern slipped away beneath the bridge and out towards the open sea, one eddy among many in a flat and turbulent cosmos.

Having left these tracks leading away into oblivion, Joel transferred some of the contents of his satchel into the canvas bag and hurried back towards Brooklyn, taking care that no one had seen him. He slipped through the streets for eight or nine blocks, a crazy Artaud lost on a midnight set, then hailed a Yellow Cab and told the driver to take him to John F. Kennedy airport, to JFK, where he would take the plane which he imagined would place him on a perfect vector, one which would pass through Cambridge and keep him for the rest of his life in an abyss of infinities, never needing to descend to earth again, like some Buddha who in his self-contemplation awaits the day that being will be sufficiently perfect for him to descend to it and slip inside.

Flying in (1)

Metric sat in his study and sweated, a memo concerning the college policy on long hair on the desk in front of him. He was worried: Kings had just appointed a new mathematics fellow, a chap called Jenson. Jenson was only thirty-eight, inconceivably young for the post. He was well enough known for his work on infinite sets and although privately Metric considered his successes to have been flukes it nevertheless introduced an uncomfortable precedent and he needed to check he had his forces around him in readiness for the year's first meeting of the Mathematics Society in Second Week. First thing was to get a note to Harping and Trenton, have them over for sherry on Tuesday and tell them he was going to organise a special meeting of the Society to welcome Jenson into the fold. That way he could pump them for whatever they knew. Who stood where on this one, that was the key thing, to ascertain who stood where.

He had lunched in hall, had had the beef, felt a little bloated. Wished he hadn't now – he hadn't seen the morning paper until he had made it to the Senior Common Room for a post-prandial and then his eye immediately fell upon an article reporting the increased dairy yields British farmers were achieving thanks to the now widespread practices of spreading sheep offal on grazing fields and feeding their animals a baked meat and bone meal made from cow carcasses. Disgusting, thought Metric, the very idea, but then, what did you expect from farmers? The report turned his stomach and lined his mouth with the metallic film that presages bile and he had need of a healthier snifter than usual to set it right. Damn college brandy, gave him heartburn, must have a word with the Dean. Then back to his rooms, a couple of hours until his lecture, no students that afternoon. Settled into his leather swivel chair, a little sleepy after the booze, he closed his eyes for forty winks. Why not?

Joel, stung awake by the brightness of the morning, looked out of the window at the sun rising high above New York. The city was a blob of molten solder oozing out along the sink lines of the

Hudson, the Harlem and the East. By putting his finger in the appropriate spot on the plastic pane he could blot Williamsburg entirely from view. *Here gone, here gone, here gone . . .* he played a child's game and built his independence. His entire world was only this, to be brought in and out of view at will. Then the plane disappeared into the clouds and he was not at all sure what had happened. For a few moments he watched a bemused mosquito caught between the triple screens of Perspex. But a patch of turbulence rattled the plane, and sudden pressure differentials constricted his sinuses and he gripped the seat arms with both hands. It felt as if someone were poking hot needles up inside his brain. He began to cry out loud, a long, dim wail, vaguely aware that what he had done was sin and what was happening now was punishment. Perhaps he was already dead? A steward rushed towards him down the aisle and reached the boy just in time to watch him snatch the Homburg from his head and fill it with a lazy vomit.

As the aircraft reached cruising altitude and levelled out the steward helped Joel from his seat. 'C'mon, son, let's get you cleaned up.' The responses of the other passengers ranged from clicks and tuts of sympathy for the pale-faced boy to a thinly veiled hatred of the disturbance he was causing, a hatred that blended with a mistrust of the clothing he wore and the cut of his hair. Although his yarmulke was back on the bridge, he still wore his black suit and white shirt. His hair was shaved short, a thin pubescent beard squirmed around his jaw and two long silky curls ran down from his ears like dribbles of music. His hat was warm from the puke which slopped inside and he carried it in cupped hands as he was led up the aisle.

Two stewardesses came up and fussed over him, taking his refusal to look on their faces as shyness. The experience of the airport and the flight had reduced Joel, for all his precocity, back into the child he was perceived to be in this new world of adults. All the rules and codes with which he had been brought up and which he had mocked in secret for so long now asserted a hold over him in a way they never had before. For in fact, although he had never heard a good reason not to look upon women, or to obey the Sabbath, or not to eat pork, or not to behold the sign of the cross, or to spend nine-tenths of the schoolday, from seven-thirty in the morning to five in the afternoon, learning the Talmud by rote, he had lived among these edicts for so long in a society of such strict convention that apart from his timid adventures in Manhattan he had never had an opportunity to disobey them. And now that the time came for him to put his midnight thoughts of logic and rationality into action he discovered that it involved the kind of emotion which could make him physically sick. The turbulence had not been the problem.

But with a child's resilience Joel sublimated the overwhelming waves of his past, rescaling his memories in order to make the most painful details invisible. He looked the blonde stewardess firmly in the eye – or as firmly as he could, given the bottle-thick lenses of his glasses – and asked her if he could have a pair of scissors please. When she looked worried and glanced at her colleague he assured her: 'Don't worry, I am not going to hurt myself. I know how to use a pair of scissors' and won her over immediately, finding with a sure instinct the susceptibility of WASPs to sassy kids. The stewardess brought a pair from the first aid box and Joel disappeared with them into the toilet cubicle. Folding his Homburg around the contents of his stomach, he stuffed it in the toilet, jamming it down until the pressure sucked it away. Then, looking in the mirror, he grabbed each of his payot in turn and with one snip apiece cut them off and bundled them into the wastebasket. He removed his collar and tie, and with a disposable razor from the dispenser hacked off what he could of his beard, though he gave this up after nicking himself badly three or four times. Then he washed and cleaned his teeth and dressed again, and emerging from the toilet spoke curtly to the surprised air staff. 'I'm all right now. Thank you, thank you. Thank you for your help, I'm all right now, I can find my own way back to my seat.' Several thousand feet below them, now emptied of its contents, the Homburg slowly spiralled through the thickening air.

Some way away a drill bit the street. The sound drifted through the open window of the professor's study and for a moment he thought it was morning and that he was in bed, listening to the noise his wife made as she snored into the stains of cold-cream on her pillow.

He came round and stumbled over to the sink, splashed some

94

water on to his face. He'd slept much longer than he'd intended and had missed his lecture. Picking up the phone he called the porter's lodge and told them to send the college car to the airport to pick up the Kluge boy. Christ! How had he slept so long?

The chauffeur dropped Joel at the lodge. He stood there by the pigeonholes examining the worn stone walls and trying to decipher the conversation going on between the two men behind the counter. But he could make out no more than a word or two and his mind soon wandered back to the journey he had just made in that strange small car through the landscape whose colours had been like those of Prospect Park, but more so. Everything was smaller here, not just the vehicles but the buildings, all these angry houses in their little rows with little gables and tiny windows, the narrow roads fighting to hold the two sides apart.

He knew England only from photographs – the pictures had shown him a world in miniature – and now he was here, in a miniature world. There were no el trains rattling high above the streets, no advertising hoardings swung out above the traffic, the pavements seemed too tiny to walk upon and the people drab, less colourful.

Throughout the drive the sky had stayed a leaden grey and a vapour of rain had drizzled down like the bronchial spray coughed out by a cancerous old smoker. The spires and parapets of the university buildings sliced into the low clouds, gripping the sky and holding it to the earth with their Gothic barbs, tenacious as a bur caught deep in the fur of some hapless animal. That the stones were cloaked in grey-green swathes of lichen and stained with the dark blood of pollution gave them a crabbed authenticity of the kind bestowed only by persistence through time. As if to remain unchanged, to stand staunch and uncaring, was a quality to be admired.

Of course, for Metric it was. The professor saw himself not as one of Joel's shoes, winding downstream in a series of mutating relationships, but as a cog in a machine that both settled into and straddled the years themselves, mechanically linking in one great computational process all the facts and details and laws that could be classified and filed away from the age of those great slave masters the Greeks, to that of those great slave masters the British, and on and on beyond into the future, the future which would be subordinated to this machine as a lumpy, yeasty liquid is subordinated to a sieve.

Metric's role in this great process, he had decided, was to become a bigger cog. And here in the porter's lodge was the tool with which he was going to increase his diameter.

He entered the lodge, stooping slightly to avoid hitting his head upon the stone lintel. He saw Joel immediately, did a double take. The boy stood there shivering with fear or cold or both. His black trousers were too short for him, his battered shoes too big. His coat was worn at the elbows and was giving at the seams. His skin was pale and sweaty as an old cheese, his hair hacked and unkempt as a scarecrow's. He peered up through the thick lenses of his spectacles; behind them his eyes were hugely magnified, black holes in the pallor of his face. Just as the professor was wondering what on earth he had let himself in for his eyes met the boy's and for the briefest moment – one he would later dismiss by refusing to remember it as anything but a wholly discrete event – Metric fell into Joel's huge pupils, seeing there spaces which folded back upon themselves and enveloped his imagination in their great velvet swamps. Then he collected himself, blinked, looked away, composed an avuncular smile and extended his hand. 'Well, you must be young Mr Kluge. Welcome to Cambridge, young man. I am Professor Metric.'

Sherry and trifles

Metric's study was on the first floor and it looked out on to the back quad. He led Joel in and Joel looked around. One wall was entirely covered with books: the boy thought immediately of Brooklyn library. The other walls were half-panelled. The room was large. There was space enough for a large desk (leather-topped), a sofa, two easy chairs and a teak coffee table. Two doors let off from the main room. One of them was ajar and through the opening Joel could see a small sink.

The windows were leaded like all those overlooking the back quad and were let into small recesses sunk deeply into the thick walls. In each recess stood an ornamental pedestal. On top of the eastern pedestal was an aspidistra; on the western a small plaster bust. The bust was of the physicist Paul Dirac. It was not clear to Joel quite what it was doing there until he moved closer and noted the small brass plaque affixed to the base, on which the following words had been inscribed:

God is a Mathematician

It was the kind of thing that Metric found amusing. The bust had been given to him by his wife, back in the days when she had still found such things amusing too. It was the only object in his study that had any connection with her. She had bought it from an antique shop in Hampstead during an afternoon stroll in the company of Peter Rogers, a research scientist based in London to whom she had been introduced by a friend, with whom she had been attending a conference on philosophy and science at London's University College. The conference was a big disappointment and she had spent the afternoon of the third day strolling with Rogers across Hampstead Heath. The weather was warm and they had ended up in Jack Straw's Castle drinking bitter shandies. Rogers invited her to a party that evening; she accepted. The party was off St James's: cocktails and a band. Rogers introduced her to various friends. He seemed very well connected, and that night she met well-known stage actors, a popular composer from France and many fashionable academics and literary types; and the philosopher Bertrand Russell, whom she knew by sight from around Cambridge, although they had never actually spoken. Russell was surprisingly witty and personable, and he charmed her immediately. Soon she found herself standing alone with him, deeply involved in a conversation about the fauna of the African savannah, a subject about which he seemed to know a great deal. Something about his manner made her suspect that he was drunk – he was indeed cradling an extremely large martini in his left hand – but no sooner did she make up her mind that that was the case than he would seem perfectly sober once again. Then, rather abruptly, he seemed to lose interest in their exchange. His gaze slipped from her face to the room over her shoulder and he began to fiddle with something in the bottom of his jacket pocket.

As she was asking a question about the mathematical ratios reified in the spiral horns of the ibex, he suddenly interrupted her. 'Come with me, my dear,' he crooned in a deep philosophical bass. 'I have something you might be interested in.' He led her over to the curtained booths which lined the walls. Most of them had their drapes drawn and as they walked past, giggles and coughs could be heard. The party was in full swing by now and they had to dodge dancers and waiters with trays overflowing with canapés and champagne flutes. Russell diverted a passing glass into Amanda Metric's hand and led her through the maelstrom and into the last available booth. Inside were a small glass-topped table and two bench seats.

Russell sat down and placed a small glass phial full of white powder on the table top. He took a slug of his martini and handed the professor's wife a tiny spoon. 'After you, my dear.' Amanda didn't know whether to be shocked or embarrassed. All Russell saw was confusion, so he took control of the situation, which was what he was best at. 'Never done the devil's dandruff before? Allow me.' He took the spoon from her, dipped it in the phial and snurfed the contents up his capacious right nostril, repeating the process with his left. 'See? Just like taking a dab of snuff.' He handed the spoon back to Amanda, who to her surprise now found herself rather excited by the chance of getting involved in such an illicit activity. She took a couple of gulps of her champagne, then ingested the powder just as Russell had done, though she was trembling so much that she nearly dropped powder, spoon, phial and all.

As the drug dissolved in her sinuses she felt first light-headed then euphoric. 'Oh, Mr Russell,' she said, 'it's just like champagne, but better!'

'I know,' said Russell. 'And call me Bertie.' And he laid a hand on her knee.

98

Metric had no idea that the souvenir of his wife's one infidelity sat on permanent display in his study; it was one of those ironies that he most assuredly would not have found funny, although as the years went by it was increasingly appreciated by Amanda, who usually remembered it when her husband was at his most pompous.

But another object drew Joel's attention more. About twenty inches long and six inches high, constructed from delicately filigreed and sumptuously engraved brass and covered with a variety of handles and wheels, it sat on the front of Metric's desk in pride of place.

Metric noted Joel's interest. 'One of Leibniz's calculating machines. An original in fact.' He sniffed. 'Designed by the great mathematician to calculate tables of data concerning the movements of the planets and the stars. "It is unworthy of excellent men to lose hours like slaves in the labour of calculation which could be safely relegated to anyone else if machines were used," to quote him directly. Quite right too. Grandfather of the modern computer. Ever seen a computer, Kluge?' Joel didn't answer, but instead stepped forward to try one of the handles. Metric moved over quickly to guide him away. 'Better not touch, eh?'

The machine was not in fact an original, although Metric thought it was, as did the dealer who had sold it to him for an extremely large amount of money. The original Leibniz calculators were built between 1672 and 1674 by a craftsman commissioned by Leibniz himself. Metric's machine, although identical in every other respect, had been built in 1821 by a very different craftsman, commissioned by one Charles Babbage.

Babbage had been fascinated by machinery of all sorts since he saw two automata at a travelling fair as a child. He wrote in his autobiography that one of the two: 'glided along a space of about four feet, when she turned round and went back to her original place. She used an eyeglass occasionally, and bowed frequently, as if recognising her acquaintances. The motions of her limbs were singularly graceful. The other silver figure was an admirable danseuse, with a bird on the forefinger of her right hand, which wagged its tail, flapped its wings, and opened its beak.' The dolls had been manufactured by an old craftsman called John Merlin, who had been touring them around Europe for many years. His audiences had included kings and queens, as well as such cultural luminaries as the German Romantic writers E. T. A. Hoffman (whose story of machinic love, 'The Sandman', was inspired by Merlin's automata) and Heinrich von Kleist, whose passion for these mechanicals burned so hot that he was inspired to write: 'Grace appears purest in that human form which has either no consciousness or an infinite one, that is, in a puppet or in a god.'

Babbage himself was a polymath. A designer – he invented a cow-catcher for trains, the speedometer, the flashing lighthouse and a pair of shoes for walking on water – a cryptologist, a founder of the Royal Statistical and the Royal Astronomical Societies and a campaigner against the playing of loud musical instruments in London (which he referred to as 'instruments of torture' and blamed for ruining his concentration) he remained something of a jack-of-all-trades until one dreary evening in 1821, when he found himself stuck in a room helping the astronomer Herschel to check over a stack of celestial calculations made by a team of human computers. After finding the umpteenth mistake, Babbage exclaimed that he 'wished to God that the calculations had been executed by steam!' And the project followed from that: collect examples of the best calculating machines ever built, use the best ideas from each and build a new machine that could be autonomously powered.

Dreaming up ways to mechanise mathematical processes quickly became the focus of Babbage's life and for the next two years he went about collecting whatever calculating machines he could lay his hands on. The Holy Grail was a Leibniz calculator, but though he searched high and low, he could not find one that he could buy and take to pieces. Eventually he gave up on the quest and began to work on his designs for a 'Difference Engine' – a machine designed to compute and print tables of numbers using the mathematical method of 'finite difference' – regardless.

Over a decade had passed since the evening with Herschel and Babbage's project was not going well. After experiencing a whole series of problems, the Difference Engine was finally scuppered by the chief engineer, Joseph Clement, who made off with all the funds. Babbage faced disaster. Then, completely out of the blue, a friend informed him that a copy of Leibniz's original plans along with the craftsman's drawings resided in the library of an aristocratic cousin. The inventor secured himself an introduction and hastened to the lady's residence by coach.

The cousin was no less than the Countess of Lovelace, Augusta Ada Byron, the one legitimate daughter of the great English poet himself, and she had more to give Babbage than a mere set of plans. For Ada Byron was an extraordinary person with an extraordinary mind. Countess, gambler, mother, mathematician, self-styled prophetess, she was easily Babbage's equal and when they met he discovered to his great surprise that she was already familiar with his work. They quickly formed an intense relationship, Ada driving Charles to be more rigorous and focused in his work and at the same time inserting her own ideas – both practical and visionary – into the design for the machine that was to succeed the Difference Engine: the 'Analytical Engine', intended to be a fully programmable computer. In particular, Ada introduced ideas taken from the Jacquard loom, which used punch cards to allow textile patterns to be preset which had the effect of putting many skilled weavers out of a job, causing riots and marches by disgruntled textile workers – Luddites – all over Britain. Ada's father, Lord Byron, was one of the few to take up the Luddite cause in Parliament, at the same time as his daughter was coming to understand the real importance of the machines which had taken their jobs. 'We may say most aptly that the Analytical Engine weaves Algebraic patterns,' Ada commented, 'just as the Jacquard loom weaves flowers and leaves.' Indeed, Babbage was later to draw a direct comparison between the structure of their 'thinking machine' and that of a textile plant: both consisted of two parts, 'Ist The store in which all the variables to be operated upon, as well as all those quantities which have arisen from the result of other operations, are placed [and] 2nd The mill into which the quantities about to be operated on are always brought.'

Spurred on by their relationship, and with the Leibniz blueprints now at his disposal, Babbage decided to have a calculator built for Ada as a gift. He wanted Merlin, the automaton manufacturer, to build it. The aged craftsman had by this time settled in London, but decrepit and rapidly losing his sight, he initially declined the commission. Babbage, however, could see that the man was poverty stricken and with no relatives to look after him it would only be a matter of offering him a large enough fee. When Merlin capitulated Babbage purchased the silver dancing doll from him as a gesture of good faith and the old man went to work on the Leibniz calculator.

It was to be one of his greatest achievements. He had in fact seen one once and, although that encounter had taken place almost half a century earlier, his skilled and trained mind could recall it clearly – certainly as clearly as he could now see the blueprints. After months of toil he managed to recreate the original machine almost perfectly. Yet the strain had been too much – as he screwed the final screw into the plate of authenticity that he had reproduced from memory as a final touch his sight gave out, and when Babbage came to pick up the calculator he found the old man wandering blind and half mad in the back of his shop, the machine lying oiled and pristine among the debris scattered across the workbench. Too ashamed to admit to Ada that he had been the cause of Merlin's decline, he sold the machine immediately and with the proceeds of the sale paid for the craftsman to be cared for in a sanatorium for the remaining few months of his life. It was this machine that now took pride of place on Metric's desk.

Metric sat Joel down, handed him a glass of sherry and welcomed him to Cambridge. He issued him with various pieces of paper, had him sign sundry others, gave him a quick run down of how the college functioned – none of which Joel understood – a quick list of people whom he could turn to if he needed help – none of whose names Joel remembered – and interspersed the whole with a series of witless jokes – none of which Joel got. Then he called for a porter to take Joel to his room and told the boy to come and see him in a couple of days, 'when you've settled in'. And then Joel was on his own.

Fast cut through Joel in lectures, scribbling notes in his own shorthand, Joel in libraries memorising proofs, Joel in tutorials writing with chalk upon a board, Joel at his desk deliberating with a slide-rule and scratching away at problems with his pencil, Joel in bed sleeping a chaste six hours. Overview: Joel growing up, Joel's Cambridge. Contrast: the Cambridge of a spoilt and self-centred aristocracy, for whom it was merely a finishing school swilling with boating, balls and champagne; contrast: the Cambridge of the middle classes, for whom it was footlights and theatre, stuttering steps on a protected political stage, walks in the country and a niche in a cosy little scene; contrast: the Cambridge of the outsider – the boy from the Valleys who starts to deal pot, the girl raped by her tutor with no recompense, the depressive discovered one morning hanging from a bridge, the fool who came to learn and is sorely disappointed. And contrast: the Cambridge of the town – long sufferings and symbioses with the hive at its centre, tarmac next to cobbles beneath the milky dawns, shirtings, suitings, averted eyes and street slang.

Joel was lucky; in the end he was saved from Cambridge by the quality of his mind. It was that mind which had got him there in the first place, and it was what gained him a level of acceptance among the monks of maths and logic that stalked the dimly lit corridors and cloisters, rule books in hand.

Metric personally supervised Joel's tuition, and it wasn't long before he was able to skim off the more useful products of the boy's agile and inventive brain. He had made the right decision: he had a genius in his care and if he prospered while he brought the boy to fruition, well, where was the harm in that? And indeed, Metric did have his work cut out, at least to begin with. The combination of Joel's youth, his personal eccentricities and his culture shock meant that trivial problems could quickly spiral out of control. The boy wouldn't eat any of the food in halls, for example, preferring to subsist on a diet of crisps and chocolate from the local grocers. He didn't seem capable of buying any new clothes, wearing his one black suit until it was practically falling off his insubstantial frame. His English was terrible and a private tutor had to be organised for him. In the vacations he had nowhere to go and special rooms needed to be made available for him in college.

The professor found all these unforeseen difficulties rather overwhelming and, unable quite to deal with them, he did something completely out of character – he turned to his wife for advice. As it happened, Amanda had been taking a quiet interest in this orphan prodigy for some time; when at her husband's behest she was finally introduced to the boy she did the childless middle-aged woman thing and took Joel under her wing. He was helpless; she could help.

So Metric got to see Joel at weekends too, when Amanda would have him over to their house and cook him some decent meals and wash and mend his clothes and take him shopping for the few things he needed. Gradually, the little lost Jewish boy jettisoned some of his incapacitating shyness, shed most of his Hasidic trappings and became an approximate replica of all the other students, if a little younger and quite a lot geekier.

On the academic side, Metric played out a clever little game. He was convinced of the truth of the last theorem of the great mathematician Fermat, the only theorem out of two hundred or so that had not yet been proved. The problem was to demonstrate the claim that the equation $x^n + y^n = z^n$ has no solutions with x, y and z all positive integers and n an integer greater than 2, and although apparently simple, it was in fact incredibly complex. Metric's great ambition was to discover a proof and so ensure that he went down in the annals of mathematical history, if not a second Fermat then at least someone who was equal to the task that the great mathematician had set. Joel knew little of Fermat and certainly wasn't aware of the challenge that this particular theorem set the world of mathematics. Metric's plan was to feed Joel various pieces of the puzzle disguised as coursework and encourage him to make the requisite connections between them, while making sure that he never saw enough of the big picture to know what was going on. Over the next few years, this is exactly what he did.

As he approached the final year of his undergraduate degree and his English became all but fluent, Joel began to exhibit a marked interest in the philosophy of mathematics as well as its practice. He would interrupt tutorials with an occasional non sequitur: But does mathematics describe the world? What are the implications for knowledge of Gödel's theorem? Doesn't Turing's universal machine demonstrate that certain problems will always fall outside the realm of mathematics?

Feeling avuncular (and more than a little mercenary) Metric encouraged his pupil. He lent him Russell and Whitehead's *Principia Mathematica* (without, of course, understanding the significance such a text would have had for his wife), Frege's *Die Grundlagen der Arithmetick*, Wittgenstein's *Tractatus Logico-Philosophicus* and even, in an adventurous moment, Lewis Carroll's *Alice's Adventures in Wonderland*, which he thought might lighten the load a little. Joel devoured them all, fascinated. He especially revered Carroll, it never having struck him before that logic could be made so quirky, so amusing. He pestered Metric about the references he didn't understand and read up on all of them. In the process he discovered relativity theory, Leibniz, molasses and mock turtles, chess and cards, Arthur Eddington, knights and courts of law and tea parties and top hats and dodos and quadrilles and . . . and something, though he wasn't quite sure what, but something about little girls, too . . . and it all fitted perfectly with what he'd thought it should be like before he had come here and it gave him a chance to fantasise again, as he used to in Brooklyn and which he'd done so rarely since he came to Cambridge. Now, when his thoughts misted over, instead of spinning yarns of dreaming spires and hallowed corridors (living here among the other students had removed those illusions for good) he invariably thought of his family and the Hasidic world he'd left behind which, in retrospect, didn't seem all that bad – at least the food had been good (he missed his mother's soups his father's breads – though not the bagels). He thought, too, of his betrayal – that's what he knew it as now, a betrayal – and with that knowledge came an understanding that he could never go back, that he'd severed the unwinding skein of return as surely as a midwife snips an umbilical cord and twists it into an atrophying knot.

Though their relationship was founded on a lie – two, in fact, as there was Metric's mixed in there as well – in Amanda and the professor Joel found something of a surrogate family. The weekends spent at their house became part of the routine and soon their place was 'home' and he could do there pretty much as he pleased. They had minor arguments, too, family-style, which brought him closer to them and to Amanda especially, since her husband, for the sake of academic propriety if nothing else, had to maintain a certain distance. As Joel was slowly integrated, his nightmares – the ones he'd had ever since leaving Brooklyn, the ones in which the prostitutes he'd met once in Times Square would catch him and hang him by his arms from a lamp-post in the street and call out to everyone what he was a liar and a traitor, call to the crowds of passers-by who would jeer and tear at his clothes with eager fingers and then, when his clothing had been shredded, at his flesh; the ones where he'd be trying to buy a ticket home, only to be confounded at every turn by the complexities of the computerised booking system; or worst of all, the ones where he'd be back and it would be normal, and he'd go to school and come home and sit down to dinner with his brothers and sisters and go to bed and sleep so well, so well, only to wake the next morning to his grey college room and the knowledge that this was the nightmare, this, what he was living, what he had done – slowly became less frequent until one day something happened and they stopped completely, never came back. That was 20 July 1969, when at Amanda's brother's house just outside Cambridge and in the company of some fifteen other people, mostly academics he knew from the college, he not only watched TV for the first time but saw the pictures come back from the Sea of Tranquillity, of Aldrin and Armstrong bouncing around in the dust. When the American flag went up Amanda's brother, a small man, almost entirely bald, who wore round wire-rimmed spectacles and smiled at everybody, took his hand and shook it vigorously and congratulated 'the American among us' and everyone cheered, *hoorah! hoorah!*, and banged him on the back. The flag had never seemed to have anything to do with him before, but now he felt a surge of pride and thought that yes, indeed, this had something to do with who he was. And as the astronauts pointed up at the rising earth, at him, for the first time he could remember he felt enormously happy.

★

Between Joel and the astronauts there was Laika, watching and whimpering, her tail tucked between her legs. This was the latest in a series of threatening events, which could no longer be regarded as isolated occurrences. It had been a mistake to bark at that spaceman she'd seen. Now they'd come back for her, they were coming to get her and she did not want to return. And worse, the world was looking through her – a strange sensation, one which wears you thin. She bounced the footage of the astronauts down to Richard Nixon and an astonished populace without interference. Everyone was watching; to try anything would be madness. To Laika, suddenly space seemed very small – and it wasn't just that she was so fat now she filled her capsule. Like Joel in his dreams, she was rigid with fear and despite the veneer of self-consciousness she'd been fortunate enough (you would think) to accrue, it was a veneer all the same and easily scratched. When the millions of years' worth of evolution salted away in her amygdala told her to cower, cower she did no matter that it made no sense. A cornered animal, she pushed her flesh into the dark corners of Sputnik II, into the tiny spaces between instrument panels and life-support systems, between transmitters and receivers, between dials and knobs, tubes and surrounds, shoving so hard and shivering so much that the hard edges punctured her skin and the differentiation between metal and sinew, dog and machine, became harder than ever to discern.

But it was more than simple fear that made her cringe – though fear, of course, is never simple, even if it often seems so at the time. There was something else mixed in, a sense of foreboding, of something dark and strange and complex unfolding just out of view. For Jennifer, Judd and Joel were all linked in, yes, they were all there, watching through her, perhaps as close to one another now as they would ever be, though Judd is only seven and is so excited, yes he's so excited, he wants more than anything to go to the moon, and he's watching it all on his family's new set, the big one in the living-room (they've got several) and he's asking Moses question after supercharged question: 'How do they breathe? Why do they float? How do they get back? When can I go?' and Moses fields these as best he can, though he's more interested in

107

the ads which are interspersed with the action, in particular one for a watch, no, for *the* watch, the Omega Speedmaster, which is the watch NASA issues their astronauts with and which is available now for the special moon landing celebration edition price of $499.99. *Omega – the true meaning of space-time.*

Jennifer is watching too. She's nearly ten now. She's watching at home on her very own set. It was, it just was the most, the most, well, just the mostest present she had ever had and she was thrilled with it, just couldn't take her eyes off it, so much so that Henry had to ration her viewing to make sure she got some exercise and did her homework. Henry had given Doreen Buerk a few pounds for it after she'd mentioned at a parent–teacher evening that it had been mouldering away unused in one of her upstairs rooms ever since her husband Donald had gone. For Doreen was a teacher now – she taught classes in a local boys' public school and in the comprehensive just down the road which Jennifer attended (she regarded the latter as her 'community service'). The set was only a black and white, but it had a very large screen and the tube was still good, and Jennifer was the only kid on her street who got to watch as much television as she liked, greatly to the envy of all of her friends.

She'd watched films and cartoons and *Blue Peter* and sometimes nature programmes, and all the music shows like *Ready, Steady, Go!*, and she'd seen the Stones on it and the Dave Clark Five and the Beatles whom she didn't like so much. Henry watched it too, though the stuff he liked bored Jennifer, who would moan at him, tell him he was dull. But Henry was happy to ignore her as he slipped into the nostalgic eurocentrisms of *Civilisation*, or rooted for Henry Cooper as he battled Piero Tomasoni (Jennifer: 'boxing, uurhg!'), or followed the domestic dramas of *The Forsyte Saga* or *Dombey and Son* ('bo-r-ing'). When Jennifer saw after ten minutes or so that she wasn't going to change his mind she'd usually leave off pestering him and go round to Shelley's or, if she didn't feel like going out, lie at his feet on the floor by the open fire (it was often too cold to sit in her room; they didn't have central heating) and doze or read a comic book or nag him to get her a cat. There was some stuff they watched together: the occasional crime series

(*Z–Cars*, *Softly, Softly*), the odd thing which Henry thought educational (*A Human Zoo*, *Wildlife on One*), comedy shows (Jennifer didn't get all the jokes but she laughed anyway) and the popular science series *Tomorrow's World*, which they both liked and which handled the BBC's coverage of the moon landing. The two of them watched the historic event with a group of friends Henry had suggested Jennifer invite over for the occasion which became, in an historic kind of a way, the precursor for the Saturday film matinée parties she'd start to hold on a regular basis a year or two later.

The week after the moon landing the BBC had broadcast a special *Tomorrow's World* show dedicated to the integrated circuit electronics which had made the Apollo missions possible. The Argyll-sweatered Hamish McCready, kids' favourite and housewives' choice to boot, held a digital watch up to the camera and removed its screen to reveal the tiny electronic muscle inside. Then he took the audience on a tour of Cape Canaveral, showed them the enormous mainframe and the new mini-computers, Digital Equipment Corporation machines, PDP–8s and PDP–9s, the same ones that Moses had been selling since he'd read a book called *The Future of the Computer Utility* back in 1966 (which had fired him up so much that he'd jumped ship from IBM to DEC), and similar to the ones that Joel would begin to work with now that he was a post-graduate – the mathematics faculty at Cambridge would buy a PDP–10 the very year he began his Ph.D.

Ecce homo

Joel was nearly twenty and first-year undergrads were younger than him now. He knew the ropes, he wasn't such an oddity any more. But for Metric the transition wasn't so happy; it meant the abandoning of his plot to siphon off Joel's talent, even though he felt that he was very close to finishing his proof. He'd published several exploratory papers, and many of his colleagues had been impressed by his progress and were beginning to expect great things of him. But Joel was a graduate student now, it wasn't so easy to pull the wool over his eyes. The professor did toy with the notion of coming clean, but there was no way he would be able to explain away those papers. Like Laika, Metric feared discovery and, like the dog, his fear was complex, an extra dimension added to it by the fact that although in theory he could stomach sharing the glory, he couldn't cope with the possibility that Joel, once alerted to the situation, would disown his tutor in disgust, proceed on his own and claim the prize himself.

And then, of course, he'd have to face Amanda. No one would have called Metric a great judge of character, least of all himself, but if he knew one thing about his wife it was that whatever Joel's reaction might turn out to be, once she'd found out what he'd been up to her wrath would be terrible to behold.

The fear did not leave him once he had made the decision to end the search for the proof. For what if he were discovered? What if Joel were accidentally to turn up those papers in the library one day? What would he do then? After all, it was quite likely. The journals in which he'd published were popular enough and what could be more natural than that the boy should want to find out what work his tutor was currently involved in (Metric always thought of Joel as 'the boy')? The more he considered it the more his trepidation grew and one night, following a particularly strenuous college dinner, while sitting propped up in the Senior Common Room, a large glass of Regoan tawny port in one hand and the *Telegraph* folded down around the crossword in the other, he decided that he had to do something or go mad with the worry.

Believing that there was no time like the present, he bolstered himself with a third glass of the fortified wine, slipped out of the SCR and, making sure no one was about, headed in the direction of the library. A tall man with a not insubstantial belly, Metric was hardly designed for covert operations. But somehow he managed to navigate the stone corridors, grassy quads and quiet cloisters without being seen by anyone save the gargoyles, who pulled faces at him in disgust as they did at so much of what they observed of the college's daily round. At this hour the library was locked, though as a resident professor Metric was in possession of a key. He approached the library door and with one last glance to make sure he wasn't being followed he slipped it into the iron lock that was embedded deep in the ancient oak. He'd never actually used the key before and was somewhat surprised when with a guilty clunk the lock sprang back and the door swung open.

A moment later he was inside. Thankfully, the night was moonlit and clear, and light enough for him to see by slanted in through the leaded diamonds of the tall, narrow windows. The room was deathly silent and Metric reflected drunkenly that he'd never realised before just how much noise there was in an average library of an average day. But the place also lacked that tension, that pressure not to make a sound, and he strolled across to the mathematics section feeling strangely free.

He knew exactly where the articles were; on his way over he'd rehearsed their position in his mind's eye. Now he went straight to them and, with a deftness that came from years of handling papers of one sort of another, tore them carefully from their bindings, folded them and placed them in the inside pocket of his jacket.

Not wanting to return to the SCR, where he might have to explain his absence, he took a circuitous route to the tutors' private back gate where he could let himself out without having to pass before the carnivorous gaze of the bowler-hatted porters. As he wound his way back through the tortuous, almost organic collection of crumbling Gothics, it struck him that the college would make a jolly good sepulchre, each of its rooms a splendid family tomb.

Removing the incriminating papers from the college library did not, however, help him to sleep any better. Now that this window on to his secret had been sealed others quickly appeared and he lay awake most of that night, and many more following, watching them sprout like acne on a pubescent face. At the very least he would have to repeat his vandalism in the faculty library and perhaps in any others which the boy frequented. When he casually asked Joel about his library habits a day or two later, he replied that he had no set pattern, that he liked to move from one to another at whim – his concentration suffered, he found, if he spent too much time in one place.

Though he knew it was completely irrational, Metric's paranoia grew and grew, and his thoughts as far as Joel was concerned became one vast labyrinth full of traps, dead-ends and pitfalls. And then, one morning while he was shaving, he stumbled across a solution so glorious in its simplicity that its discovery was almost as satisfying as he imagined the finding of the proof of Fermat's Last Theorem itself might be. If he couldn't take the evidence away from Joel, he would just have to take Joel away from the evidence. The only question which remained was how that was going to be achieved.

An opportunity presented itself one summer afternoon, when the quad outside Metric's window was noisy with students languishing on the grass. Joel appeared for his fortnightly tutorial, prompt as ever, dressed in his usual jacket, tie and round-necked pullover despite the warm weather. He knocked and entered, delivering his greeting in that familiar tone of his which, as Metric had noted on many occasions, was simultaneously belligerent and self-effacing. As the boy sat down in one of the two wicker chairs and took his papers from the satchel that he carried, the professor watched him from the window from where he'd been gazing, just a moment or two before, at the young men strewn across the lawn. Why couldn't Joel look more like one of them? The huge lick of greasy black hair, the heavy spectacles, the skin tormented with boils and that nose which seemed to suck up most of his face . . . there was no doubt about it, he was an ugly one. And yet . . . and yet there was something about him which shone through, something which made you want to be near him . . . Amanda could see it, presumably, more clearly than he could.

He started the session by asking Joel to take the initiative (he'd forgotten what it was the boy was supposed to be working on). Joel read out a few paragraphs summarising his proposed solution to a particular problem in set theory. Metric saw which way he was heading and interrupted him to sketch some figures on his blackboard. As he drew he talked, and when he turned back to face Joel he was surprised to see that the boy was not paying the slightest attention but was instead looking across at the window where he himself had previously been standing. This was most uncharacteristic!

'Ah, Mr Kluge, I don't want to spoil your enjoyment of the fine weather, but do you think you could apply your attention to the matter in hand?'

'Uh, I beg your pardon?' said Joel, still locked into his reverie.

'The problem, my dear boy, is located here –' he tapped on the blackboard with the chalk '– not, I believe, in the quad, though I must confess that on such a beautiful afternoon as the good Lord has offered us today I would as soon, I believe, be out there myself as . . .'

Quite suddenly Joel interrupted. '*God is a mathematician*. Do you believe that yourself?' Metric was startled. 'Your bust of Dirac, sir. The inscription reads *God is a mathematician*. I wondered if you believed that yourself.'

It took the professor a moment or two to realise that Joel had not been looking out of the window, as he had assumed, but had in fact been staring at the bust of Paul Dirac which occupied the plinth in front of it. He was about to tell Joel that they should really get on with the tutorial and that this was a side-track best saved for another occasion when the thought struck him that here perhaps was an avenue worth exploring. 'Hum,' he mused and, placing his piece of chalk carefully into the gutter at the bottom of the blackboard, walked thoughtfully across the room to the bust. With one hand he picked it up and held it at an angle appropriate for contemplation and with the other – as if as an afterthought – he carefully pulled the window to, shutting out the distracting hubbub coming from outside. The room became soft and still. 'I'm not sure,' he said. 'It's an interesting question. Something I've thought about often. The first question to ask, I suppose, is what exactly does that statement mean? Presumably, it means that the world adheres to the precepts of mathematics. There are problems with this position, needless to say – you must have come across them in the books on philosophical logic I gave you to read: the

Wittgenstein, the Frege and so on. Naturally, even asking what our sentence means already embroils us in debate. For example, one has to ask: How exactly do we ascribe meaning? Maybe that is where we should begin, with the problems of meaning. Quine's rather good on this. Have you read Quine?'

'I've read *Word and Object*, obviously,' said know-it-all Joel, putting down his papers and crossing his legs, 'but I'm thinking about things in a far more general sense. That is to say does mathematics describe *this* world, or does it describe some other, more ideal, perhaps transcendent realm?'

'Aha! Neo-Platonism. Well, it has a long and glorious heritage, and you'd be in fine company, though it's somewhat discredited today, I fear.'

'I was thinking more of Leibniz actually, and his idea of the monad, which as an idea I feel manages to make the leap between the transcendent and the material somewhat better than Plato's essences, or those of Plotinus, if you prefer.' (It was unfortunately true that Joel – as part of his attempt, both conscious and unconscious, to paper over his past – had picked up many of the accents and mannerisms of upper-class Cambridge English. Metric, of course, thought this was splendid, the horror of it completely escaping him.)

'It seems, my boy, that you are moving somewhat out of the precinct of pure mathematics here, but go on, go on.' Encourage him, encourage him, thought Metric, mentally rubbing his hands, then catching himself and physically straightening up.

'Well, according to the Jewish Kabbalah . . .'

'I'm afraid I'm, ah, not familiar with that particular tradition,' said Metric hastily.

'Oh?' said Joel, a little surprised to have found such a glaring gap in his tutor's knowledge. 'Well according to that or, at least, according to the version known as Lurianic doctrine, although it is only one of many, the universe is created when Ein-Sof, which according to classical Kabbalah is not at all identical with the revealed divine creator but more like eternity, or infinity – the absolute perfection, if you can imagine the difference – well, the universe is created when Ein-Sof withdraws into itself and opens a space of possibility, as it were.'

'It reminds me a little of Hegel, though it's a long while since I've read him,' Metric murmured, unsure as to where this might be heading.

Joel ignored him. 'The process by which it does this, which is most interesting, is also most strange. You see, the problem is that Ein-Sof has no will, no volition at all: it just is, you see. It's perfect and undifferentiated and it just is. So how is this withdrawal initiated?'

'God?' said Metric hopefully.

'Aha, no, that's just where you're wrong! And anyway, it wouldn't work for popular Kabbalah, which conflates the notions of Ein-Sof and God. No, what happens is this: the perfection of Ein-Sof is such that it begins to shake with a kind of "self-satisfaction", though you must understand this as an anthropo-morphism and not a true description.'

'Naturally,' said Metric, thanking his stars he was a Christian.

'Well, as a result of this shaking, a series of what are known as "primordial points" are engraved in the essence of Ein-Sof, and as a result of this engraving the primordial space, in which the world can be formed, comes into being. The interesting thing about this engraving is that it is actually a *linguistic* phenomenon. The engraving forms a malbush, or a garment, though a garment that is part of that which it covers – like the exoskeleton of a grasshopper, according to one tradition – and this malbush is made up of the twenty letters of the Hebrew alphabet and their two hundred and thirty-one possible two-letter combinations, or 'gates', as specified in the Sefer Yezirah. In fact, the malbush is the primordial Torah itself, though that is beside the point.

'So, in mystical Jewish thought the world is intended to be built about this linguistic structure, very similar in certain ways to the ideas laid out in the *Tractatus* or in Leibniz's essay on Monadology. But something goes wrong. In the primordial space ten vessels come into being, vessels whose interrelations and structure will format the world. But in the process of world-building the vessels are broken and the world we end up with, this one, is the result of that catastrophe, although at all times it is striving to return to perfection and will eventually do so. In all, then, there are three processes at work. Zimzum is the movement by which Ein-Sof originally withdraws into itself, thus opening up the space in which the vessels are created. Shevirah is the chaos that ensues once the vessels have been broken. And tikkun is the restructuring process by which the world reattains perfection.'

Joel stopped and Metric delivered a slow 'I see'. Then, as no more seemed to be forthcoming, he prompted: 'And so?'

'And so, according to Jewish tradition there would indeed seem to be a link between our apparently chaotic and unintegrable world and the perfect mathematical linguistics of the primordial space. In a way it's sort of proposing a link between Wittgenstein's later work and his earlier.'

'Well, it's one thing to propose it and another to find it. And I wouldn't set too great a store by the later work if I were you.'

'No, obviously, I couldn't agree more. But I do think it's worth trying to find that link.'

'You do, do you? I never knew you were so religious, my boy.'

'Oh, no! This isn't a religious problem at all! It's a logico-mathematical one. I just wanted to illustrate ... after all, even Russell agrees ... well what I want to say is, oh dear, you've been so kind to me ...'

Metric smiled indulgently. 'What exactly is it that you're trying to say, my boy?'

Joel had another go. 'What I want to say is that I think the answer lies with the structure of chance and I'd like to change my thesis in order to study it.'

Metric drew a deep breath. He certainly had not expected it to be this easy. 'Probability theory, is it?'

'Er, yes and no. Yes as far as the maths is concerned. But the thing is that there is a strong empirical aspect to the whole, er, the whole thing, as it were. I mean, what I need to do I think is to study probabilistic mechanisms in relation to quantum theory in order to ground my thesis, which will, I think, entail, if my understanding of the workings of the university are correct, and I'm not quite sure that they are –' Joel was sweating now ' – that I will have to transfer out of the Mathematics faculty and into the Physics. I think. Especially since I'll need to spend a lot of time with the computer, because I'll have to run models and compile masses of data.' There. He'd said it. Joel held his breath and began to count.

'So what you're saying is that you don't want me to teach you any more?' Joel couldn't speak. He sat there waiting for Metric to explode, perspiring frantically. He bit his bottom lip, drew blood. At least when he'd left his parents he hadn't had to confront them. 'Well, I can't say I haven't seen it coming. It's about time you moved on. You're a very clever chap, I dare say you've outgrown me. I'm not convinced by your thesis, I have to say – I think we're going to have to hammer that out a little, maybe some outside help is called for. But I don't think that what you're proposing is impossible, not by any means. No, I don't think it will be impossible at all.'

Going . . .

So Joel made the switch and moved out of maths and Metric could breathe easy again. The new thesis went well and the boy (who by now was pretty much of a man) felt at home in his new discipline, not least because he had consolidated the first proper friendship he'd managed since he came to England. The PDP-10 made a fine companion: straightforward yet complex, patient yet temperamental, promiscuous yet focused (access was only possible on a time-share system). Because he could get in more time with the machine that way, Joel became almost nocturnal and the small hours invariably found him hunched in semi-darkness before the small round screen, punching in his programs and hunting for statistical significance in oceans of quantal data.

He liked Cambridge by night, even in the winter. It was a peaceful place; with most people in bed, the countryside seemed to take over the town and suddenly the trees bushes lawns took precedence over the crumbling, blackened buildings. And the air seemed more straightforward after dark, less ambivalent. Among the other students

Joel acquired a reputation as something of a ghoul – first years used to call him 'the vampire', but soon changed that to 'the glumpire' because he never smiled. They'd run from him in mock terror when, at the tail end of an all-night bender, they encountered him wandering home from the computer labs at four or five in the morning. Although vaguely aware that he was the object of their mirth, Joel failed to comprehend this behaviour and generally ignored it, but he did get angry one night when some students lay in wait and drenched him with eight pints of stale ale that they'd salvaged from the dregs bucket in the college bar and had no doubt pissed in too. Screaming at his assailants as they disappeared into the shadows, he woke the Proctor who, in the best traditions of British justice, disciplined him for causing a disturbance.

But though Joel generally preferred his nocturnal existence, as summer came around again even he began to feel pangs for the touch of sunlight on his pallid skin, and every now and then he'd take a day or two's break from the lab, reboot his body clock by sleeping a full twelve hours and venture out into the daylight for a pastoral afternoon spent in Grantchester meadows or a short hike through the Cambridge countryside.

. . . *going* . . .

Laika had been up there a decade before her erratic orbit carried her above the clear summer skies of Cambridge. Stoned students caught her glint as they made out in Grantchester Meadows, an extra star to wish upon – though more often than not they put it down to the drugs. As usual, the town smelt of mown grass and traffic exhaust, Pimm's and bitter, stagnant river water and student sweat. At every possible opportunity ragged bands of youths collapsed in the parks and quads to drink away the day and boast pompously about how much work they were not going to do. Meanwhile the rest of the country tried to come to grips with what the dons condescendingly referred to as 'social change'. The colleges were still heavily segregated, but the warm weather had turned the parks and lanes into rustling zones of fornication. It was impossible to walk along a river bank without disturbing couples copulating in the cow parsley.

Joel picked his way along the Cam until he found a vacant patch that was relatively clear of used condoms and cigarette butts. He took off his jacket, folded it into a cushion, sat on it and opened his well-thumbed copy of *Principia Mathematica*. Picking up where he had left off in the library, he began to read. For him it was like poetry: the ideas clicked through his mind with the certainty of a well-oiled clockwork mechanism, beautiful in their elegance and logic. He read avidly for about twenty minutes, quickly digesting each clause and each proposition, his greasy hair stubborn against the breeze, until his concentration was broken by the raucous sounds of a punt full of people moving downstream towards him. A sharp meander in the river's course prevented him from seeing the party, but they were definitely drawing closer. The noise increased in intensity until individual words became discernible between the cackles of laughter and a moment later the nose of the punt appeared from around the bend. Packed with people, cans of lager and half-consumed bottles of wine, the craft drifted past, trailing marijuana smoke in its wake. It was a smell he recognised from the streets of Crown Heights and Williamsburg, and although he had never been sure what exactly the odour signified, it nevertheless triggered a sudden and violent memory of his home.

Some of the boat's occupants he had seen before. The puntsman – a fairly nominal title, earned by the fact that he was holding the pole rather than doing anything constructive with it – was an Irish fellow who lived on the same staircase as Joel in college. Short and squat, with a blob of bronze hair, he fancied himself a poet and drinker, and was never to be seen without a collection of Yeats, or at least a Malcolm Lowry, stuffed into one of his pockets (which he would pull out and quote from at regular intervals). Joel knew none of the girls; in fact he didn't know any girls at all. The mores of his upbringing were still set within him and even now he could not bring himself to look at any of what he thought of as 'the females' in the face. The constant tides of flirting and fornication which sucked at the groins of his peers passed completely over his head and he was barely aware of the curious rites that went on around him day in, day out. Now that the summer was here and they were becoming more obvious, he found himself uncomfortable when forced into any kind of close proximity with his fellow students. When all was said and done, Joel was most definitely a loner.

He caught the eye of McGuigan, the Irishman, and immediately dropped his gaze and tried to return to his book. But McGuigan had seen him and began to sing, cheered on by his companions:

Oh Booky, Oh Book Book, Oh Booky my dear,
Why is it I always keep you so near?
Oh Booky Oh Booky Oh Booky my love,
No use as a brolly no use as a glove,
Oh Booky Oh Booky Oh Book Book my heart
You've given me nothing and now we must part.
Oh Booky Oh Booky Oh Book don't be glum,
You've lived off my weakness but now we are done
Oh Book Booky-Booky Book Book don't take it so hard
That I've gone and replaced you with ten pounds of lard –

He broke off to take a breath, then sat down with a thump on the end of the punt, doubled up with private laughter. Everyone applauded, except Joel. A girl threw a bread roll at him; it glanced off his shoulder and disappeared into the cow parsley, and he tried not to react. The punt fell silent for a moment but then McGuigan, who had been swigging from a bottle, continued his address. 'That's Joist, that is. That's Joist, you know.' Thankful for an excuse to turn their eyes from Joel, the others looked up at him.

One of the other men said in loud, Home Counties tones, 'I say, McGuigan, what the fuck are you on about now?' and the girl languishing on his arm tittered at the obscenity.

'No, it's Joist, I say. Have I not told you the one about Joist then?'

'You most certainly have not,' said the Englishman, Kendricks, trying to retain the upper hand.

'Well, then. It's like this. There's this Kerryman, y'see . . . no, shhh, listen, it's a good story . . . there's this Kerryman and he's out of work, down on his luck like.'

'Ooo, Tommy, I do like your accent,' said the girl who had thrown the bread roll.

'Carol, ya hussy! Are you gonna shut up or am I gonna tip you in the river!' McGuigan cried, grabbing at her ankle. She shrieked and scrabbled away from him towards the bows, rocking the boat dangerously. When she reached safety she tucked her lips between her teeth and nodded.

'OK then, I'll continue. But no more interruptions mind.' He had his audience now. 'So there's this Kerryman who's out of work . . .'

'We've heard that bit,' said Kendricks funnily, but no one took any notice.

'. . . and he's generally down on his luck. He's in Dublin, see, and if he doesn't get work soon, he won't meet his rent and he'll be out on the street. So he's hangin' aroun', hangin' aroun', asking his mates, "Have ya heard anything, have ya? No news is tha'?", until one morning one of his mates tells him of a building site he knows of where they're hiring. So he gets hisself along there and goes up to the foreman and presents hisself. The foreman looks him up and down and feels sorry for him, 'cuz he's a skinny little runt, and says all right then, you've got yerself a job if yer can make yerself useful. So our hero, he's over the moon, and he's like "where can I start, where can I start?" So the foreman says to him, "Go sort out that stack of lumber on t'other side of the yard." ' Carol started to giggle again, but McGuigan shot her a look and she clammed up. It was a sub-routine of one of those rites so alien to Joel. 'So he goes over and starts moving and stacking and moving and stacking, and he's been at it about an hour when the foreman walks up to him and taps him on the shoulder. "What's the matter?" the foreman says. "Don't you know the difference between a girder and a joist?" "Oh that's easy," says the Kerry, turning round and mopping his brow. "Joist wrote *Ulysses*, and Girder wrote *Faust*!" '

The party collapsed with laughter and McGuigan hurled the bottle he'd been sucking on high into the air for emphasis. It came down with a splash and frightened two moorhens, who took to the air with a clatter. Flying low over Joel's head one of them let loose a crap and the runny lime landed splat in the middle of page 131 of *Principia Mathematica*. This caused even greater hilarity among McGuigan's group, but fortunately for Joel at that point the boat passed out of sight around the next bend where, owing to the pilot's lack of concentration, its bows snagged on a large clump of water weeds that extended out from the bank.

Now that they had gone Joel's fury boiled over. 'Bertrand Russell himself used to sit here and read, you know!' he yelled after the party. 'And Lewis Carroll!' But his words were lost to the river. He tore out a clump of grass and wiped down the soiled page, cleaning off the last stubborn dregs with his handkerchief, and tried to turn his attention back to the text. But it was useless, and soon he flung the book aside and lay back in the grass. The light poured down through the simmering leaves and splashed across his face, dappling him with shadows. The photons sparked on his retinae and tiny currents buzzed around to the back of his brain, setting up interference patterns in his cortex and making spirals dance in his vision. He blinked and rolled on to his side. Despite the breeze it was warm, and as his carooming thoughts began to gyre more slowly and lose their points of reference he drifted in and out of sleep. A blonde girl lay face down in the meadow about ten yards from him; she had taken off her blouse and her bra lay unclipped on the ground beneath her, forgotten as an ancient obligation.

She dozes there, her back pink from the sun, her face in shadow but already browned, her hair nattering with the zephyrs that twitch to and fro across the field. A fly comes down, alights upon her shoulder and the local muscles spasm of their own accord. Like an animal, thinks Joel, remembering the girl in the boat who had hit him with the bread roll and at whom he had stared. Disturbed, the fly lifts into the air, buzzes around for a bit and lands again, a few centimetres from its previous position. Joel has noticed before how a movement from beneath will serve only to unsettle a fly, make it take off for only a second or two, after which it will invariably return to feast once more. But by bringing a hand down in a swift feint, a rush of air disturbs the cilia on its back and the fly infers a much greater sense of danger than from a movement sensed through its legs. Now it will fly off to pester someone else. Of course, Joel reflects, it's preposterous to think of a fly as being capable of inferring anything, in the true sense – it's far too primitive a creature. The point is that a fly's actions are triggered directly by its nervous responses to stimuli. If I had a big enough computer, he thinks, one that took up two or three rooms, I should be able to model that fly completely. He is somewhat mistaken, as it happens, for great mathematician though he is, Joel knows little or nothing about physiology or neurology or biochemistry and the rest of it. How could he, when even he can never hope to command more than a fraction of the material that has been written on his own subject, let alone acquaint himself with the rolling hills of data that stretch further than the eye can see in all directions in each of the other disciplines?

Too late he looks back towards the girl, or perhaps just in time. She is sitting up, having risen to swat the pest away, and one large brown nipple is hanging free in the air. Musty from her snooze, she rubs her nose to clear it of pollen. This makes her sneeze, a cute sneeze, *a-tissoo*, and her breast trembles nicely. We turn to Joel, expecting some reaction: a leer, a line, even a darkening of the eye . . . but no, there's nothing. Not a tremor. The smile upon his face is one of simple fascination – he's still contemplating his digital fly (so to speak) and gazing blankly at the girl's breasts while doing it. Naturally she spies him, gives him a dusky look, picking up perhaps on the strange magnetism Joel has that Metric also recognised (if only he'd do something with his hair . . .). She waits. But there's no reaction at all. With a loud 'tut' and an exaggeration of her movements the girl pulls on her blouse and moves away, swinging her bra behind her as she goes. She'd heard of a cat without a smile, but a smile without a cat?

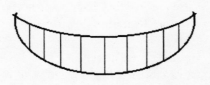

Joel was lost in space. He was with his one true love, the only love he'd ever known. Click click whirr went the limbs of this love, limbs which could hardly be described as languid. Her tendons were of wires and pulleys, her joints made of gears, her vital organs of transistors and valves. Her eyes were made of *and* gates, her mouth of *ors*, and her cunt was made of *nots*. *Not not not not not.* And in that lay her charm. Her brain was made of slide-rules and her flesh of logarithms, tables and matrices. Her breasts were sets, her hair had square roots and her clothes were quite transcendental. In short, she was perfection and all the more perfect because Joel could attain her, in a glorious jouissance of integration, whenever he wished. Logic is its own reward and Joel liked nothing better than to trace out its many branches until his brain felt ready to implode.

. . . gone

On finishing his Ph.D, Joel was offered a position as a research student at CERN, the European Centre for Nuclear Research, situated on the French–Swiss border. He took the job and was glad of it. It was time to move on and he was not sorry. He had been in Cambridge for the best part of a decade but apart from the old PDP–10 and the kindness of the Metrics, he'd put down no roots there, none at all, and he had no fondness for this place which could never in any event have survived being the realisation of such a fantastic dream.

4

A handful of pixels

Jennifer lay with her nose about three inches from the dusty screen of Donald's old TV and watched *The Partridge Family*, *Roadrunner* cartoons, *The Osmonds*, sitcoms, soaps and reruns of *Lost in Space*, the signal of which, it just so happened, was also being picked up by Laika in her satellite. Both dog and girl had a thing about the robot. He looked so useless with his goldfish-bowl head and flexi-tube arms, and yet the flashing lights suggested that a keen and even tender intelligence lay within. It was 1972, six years after Doreen had had her husband committed and the year that Joel had left Cambridge for CERN, and Jennifer had just turned twelve.

Eager to explore all possible watching habits, she had recently begun to hold TV parties on Saturday afternoons, an idea that grew out of the original moon-landing gathering three years before. After lunch about ten children would come over to watch the afternoon matinée, which was as a rule either a Western, a musical or a Hollywood epic of great scope and grandeur.

If the weather was fine, Henry would retire to the garden while they watched and potter about. He would mow the lawn, or do a spot of weeding, or just read the paper. What he would never do was stray very far from a regularly refreshed squat crystal tumbler full of gin and tonic mixed half and half which he would bring from the drinks cabinet in the living-room, set down on the chipped metal filigree of the garden table and return to at intervals which grew shorter and shorter as the sun sank lower and lower in the sky. Every refill meant confronting the gathered children, and with each one he would smile a little more and see a little less. By the time evening came, nothing much would exist outside of the three sides of fence that boxed in his plot and the sunset, whose great burning orb would begin to seem to him like a giant lemon sliding into the bottomless cocktail of the night. When it dipped out of sight it was time to go in for a sweater, a top-up and some dinner for which Jennifer – whose friends, called home by their mothers, would have left by now – would now be clamouring.

In the winter he would cook lunch for her instead (chops under the grill and frozen peas and mash) pick at his own portion until she finished eating, greet the children who spewed in through the door, all sticky sweets and sweaty hands and screaming for the movie, leave the dishes in the sink and disappear off to the local or perhaps the golf club to play a quick round and hover in the bar for an hour or two before returning. When he got back, Jennifer would no doubt have raided the biscuit tin and be curled up asleep on the armchair by the fire.

He thought at the beginning that he enjoyed the children's company and for the first few of those TV afternoons he sat with them, on the pretext of making sure that they got up to no mischief. But the hot mess of rapt faces, wide eyes, lips wet with sucking and chewing, and half-clad young limbs opened him to something that the booze had long kept subdued. The soft nap of a pre-pubescent thigh, the bud of a breast pressed up against the arm of a chair, a young boy's erection brought on and sustained by boredom; these things did not fail to come to his notice. He was a man of the world, or so he thought, he had read *Lolita* (several times) and while he was aware of the dangers, he believed they could be contained. So he did not see it as a problem when Judd – whom Henry regarded as a presumptuous boy (and certainly exotic) but whom Jennifer seemed to like – pulled the hair of Alice, the youngest of Jennifer's friends, and Alice started to cry and insisted on sitting on Uncle Henry's knee before she would stop. If Henry's hands did not stray and everything was good and proper it was only for a while, because desire will always disrupt, and before long Henry was silently giving thanks that the girl did not notice – or did not seem to notice – the extra muscle that ran along his thigh and remained there until just before the film was due to end and the parents due to arrive, when he had to place his charge back down on the floor and shuffle upstairs to relieve his aching testicles and rearrange his damp and ruffled clothing.

From then on Alice regarded Henry's lap as her domain. Capable of generating the precise amount of emotional upheaval needed to get her own way (even that first time there had been some debate in the group as to whether Judd had pulled her hair unprovoked or whether she had driven him to it) she had also noted with her sure child's eye that the staking of her claim had aroused not the slightest jealousy in Jennifer. Indeed, Alice was slightly disappointed, as this had been part of the desired effect, but she was not to know that Jennifer did not regard her putative father as in any strong way hers. They lived together like earth and moon, bound together by circumstance, ritual, habit and the gravitational pull of normality, into the pit of which all things eventually slide. But they never really touched. This suited poor Henry, who was more intimate with the shades and moods of his cocktails than those of his daughter, and it suited Jennifer too, who with perfect precociousness knew that if the relationship functioned at all it was because it was she who was responsible for her father and not the other way around. She had been flipped into self-possession at a tender age by the circumstances of her mother's life and the catastrophe of her death, as if, even as an infant, various behavioural modes had lain latent within her, one of which – the one she'd settled into – was able to accommodate the stresses of her childhood. So she was happy that Alice should be dandled from Henry's knee because he would never dandle her, Jennifer, again and she felt no regret over this. Although she knew something of boys she did not know enough to make a conscious connection between these afternoons and the stiff, sweet stains on Henry's underwear that she sometimes found when it was her turn to do the wash. Yet she got from them a flush and a tingle in her stomach that came from the awareness of having seen something forbidden or, at least, never spoken of, and which promised that the world was a bigger place than she yet knew. And she was aware also that at these times she thought of her friend Rever and of running in the woods behind the houses after school, and of Mr Kinever, who taught her science, and who was lithe and firm.

So for a few weeks Alice sat on Henry's knee, and Henry got up now and again and disappeared upstairs, the amount of bare flesh that he managed to graze with his fingertips directly proportional to the number of times he had to leave the room. After a while, the experience began to seem quite safe and Henry found himself getting a little bit more drunk and a little bit more brazen, until one wet Saturday afternoon, as *Seven Brides for Seven Brothers* flickered across the screen, his hand reached that little bit too far. Suddenly Alice's giggles became sobs. She didn't climb down from Henry's knee but sat stock still and demanded to be taken home, as if unaware of the origin of the offending sensation. Something was wrong, something was most definitely wrong, her mind was all confusion, something had happened which didn't fit with the way things were, the way things should be. Henry got up and pretended to fuss, and Jennifer came over and shushed and cooed until Alice was calmed by the attention. But she still insisted on being taken home, and Henry was put in the awkward position of having to call her parents and ask them to come over and pick her up.

The group, minus Alice, watched the rest of the film in silence, then trooped off out of the house. Jennifer left with them. All in all, it had been an unsuccessful afternoon: the crying business aside, except for Alice everyone had been bored by the film and they were left listless and in need of something to do. The rain had stopped, so they went down to the park to smoke cigarettes and scratch their names on the benches. Judd didn't smoke and he didn't really know anybody either, and everyone was a little wary of him because there weren't too many black boys about in Stratford at that time. He charged around the sodden lawns, his arms outstretched, making the sound of a propeller under his breath and saturating his expensive leather shoes with moisture, banking and diving in between the benches, making up his own movie inside his head. It was easier for him to follow the plot this way anyway

– when he watched TV, even when he was with all the other kids at Jennifer's – he often blanked out and missed crucial events. Too embarrassed to ask what he'd missed, and often not realising he'd missed anything at all, he kept quiet which, in the eyes of the others, made him more mysterious still.

In the park, then, they left him to play aeroplanes, to take off from a bench, fly around, return to the same bench to take off again. In 1938, four years after Jennifer's mother had been told by her dance instructor about Wilbur Wright, the billionaire Howard Hughes had taken off from Floyd Bennett airfield in the United States, spent four days flying around the world in a single circular arc and returned to park his aeroplane in its hangar in the exact same spot in which it had been parked before his departure. If Nadine had been entranced by the image of Wright taking off in his biplane and flying in a circle to return to the same spot again, then perhaps she would have been charmed by watching Judd, this little Howard Hughes, flying in circles in order to disappear himself from the crowd of onlookers, running in order to stand still, speeding across the earth in order to experiment with time.

Her daughter was certainly intrigued. Jennifer couldn't keep from glancing at Judd between hot puffs on the carrot-ended cigarettes that were circulating, annoyed by the childishness of his game and drawn to it at the same time. Judd, by the way, was thinking about her too: while the other children blurred into the background he did not want to disappear Jennifer. Not because of who she was – they'd hardly ever exchanged a word – but because the TV afternoons were hers and they reminded Judd of the home he missed so much. If his father represented for Judd the logical power of machines, then Jennifer had come to mean access to the TV land of his childhood California. He wasn't bothered by not always being able to follow the plots of the films they watched, because the plots weren't what he was there for.

Left alone back at the house, Henry turned over the Alice incident in his mind, looking for a way to lie to himself. It wasn't clear, he finally decided, that he'd had any intention of interfering with the girl. For blame to be apportioned there surely had to be intention, there had to be a moment in which he had made the decision to act. But if such a moment had existed he could not remember it. The drink no doubt had something to do with it – he had certainly drunk more than usual. But now he thought about it he'd had a touch of cramp in his arm, yes, that was it, and he'd needed to flex it. A man gets stiff with a child on his lap for that long and she was no feather; yes, he was often surprised how heavy these kids were, they didn't look it, skinny as alley cats, some of them. And the whole affair was probably nothing to do with him anyway. It could have been something in the film that had upset her. Or how did he know one of the boys hadn't whispered something malicious to her? The little black boy, no doubt: he'd pulled her pigtails before, after all. For God's sake, it could even have been the weather, the rain beating a bit harder on the window than before, a change in air pressure (he'd better check the barometer in the hallway), a conjunction of the planets. Perhaps the house stood on the intersection of ley lines.

Whatever the reason he finally came up with, from then on he kept out of the children's way during those cinematic Saturday afternoons. Jennifer didn't mind. Although she worried about her father, she knew she was quite capable of running things without him around. However many kids turned up of a weekend to watch her TV she was always quietly in control and none of them, even the older ones, had ever taken any liberties with her or her house. And anyway, without Henry around it was easier for her to test her power over the boys who came over: the world of males had fascinated her for a while now and, like a restless sea lapping discontentedly at the shores of some pre-biotic land, she wanted to colonise it. Henry's presence had made the environment too arid for her exploring tendrils to make much progress, but with him out of the way the atmosphere changed and she was at liberty to use words fingers glances like lichens and mosses, hyphae and rhizomes. With these tools she began to inch her way across the skins of these boys and slowly weave a psychic mat of mild exploitation.

A month or two later . . .

Now the summer evenings were stretching themselves out beyond the end of the school day; now the breezes that accompanied them were warm and inviting and the birds provided an extra dimension to the bushes and the trees; now Jennifer could trip home from school glowing with the innocence that radiates only from a perfect depravity freed from all external perspective. She could loll on the hot stones of the low wall that defined her tiny front garden, sip at a lemonade and call to her friends as they passed her on their way back to their homes on the estate.

At the end of the day the school spat them out and they passed into small groups, volatile molecular knots bonded by the juxta-positions of geography, age, smell, money, looks, peer pressure, the disguised dictates of desire and the hidden agendas of the vast yeasts of the future. Each child formed a nexus, a series of points of intersection for a tumult of factors, and each child resonated accordingly.

Shelley was Jennifer's best friend and she straggled along Hunt's Crescent, all scuffed shoes and stretched socks and stained cuffs. Dog-eared exercise books poked from the top of her bag, crammed in among toiletries stolen from Boots and odd bits of jewellery and a broken watch Lewis had given her, and sweet wrappers and crushed chocolate bars and half a pack of Embassy Filtered, two of which had been half smoked and pinched out, and a packet of mints and a box of matches, both live and dead, and one gymshoe (Shelley was still hoping the other one was going to turn up) and last term's report card which she had not passed on to her parents for obvious reasons, and a biro drained dry of ink, ink which now formed a dark decoration along one of the bag's lower seams. All this was immersed in the smell of rotting canvas, the cloth still muggy from having trailed round behind its owner throughout the winter months.

So Shelley came first and after Shelley came the bag, that theatre of the ongoing war between the concerns of a burgeoning social life and the discipline of school, and after the bag came Rever, who had just been given the brush-off by Shelley and was trying to look cool about it. Shelley spotted Jennifer sitting on her wall and crossed the road to join her. Now she had an ally and Rever was defeated and had to carry straight on, scoping the girls from behind his plastic Ray Bans and adjusting the Aston Villa sweatbands that he always wore around his thin wrists as he went.

Immediately suspicious, Jenn questioned her friend. 'What you doing with Rever?' she demanded.

'I wasn't *with* him, you idiot.'

'Well pardon me for breathing.'

'It's all your fault in the first place.'

'What? What have I done?'

'You told him I wanted to go and see some poxy play at the theatre.'

'So what?'

'So he's gone and brought me tickets, that's what.'

'So what's the problem. Why don't you go?'

''Cuz he's a creep. We don't all have the same tastes as you.'

'*I* don't fancy him.'

'You do an' all. You fancy him rotten. You told me so at New Year's.'

'Yeah, well that was New Year's. I've gone off him now.'

'Lewis said you did it with him.'

'Yeh, well, Lewis doesn't know shit. How does Lewis know anyway?'

Shelley feigned loss of interest and changed the subject. 'That lemonade?'

'Yeh.' Twirling the liquid around in the glass. 'You want some?'

'All right.'

'Come on then.' Jennifer slides from her perch on the wall and Shelley follows her into the cool of the house. From outside their giggled conversation is still audible, although individual words cannot be distinguished. It is balmy, it is summer. A dragonfly flits across the screen. Two or three people walk past the house: pedestrians. A young boy on a bicycle crosses, right to left. A few moments later another boy chases after him, yelling. Peace for a moment. A brown mongrel dog wanders along the pavement, sniffing at the wall. It stops, cocks its leg and pisses up against the stones.

Shelley emerges from the house just in time to see it run off. 'Oi, Jenn! That mangy dog from next door's been slashing up your wall again!'

At her shout, Jennifer reappears. 'Oh, shit! That little fucker. It does it deliberately, you know.' She yells abuse at the dog, which canters away down a side road, then locks the front door behind her and walks off down the road with her friend.

Half an egg

Deep in Jennifer's matrix. Being a catarrhine primate (Old World Monkeys, anthropoid apes, humans) Jennifer has a modified oestrous cycle, aka a menstrual cycle. Unlike many mammals, the catarrhine primates do not exhibit a well-defined period of oestrus or 'heat', coinciding with ovulation, when the female will copulate with a male.

Preceding and succeeding oestrus there are various changes that take place throughout the body, particularly in the uterus. These may be regarded as preparations for pregnancy. The whole set of these changes is controlled by hormones. The first phase of the cycle is known as follicular. Stimulated by the pituitary hormone, Graafian follicles begin to grow inside the ovary. At the same time there is an increasing secretion of oestrogen by the ovary and a proliferation of the lining of the uterus (endometrium), paving the way for the next stage, ovulation. Eventually the ripe egg will burst from such a follicle. The egg is discharged on to the surface of the ovary and thence passes into the oviduct. There is also an activation of mating reflexes.

The third phase is known as the luteal stage, and involves the formation of a temporary organ of internal secretion, the corpus luteum (yellow body), in the interior of the ruptured Graafian follicle after ovulation by the ingrowth of the follicle wall, which becomes yellow secretory luteal tissue. The secreted hormone is progesterone. Formation of the corpus luteum occurs as a result of action of the luteinising hormone and its secretory activity requires the presence of the lactogenic hormone of pituitary. At this time oestrogen production decreases, while there is a great development of the uterine glands. If ovulation does not result in fertilisation then the cycle goes into phase four: the regression of the corpus luteum, the beginning of new follicular growth, a return to the unproliferated state of the uterine lining, the diminution of oestrogen and the cessation of progesterone secretion. In the special case of the menstrual cycle there is a sudden destruction of the mucosa of the uterus at the end of the luteal phase of the cycle, producing bleeding. If, on the other hand, fertilisation does occur then the corpus luteum persists and continues secreting during part or all of pregnancy. On the morning of 15 May Jennifer had entered the second stage: ovulation.

As for the egg which was released, it was large and complex – nearly one hundred thousand times larger than the sperm that would one day penetrate it. And while those sperm would carry only chromosomal information with them when they came, the cytoplasm of this egg was packed full of mitochondria. Containing DNA and oxidative enzyme systems, mitochondria are the energy factories of every living cell. Once, billions of years ago, they were bacteria; free-living and vicious they entered other cells and multiplied like viruses until they split their host asunder, so releasing multiple offspring into the world. But somewhere along the line a host cell captured this parasite and tricked or coerced it into a symbiotic relationship. With this tamed and rapidly respiring organelle inside of it, the host could now breathe and metabolise much greater quantities of food into adenosine triphosphate, a molecule crucial to many cellular processes. The eukaryotic cell – the cell which makes up all multicellular organisms – was born.

Mitochondria do not reproduce like nucleated cells. They do not exchange DNA with other organisms; rather they divide and multiply like bacteria, according to their own rules. Mammalian mitochondria is passed only down the female line; the male sperm introduces no new mitochondria into the ovum. Which begs the question: what are men for?

Rubble in mind

Saturn V is launched, Judd's ruler twangs, the pellet arcs across the room and hits Lewis on the neck. Doreen Buerk spins around on one heel and stares at the small American down the length of her nose, fixing him like a doomed field-mouse with the ball-bearing pupils of her grim stoat eyes. She lets the silence gather, creating maximum dramatic tension for the opening of her speech. When she senses that the time is right she starts to yell: 'That's it! Out! Out you go! I've told you and I've told you I won't put up with this kind of behaviour. You will be penalised after school. Outside the door! Go! Now! I'll deal with you after class. It may come as a surprise for you to learn that some of us would like to continue the lesson without interruption.' Judd opens his mouth to protest but she shouts him down and expels him from the class, to the great amusement of his peers.

Out in the corridor, lonely and upset, Judd fiddled with the buttons of his digital watch, a present his dad had sent him only a few weeks before and the only one in the school. But he'd played with it a lot recently and was soon bored with it. He looked around the hallway for something else to focus on, something to bind the random rush of thoughts that tumbled through his head. The building was old, older than most things in California. He stood at the foot of a stone staircase that wound upwards for three or four flights. Daylight spewed into the darkened vault from the western landings. He let himself imagine that one of the landings led on to the street on which his father's house stood, thousands of miles away, back on the Pacific Rim. He had one chance to take the right doorway, and one alone. Which one would he take? Another door led into Pioneer 11. Pioneer 11 had been launched the previous month. Judd had read about it in *National Geographic*; it would be somewhere out by Mars now. He'd be stuck inside the probe with no way back and not much air. Out of the window he'd be able to see the huge peak of Olympus Mons, which he remembered because it was the biggest volcano in the solar system. He'd probably be able to find some freeze-dried ice-cream in the supply lockers; he'd had some at Christmas, when his father had taken him to the space exhibit at the Smithsonian when they'd all been in Washington DC because his mother had been invited to an important party. It was all hard like polystyrene until you bit it, then it foamed up in your mouth and was kind of like ice-cream, but in a weird way, because you didn't taste it until after you swallowed. That was when Apollo 17 had just landed on the moon, and the man at the museum had said that the astronauts were probably eating the ice-cream right at the same time Judd was and Judd had asked him if it was true what the *National Geographic* said, that there weren't going to be any more men on the moon for a long time, and the man said that he was sure that there would be. Judd said that he would like to be an astronaut and fly there and his father patted him on the back, and the man said: 'Maybe you'll be next then' and Moses thought a black astronaut? and remembered the ghettos that made up the bulk of the city and forced a smile.

Tired with the demands the punishment was making on his imagination, Judd mentally stamped his foot. Why had his mother brought him here to these English Midlands which lay about him now like a river fog that would never lift? Eight months previously, when they had first arrived, he could still invoke the forest tang of the pine trees, the sound of the tyres of his father's Lincoln drawing up in the driveway, the hollow knock of basketballs in the courts at the foot of the hill, the low-res blither of the ever present television. He could use these gentle demons to open portals to the long evenings and the bored sun and the roller-skating and the easy food back home. But the access gates had dwindled and finally disappeared as his reference points had all slowly been replaced and he had grown, faster than he ever could have imagined, into this different place where no one had ever eaten a Twinkie bar or even knew what root beer was. And to make matters worse the new culture had infected him despite himself, using as a bridgehead his dim memories of his visits here as an even younger child, and now it prickled his skin like a rash. He was in a no-man's land of change and uncertainty and, although he longed for it, California somehow seemed as alien as the surroundings into which he had been thrust.

The train of thought exhausted itself; Judd gave it up and listened for the tractor, but its rattlings could not be heard from inside the hallway. Instead there was only the velvet hum of children organised behind walls and the echoes of his own small movements in the cavernous space. He coughed and listened to the reverberations, but they brought comfort and fear in equal doses. The feeling connected with one which came to him sometimes as he lay on his bed at night waiting to fall asleep. He would be looking down the length of his body when abruptly the twin peaks his feet made in the blankets would seem an incredible distance away, as if he were looking at them through the wrong end of a telescope. This stretched perception was not so much accompanied by as actually a part of a sensation he felt in his feet, in his almost hairless groin and around the back of his skull. It was a tingling, but a tingling which always seemed to be drawing away, like an ebb. It was as if the tides of all the things that were within him, and which he neither understood nor knew how to number, were ebbing away into the bed and into the room around him. It was that ebb which was both frightening and comforting simultaneously.

He began to worry that the duty master might happen by and further chastise him, and his testicles grew warm at the thought. He wondered about this word the Buerk had used, 'penalise'. In his mind it became linked with another word, one that was austere and technical, and which adults used with caution. Back home the teacher would have said 'punish', and to be punished was OK, because it would happen and then be over, and did not threaten to go on and on in the background, day and night for ever, interminable.

To escape he would make himself invisible. How would he do that? Easy – by making time stand still. Across the hallway from him was a door . . . it was simple to imagine that this was the only door through which any threat to him could come. He just had to fix the door in time as it was – closed. He narrowed his eyes and contemplated the view before him. Now, all he needed to do was click his eyelids down and up like a camera's shutter to foreclose the possibility of the door's ever opening. It would take only a moment . . . and yet he hesitated. For to take possession of the world in this way was also to allow the world, in its tedious materiality, to take possession of him. A shiver went down his back as he became aware of the threat presented by the cold stone wall behind him. What if, in the instant that he closed his eyes to cement the door, the wall took advantage of his distraction to cement him? It was a possibility. Yet which was the greater, his fear of the duty master or his fear of the wall? Perhaps if he was quick he could catch the wall off guard. He decided to go for it.

While Judd bent space–time and dreamt of escape, inside her Cartesian classroom Doreen Buerk seeped on in nasal tones about glacial erosion in mountain regions. With the unbreachable wall of her knowledge erected around her she issued edicts to the class full of pingos and mud-flat polygons, permafrost and outwash, arêtes and bifurcations. But the concentration of her pupils was undergoing pre-glacial unstratified drift: there were only five more minutes left before the dinner bell rang, and though they yawned before the children like the largest of underground caverns it was not within their capacities to fill them with what Doreen Buerk might have regarded as useful deposits.

But wait a minute. Something was permeating the hard crust of Lewis's brain and forming stalactites of some description. The closed system of the geography lesson had been breached with the expulsion of Judd to the corridor and, with the usual dampeners on lateral bleed short-circuited, Lewis's mind was meandering. It had indeed meandered all the way to the great ocean of the guilty conscience, a sight he had not witnessed before.

Doreen had been telling the class how glacial action had inspired

Percy Bysshe Shelley's poem, 'Mont Blanc', calling it 'one of the most wonderful of poems about nature' and 'the birthright of every Englishman'. It was at this point that the ten-and-a-half-year-old hand of Jacob Hethlethwaite shot up into the air, quickly followed by the sound of him reciting from memory: 'Thus you, raven of Arf – dark, deep raven – you multicoloured, no, multivoiced vale, over which pins and crags, and caravans sail like fast cloud shadows and sunbeams which seem, er, powerful lightness in the arm which, comes down . . . I know it I know it . . . er, comes down from the ice gluphs that grid his secret throne, and, and . . . bursting . . .' Jacob stood and trembled, transported by the emotion of the piece.

Doreen Buerk watched him with a dalek's steely eye, boring a hole into his forehead with her gaze and forcing him to shut up and sit down. 'Yes, thank you very much, Jacob, that's very good,' she buzzed in an even and metallicised drone, 'but I think we can save it for the English lesson, can't we.'

Eddie Richmond called out from the back, 'What's a gluph, miss?'

Doreen's face reddened just a shade. 'What did I just say? Are you asking me to repeat myself, Master Richmond?'

'No miss.'

'No. I didn't think so.' She returned to firmer ground, to perma-frost and solifluction, leaving plots against Jacob Hethlethwaite to coalesce in the imaginations of most of the class. One of the exceptions was Lewis. The poem reminded him that he had filched his father's best Mont Blanc fountain pen, which his father thought he had just mislaid, much to the annoyance of his new girlfriend who had given it to him the previous Christmas, and it was very expensive and how could he have lost it? At which point his father hit his new girlfriend in the mouth and said, 'It's only a fucking pen, shut your fucking gassing for five christing minutes, will you?' As a result of which Lewis thought it was probably best that his father did not discover that he, Lewis, had stolen the pen and given it to a girl he wanted to impress and who went by the name of Shelley.

Lewis was the oldest boy in his year. He had been put down two years running (and once a few years before) because he was obsessed by girls. It was all he thought about. He was the boy first discovered keeping porn mags in his desk; who blew up condoms like balloons in the playground. He was one of the few boys in the school who was thought by his peers to have had sex, and it was true, he had. With his father, with a sixteen-year-old girl who was drunk at a party that his elder brother Rever had taken him to and with Jennifer, Shelley's best friend (who had slept with Rever as well). And right now he wanted nothing more in the world than to have sex with Shelley. He had given her the pen to help her make up her mind about letting him finger her. Jennifer had done it for three B&H, but then Jennifer had done it with everybody. Shelley on the other hand, was class.

Shelley's 'Mont Blanc'. It was a too much of a coincidence. Maybe the Buerk knew? Maybe she'd seen Shelley with the pen? It was a terrifying thought and once Lewis had entertained the idea he found it difficult to get rid of. He squirmed in his chair, made a pyramid with his arms and tried to hide his head in the shadow that they made. He hoped that everyone would think that he was intent upon following the lesson in his textbook (although that alone was enough to arouse suspicion). He could feel Doreen Buerk's words; they were spread across his back like the tentacles of so many malicious octopi and they curled the suckered tips of their podia together so that they might form a powerful web with which to keep him down. With his head lowered he imagined he could feel her eyes prowling around him, the cold eyes of a cephalopod searching for a way into all those juicy thoughts.

The bell finally rang and Geography ended, and the kids thundered from the room. Lewis walked out slowly, lagging behind the rest and loitering outside the door, while Judd was called back into the classroom and chastised by his teacher. When the young American was released, Lewis followed him out into the playground and tailed him out along a line of poplar trees and on to the playing fields. Then he increased his speed until the two of them drew level. 'Hey, Judd!'

At the sound of Lewis's voice Judd turned and punched the older boy square in the face. Then they were both on the ground, wrestling in the dirt. Having taken Lewis by surprise, Judd had the upper hand, but he didn't have it in him to hurt the older boy. Partly he didn't want to and partly he was afraid that however much he hurt Lewis, Lewis would hurt him back two-fold. What he really wanted was to humiliate him, to make him feel as wretched as he felt himself – that would be the only way to repay him for snitching. Lewis, as Judd had suspected, had no such qualms about inflicting pain. He knew how to hurt and was ruthless about it. So Judd quickly lost his initial advantage and took a series of hard blows. Clothes were ripped, hair was pulled, palms and knees were grazed as the two boys rolled over and over. Then the American's anger returned and suddenly he had Lewis's head in a decent grip and was grinding his face into the soil and trying to tear off his ears. Lewis was experienced enough to know that if your enemy hasn't gone down after you've given him the best that you've got then it's time to get out while you still can. He broke away and scrambled to his feet, with Judd not far behind.

By this time a crowd had gathered around the entertainment. As the two fighters squared up to one another for a second bout someone at the back yelled 'Pinkerton!' The Deputy Head was approaching. Suddenly there was an enormous dissipation of tension. The crowd, previously a solid group bound by a common interest, now changed state and became liquid, the pupils rearranging themselves in mobile molecular clusters of twos or threes. By the time Pinkerton had motored up a second change was underway: two boys were picking football teams in an attempt to give the illegal gathering the appearance of a kind of order that authority would approve of.

Pinkerton was a short, stout man with an elliptical face and unkempt khaki-coloured hair that he scraped across his expansive bald pate. His tatty suit was the same mottled khaki as his distressed locks and as he walked he swayed from side to side, his thighs too large to let his legs swing perpendicular to the ground. Under one arm he clutched a file bulging with papers. He drew up to the crowd and stopped, removed his glasses with his free hand and rubbed them on his shirt before replacing them, then gave the group a hard stare, his mouth set like a toad's. 'Hum. Football. Good show,' he said. 'But keep the noise down, will you, or move away from the buildings.' Then he waddled off towards the staff canteen. Behind him, the excitement and the danger over, the liquid crowd became a gas and dissipated across the playing fields. Precipitated out was the original catalyst, Lewis and Judd.

Judd's heart was racing. He'd never done that before, hit out first, but his anger against Lewis had been building for a long time now. Lewis was the one who whispered 'nigger' to his cronies when Judd could overhear, it was Lewis who'd knocked a bottle of ink over his new satchel in the first week of term, who'd spat in his sandwiches the day they'd grabbed his lunch-box and thrown it around the room.

It had made him feel good to hit Lewis, like a hero, like an astronaut. But he didn't know if he could do it again. He hadn't known he was winning the fight when Pinkerton arrived; even while he'd been rubbing his opponent's face in the dirt he'd been thinking that at any moment the tables would be turned and he was going to have to run. Now he was elated and scared, both.

Lewis was, too. He hadn't expected a kid a couple of years his junior to hit him so hard. His nose was bleeding and he could still feel Judd scrabbling at his back in a manner not dissimilar to the octopoid words of Doreen Buerk. He felt a little dizzy. Across the fields the tractor engine stopped and, though neither of them noticed, it seemed there was something missing from the day. Everything shimmered. Lewis had been here before, but he hadn't. And then he did something very strange, something he definitely couldn't remember having ever done before, something that went against everything his father had taught him. He apologised.

'Fuck you,' was Judd's response.

'No, you don't understand, I'm sorry. I really mean it.' From where Judd was standing, something was wrong. Here was this boy who was older than him, who was taller and harder, and he was apologising. To him. For his part, Lewis was going red with the effort. 'I mean it.'

'Yeah, as if it means anything coming from you,' sneered Judd, suddenly buoyed up on a wave of memories of American television shows. He had not been in this situation before; he had to draw on what he could in order to know how to behave. Lewis on the other hand rarely got to watch TV at all. He wasn't aware that he was now dealing with a simulacrum, a montage of melodramatic behaviour. But Judd was black and beneath that tag a lot of weirdness could be brushed. Like cowboys at a gunfight, the boys wheeled around one another.

'I said I meant it. I've never said that to anyone before. You can't say fairer than that.'

'I don't scare easy,' spat Judd.

Stumped, Lewis tasted blood on his lips and reached up to touch his nose. His fingers came back wet with blood and he held them out to Judd like an offering. 'Look, I could help you out.'

'You ain't got nothing I want,' said the lone rider.

Lewis thought about this for a moment, then his face brightened. 'I can get you a girlfriend.'

Over the last few months, out on a limb in England and separated from his friends, Judd had plenty of time alone, time which needed to be filled. He read a bit, but he was not much of a reader; he watched English television, but it was not the same. And he didn't like the cold, so long walks exploring the countryside were out too. He had reached puberty early and, although only ten, already had a fuzz around his testicles. And among that sprouting down he had discovered the perfect toy with which to while away the long evenings spent waiting for his mother to come home from the theatre.

To begin with, odd things aroused him. The shape of a kitchen utensil, the angle of a spade sticking out of the garden earth, the silence of a room, the syncopation of a dripping tap. Almost anything, it seemed, could conjure an erotic adventure from a lonely mood. Then blood would start pumping into his member and he would slip into a soft, drugged state from which he could not emerge until he had ejaculated.

Soon he began to get turned on by anything mechanical. Cars, bikes, trucks; the old hand pump that stood out behind the house, left over from when there was a well; roundabouts and swings in public playgrounds; the clockwork viscera of a wrist-watch, which he knew how to take apart but not how to put back together;

143

strange machines he built with Meccano; an ageing chair that smelt of damp and worm dust, the seat and back of which slid to and fro along a complex ratchet. All these things would lead him into an erotic dream of process, of the road to consummation, but despite being always keen to take the first few steps along the way, consummation was almost never reached: instead, Judd would find himself overwhelmed with the narcosis of arousal, which would blend with his picnoleptic experiences to produce a state in which change was like the pressure of the air, no longer orchestrated by clock hands and numbers, but a part of the planet as it breathed its crusty breath. Now his senses were plugged into a vast field of time and sensitive to every potential that flickered across it: each fluctuation at the world's boundary some ten billion light-years away was linked to every movement of his hand, every swirl of his fingerprint, every fold of his foreskin.

But, fickle youth that he was, he soon tired of making love to the universe and refocused his desire on the glory of flesh. He pored over the lingerie advertisements in his mother's magazines, trying to decipher the glyphs of the female form. He went through her wardrobe, fascinated by the way her clothing differed from his own: the awkward cuts, the peculiar materials, the rows of tiny buttons that opened the wrong way. He began to stare at girls, to sneak looks down their shirts and up their skirts, to realise that their skin and hair had a different quality from his own. Sometimes he found differences and sometimes he did not. But the upshot was that when Lewis spoke to him he was ready.

Lewis told him to meet him by the bus-stop the next day after school.

'But I can't!' Judd protested. 'Michael always picks me up and drives me home. My mom says so.' Michael was his mother's personal assistant; a camp Los Angeleno, she'd insisted he accompany her during her sojourn at Stratford.

'Tell her you've joined the chess team or something.' Lewis. Always ready with an answer.

Boys and girls

At four the next day the final bell rang as usual – that bell that in the summer more than ever sounded the change of segregation, order, captivity, purpose into freedom, enthusiasm, unfettered desire. With the quick switch of affiliation familiar to wars and childhood, Lewis and Judd were now thick as thieves, bound with the special bond that conspiracy confers. They ignored the bus and together walked towards the estates that bordered the town, Lewis leading Judd into the curved culs-de-sac, down the short-cuts made into tunnels by the early summer foliage, along the backs of bulging garden fences, over railings and through a bush or two, across a culvert with a stretched-leg leap (and into which a library book fell unnoticed from Judd's satchel). Finally they arrived in a small playground on the edge of town. Fields stretched out before them and away to the right were some woods. It was hot, late afternoon hot, and mayflies and bumblebees gyred in the air around them. Lewis sat on one of the swings and lolloped to and fro, scuffing his shoes in the dirt. The leather on their toes had already been worn down to a cardboard grey.

'D'you fancy a tab?'

'What's that?'

'A smoke. A cigarette.'

'I don't know. My father says it's bad for me.'

'One won't hurt you, will it?'

'We used to smoke cornpipes at camp. Like Huck Finn.'

'Who's that then?' asked Lewis, puzzled, and Judd began to explain all about Finn and Tom Sawyer and Mark Twain and the Mississippi and freed slaves and hiding out on islands and dressing up as girls.

'Dunno if I'm too keen on that last bit.'

'But they were trying to escape, don't you see, and it doesn't mean they were weird or anything, they were just doing what they had to do. But Huck got himself found out because the old woman made him thread a needle and she saw the way he did it wasn't the way he'd have done it if he was a girl.' Lewis didn't see how there could be different ways to thread a needle and Judd started to explain, but then it didn't matter because the real girls had arrived, Jennifer and Shelley.

The girls approached, the glare of the late afternoon sun above and behind them. They'd come from that direction because they knew that the light would make the fabric of their shirts semi-transparent and allow the boys a glimpse of the outline of their slim young torsos and developing breasts. When they got close Lewis said, 'Uh, hi, uh, this is Judd.'

'We know,' said Jennifer sarcastically.

'Oh, right, you do?' said Lewis, confused.

'Judd comes round Jenn's to watch TV on Saturdays,' said Shelley. 'Doncha, Judd?'

Judd said 'Uh huh' and looked down at his shoes, feeling awkward because he knew that Henry had banned Lewis from the TV afternoons.

Lewis was in a difficult situation. He had been going with Jennifer, but then he'd started seeing Shelley instead. To his surprise, Jennifer had not seemed particularly bothered by this blatant betrayal and still insisted upon hanging around with him. He felt that he had to be nice to her, not so much to assuage his guilt – because he didn't feel particularly guilty – but because his experience of girls told him that an emotional explosion was eventually due either way. He figured that his best policy was to try and forestall it for as long as possible. This involved being relatively pleasant to her and letting her bum a lot of cigarettes.

Shelley was becoming worried by Lewis's continual niceness towards Jennifer, because Lewis wasn't nice to anybody. That was why she liked him, because she thought that was cool and this unusual behaviour was making her uneasy and jealous. She certainly thought that now Lewis was seeing her he should be a little less attentive to her best friend – who wouldn't be her best friend for much longer if things didn't change. She assumed that he was feeling guilty about dumping Jennifer and the fact that Lewis had brought a friend along for her bolstered this analysis.

Jennifer was not impressed by the fact that Lewis had brought Judd with him; presumably he was meant for her, so that Lewis and Shelley could disappear off on their own. Was he trying to be funny? The kid couldn't be more than, what, ten? She knew that Lewis had been put down a few years, but she didn't know he'd started socialising with the babies he was forced to take classes with. Or was this solely for her benefit? Was this the only person he'd managed to convince to come along?

Shelley had to admit to herself that if she were in Jennifer's shoes she wouldn't be best pleased. Judd was pretty young.

Before her thing with Lewis the youngest bloke Jennifer had slept with had been seventeen. She should have stuck with the older ones, she told herself. She should never have let her form drop. Secretly, though, she had a soft spot for Judd. That afternoon in the park when he'd been playing aeroplanes she'd had an almost uncontrollable urge to hold him, to stroke his hair. She couldn't be getting broody, could she? Not at her age?

The four of them walked off across the fields. Jennifer sulked along behind the others until Lewis dropped back to see what was the matter. As soon as they were out of earshot, she let rip. 'What's the big idea of bringing that kid along?'

'It's all right. He's American.'

'What's that supposed to mean? I hope you don't expect me to baby-sit while you and Shel go off and enjoy yourselves.'

'Yeah but he can come and watch TV.'

'That's different. Loads of people come then. I don't know half of them.'

'You never asked me.'

'You're too old. Dad won't let you come.'

'Never stopped you before.'

'Fuck off, OK!'

'Look, I said it would be all right, didn't I? It's just for half an hour. How would you like it, being all on your own in a foreign country? How would it suit you? He needed a guide and that's me. I'm showing him the ropes.'

'Like what? What are you showing him?'

'The way we do things around here.'

'And how would you know?'

'Look, you can help if you want, but you don't have to. He doesn't need me or you or anybody. He's a tough kid.' Lewis saw his words weren't having much effect, so he tried a different tack. 'He's from Hollywood, so if I were you I'd be nice to him. Aw, c'mon Jenn. I'll make it up to you. How many ciggies do you owe me? Do us a favour. And look how pleased Shel is 'cause she thinks she's going to get me to herself. It's just this once. Look, if you do it I'll give you this.' He fished a crumpled joint out of his pocket and handed it to her.

'What's this?'

'What d'you think it is? It's a spliff of course. Never seen one before?'

'Course I have.' She hadn't. 'Just wanted to know exactly what type it is before I agree.'

'Er, it's blackash I think. Yeh, blackash, definitely.'

Jennifer stared at his hopeful face, his shit-eating grin, the glossy curls which crowned his head. Then she looked ahead at Judd, who was stumbling along next to Shelley. His hands were thrust into his pockets and he was kicking at stones. He looked bored. Then she looked down at the joint. It was bent and badly rolled, and it tapered in all the wrong places. All in all it was a far cry from the perfect cone that she had imagined a joint to be. But it was a joint. Therefore it was something new and its power was strong. 'Oh,' she sighed, 'OK. Fuck off then. I'll see you back here in an hour.' She dashed ahead and grabbed Judd's hand. 'C'mon, kiddo, we're going this way.' And with that she marched him off in the direction of the woods.

Spermatogenesis (1)

Lost in the tangle of Judd's testes, which had recently jumped hand in hand off the cliff of puberty. All around, gametes with reduced cytoplasm are forming. Within the nuclei of spermatocytes, chromosomes start to appear as very long fine threads with chromomeres spread like beads along their length – this is the leptotene phase. Gradually the zygotene stage begins, and each pair of chromosomes (such a pair is known as a bivalent) aligns itself and starts to twist and thicken, each chromosome doubling in the process. Each bivalent now consists of four chromatids which remain paired but as pairs separate from the two chromatids derived from the homologous chromosome (diplotene). Diakinesis follows: the chromatid pairs – still linked by chiasmata, the visible expression of the interchange of genes (there are usually one or two chiasmata per chromosome pair per meiosis) – move to the periphery of the nucleus, close to the nuclear membrane. The nucleoli – the small, dense bodies containing RNA and protein which reside in each resting nucleus – disappear, as does the nuclear membrane. As a result of the effects of the chiasmata, the bivalents usually end up as mixtures of one or more pieces from the original chromosomes. The chromosomes at this stage are still diploid; for them to become gametes a second meiotic division must occur, which in most cases happens almost immediately. The two chromatids separate, one going to each daughter cell; which goes where is again a matter of chance, as long as the two from each chromosome go to opposite poles. Division spindles appear and the united chromatids gravitate towards either end. There are now two pairs of two daughter cells, in this case spermatids, each pair joined together by a spindle. Each cell is now haploid even though the original cell was diploid, and this reduction is the basis of genetic segregation. Now the chromosomes uncoil, elongate and eventually disappear, new nuclear membranes form and the spindle also gradually disappears. It is at this stage that the cytoplasm begins to divide. Extensive changes take place; at the same time the nucleus condenses.

A flagellum forms. This consists of eleven microtubules arranged longitudinally, the whole being surrounded by an outer membrane which is continuous with the plasma membrane of the cell. The sections of the flagellum are known as basal body, blepharoplast, kinetoplast and kinetosome. Each flagellum is around a quarter of a micrometre thick and several hundred micrometres long. By undulating in a wave-like manner, the flagellum propels what is now a gamete, or spermatozoon, along. There are some mitochondria in the flagellum, but they don't make it into the egg.

Into the trees

'Ow!'

'What's the matter?'

'I'm caught on a briar. It's tearing my pants.'

Jennifer sighed and went back to free him. By turning to try and see where the thorns were stuck he had unbalanced himself, and she took his thigh and locked it under one arm to steady him while she extricated the bramble from his clothing.

Goose-pimples sprang up Judd's leg at her touch. Except for his mother, he couldn't remember anyone touching him there before. He was feeling very different from the way he'd felt the day before, just after he and Lewis had been fighting. Then he'd felt like a hero. Now he felt . . . he wasn't sure how he felt, but he knew he wasn't in charge. 'What about Lewis?'

'He's meeting us later. He has to talk to Shelley about something.'

'Is that her name? Shelley?'

'Yeh.'

'She's nice.'

This was not what Jennifer wanted to hear. 'What about me? Eh? What about me? Is she nicer than me? Is she?'

'I-I don't know. I hadn't thought . . .'

'Well think! Who's the nicest?'

Judd thought about it and decided policy was the best honesty. 'I dunno . . . you are, I guess.'

At this, Jennifer seemed satisfied. 'C'mon,' she said. ''S this way.' They pushed on along a narrow path that led deeper into the woods.

'Where are we going?' Judd asked. Not scared, just inquisitive. Jennifer was close now. She smelt good.

'Just over there. See that tree? That's where we're going.' She freed him and they picked their way through the undergrowth towards it. Its roots formed natural seats where the soil around them had been eroded away by wind and rabbits and they sat on these, quite comfortable. It was a favourite spot of Jennifer's. She reached into an abandoned rabbit digging beneath one of the roots and pulled out a cigarette lighter. Judd watched her in silence. She lit up the joint and puffed on it in silence for a while, getting used to the peculiar flavour. The smoke got in her eyes and made them water, and her head began to swim a little. She winced and passed the reefer to Judd, the way she had seen teenagers do it in the parks. 'Want some?'

'I mustn't smoke cigarettes. My pa says they're bad for me.'

'It's not a cigarette, stupid. It's a spliff.'

'What's the difference?'

'Try it. It'll make you feel nice. Like me.' She giggled and put her hand to her mouth.

'Why're you laughing?'

''Cause I feel nice. That's what it does, it makes you laugh. I'm nice, I'm nice. Don't you want to laugh? Don't you want to be nice like me? I thought everyone in America took drugs.'

'Not anyone I know.'

'Well, be different then. It won't hurt you.' She held out the joint towards him and he looked at it. There it was, something he shouldn't do. He took it and puffed on it. The smoke was soft. Sweet and heavy. He didn't cough. He took a few more puffs. 'Hold it in,' said Jennifer. He did and his lungs were hot like bellows. As he passed the spliff back a glowing blim of hash tumbled out and landed on his leg. With a start he brushed it away. It landed in the grass and burnt itself out, a tiny dying star. Where it had landed on his skin a blister came up. He had been marked, but he didn't seem to feel it. Soon he and Jennifer were rolling around in the shade of the tree, laughing uncontrollably about nothing in particular. Speckles of sunlight dappled young skin.

Now that Jennifer had lapsed out of her pose, the age gap between the two of them seemed to narrow considerably. She began to tickle Judd and her thighs heated up, these two events acting as lenses through which her desire became focused. The heat channelled out the noises of the woods and swamped the area beneath the tree with libidinal energy. Judd was far too artless to resist. For him, everything was as it should be. It was only afterwards, when he put his trousers back on and his little world flooded back in along with the sounds of the leaves and the cries of other children playing over on the estates, that he became afraid of what had happened and began to cry. Then Jennifer comforted him and told him not to tell. She was his film idol, his silver dream. He promised her he wouldn't.

5

Another kind of fold

It was dark by the time Michael dropped Judd home, summer dark, and everything around had been beaten blue by the onset of the night. The Axelrods were renting a house just outside Stratford, one which had been popular among the better-paid members of the casts of the Royal Shakespeare Company for many years. Situated in a small hamlet, the building was something of a folly. It had been built in the 1930s by a random member of the Midlands gentry and stood apart from the farmhouse and labourers' cottages that made up the neighbouring buildings. The architect had mashed too many styles into too small a space: the front porch was art deco; at one end of the pitched roof there was a squat, castellated turret; there were gothic windows, French windows, portholes; the northern walls were pebble-dashed, the southern painted; there was a carport to the east and a small indoor swimming pool whose sides were constructed from marbles taken from decommissioned churches to the west. Moses had chosen the house because its mongrel style reminded him of California. Melinda liked it because the unusual pool made the perfect focus for her social gatherings. She had held several over the summer, all highly fuelled with Pimm's, gin and various other drugs, and all of which had threatened to tip over the edge from party into outright orgy. To Moses's secret disappointment none of them ever did, all the guests being that little bit too neurotic to let themselves go completely.

The garden helped considerably in creating an atmosphere for these parties. It ran to the edge of a cliff which dropped straight down for a hundred feet until it hit the flood plain below, where the fields scanned out flat away for miles and half-way to the horizon the town of Stratford stood. On the cliff top itself there was a small raised circle edged with stones, in the centre of which stood a seat with long legs like stilts. In this Judd liked to sit, his face against the sky, his eyes roaming across the earth and the wind blustering in his hair. Back home you could rarely see this far – even in Beverly Hills which was high up like this – because of the smog trap created by that basin of a city.

Moses was back in the States on a business trip and Melinda had a show that night, so Judd had the house to himself. He pushed open the front door and tingled as its draught excluder wooshed against the rubber bristles of the mat inside (it was another of his favourite sounds). Then lights on and straight to the well-stocked ice-box for some milk – the suck of the seal, the delight of this cool, wonderful space – which he gulped down straight from the bottle. He pulled over a chair and stood on it so that he could reach down the Cheerios from on top of the wall cabinets. Poured himself a bowl, ate the cereal, the spoon fist-gripped in his right hand, drew moustaches on the model adorning the cover of his mother's *Vogue* with his left. He finished the cereal, poured himself a glass of juice, took the tub of ice-cream from the freezer and while he waited for it to defrost enough to get the spoon in he continued to decorate the cover of the magazine. Then he started to examine the lingerie advertisements inside. The waif-like models immediately brought to mind his earlier fumblings with Jennifer and he began to draw onto the pictures the parts that they did not show in the same spirit that he embroidered reality to cover up for the parts of it that he continually missed. As he sketched, his groin and thighs grew hot and he felt again the hard, smacking kisses she had given him and the strange, numbing clutch of her insides, but then, just as he was becoming fully aroused, he lost interest in the promise of an orgasm and became fascinated with the memory of the way that Jennifer's body had disappeared inside of itself at the top of her legs in a manner which was both totally unexpected and totally perfect at the same time. He examined the magazine photographs most carefully, but while they promised to reproduce this effect they didn't deliver, and his crude addendums were little more successful. Eventually, after experimenting for a while, he folded a page down and back on itself, so creating a hidden crease which proved more satisfactory than all of his inky scrawls and blotches.

He blinked out for a while and when he returned to himself the ice-cream had softened, so he took it into the living-room and ate quite a lot of it in front of the TV, then fell asleep on the sofa. While what was left melted to liquid beside him, he dreamt of the trees that afternoon and of something chasing him, chasing him, but he didn't know what. The sound of his mother's car in the drive woke him up and at the last moment he remembered the magazine, retrieved it from the kitchen and charged up the stairs to his room to hide it before she came in.

Fuck logic

Out at the far end of the school fields there was a hole in the thick hedge that served as retaining wall and boundary marker, and through the hole and beyond the hedge was a patch of wasteland, a forgotten zone which lay between the school's borders and those of the industrial estate that backed on to it. This is where Lewis and Judd spent their lunch-hours, picking among the leaves and rabbit holes like leucocytes, smoking, kicking at the odd bits of dead machine that poked up from the scarred ground, itself a festering scab of metal, rust, broken concrete, litter and clay. Hanging out with Lewis here, talking about girls and teachers and TV, doing what he wasn't supposed to be doing, Judd was really happy for the first time since he'd been in England. Lewis, it turned out, was actually quite shy and withdrawn, not at all as Judd had thought him to be, and the two boys quickly warmed to each other's company. There was something else, too: Judd had noticed that

Lewis also blanked, as he did, that Lewis would stare at something and disappear into it for a while – a few seconds, a minute – and this filled the young American with an immense joy because for the first time he felt that it was OK to be like he was. With Lewis, he didn't have to make things up, to pretend that the past was a logical continuum; he didn't have to feel guilty for not being there one hundred per cent of the time. Often, the two of them could spend a whole hour kicking around in their private playground and not say a word, just phasing in and out of their thoughts, alone together until the bell rang to signify the end of free time.

They could hear the school bell from where they were; borne by the wind, its needle vibrations bounced like hailstones off the walls of the buildings beneath which they played. A few last drags and they headed back through the hedge and across the playing fields, sucking on mints as they walked – a precaution which was no defence against the bomb-dog nose of the Buerk but which was enough to deceive the spavined and manic Mr Pincer, who was taking them for maths that afternoon.

Inside the huddle of school buildings loose packs of kids headed for the washrooms and hollered against the enamel latrines, bouncing urine-laden echoes down the corridors as they relieved themselves and scrubbed at their grimy hands and knees. One or two slunk out from the cubicles in which they'd been wanking and rinsed the smell of cheese from their hands, lest anyone should smell it and target them for abuse. Fat boys took pinches with resignation and red faces, thin boys took shoves and elbows in the ribs. Boys with books got tripped and jeered at, narcissists combed their hair and squeezed a zit or two. Rumours flew that two boys had been caught at it in the headmaster's garden, but then there were always rumours like that. Lewis and Judd threaded their way through it all.

Mr Pincer, bright enough to detect that his class found his lesson less than thrilling but not to realise that his own obsessions would bore them more shitless still, had decided to spend a few periods giving the boys a primer in computer science. He thought it would make a change from ordinary maths and besides, he said, standing at the front of the class, the scrawl of his face twisted round like

156

an @, 'computers will soon be a part of all our lives and it will be very useful to you all to know about how they work'. Behind their pursed lips all the boys were laughing at him, but mockery had been part of the scenery for many years now and Pincer no longer seemed to care. After all, his fellow teachers laughed at him too; he knew that everyone thought he was a crank. But beneath the blasé exterior it got to him anyway and the effect was to make him as temperamental as the circuit boards with which he tinkered in his workshop at the weekends.

'Who saw the moon landing on television?' he asked his unen-thused class. A few hands, including Judd's, went up. 'Well, then you may remember that an entire roomful of computers was needed back on earth in order to control that mission. These days, though, just four years on, we can fit the amount of processing power provided by that room into a few small chips that you can hold in the palm of your hand.'

'Hold the vinegar on mine!' someone called out. The class tittered.

'Yeh, and kin I 'ave a pickled onion wiv mine?' muttered some-one else.

Pincer tried to remain good-humoured. 'Yes, yes, of course, very funny, ha ha, but I'd like to get on if I may. The first computers had no chips at all. The first computers had cogs and gearwheels, and would have been powered by steam if Charles Babbage, the chap who designed them, hadn't died before they were built. Babbage's work was all but forgotten until this century when – no, Whiteford, just listen, no need to write all this down, I just want you to listen for the moment. What was that? No, no you're not going to be tested on this, just listen – when certain ideas of his began to be worked on again. For this we have to remember a very famous mathematician called George Boole, who in fact was an acquaintance of Babbage's, though the two men never became friends.'

'Why not?' asked Lewis.

'I don't know why not, Lewis,' answered Pincer icily. 'But it's not that implausible, is it? After all, we've met on several occasions and I somehow doubt we're destined to be friends. The point is, everybody, that Boole was the father of modern algebra and he developed the symbolic logic which all computers use today. We won't go into that logic now, although later on I'll set you a few puzzles and problems so that we can have a bit of fun and get the basic idea.' The class groaned with horror. Suddenly, Pincer remembered an anecdote. 'Oh, yes, there is quite an odd story connected to this. Boole died in slightly peculiar circumstances.' At the mention of death the class perked up and a few pairs of eyes flickered in the teacher's direction. 'His wife, Mary Boole, was one of those mystical types. She wrote some book on the supernatural and was very involved in strange medicines and healing practices, and was a devotee –' ('That means she was devoted to him,' Lewis hissed at Judd) '– of a doctor who was obviously a bit of a quack and who thought that cold water was the magic cure-all for any disease. Poor old Boole caught a cold one day and his wife insisted that he be wrapped in sheets soaked in icy cold water, in order to shock him back into health, I suppose.'

'Did he die?' called out Lewis, who was somewhat perturbed by all this.

'Yes, Lewis, he died, poor fellow.' The teacher pushed on, a schooner sailing through treacle. 'And it wasn't until after the First World War that an American called Claude Shannon, another American called John Atanasoff and a German by the name of Konrad Zuse all realised independently that Boole's logic, what we now call Boolean logic, could be combined with binary numbers – remember, those were the numbers made out of zeros and ones that we looked at last week – and built into electrical switching circuits in order to make an electronic computer.'

'What's an electrical switching circuit?' someone asked, hoping to delay the arrival of Pincer's problems for a few minutes more.

'Just what it sounds like. It's a series of switches, which can be either on or off, one or zero, powered by electricity. You see, Babbage's computers were all mechanical, made out of metal cogs and gears which had to be built to very precise specifications in order for the machine to work. But Zuse, Shannon and Atanasoff all realised that it was much easier to build a computer using Boolean logic and electrical switches. In fact, Zuse went on to build electromechanical calculators which were used in the guidance systems of the V2 rockets that were fired on London by

Hitler.' Rockets and bombs. Now that *was* interesting. 'The war came at a crucial time. Only this year the government revealed that Colossus, the first electronic computer, was built in Britain in 1943 as part of the effort to break the Nazis' secret codes. The Americans built computers to help them design the atom bombs that were dropped on Japan. A lot of very complex calculations are involved in trying to get an atom bomb to explode – it's a bit like trying to work out the way every molecule of water will be moving in a kettle when it's boiling away very hard – and you really need a computer to work all these problems out for you.

'After the war the American Army's Ballistic Research Laboratories built an enormous horseshoe-shaped computer called ENIAC – that stands for Electronic Numerical Integrator and Computer. ENIAC was incredibly complicated: it had 17,468 vacuum tubes, 70,000 resistors, 10,000 capacitors, 1500 relays and 6000 switches –' Pincer smiled at his own powers of recall, but he had lost the class again ' – and it was one of the few computers to be decimal, rather than binary. One of its very first tasks was in fact to simulate the explosion of an atom bomb. ENIAC couldn't be programmed like a modern computer; instead it had to be rewired every time a new problem needed to be solved. A brilliant chap called John von Neumann, who'd worked on the original atom bomb project, joined the ENIAC team in the late 1940s and basically designed ENIAC's successor, the EDVAC – the Electronic Discrete Variable Computer. Now, you need to remember von Neumann's name because,' Pincer paused to watch Whiteford start to scribble away in his exercise book, 'because what he came up with has been used as the blueprint for computer design ever since. OK, that's enough chat. I think it's time for everyone to do some writing.'

Pincer turned, picked up a piece of chalk, wiped a few marks from the board with the heel of his palm, and began to write out some sentences in a looping hand. *Logic gates are digital electronic circuit components that perform a given operation on one or more input signals to produce an output signal,* he scrawled. *The signals these circuits operate on are either voltage or current levels which are separated into two binary states, logic zero and logic one, also referred to as high and low states.* So far, so good. *Since logic gates operate on binary values, they* can be used to represent Boolean operations. Boolean functions can be constructed with these gates to form 'combinational' circuits. There are seven main types of logic gate.

While the class struggled to copy all of this down, the teacher drew the first three types of gate on the blackboard:

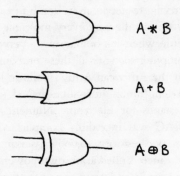

Of course, in the hands of a group of boys just edging towards puberty these diagrams all too easily suggested something else. Lewis and Judd sat together, comparing notes and egging each other on, and pretty soon they both ended up with a page full of symbols that looked rather more like this:

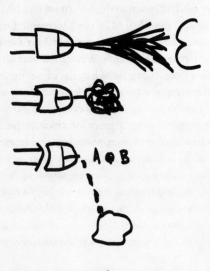

And so it was that at the rear of Mr Pincer's classroom logic got subverted by desire.

As the boys scribbled, Pincer took up his main theme once again. 'The key development in computing', he blithered, 'was the idea of storing both the data and the operating instructions in a centrally located memory, allowing the machine's function to be changed merely by rewriting its operating instructions. This leads us on to the distinction between software and hardware, software being the instructions and hardware the actual switches and circuits. Although Babbage came up with this idea, borrowing it from an automatic loom that was around at the time which used a punch-card system to allow you to set what kind of pattern you wanted it to weave, it wasn't made a general principle of computing until Alan Turing, that's t–u–r–i–n–g Whiteford, said that in theory, the computer was a machine which could do the job of any other machine by being programmed in the appropriate way. You'll no doubt have come across the phrase "Universal Turing Machine" –' of course, no one had '– well, now you know where it comes from.

'Turing had been one of the key people behind the Colossus, and after the war he and von Neumann worked together on the EDVAC and another machine called the ACE. Up until 1955 all computers were built using glass valves as switches. Moths and other insects used to be able to climb inside these and short-circuit them, which is where we get the term "computer bug". And the operators communicated with these machines by means of punched cards or paper tapes, just like the old looms that Babbage had stolen ideas from. Lots of money was being put into computer research at the time in America, because they were seen as the key to countering the threat that had been posed ever since the Soviets put the first satellite, Sputnik, up into orbit in 1957.'

'Why was it a threat, sir?' asked Hethlethwaite.

'Well, Jacob, it wasn't really. All it did was broadcast a few beeping sounds from a radio transmitter, but the Americans got very worried about it and thought that maybe it could do much more than that, spy on their military bases perhaps, or beam down communist propaganda or something. Anyway, in the computers of the time transistors were gradually replacing valves and magnetic disks and drums were gradually replacing punched tapes. There was a big step forward in 1959, when a researcher working for the company Texas Instruments invented the integrated circuit.' Pincer turned and wrote the phrase up on the board. 'Thanks to this innovation, *thirty million* switches and logic gates could be fitted into one square foot of space, sixty times more than had previously been possible. And two years ago a chap called Marcian Hoff at a company called Intel,' again he wrote out the names, 'came up with the idea of trying to fit an entire computer on a single wafer of silicon, called a chip. The first chip was called the 4004 and it had 2250 transistors, could carry out 60,000 operations per second and process four different pieces or "bits" of data at a time. Then came the 8008, and this year Intel have brought out the 8080. The 8s mean that it can process eight bits of information at a time, so it's twice as fast.' Pincer took a small cardboard box from his desk drawer, opened it, and walked up and down the aisles showing its contents to the boys. 'This is an 8080 chip,' he explained proudly. 'With it you can build a microprocessor, the heart of the modern computer.'

At which point Martin Martins, the hated corridor monitor from 2B, knocked on the door. Pincer waved him in. 'Yes, Martins, what is it?'

'The Head wants to see Axelrod in his office right away, sir. At once, sir.' Martins was like some kind of pre-pubescent squaddy, one that had been squad-bashed into total submission.

'Very well,' said Pincer. 'Axelrod, go with Martins. And don't slouch, boy!'

Discovery

Melinda had woken late that Wednesday morning and, unusually, had found herself with nothing to do. No lunch dates, no hairdressing appointments, no rehearsals, no discreet liaisons, nothing much of any kind. She got up, made some coffee and took a long sauna. Then she wallowed in the pool for about half an hour, switching the jets on full and letting them play across her clitoris until she reached orgasm and her identity was fused for a few brief moments with the chopping surfaces of the water. Rejuvenated, she ate brunch and decided to do a spot of housework. She pottered around downstairs for a while, sorting out old magazines and dusting to the sound of an Isley Brothers album that Moses had brought over from LA, then she went upstairs to sort out her washing and tidy Judd's room. It was a mess: half-read comics and discarded school books littered the floor, a toy baseball game was laid out in the middle of the carpet, dirty mugs and plates were balanced precariously on various shelves, and crumpled clothes had been thrown into corners and stuffed down the side of the bed. A soiled gym kit was draped over the back of the chair and on the window-sill a bird's nest that Judd had found in a tree a few months before was slowly disintegrating into its component parts of twigs, dried mud and dead moss.

Melinda let out a motherly sigh and went to work, stacking the crockery and recovering all the clothing which she sorted it into a pile to be washed with her own. It was when she pulled the bed away from the wall and stripped the sheets that she discovered the annotated magazine, hidden by Judd between mattress and base. It was a *Vogue* she hadn't read, so she sat down on the naked bed in order to have a quick flip through.

She could hardly miss Judd's drawings: they were very explicit. The models, usually so demure (at least on the face of it), had been cross-sectioned so that their internal organs were now in plain view. Exaggerated vaginas abounded, most of them about to be entered by disembodied penises; breasts were splashed with spurts of what she supposed was semen. To make matters worse, a sheet of graph paper torn from a school book fell out from between the pages. With trembling hands Melinda picked it up and discovered a chart that had been drawn up by Judd in order to keep track of his early sexual investigations and impressions. *6 June 1973*, it read. *First did it with Jennifer. Weird. Didn't feel much. Kind of slimy.* And it went on from there.

Melinda was horrified and she rushed downstairs to the drinks cabinet where she poured herself a slug of brandy in order to stay her tremblings and cool the heat in her loins. It worked until she remembered the old joke, *Come upstairs, I'll show you my etchings*, then she started shaking some more.

How . . . ? Why . . . ? What . . . ? she thought. Then, a series of flashes: led astray . . . evil girl . . . little Judd . . . outrage . . . reputation . . . my own son . . . the papers never . . . scandal . . . ohmygod . . . nipinbud.

She picked up the telephone and rang the school.

Head games (1)

Scene: the headmasters office, St George's Grammar for Boys, mid-afternoon. The office is situated in the front rooms of a Queen Anne house, foundation stone laid 1812, used as a private dwelling for one hundred and fifteen years until it was put up for sale and purchased by the expanding school next door. The windows are divided into two vertically sliding frames of nine panes apiece which slice the afternoon sunlight into segments that shine so brightly on the opposite wall that the rest of the room is thrown into shadow. His bald forehead emblazoned by a lower central segment of the matrix of light (2,5), the headmaster sits like Christ about to pass judgement. In the shadows Judd Axelrod, Melinda Axelrod and Doreen Buerk cower like prodigal apostles.

★

Doreen was badly shaken. As if it were not enough for one afternoon to be told that one of her pupils – a mere ten-year-old – was having a sexual relationship with a thirteen-year-old girl from the comprehensive, she had also had to discover that the mother of this negro was not only English and not American as she had assumed but white! What was the world coming to? She made several cross-referenced mental notes to remind herself to write to the board of governors and recommend that they take no more of these short-term foreign students. The whole thing genuinely frightened her: whatever her pupils and her colleagues thought, since Donald had been committed to Hatton Central Hospital six years previously (where he still remained, writing out long-hand volumes of the Word of God, which he scried from the images that played across his many televisions) she had been a woman plagued by deep insecurities. Now that madness had apparently come to visit her again she was forced to reconsider her whole role in the social machine. What if, she thought, what if this is all down to me? What if I attract them? What if I am cursed to spend the rest of my days threatened by half-wits and degenerates?

Melinda, meanwhile, was on top of things. The session had begun with the headmaster questioning Judd in order to ascertain the extent of the damage and searching for loopholes through which he could slip free the knot of the school's responsibility, and Melinda had quickly cottoned on to this and refused to let him get away with it. She was a celebrity of untarnished reputation, she reminded him, and there was no way she was going to allow him to question her abilities as a mother. She had come across this kind of thing before, she said, her child being badly treated because of the colour of his skin. She didn't understand how this could have been allowed to happen. Didn't she send a car every day to pick up Judd from the school gates? How had he been able to meet this girl? Had the school no idea at all when its pupils were on or off the premises?

A cloud covered the sun and the halo disappeared from the headmaster's head, and the differentials of light and dark in the room became less extreme. By contrast, the adults had begun to argue more intensely, Doreen Buerk having decided that she was not going to let Mrs Axelrod or anyone else impute that she, a member of the Women's Institute and the Rotary Club, and a pillar of the local community, might be a racialist.

Judd sat among them, now ignored. To begin with he had been terrified, embarrassed, frightened, totally exposed by the Head's questioning. Under the assault, he had started to understand that his crime embraced not just the events of the previous few weeks but his behaviour throughout most of his life. They'd kept asking him *why? why did he do this?* but he didn't have an answer and searching for one now it wasn't surprising that he made a link between the sex and that for which he had most often been chastised in the past – his picnolepsy. His father had been proved right, it seemed: if he weren't always blanking out, if he paid more attention, if he had more common sense this would never have happened. Silently, he began to shiver and shake.

It frightened him more than anything that he had never seen his mother like this, burning like a torch of self-righteousness. He couldn't guess that her reaction in fact had little to do with his own indiscretions and more with a battle that she had been fighting with the country of her birth ever since she had been a little girl. She had always hated England, had always found its inhabitants snotty and self-centred. Ever since she had been at drama school she had watched girls with the right accents and the right backgrounds get the preferred parts, girls who were as a rule far worse actresses than the ones that were passed over. Fighting her way up the professional ladder she'd lived a squalid existence, out of work for most of the time, the temptations of prostitution flickering above her like a badly wired light bulb, the names she despised emblazoned across the West End. Then, by complete fluke, she'd been spotted by a Hollywood talent scout who got her a screen test, an agent and finally a part: an 'English Rose' cameo in a Sophia Loren vehicle being made by Paramount. She had never looked back. After a series of slightly grotty affairs with producers, minor directors and other actors, in 1962 she'd met Moses, who had been in Hollywood on his industry convention. Within six months Melinda was pregnant; they had just decided to stay together and have the child when she miscarried. But the bond didn't break, they stuck it out, in the end it brought them closer together. Moses had never felt this much for anyone before, he didn't know it was possible. A year or so later Melinda was pregnant again and this time there were no complications and the couple married the year after Judd was born. A child out of wedlock and an interracial marriage would have wrecked the career of an aspiring actress at any other time, but this was the sixties. Rather than impeding her progress it hastened it, hooking her up and depositing her on a higher conveyor belt. Judd was born without complications (apart from the Ouija board) and became a symbol of his mother's new life. Everything was rosy. There were parts and parties, she and Moses remained faithful within reason, everything was a success.

Except . . . except that she wasn't quite getting the parts she wanted. The landscape of her desire still vibrated with the dull wave of an urge to play those roles which the girls from good homes had always been given. She wanted to prove that she was not simply a good actress, but a great one, too. She began to look around for projects that were more 'arty', more cultured, but apart from a couple of workaday adaptations of Jane Austen novels she found nothing that she really liked until her agent mentioned that a chance had come up of a season back in England, playing in *King Lear* and *Twelfth Night* with the Royal Shakespeare Company in London and Stratford-upon-Avon. It was ideal – she could return home triumphant and boost her career in the States simultaneously, the perfect revenge and the perfect career move in one.

Unfortunately, the reviews had been lukewarm and the whole thing, rather than being a triumph, had turned into something of a battle of attrition with her countrymen. She'd already begun to regret returning to England at all but now, now that she had so damaged her son by coming here, well what was left? This is what her thirst for revenge had brought her. Now she felt really Shakespearean.

Torn between her feelings of personal guilt and anger that the years of struggle and abuse should bring her to this she raged at Doreen Buerk and the headmaster, almost peeling the plaster from the walls with the turbulence she projected. But at the same time, and almost despite herself, she began to construct from the elements of this storm an enormous edifice, one in which she was to live for the rest of her life, and which was supported and reinforced with struts and boards fashioned from the feelings that the cold and clinical light of her anger had illuminated.

From where he sat on the old leather settee, his feet barely touching the floor, Judd gazed up at his mother's towering construction. Tall and new, it caught all the light now that the sun had reappeared from behind its cloud. If he were to be saved, would he have to build one of these for himself?

Blood baked in concrete

While Jennifer lay awake in bed, having given up trying to cry herself to sleep, all the soft lights padded Henry from the night as he stumbled home. He had barely been conscious when the landlord from the Falcon had yelled in his ear: 'D'you need a cup o' coffee, Henry? Eh, I say d'you need a coffee or summat? Or a glass o' water?'

'Oh, leave 'im be. The ol' fucker's so soused he can't even 'ear us. D'you wan' me ta purim out fur ya?'

'Nah, I'll see to 'im. You geroff. We'll need you in sharpish termorra. We've gorra party in fur lunch in the ba' room.'

'Awright then. Tarra.'

'Tarra.' Simon the barman disappeared through the back of the bar. Nigel – the landlord – stood and polished glasses and replaced them on to the dark wooden racks where they'd be ready for the next day's drinking. The shelves, the bar itself, the chairs with their worn red seats and perimeters of brass studs, the windows with their leaded panes of glass, the fireplace, the horse brasses, the skirting board and the dado, all these were stained with sweat and farts and smoke and ale and varnished with a thin veneer of sticky conversation. From the back corridor came the sounds of Simon trying to get his bike out.

'Watch that new paint, you clumsy oik,' Nigel yelled, and then in lower tones to Henry (who wasn't listening) said, 'Careless little sod.'

'I heard that!' Simon yelled back.

'Geroff wi' you!' The door slammed. 'Christ, you can't get the help these days, can you? I SAID CAN YOU!' Then quietly, 'You can't 'ear a bleedin' word I'm saying.' He finished drying the last few glasses, put the beer mats into soak and went out back to empty the bins. When he returned, Henry's head had lolled over to one side and he was slumped even further down into his chair. Nigel began to lose patience. 'Awright, this isn't a goddamn 'otel. Time to go. OY! WAKEY WAKEY!' He shook Henry by the shoulder and the drunkard came to, looked up through red and rheumy eyes. Tried to speak, gave up. Was not sure. Nigel helped him to his feet and took what was left of a burnt-out Dunhill from between his limp fingers. 'That'll hurt in the morning, for sure,' he said to no one in particular. 'C'mon. Up ya get. D'you want me to call you a cab?'

'Nuuuuhhh.' The negative rattled from Henry's throat along with a stringy gobbet of bronchial saliva.

'Ya sure, are ya?'

'Uhhhh.' Nigel pulled back the iron bolts that secured the heavy oak front door and gently propelled Henry out into the street. He felt like a boy pushing a toy boat out on to a pond, vainly hoping that the wind would fill its sails and carry it away. Publican and patron had known each other for many years and it was a long-standing joke that without Henry the pub would have gone under long ago, although it was a joke that nobody but Henry laughed at these days. If there were any more evenings like tonight, Nigel thought to himself, he might have seriously to consider barring the man. There was a point at which even the most valued customer became a liability. 'Goan out with you, y'ol' pisshead,' he said. To his surprise Henry was indeed caught by the wind and stumbled off to the left. 'Hey!' called Nigel, 'where the fuck're you goin'? Don't you live that'ur way?'

Henry stuttered to a halt, turned round – his hands clutching at the air for balance – and made ready to set off on the appropriate trajectory. For a moment he found his voice. 'G'night Arthur. It was wonderful.' And with that he lurched off down Sheep Street, the Elizabethan buildings leaning over him like interested ogres, no straight lines or right-angles among them, a scene from *The Cabinet of Dr Caligari*.

Henry felt the street close in behind him and he pushed on, taking his bearings from the tourist lights down by the river. As he neared the bridge it occurred to him that it was time for a cigarette and, narrowly avoiding a lone car, he weaved across the road towards the tall poplars which line the small park that stretches between the bridge and the boathouse. He sat on a bench and searched through his pockets for a fag. They felt voluminous, the pockets, like sacks. He worked his hands through them, brushing past cigarette packet and lighter several times before managing to grab them. Eventually he got them out and placed them gingerly in his lap, taking a few moments to pick flakes of tobacco that he'd dredged from his pockets out from beneath his fingernails. Trying to get a cigarette from the packet and into his mouth was the next trial, and as soon as he'd managed it he dropped the pack on the floor, then lost hold of the cigarette while bending to recover the pack. But finally he was ready to attempt ignition. It was a clear night: to his intoxicated gaze street lamps headlights stars seemed equidistant. He sparked up the lighter and its flame floated out there with the satellites, out there with Laika (who was quietly scrolling across the night sky, of course). He was concentrating so hard on bringing it to bear on the tip of the fag he might as well have been trying to guide the various parts of Skylab in to dock.

Back home, Jennifer tossed and turned in her small bed and stared at the walls and the ceiling, taking her father's late return as a sign of trouble. She had not met Judd's parents, but she knew what his mother looked like because she had seen one of her films once, in the Odeon by the hospital. Yet although she could quite clearly recall Melinda Volitia's face she couldn't remember the film's title or much of the plot, because it was during that movie that a boy had touched her up for the first time. The boy was Damon, a swarthy nineteen-year-old, and Jennifer had ended up going to the film with him because Shelley had ducked out of their date at the last minute, pleading something about a dentist's appointment. For some unfathomable reason Jennifer had fancied Damon a bit and had agreed to go along in place of her friend.

It was a Saturday afternoon and they'd both been early and had stood uneasily on the cinema steps together, waiting for the usherette to unlock the doors, while a greasy rain whipped down inches from their noses. Finally, the doors were opened.

'Let's go inside then,' Damon had said flatly.

Jennifer suddenly had cold feet. 'I dunno. I'm not sure I want to see this one that much.'

'Might as well. Look at it.'

'Look at what?'

'The rain, stupid. What else you gonna do?' So, spoilt for choice, they'd gone in. Damon had belched as the usherette took their damp pink ticket stubs and led them into the murk.

Jennifer had giggled. ' 'S all right,' she'd said, 'we know the way.' Inside, the cinema was almost empty. A couple of men were already asleep in the stalls and in the drool of silver light Jennifer was able to make out the heads of two scrawny women, both of them still shrouded by their rain bonnets. She balanced on the edge of the folded seat and eased her weight forward until the chair snapped open and swallowed her. The tiny mites that feasted on the stuffing and velour rumbled away to themselves as their world was compressed. Damon sat down and almost immediately put his arm around his date, who just as quickly struggled free.

'Wait a minute,' she whispered nervously, not really sure what to do. 'Let me get me coat off.' She stood up and slipped off her mac. Underneath she wore a tan miniskirt, short black felt boots, a white nylon top.

The film was not particularly engaging; at least, it did not engage Damon's attention, most of which was taken up by Jennifer. By her lips, her small breasts, her thin, almost hairless legs. His left arm curled around her tiny back and crushed her to him. With his left hand he pummelled her right breast and occasionally pinched her nipple in what he imagined was a tender squeeze, while snaking the fingers of his right hand up her skirt, around the elastic of her panties and down among the fine hairs that curled across her groin. He hadn't stopped to consider that she was not wet, that he would have to force his index finger up inside her. He was completely engrossed in his own fantasy by now, her body merely furnishing the tactile feedback. His imaginings even provided for the way she was feeling, for the idea that she was being stimulated by a sweet pleasure pain.

But the feel of his fingers grubbing up against her hymen had merely sent raw sears shooting up from Jennifer's groin and into her stomach. For a moment she had wondered why she was doing this, why was she letting this sweaty oaf with his clumsy mitts scrabble away at her? But she was so hungry for experience that the thought remained an abstract one and gained no purchase on the situation unfolding before her.

Damon broke into her during Melinda Volitia's big love scene. Some blood was released and he took it for lubrication and set about with renewed vigour, frigging away at her while semen leaked from his boy's cock and diffused through the fabric of his Y-fronts. A hundred million sperm caught in a fishing net; an actress's face fixed for ever in the mind of a young girl.

After the show they'd stood at the bus-stop, and the bus had come almost immediately and Damon had got on. Jennifer had remained on the pavement and they'd waved a casual goodbye, neither wanting to see the other ever again. The rain had stopped and the clouds had evaporated, or so it seemed, and Jennifer had walked across the town in search of Shelley, her panties encrusted with blood. Someone wolf-whistled at her from the opposite side of the street and she did not turn and yell a *Fuck off!* as she normally might but kept walking straight ahead, overwhelmed by a feeling of utter neutrality.

A few weeks later she lost her virginity proper. She was chasing Rever – it was a matter of proving herself to the girls she hung out with, most of whom were at least a couple of years her senior. At the time, everyone had a thing about Rever. He was tall, wore black, had an angular face. He seemed very withdrawn, very cool.

He was the singer in a band and they said he wrote poetry. At a house party, the house of someone she didn't know, the parents away, she saw him with a book in his hands. Without him noticing she sidled over and took a peek at the cover. It was a pocket edition of Blake's *Songs of Innocence and Experience*. She knew it well: Henry used to read aloud from it when the profound mood took him. She confronted Rever and recited 'The Sick Rose' straight off, then bullshitted him for a while with knowledge that she'd taken from the paragraph on the back cover of the volume and nurtured in the rich soil of his comments and his ignorance. Pretty soon they were snogging in one of the bedrooms.

The summer holidays came and she would go round to his house afternoons. His family was liberal and they were quite happy that Rever should have a girl spend time in his room, though they would perhaps have been less happy had they known how young she was. But she hardly ever saw them anyway – when she called at the house a voice would just yell from deep inside, 'Who is it?' and she'd shout back, 'It's me, Jennifer, is Rever in?' and the voice would shout back either, 'Yes, love, he's upstairs, go on up,' or 'No, he's out, but you can go up and wait if you like.'

They tried without success on four separate occasions before Rever managed to penetrate her fully. Finally he had worn a condom and that had made it easier; before, she had always had to tell him to stop because the pain was too intense. But she wanted him and she was going to have him. She'd known from the start that if she went out with him he'd expect her to sleep with him and she wanted that. When they finally succeeded and he was on top of her and inside her, she couldn't feel anything except the pain. He moved to and fro for a while with a kind of rocking motion, then gasped, 'Jenn. Oh, Jenn, Jenn, I'm going to come, Jenn, I'm going to come,' and she'd had no idea what he meant by that. Afterwards she ached a bit and she didn't stay long, but it wasn't too bad. Mainly she felt numb.

Shelley had been away at the coast with her parents and when she got back she rushed straight round to Jennifer's house. 'Jenn, Jenn, I thought of you on Tuesday!' she gasped, 'I honestly did. It was Tuesday, wasn't it? I thought of you.' Her face was puffed with excitement and she kissed her friend all over. Jennifer told her all the gory details. She saw Rever perhaps another half a dozen times before he tired of her infatuation with him and told her he didn't want to see her any more. She cried and was angry that she still didn't understand about coming, deciding it was something that only men did.

Judd certainly did not make her come, although being smaller – and younger and therefore less concerned with his own prowess – he managed to hurt her rather less. She rarely touched herself and did not, then or later, come properly to associate sex with pleasure. No, it was about something else, sex was. Power, perhaps. Gaining authority. Being liked.

Hardly had their illicit liaison been discovered than Judd was whisked back to the States without being allowed to see Jennifer again. This hurt her very much. She'd never met anyone like Judd before; he was so different from her. She was all motion, all movement, plastic and tactile and liquid and vital, fazed by nothing because there was nothing to which she couldn't accommodate herself. But Judd was strange. He was black, of course, so that made him special, but he was also so quiet, so composed. He could do stupid things, childish things, like pulling Alice's plaits or playing aeroplanes, but that way he had of sitting motionless for minutes at a time, apparently not looking at anything at all, just thinking . . . it seemed to Jennifer that he was like a Buddha or something, so composed, so divine. If she was the sea then he was an outcrop of land, a continent contemplating itself, an opportunity where previously there'd been none. She'd not thought much of him when he'd first arrived in her life, invited to her TV afternoons not by her but by a neighbour, the son of one of the costume designers that Melinda knew through the theatre, but he'd ended up opening up a whole new realm of possibility for her. Maybe his being American, maybe it had something to do with it, maybe this was how Queen Isabella of Spain had felt towards Columbus when he'd brought her the New World, because Jennifer certainly thought about the rest of the world and its immensity more as a result of meeting Judd than she ever had done before. That's what

Judd was for her: he was the world outside the little English suburbia in which she lived and dreamed, outside of a mother that she could never imagine except as a naked shoot peeling and peeling itself forever further back into insanity and a father who had only bloomed inside the hothouse of a bottle of gin. Judd was the desert, unclaimed and alien, and by the time he was taken from her she'd wanted him so much that she'd have invented new forms of life to get to him, would have flowered herself, would have engendered a new ecosystem in the spaces where she and he touched, a hypersea of mycobionts and phycobionts, pentastomes and arthropods, parasites and plants, a symbiotic biophysiology with which she'd extend herself and place herself in permanent contact with his skin.

The day following the one on which Judd had been pulled from class and taken home Jennifer had answered the telephone to a choking female voice.

'Is this the correct number for Mr Henry Several?'

'Yes.'

'May I speak with him please?' The three words *speak with him* jittered like coffee cups in an airliner flying through turbulence. Jennifer intuited immediately that it was bad news and that it concerned her; she laid the handset down on the telephone table and called her father. As Henry emerged from the living-room, drink in hand, she disappeared inside the kitchen and stood as silently as she could behind the door. Through the gap between door and frame she could see the hallway mirror; in its reflection, as he picked up the plastic handset and put it to his ear, was Henry.

'Ah, yes? This is Henry Several. What can I do for you?' He began by swilling the ice around in his glass and was just about to take a sip when he changed his mind and put the drink down on the telephone table, picking at a loose patch of veneer that had begun to rise up from the underlying wood instead. It was when a large chunk of the old, shrivelled surface came away in his hand that Jennifer knew she had been discovered. She watched Henry sag under the attrition of the winds which blew down the phone line; she saw the final coherence of spirit that remained to him fissure and tumble as if the collection of parts which was her father was no longer capable of generating a rhythm by which the whole could live and face the world. The pieces, hitherto held apart by tension and intensity, collapsed in against each other as their micro-fields were shorted out and suddenly Henry occupied that little bit less of the world. '. . . Yes, I think so, yes, no, yes, whatever you say, I'm terribly sorry, of course, at once, I cannot understand how . . . I cannot apologise enough, Thursday evening then, yes, anything I can do, of course, may I just say how sorry I am . . . yes, no, of course, yes . . .' And then the phone went dead and the house rang with the dreadful silence that annexes the world after a storm has passed through. Henry shuffled into the living-room, leaving his drink in the hall.

Jennifer sat huddled behind the kitchen door, wondering what would happen next. For a long time she didn't breathe, as if by refusing to use her orifices she could metabolise herself into a new state, one in which all the pain was spread so evenly throughout her body that it became merely another form of wave, meaningless and simple. Soon, of course, she had to exhale, and when she did the dead air came out in a rush, stripped of its oxygen by her vigorous lungs. She started to worry about her father and walked along the hallway, scared that she would laugh from fear and shame. Every nerve end tingled and her groin throbbed. From her stomach to her vagina she flushed hot with desire. She reached the living-room door and when she pushed it open she saw her father, a station-ary man in front of a blue-white television. The burning twitched out and her legs flooded with fear. 'Daddy?' Henry did not turn to look at her, but his head fell forward just a little. 'Daddy, I'm sorry, I didn't mean to hurt anyone.' He turned now, just enough to see her. She checked his brown eyes for anger but could see none, so turned on the tears and ran to him. He held her to him and stroked her dark hair and told her how like her mother she was and how just as he had loved her mother he loved her too and that to him what she had done was not wrong, that she would always be perfect in his eyes, that it did not matter what people might say, that people were stupid and they'd never understand.

★

Thursday came around, evening turned to night, and Jennifer's mind rustled too much with what she could remember and what she thought might come to pass to fall asleep and Henry sat drunkenly on a bench by the river and smoked cigarettes down to his knuckles. It was a warm night by English standards. The Midlands was a week into one of those brief English heatwaves that induces men to strip down to shorts and T-shirts, women to sunbathe in their lunch-hours. Sweat gathered under arms, in navels, at the backs of necks and knees, in shoes and folds of fat. White skin had already turned pink and tight. Everyone could smell themselves, feel themselves. They were not used to this. The headaches were about to begin, the tempers to wear thin, everyone found themselves wishing for a cloudy day, a spot of rain. Whole towns couldn't sleep, noises carried at night, the cities sounded hollow as old sherry casks. No longer damped by moisture, the cries of whirring tyres coughing engines sudden horns and brakes slipped out from between the buildings and echoed free across the rooftops, playing with the cats who'd left the streets to the shoppers and the dogs. Windows were left wide open, doors unlocked. The rivers had grown warm and begun to stink. Groups of tourists were drifting in like migrant tribes, to feed and to be fed upon. Stratford was no longer a network of thoroughfares but a patchwork of spaces.

Jennifer slipped out of bed, walked over to the window and climbed out on to the sill, letting her legs swing free and her heels rub against the brickwork. She could easily see the town centre, only half a mile away and glowing in the blue night. Stratford was an encrustation, a slow conglomeration of wood and wattle and stone and bricks and cement and steel and asphalt and oil at the point at which water and this way and that all met and afforded the necessary conditions for such a parasite to gain purchase and prosper. The town grew like lichen, symbiotic pairing of flesh and rock, sacs of blood moving within their thick shell walls like hermit crabs, the encounter a prerequisite for the emergence of the new form of 'cultured man' whose English archetype had been run out of town on a poaching beef, four centuries before. Henry sat and contemplated the red-brick theatre, his new and massive shrine. Another cigarette burnt down to the filter.

Jennifer climbed back into her room and got dressed, for once donning clothes which made her look like the thirteen-year-old that she was. She went downstairs, out the front door and through the estate until she reached the main road that led across the bridge and into town. Off in search of her father. She passed the garage, the Alveston Manor Hotel, the line of the old tramway, the jetty crowded round with rowing boats for hire.

Crossing the bridge, her footsteps echoed on the metal grille; through it she could see the reflection of the street lights on the gently popping surface of the barely moving river. She spied Henry before she was even across, went up to him, took his hand and helped him up from the bench, led him home. As they walked back he began to talk, though not of the meeting that he'd had with the Axelrods earlier that evening. Rather, he told her stories of her mother, whom she had never known. He told her, as if he were talking to himself, what her mother was like when she was young, how she'd been a talented computer, how it had come to nothing. He told her how he'd met her during the war and loved her from the first moment he'd seen her though she'd been too busy with the soldiers to spare a thought for him. He told her how they had met again a few years later, how he'd won her heart and how they'd married. He told her about their first few years together and about his infertility. He told her, as she led him deeper into the maze of streets that made up their estate, about Nadine's illness, about her drinking and her visions, about the voices in her head, about the letters she used to write him while he was standing right there in the room with her. In faltering tones he told her how Nadine's family had shunned her, about how she'd nobody left but him, about how she'd abused him with threats and lies and conceits, about how little by little he had failed to cope. And he told her about how one day he had no longer been able to find a way through it all and had called the hospital and had her committed.

It was not until they reached the house and Henry stood upon the doorstep fumbling for his key that he told Jennifer how it had been discovered that one of the orderlies had been pimping out her mother's soulless body.

'How did they find out?' Jennifer asked quietly. It was the first question she had asked, but she already knew the answer. Nadine had become pregnant. The child was healthy but there were complications and physically Nadine was never the same again. She'd stuttered on until John Glenn became the first American to make it into orbit – aboard Friendship 7 in 1962 – at which point she no longer had the strength to eat. Then it was only a matter of days.

'And that's why your father is such a sad man and such a bad man and drinks such a lot and why, you see my darling, he is not your father at all, but just the man who looks after you and who tries to care for you and he is sorry because he was not strong enough for your mother and he is not strong enough for you.' But Jennifer was no longer listening. As tears began to run down Henry's purple cheeks she was remembering as clearly as if it were yesterday the faces the dark ward the screams and the gibberings that greeted her as she was sucked out into the world. She pulled in her cheeks and bit them, tried not to cry.

Shrink

Within days of the discovery Moses had flown to England, collected Judd and returned with him to California. Melinda was to join them when she had fulfilled the terms of her contract with the RSC, which included a further six months in London after the Stratford run was over. Until then, the family would communicate by telephone and Moses would fly over to see Melinda whenever he could. The Axelrods had decided 'for publicity reasons' not to press charges against the school or against Jennifer and Henry.

Back in LA, the search for a good shrink was top priority. Eager to atone for bringing Judd with her to England, Melinda called Donna long distance and asked her advice on a psychoanalyst. Donna quickly warmed to the task. 'Well, I'm no expert, but if I were you I'd get in touch with Schemata.'

'Schemata?'

'Uh huh. My sister's been seeing him for five years now and he's done wonders like you would not believe. And this friend of mine, Marie, you know her I think, yeh you do, Marie, you met her over at that pool party of Allan's summer before last, you know, the one where Oscar got thrown into the pool with all his clothes on and ruined six grams of uncut toot and Raymond got caught in the sack with Allan's daughter who was only fifteen at the time, yeh, that's right, *that* party, yeh well, Marie says he is like a specialist where kids are concerned and I know for a fact that he sorted out Allan's daughter after, you know, after that *event*, Opal I think her name is, yeh, Opal, or Amethyst, or Sparkle or, something, you know, glittery, and now she's doing fine. She's seeing Raymond again though she's seventeen now so it's OK an' all, and I hear they're getting married in the fall. Apparently they're gonna have a pool wedding, with the guests and the priests and everyone in swimmers and an underwater altar. Have you ever heard of *anything* so groovy?' Melinda was convinced and it was all settled very swiftly: Judd would be returned to his old school in Beverly Hills and would also undergo an intensive no-expenses-spared course of treatment with Dr Hinckley Schemata.

Judd was in a state of mild shock. He'd wanted to come home, but not like this. For two weeks his father wouldn't talk to him. He thought sometimes that he was being punished for wishing for change, for not being happy in England. He thought a lot about Lewis, about how their fight and then their friendship had made him feel special and in charge of himself, like a hero. How embarrassed was he now, that he'd ever felt like that? Now he felt transparent. The hot Californian sun and high blue sky of which he'd dreamed so often seemed not to welcome him but to swallow him. Beneath the glow of the identical days it no longer appeared to matter where he was or who he was, and he spent the first few evenings at home sitting cantilevered out over the Malibu cliff side on the edge of the balcony, feeling lonely and scared, watching the sun turn the sky to nicotine before melting into the clicking waves and desperately trying to concentrate, to keep his mind on this view.

Because now whenever Moses caught him 'day-dreaming' he would take his belt to the boy, fetch him a few sharp lashes across the backside, *Knock some sense into him*, he said. This was a new experience for Judd and the thick leather seared his mind, left raw welts along which ideas could run, around which decisions could form – decisions and ideas not his own, that would be loaned to him and on which he would pay interest for years to come.

He was restricted to the house, too. The open and relaxed network of friends and haunts that had previously characterised his life in LA was now replaced with a series of concentric and paranoid structures that had at their centres study, the wisdom of elders, the irresponsibility of children, the danger of experience. He was continually questioned about his personal habits and when the time came for him to return to school he was restricted to talking to certain friends and was repeatedly warned off having any contact with 'members of the opposite sex'.

In the beginning he thought of Jennifer a lot. Often she was the only thing he could hold in his mind. But within weeks of leaving England he found he could already hardly remember her. Her face was the first to go, washed out by the afternoon sun of the ever expanding distance between them. He found to his dismay he could impose almost any features he wanted upon the haze of flesh she'd become. Then her voice began to fade and when he reconstructed it in his mind it could have been Shelley who was speaking, or Lewis, he could no longer tell. Her hair remained, the shape of her hair, but the feel of her was gone altogether and in many ways the sex might as well never have happened. He'd lost interest in that anyway; he'd only been curious to begin with, not driven. It was her, always her. Who was she anyway? The lines the belt made across his back seemed to eradicate her smile. It was *her* fault. It was *she* who had done this. He screamed this to Moses often when punished. But he wanted to be with her anyway. He didn't know what he wanted. His mind was a blur.

He began to schedule his television viewing according to the times he knew Jennifer liked to watch, setting a clock to GMT and sometimes getting up early, sometimes staying up late. Voodoo space, TV space could connect them, he figured, rehashing ideas from his comic collection. That's where the power was. Here he was, then, sitting alone in front of his screen, projecting his mind 6000 miles across the earth, casting a spell . . . she was there, just on the other side of the glass, he could feel her. Maybe if he half closed his eyes, meditated like the Buddhists did, looked through the images, maybe then she'd emerge from the play of pixels and he'd see her, watching the same flat figures dash about in the frame, zooming in and out with the camera. He hadn't spotted her yet, but he'd heard her, he'd caught the timbre of her voice in some random phrase more than once, and he was sure it wouldn't be long now before she'd appear.

0 1 0

What if Brother Jack were wrong? What if history was a gambler, instead of a force in a laboratory experiment, and the boys his ace in the hole? What if history was not a reasonable citizen, but a madman full of paranoid guile, and these boys his agents, his big surprise!

Ralph Ellison, *Invisible Man*

6

Over mandrake they met

Henry didn't need too much persuading, from Moses or anyone else, that it would probably be better for all concerned if he took Jennifer away from Stratford while things had a chance to quieten down. Switzerland was the obvious choice – his father had been a Birmingham banker who looked after the international interests of his firm and Henry had spent many of his school holidays in and around Zürich, Geneva and Lausanne, back in the days when skis were great planks of wood that only farmers and woodsmen found uses for. When school term ended Henry would take the train to Birmingham, where he would be met at the station by his father's man. He'd spend a night or two alone with the small staff who lived at the Edgbaston house and then, with his school trunk replaced by holiday suitcases, he would be taken back to the station and placed on another train, a ticket and an itinerary and a tip for the guard in his pocket.

It was a ritual which ended with the Great Crash of 1929 and his father's ensuing suicide. Henry was brought up by his mother, who returned to live in Birmingham permanently, and he did not see Switzerland again for many years. But the family still had contacts out there and the country always retained a mythical air for him, that special aura that is bestowed only by the memory of idyllic childhood moments – a road in summer, an unfamiliar smell, a soft, repetitive sound, the pattern of light on a window, a shiver of rain from a cloudless sky. What with the personal pressure and the Axelrods' insistence on avoiding a scandal, it was the logical place to which to beat a retreat.

It was some time before Jennifer realised that she had gone without a period ever since Judd had been taken back to America. But by then she was squatting on the shores of Lake Geneva and digging her fingers into the sandy dirt. Not wanting to spoil her fun, she banished the disagreeable thought to the back of her mind.

Henry lay on the ground some distance away, snoring gently. He was wearing four watches, two on each wrist, and Jennifer could see the sunlight glinting off their bevelled faces as she moved her head from side to side. The watches lived on his arms like an infestation, increasing or diminishing in number but never quite disappearing entirely, the physical manifestation of the trauma he'd experienced with his wife's madness and death. It was somehow apt that he should have such a strong familial connection with Switzerland, that country of the clock, that crucible of mountains within which the disease of timekeeping had managed to concentrate itself and mutate until it was sufficiently strong to infect and enslave the globe.

The wind whipped across the water, coming up from the south and furrowing the lake's surface with waves, making a noise like a great canvas sail suddenly catching the breeze. Around the curve of the shore Jennifer could see the grey concrete buildings of the city, square and stark beneath the bright autumnal sky. She did not like Geneva, she had already decided. In fact, she didn't like Switzerland much. She didn't like pine trees and mountains, she didn't like Swiss television – which she couldn't understand – and she didn't particularly like the Swiss, at least those she had met, who were all too smartly dressed. But Henry seemed to like it here well enough. The beer suited him better than that he drank at home and in the two weeks that they had been in Geneva his face and eyes had grown less bloodshot than they had been in years.

Jennifer went over to him and pummelled his shoulder. 'Wake up, Dad! Dad! I'm bored. Wake up!' But he murmured thickly that she should go away, he was sleeping. She picked up first one and then the other of his thick pale arms and let them flop like severed limbs back on to the lush grass. Then it struck her that it might be more fun to have him asleep than awake and began to remove his watches. Two of them had buckled leather straps: they were easy enough. But the others had elasticated metal bracelets and she would have to ease them over Henry's hands while taking care not to trap any of the hairs on his arms.

He hated her taking his watches. She could never work out why he wore so many. When she asked him he always said that it was so that if one of them went wrong he'd still know what time it was. But they never seemed to be synchronised at all and he fiddled with them so much – he was forever removing the backs to tinker with the mechanisms – that it was a miracle any of them ever worked at all. (And how would you know anyway, she reasoned, which of them was showing the right time, unless you knew the time already?) The only time they ever seemed to be properly set was at Christmas or at the birthday parties that she used to have when she was younger when, as a party piece, Henry would wear his entire collection of seventeen wrist-watches and eight pocket watches and walk into the living-room ticking like a beam full of death-watch beetles and saying, 'Here comes old Father Time.' Jennifer and her friends would roll up his sleeves and trouser legs and go through his pockets trying to find them while they were still synchronised, because fifteen minutes after he had set them all there would already be wild variations. Some of the timepieces would be gaining time, their minute hands sweeping around the dial, others would jump their gears and bounce backwards, others would stop altogether. Like some cultural microcosm, within minutes of starting Henry would be a patchwork of different times and speeds.

With the watches removed and jangling on her own little wrists Jennifer went back to the hole she'd been digging. She pushed them right up above her elbows and twisted the straps around to make them stay, freeing up her hands so that she could remove more soil. Soon her fingers found a root as thick as a cable and, pleased to have something to focus on, to have an aim in the midst of that most aimless of afternoons, she gradually dug away the earth from around it. The root was covered in tiny hairs which wobbled under the weight of multitudinous particles of soil. She had uncovered about twelve inches of it when she discovered a fork, and just beyond this she found a large tuber growing from one of the branches. She began to dig away at that too and before long had exposed the top of a round, turnip-like vegetable. She wanted to uncover it completely but the clayey soil made digging down around it difficult and her fingers were already beginning to ache with the amount of compacted debris which had built up beneath her nails. Eventually she had an idea and went back to where Henry was still sleeping. She nudged him hard in the ribs with her foot but the rhythm of his breathing barely altered, so she felt in his pockets for the penknife she knew he always kept about his person. Once she'd found it she returned to her excavations, scraping away now with the little blade, taking care not to damage either the tuber or any of the subsidiary roots which branched from it at intervals.

By the time she had uncovered two-thirds of the mandrake – for that is what it was – most of the afternoon had passed away. But now that she could see most of it she lost patience and clasping the vegetable with both hands began to tug. It still wouldn't budge so, placing both feet beside it in the hole she braced herself against the planet and pulled. This time she was sure she felt it shift. Adjusting her stance like an athlete she gave the thing a final, almighty heave.

A lot of things happened at once. The root exploded out of the ground; there was a terrible shrieking sound; Jennifer rolled over backwards, the tuber all over her; someone stepped out of the trees. Panicking now, she tried to see who the newcomer was and simultaneously to fight off the system of roots which had tangled itself in her hair. She got to her feet and fell over, pulled down by a strand that was still stubbornly attached to the ground. The stranger ran over and disengaged the struggling vegetable, then helped Jennifer to her feet. As soon as she was up she was cross and twisted away from his hands where they held her.

She turned to face a man, tall and gaunt, in his mid-twenties. Unkempt stubs of black hair stuck out from beneath his blue woollen hat, he wore heavy walking boots, and his clothes were dirty and torn. His thin face bristled with something that was half stubble, half beard, and behind jam-jar spectacles two dark irises tunnelled their way back into his skull. On his back he carried a small army-green pack which rattled when he moved and which was marked with stains that Jennifer found quite unfamiliar, and he also carried about him a strange aura of distress, as if he were both present and yet somewhere else, and not quite sure how this impinged on the situation. This last reminded her of Judd, but whereas with Judd it had seemed a source of strength, this man oozed vulnerability.

Jennifer caught a whiff of it immediately, took it for weakness and seized the initiative. 'Why did you scream?' she demanded in English, without thinking. 'You frightened me.'

He answered her in English, also automatically. 'Me? But it was you who screamed. That's why I ran over.' His words were quite precise, his accent posh, like Doreen Buerk's. He wasn't Swiss.

'Well, it wasn't me,' she said. 'And if it wasn't you and it wasn't me, then who was it? Because my father's asleep on the grass over there and there's been no one else around here all day.' She stuck out her arm and pointed to the prostrate figure on the other side of the clearing. 'See?'

The man shrugged and said nothing. He noticed the mandrake which was lying where it had been dropped in the confusion. He took out a pocket-knife and cut the tuber from the last restraining root. 'Why were you digging for this?' he asked Jennifer.

'Dunno. Something to do, I s'pose,' she shyly stropped.

'Do you know what it is?' He turned the tuber over in his hands, flicking the dirt from it with grubby, nail-bitten fingers.

'Yeh, course I do. It's a turnip, anyone can see that.'

'No.' He laughed. 'This is no turnip. It's a mandrake. Some people say that they scream when you dig them up, although that's only supposed to happen if you do it at night.'

Jennifer looked at him incredulously. 'Plants don't scream. *Everyone* knows that.'

'Well, I'm just telling you what they say, that's all. Though it seems to me that we both heard something like a scream and unless it was your father having a bad dream . . . Perhaps it was an animal in the forest. I hope so. It is not such good luck to hear the mandrake scream. It can send a man mad, apparently.'

'And what can it do to a woman?' said Jennifer, refusing to be impressed.

Confused by her question, the man offered Jennifer the tuber and she took it back from him. 'What are you going to do with it?' he asked.

'Eat it, of course. Take it back to the hotel and get them to cook it for me in the kitchens. If you stop being so rude I might even save you some.'

'Well, usually it's dried and used as a medicinal herb. I've not heard of anyone eating it whole before.'

'Yes, well, now you have. The world's full of big surprises. It's something we all have to get used to. Even someone as clever as you.'

But her sarcasm was lost on him. He scratched his nose thoughtfully. She hadn't noticed before how large it was. 'Well, people *have* told me I'm clever. But I'm not sure it's so easy to tell the difference.'

'Between what?'

'Between very clever and very stupid.' He smiled and showed faintly yellow teeth, aware that he was talking down to her but not sure he knew how to do anything else.

'You ain't half full of yourself,' said Jennifer, who also couldn't think of a better reply. She sat down on the grass and the stranger copied her. 'Who said you could sit down?' she snapped. 'I don't remember you asking me! Is that how you treat a girl? Clever or stupid, you're still damn rude.'

The man leapt to his feet. 'I am sorry, but are you a girl?' he exclaimed. 'But I thought . . . but I did not . . .' He looked at the watches on her arms. They read 3.15, 4.25, noon and 8.18. 'Is that the time? I have to go, I am going to be late . . .' He turned to leave but she grabbed him by the sleeve of his jumper.

The shyness that had overtaken him boosted her confidence, and she giggled at him to stay. 'Did you think I was a boy?' She laughed when he turned back to face her, his cheeks red. 'Why?

Is it my short hair? But it's not that short.' Puzzled, she held her arms out and looked down at herself. She was wearing jeans, tennis shoes, a baggy cagoule. This last she unzipped so that the stranger could see the curves of her small breasts through her T-shirt. 'Do I look more like a girl now?' He blushed terribly. 'You're not Swiss, are you?' she demanded. 'Where are you from?'

'The United States.'

'But girls have short hair and trousers there!'

'Can we drop the subject please. I am very sorry, I made a mistake. Please let us talk about something else.'

'OK! Don't get upset! How old do you think I am?'

'I don't know. Please, I don't want to embarrass myself again.'

'Go on! I won't mind. I think you're thirty. Am I right?'

'Twenty-four actually,' he said, brightening a little.

'You see! I can be wrong too! Now, your turn.'

'I don't know. Maybe eighteen, at a rough guess,' he muttered.

'Bang on!' Jennifer exclaimed, delighted at his miscalculation. 'You see, you were right.' Encouraged, he asked her where she came from. 'England. Birmingham. Stratford-upon-Avon.'

Joel made an attempt at a joke. 'Which one?'

'All of them, sort of. Stratford is the town where I live, Birmingham is the nearest big city and England is the country.'

'I know,' he said hurriedly, angry that his joke had backfired. 'I used to live in Cambridge.'

'Oh,' she said, excited that they had something in common. 'I've been to Cambridge. It's nice. It's very pretty. When I'm old enough I'm going to go there to study.'

'But you're eighteen, that's old enough.'

'Er, yeh, but I want to . . . I need to see the world a bit first. Travel, you know.'

'Yes. I wish I had done that. I joined the university when I was sixteen.'

'Wow! You must be really clever.'

'I thought you'd already decided on that.'

'No, but I mean *really* clever.'

'So what did you mean before?'

'Before I thought that you just thought you were clever, but weren't really.' There was a slightly embarrassed silence, which Jennifer broke. 'What did you study?'

'Mathematics.'

'Oh, I want to study maths,' she lied. This was fun. 'You can sit down now, by the way.'

'Thank you.' The stranger sat on the grass beside her. 'I wouldn't.'

'Wouldn't what?'

'Study mathematics.'

'Well, I hadn't completely made up my mind . . .'

'It's a waste of time. I quit in the end.'

'What do you do now, then?'

'I'm a researcher.'

'What do you research?'

'Physics.'

'Oh.' At a loss. 'What sort of physics?'

'Quantum physics.'

'What's that?'

'It's to do with things that are very very small.'

'Like atoms?'

'Smaller than atoms.'

'Nothing's smaller than atoms.'

'Some things are.'

'Like what?'

'Like the things atoms are made up of.'

'Like what?'

'Protons, neutrons, electrons, neutrinos, quarks. The quark is very new. Its existence was only demonstrated a few months ago.'

'I know. I heard about it on TV. But I don't understand how you see all these things if they're so little?'

'Well, you don't really see them, not with your eyes at least. We do certain experiments and depending on the results we try and deduce what might be there. We use something called a particle accelerator.'

'What's that?'

'It's a huge circular tube that we fire atoms down, very fast, so that we can smash them into little bits. Using very sensitive detectors we can then find out what different kind of bits there are.'

'It sounds weird.'

'It is weird.'

'Can I see it?'

'What, the particle accelerator?'

'Yes.'

'Perhaps. I'll have to ask.'

'Where is it?'

'Not far from here. By the border. A place called CERN.'

'Is that where you work?'

'Yes.'

'So why aren't you working now? What are you doing out here?'

'I'm taking a holiday.'

'Why?'

'You ask a lot of questions.'

'Do I?'

'There's another one.'

'I suppose I do.'

'That's better.'

'What's better?'

'Better schmetter. You made a statement instead of asking a question. But then you ruined it by asking another question.'

'What's the difference?'

'A statement tells me something. A question asks me for something.'

'Sometimes questions can tell you something too.'

'That's just the problem.'

'With what?'

'With mathematics. With logic.'

'Is physics better then?'

'Sometimes. Perhaps.'

'When?'

'That's what I'm trying to find out.'

'Will you tell me when you do?'

The stranger laughed. 'If you want.'

'Do you think you'll find out soon?'

'I doubt it.'

'I hope you do. We're only in Switzerland for a short while. We're staying at the Hotel du Lac.'

'Well, if I find out I'll be certain to let you know. Who should I ask for?'

'Ask for me, Jennifer. Jennifer Several. And you haven't told me your name.'

'My name? My name is Joel Kluge.'

'Pleased to meet you, Mr Kluge.'

'Pleased to meet you too, Mademoiselle Several.'

Mademoiselle Several. Jennifer liked that. 'You don't sound American,' she said.

We don't see them with our eyes

She was probably the first female with whom he had held a proper conversation, if you didn't include his mother and his sisters and Amanda Metric and sundry administrative staff in the academic institutions he had attended. The girl he had thought was a boy, with her bobbed hair and frail limbs and the watches on her arms. She reminded him of a dream he had had a decade before, lying on the bank of the Cam, a dream of a perfect girl with mechanical arms, a dance of a dream on the bank of a river, a dream made flesh where water meets land on the banks of a lake. It was quite unheimlich – a German word he knew that meant 'uncanny'.

Joel turned the coincidence over in his mind as he hiked the few miles back into Geneva. He started by keeping to the water's edge, but after a while the going got too rough so he cut inland a few hundred yards and joined the highway. Cars and trucks rattled past him as he walked, and dressed the pine and spruce with fine sprays of lead.

He reached the hostel where he had been staying while his usual room on the CERN campus was unavailable and asked the receptionist, a balding Frenchman in his early thirties who was dressed in a white T-shirt and motor-cycle trousers, for his key. Then he went upstairs, dumped his pack on his bed, undressed and went down the hallway to shower. On his return he took from his backpack half a packet of crushed wafers, a tin of sardines, a textbook, a notebook and a flask of water, and sat there on the bed wrapped in his damp towel, a table in front of him, making himself a meal while he read. He had soon covered the thin red blanket with crumbs. With a pencil stub he scrawled some figures in the notebook.

When he had finished eating he threw the can and the plastic wrapping from the wafers into the bin, and with the cuff of his discarded shirt wiped up a few drops of oil that had been spilt when he'd opened the sardines. With the table now clear except for the notebook, he reached again into his haversack and extracted two red dice. He weighed them together in his left hand, rolled them around with his fingers, listened to the clicks that were made as each struck the other. Then he let them tumble on to the table, where they bounced and quickly came to rest. He sniffed and scratched his five-day beard, then recorded the scores and repeated the process. He did this for an hour and a half, then broke off to take a piss. By now he had long forgotten the encounter with Jennifer. Around ten he stretched out on the bed and fell asleep.

He was lying on the bed and the door opened and he floated towards it, worrying about banging his head. His room was bigger than it had been. He was no longer looking out from within himself but was watching the whole scene from above, as if he were on the roof of the building and all its walls and floors had become transparent. The body he had left behind floated out of the door of the room, both hitting its head and not hitting its head. There were others in the hostel, but they quickly became thinner until they were stick-like, at which point they were absorbed into the pulsating, gelatinous walls. The hostel trembled, all around it was white, there was no city. It trembled and dissolved, and the levitating figure was now a swimmer swimming upwards through the vitreous humour of an eye. His own eye. Joel swam upwards through his own eye, towards its cornea. His eye was not for seeing but for swimming. He seemed to have no trouble breathing. It had to do with waves.

Hypercycles

Haunting the night was another homunculus. Laika now filled her capsule so completely that apart from perception she had few functions left. With one eye on her monitor, the other on her porthole and two ears for the little speaker, she had become an almost entirely mediated being. It was no longer possible to distinguish between her and the machine. In came the plot lines, newscasts, pop songs, weather maps, planet views, co-ordinates, troop movements, flight paths, football results, lottery wins, share prices, tax figures. Out went very little apart from carbon dioxide and shit. But there was a regularity about the latter, about the waste products, that distinguished them from the information. Passive, partial, larval, contemplative and contracting, Laika bound the distributed excitations of data that flooded in through all her channels. She drew nourishment from them, a nourishment which sustained her long after her rations ran out. This was her secret, her creative work. Locked in her capsule in pure contemplation, a whirlwind of consciousness, a cinema-goer, again and again Laika remade her image, her self, from a synthesis of the differentials and potentials inherent in the incoming noise. On every level of her being, from the most ethereal operations of imagination and mind to the chemical susurrations of her fluids and cells, she exploited hypercycles and auto-catalytic loops, turned information into energy, let such a habitus unfold that could synthesise the present itself. Photon thought vibration disappeared into her and from this coarse grain of difference the processes of body and mind made the day.

She made a motor, powered it with the mediacasts she picked up, which were powered in turn by the motors of cameras, the capstans of tape recorders, the engines of newspaper presses and television studios, of space ships and particle accelerators, of fashion shows and wars. Like a billion gear wheels, these all intermeshed and drove one another, the whole a great machine fuelled by the perambulations and communications of Jennifer, Judd, Joel and millions like them. The result was an environment into which an unlucky parasite could be thrown and might yet survive, thrive even, breed perhaps and evolve.

Like the eukaryotic cell a billion years before her, like the lichens which conquered the land, Laika found herself in such a position, one which called for synthesis, for true creativity. And she rose to the occasion, finding new attractors, new degrees of freedom, new biological spaces in which to squirm and bulge. A rogue bacterium trapped inside a cell, in the normal course of events either she or her host would have died. But earth's atmosphere had changed, there was a mediascape now which, like the Oxygen Revolution before it, allowed new possibilities for life. And Laika was to be the exploiter, the dark precursor, the multiple starting point for a whole new plot line. She and Sputnik II melded together, became symbiotic, photo-autotropic, and in this way they fed and survived and continued their orbit, marking their wake with a crumbling stream of data-desiccated faeces that in doses measured out meanly by the once-dog's pulsating sphincter spilled down a tube, out of a valve and far off into inconceivable space.

The restaurant

Victor was heading for the tradesman's entrance in the hope of nipping outside unseen and having a quick smoke. He'd just put his right hand on the door handle when: 'Victor! Wohin gehen Sie? Die zwei Männer warten am Tisch fünf! Schnell!' Furious at being spotted by Schöllhammer, the Austrian headwaiter, Victor changed direction and headed back through the kitchens towards the restaurant, grabbing a tankard full of breadsticks as he went. He flapped through the swinging doors and headed over to the far table in the front window at which two corpulent businessmen sat, both of whom were wearing expensive steel-rimmed spectacles. They accepted the breadsticks without looking up. The paler of the two – and they were both pale – immediately reached across, pulled out one of the tubes, broke open its plastic wrapper with his teeth and ate the crisp, powdery stick in one long, mechanical, unbroken movement while his companion continued to talk.

Returning to the bar area, Victor stood and uncorked a bottle of Riesling and watched the cud-chewing movements that the man made as he masticated. Then the front door opened and in out of the rain stepped a bedraggled-looking Jew. Victor ignored him and wondered if there were any way he could get out of having to serve him. The restaurant was not particularly busy and all the tables apart from that at which the two businessmen sat had their food. He took their Riesling across and poured it out with a flourish, taking pains to make plain the kind of service a real Swiss could expect. But the businessmen ignored him and Joel had not noticed either, being too busy removing his coat and hat.

Victor darted down the far end of the restaurant, away from the door, asking at the occupied tables if there was anything anybody needed. Eventually, tired of waiting for assistance, Joel chose a table for himself.

Instantly, Victor was upon him. 'Excusez-moi, monsieur, mais celle-ci est réservée. On ne peut pas s'asseoir ici.'

'Er, sorry, ne parle pas français, je suis American. Can you parler anglais? English?'

American Jew, thought Victor. The worst sort. Probably related to the one who beat his cousin to that job in New York last summer. Salaud. 'You can nort seet here, see? Ist reserved. Taken. Pleeze to move to back of ristiran.'

'Uh, OK.' Too polite to protest, Joel stood and followed Victor towards the kitchens. There was a table there all right, just behind the swinging doors. It was disturbed by a constant draft and the smell of the stoves, and whoever sat there stood a good chance of having someone else's meal spilled all over him as waiters rushed in and out with their trays full of food. To engineer a disaster along these lines was exactly Victor's intention. It would cheer him up. But as he pulled out a chair with an elaborate flourish Joel caught his eye and clocked what was going on. He looked from the waiter to the chair, from the chair to the waiter, awkwardness and anger alternating in his chest like a strobe and making it impossible for him to think of a way to sidestep Victor's little manipulation.

Fortunately for Joel, just at that moment Schöllhammer swept out of the kitchens and nearly bumped into him. The headwaiter saw immediately that the customer was an American, gave Victor a black look and addressed Joel in English. 'Monsieur, I am terribly sorry, I did not see you there. Welcome to the Café Alsace. I trust you are finding everything to your satisfaction. Where would you like to sit? I'm afraid the weather is a little inclement today, but still the window tables are worth it, I think. Victor, sit the gentleman over there, table four, in the window. Can I get you anything to drink, sir?' Joel ordered a mineral water and Victor, fuming and unapologetic, led him back to his original seat.

'He's in Geneva again on Sunday and I said we could meet him in that restaurant in the square, the one you said you wanted to try. Oh, please, Daddy! He says he'll help me with my maths homework. It'll make up for me missing school. Please!'

Henry toyed with the idea. His first instinct was to say no, but he had long ago passed the point where he could refuse Jennifer anything. But what he could do was prevaricate. 'I'm not so sure. After what you've just put us through I don't see why I should let you at all. I'm not at all sure I shouldn't punish you just for attempting to set this thing up.'

'But Daddy, it's not like that. He's older, and he's . . . he's a *scientist*. And anyway you were asleep.' She was calling him Daddy, a clear sign that she knew she was going to get her way.

'Well, perhaps you should have woken me.'

'But I *tried*!' Henry had to agree that she might be telling the truth. The day had been warm, the lunch had been big, the beer had been drunk. 'What's this sudden interest in maths, anyway?'

'You *know* I've always been interested in maths. It was my best subject last term.'

He honestly couldn't remember if this were true or not. 'And you say he has offered to tutor you?'

'Yes. Oh, Daddy, I'm so bored here. There's nothing to do. *Please*. It is school work, after all.' Oh, such a sweet smile. There was a pregnant pause, although Jennifer was pretty sure of the sex of the imminent progeny.

'Well, I suppose the least I can do is meet him.' She leapt up, threw her arms around her father's neck and planted a big kiss on his cheek. He stumbled to keep his balance; he was no longer young. 'I'm not promising anything, mind you. We'll have to see.' Holding her in his arms his ears rang a little. He felt the cartilage between his lumbar vertebrae twinge under her weight, and he gripped her beneath the arms and eased her from him. When she ran excitedly into the adjoining room he sat down on the edge of the bed just to rest and breathe, and when he had begun to recover he adjusted the position of the watches on his wrists and synchronised them, for yet again they had run away from one another.

Sunday came and they walked out through the town together, heading towards the square in which the meeting with Joel was to take place. It was raining lightly, but Jennifer was ignoring the fuzz of water in the air and concentrating instead upon not stepping on the cracks in the pavement. Henry walked slightly behind her, puffing on a cigar and holding a golfing umbrella up against the drizzle. They had been walking for about ten minutes when they rounded the final corner and entered the square. Five or six large cafés occupied its four sides and their chairs and tables spilt out beyond the huge awnings, completely colonising the plaza. Today, however, the chairs were leant up and the umbrellas closed down as a precaution against the weather.

Jennifer ran on ahead towards the Café Alsace and pushed her face up against a window made soft with rain. 'He's here, he's here,' she called to Henry. Turning round to face the glass she pushed her hair back and into place. Within a split second she was in adult mode. They pushed the door open and went inside.

Joel, already half-way through his soup, looked up as father and daughter crossed to his table. An open pad, a pencil and the two red dice lay on the table next to the cruet. 'Hello,' he said.

'Hello,' said Jennifer. 'I bet you didn't think I'd come.' She flashed a shy smile at him and for a moment it looked as if he might smile back. 'This is my father, Henry Several. Dad, this is Dr Joel Kluge.'

The two men simultaneously sounded a greeting which was immediately followed by an awkward silence during which Joel remembered that he should stand up, which he did. Next, he offered his hand to Henry. Henry took it.

Victor arrived and laid the extra places perfunctorily, maintaining his ridiculous accent (he could in fact speak English perfectly well). ''Allo, 'ow ar yu? Plis mek yourself cum-furt-uble thank you? Wud you like these menu?' Jennifer and Henry sat down, took the menus from him and thanked him, although Henry couldn't resist making a comment about crazy foreigners beneath his breath which unfortunately for him Victor overheard. He ordered a beer for himself and a lemonade for Jennifer, who scowled slightly when she thought no one was watching. The preliminaries over, nothing was left to be done but for the three of them to look at each other across the table. No one said anything.

Finally, and to Jennifer surprisingly, it was Henry who broke the ice. 'So, Dr Kluge. I gather you met my daughter by the lakeside last week. I'm afraid it seems that I was fast asleep, but Jennifer has told me an awful lot about you.'

Across the table, Jennifer grinned. She was pleased to see that Joel had shaved and brushed his hair. 'Did you think we would come, Joel?' she asked.

'Please, Jennifer, I think you should address the gentleman as Dr Kluge.'

'*Dr Kluge*, did you think we would come?' Beneath the table she rotated her feet to and fro on the heels of her shoes.

'Well, I didn't know, but I suppose I thought you might, yes. I don't want to be rude,' he said turning to Henry with what he hoped was a smile, 'but would you mind awfully if I continued with my soup? It's getting cold.'

'Please, dear boy, go ahead. It looks good. Think I'll have a drop of that myself. Cold day and all that. Good drop of soup warms you up.' Underneath the table, Jennifer nudged his shin, prompting her father to remember his lines. 'Jennifer tells me you have offered to give her some tutelage. That's very gracious of you. She's missed a lot of school.' The reason hung in the air like a raincloud and Henry quickly shone upon it the sun of a lie: 'She's not been well.'

For the first time in years, Joel thought of Millstein and how hard it must have been for the teacher to approach his own father that first time. At least Millstein's motives had been purer than his own, he thought. 'I thought perhaps I could help her out with her maths,' he said quietly and was saved from further elaboration by the arrival of the drinks. Brusquely, Victor took the Severals' order.

'So what part of the United States do you hail from, doctor?' enquired Henry, while Jennifer was pointing out to Victor what she wanted from the menu. At the question Joel started and the spoonful of soup that he had been in the process of swallowing went down the wrong way. Trying to keep the liquid in his mouth only made it worse; it backed up his oesophagus and into his nasal passages. A fine spray of broth came out of his nose and peppered the table-cloth, dark spots bright against the white. Like niggers in a good Swiss town, thought Victor instantly. A minor coughing fit followed, which Joel exacerbated with his repeated attempts to apologise.

Jennifer passed him a glass of water and assumed a worried expression, and Henry leant over and pounded him on the back. 'Come on old chap,' he barked encouragingly, 'no harm done!' Victor disappeared and after some delay reappeared with a cloth and a jug of water, the contents of which he thought he might manage to slop over Joel. But as he moved towards him Joel, one step ahead, pushed his chair well back out of the way. 'Nothing to worry about,' said Henry cheerily, as Victor finished wiping the table, his assumption of command coinciding with the moment that the lager he had already drunk began to have an effect. 'It's all over now. Another beer for me, a lemonade for my daughter and another of whatever Dr Kluge was drinking if you please.' Returning to the table, his throat still aching slightly from the recent convulsion, Joel slowly drank the glass of water that Jennifer had given him, holding up his free hand to fend off further sympathies. Then he sat back in his chair and wiped away the beads of sweat that had pearled at his hairline.

Over at the bar, Victor had set a glass beneath the lager tap. As the beer puddled in the bottom of the stein he glanced around to make sure that Schöllhammer wasn't watching, then poured himself a schnapps beneath the counter, dropping down on his haunches to knock back the drink. All of a sudden he was struck by a particularly mischievous thought. He quickly poured out another schnapps and then, checking that the coast was still clear, he tipped the measure into the foaming glass of beer. A quick stir with a cocktail stick and no one would tell the difference. Then he poured out a lemonade for Jennifer and a mineral water for Joel, placed all three drinks on a round brass tray and delivered them to table four before returning to the kitchen to pick up the starters.

No sooner had the drinks been set down than Henry took a large draught of his lager. 'Fine beer,' he remarked to Joel, eyeing the man's mineral water. 'You not a drinker yourself?'

'It doesn't agree with me,' replied Joel, who had just about recovered his composure.

When the starters arrived Henry tucked into his soup with gusto and indeed ordered a bottle of Chablis to accompany it. As the wine was being poured, he turned again to Joel: 'So are you a mathematician by trade?'

'No, Dad, he's a physicist,' hissed Jennifer.

'Aha, well, you know me. I'm just an old accountant, it's all the same to me. As long as you're not one of those maths chappies with a practical streak.' He winked as he said this and gestured with his chin towards the dice that still lay by the cruet.

Joel followed Henry's gaze, but the reference was lost on him. 'I'm sorry?' he said.

'Practical. A practical mathematician! Putting those numbers to work! In a casino old boy! You know –' and here pointed with a long finger at the dice Joel had placed on his side plate when he had first sat down, ' – *gambling*!' He rolled out the word with an even rhythm, giving it three syllables. Joel looked to Jennifer for a clue. He didn't understand what Henry was talking about. It was difficult to say which of the two was the more confused: Joel, for not understanding, or Henry, for understanding that Joel was not understanding.

'Don't tell me,' said Henry finally, 'that you've never been to a casino.'

'No, I don't believe I have.'

'Well, I have to take you to one! It's something which anyone with an interest in numbers simply can't pass by. Don't go often myself, of course, not my bag, as they say, but it's something you definitely must see. If you're handy with the dice then we should at least get you into a game of craps.'

'Dad . . .' complained Jennifer.

'Craps?' asked Joel.

'Craps. Playing dice. For money. You roll two dice and bet on the various possible outcomes.'

Playing dice for money? The idea struck Joel as novel. He thought of his notebooks and their dense forests of probability trees. 'That sounds like fun,' he said, mostly to himself.

'In that case I shall most definitely treat you to a visit to the casino. I'm sure you'll find it most exciting.'

'My research work is not particularly exciting,' rued Joel. 'I mainly work with computers.'

'Ah computers. I was a code cracker, you know!' said Henry pompously, taking the non sequitur in his stride. 'I knew Alan Turing, way back when. Is that what you do? Code cracking?'

'Did you?' Joel exclaimed. 'Really? I know something about his work with computers, but not a great deal. I don't suppose you happen to know what inspired the idea for the Universal Turing Machine, do you?'

Pleased to have found a common subject, the two men chatted enthusiastically for a while. Although Henry didn't know a great deal about modern computers, back at Bletchley he had had one or two conversations with Turing about his ideas for a logical machine that, by dint of being fed its instructions in binary form on an effectively infinite tape, could theoretically perform the function of any other logical machine. As for what had inspired it . . . well, he did seem to recall something about the work of Charles Babbage and Ada Lovelace, and the old Jacquard loom, 'which was programmable, you know, yes, punch cards and all that'. Joel mentioned John von Neumann, about whom he knew more than he did about Turing, and Henry told him an interesting anecdote. 'Turing and von Neumann worked together, of course, on EDVAC, after the war. You know, don't you, that von Neumann was Hungarian by birth, but did you realise that back in Hungary his father was a banker, who had financed the introduction of those very Jacquard looms into his country years before? Some coincidence, hum?' Joel was suitably impressed. Henry asked him just what it was he did at CERN.

'I work on the particle accelerator. It's code-cracking too, of a sort. We try and crack the codes of atoms.'

'Atoms, eh? Darn me!' Henry clanked his spoon down into his empty bowl and sat back to take a swig of his wine. 'Like a drop of this, my boy? No? You should try it. Damn fine.' He refreshed his glass and reconnected with the thread. 'It all seems a bit highbrow for Jennifer, mind you. She can hardly even add up straight.'

'Dad! Don't listen to him. Anyway, Joel – Dr Kluge – isn't going to teach me about computers and physics. We're just going to do some basic maths, aren't we? Algebra, and equations and stuff.'

'Yes, of course, although –' Joel turned to Henry, his face seared a bright red, ' – I was thinking of inviting Jennifer out to the Centre, with your permission. It's not far, it's just out past the airport, near the French border. We can take a train there. Jennifer asked if she could see the accelerator and I think she will find it, uh, educational. Perhaps you would care to join us, Mr Several?' Henry tried to gain purchase on the use of the first person plural by this young man; there was something about it that . . . But the alcohol had got the better of him and the impression morphed itself into the idea that it would be nice for Jennifer to be able to go somewhere without him for a change. She should be safe enough with this fellow, he seemed responsible, he was a scientist after all and God knows they're a dull enough breed, not likely to come to any harm there. One heard of girls being seduced by music teachers, they were positively famous for it, but by a maths teacher? It was out of the question. So Henry convinced himself, and for the remainder of the meal he acquiesced to all his daughter's requests. It was eventually agreed that as long as Joel was available he should come to the hotel each morning and tutor Jennifer between eleven and one. They would start the next day and she would visit CERN on the following Saturday.

By the time they left the Alsace the rain had stopped. Jennifer soaked her shoes through by jumping in and out of the puddles.

'What a charming young man,' Henry remarked to his daughter, who wasn't paying him the slightest attention. 'And never even been to a casino.' To emphasise his disbelief he puffed hard on the large cigar he was smoking. Like others before them the clouds of smoke he exhaled hung on the damp Sunday air like dirty cotton swabs. Together they formed a septic trail that marked the couple's course through the labyrinth of streets and back to their hotel.

Initiation

Joel sat on the teak toilet seat in the second cubicle of the first-floor gentlemen's rest-rooms in the second-largest casino in Geneva and clutched his ankles with his hands. His colon was empty but he sat there none the less, his chest folded on to his lap. The position was not one of pain or strain, but of an arrested thought process. He was overwhelmed by the casino, by this crazed house of numbers, so much so that his bowels had loosened. But once he'd dumped a nervous quiver of faeces into the gleaming bowl he found himself distracted, wondering just to what extent the tangle of sewers, pipes and processing plants that formed the substratum of the city mimicked the workings of his own viscera.

Back in the main room Henry was wondering what had become of his companion. He crossed the floor in the direction of the bathroom, weaving his way between the baccarat tables and eyeing the fall of the cards and the movement of counters as he did so. But just as he was about to open the mahogany door – the one with the word *Hommes* embossed across it in gold – it swung back and Joel stepped out. 'Ah ha! Just wondering where you'd got to. Not in any trouble, I hope?'

'No, no, I'm fine,' Joel replied, warily peering out into the hall. The low chatter, the dark booths and thick carpeting, the clink of glasses and chips, the flash of jewellery and teeth; that this cosseted environment should be laced with so much adrenalin completely bewildered him. The contradictions reminded him of his barmitz- vah and the palpable disjunction he'd felt at the time between his own anticipatory excitement and everyone else's radical calm. The memory was intensified by the impression all these people gave that they were here to worship. Standing or sitting at the tables, they had the same rapt expressions as rabbis locked in prayer and contemplation, their faces a peculiar mixture of fervency and des- peration.

Henry led him through the club, explaining the different card games – chemin-de-fer, baccarat, blackjack. He described the role of the croupiers, the use of the shoe, the value of the chips, the workings of the bank, the etiquettes of betting, the security arrangements.

Joel took in everything, thinking all the while that these were the preliminaries. 'And so where are all the dice players?' he eventu- ally asked.

'No craps here, old boy,' said Henry, ruefully swilling the ice around in the bottom of his empty gin and tonic. 'You don't see so much of that over in Europe. You're better off back in America if you want to use your dice.' Slightly disappointed, Joel pointed across to the far end of the room where thick clumps of people were gathered around several long, thin tables and asked what was going on there.

'Aha, roulette! Game of princes! Let's go take a look, shall we?' They moved across to one of the quieter tables and stood at the wheel end and between spins the Englishman sketched out the rules for Joel, showed him how to admire the silent, seemingly frictionless twirl of the wheel, the deft movement of the croupier's wrist which sent the ball scudding against the direction of rotation, the clack of the chips as the players placed their bets. Joel was particularly moved by the way a hush fell on the group as soon as the ivory ball was released, its tik-tiketty-tak emerging clear from the previous commotion, the sound gradually dying away as gravity's basin guided the ball to rest in one of the cups. It reminded him of the sound of the pellets of freak summer hail which had fallen on the tin roof of an old shack he had sheltered in one night on the first hiking expedition he had taken after his arrival at CERN. A high wind had blown up and he hadn't been able to sleep because of the clatter of the trees. The hail came down, the wind dropped and behind the percussive rhythms of ice on metal the forest fell silent, as if to listen. As the storm moved away and the hail fell off, Joel could remember being overtaken by the most extraordinary feeling of peace. It was something akin to this that he was experiencing now, but he could not see yet that the peace that was promised by roulette would never arrive, that in a strange eternal return the wind would pick up again and again, and that there would always be another spin of the wheel.

His attention was also drawn by the rituals of preparation and consumption, the spell of the etiquette, the heady combination of euphoria and proscribed behaviour. He gripped the chips that Henry had bought to give him a start so firmly that when the time came to use them they were glued together with sweat and the mucilaginous gunge secreted by his palms. He watched Henry play the table with the intensity of an amateur assuming the cloak of a professional, pretending that his mistakes were deliberate attempts to educate Joel in what not to do. But Joel was in no mood to judge. It did not occur to him that one might play well or badly; one just played. It seemed to him that roulette was a way to let your personality be moulded for a time into shapes dictated by mathematics alone and he thought of the numerical vistas he'd roamed as a child. Here in the casino, in a strange, miniature and quite perfect way, was that Cambridge of the mind he had sought when he had deserted his family and boarded the plane bound for England. Here was a world in which people, for a period at least, gave themselves over to the Number. To Joel it was obvious that money was the excuse, not the reason.

More people gathered around the table and soon he stood in a crush, his shabby figure curious against the shimmering dresses and the crisp, dark suits. The table hovered level with the players' groins, a tense plateau of energy drawn out from their genitalia. The yellow betting grid etched upon this larval surface reminded Joel of the periodic tables that hung in the labs and lecture rooms of CERN, and he wondered if their functions were complementary, the periodic table merely representing the bets that had been laid on the spin of the wheel that was the birth of the universe.

Here was something so much more satisfying than the dice he was using. He'd been working away at chance for some time now, figuring that if – as he had explained to Metric several years previously – the universe was indeed rebuilding itself in the image of perfection, reconstructing the shattered vessels, then there should be traces of this process to be found. But where should one begin to search for them? Joel had spent the first year of his time at CERN pondering this, until the answer had suddenly come to him, somewhat significantly he thought, on a ragged mountain top during one of his walks. Chance! Chance was the key! If the universe was perfect then randomness – chance, probability – should be perfect too: analyses of random samples would prove them to be just that, random, and there would be no statistical significances to be found in the data. But if the universe was imperfect, as it was, then there would be flurries and eddies in chance, rivulets and rifts, patterns and predictabilities. It should be possible, to a limited extent, to map the future. The idea had taken shape like cracks across a windscreen, and on his return to the town he immediately bought himself several sets of dice and began to compile data.

It was a grand design. Not only would he be looking for localised effects but ultimately he would be trying to track changes over time – to see if there was some kind of generalised trend. It was an insane project, he knew, one on which he could spend his whole life and still have nothing to show for it. But now, with this game of roulette, it seemed as if there might after all be a way to get tangible results. Here was a chance machine that ran twenty-four hours a day, seven days a week, all over the world. If there were indeed results to be measured, if the world was actually evolving towards some higher realm of total perfection, then how much more keyed into that progression would this meshwork of gamblers and wheels be than he himself, alone in some room with his dice? This, then, was the way to proceed. It was beautiful. It was the most beautiful thing.

'I'm all out of chips,' said Henry, in what he imagined was the accent of a whiskey-drinkin', horse-ridin', whore-whuppin' and hard-gamblin' frontiersman from the American Wild West. He looked down at the chips in Joel's hand. 'You not goin' to play then, pardner?'

'Er, no,' said Joel, emerging from his reverie, 'not tonight, I don't think I understand the game well enough yet. Perhaps you'd better play for me.' He passed the gummed-up clump of counters back into the older man's hands, the colour beginning to seep back into his face as he did so. For the first time that evening since he'd been getting ready to go out it struck him that instead of philosophising about roulette he should be worrying about whether or not Henry suspected him of wanting to have sex with his daughter.

Spermatogenesis (2)

For activity in Joel's testes, please refer to Book 001, Chapter 4, *Spermatogenesis (1)*.

Dark matter

Most of all, Jennifer was impressed with the sheer size of the accelerator. She couldn't quite conceive of the size of the ring itself, the Super Proton Synchrotron, twenty-seven kilometres in circumference, but the massive detectors in their deep underground bunkers made the scale of the thing plain enough. Joel gave her a guided tour: he showed her the SPS control room, with its computers and banks of television screens which let the technicians monitor every part of the gigantic structure; also several of the experiments, driving from one to another in a car he had borrowed for the purpose.

It was a clear day and they could see the Alps in the distance, away beyond Geneva. They crossed the border into France and back again. Some of the experiments were housed in hangers thrown up on hillsides where sheep and cattle grazed, others were buried as much as six storeys down into the ground, two thousand tonnes of superstructure and electronics. These great pits swarmed with cables thicker than Jennifer's legs, cables which puddled on the floors and levels and tumbled down the walls like enormous earthworms in a giant fisherman's bucket. White cubes as big as caravans and stuffed with integrated circuits were stacked up one on top of the other like so many fridges in a reclamation yard; blue metal walkways ran between them and around them. Cooling fans as loud as aircraft jets roared constantly and the din drowned out everything else. On one of the cabinets were painted the words: 'Hands off. You will be shot.' A sign hung above a door on the second floor; it read: 'If you have nothing to do, don't do it here.'

'THIS IS THE BRAIN OF THE DETECTOR,' Joel yelled above the noise. 'WHEN THE COLLISIONS TAKE PLACE INSIDE, THE SHOWER OF PARTICLES IS TURNED INTO A SERIES OF ELECTRONIC PULSES, WHICH ARE FED INTO THESE CIR-CUITS – THERE'S ABOUT THREE OR FOUR MIL-LION, I THINK. THESE WORK OUT WHETHER THEY'RE INTERESTING ENOUGH TO BE

STORED ON THE MAGNETIC TAPES SO WE CAN LOOK AT THEM LATER.' He grinned and nodded wildly as he shouted, gesticulating at various parts of the space. Jennifer nodded back, unable to make out most of what he was saying. But she didn't need to know the facts in order to learn: the very sight of this vast complex, buzzing with people and completely dedicated to tending this even vaster and mostly invisible machine was entertaining enough. It was as if some benign alien presence had taken root up here in the mountains and had attracted a colony of humans both to interrogate and to be interrogated by, and when she saw *Close Encounters of the Third Kind* at the cinema four years later it would bring this visit to CERN back to her so immediately that she cried all the way through the final scenes.

'ARE THESE THE ONES WHO FIND OUT WHAT ATOMS ARE MADE OF?' she yelled.

Joel, pleased that she had asked a question, started nodding even more furiously. 'YES, BUT THEY DON'T EXAMINE THE DATA HERE. TOO NOISY. AND IT'S NOT ALWAYS THEM WHO MAKE THE DISCOVERIES. THE FIRST SUB-ATOMIC PARTICLES WERE IN FACT DISCOVERED BY WOMEN – THE PHYSI-CISTS INVOLVED WERE TOO BUSY FLYING OFF TO CONFERENCES TO BREAK DOWN THEIR OWN DATA, AND THEY GOT THEIR WIVES AND GIRLFRIENDS TO DO IT. BUT GUESS WHO TOOK ALL THE CREDIT?' The idea intrigued Jennifer and she wondered if Joel would ever let her examine any of his data.

They had started the lessons that week as planned and things had progressed well enough. Jennifer's grounding in maths was more basic than Joel had dared to think, but she was bright and she quickly picked up new ideas. If anything was going to hinder her progress it was her propensity to lead Joel off the subject: she loved to chat and wanted to know everything about her tutor. Joel found the attention quite disconcerting – enough to render him almost incapable of parrying her questions – and he had a hard time keeping the proportion of maths in their sessions to over fifty per cent. And not only did Jennifer grill him, but she criticised him too. She found out that he'd never had a girlfriend, had never bought a record, didn't own a car, didn't watch TV. She teased him that he didn't have a life. Didn't he do anything but work? She lent him some cassette tapes she'd brought with her from England: *The Rise and Fall of Ziggy Stardust and the Spiders from Mars*, Leonard Cohen, *Sticky Fingers*, *Electronic Meditation*, some Crosby, Stills & Nash. He listened to them all, but only once.

After he had shown her around on the Saturday they went for lunch in one of the refectories. Jennifer rattled on happily about her morning, too busy talking to do more than pick at her sandwich, although she ate the whole bagful of potato chips which she was supposed to be sharing with her new friend. Joel sat there, munching on a baguette stuffed with Emmenthal and sliced salami, and watched her as she told him about everything that they had just seen on their tour around CERN. He felt displaced. Hearing the descriptions fall from her mouth: 'all those maggoty wires and cables', 'so noisy it was like standing in a weir', 'like being inside the theatre, but full of these kind of caravans' – images taken from the town in which she had grown up and reconfigured in order to help her comprehend this new experience – it seemed to him that he didn't know what she was talking about, that she was chattering about somewhere he had never been. He listened, fascinated.

But soon even Jennifer ran out of things to say. Remembering her hunger, she applied herself to her sandwich while Joel sat and looked out of the window, embarrassed now to watch her and trying to think of new topics of conversation. Getting Jennifer to come out to CERN had filled his thoughts for the previous fortnight, and even after it had proved easy to get her and her father to agree to the visit it had still obsessed him, worried as he was that something might go wrong and that she wouldn't be able to come. But for all that, he hadn't thought about what they'd do beyond him giving her the tour. Now that he'd shown her the main attractions he was all out of ideas.

'Whereabouts do you live, Joel?' Jennifer piped up. She'd swallowed the last desirable piece of her sandwich (she left the crusts) and was beginning to unwrap a chocolate bar. Joel mumbled the name of a residential block, but was no more forthcoming than that. Earlier in the week her probings had revealed that although her tutor did not have a TV he did have coffee-maker, and now she used the knowledge as a crowbar to lever his private life a little further open. 'I think I'd like some coffee. Why don't we have one in your room? I want to see your coffee machine.'

Joel, suddenly scared: 'Well, I er, I don't think so, it's a terrible mess, and it's too far away, it would take us ages to walk there. And shouldn't you be getting back . . . ?'

'We've still got the car you borrowed! And I don't care about the mess. And Dad's not expecting me back till this evening anyway. Come on! I want to see where you live!' She dragged him from the table and out to the car, and they drove the short distance across the campus to Joel's block.

He had a room on the fourth floor at the back. They climbed the concrete stairs and came to the door; Joel unlocked it and pushed it open, letting Jennifer in first. She walked into a large double room with one big window that looked out on to a sky freckled with low grey clouds and, beneath it, the drab town of Meyrin. There was a bed in the corner, a desk, a coffee table and some chairs, a kitchenette, a small bathroom equipped with toilet and shower. It was not dissimilar to Henry's room in the hotel (she had only a small single further down the hallway). But what made the room distinctive, apart from the bookshelves overflowing with daunting-looking volumes, the stacks of papers and computer equipment, the piles of clothes and the fairy rings of dirty cups, were the pictures on the walls.

Photographs and maps had been pinned up haphazardly and covered every available space. While Joel made excuses for the mess, and washed mugs and filled the coffee machine, Jennifer peered at some of the pictures. Photographs of piles of objects. Piles of shoes, so many shoes that they filled a whole room, piles of spectacles, piles of suitcases. Piles of trousers, hats, shirts. Banks of cabinets and boxes full of smaller objects – cigarette cases, rings, wallets, small odd-shaped pieces of some dull metal that Jennifer could not identify. There was a map of what must have been Europe, but it was completely black and had no features – no coastline, no national boundaries. All it had were place names and under each name a number, usually in the thousands or hundreds of thousands. Jennifer moved around the room; behind her Joel panicked over the coffee.

Photographs of lampshades made of some curious parchment and etched with complex designs that looked like tattoos. Long ropes next to piles of what she thought were horses' manes. Many many pictures of empty shower rooms like the ones at Stratford rugby club; others of rooms that she recognised as slaughterhouses from the meat hooks set into the ceilings and the dark splashes of what must have been blood on the walls. (She winced – the fact that the pictures were in black and white made them somehow worse, because they activated the imagination.) Furnaces like the ones she had seen in pottery museums in the Black Country on school trips, forest clearings that had been excavated and strewn with a strange, coral-like shale.

She couldn't make the connection between all the pictures. This was a part of himself which Joel had not revealed to her; in all of their talking he had not told her that he was into photography, especially of such a weird kind. A frisson of fear made her tremble like jelly. Who was this man with whom she was spending her time?

'How do you have your coffee?' he asked her.

'White with sugar, please.' She turned round to face him, to ask him about the photographs, and he handed her a cup. 'Joel . . .' But the wall behind him was full of pictures that she had not yet properly seen and for a second she focused on them and in that moment everything became clear. At the sight of the people, hollow like ghosts, she dropped the cup; it fell to floor and splashed scalding coffee up her jeans. 'Oh, Joel, I'm sorry, I'm so sorry, oh, God, it was . . . it was the pictures, I . . .'

Joel dashed around her with a tea-towel, swabbing up the mess and dabbing the worst of it from her trousers, forgetting that he was touching a girl's legs for the first time. 'I should have warned you,' he apologised. 'Nobody really comes in here and I forget about them, about what other people might think, coming in here, you know, unprepared. Awful, aren't they.' He refilled Jennifer's cup as her eyes roamed the wall, trying to construct a meaning out of the bodies stacked like wood, the walking corpses next to the stunned and embarrassed Allied soldiers, the heaps of babies all with their skulls caved in and cortical matter dried into waxy rivulets on the walls above them, the crude torture chambers with their pincers and rheostats and the laboratories filled with samples, the hills of ash whose contours were broken by protruding skulls and femurs, the naked women standing in circles or being set upon by dogs, the mattresses waterlogged with diarrhoea, the two stick-like children sitting astride the bloated corpse of their dead mother and playing with a die, the photographs of the Nazi officers smiling with their wives. The content of all the previous pictures, the ones she had misunderstood, became horribly clear.

'Where are these pictures from?' Jennifer asked, trying to keep her voice steady, more afraid than ever.

'They're from the Holocaust. During the Second World War, the Nazis tried to wipe out all the European Jews. They nearly succeeded.'

'Why?'

'Ha!' It was only the second time she had heard Joel laugh. 'I don't know. There are reasons given in the history books, of course, but they don't really mean anything. It seems to take more than logic to understand why a particular group of people should go completely out of their way to eradicate more than six million . . .'

'Six million!'

'I'm surprised this is all so new to you. Don't they teach you history in school?'

'Yes, but I've never much liked history. Our teacher, Mrs Pettigrew, is awfully dull and I think she mentioned some stuff about it once when we did the Nazis and Churchill and stuff, but I never really realised . . . I mean, we didn't see any photographs like this or anything.'

For the next hour they looked at the pictures together, Joel telling Jennifer the stories behind each one, simple stories made up of where–when–what, because the images were too stark, their content too clear, for them to need the padding of human detail – of whom. Jennifer listened in silence, really learning something for once, Joel really teaching. As he talked she was surprised at how empty she felt, hollow as the emaciated Jews who staggered blinking from the dormitories. It was shock, of course, brought on as the planes of her being began to rotate making her strange to emotion until a fresh configuration was reached, one which would bring with it a whole new array of intersections, interstices and possibilities.

She asked him how he'd got interested in all of this.

'Well, of course, I'm Jewish myself, so that's part of it. But like you, it was never real to me when I was told about it at school, or when my parents mentioned it, even though my Uncle Isaac and most of his family died in one of these camps, this one –' he pointed to one of the pictures on the wall, '– Treblinka. No, it never came home to me until I came here to CERN, in fact. An old physicist here, a Jew, one of my supervisors . . . well, we were in one of the laboratories the summer before last and it was terribly hot, and he rolled up his shirt-sleeves – something I'd not seen him do before, he was very neat and proper. And on his arm was a tattoo, like this.' He pointed to another picture, this time of a serial number etched on to a woman's arm in an inky, ragged blue. 'I asked him about it and he told me. He'd been in one of the camps, not Treblinka, another one, Dachau, it's near Munich. I told him about my uncle, and he told me all about the war and what had happened to him. He gave me a lot of these photographs. I didn't want to take them at first but he told me he was dying and he was right – he died last year, of lung cancer; he'd thought that since he'd survived the camps nothing could kill him, especially not something as ridiculous as tobacco. He smoked right up to the end, even after he knew it was coming. But I don't think he really cared by then.

'The terrible thing is, of course, that this is nothing new. Humans have been involved in the systematic destruction of each other ever since history began. You can go right back to classical mythology and find accounts of concentration camps. Scratch at the history of any country in the world and you'll soon uncover the layers of blood on which it was founded. Take America, for example, land of the free, right? Except for the native tribes who were wiped out by the early settlers and the black slaves who were imported in vast numbers from Africa – mostly by British companies, I'm afraid – and the Chinese immigrants who were treated no better than slaves and worked to death laying railway lines. Look at Stalin's massacre of the Kulak class, or his starvation of Ukrainian peasants in the thirties – that killed as many as the Nazi Holocaust. Or the destruction of Tasmanian aborigines by European immigrants, or the modern Chinese attempts to eradicate the Tibetans.'

'But why are you so obsessed with this stuff? Don't you find it gruesome? There are good things in the world too, you know.'

'Maybe. But I don't know if they outweigh the bad things.'

'But Joel, that's ridiculous! More people are born than die! The number of people in the world is still going up! And that means that there's more love than death, doesn't it? Doesn't it?'

'I don't know. Do children always spring from love? How many parents do you know who are really happy? Who truly love one another? Who love their children?'

This touched a nerve and Jennifer suddenly found herself battling against pain, refusing to accept that her argument was invalidated by what Henry had told her of her own conception. 'But love isn't that simple . . . i-it doesn't mean that you always walk around with a smile on your face, that you are never unhappy. It's more than that. I mean I know my dad loved my mum, e-even when she went mad and, I don't know how to explain it to you, but it's not like you think . . .' Tears of frustration began to form in her eyes as she failed to think a way through the moral conundrum. Instinctively, she changed tack. 'I mean, haven't you ever fallen in love?'

Joel looked at her. 'No. I don't think I have.'

'What? You've never had a girlfriend?'

'No.'

'Are you gay?' Joel looked blank. 'Are you a homosexual?' She demanded the information, letting herself get angry with him now, widening the channel down which she could escape from the thought of her mother's rape.

'No, I don't think so.' Joel knew that such people existed, but he had never given them much thought.

'Well, haven't you ever even had sex?'

'Er, no, not that I remember.'

'God! You're a *virgin*?'

'I suppose so.' Joel was by now acutely embarrassed.

Jennifer's anger vanished and she began to giggle. 'Really? That's amazing.' She allowed herself to start laughing properly – it was hilarious, wasn't it, the idea that this man, a good ten years older than her, had never slept with anybody? It was too much. Of course, Joel didn't see the joke. He suddenly felt incredibly self-conscious, painfully aware of his body extruding itself into the room like some ungainly piece of scaffolding – temporary and purely functional. By comparison, Jennifer seemed like an alien being, an angel complete in her physicality. It suddenly struck Joel that the ethereal wasn't a realm of pure mind, divorced from the strictures of the material; it was a realm of pure physicality, pure expression. Freedom had nothing to do with being released from the confines of substance. It was to do with being released from the confines of form, of designs generated like the by-products of a chemical process by the operations of thought. Perhaps form wasn't imposed on matter, perhaps human beings had it wrong when they tried to understand the world in terms of abstract schemata imposed from above. Perhaps form grew out of the way things collided, the way they connected, the way they moved. But then, wasn't logic itself such an outgrowth? The thought seemed contradictory and Joel felt confused.

Jennifer saw all this flash across Joel's face and took it for straightforward sadness. She stopped her false laughter, stood up from where she had been sitting on the edge of the bed and came over to where he was kneeling. Shaking a little she put her arms on his shoulders, then bent down and kissed him on the forehead. She felt nervous, tentative, like a stream finding its way down a mountainside, daring to try and erode. She thought of Judd and his arid body, slow and absorptive, so different from Joel's, which was sensitive as a scree-littered slope. She pulled him towards her and bound his fragments with her moisture, her warmth, cloying them into a malleable clay. Sex wasn't anything out of the ordinary for Jennifer. It wasn't transgressive, it was merely an obvious corollary of the world as she experienced it – as a tactile and heterogeneous place, riven with channels but never ruptured, marvellous and occasionally brutal, but never alien or cold. Maybe this was a result of her shattered family and peculiar upbringing, maybe it was something she was born with, it's impossible to tell, but perhaps this is why she was so shocked by the Holocaust images and, ultimately, not as deeply affected by them as Joel.

Joel remained motionless, so she bent down a little further, locked her arms around his neck and began to kiss him instead on the lips. It was a strange feeling, from which he could not generalise. Then slowly she began to undress him. He couldn't generalise from that, either.

It was a total shock, the sex, an overload of every sense. Even to have someone else touch his clothing, unbutton it, unzip it, made him shake. He flushed hot and sprang goose-bumps simultaneously. When she was naked and he saw her skinny limbs he couldn't help but think of the wraiths on the walls, the camp survivors. He tried to block them from his mind, but then he thought of home and that was worse – all the old moralities came flooding back, here he was in the forbidden zone, he wasn't even married, how could he think of such a thing? His mind reconstituted the whores in Times Square, the electric shock of that crotch, the mugging, the bridge . . . the accelerator, the particle ring, the news that another section of Skylab had that day successfully docked. Her skin was like flames . . .

She felt it and placed his hand on her breast and that calmed him.

Afterwards, he couldn't remember coming; he could barely remember any details at all. The whole thing was a blur, but a vivid one, a fast-forward video trace. For weeks he couldn't think of it without shuddering, as if someone had dabbed ice on his nipple, but at the same time he was proud, he had managed it, he'd crossed a threshold and nothing would be quite the same again . . . The area of skin between his anus and his scrotum seemed permanently tender, but on the inside, as if a cat were licking away at the very fronds of the muscles down there. In a way he had come to life, he felt totally alive, it was like a drug. It was a good month before he wondered if this was how a computer might feel, if you flooded it with data.

As for Jennifer, while they'd been making love she'd thought of algebra, a special kind, though derived from what Joel had been teaching her. *This plus this divided by this over this equals what?* she'd mused, as she'd scrawled her calculations across the tablet of his skin.

Life as we know it

In retrospect, 1973 became known to scientists as the annus mirablis of physics. Joel's insight apart, breakthroughs that year included the discovery of neutral currents (which lead to the final establishment of the existence of the quark). Nor were the other disciplines left out. IBM engineers discovered the group of alloys known as Rare Earth, which enabled the development of rewritable optical media, the first practical steps were taken in the science of genetic engineering and tape capstan motor acceleration reached a new rate of 0 to 200 inches per second in 750 millionths of a second.

But the year's real first, its most exciting and unprecedented event, took place far from prying eyes and Nobel prizes. It happened deep inside the body of Jennifer Several, where a single ovum was busy being fertilised by spermatozoa from two different males, Judd Axelrod and Joel Kluge. This had happened before, would happen again: the result was generally twins. But in the strange case of Jennifer Several the progeny would not be two children but one and one alone – one child parented by three distinct sets of DNA. In 1973 in Jennifer's womb a three in one – a thoroughly materialist and thoroughly unholy trinity – was being gestated. And this is how it happened.

Shortly before Jennifer had intercourse with Judd for the last time an ovum was released from her right ovary and started its slow journey down the corresponding fallopian, propelled along by the tube's muscular action and the efforts of the tiny cilia on its internal surfaces. Then Judd's spermatozoa were ejaculated into Jennifer's vagina, and a few of these managed to work their way up past the cervix and into the uterus. A significant number died then and there. Of the survivors all but one chose the left-hand fallopian.

Jennifer had heard about the quark's existence shortly before she and her father had left for Geneva: the breakthrough had made the nine o'clock news. It's fair to say that she didn't take much notice – her mind was on other things at the time. But she absorbed the information anyway and it kicked around in her subconscious, where it was processed and puzzled over. Her subconscious couldn't quite put its finger on it, but something about the quark worried it. It did a bit of research into quantum mechanics and that was when it learnt about Heisenberg's uncertainty principle, which stated that it was impossible to know both the position of a sub-atomic particle and its momentum at the very same instant, the upshot of which was that the behaviour of particles could not be predicted. Disaster! If the scientists had shown that the world was fundamentally incoherent, the subconscious would be out of a job! This was terrible! It told the body its concerns (as it always did, the two of them being extremely close) and the body was no less worried, knowing full well that without the subconscious to anchor it, the conscious mind would have taken off on its own long ago, leaving the body behind to rot like so much senseless meat (being no different from anyone else, the body too languished in a world of Cartesian delusion). There was danger here, it thought, a great deal of danger, and the cells of the spinal column (who'd heard the news first and regarded themselves as somewhat more sensible than their brethren) decided to keep a lid on the information and forestall widespread panic. But the body is a hot-house of gossip at the best of times and it didn't take long for rumours to start, which soon spread like viruses to every fingertip, sebaceous gland and hair follicle – and, inevitably, to one little protoplasm on the end of a cilia, who whispered the secret to the ovum as it passed by on its journey to the womb.

Well! That changed everything. The ovum wasn't at all sure that it wanted to be fertilised now! Go out into an uncertain world? Not likely! It quickly decided that with all these great changes afoot it would be far better off staying inside, at least until the situation had been clarified, so it fastened on to the wall of its tube and hunkered down.

Meanwhile, nobody had told the lone spermatozoon about the quark. It was just wandering around at the bottom of the right fallopian wondering if it shouldn't have gone up the left-hand one with the others when Jennifer's period began and she started to eject the detritus of another menstrual cycle. This disorientated the little spermatozoon so much that when the tempest was over and, by some miracle, it had survived, it decided to stay put for a while and recover its strength.

Jennifer's next two cycles were cancelled, as the body felt that it needed to make an example of the fallopian tubes and penalise them for having let one of their cells break the news to the ovum, so the ovum and the spermatozoon were left undisturbed for a couple of months. And while they were both sitting there it just so happened that a large dose of cosmic radiation that had been travelling for aeons from some distant galaxy streamed through Jennifer's body, causing mild chromosomal mutation in these two somewhat disoriented little gametes (inversion in the ovum, translocation in the sperm).

Then Joel's semen was injected into the situation and Judd's one surviving spermatozoon thought it had better get moving. Meanwhile, back at the top of the tube, the ovum had been persuaded that life must go on (the body had made the case to it that quantum uncertainty only held on the sub-atomic scale and that the traditional heuristic values of truth could still be maintained in the macro environment). With a heightened sense of its own importance (it now regarded itself as the world's first philosophically adept egg) it began to move on down; there was a spermatozoon waiting, the cilia had said. With Joel's spermatozoa fast bearing down on them, the ovum and Judd's spermatozoon crept closer and closer together. The little sperm knew full well that if it was discovered by the enemy hordes they would destroy it immediately, so it thrashed upwards with all the force it could muster. It caught sight of the ovum up ahead just as the first of Joel's spermatozoa rounded the bend behind it, gaining fast. Judd's sperm swam as fast as it could but little by little the Joelean leader drew level. Side by side they raced the last few millimetres towards the ovum. But the ovum had not detected them yet. It was far too busy thinking about how important it was, carrying the torch of the body and the unconscious out into this uncertain new world. It completely forgot about its sacred duty to let one sperm in and one alone. When the two spermatozoa arrived and burst through the vitelline membrane together, their flagella practically entwined, it was a moment or two before the ovum realised just what was going on. And by then it was too late: the haploid nuclei of the three gametes had already started to fuse together (helped by another handy burst of cosmic radiation) and the ovum's identity was lost in the flux as it and the two spermatozoa became a zygote. In a normal human embryo this process takes about a day, but having three gametes involved complicates everything and it was two days before the new nucleus underwent mitosis.

The process of mitosis, or cell division, begins when the chromosomes in the new nucleus start to duplicate themselves. Long threads of these duplicates coil into close spirals, shortening and thickening as they do so. The nuclear membrane dissolves and a spindle forms, with the chromosomes attaching themselves to its centre. They pause for a while in this position, then the duplicates move towards either end of the spindle. At the same time the spindle elongates and when the two sets of chromosomes are a sufficient distance apart they begin to uncoil. New nuclear membranes form around them, and eventually both spindle and chromosomes disappear, leaving two cells with their own nucleoli, which in turn start to divide.

Now that this processes had begun, the fallopian tube gasped a sigh of relief and pumped the expanding cell mass down into the uterus, where it fixed itself on to the uterine wall and continued to grow. But the complications experienced during fertilisation had a knock-on effect and every cell was taking longer to divide than it should have done. It was a full two weeks before the blastocyst appeared, and two months before the embryo reached the stage achieved by a fertilised bird's egg in three and a half days.

The human genome does not operate like a computer program – it is not a straightforward set of instructions which are faithfully followed. Rather, the genes work in ensembles (cistrons), and act in multi-dimensional inter-connected circuits that include cis-acting regulatory elements (which influence nearby genes on the same chromosome using various promoters and operators, hormone-responsive elements, chromatin-folding domains and facultative heterochromatin) and trans-acting elements (which influence distant genes belonging to other chromosomes by creating diffusible products such as RNA, proteins and metabolites) (Kauffman, 1993). This means that the project of isolating the gene for a particular type of human behaviour (the gene for crime, the gene for homosexuality) is fundamentally misconceived. Rather, the tangle of genes and regulatory products – in effect a sparsely connected network – creates a kind of dynamic arena in which cells can form, and within this arena are various basins, or attractors, towards which the behaviour of the network tends. Each of these attractors is a motor for producing a different type of cell, and whereas the normal human genome has two hundred and fifty-four of them, Jennifer's mutated genome had cathected two more and so had two hundred and fifty-six. If the genome, then, is like a computer at all, it resembles less a Universal Turing Machine, which processes information in a serial fashion, than a dynamic Boolean network (or parallel processor, or neural network), in which a collection of inter-linked switches process information in concert by altering their behaviour according to that of their neighbours, rather like a flock of birds or a swarm of bees.

In the genome network each cell type is one of the possible outputs of the system. As it forms, each receives information from the surrounding cells via their regulatory elements, and structures its future differentiation and mitotic behaviour accordingly. Different cells receive different information and develop different characteristics. To a degree, the mechanism is an oppressive one: any cell is capable of an extraordinary range of functions, but in the genome system the peer pressure exerted upon each individual by its neighbours means that it promotes one particular function and specialises in it, to the neglect of all the others.

Having three sets of genetic material within, the blastocyst which was to become the daughter of Jennifer, Judd and Joel produced rather more cells of a rebellious variety than was usual, but the end effect was pretty much the same: as more and more cells were produced they formed themselves according to type into spatially ordered arrays which eventually would become tissues and organs.

Even at this stage, though, the DNA inside the cells is not doing all the work. The shape of the organs (and indeed of the cells themselves) depends to a large extent upon certain fundamental features of polymer chemistry. Surface tension, gravity, pressure, all these things play a role, as do occasional cascades through the system of regulating variables (once cells form into the sheets that make up tissue they continue to act as regulatory networks) and the fact that dissipative chemical systems of any kind can – if they have the appropriate activation and inhibition mechanisms – spontaneously order their components into spatially ordered patterns such as stripes, spots or zigzags. These patterns are called Turing patterns, again after Alan Turing, Henry's friend from Bletchley Park, who was the first person to model them.

After about twenty weeks the embryo became a foetus and the macroscopic effects of the extra genetic material and the chromosomal mutations in the gamete stage began to become apparent: the child had two hearts (one dominant, positioned in the left-hand upper chest cavity, and one subsidiary, positioned slightly lower and to the right), a slightly elongated skull, and a new gland in the brain that was growing out of the pineal apparatus and which housed two novel types of neuron.

7

In which ego battles superego

'Do you miss her?' That was the first question Dr Schemata asked
Judd. By way of reply the boy stared rather blankly at the wall. A
Kandinsky hung there, stark and prime. 'How often do you think
of her?' the analyst continued. 'Come on, Judd, I'm here to help
you. Do I frighten you? If I frighten you, tell me, and we'll see
what we can do about it, shall we?' Judd kicked his heels on the
floor and thought of the swings in the playground on the edge of
a town six thousand miles away. Schemata addressed himself to
Moses, who was still in the room. 'Perhaps you had better leave
us, Mr Axelrod. It might be a better idea if Judd and I spoke man
to man from the start.' Moses nodded a slightly hesitant approval
and allowed the doctor to guide him from his chair and out of
the door. The doctor's polyester flares swished together as he
walked, making a quiet whipping sound. 'I know you understand,'
he said to Judd's father earnestly. The dark man was several inches
taller than Schemata and almost twice his body weight. 'Make
yourself comfortable here in the waiting room. Ms Klixen!' He
called for his assistant, one leg stuck straight out into the air behind
him to counterbalance his body, the weight of which was supported
only by the friction of his right palm against the burgundy leather
panelling of the open door. The woman appeared from around
the corner. 'Ah, Ms Klixen. See if Mr Axelrod would like some
coffee, would you?'

The doctor smiled at Moses and vanished back inside his office, easing the door to behind him with an oh-so-careful *whupp*. Moses watched as the handle was turned back into position from the inside, rather than simply released.

'How would you like your coffee?' Ms Klixen's voice was loud in his ear. She was very close. He turned to her and found himself gazing into her cleavage, for all his height. Her perfume gripped his nostrils and prevented him from turning away. It was a very fine cleavage, and it was a moment or two before he pulled himself together and managed to come up with an answer.

He grinned at her, looked her in the eye. 'Black as night and twice as dark,' he said.

Returning to his desk, Schemata began again. 'OK, Judd, it's just you and me now. Just you and me. I want to make it clear that whatever you tell me goes no further than the inside of these four walls. And they don't have ears, I can promise you that. No one else will ever know of the conversations that you and I may have. Not your father, not your mother, not anyone. Do you understand that?'

Judd managed a nod. He suddenly wished for bangs, for hair that he could tip forward and hide behind. But his tightly curled fuzz stood up on end and all he had to help him dissemble in the face of the cold gaze of this peculiar man were the coffee-coloured pigments of his skin, a defence he would need to call upon again and again as the next few minutes turned into days, and those into months, which would in their turn stretch first into seasons and then into years in a way, sitting here now, that he could neither expect nor imagine.

Nor could he foresee how those years would be ticked off by the minute hand of his visits to Schemata and how his life would be ruled by a temporality quite different from that of the majority of his peers. For the gregarious rhythms of his childhood were about to be stalled and Judd would be geared up instead into that calculated zone of adult time which charts the globe with a regime founded on clockwork, migrated into quartz. In 1714 the British Government's Board of Longitude did far more for their country's expansionist cause than many a military division: by offering a prize for the construction of a portable chronometer – a prize won

228

by John Harrison of Hull in 1763 – they managed to subsume even the leavening doughs of the day beneath the drifting structures of their empire so that it too could be specified, ordered, digitised, filed. It was this order which Judd had unknowingly transgressed and to which he would now be made to conform.

'How often do you masturbate?' Schemata asked. Judd had never thought to count. Schemata had him by the balls, so to speak. 'OK, try this one. What do you think of when you masturbate?' Sugar and spice and all things nice. 'Of what do you dream?' Of mountains and horses and bees and blood and packs of hot wolves all acid at the edges. Sometimes the moon, sometimes red rooms with dark gables so high that all smoke is lost. Laughs and doors and words in white bubbles. Batman, the Joker, school desks, nakedness at the end of long corridors, doors opening on to rooms of peering folk. Catwoman, punishment. The soft washes of the sea. Into the forest, into the trees. Control. 'Ah hah!' Schemata licked his lips and formed his fingers into a temple. 'What thoughts do you have regarding your mother?' Judd crying, very upset. 'Your mother is an actress, is she not? Quite a famous actress. I have never met her, but we deal with many actresses here and I believe I have seen several of her films. Do you like her films?' He never thought about it, he didn't know. He thought of his mother, of his last week in England, of whispers strained voices behind closed doors, of odd words and phrases seeping down to him from the adult world, Jennifer's name, his mother crying, his father hissing. How had he sat during those conversations? With one hand always touching at his nostril lip cheek, the other clutched in the warm space between his tightly closed thighs while outside the window the heavy Midlands clay rolled away in low hills until it met far off with the thick, low sky, a sky that seemed to shave the chimney pots off the houses, a sky so weak it almost seemed to rely on the upper branches of the trees and the slate-grey village steeples for support. Nothing at all like the sky he'd longed for, a sky so high and round that the greatest towers in the world could rise to challenge it and yet never make a mark, so high that even when great basin smogs hovered for days across the city it was still there if you scrambled high enough up in the hills to find it, high up through spinneys of Californian pine and cedar, high up past the millionaire lots with their half-finished houses which pinned back the boulevards that crept up the hillsides beneath you, tentacles of tarmac, oily and broad.

It did not take Judd long to decide that he did not like this doctor Schemata. He quickly learned to fear him, too. His father approached this man with caution, and his father did not approach *anybody* with caution.

'I've been reading a little Freud,' said Moses brightly at the beginning of the next session. 'Thought I'd try to keep up.'

'Oh, no one reads Freud any more,' Schemata said curtly.

'But I was under the impression that you were a neo-Freudian. Is that not correct?'

'Of course it is. Exactly why we no longer read him,' replied the doctor darkly. 'This isn't nineteenth-century Vienna we're living in. Things have moved on.' Browbeaten, Moses thought he'd probably better move on as well; he stuffed his hands into his pockets and retreated into the waiting-room, where he hoped he would be consoled by Ms Klixen, Ms Klixen's coffee and Ms Klixen's cleavage. But Ms Klixen was not particularly interested in being consoling. She was engrossed in a telephone call, strains of which Moses caught as he thumbed through the magazines that had been strewn carefully across the low marble coffee table. Bored, he lit a cigarette, the paper crackling up as he inhaled. Ms Klixen finished on the telephone.

'Ms Klixen? Er, excuse me Ms Klixen, but do you think I could have a cup of your fine black coffee?' But, for whatever reason, Ms Klixen ignored him. He got up and wandered over to her desk, where he repeated the question in a lower voice.

Now she looked up brightly, too brightly. 'Why, of course Mr Axeljob, I'll get you one right away. You take it white, ain't that right?'

He took it in his stride; it was an opener. 'No, black, if that's OK.' He smiled his best, most sweetest smile. 'Though I do enjoy a touch of cream now and again. And it's Axel*rod*.' Ms Klixen returned his gaze as coldly as she could and left her desk to go to the coffee machine, smoothing her skirt as she went. Moses was convinced he had caught the merest glimmer in her stare and strolled back over to the white leather sofas well satisfied. The room was really two rooms of approximately equal size that had been knocked into one larger space. Some of the dividing wall remained in the form of an arch, each side of which was still solid partition. Thus there were certain areas in Moses's end of the room – which contained the grey marble coffee table, the white sofas, the magazines and a yucca plant – that formed blind spots with regard to certain areas in Ms Klixen's half – which contained the reception desk, the coffee machine and the hatstand. From his position on one of the sofas Moses could hear but not see Schemata's assistant pouring out the coffee. After a moment he heard her replace the pot on the stand and click over the wooden floor towards him in her heels, the cup and saucer rattling in her perfect and efficient little hand. She came through the arch and he looked up and smiled. Then, as she rounded the coffee table, she turned her heel and stumbled. The hot coffee sloshed over and out of the china cup and down to where Moses's long left leg lay extended alongside the coffee table.

'Jesus Christ!' Moses screamed, leaping to his feet.

Ms Klixen immediately started fussing. 'Oh Mr Axeljob! I'm soooo sorry, let me get you a napkin, oh, I'm sooo sorry, I'd made it black for you as well, oh, I do hope it hasn't ruined your suit.' Moses tried to hold the scalding fabric of his trousers away from his leg, but by the time the woman returned the coffee had cooled enough to allow him to divert his attention from the pain and take the opportunity to brush her breasts with the back of his hand as he reached across her to take the cloth which she had brought him.

Once back in his seat, a fresh cup of coffee before him and Ms Klixen safely back behind the fortifications of the reception desk, Moses turned again to the magazines. He picked up the latest *National Geographic* and leafed through it, flicking past articles on the oil crisis and British farming techniques, on pictures of deep-sea submarines exploring deep-sea trenches, on diagrams of the new generation of communications satellites, on a jokey report about a scientific cargo cult which apparently believed that Sputnik II was still in orbit, all systems go, Laika still alive.

One article that did command his attention focused on a new networked computer system known as the ARPANET. According to the piece, back in the 1950s the US Department of Defense had commissioned the RAND corporation to look into the possibility of designing a computer communications system capable of surviving a nuclear attack. The investigation had concluded that only a network of computers with no central point of control would do the trick, the idea being that by using a collection of interconnected 'nodes' each of which would contain the necessary information to route packets of data to their destination, the system would be flexible enough to continue to operate despite high levels of disruption and damage. The first node had been installed at UCLA in 1969 and at the time of going to press, thirty-six more were in place all over the country.

Sexy, thought Moses, immediately beginning to wonder about the possible commercial applications. He was a marketing man, not an engineer, so to him the possibilities were potentially limitless – not that he could actually think of any right now.

But the magazines couldn't keep Moses's mind off his troubles for long. He found it hard to believe that all this was happening to him, that he was here in an analyst's office waiting for his son. If it had happened to a friend of his he would have laughed in his face, would have thought it so improbable as to be a joke. Older boys were supposed to seduce younger girls for chrissake, not the other way around. And both of them were so young. At Judd's age *he* wasn't thinking about pussy. Was he? He couldn't really remember. But he didn't think that he was. What he did know for a fact was that he was seventeen before he got inside a girl's panties, not *ten*. God, he was jealous. Jealous! Of his kid son. Unreal. If Melinda hadn't found the drawings and the diary he wouldn't have believed it. He was mostly glad that they had gotten him out of that godforsaken country before anyone had gotten hold of the story. To have had it splashed all over the press would have ruined Melinda's career and it wouldn't have done his own a lot of good either. The two of them got enough bullshit from every angle because of their marriage; they didn't need this as well. It would really prove all of them right, all the bastards who had sneered, who had said by the looks in their eyes that the two of them would never be able to make it work. What in Christ's name had gotten into Judd's head? When he'd met the girl's father he'd had to fight back the urge to slam him up against the wall of his sad little English house and beat him upside the head. The only reason he'd managed to restrain himself was that the man was such a sorry little fucker that it wasn't worth it, it would have been too easy. He'd towered above Henry as the accountant gasped endless cloudy apologies on the winds of his caustic alcohol breath and desperately tried to focus his rheumy eyes upon one thing, one solid object that wasn't Moses, while Melinda had sat on the edge of a threadbare little sofa and cried. Afterwards she had actually felt sorry for him! Had actually felt pity for this man who couldn't keep his hot, whoring bitch of a daughter under some kind of control.

It was the snake in the grass, the accursed share, the return of the repressed. It was exactly what Moses had slaved all these years to escape. This was the kind of thing that went on in the Projects, where his people lived herded together in crates like cattle, like chattel still. And he had pulled himself up out of it by his own bootstraps, become a (*very*) successful businessman, married a white woman, God bless her. Yes, that's right, a white woman, an actress, not some two-bit hooker out for some black cock but a real successful white woman. Even today, maybe especially today, that was almost impossible to carry off, to make a success out of. And they had held it together all this time, through Melinda's miscarriage, through his mother telling him that he was insulting her in it and through it, they had held it together only to be tripped up in a way that he could never have foreseen.

Yeah. Yeah? *Yeah*! Well this was not going to be a problem. He, Moses Axelrod, was not going to let it be a threat. Like every other problem he had ever had to face – and there had been plenty – this was going to get solved. He had the position, he had the money, it would get solved. *Bang*. Just like that. This Schemata was said to be the best, *bang*, we'll have him, no expense spared. Nylon trousers or no nylon trousers.

233

Feeling more cheerful, Moses looked up from the magazine and glanced around, started to hum the melody line from Curtis Mayfield's *Futureshock*, which had been released that year. He stubbed out his cigarette in the ashtray but flicked the butt at the yucca plant standing in its white pot in the opposite corner of the room. It thwacked against a leaf and Ms Klixen glanced over. Having thus renewed their relationship, Moses decided to test the limits of the assistant's interest by playing a little game using the sightlines of the office. He stood up and pretended to become absorbed in a series of large abstract artworks which were arranged on the walls. He coughed and moved towards the first of them, contemplated it for a minute or two and quickly crossed the room, shooting a glance at Ms Klixen as he did so. She was not looking at him. He paused briefly to pick up the ashtray from the coffee table, then continued over to the next blind spot where he tipped its contents noisily into a wastepaper bin that had been positioned just behind it. On the other side of the partition Ms Klixen sat and quietly fumed. She was considering how she could make it clear to this man who thought so much of himself that it was he who required psychoanalysis and not his son.

'Ms Klixen,' Moses sang out, 'I believe that your yucca needs repotting. I can recommend an excellent man in Beverly Hills.'

'I don't think that will be necessary, thank you Mr Axeljob. We had it done just this last year.'

Moses moved out of the shadows and stood in front of another picture, his back to the assistant. 'Why is it you insist on mispronouncing my name, Ms Klixen?' It was a bold thrust, but it was deftly parried by the clatter of keys sent forth from Ms Klixen's electric typewriter as she powered her way through a letter.

On this occasion, Moses (ego) is getting the better of Ms Klixen (superego). In order to do this, Moses has established a position by describing the shape of a three-point limit attractor. He holds this position until the system is rendered inflexible by repetition. Thus destabilised, he will begin to move around the room more quickly, gradually converging upon a vulnerable centre.

Moses was moving across to consider another picture when he passed the heavy door which led into the psychoanalyst's office and had a sudden – and uncharacteristic – crisis of confidence. Behind it, what was the doctor saying to Judd? And what – potentially more worrying – was Judd saying to the doctor? Could they separate children from their parents if the parents were deemed unfit? God, had he been a good father? It occurred to him for the first time that a mixed marriage was grist to the mill of blame and suspicion where the social welfare were concerned. What kind of power could be exercised by the man behind the heavy door? He had always felt that he enjoyed a good relationship with his son. They did things together: he took Judd to ball games, they flew kites together on the beach, shot baskets in the yard of an evening. He'd tried to be around as much as he could when he wasn't away on business. But it was still true that he'd had his suspicions that something wasn't quite right with his kid. Melinda liked to think that it was because Judd was special, a cut above as she'd say, but Moses had always thought there was something odd about the way the boy found it hard to pay attention, the way he wandered off on his own, the way he seemed to lose track of time. Hey, he was a good father, he had always taken it for granted that he would be. Shit, he was there more for the poor kid than Melinda was. More likely it was her and her fucked-up Hollywood friends who had done for him. That junky Donna bitch always hanging around and putting ideas into Judd's head. He wouldn't be surprised if the woman had been fooling around with him, that's the kind of sickfuck thing she'd be into. Christ, and she'd recommended this shrink, who was probably in there right now, reprogramming the little sucker!

Ms Klixen stopped her typing and Moses turned round to look.

Then the handle of the heavy door rotated and Dr Hinckley Schemata came out, ushering Judd before him. He beckoned to Moses. 'You wait out here, Judd, your father and I will only be a minute. Ms Klixen, could you look after Judd for me? See if he would like something to drink. Mr Axelrod, could I have a few words?' Ms Klixen tottered over and began to fuss over the boy, demonstrating to Moses that Judd, merely by the nature of his being, merited more attention than his father ever would. Schemata smiled a saccharine smile and held out his arm in a move designed to annex Moses's space and draw him into the surgery. The initiative worked and Moses found himself back in the large room which was now only dimly lit by the little sunlight that filtered through the bank of Venetian blinds which formed a chic backdrop to Schemata's glass Mies Van der Rohe desk. 'Please take the couch Mr Axelrod.'

'No, really, the chair is fine.'

'As you wish, but I would prefer it if you would take the couch.' Moses sat down in the chair. Either way, he realised, he had already been placed at a disadvantage.

The doctor sat behind his desk. With the only source of light now to his rear, his face was almost completely obscured by shadow. His teeth gleamed briefly as he drew back his lips to speak. 'I would just like to ask you a couple of questions, if that's not too much of a bother.'

'Shoot.'

'But before I do, would it be possible for you and your wife both to come and see me at any juncture? I really do need to see the two of you together.'

'That's, er, a little difficult at the moment, I'm afraid. Melinda is working in England right now. She won't be back in LA for at least six months.'

'I see.'

Pause.

'Has Judd ever seen the two of you naked?'

'Sure, when he was younger, I guess. Maybe not for a while.'

'So nudity, while it used not to be a problem, has recently become an issue in your household?'

'Well, I wouldn't say that exactly . . .'

'But at some point you and your wife stopped undressing in front of him?'

'I guess so.'

'Has he ever been present while you and your wife have been engaged in intercourse, Mr Axelrod?'

'Now look, doctor, I don't know what you're getting at . . .'

'I am insinuating nothing, I can assure you. It is a standard question. Please answer it. There is no need, I'm sure, for me to add that this conversation is being conducted in the strictest confidentiality.'

'No.'

'No you will not answer me, or no he has not been a witness to the carnal act?'

'The latter.'

'Are you quite positive?'

Moses looked around the room. Motes of dust journeyed tirelessly through the thin beams of light, glinting satellites set loose from the tug of the planet. To them the habits of the world seemed not to apply, operating as they did without any apparent concession to gravity. 'Maybe, when he was a child. You know, when he was very young, we used to have his crib in our room. We thought he was too young to notice. Do you mind if I smoke?'

'Please. Children are very aware, Mr Axelrod. There is an ashtray to your right. I am not looking to apportion blame.' Moses lit the cigarette with the silver Zippo that Melinda had given Judd to give him for Christmas the previous year. The blue smoke curled upwards in the still air like the smoke from a gun (he thought), winding itself in and out of the rays of light like a creeper scaling a trellis. Driven by the motor of the thermals the smoky orbits trapped flailing motes within their spinning whorls. Took them up, upwards, up, up to the ceiling and the darkness that cowered there.

Moses emerged and blinked in the bright light that flooded the waiting-room. Ms Klixen appeared from around the partition. 'Judd will be just a minute. He is using the bathroom.' She had an expression of triumph on her face, as if she had overheard the men's conversation. Schemata busied himself with some papers that were stacked on the reception desk and Ms Klixen stood and cleaned the leaves of the yucca. Again Moses had to wait, but this time the waiting was no fun: with the doctor there he had no room to manoeuvre. Still smoking, he made the circuit of the artworks once again, forced to look at them properly this time. But there was something threatening about their primary colours and geometric patterns and spiral motifs, and he realised that he really didn't like these pictures and moved across to the window instead.

The slats of the white blinds were tuned to the sun and light flooded through. He lifted his right forefinger to face height and placed it on one of the aluminium ribs, kinking it down as he imagined a private detective or an assassin might do. On the street below almost nothing was happening. Two or three cars rolled by, their tyres squeaking on the asphalt when they turned off the main drag. An old bent man in a brown suit sat beneath his hat on what was left of a broken concrete bench. The afternoon shimmered, threw Moses's gaze back at him. He let the slat unbuckle and return to its remembered shape, but the day still poured through. Turning, he was frightened by the leaves of the yucca, which shone so vividly with the chemical sheen that Ms Klixen had so doggedly applied that he could almost see his face in them. He passed beneath the centre arch, but there was still no sign of Judd. Schemata had disappeared back inside his surgery; Ms Klixen had found some other task with which to engross herself. Returning to the sofas he circled them slowly, running his left hand along the leather backs and smoking with his right.

The bathroom door opened and Judd wandered out, looking lost. 'Dad?'

'OK, son, let's go.' Moses spun into the space between the sofas and leant over the coffee table, stubbing out his cigarette in the ashtray placed at its centre. Then, circumnavigating the furniture for the last time, he beat a path to Judd, whom he took by the hand and led out the door. He muttered to Ms Klixen that she should send the bill on; she ignored him but exuded self-satisfaction none the less.

When they had gone, the room was still. Schemata emerged from behind his door, passed some paperwork to Ms Klixen, then disappeared again. Ms Klixen took an apple and a magazine from her desk and applied herself to both. The yucca nestled in the corner and tasted the air. When it was satisfied that it was alone

238

it began to relax. It flexed its newly polished leaves and slowly stretched them out towards the window. It was not pleased about the cigarette butt lodged among its roots. But there was not a great deal it could do about it.

Tidal action

Several months have passed and things have calmed down. Moses is no longer beating Judd and the child has been synchronised with a routine of school and psychoanalysis and not much else. Despite his magic, Jennifer has receded even further into the distance. But magic, like drugs, has its side effects. There are debts that have to be paid for pulling information from the ether, for creating new possibilities and channelling flows, for reshaping the world with no other tool than desire. Use the television and the television uses you – it takes a part of you, reconfigures you, infects you: you take TV on board. So it was with Judd – the TV was in his life now and he couldn't shake it, even when he switched it off. Idle moments (when Moses wasn't around) were all spent acting out his favourite shows, the house his set. He was a secret agent in action, he crept along a wall, fled up a staircase, the lens always behind him, the audience unable to get a glimpse of his face. Then, *caboom*, he kicks open a door, enters a room (gun in hand, scoping). Exposed, he surveys the scene, the camera still behind him but now seeing what he sees, the audience checking things out as if through his eyes: a neatly made bed, a wardrobe full of clothes, an open door on to a balcony and beyond an abyss. In the room, stuffed animals, many many stuffed animals, on the bed and on the chairs and on the window-sills, watching him, staring back at the lens like a room full of bandits. *Bang! Bang! Bang! Trchrchrchrcht!! Caboom!!* One by one he takes them out, executing a faultless sequence of bullet dodges as he does so, just like Shaft, or Paul Michael Glaser in *Starsky and Hutch*. 'Yo, Huggy Bear, you got yours, brother!' he calls as Huggy is caught in the cross-fire and falls face down on the floor. Once the room is secured our hero collapses on to the bed, exhausted. Splayed out, eyes closed; the camera moves across the floor and up the divan. As we see the first glimmers of the agent's profile the audience holds its breath. But each time we come in for a closer look his eyes flicker open and we flinch back – he is still suspicious, still on his guard. Then, finally, we swoop round and see him full frontal, his face in repose. He wakes, he blinks, his face twists into a grimace, his mouth lets out an anguished gasp. He fills the screen, twenty feet from chin to brow we feel his pain. Cut to camera two, positioned over by the door: we see that camera one is not a camera at all but another agent. And not just any agent; camera one is our hero's double, the only difference being that over one eye he wears a patch. His face is quietly attentive. Eye meets eyes, self sees self, everything is frozen in this final moment. The shot fades to black, leaving us in the domain of pure terror. This is television. The credits roll.

Back in Stratford, alone in the house on the hill, Melinda had started to drink. Often she'd come back from a show and lie in the pool for half the night, a bottle of gin and a bowl of ice next to her on the tiles, ice slowly melting, gin slowly disappearing, the house in total silence. She wouldn't even have the waterjets on – she couldn't bear the noise, the way they disrupted the surface of the water. The skin-like film of the pool made her feel calm, continuous with this giant meniscus that sucked at her waist and pulled her out into a plane. If she'd erected a psychic structure for herself in the headmaster's office that day the effort of supporting it exhausted her now; she no longer wanted to be monolithic but was desperate instead to collapse, to let herself be saturated and dissolved, to transmute her grand plan into the nets and tracings of bacterial action, into the suck and slide of the tides.

Something had to give. When, weeks later, she crawled out of the pool of chlorine and alcohol, she knew it would be the acting. Let England have it – it had won. It was a worthless prize in any case. She had chosen her husband and her son; she would go back to Los Angeles and slip into an easy life, a new act. Moses made plenty of money, more than enough for them both. They were rich for chrissake. She didn't need to work.

She thought at that moment that it would be fun; that it could, in fact, be delightful. But what she did not realise was that though she would banish the bitterness and hang on to her husband, she had already lost Judd. Unable to place trust in herself she'd relinquished responsibility before she'd had time to think, at the moment she had passed him over into the welcoming arms of Dr Hinckley Schemata.

Spaceman

At the end of each of the countless visits to Schemata's surgery which followed, Judd always made a point of visiting the bathroom. Once safely locked inside he would stand up on the toilet seat and look himself all over in the mirror, as if to check that he was all still there, that he had not left any part of himself behind in the doctor's consulting room. Despite the hours that he had spent in there it still seemed as if there were areas of it that he did not know, could never know. The room was always so dimly lit that the walls appeared not to join at the corners but to bend outwards and stretch away for ever, like the warp drive portals in *Star Trek*. Judd would lie on the analysand's couch, the nexus of these gateways, and stare up into the gloom, wishing he could find his communicator and instruct Scotty to beam him up out of there.

But after a while he got used to Schemata. Occasionally it would even seem as though the analyst was not in the room with him at all. He would lie there and recite his thoughts and dreams without even thinking about it, giving voice to whatever bubbled up from his memory, reconstructing the experiences with whatever shapes and tools were at hand. Thus a dream which, the first time around, might have been coloured in shades of grey with limey lights and odd gasps of red here and there would be remembered in sharp black and white. Or characters from old dreams, long ago, folks who lived down there and never normally saw the light of day, would surface and take shape among the heaving flows of Judd's imagination, only to speak with the doctor's voice when they finally emerged. Sometimes things he'd never known came together for him, right before him, and he told Schemata those too because in the end it was all the same.

By then the consulting room no longer seemed one simple space. Not only was it strung out, extended and suspended like a gob of spit hanging from a railing, like an amoeba beginning to divide, like an axon laced across a cortex, like a starship stretching into hyperspace, but its component parts – Judd on couch, Schemata at desk, filtered light, mahogany bookcase, another yucca – had internal coherence but little apparent relationship to one another. Each object seemed to float in its own universe and be subject to its own laws, the fractal boundaries of each mini cosmos vying with those of its neighbour like crosswaves in a harbour. The combined effect of his father's disapproval, his mother's hysteria and Schemata's probings had made Judd fear the escape hatch of his childhood, despise the strange realm of dilated time that he'd disappeared into every day, and it got to the stage where he was terrified to step down on to the floor at the end of each session lest he slip through and back into the picnoleptic experience and keep falling for ever. There was too much freedom in there, he didn't understand it, he wasn't to go there any more; so whenever he entered the consulting room he would wait at the door until Schemata's back was turned, then close his eyes and run for the comparative safety of the couch lest the monsters that lurked in those interzones grab him by the ankles and pull him screaming under.

As for Hinckley Schemata, he could never quite understand why it was that Judd seemed so keen to get on with it. No sooner had he crossed the room to sit at his desk than the boy was prone and passive on the couch, if a little tense. None of his other patients was this pliable; most of them liked to play out some little head game before the session 'officially' began, although, as Schemata occasionally smirked to himself, the session began as soon as they opened the door to his office, even if they often did not realise it. But while he had the upper hand on the majority of his patients, there were a couple who were playing a double bluff. The tactic of these two women was to give the analyst the illusion of control, letting him think of them as foolish neurotics who doted upon his guiding light, in order to use him for sex. After all, it was so much cleaner and more respectable than trawling hotels and singles bars for a gigolo, and it had the added bonus that their husbands were happy to pay for it. Imagine how horrified the psychoanalyst would have been to discover that these two ladies knew each other and often compared notes.

Judd, on the other hand, became something of a test ground for his theories. *It's all in the way the patient's fantasy life is structured. If this is askew, life itself will be askew. If it is straight and pure, life itself will follow. Life always follows fantasy. Making fantasy perfect, this is what we need to do.* If this was his goal, the doctor achieved it almost by accident. Because lying there, his own voice lost in the darkness, his sight disembodied, Judd learned to be afraid of the way the objects around him were dispersed and stretched out in this manifold, curved, relativistic space which outwitted global order. He came to rely upon the voice of the analyst to orientate him, to give him some kind of certainty, and thus was turned to Schemata's will because the man's sotto voce tone was the only thing which filled the room and linked one point to another. In this manner that Riemannian surgery, the last remnant of Judd's picnoleptic imagination, was transformed into a nice Euclidean cube: linear, logical, x, y and z.

By the end of the second year Judd was convinced that what he had done was wrong. By the end of the third, he knew that it both was and was not his fault. It took him a further twelve months to come to understand that he was split into parts that wanted, parts that were to be trusted and parts that held it all together, and by the end of that fourth year the Judd who had been all on one plane, the Judd who had ebbed and flowed was no more and in his place there was a new Judd, a Judd–Schemata, a Judd who had hidden depths and dizzy heights and common sense and *feelings*,

feelings that had been precipitated out from actions, reified and abstracted. Oh, the agonies and the joys! This new Judd thought for a while that he might like to grow up to be an analyst like Schemata and did not notice how his father's eyes looked sad when he told him this over dinner one evening. For this new Judd spent his whole time looking after the structures that had been erected inside him.

In this phase of things Judd discovered earnestness. He became 'serious' and 'involved with things'. The analysis had made him feel mature beyond his years and more 'experienced' than his peers. At school he got himself a reputation for being aloof. He now looked upon his early sexual activities as having enabled a leap in his development; he understood that he had 'jumped the queue' in growing up, as Melinda would put it when she was feeling sympathetic, which these days was most of the time.

Annoyed that he had lost control of his son, Moses began to nag him. What was he going to do with his life? If he didn't think that being a businessman like his father was good enough he'd better start studying hard – it was no easy task being a doctor, especially if you were black. Had he thought about this? He hadn't done so well in his exams this semester. Did he think he was good enough? In a white world you couldn't afford to take on something and then fail – coloured people got no second chances. Judd should take a leaf out of his book – know your limitations, decide what you can achieve, then do it. No looking back, no second thoughts. Did he think he was good enough? Did he? His results didn't look too hot. Was he letting his concentration drift again? Did he have any idea how much his analysis cost? Four or five kids from the Projects could be put through school on what he paid Schemata. He hoped Judd appreciated it.

In times gone by Judd would have let it all drift over him – maybe that's how Moses had got to be this way, because before it hadn't made any difference. But now it did, he took it all to heart, let it make a turmoil in his brain. He got so guilty, it all got mixed up with his colour, Pop was right, he didn't do so well at school, maybe he wasn't so bright. The precociousness he'd experienced for a while back there gradually melted away and he was left with a clutch of insecurities that clattered around his head, rusty mechanisms driving a shooting gallery full of rotating and accepted desires: steady job, consumer goods, good name, nice neighbourhood, maybe a wife (if he kept quiet about the transgressions of his youth).

Melinda stood by, trying to convince herself that this is what she'd wanted. This is what they'd paid for, right?

The seventies were drawing to a close. Both Viking landers had reached Mars and the first pictures of the surface of a planet which was not our own were circulating in the news. A test-tube baby had been born and genetic engineering was a household concept. The Voyager probes were on their way to Jupiter. Judd, still interested in space exploration, plotted their progress through the void. Pioneer, he noted, was nearing Saturn. Saturn is a very long way away. It's dark out near Saturn, dark and cold.

Somewhere high above the earth, Laika howled.

8

School's a beach

For Jennifer, on the other hand, the seventies were far from over. After they had met up with Joel, she and Henry stayed in Geneva for a further six weeks, then Henry began to feel that he had been away from the office long enough. Not only that, but the school year was about to begin and while he had the greatest faith in Joel's tutoring skills he felt that two hours of maths a day was not going to compensate for his daughter missing any more class, especially as on her return she was to start at a new school.

Jennifer supervised the packing, a complex affair due to the amount of shopping they had done over the summer and the gifts that had been heaped on them by the old family friends whom Henry had insisted they visit. She remembered them vaguely as a repetitive series of smooth-skinned Swiss spinsters and robust couples with grown-up children all of whom lived in well-furnished and supple apartments, which, had they been people, would have been ski instructors or tennis stars. Henry would force her to wear one of her 'best' outfits, usually a razor-creased skirt and a fussy blouse and perhaps a jacket to match that gave her difficulty breathing. But she enjoyed it in a way, it was a kind of dressing up, and the clothes made her feel professional and efficient and conspicuously adult (though exactly for this reason slightly ridiculous at the same time). The paradox was emphasised by the patronising way in which her hosts invariably addressed her, with their high-bourgeois determination to take even a thirteen-year-

246

old seriously. They would ask her terribly dull questions in clipped and perfect English, their words shaped by a determination that was frightening, while she sat on some uncomfortable, overstuffed chair with her legs together (an unusual occurrence, she thought to herself), answering with an affected shyness which she hoped hid her boredom, and feeling like a prat.

The dismalness of the whole experience was always accentuated by the fact that Henry hardly knew most of these people himself. The older ones had been his parents' friends, shadowy 'aunts' and 'uncles' whom even as a child he had known only vaguely, the younger ones his playmates of those pre-war lakeside summers, and the meetings were always tainted with the forced atmosphere that attends reunions between old friends who no longer have anything in common. All interaction would take place on a rarefied plane of politeness so awkwardly constructed that the conversation could at best take faltering steps and could certainly never flow. Jennifer was often treated by the grown-ups as a lubricant with which to oil the gears of this intercourse but it was a tactic which was rarely effective. Part of the problem was that everybody had always to be seen to be in command of the situation. At least she could not understand them when they talked tactfully with Henry in French or German about how terrible it had been about her mother.

It struck Jennifer as odd, when she emptied the toiletries out of the cabinet in the bathroom, that the packet of tampons she had brought with her from England had not yet been opened. Her periods had begun around the time she'd lost her virginity but Henry, of course, had not thought to educate her on the subject at all and her school had not been much better. The first time she saw herself bleeding she thought she had hurt herself inside, that it was a result of letting Rever penetrate her. Suddenly all that they had drummed into her at school about God, about good, about purity seemed as if it might be true and she thought for several terrifying weeks that God was punishing her for her actions, especially when the bleeding recurred a month later. She felt terribly alone in a way that she hadn't before, even at those moments when she missed her mother. Then she read something about the

247

phenomenon of the stigmata and this got muddled in her mind with what was happening to her, and for the next month she wondered if she were perhaps a saint, whether the bleeding was God's call. Several times she went by the convent school and hid in the trees overlooking their grounds, watched the girls come out in their straw boaters and gloves and neat little tailored outfits, and imagined that that's what would happen to her if anyone should find out about her holy nature. But the more she looked into it the less the idea of being a saint appealed to her, especially when she went into the local church and looked up at them writhing away for eternity in their stained-glass flames. These images disenchanted her so much that she decided to search for a more prosaic explanation. She found a medical encyclopaedia in the school library, but since she did not know the correct biological terms for the parts of the body which were troubling her she had little luck until thanks to its signatures of wear the book fell open on pictures of a naked couple with accompanying anatomical diagrams. The genitalia had been heavily censored by some bowdlerising librarian and thickly annotated by the many subsequent readers but fortunately for Jennifer, despite a few crude sketches and various scribbled words and arrows, the cross-sections of the plastic-looking 'internal workings' and their accompanying text remained legible, and she learnt enough to be able to reject her religious theories.

Once her shame had evaporated she felt able to approach one of the few teachers whom she liked and the woman had the sense to tell her how to look after herself. She also gave her a book to read on the subject and a packet of sanitary towels. What Jennifer remembered as remarkable about these events was that they seemed to mark – by way of the triangulations formed between the physicality of her sexual encounters and the blood that ran from her, her loneliness and her fear and awe of a vengeful, then ridiculous, God, and her discovery of a new set of words that adults used among themselves – the expanded moment in which she first began to think of herself as a discrete person, distinct from those around her, with a shape and momentum all her own. She was fascinated, too, by the way in which her coming of age was linked in to the phases of the moon and the tides, as if adulthood, womanhood, tied you into the rhythms of the whole world, ending the isolation of childhood.

Then, that summer in Geneva, the periods had stopped and she hadn't confronted the fact until she'd found the unopened packet of tampons, partly because she still hadn't become fully attuned to the rhythms of her menstrual cycle and also because she'd pushed the disagreeable thought to the back of her mind that day by the lake. She had worried about it on the train back to London and absent-mindedly bitten her nails down to the quick, but by the time they'd got back home to Stratford (at which point Henry had noticed her fingers and told her to stop) she'd buried the topic and it ceased to concern her. She had decided – with that absolute finality of judgement that mars all logic and marks out the limits of its usefulness – that she was not pregnant and that there was another explanation. After all, the book Mrs Giddens had given her said that periods could often be erratic in early puberty. Once one potentially frightening situation had been discovered to be merely normal, others could quickly be assumed to be that way too. It was an easy trick to learn.

Finding another school for Jennifer had been a complex business. In theory, the comprehensive could not expel her, but Mrs Craven, the new headmistress, felt rather strongly that it would be best for her if Henry found her a place somewhere else.

'It is not simply the good of the school we are considering here, Mr Several,' Craven hummed, 'but the best interests of Jennifer, and of course those of the other children. I'm sure you appreciate how difficult it could become for her should she stay on here. Children can be merciless, you know, once they get wind of the fact that somebody is a little different.' Henry gazed around the office as she spoke, only looking at her when she rose to refill his glass with cream sherry. Two of the room's walls were shelved and covered with box files; the third was smothered with timetables, all meticulously written out by hand. The fourth was taken up by a large, classroom-style window, the lower panels of which were filled with frosted glass, opaque as the meeting he was having. Craven recorked the bottle and returned to her seat, tucking her skirt modestly under her arse as she sat down to face him across the great expanse of her tidy desk. She looks like a newsreader, thought Henry to himself as he sipped at the sickly liquid she'd poured him.

When he told Jennifer that evening that Mrs. Craven thought the best thing would be to try and persuade the convent school to take her she burst into tears and screamed at him, 'I won't go, I won't go, I won't, you can't make me go there!' Henry lost his temper and reminded Jennifer in no uncertain terms that it was in fact her fault that he was now going to have to start paying for her education. Not only that, but it was an opportunity which many girls would jump at – she should be grateful. She retorted that she couldn't go to that awful school because she didn't believe in God, and if he tried to make her go she'd telephone the head-mistress and tell her in great detail exactly why it was that she was being expelled from the comprehensive. Henry told her that she wasn't being expelled, that she was leaving because everyone agreed that it was in her own best interests to do so. She called him a sap. He went red at this point and although he tried to remonstrate with her further it was pretty clear to both of them that once again he had lost. Jennifer ended up being sent to St Anne's, a small public school for girls a little further away than the convent, but which ran its own special school bus that she could catch from Stratford High Street. Henry was secretly relieved because the fees at St Anne's were rather less than those at the convent and the uniform was cheaper too. And he didn't believe in God, either.

At the new school she was treated very differently. The other pupils, infected with the half-baked prejudices of their parents, sneered at her for the most part – and feared her too because she had been to a comprehensive. Most of the girls were fair but Jennifer was dark and slightly swarthy, and her eyes had a fire in them that the washed-out moonstones and opals around her could only reflect (or so she liked to tell herself). The teachers took a great deal of trouble over learning her name, sitting her in the correct place in the class, helping her to Fit In. Whenever anyone asked her what she would like to do she simply said maths, and she covered all her exercise books in largely meaningless figures and invented algebraic formulae. Since none of the other girls could even imagine *wanting* to do maths, this set her apart further still.

She still saw some of her old friends after school, though not as much as she would have liked as she now had to do a great deal of homework, but they too had become suspicious of her and would make occasional remarks about her being too posh to keep company with the likes of them. This hurt. Her first term was one of the quietest, most solitary periods of her life and it set the pattern for what was to come. Most of the time she felt neither happy nor sad and had nothing to say to anyone. During break times she sat alone on the benches skirting the playing fields – much larger and grander than those at the comprehensive – and gazed vacantly out over this pale beach at the ocean of cabbages that filled the farmland beyond. She thought of her mother a lot and fantasised about what she had been like. She wondered too about her real father, whose skin and hair she bore (her mother had been fair, like these dainty St Anne's girls), about who he was and what he was like, and whether she could regard what he'd done as a crime, since she was the result.

Her periods had most definitely stopped and she'd put on some weight, despite not wanting to eat in the limbo which was her life in this place. Like a wary Proserpina she was conscious that every mouthful swallowed would bind her closer to the new school, almost as if the school was a mycorrhizal fungus that was offering her nutrients in exchange for a symbiotic relationship from which she would never escape. She wanted to resist, but her appetite had increased in inverse proportion to her desire and she found herself ravenously hungry almost continually; like the Cambrian algae devoured by the first metazoic predators, she was being forced up on to the shore where, like her mother before her, she would be faced with the choice of extinction or of finding some way of becoming plant. The land, so tempting when she'd only regarded the part of it that was Judd's skin, was proving somewhat harder to colonise than she'd imagined.

If anything, the food was worse than at the comp but she ate her portions greedily and took left-overs from the plates of her

peers, whose delicate stomachs had been raised on mother's cosmo-
politan home cooking and the à la carte menus of restaurants. For
this they hated her even more, called her *dustbin*, *pig*, were disgusted
that she should so relish what they regarded as little more than
slop (and they were right, it was little more than slop). Lunch-time
was for them a chore: they pushed the food around their plates
and felt nauseous, all the time discussing fashion and dieting and
how – like their mothers, whom they both hated and admired –
they had to keep an eye on their weight.

Fun is bathing in steel

October was dreary and the drizzle seeped through the days as
they segued into winter. Even the trees dropped their leaves half-
heartedly, tired of waiting for the sun – which seemed to have
retired hurt into the dismal sump of clouds that sulked for ever on
the winds – to turn them to their proper auburns, bronzes, golds.
Foliage became mulch while still on the branch. The summer and
the winter proper both seemed as far away as if they were figments
half-remembered from a book. The girls all moaned constantly
and some of them began to talk about their skiing holidays, and
Jennifer found herself thinking that she, too, would like a skiing
holiday. But she didn't think it wise to ask Henry if she could
have one.

Then the winter came and stayed. She and Henry weren't talking
much. He had shown an interest in the new school for a while
and was especially taken with the way that Jennifer looked in her
crisp new uniform, but once term was underway his interest waned.
Apart from a few sessions in Geneva he had managed to cut back
on his drinking – ever since that night, in fact, when he had told
Jennifer what she should never have known – but by Christmas
his intake was up again. His business affairs had not recovered
properly from the neglect they had suffered over the summer and

the other partners were starting quietly to manoeuvre any sensitive clients out of his care.

He and Jennifer spent the festive season with some cousins from the north-west, the closest family the two of them had. Henry had been an only child, as had his father, while his mother had a sister who'd married a Liverpudlian shipping clerk, a union which had produced two children roughly Henry's age. It had become a kind of ritual for them all to spend at least one weekend a year in each other's company.

Henry spent most of the holiday tipsy and Jennifer spent most of it disaffected, a new mode she was testing out with the intention of using it back at St Anne's in order to cultivate herself a reputation as an existential outsider. On Boxing Day she made a half-hearted attempt to seduce one of her cousins, a ginger-haired boy called Geoffrey who was two years her senior, but he was completely oblivious to her advances and kept pushing her away, preferring to play with his new Scalextric by day and his new telescope by night. He used the latter to scan the skies for satellites and on one occasion tracked Laika for an hour, although neither of them knew it.

It was the same story with most of the teenagers Jennifer was meeting now. The other girls at St Anne's were clean and delicate, and shocked even by the thought of masturbation, let alone the fact of intercourse. Yet all of them were fascinated by their maturing flesh and the onset of menstruation. The handful who had kissed a boy wore the experience like a medal. For the first time in her life Jennifer began to fear notoriety, something which she had hitherto always revelled in (and considered unimportant) and so she kept quiet about her past. The other girls with their giggles and their blushes made her feel unclean and she began to be embarrassed about her body in the changing rooms. She felt that a stigma hung around her in the form of an invisible but still perceptible mist; she could see her class-mates shiver with the dampness they felt when they came too close. They began to tease her about her weight and she became terrified that they would discover that her periods had stopped, so she made sure she carried towels in her bag the first week of every month and wore them on days when they had Games.

The feeling of being tainted slowly ate into her, until she carried it with her even when she was away from St Anne's. With it came guilt, which had always been alien to her but which she wore now like a mantle, a heavy fur which bent her and insulated her, warmed her and disgusted her. As the spring rolled in and her father slipped further and further into his whisky blend of blurred lights and memories of what might have been, she started torturing herself with the idea that his decline was her fault, that she, by dint of her very existence, was a constant reminder to him of her mother's madness and rape.

Her breasts ballooned and she grew taller, but at the same time she started to stoop. For the first time, she thought herself ugly. When spring evaporated into a short, tense summer full of foul winds and bad moods, she was as alone as she had been in the autumn but could not shake the feeling that someone was constantly with her, peering over her shoulder.

The summer – which seemed to her in retrospect like a small, dry scab on a wet graze of a year – came and went quickly, and at the end of it Jennifer put on yet more weight. She put it down to her dread of returning to St Anne's but in the mornings as she walked to the bus she was often overcome with bouts of extreme queasiness. Two or three times a week she would wake before the autumn dawn had begun its slow limp over the horizon and sit up in bed clutching at her stomach, the two thin bars of the electric fire a hot grimace in the darkness of her room. Comics, magazines, chocolate wrappers lay strewn across the covers, left from the night before when racing thoughts had kept her from her sleep. Soon she found it impossible to eat breakfast, throwing up whatever she did manage to force down for the sake of appearances.

Because she'd be bound to meet a crowd of the comp kids, ex-friends among them, she began to hate the walk to the bus-stop even more than the school day which lay ahead. The previous year's taunting and the jibes about being posh were nothing compared to the silence they met her with now – it meant she was just another St Anne's girl and therefore merited nothing but resentment. In her most depressed moments she sometimes wished that Henry had made her go to the convent; at least then she'd only have been laughed at.

In one of her magazines she read about anorexia nervosa and she thought she had caught this like a disease off one of the girls at school and that this was why she ate chocolate at night and then vomited in the morning. Eating disorders, the article had said, disrupted the menstrual cycle and Jennifer assumed that this must be why she still hadn't had a period. She'd lost all interest in sex, but Judd and Joel were in her thoughts constantly, like ghouls.

Maths was now her best subject and she still structured her comprehension of the numbers and their fields around the vivid, simple concepts Joel had sketched for her during those tutorials in Geneva. But she kept catching Judd's face out the corner of her eye, seeing his profile in the fold of a uniform or in the shadow of a door, his skin, even darker than she remembered it. She often heard his voice rising out of some general hubbub, calling her name when she was listening to music or standing in the dinner queue or sitting in the main hall waiting for assembly to begin. She missed him and wondered why he hadn't written to her. When an old mini-series starring Melinda Volitia was repeated on the television she watched it avidly (from her vantage point in the heavens, Laika watched it too: it was one of her favourites). Her TV watching had fallen off since she'd been at St Anne's; the mini-series, awful though it was, piqued her interest and she began to switch on the TV more often. She favoured American films and series, especially ones with black actors. She day-dreamed herself into cop shows and thrillers, conjuring up situations in which she would be kidnapped or raped or marooned, only to be rescued by a grown-up (and rather hunky) Judd. Her fantasies ignored the fact that Judd was younger than she was, but one of the things that the imagination knows is that time neither flows in a straight line nor radiates out from a simple centre, but evolves at different speeds in different places with scant regard for con- sciousness, which it regularly sidelines and confuses.

But although, for Jennifer, things had always been complex, this did not prevent her from harbouring a dream of clarity, a dim hope that some day she would be able to understand her actions and explain them. While she had always imagined that growing up would involve a transition at the end of which she would come to understand the world and its permutations, giving her at least some semblance of control over most eventualities, she now discovered that as she edged towards the socially accepted age of maturity all she wanted to do was relinquish responsibility for anything and everything. The confidence and assertiveness which had seemed to be her birthright were deserting her, evaporating like moisture from her pores.

In frustration she began to use the sharpened point of her school compass to scratch and pick at the blemishes on her fingers and arms. But the real damage started in a maths lesson when, lost somewhere in the wild terrain of her dreams, she felt a dull pain and looked down to find the point of the instrument buried a full centimetre into the pad of her thumb. Blood fled from the wound in great purple spheres which exploded like dying stars across the striated cosmos of the pieces of graph paper strewn across her desk.

In her day-dream Judd had been saving her from a burning building in which she had been tied naked to a chair and left to perish for no apparent reason by an evil, faceless madman. Her hero had broken down the door, risking backdraft and flash-over with only an oxygen mask to protect him. He strapped the mask to her face just as she was about to breathe her last, gathered her in his arms and carried her through the inferno, leaping to safety from a seventh-storey window beneath which his trusty team had inflated an enormous crash mattress. And then he was fucking her on a cool patch of grass hemmed in by lush willows and rhododendrons, the spray from the hoses gently weeping over them. As he plunged into her for the final time and exploded she'd rammed the metal point hard into her flesh.

The girl sitting next to her fainted and the class erupted and the maths teacher sent Jennifer off to see the nurse, who admonished her for being so careless and fixed her up and let her stay in the surgery for a while to recover. She sat alone on the hard bed, the tips of her shiny black shoes brushing to and fro across the white tiled floor. Beneath the bandage her thumb throbbed. The nurse was at her desk in the adjacent office writing something, her wide back visible but her face obscured by the half-open door. Bored, Jennifer began to examine the skin first of her good thumb –

noting the vortex of her fingerprint – then of her other fingers, of her palms, of the back of her hands and of her forearms, half slight tan and half hairless white underbelly. She marvelled quietly at the rippled lines that ebbed across her palms and the mesh of tiny interlocking creases that ran from her knuckles all the way up along her forearms. She scrutinised the dark hairs as they disappeared into her epidermis: each one seemed made to take a compass point, to be a tiny vagina awaiting a metal penis. Why weren't they bleeding? Why wasn't she bleeding? Every other girl in her year was bleeding every month. Why wasn't she? All these pores should seep blood to make up for it, to show them all that she could do it. She looked around for something sharp. On a metal trolley at the foot of the bed was a box of tissues; protruding from behind it were the slim curves of a pair of suturing scissors. The scissors lay in a stainless-steel kidney bowl and a pile of cotton swabs was mounded up on top of them.

Jennifer looked over at the nurse, still ensconced at her desk. She could hear the soft scratching of the fountain pen the woman was using to write with; there was something terribly exciting about this sound, this rasping. It was like hot, dry breaths heard from a distance, quick gasps and gulps, the travelling companions of pleasure. Tingling, she leant down the length of the bed and stretched out towards the scissors with her good hand. She didn't want to move in case the woman in the next room heard her; she could just reach if she stretched . . . but as she grabbed at the scissors they overbalanced the kidney bowl with a clatter and the noise brought in the nurse. 'I was just trying to get something to blow my nose with,' Jennifer smiled, sweetly.

That evening at home she picked at her skin with the points of the kitchen knives but they were all too blunt and only made deep puckers which hurt but drew no blood. Giving up on the knives she went upstairs to the bathroom where, among the detritus in the cabinet – old tubes of shampoo, half-used bottles of cheap aftershave, a pair of tweezers turning green with age, oily tubs of moisturiser and Henry's spare spectacles, bottles of crumbling pills with faded labels – she found a packet of Henry's razor-blades. She slipped one out of its greased paper envelope and held it up to the light. It was much thinner than she'd expected. Taking off her shirt and bra she pulled at the skin on her torso and arms, searching for a place to try it out. She wanted somewhere that wouldn't show and after much consideration decided on the area just underneath her left breast. Pinning her hair up and back, growing more nervous by the minute, she took up the blade from where she'd placed it on the edge of the wash-basin. What was the best way to hold it? She experimented, eventually deciding on a grip which involved her thumb, her middle finger and her little finger. To test the blade's resilience she flexed it slightly. But she was shaking and the grip was more awkward than it looked, and the blade slipped down and across, slicing through the tip of her finger and embedding itself in the nail. For a moment nothing happened, then blood started gouting out in great rhythmic swells. She stared at her finger in shock, as if amazed that this was all she was. Her hand and arm went cold and began to tingle, and when she tried to shake the blade loose she only succeeded in spotting the bathroom walls with blood. Gingerly, as if it were red hot, she pulled the blade free, staining crimson the dressing that the nurse had put on her thumb, and dropped it into the sink as if it were a bug that she'd picked out of her hair. She ran her hand beneath the cold tap for some minutes, drawing comfort from the water which ran so freely and gazing blankly as it swilled the blood away and the sensation began to return to her arm. But as soon as she took it out of the flow the bleeding returned. Eventually she managed to staunch the blood by wading toilet paper around her finger and binding it with strip plaster.

Later, after the situation had been brought under control, she made the planned incision beneath her breast. It was just deep enough to cut through the seven layers of skin, it didn't hurt much and the blood ran prettily down across her belly. There was an enormous tension in the act. On the one hand, the cut threatened to tear her apart, to unpick the locks of her skin and let her blood, that internal sea, rip her apart in a liquid eruption. But on the other, the cutting made her feel in control, as if by daring this dangerous incision she was, for an instant, once again mistress of herself.

When she awoke the next morning she examined the damage with detachment. The finger and thumb she re-dressed: the thumb was OK but the finger she was not proud of and it still bled. But the chest cut had scabbed over and she stood naked in front of the mirror and stretched her hands above her head in order to admire it, the confidence she'd felt at the moment of incision reinforced by this proof that she could heal. It was then that she noticed that her stomach was more protuberant than usual. She wanted to put it down to her general weight gain, but when she stood sideways on to the mirror and stretched and probed and prodded it was undeniably firm. She sat down and wept, then ran to the toilet and was sick.

Once again she found herself in the school library, but she could discover nothing that was of much use and soon gave up, skiving the next day off school in order to check out the public library in Stratford instead.

Fishfingers can be fatal

The reference department was in the older part of the building, at the top of a set of worn wooden winding stairs. Jennifer had never been up there before; she had only ever used the ground-floor fiction sections with their high ceilings and strip lights. But the first floor was a different story. Here was a space that reeked of oak panelling, of the damp musk of decaying books, of the rust tang of pipe tobacco escaping from the fibres of the tweed jackets of the old men who sat all around, sagging into their quiet old age.

Anita O'Bray, the librarian on duty, felt eyes upon her, but when she looked up from the card files she was cross-referencing there was nobody looking her way. The reference room was as it had been for the last half-hour: nine people sitting at the reading tables and old Mr Keighley slumped fast asleep in the chair by the radiator, his head back and his mouth wide open. He had been coming here to sleep for over a decade, as much of a fixture now as the books themselves, and the librarians generally left him, his gentle snores and his clothes that smelt of naphthalene to their own devices. As Anita O'Bray watched him a thin string of saliva dripped down from his jaw and pooled upon his collar. Suddenly he disgusted her and she found herself thinking that he was a filthy old man who should be put in a home. She shuddered and turned back to her work, but as soon as she did she felt the eyes on her again, manifesting themselves as a hot patch on her cranium and a strange tingling at the top of her spine. She tried to dismiss it but the sensation became stronger and stronger and when she finally gave in to it and looked up, standing there in front of her was a short, plump girl, probably aged about fifteen or sixteen. She collected herself. 'It's that way,' she said. 'If you go to the last stack and look on the third shelf down there's a whole section there.'

Jennifer turned round, thinking that there must be somebody standing behind her. But there was nobody else. She turned back to face the librarian. 'But I haven't told you what I want yet,' she said.

Anita O'Bray was confused. Hadn't she just answered this girl's question?

'This is a library, young lady, not a playground. If you think it's funny to pester the staff I'll have you sent outside. Last stack, third shelf down, half-way along.' Jennifer opened her mouth to protest but thought better of it. Instead, she backed along the line of Anita O'Bray's stare until she reached the final stack. Half-way along, on the third shelf down, was the section on human reproduction. Surprised but too intimidated to question the librarian's apparent telepathy she selected some books, sat down at the small study table that was built into the wall at the end of the shelves and did not emerge again for over an hour. When she finally did leave, it was a full two minutes before Anita O'Bray could contain her curiosity no longer and went over to the stack to see to just what section she had sent the poor girl.

The books that Jennifer had found there both informed and

confused her. They convinced her that she was pregnant, but also that she couldn't be, since the human 'gestation period' – as the books called it – was supposed to be at most nine months and she hadn't had sex for well over a year. She bought a pregnancy tester from the chemist's – telling the assistant that it was for her mother – but when she got it home and it tested positive she took out the razor-blade that she kept hidden in her room and carefully made a three-inch incision in the flesh of her upper arm.

The curious pregnancy progressed at an unbearable speed, so slowly that it was almost impossible for Jennifer to keep track of the changes that her body was experiencing. She would follow a symptom like an ache or a swollen gland for a few days, hoping that it was indicative of something, only to find that while she had been concentrating on that something else of apparent significance had occurred, such as a darkening of the veins in her thighs or an increase in the size of her breasts. She let out her clothes as much as she could – which got her a reprimand from the deputy head for looking 'a disgrace to the uniform' – and she badgered Henry endlessly for sick notes to exempt her from Games. As a precaution against the discovery not only of her increasingly imminent parturition but also of the fine lines of scar tissue which now webbed their way across her chest and her upper arms she did everything possible to ensure that no one should see her naked.

She became increasingly obsessed with the scarification and soon developed it into a strata of ritual that concentrated and steadied her in the face of these unexpected events, in some way hoping to construct a net of scars that would contain her body and its fluids in the face of the expansion it was experiencing. Every other night after her bath she would clear the condensation from the mirror and standing naked before it cut herself until her reflection ran red with blood. She had assembled a small kit comprising razor-blades, cotton wool, a tube of antiseptic cream and a phial of Cicatrin powder to hasten scabbing, all of which she kept in a metal tin that had once contained throat pastilles. These tools formed one axis of the ritual, the controlled flow of blood a second and the soft elasticity of her skin, which grew with the child and gave with the blade, a third. In this manner she erected a map which trapped the changes taking place and ordered them in a landscape of pain – a geography which stretched from the dull, languid valleys of the burgeoning foetus sapping away at her insides to the sun-scorched slopes of embarrassment that she traversed at school, trying to hide from the glares of the teachers and the tongues of the girls, and right up to the peaks of pain she climbed alone in the evenings, shut away in the bathroom.

But this fragile peace was constantly threatened by the dreams that shivered their way into her mind at night. Her descent into sleep was often via the smarting route of her freshest wound and her slumbers were sensitive and raw as a result, her cortex trembling at the slightest resonance nearby. Henry's quiet insomnias, invoked like demons by years of alcohol abuse, dissipated his increasingly despondent and incoherent moods into the structures of the house, and they saturated Jennifer's sleep like the fragmenting banks of methane that sweep across Titan, Saturn's moon. A domestic row further down the street glimmered in her night like a blinking buoy. A truck trundling down the main road drew fuzzy tracks across her dreamwork; a fox foraging in the dustbins produced a mirage in the middle distance; two copulating cats drilled worm-holes through her cortex. The beating of her heart was woven into the rhythms of her brain as the tides are woven into the fabric of the oceans, the yellow moon pulling them slowly this way, slowly that.

Were this all, Jennifer would have found rest enough among the slumberous maps of the neighbourhood she nightly drew, but other planetoids were ascendant in her system. One other moon would have been disruptive enough yet she might have become attuned to this, thanks to latencies in the accumulated layers of genetic deposit that were the helices of her DNA. But the object that now spun in her zenith was a double system, a maelstrom, a flexing wrinkle in her gravitational field that made the patterns of her sleep unintegrable and could force her from her slumbers and bring her gasping into the still and silent room, where the wind nibbled gently at the cheap print curtains and the blood coursed in hot currents around the conch spirals of her ears.

As the foetus grew, the effects which had so far been confined to her dreams began to seep out into her waking life. She would become suddenly aware, sitting in the classroom, of traffic moving in the remote distance, miles away, far out of earshot. Walking down an empty street she'd hear snippets of disembodied conversation. She heard the workings of machines when they were unplugged, the hum of televisions that had been switched off, the clattering of typewriters that lay idle. She asked a teacher during an essay-writing class if she could shut the windows because of the racket outside and got threatened with detention. The other pupils giggled and hissed quiet phrases among themselves like a box full of vipers but she could no longer tell whether the snatches of conversation she overheard were real or imagined. *That's Jennifer Several*, they said, *stay away from her. She's crazy and she stinks.*

'Do I smell different?' she asked Shelley a couple of days later on the verge of tears.

'What?'

'How do I smell? Tell me!'

But Shelley wouldn't tell her, wouldn't admit that she smelt of something to come, of solitude and plenty. Instead she said: 'I don't understand you any more. You're not the same these days. Ever since you've started going to that posh school you've been different.'

'But it's not my fault! It's not my fault! You've no idea what it's like!' Jennifer screamed, her self-pity transformed immediately into rage. 'I thought you were supposed to be my friend!' She launched herself at Shelley, arms flailing, and caught her a punch on the cheek and the shoulder.

Within moments the two of them were tussling on the ground, biting and scratching and thumping, until Shelley shoved her hand into Jennifer's swollen belly. Reacting to the harsh contact, the child inside squirmed like a drowsy marmoset – at which point Shelley let out a scream and recoiled in horror. 'God, Jenn, what . . . what's wrong with you? I thought I felt . . .'

'What do you think's wrong with me?' Jennifer spat. 'Why do you think I look like this? Why do you think I'm so fat all of a sudden and can't talk to anybody and everything?' She started to

263

cry and sobs cracked from her lungs in great fists of wet sound.

'But have you seen anyone? Have you seen a doctor?'

'I don't want to see anyone. I just want to be left alone.'

'Who did . . . y'know, who's responsible?'

'I don't know . . . Judd, I think. But there was this other bloke when I was in Geneva.'

'Oh Jenn . . .'

'Don't!'

'But Jenn, that was so long ago. It was over a year ago. It can't be right. There must have been somebody else.'

'Don't tell me there was somebody else! Don't you think I fucking know? I know what it fucking well is! I know all right. I can hear it. It makes me hear things.'

'I think you should see a doctor.'

'I'm not seeing anyone, you understand, no one. This is my problem, it's nothing to do with anyone else. And if you ever tell anyone, anyone at all, I'll kill you, do you understand? I'll kill you!'

'Yeh, yeh, OK, I get the message,' Shelley said, shocked.

Jennifer stood up and tried to brush the mud from her skirt. 'I'll be seeing you then,' she said, more calmly.

'Yeh, whatever,' Shelley replied, nonplussed. 'Be seeing you.' And she watched as Jennifer turned and walked off, not quite into the sunset, which was to her left, but almost.

That evening, after Henry came home from work, he got the hiccups. They came on over dinner, after he tried to wash down a piece of fishfinger that had got stuck in his throat with several hasty gulps of lager. Jennifer's mood – which had been sour up until then – suddenly lifted at the sight of him jerking up and down in his seat, face red as a beet.

'I don't . . . hic . . . understand what you thi . . . hic . . . hink is so blood . . . hic . . . y funny,' he gasped when he saw her reaction, the veins on his forehead already standing out in a quite alarming fashion. Jennifer ran to get him a glass of water and told him to drink it upside down, but he thought she was making fun of him and although she tried to demonstrate – and ended up getting most of the water on the floor – it just made her laugh even harder and nearly gave her the hiccups too. Eventually he managed to do what she instructed and the spasms in his diaphragm subsided enough for him to be able to finish his dinner, although he kept having to force a belch in order to buy enough time to chew and swallow a mouthful.

After dinner the hiccups did not go away and he sat in front of the TV all evening nursing a gin and tonic in the vain hope that the quinine and the bubbles would cure him. Several times Jennifer leapt out at him like a mad thing, screaming at the top of her lungs, the idea being that she might shock the hiccups into submission. But to no avail – they were still going when he went to bed and they kept him awake in a twilight world of percussive torture until he gave up and came downstairs to try to read a book. By the time Jennifer came down for breakfast he looked ten years older. Seeing him with his eyes even more bloodshot than usual and the skin drawn tight across his skull, for the first time in over a year she felt more concern for him than for herself.

When she got in from school that day he was already back from work and still hiccuping several times a minute. That evening he ate nothing. The fiery hilarity of the previous night had disappeared, leaving only the dark coals of worry glowing hot in Jennifer's heart. Henry had decided to try and drink the hiccups into submission and by nine o'clock he was paralytic, having finished his first bottle of Scotch and started on a second. But the spasms still racked his body and at a quarter to ten he began to cry, the continual eructations turning his saliva into a fine foam which dribbled from his mouth and nostrils. He lay on the sofa and Jennifer came to him and cleaned his face and held him in her arms as best she could. He bobbed in and out of a drunken slumber between the spasms and there was a Charlie Chaplin movie on the TV which she half watched while she stroked his head until she fell asleep herself, lulled by the rhythmic pulsing of the old man's body and the bleating music coming from the set. While she slept, the four hearts beating within the confines of the room vied with each other for control over the patterns of her dreams. On the television a cocaine-fuelled Chaplin charged around the factory floor of *Modern Times*, desperately trying to keep up with the machines.

She awoke at three to a room filled with white noise. Henry was in the same dreary stasis, intermittent tremors still running the length of his body. They appeared less powerful but then he was offering them less resistance. When Jennifer eased his head out from beneath her lap she found that a thin pool of acidic bile had gathered in the dip formed by her skirt and run down over the edge of the sofa. She fetched a cloth and cleaned up, and as she wiped away the scum from his mouth she checked his breathing: it was weak and irregular, and when it came it came in a soft, low curdle.

She switched off the television, brought the blankets down from her bed and laid one over him, then made a bed for herself on the floor. When she awoke again it was early morning and raindrops pullulated on the window-panes. The little light which had found its way into the room was so stale and colourless that it seemed to have been trapped in there for weeks. It was cold, too, so she put on a couple of panels of the fire and, yawning, went into the kitchen to make a pot of tea. We, however, stay in the living-room, our camera fixed in one position, our film dividing the scene into twenty-four segments every second, each one of which opens out like a monad on to all the others, each one of which is a bitter shard split off from the vast spinning plane of heterogeneity that is the cosmos. The sofa is turned away from us; we cannot quite make out Henry's recumbent form. The curtains are not fully closed and the only movement comes from the raindrops running down the glass and the flicker of heat above the fireplace. The hiccups have stopped and from the kitchen come the sounds of Jennifer making the tea: the cups are rinsed, the kettle boils, a cupboard is opened and closed, there is the sound of pouring water and metal on china. A few seconds later, an infinite interlude, Jennifer comes back into view with a cup in each hand. She sets one down on the television, dipping at the knee with the awkwardness of the schoolgirl that she is, not altering the angle of her wrist. A biscuit is clamped between her teeth and she has her lips drawn back so as not to dampen it with her saliva. One hand

266

now free, she removes the biscuit from her mouth and turns to Henry. 'Wake up, sleepy. I've made you some tea. Wakey wakey!'

She puts a hand out to shake him but his eyes are already half open and he offers no resistance. She puts the tea and biscuit on the floor, tucks back her hair behind her ears and runs her fingers across the ripples of his face. She touches his forehead and eyes, and lets out a series of small involuntary gasps as she does so. She puts her fingers on his lips for a minute or so, then bends down and touches his mouth with her ear. Then quietly she gets up and needles into the space behind him on the sofa, spooning him and trying – abstractly – to warm his body with her own. From above the outline of his neck ear hair she can see the gas fire dance. Within the confines of the room three hearts now beat.

It took about an hour and a half for the ambulance to arrive and she made tea for Wayne and Guy, the ambulance men, while they consoled her and dealt with the body. She hadn't cried yet: everything so far had seemed very matter of fact and routine.

At the hospital the doctor, who was tall and Indian and very slim, told her rather earnestly that it looked like a heart attack. He listened to what she had to say and noted the smell of alcohol on the body, rubbed his chin and said: 'Hum, acute singultus, very rare. Only ever heard of one or two cases. Most unfortunate. Looks like the old boy's heart couldn't take it.' He didn't react when Jennifer told him that Henry wasn't her real father and while they were talking he noted the shape of her belly and the miscoloration in the whites of her eyes. She signed the appropriate forms and they ordered a taxi to take her back home, which she paid for with money from Henry's wallet. She started to tidy the living-room and it was only when she realised that she was supposed to be at school that the tears came.

Later that day she understood she had to start telling people. She rang the school and also Henry's office and pretty soon everything was taken out of her hands.

Home alone

The firm of Hedges Hedges and Bentley occupied small premises in Cannon Street, between a pub that did most of its business in the lunch-hour and a restaurant that changed hands at least once every eighteen months. Michael Hedges (one of the Hedges of the firm's title, the other being his father who had long since gone to that great ledger in the sky) stood at the single window of his office staring out at the view across the twelve-foot shaft on to which the window let and which acted as a sinkhole for pigeon shit, exhaust fumes and something which only vaguely approximated sunlight. Behind him was a space that was barely more cheery. Green filing cabinets heaped with overstuffed portfolios lined one of the nicotine-hued walls, a dark bookcase crammed with reference books took up most of the second, and a gas fire and a few framed photographs that had faded to the point of anonymity embroidered the third. The brown door was chipped and the tape which adhered the fire regulations to the back of it was yellowed and peeling. The skirting board, where you could see it between the stacks of papers happily spawning across the floor, had been left undusted for so long that the tiny particles of atmospheric urban dirt had compacted into a greasy stratum that would by now be all but impossible to remove should anyone care to try. The frieze of plaster fruit and flowers which made a circuit of the ceiling had been painted over so many times that none of the original detail was discernible. The impression was that the ceiling was melting, and would at any moment begin to drip heavy boiling globules down upon the occupants of the room.

Jennifer heard Hedges sigh and looked up just in time to see him turn away from the window. The funeral had been the day before and the programme lay on Hedges's desk beside the buttonhole he had worn. He had come straight into the office after the service in order to do some work, even though the rest of the firm had been given the day off. The dark suit he had worn hung from the hatstand, wrapped in a cellophane dry-cleaning bag. 'Very sad,' he said, looking at Jennifer. 'A tragedy. Your father was not only an invaluable asset to this firm but was also one of my dearest and oldest friends.' His words echoed the address he had given at the service and now, as then, Jennifer regarded them with suspicion. She had heard Henry mutter to himself on several occasions about how Hedges was deserting him.

The senior partner smiled at her. 'You have been a very, *very* brave young girl.' His eyes were tired and his face heavily lined, and the articulations of his body seemed peculiar to someone like Jennifer, who hadn't spent the best part of thirty years sitting in a chair. 'But we have to decide what we are going to do with you. Where are you staying, at the moment?'

'With my best friend. Shelley. Walters.' Although she felt that Hedges was patronising her, Jennifer answered him shyly and automatically. She both trusted and mistrusted him, respected and disliked him, but such feelings seemed to belong to a plane quite distinct from that upon which their conversation was taking place. As far as that went it was as if she were five years old again: when asked questions by someone in authority you answered them, because that is what you'd been taught authority meant.

'There are many things, many practicalities, that you and I have to discuss.' He spoke his words in a ponderous, flavourless monotone. It was the voice he always used when emotion impinged upon money. 'Your father did leave a will, of course. He left everything to you, but there's not much, I'm afraid.' For a moment he dispensed with the patronising attitude. 'I'm sure you're aware of the reasons for that.' To Jennifer's surprise she nodded. It made her feel like a traitor. 'There's the house, of course, which your father owned outright: the mortgage was paid off several years ago. And there's a small amount of money left in trust for the payment of your fees and upkeep, should you decide to stay on at St Anne's. But apart from a few odds and ends that's pretty much it. It's not a disaster, but neither is it going to be plain sailing.' He looked at her again, the small, fat girl wrapped up in a vast brown overcoat and curled, insofar as it was possible to curl, into the unforgiving chair which faced his desk. His mind conjured several possible futures; two of the options he immediately repressed (one not quite so completely as the other, so that he could retrieve it for use at a later date). 'Your father's will specifies me as your legal guardian. I'm the person who will be acting for you until you are old enough, in the eyes of the law, to take your own decisions.' The scandal that Jennifer had been involved with two years before flickered into Hedges's mind and he tried to banish it to the same realm as the dark possibility he had imagined just a few moments before. 'I think the best thing would be for you to stay on with Shirley for the time being . . .'

'Shelley,' interrupted Jennifer. 'It's Shelley.'

'. . . er yes, that's right, with Shelley, for the time being, while I deal with the Social Services and make the appropriate arrangements for the longer term. Unless you want to come and live with me, which you probably don't think is a very good idea.' He laughed nervously, all the time watching Jennifer's eyes and trying to gauge her. She shook her head. 'I suppose we'll have to see if we can sort something out with the school, see if they will take you on as a boarder. I think you'd probably prefer that to a foster home. The other option is to go up to Manchester and live with your cousins there. They have made the offer, which is really very generous of them.'

'Why can't I live in my own house?'

'Well, you may be able to in a year or two's time. There is a proviso in your father's will that says if anything should happen to him you be allowed to stay on in the house if at all possible. But at the moment you are still officially a minor and I doubt that the local authority will be particularly enamoured of the idea.'

'But I'm not alone,' the girl protested. 'There's my cat. He still lives there. He can't move. I have to look after him.'

'Well,' said Hedges, pleased that he was able to make a concession, 'you've still got your keys, haven't you? Just because you're staying with Shelley it doesn't mean that you can't go back to your house. You'll just have to go in and feed him every day and make sure that he's all right.' Jennifer nodded at this, pleased with her invention of the cat, and Hedges continued evaluating for her benefit the legal technicalities of the situation. Eventually he brought the meeting to a close and told his secretary to put Jennifer on the next train back to Stratford. When she had gone he felt a pang of sympathy for her; he judged her to be something of a dullard, a 'natural victim' lacking in 'spirit', and imagined that organising her life was not going to be an easy task. Then he chastised himself for being so quick to judge. She was probably still in shock, poor thing. What a terrible thing to have happened.

Shelley's house was only a few streets away from Jennifer's own and it wasn't long before the Walterses were letting the orphan spend most nights there on her own. They had never had a particularly high regard for Henry and, unlike Michael Hedges, were quite convinced of Jennifer's self-sufficiency. They had liked the girl a great deal when she was younger but were surprised by how heavy, shy and morbid she had become over the last couple of years – and while they wanted to help her out, they were pleased not to have a heavy morbid shy teenager in their home more than was absolutely necessary. Once the initial wave of official grief and shock had passed through the rather vague and diffuse community of which Jennifer was a member, most people were inclined to let her get on with it, offering help only when the need for it was obvious and apparent. And this suited Jennifer just fine.

The lie about the cat had been a good one; she maintained it with everyone except Shelley and it gave her the perfect excuse to go home almost as often as she wanted. But she felt more than ever that eyes were upon her and she developed various subconscious strategies for avoiding them. Whenever she visited the house she went around the back, and she hung double thicknesses of muslin or net curtains across all the windows so that no one could see in from outside. She adopted clothes which were as voluminous as possible – in particular an old overcoat of Henry's which she wore continuously, despite Mrs Walters's constant exhortations for her to take it off – and took to hiding beneath headscarves and wide-brimmed hats. She avoided main meals and snacked instead, so that she wouldn't be obliged to spend regular periods of each day in a predictable place. She used roundabout routes wherever she went.

In one sense these evasive tactics brought her more attention:

the girls at school noticed and despised her more than ever, and even the younger pupils began to ridicule her. But the net effect was the one that she desired: people kept away from her. From their cold, slowly moving faces, blank, flat eyes and the way they darted away from her as she swam through the shallows of her life, she often imagined them now as so many little fish.

She had now been pregnant for over two years. Six months earlier her belly had stopped expanding and the fat she had put on disguised her condition. But in contrast to her situation at thirteen she now looked young for her age. The house was the only place where she felt safe enough to expose herself at all – its shrouded and dim interior became her holy place. She would stand in the half-light, large patches of her chest and upper arms shining with a luminosity that skin does not usually possess. These were the razor scars, the results of the blood-letting through which she released the genital quality of her skin. The areas were each about three or four inches across and roughly square and each was a lattice of finely drawn lines, a net drawn to reinforce her body. It was as though she were a single cell whose internal processes were undergoing mitosis but whose cell wall was terrified of rupturing. She began to be haunted by the fear that the child would never come, that her body would never be returned to her, that the fruits of the pregnancy would not be some bloodied infant but the eventual entrapment of her body in this expanding mesh of scars. At these times she projected an image of herself as a wicker woman, woven with scars from head to toe, silent, solid, cold, immortal, impregnable, mother and child locked away inside a basket work for all eternity. Yet she could not stop using the blade on herself.

The house had become an eddy in time, slowed and linked to things alien to the homogeneous suburban region that surrounded it, which marched stoutly onwards to the rhythms of the ticking clock, the commuter train, the school bell and the television news and sport. Within Jennifer's four walls time's only ally was the sequence of cuts she was making on her body; a prisoner in solitary, hatching off the days.

She was by now regularly experiencing bouts of pain in her

abdomen and around the time that the pain became continuous the school holidays commenced. When she felt up to walking she spent the days wandering aimlessly around Stratford; when she didn't she lurked in the house, battling with her grief over Henry and only turning up at the Walterses' for the occasional meal. She had several more rows with Shelley, who was by now determined that her friend should see a doctor and kept threatening to tell her mother if Jennifer didn't do something. But this attitude just sent Jennifer into a rage – she remained convinced that fate was at work and that its trajectory should be interfered with by no one. If Shelley tried to get her to give reasons she just snapped back that it was obvious, or that it was too complicated to explain.

Soon, though, it became clear that people were becoming suspicious and even Jennifer began to be aware that a crisis point was being reached. Her dreams, which had been getting increasingly vivid, had started to spill over into her waking hours and she had begun to see things which were not there. Flashes of colour and brief waterfall effects in her peripheral vision mutated into small, indefinable creatures curling up beside her, cats and squirrels darting across her path, men in overcoats sitting on rooftops, dragons in the clouds, curtains of rain on a fine, bright day. At night she felt that the house was surrounded and the fear was so powerful that she occasionally slept at the Walterses' again. The hunted look she carried in her eyes deepened and she was permanently on the verge of tears. More often than not there was a murmuring in her ears, a chthonic babble, as if a tribe of dwarves who dwelt in the earth beneath her feet were speaking together in tongues.

She was alone in her house when the first contraction came and the pain was so intense that she fainted. She would have remained there on the living-room floor if Shelley hadn't stopped by to apologise for some of the things she'd said during the row they'd had the previous day. The front door was locked but she knew that Jenn kept it that way and when she came around to the back door it was ajar. She entered nervously, calling her friend's name. When she saw Jennifer sprawled unconscious on the floor, she was immediately scared, partly for her friend, but also for herself, in case this was her fault for not having taken action sooner. She called for an ambulance and sat bathing the pregnant girl's forehead with a damp cloth and whispering her name, while she waited for help to arrive.

The caesarean section

In the emergency ward the doctors and nurses perform for each other, so obsessed are they with the many hospital dramas that now fill the television schedules. Indeed, it's difficult to see how any treatment actually gets done with the staff constantly sloping off to catch the latest instalment of *Hospital Ward* or *The Young Nurses*. But it's not all wasted time. Bedevilled with cuts in funding, many now learn their jobs from these medical soaps. How else are they to know the correct level of urgency required for three violently haemorrhaging car crash victims as compared with that needed for a single endoscopic retrograde cholangiopancreatography? Or how to talk to the little boy who has trapped his penis in his fly zip or the bag lady who's lost her marbles and won't sign the release form that allows the hospital to carry out the heart bypass operation that could save her life? Or how to deal with that wrong decision that cost the life of a two-year-old child or, most important of all, how to cope with an on-ward romance that's gone horribly wrong?

Recognising the importance of TV in modern medical practice, Ms Shanahan, the surgeon in charge of Jennifer's case, has made the decision to use the caesarean she is about to perform as a marketing opportunity. The houseman she has chosen to assist her in this is none other than dishy young Dr Parker, darling of the ward, chosen for his photogenic appearance. In one corner of the operating 'theatre' Ms Shanahan has had installed a video camera which will distil the events of the next half-hour or so on to a tape, which will then be rushed straight out of the door and into the hands of a waiting motor-cycle messenger, who will speed to

the city of Birmingham and the studios of the television company
with which at that very moment Ms Shanahan's assistant is negotiating terms. Jennifer's thumb print at the base of a form assures
her consent.

Roll it.

'OK, we've got a severe dystocia possibly caused by a breech
presentation. No indication of foetal distress, so we're going to
move straight into a hysterectomy procedure. Nurse, are you
ready?'

'Yes, Ms Shanahan.'

'Parker, can you see? I want you in on this one.'

'I can see.'

'Good. Then let's go. We're going to make a lower segment
transverse incision. Why do we prefer this over the so-called classical caesarean. Parker?'

'The transverse has the advantage of requiring only modest dissection of the bladder from the underlying myometrium.'

'And?'

'Er, and there's always a danger with a vertical incision that it
may extend too far downwards and tear through the cervix into
the vagina and bladder. And a transverse incision is much less
likely to rupture than a vertical incision during any subsequent
pregnancies.'

'And a transverse incision results in less blood loss, is easier to
repair and does not promote adherence of bowel or omentum to
the incisional line. Good. Nurse, scalpel, please. Thank you. Now,
I'm making an infra-umbilical midline vertical incision. It's got to
be big enough to deliver the foetus through and this is a big baby.
Listen to that skin pop. Good. See how I draw the knife down in
one clean movement. No hacking or sawing. If we do it right it
should heal up with minimal scarring. We're cutting down to the
level of the anterior rectus sheath . . . now we free the area of
subcutaneous fat – like so – to expose a strip of fascia in the midline
about an inch or so wide. See? You'll see some surgeons incising
the rectus sheath with the scalpel throughout the length of this
incision, but I prefer to make this small opening and then incise

the fascial area with scissors. Scissors! Like this. I think it's safer and cleaner – and for the time being at least I don't want to see you doing it any other way. Good. Here we go. Now what am I doing?'

'You're separating the rectus from the pyramidalis muscles using sharp and blunt dissection, exposing the transversalis fascia and the peritoneum.'

'Good, Parker, good. You've obviously done this before. Now, here, I just have to dissect this preperitoneal fat like so and . . . swab please . . . excellent, so we're now ready to open the peritoneum. How are we going to do that? Um? Come on, she'll have gone into labour by the time you've thought about it! Elevate the . . .'

'Elevate the peritoneum with two haemostats placed about two centimetres apart, then visualise and palpitate the tented fold to ensure that the omentum, bowel and bladder are not adjacent.'

'OK, so why don't you do that for me. That's right, apply them there and there, good . . . by the way, I haven't done a Pfannenstiel incision – you do know what that is, I presume?'

'Er, it's where the skin and subcutaneous tissue are incised using a lower transverse, curvilinear . . .'

'Yes, yes – well, we haven't done that because I want a good exposure of the uterus and appendages so that we can get a good look at what is going on in there. This amount of fat would make that difficult with the Pfannenstiel, and we're expecting complications, so better to play safe. Are you satisfied with your fold?'

'Yes.'

'Good. Then let's open her up. OK, so we incise to the upper pole of the incision . . . ah, like so . . . and downwards to just above the peritoneal reflection over the bladder, here. And there's the uterus, underneath. Now immediately we see, what?'

'That it's slightly dextrorotated?'

'Right! So?'

'So we lay a laparotomy pack in each lateral peritoneal gutter.'

'Excellent. Especially wise in this case, because one possible complication may be infected peritoneal fluid. Nurse, would you do that for us, please? Good. Now if we take the forceps – thank you – we can grasp the vesicouterine serosa in the midline like so and make a small incision with the scissors. By pushing the blades through and opening them we can separate the serosa from the myometrium and then incise it properly. Now the best tool for the next bit is the fingers . . . we want to slide in under this flap of peritoneum and gently separate the bladder from the myometrium . . . it's a bit like skinning a rabbit . . . ever skinned a rabbit, Parker? No, I didn't think so. There we go. You have to be careful here because it is possible, especially if the cervix is dilated, to dissect downwards too deeply and enter the underlying vagina by accident, missing the lower uterine segment, so we only want to separate the bladder back by about five centimetres.

'Now we can open the uterus through the lower uterine segment about two centimetres above the detached bladder. We're going to do this carefully, a small cut at first, and we have to judge it so that we get all the way through the uterine wall but don't harm the foetus. OK, here we go. And that's fine. Now we're through we can extend the incision using bandage scissors . . . OK?'

'Uh huh.'

'In fact, this segment is so thin that I could do this simply by pulling the incision apart with my fingers. We have to make this wide enough to allow delivery of the foetus without having to disturb either of the lateral uterine arteries here and here. Now, look there, that's the placenta – that's why you have to use bandage scissors. It's easy enough to detach it . . . like so, see? . . . but if you cut it by accident you're looking at severe foetal haemorrhage. There, there's its cranium, can you see there?' Cut to Parker. Nods. 'Doesn't look like a breech position after all, which is going to make all our lives easier.

'So, we're ready for delivery. The vertex is presenting so I can slip my hand into the uterine cavity here between the symphysis pubis and the head, and elevate gently through the incision. You can help me here by applying a moderate transabdominal fundal pressure . . . not that moderate! Come on, this is a hefty baby here! That's better . . . OK, here it comes . . . nurse, aspirate the nose and mouth please . . . thank you . . . don't want you drowning in

277

the amniotic fluids now, do we, darling? OK then, more pressure
. . . here it comes . . . here it comes . . . here *she* comes . . . wonderful. Nurse, take this, please, Parker, 20U of oxytocin intravenously,
10 millilitres per minute, nice and quick now, please. Keep your
eye on the uterus and when it's contracted back in you can slow
the flow a little. While you're waiting you can apply some fundal
massage. That should help reduce the bleeding and speed up the
delivery of the placenta. I'm going to clamp and sever the umbilical
cord, just quickly, like so . . . now, nurse, she's all yours. Parker,
you're still with me, we've got work to do despite the miracle of
birth. Can you handle the delivery of the placenta while I put on
some fresh scrubs?'

It's a wrap. And it looks like Parker's landed himself a role in the
forthcoming movie.

The eyes have it

From the start, they weren't going to let her keep the child; she
was still officially a minor, if only just, and then there was the
scarring of course – very worrying. But when they discovered that
the child had two hearts and other more subtle abnormalities the
case was referred to a higher authority, who immediately decreed
that the child should be kept under close supervision at all times
and that the mother should be told it was stillborn.

The birth went out on *Living Eye* that night, right after the local
news. Laika tuned in from her vantage point, catching the show
on the satellite relay. An eye in the sky, she looked down, but she
didn't pick up on anything strange.

Check out

For months after the birth Jennifer refused even to acknowledge the experience. Michael Hedges knew, of course, as did the Walterses, but they were very careful to keep any mention of the whole affair to themselves. The school was told that Jennifer had suffered a burst appendix and that became the accepted version of events.

They kept her back for observation and she spent a week or two in hospital, on a drip. Her moods were jagged so they smoothed them out with lithium, but she made no further attempt to cut herself. They had her removed from maternity for fear she'd upset the other mothers and put her in a spare bed in the geriatric ward. She spent the days crying quietly to herself, her face turned to the wall, while the old women in there with her juddered around the room, dribbling and scraping at the air like desiccated trees fidgeting at the onset of storms that will bring them, brittle and cracked, to the ground.

She lost weight rapidly. Of course, she was no longer carrying and there was the concomitant fluid loss, but her bingeing had ended and now she ate more regularly again. Throughout that period, whenever she looked at herself in the mirror she had a strange sense of juxtaposition, as if she were all at once standing upon the crests of two waves of time, the period of the pregnancy sunk out of sight into a trough, what she was before and what she was now crushed together into a single bastard bloom of flesh. There was something else, too, something that was at first obscured by this shimmering duality, something which took a good while to filter through: the feeling of being watched was gone. She no longer felt those cool patches slither down her cranium and inside— outside her spinal column. Those dewy disembodied eyes that seemed to coalesce out of the susurrations of her own blood and tissue were no more.

By November she was ready to return to school. In the wake of the birth she insisted on being allowed to live in the house, and after consulting the Walterses, who promised to keep an eye on her, Michael Hedges capitulated, thinking that she'd probably been through enough. The following summer she took her O levels, and when her results were below average she announced that she was going to leave St Anne's and get a job. Nobody really wanted to try and stop her, especially as she seemed largely to have recovered from the traumas of her early teens and returned to something of her former self, and by the end of the summer she was employed as a check-out girl in the Woolworth's on Stratford's Bridge Street. She worked at this and other similar establishments for the next few years, hanging out with the town's first wave of punks and experimenting with drugs.

9

Oedipus wrecks

Cars cruised Hollywood Boulevard; their hot tyres on the soft asphalt made the sound of long strips of damp cloth being slowly torn apart. Small knots of men snarled every street corner and women clad in tight, low-cut tops and short skirts stalked the pavements or sat, legs akimbo, astride fire hydrants, their hard breasts jutting up and out. It was eight o'clock in the evening and still hot. The city lay like coals and the sky flickered with the shimmer of a barbecue that's given out its best cooking heat. Thick skeins of grey smoke wound like ivy around the seething purples of the sundown clouds. Up and down the strip the telegraph wires sweated and hummed with the voices that were stretched along them, thinner than hair. There was a wax museum whose air-conditioners roared front and back day and night to keep the occupants from melting away. Next door in the arcade the chimes of the one-armed bandits sang louder even than the fans: from across the street you could hear their levers and dials clanging like a pen full of terrified cattle.

Above the arcade was a floor of offices and above these – and you had to go round back and up a metal stairway if you wanted to gain access – were a couple of apartments. Inside one of them, Judd dropped his telephone handset back into its cradle and broke his connection, the intensities of the sexual fantasy he'd been having folding themselves away like electrons in the tube of a cooling television. He got up from his bed, wiped himself and pulled his pants up over his detumescent penis. He lit a cigarette. He felt no more relaxed than he had before the phone call and for a few minutes he paced the room nervously, sure that he had something important to do. A small quantity of cum seeped from his urethra and formed a damp patch on his thigh. He couldn't decide whether he liked the soiled feeling this gave him or whether he would rather be clean, showered, sterilised.

He'd done telephone sex several times now, numbers from the back of a magazine. It wasn't exactly satisfying but until he'd discovered it he'd found it very hard to masturbate. Since the scandal eight years before he'd only had sex with one person, a tough girl from South Central who'd picked him up and slept with him for a while because she'd needed a place to stay. That had been the previous summer, just after he'd left high school and moved into the apartment. (The significance of the date they'd first fucked didn't escape him – 4 July 1980, Independence Day.) But apart from that he'd come through puberty with little or no sexual contact, which would have been bad enough even if Schemata hadn't reconfigured his imagination to such a degree that it was difficult for him to enjoy the company of his left hand. Every time he tried to turn himself on his mind would vault over a precipice of logical implications, psychological profiles and political prerogatives and hurtle down a wall of consequences, the psychoanalyst's voice sounding in his ears like the rush of air itself, drowning out any mustering desires.

It drove him half crazy. It was as if Schemata had set up an irrigation system around the mountainside of his mind, insuring him against any ill effects that might have come from his encounter with Jennifer, yes, but at the same time completely subordinating him. Seamlessly integrated into this system of psychic hydraulics and unable to remember what he had been like before, Judd found it impossible to get any kind of perspective on his own personality. The only real refuge was his dreams: while he'd remained in the analysis they too had been affected (like Rod Serling in *The Twilight Zone*, Schemata would always appear at the end in the role of narrator, to bracket and interpret the preceding dreamscape, give it some awful moral), but once the sessions had ceased his

imagination had used the cover of the night to begin to shake itself
free of the doctor's influence, temporarily flooding and disrupting
the network of pipes and pumps that he'd laid. Although a welcome
relief, the downside of this was that Judd awoke almost every day
to a semen-soaked bed – which meant that he suffered from acute
embarrassment whenever he came into contact with his parents'
live-in Filipino housemaid.

As soon as he moved into the apartment on Hollywood Boulevard he took advantage of his new-found privacy by paying a
visit to one of the local adult shops and buying himself a few
magazines. Carrying them home inside their plain paper bag, positive that everyone on the street was watching and remembering
him, he was as excited as if he'd been going on a date with the
prom queen. But to his surprise the pictures left him cold. He had
to ask himself why had he gone and bought magazines full of white
women. He'd done it without thinking, it was a cultural reflex.
But that raised the question: being black physically but half-caste
technically, which colour of girl was he supposed to prefer? Jennifer
had been white, of course, but as an isolated case it was hardly
conclusive. Why couldn't Schemata have helped him sort that one
out? He'd talked a lot about the Oedipus Complex, and that was
all very well, but he'd never made it clear whether one should
give in to the psycho-sexual channels it created or resist them.
Would only a woman like his mother make him happy? Or would
a woman like his mother destroy him? His subsequent affair with
Annette, the girl from South Central, did not make things clearer.
Superficially, she'd not been like Melinda at all – she was black,
for a start. But then Annette had been hard, self-motivated, not
prepared to let anything get in her way, and he knew his mother
was like this too, or could be. He stayed confused.

Telephone sex removed all these questions. It was easy, anonymous and it had no visual element. It made him feel like shit, but
it got his rocks off, so it was some kind of solution.

The room was a reasonable size and all his own. He could think
there, or more than he could at his parents' at least. There were
the bed and a few other oddments of unremarkable furniture.

283

Stacked around the place were a few books: self-help books mainly, a few soft-porn novels, some black-consciousness literature (most of which had been recommended to him by Annette), several Mickey Spillanes (Mike Hammer: 'Fastest with a Gun, Hottest with a Girl') and one or two cheap classics. His copy of *Moby Dick* had been awarded as a school prize, and the fine cracks along the spine revealed that he had got about a third of the way in and given up. He deliberately hadn't put any pictures up on the walls – he liked them white, anonymous, he liked the feeling of transience they gave him, the feeling that he was just passing through. But there was something about the bare plaster too . . . he had a dim idea that he wanted as much of it exposed as possible. It comforted him. Annette had turned her nose up at this decision, said he was being pretentious, that he should decorate. He told her it was typical of a girl to say that, a comment which sparked a minor argument in which he'd been backed into a corner by refusing to explain why he liked the walls bare ('I just do, all right? I just do'). But it wasn't that he hadn't wanted to explain further; he had, it was just that he couldn't untangle his thoughts about it all.

He was supposed to be looking for a job: his father had put him on an allowance, which was how he could afford the apartment (Moses didn't want him to go on welfare) but he'd given up scanning the small ads in the newspapers months before. He had no idea what he wanted to do. Every time he spoke to Melinda she pestered him to try for college; his father on the other hand still had this idea that he could make it in sales. Judd wanted to do neither. He couldn't bear the idea of following in Moses's footsteps – for one thing, it was all too Freudian. But neither could he see the point of going to college. He'd already had his head filled with enough crap, he'd decided. Why cram it fuller still?

So he drifted, hung out in cafés, had telephone sex, wandered the streets of Hollywood, read, listened to music. He became furious and morose. He started to build models again, from plastic kits – he'd done it as a kid, especially in England, had assembled them as a way to cheat wet weekends of boredom. Before he'd built anything he could get, but now he only wanted to build aircraft. Helicopters, fighters, passenger jets. Gluing together the grey plastic wings and fuselages helped him to cut his imagination loose from reality. If he couldn't return to a time before Schemata then perhaps he could recreate himself anew, dream a dream of flight, put himself up there with the clouds, roam with those giant patterns as they dragged their shadows across the earth, touching the ground only in order to prove to it that he was free.

He didn't see too many people. Most of his friends from high school were either in jobs already or had gone off to college or were thinking of going or were concentrating on their sports or whatever. Most of them, in other words, had some kind of a goal. He didn't and it singled him out.

Before the year was out Moses grew bored with trying to nag his son into activity and found him a job working the front desk in a used-car lot owned by a business contact who owed him a favour. The deal? Take it or lose your allowance. Judd took it. It didn't liven things up much, at least not to begin with. It made him depressed, too, and tired (so no change there). Most evenings he came home and just sat in his front window and smoked, watching the street below, switching on the TV when he got fed up with that. Having a job, though, did mean he had something to talk to his school friends about and sometimes he met up for beers with a group of them. For a while he got quite sociable and for a few months he even started going regularly to night-clubs, at one of which he met another girl, Marsha. This time it lasted a while, and she was in it for him and not just his place. They spent weekends together, smoking dope, listening to music. But when it came to making love there were problems. It had been fine with Annette, but the fact that Marsha actually cared for him seemed to make it impossible: either he wasn't interested and couldn't get hard or he was overwhelmed by emotion and came too quickly. Pretty soon she left him for somebody else. After that it was back to TV, telephone sex and a fridge stocked with fully readjusted American beer. Later on, as an experiment, he tried fucking a couple of call-girls. That was OK, but expensive.

Although when he started the job he was kept pretty busy, trade

285

quickly began to drop off. With nothing better to do he was soon spending most of his time hanging out in the repair shop with the two mechanics, Lionel and the Bomb. The Bomb was a DJ – he had taken his tag from the name of a drumming technique invented by the bebop drummers. He played at parties at the weekends and was always terrified of staining his hands with oil. Lionel was a high-minded dread, a Rasta. He was Jamaican; he'd come to the States ten years previously to find work and he sent most of his wages back to his baby-momma and daughter in Kingston. He and Judd talked politics a bit, discussed Marcus Garvey, Martin Luther King, the Black Panthers. Lionel had plenty disdain for it all. He told Judd about the hopeless situation in Jamaica, about how two white politicians, Seaga and Manley, had the island sewn up between them. He called it 'the shitstem'. 'Rasta ha' no part in it,' he'd say to Judd, who'd nod vigorous encouragement, keen to improve his political credentials.

The lot was on a busy feed road that ran past a housing project before it joined with the freeway. There had been a couple of gang killings in the area the previous year but the kids who hung out on the corner and occasionally came into the lot to look over the cars never gave Judd any trouble, except for the occasional remark about being a coconut and a lot of lip about the prices of the cars in the showroom. The business didn't smell of money and it only ever got broken into out of boredom, and even then there was never too much damage done, except for the night when some joyriders hot-wired a Buick and drove it out through one of the sheet-glass showroom doors. That afternoon Lionel had been giving the car an oil change and had left the sump to drain overnight, so the kids didn't get very far before the engine seized up on them and the Buick ground to a halt. Word got around among potential thieves, who weren't interested in stealing some heap of junk that was going to break down after a couple of miles. So crime fell off. Unfortunately, however, sales did too: word also got around among potential clients; perhaps the two sets overlapped. Business got slower than ever.

Irving Scofield was perfectly aware of this and completely untroubled by it. Scofield was the lot's owner and the friend whom

Moses had touched for Judd's job. An entrepreneur, no one really knew quite how he made his money but he seemed to make a fair amount of it. Speculation about him constantly circulated in one guise or another, and there had at one point been some nasty rumours going around about a link between Scofield and a missing shipment of DEC computers which had been under Moses's jurisdiction, but nothing had ever been proved. Whatever, the point was that Scofield didn't care that the lot wasn't doing so well, because he kept the business open as a tax dodge.

So as Judd's flow of paperwork became a trickle and the backlog of repairs for Lionel and the Bomb dwindled and then disappeared, the three of them found themselves with entire days full of nothing to do. By now, Judd had learnt a bit about cars and some days he'd fine-tune one of the vehicles parked out front, taking it around the block and running it with the hood up, trying to spot problems that he knew how to solve. The rest of the time he mostly spent building models, though he'd moved on from aircraft now. His unsatisfactory sexual experiences had made him question more strongly than ever the effect that Schemata had had on him, and he soon came to the conclusion that he needed to free himself from the analyst's influence and reclaim his personality for himself. As a first step he decided to try and remember what he'd been like as a child, and to this end he went out and and bought a stack of new kits in an attempt to rekindle the old obsession he'd had with space. Rockets, satellites, landers, starcruisers, he built them at his desk, immersing himself in the simple poetry of part and plan, glue and sprue in order to kindle a more complex experience of memory and dream. In space anything was possible; the concept itself was fairly abstract. Time worked differently too: out there where the stars marked passing aeons with the comings and goings of planets, solar systems, entire galaxies, Judd's own life seemed irrelevant enough. And if his life was irrelevant, the scribble of a shrink upon it was more irrelevant still, of no consequence. It was pleasantly contradictory, this fantasy, which was what made it so complete: on the one hand Judd needed rockets and boosters, he needed a massive increase in speed to escape the gravitational pull of planet Schemata. But on the other hand, his ultimate destination was the depths of the universe and the total stillness, the absolute self-control, that his arrival there would bring.

Soon he had miniatures of the Sputniks, the Saturn V rocket, Space Lab, Voyager, Apollo, an X-Wing fighter from *Star Wars* and a carrier ship from *Space 1999* cluttering up a table in his office. That April the space shuttle Columbia had made its first manned flight and Judd constructed a giant model of the craft and the rockets which carried it into the sky. He was very proud of it and was going to give it to Lionel and the Bomb to put in the repair shed, but before it was finished there was a picture of Columbia on the front page of the paper one day, and when he saw it Lionel started venting his spleen at Americans in general for pissing money out into space and not being able to house or feed their own people properly. Silently embarrassed by his inadvertent political incorrectness, Judd stopped making models after that.

In camera

By monitoring the Russian media Laika knew now to what extent they were exploiting her, erecting statues in her honour and putting her face on to stamps. She was famous and everyone was getting something out of it (everyone but her). Still, she liked the attention, even if she pretended to disapprove. Her main competition, the only serious threat to her status, was this cosmonaut Gagarin. Annoyingly she'd missed his little sojourn in outer space – it just so happened that he'd been launched into an orbit similar to her own, but a little bit ahead, so they raced around the planet together, dog in pursuit of man. She'd hoped to catch up with him, freak him out a little, the greenhorn, but he disappeared back down through the clouds to a hero's welcome without the gap having closed.

It was sickening, watching it all on TV, though she had to admire the bureaucrats – they milked it for all it was worth, renaming the square where he first addressed the crowds Gagarin Square and erecting there a huge titanium statue of space android Yuri jetting through the atmosphere, a future perfect man all aerodynamic efficiency, his arms out like Christ's, his trusty cannonball-like craft at his feet like a . . . like a faithful dog. Here he was, the icon, the crucifix that Soviet reason had claimed to stamp on the twentieth century, and meanwhile where was she? Female, canine, victim of prejudice, all her achievements subjected to a cover-up. She'd made a life up there, after all, while he'd just come on a day trip, a glorified lost weekend. Talk about a glass ceiling!

Well, what did it matter to her? He'd merely been adjunct to the operation, a twist of cortex and skin inside his machine, a circus boy fired from a gun. But she had achieved proper integration – she felt through her craft, its exterior her exterior, its controls and her nerves co-extensive. So sensitised had she become to the behaviour of the capsule that she now felt the impact of space dust as if it were hail on her back. Her changing relationship with the earth's electromagnetic field was as noticeable as the first quiver of a distant front of rain across the fields on a humid summer afternoon, the slight gravitational tug of a passing satellite as tempting as the odour of a prowling male.

Until 1968 she remained secure in the knowledge that whatever Gagarin did, she had one unassailable advantage in the race to be the world's greatest space icon – she, at least, had died young (and only two years after James Dean). But then the cosmonaut went and nose-dived his test plane and even the Western media rumour that the crash had been engineered by an over-enthusiastic publicity department couldn't reconcile her to the fact that there was no stopping him now. Mankind would choose him over her as their emblem – him they could manipulate. Yuri Gagarin had been launched into the space of the symbol and this time he wouldn't return.

Craps

The summer drew on and if you stood out in the street on any day that you chose – it made no difference which, they were all the same – you would see the silver-grey band of the tarmac that stretched away underneath the freeway and all the way down to the sea vibrate and shimmer with heat. The light was always so bright and clean that you could hardly see the sky, even when the pall of smog was not present (which was rarely) and no one walked anywhere any more except for those, like the bums, who had to (and they stayed put when they could). The heat wore tempers as thin as the membranes of boils over-swollen with pus. Occasionally these pustules burst and there were shootings on the highways.

With his model building abandoned, Judd had nothing to do. It was too hot to fool around in the forecourt; any tinkering had to be done in the showroom where you could have the air-conditioning on, and this meant that you couldn't run the engines for more than a couple of minutes because of the fumes. It was cooler in the repair shop, but that was the domain of Lionel and the Bomb, and no work was to be done there unless they sanctioned it – and they wouldn't sanction it unless it was 'real' work, which meant work that they were going to get paid for or which would improve their immediate environment, such as fixing up the refrigerator or the sound system, jobs which could take days if handled properly.

It had indeed begun to seem as if the two mechanics did no work whatsoever. When they weren't playing their newly acquired records to each other they would play dice, their overalls folded down at their waists and their dark torsos glistening with sweat. They used the upturned hood of a 1973 Chrysler as a craps board, having drawn markings on it with a waterproof pen, and played each other for quarters and dimes.

On this particular day they both sat there like princes on seats ripped out of a Porsche Spider, cigarettes glowing in the shade and beer cans at the ready, admiring the view of the freeway flyover.

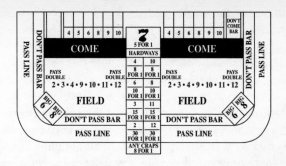

'Ah, dis is de life, ma man,' drawled Lionel, broadening his accent to emphasise his contentment.

'Sho' is, brutha, sho' is,' replied the Bomb, who was concentrating on rolling a small joint using only one hand, a trick which he had not yet perfected.

At that moment, unbeknown to either of them, Irving Scofield walked into the showroom. Judd was sitting on the main reception with his feet up on the desk and his chair tipped back, reading in the paper that the space probe Voyager 2 was just passing Saturn, that IBM's new product, the Personal Computer, was selling well (he tried to remember if that was the thing his father was working on now) and that a deadly new disease called Acquired Immuno-Deficiency Syndrome was killing homosexuals. The air-con was on full and the noise of the fans drowned out Scofield's approach. It was not until the owner stood right in front of the desk and coughed that Judd looked up. For a second he froze, then tried to get up so fast that his chair fell over and a pile of empty plastic sprues stacked up on the edge of the table behind him clattered to the floor. Doing his best to ignore all this he hurried round to the front of the desk, hand outstretched.

'Mr Scofield, ah, Mr Scofield, what a surprise. It's been pretty quiet around here, I was just taking my lunch break . . .' Judd tailed off as Scofield stood there impassively. He was a big man, very dark-skinned and broad. His hair was fringed with tidy grey curls that slowly blended into black as they spread across his crown. He looked down at Judd through hooded eyes, the folds of skin only hinting at the small, hard irises and yellow whites that lay back in there somewhere. The deep creases in his forehead and heavy jowls gave his face the look of a stump of wood turned to charcoal and pulled from the fire, the fine threads and patterns of the living tree having been transmuted into thick perpendicular scorings more reminiscent of the patterns of erosion in a permeable rock than of anything organic. It was a difficult face to read.

But then it broke into a broad smile, the cindered bark stretching back to reveal the living sap beneath: bright, bright teeth adorned with gold, the pulpy red flesh of a well-tended mouth. The man ignored Judd's outstretched arm and seized him instead by the shoulders. 'No need to apologise, my boy! You're entitled to put your feet up now and again! I was just thinking how fine the old place looks! Seems like your father was right to get me to take you on. Fine job, fine job.' His voice was massive and soft.

Judd brightened immediately. 'Thanks, Mr Scofield. Is there anything I can get you? A 7-Up? Some water? A coffee?'

'Ah, water, if you please. It sure is hot out there today.' Judd loped over to the cooler, cracked down a paper cup and filled it. Inside its plastic drum the water belched and rumbled.

'I just want to have a quick look round back, check out the repair shop,' Scofield called, heading for the door. 'How those boys doing out there anyway?' Immediately, Judd's panic returned. Lionel and the Bomb were undoubtedly playing craps, as they did almost every afternoon now. Judd rushed to his desk, meaning to grab the phone and call them on the internal exchange, but Scofield had stopped at the showroom exit and was waiting for him. 'Come on, son! I haven't got all day!'

Judd crossed his fingers and joined the boss, handing him his drink. Scofield took the water, downed it in a single gulp, crumpled the cup with one flex of his enormous hand and tossed the remains into a drain before leading the way round to the repair shop. Judd followed with trepidation, almost shaking with fear – what would happen when the boss found out, what would his father say? Schemata was suddenly back with him again, whispering consequences in his ear, apparently more powerful than ever. The three of them headed around the edge of the building and disappeared out of the flat hot sun into a rhombus of shade. Judd could already make out the sound of the dice rattling against the metal of the Chrysler hood. Even worse was the musk of marijuana hovering on the still air.

'Hello, boys!' bellowed Scofield. Lionel and the Bomb turned around, but instead of the blanched faces that Judd had expected to see they both broke into smiles and came over to greet the owner.

'Hi, Mr S!'

'Hey! How ya doin'?'

'Pretty good. You boys shootin' a little craps there?'

'Yeh, jus' somethin' we rigged oursel's up to pass the time. Bin pretty quiet roun' here. Can I get you a beer, Mr S?'

'No, that's all right. I can't stay long. Just came by to ask a favour. Tell me, can you boys fix up a vehicle for me, soup it up a little, stiffen out the suspension, reinforce the hood and trunk, that kind of a thing?'

'No problem,' said Lionel, looking at the Bomb.

'How long would it take?'

'Well, depends on what it is, but unless it's something really weird, then a week, max.'

'It's a '76 Lincoln. Reckon you could start on it over the weekend? I'll give you double time.'

The mechanics looked at each other and shrugged. 'Sure, no problem.'

'Fine. I'll get Jacob to drop it by, last thing Friday. He'll call you tomorrow, run over what you'll need. OK, that's all. Everything else OK?'

'Jus' fine, Mr Scofield.'

'That's what I like to hear. You boys get back to your game now. And don't smoke too much of that there reefer – that stuff rots your mind.'

An astounded Judd walked Scofield back around to the front of the premises and watched him vanish behind the smoked glass of his Cadillac. When the car had driven away, he hurried back to the repair shop and demanded an explanation. Lionel and the Bomb pulled up an oil drum, sat him on it, put a cold beer into his hands and gave him the low-down, which as far as Judd was concerned amounted to an object lesson in the fact that not everyone in the world adhered to the same principles that had been drummed into him by his father and analyst. Then they taught him craps. The few customers who called in at Route 66 Autos over the next few weeks found the front door locked and a cardboard sign directing them round back taped across the glass.

Lizard me this

Lionel and the Bomb were lazy players. They thought they could get on top of the game, that they could spin it one way or another just by thinking about it. They were forever wishing for the perfect series of throws from the worn wooden dice that clattered across the Chrysler hood a thousand thousand times that summer. Lionel's game was one of austerity followed by binge: he would carefully place bets calculated to insulate him against cruel streaks of misfortune and in this way he would inch his winnings upwards. Yet he could only hold out for so long before he tired of his cautiousness and with the sweat building on the sandy palms of his fine, long-fingered hands he would hazard a large stake on a single round and blow the lot. But if Lionel's game was a (failed) attempt to outwit chance, his friend's was an exercise in will. The Bomb would sit stripped to the waist with his feet drawn up beneath his round thighs and a beer can balanced on the folds of his belly, trying to divine or influence the next result (which of them it was wasn't quite clear). To help him in this task he used any number of signs coaxed from the immediate surroundings: the number of flies that settled on the rim of a coffee cup, the number of cars that came down the street, the number of motes in a ray of sunlight that had found its way into the workshop through a chink in the panels of the metal walls. When no obvious signifier was at hand he would close his eyes and try to conjure the numbers on the insides of his eyelids, or picture the dice in the position in which they would come to rest. And then, having decided upon the result, he would lay his bets in the appropriate manner and throw. Most of the time he was wrong, of course; but when he did win he won big, usually just enough to allow him to continue to play.

It was inevitable that this idle pastime with its easy lack of focus – really an excuse for long, languid conversation – would be disrupted somewhat by Judd's inclusion in the system. It was a classic example of the three-body problem. The behaviour of a gravitational system with only two bodies – a double star for example, or the earth and its moon – is easy to predict if you know a few basic things about the objects involved, such as their mass and their relative positions at some point in time. But introduce a third body and however much information you have it is impossible to predict exactly what will happen. You know what outcomes are possible – Judd wins, Lionel wins, the Bomb wins, or there is a combination of draws – but beyond that, nada. The equations are no longer integrable – they no longer converge upon a single solution but offer only alternatives, separated by infinitely complex fractal boundaries.

To counter this problem the trio dispensed with cash for the time being and played instead with nuts, washers, piston rings and spark plugs, the idea being that they would go back to money when Judd had learnt the ropes, at which point major fluctuations in the game would, they hoped, have more to do with skilful betting and less to do with chance.

Although keen to enter this new arena with its promise of an alternative to the moral world with which he'd been programmed, Judd played hesitantly at first. He felt out of place sitting on his drum in his brown stay-pressed suit, while Lionel and the Bomb slumped back in their car seats, looking as if they had grown into the oil-stained overalls that hung about their bodies. But he soon got used to leaving his jacket hanging on a nail behind the door and loosening his tie, liking the feeling of jaded respectability that the look gave him even though he was still too young to carry it off properly. His face was smooth and glowed like a polished stone as he sat perspiring in the shadows of the repair shop. His skin had darkened even further as he had left adolescence behind: over a period of years it had turned him from the dirty brown he'd been in England to a hue that seemed to contain all the colours of the dusk, sifted into one another and banded together tight.

He played cack-handed and concentrated too hard, hurling the dice across the hood as if any wrist action would curse the throw. 'Loosen up man,' the Bomb would drone, flopping and flipping his pudgy hand in the air to demonstrate. 'Let the dice *flow* out of you.' He watched his opponents carefully, asked them questions and tried to imitate their techniques, but he found both approaches next to useless and eventually it dawned on him that he was trying too hard and that this was a simple game that required little effort. All the possible combinations of the dice were fully refreshed each time you scooped them off the board; you did not have to concentrate except on the betting, that was the point. He got into the habit of placing a pass bet every time and only rarely laying the odds or placing a come.

With little to contribute to the interminable conversation that went on between Lionel and the Bomb, he began to watch the dice – not just when he was throwing them, but all the time – to see how they fell. He would have thought it would be hard to concentrate on the game like this, but on the contrary, he found that the progress of these numbers across the Chrysler hood was the perfect thing to help force the presence of Schemata from his mind.

Before long, the dice started to fascinate him for their own sake, not simply as a displacement activity. Most important, he'd noticed that as soon as he'd stopped trying to bend the outcome of the dice to his will, or place overly strategic bets, the sequence of results began to seem less erratic, no doubt in part because he was no longer only concerned with the small proportion of them that gave him some return. He began to take a mental note of all the throws, including those made by his opponents, and to see if could spot when the numbers formed little orders and patterns over time. He noticed how when he did win he won in streaks, as if the shape marked out by the dice had moved across the board to occupy the area circumscribed by his bets, forming itself around them, hugging them. It seemed as if the dice traced out the movements of a small creature. Something cold-blooded, he felt, a desert creature perhaps. Maybe a scorpion. Or a gecko.

He spent the whole summer this way, sitting drinking beer and rolling blunts with the two other softly sweating men in the dusty, shady repair shop, and watching the movements of an animal created by chance. 'Do you see that?' he said to Lionel and the Bomb one time.

'See what?'

'It just put out its tongue.'

'What did?'

'The dice lizard.'

'What you talkin' about?'

'All the throws, they make a shape. Looks like a lizard. I've been watching.' The two men exchanged glances. They'd thought him weird when he started making those plastic models; now they knew he was crazy.

The Bomb put a fat index finger up to the side of his forehead, rolled his eyes, and slowly screwed the finger back and forth. 'Whew, brutha, what you bin smokin'? Let me at some of that. Or you jus' bin lying out in the sun too much again?'

Judd opened his mouth to explain and then thought better of it. 'Yeah. You're right. I'm going nuts.' He lifted up the beer he was holding in his left hand and looked at it. 'Too much of this in the afternoons, I guess.' He drained the can and they all laughed, then he stood up. 'I'm going outside to get some air.' He walked out through the baking metal doors and round into the forecourt, just as a green Chevy pulled in. Quickly, Judd took the keys from his pocket, opened the side door to the showroom and slipped inside. While the driver was opening the door for his passenger, Judd unlocked the main entrance and walked back out into the sunlight to greet the two customers. As he moved towards them it struck him that Schemata's voice hadn't sounded in his head for weeks now. He quietly cleared his throat and looked for somewhere discreet to spit.

The conspiracy theory

They circle the child as she lies in the crib, the tubes and sensors trailing from her limbs torso head the articulation of an extended nervous system. Their starched garments rustle in the surgical silence of the room, provide a brushed high-hat to the toms of the ECGs which are meeping the child's two heartbeats in a long cycle of strange delay. The room is the logical conclusion of cleanliness – so white it shimmers – and utterly deadly. All is concealed except for the machines, the mutant body in its metal bed, the eyes and ears that escape the masks and caps. The child lies sedated; beneath their lids her eyes violently saccade. For some time now the doctors have been here.

Earlier: an oxygen tent, the child is prone, barely breathing. There are other children; it is a nursery. No outward signs suggest the unusual internal organisation. There is some doubt at this stage as to whether or not the child will ever attain consciousness; she has been in a coma since birth. The nurse arrives to take a blood sample. She peels a tiny blade from the sterile casing in which it has been packed by a clean and busy machine far, far away and clasps it in her right hand, using a grip which involves her thumb, her middle finger and her little finger. She feels a tremor in her wrist, as if a nerve has been trapped, and shakes it out. With her left hand she lifts and secures the plastic flap of the isolation tent, and takes the child's arm. She crouches and manoeuvres the tiny thumb of the tiny hand into a suitable position. On the trolley beside her is a small phial in which she will collect the blood. She places the tip of the blade against the soft pad of flesh and prepares to slice a small and shallow wound. But before the metal even penetrates the epidermis the child bucks violently. The blade falls to the floor and the nursery is fractured by a fine, fine sound. The windows that separate room from corridor suddenly burst. Immediately the other infants are awake and they pummel the frightened air with their screams.

They move the child to the white room. Tests are carried out. Eventually the three doctors emerge.

'Inform the mother that the child was stillborn.'

'What if she asks to see it?'

'We had a stillborn late last night. The Fodor child. It will still be in the morgue. If she insists, show her that. But impress upon her that it is against hospital regulations.'

'Doctors! I'm sorry, but I find it hard to believe my ears! I must protest in the strongest possible terms!'

'Ms Shanahan, you saw the damage done to the nursery. We have no idea what it might be capable of . . .'

'It is not an it but a she, and she has a mother.'

'The mother is only fifteen years old. The likelihood is that the child would be put up for adoption in any event, especially considering the circumstances.'

'Yes, she is fifteen, and that is quite old enough for there to be a significant debate on the subject before a decision is reached. And the fact remains that such a decision is quite outside your authority.'

'She has a point, Alan.'

'She may have a point in normal circumstances, Scowcroft, but need I remind you that these are not normal circumstances? I want you both to understand that it is not I who have authorised this. There are higher powers involved. The instructions I have are quite clear. This is far from being an isolated case. I do not find what we have been asked to do particularly pleasant, but there are times when the greater good dictates . . .'

'The greater good? What about the good of this child?'

'It will be quite safe in our hands. If it . . .'

'If she!'

'. . . if *she* lives, and all goes well, there is no reason why she should not be put up for adoption at a later date. I can't believe you have a problem with this. We should have got used to it by this time. After all, Bindoon . . .'

'The Bindoon project was terminated nearly a decade ago. And how you can stand there and bring that up with the stories that have been emerging from that place . . .'

'You shouldn't believe everything you hear. And the case still remains that even were these abnormalities not exhibited the wounds the mother has inflicted upon herself are reason enough to have the child removed from her care.'

'We don't know that they were self-inflicted!'

'Ms Shanahan, please! I am prepared to discuss the situation to a certain extent, but I will not argue the toss over conclusions that are staring us in the face!'

Ms Shanahan fell silent.

'What do you . . . what do your instructions suggest that we do?' asked Scowcroft.

'Thank you, doctor. A sensible question at last. For the time being at least *she* is to be kept here under observation. Ms Shanahan, since you are obviously so concerned over her fate I will put you in charge of organising that. But don't get too involved. You must realise that in the final analysis it is out of our hands.'

The child survived and grew like a creeper into the corners of its room. When she touched her face she felt dry wall of plaster breeze-block brick and flaking paint. When she put her foot upon the ground she felt foundation, piles sunk deep into the earth, the rust and worm and clay that gripped and seeped about them. When she looked she saw light, surface, colour, texture. When she listened she heard the sounds that underpinned the silence: the footsteps in the corridors, the wails that pained the wards at night, the reassuring clink of glassware, the soft pops of hypodermics puncturing skin, the dry rasp of cells as they died and coagulated to scab a healing wound. When she ate she tasted the yellow mark of Africa, the bark of foreign valleys, the cloches of the Home Counties, the old earth of the Midlands, the rum-dark minerals of the steppes, the seething heat of Hyderabad, the sharp quick yeasts of German forests. When she bit she bit the bursting globe, when she pissed she pissed the oceans and the clouds. When she shat she shat the cosmos, her sphincter both channel and interrupt.

There was a wet-nurse whose milk was full of notes and chords. She talked to her but the words were very loud to her and she found each expression difficult to grasp so much did it speak of simple, discrete and alien things — for in her world there was nothing but relationships; it was a sponge of complications. Everything moved and nothing moved, except her limbs which grew almost as she watched, the baby wrinkles disappearing as if warmed from underneath. Sometimes she lay there floating in the brightness, sometimes it was dark, so dark she could feel the glint her eyes made in the void. Sometimes she spread faeces on the walls, writing herself in the spiral waves and patterns of the Belousov-Zabotinski reaction. Other times there was nothing to look at and she would amuse herself by running cross-catalators on her retinae and watching their pretty patterns.

She left her smells around the place, hid from them, followed them. The tracks she liked best were the ones left by the heat of her palms and soles upon the frigid linoleum. By lying on her stomach she could apperceive the differentials thus created fizz and hum to nothingness, segue back into the cool metastratum of the floor.

Big bang

By the time Route 66 Autos was shut down Judd thought about little except the dice. For whatever reason, the lot's financial usefulness had finally come to an end and Scofield sold all the cars to another dealer across town. After three days spent delivering the vehicles – more work than they'd done in months – the three employees all found themselves out of a job. The Bomb wasn't particularly bothered as his career as a DJ was taking off – he'd been doing three or four gigs a week for some months now and he no longer needed the day job. Lionel and Judd hung out together for a while, until Scofield found Lionel work fixing up the small fleet of delivery trucks that he had just purchased for the service laundry business that he was starting up in Venice Beach.

'If I hear of any kind of opening I'll call you right up,' Lionel promised Judd over lunch in a diner two streets from the ocean. 'I'll even mention it to Mr S. A lot of people work in that place. Something'll come up. Don't worry about it. Lionel'll sort you, mon, no problem.'

'Yeh, thanks, man. I knew I could count on you. Something'll come up.' Judd stirred sugar into his coffee with a plastic spoon and what Lionel had once told him about the history of sugar – that there was as much (if not more) blood on this white powder as there was on cocaine – flashed through his mind. He was going to miss working with the dread.

'What about your folks, mon? Can they help you out?'

'I dunno. I mean the old man got me the job at Route 66 in the first place. He's a friend of Irving's, see. I don't want to ask him again. I figure I want to sort something out for myself.' He hadn't told Lionel about the years of analysis, or that his mother was Melinda Volitia, and he had no intention of letting him or the Bomb find out about either. But it was true, he didn't want to turn to his parents. He had been avoiding them ever since he had moved out the year before and he didn't miss them too much. When he talked with his father on the phone Moses sounded shiny and busy. He spoke to Judd now as if Judd were finished with, a business deal that had been completed. Judd felt as though he had been turned out of the house in the same way that a washing machine is turned out of the factory – new, efficient, desirable, functional, designed to sit in its place and do its job. Fully readjusted.

As for his mother, she'd retired from acting and had taken up a full-time career in shopping. Whenever he spoke to her she always seemed to be just back from Rodeo Drive or somewhere like that, or off to have coffee at the latest café or for lunch at some little place down the coast. She seemed happy, though he wasn't really sure that he knew her well enough any more to be in a position to judge. She had become carefree, but in a studied way. He missed her moods, her mild depressions.

She and Moses had moved from Malibu to Beverly Hills and on the last occasion that Judd had paid them a visit Melinda had been throwing one of her 'infamous' pool parties. He had been troubled by the new crowd that his parents were mixing with; he got the feeling that many of their current acquaintances weren't altogether comfortable at the idea of a mixed-race family in their midst. Too many comments from behind the vodka tonics. But in some ways this was easier to cope with than the behaviour he'd sometimes encountered in the past when his mother's friends, enchanted as they were with his 'exoticism', had made occasional drunken efforts to seduce him. It had begun when he was about sixteen: hands – male and female – brushing his arm or butt a little too often, brazen stares, blown kisses. Melinda, when she witnessed it, had thought it wonderful that her son was this attractive and she teased him about it, but perhaps she wouldn't have been so keen if she'd been around the night Donna had got drunk and lured Judd out to the pool house where she'd practically assaulted him.

He sipped at the sweet coffee and looked out into the street, thinking to himself that fall didn't really happen in LA, that the seasons just moved from summer to less-summer and back again. 'I miss shooting craps already,' he complained to Lionel. The truth was that without his regular fix of the game, Judd was finding it difficult to continue to keep the psychoanalytic imprint that had been left in his brain subdued. With each additional day that passed Schemata's presence loomed a little larger in his thoughts. He was frightened. He didn't want to go back.

'Yeah. Me too. I have to work afternoons now. I've no use for that, mon.' Lionel grinned. 'You were just getting to be good, too.'

'Well, I reckon I'd learnt the ropes all right, but not much else.' He took another sip of his coffee. 'You seen the Bomb?'

'Yeh, saw him Sunday. He's got a gig this weekend, some party over in the valley. Great flyer – it's a picture of a nuclear warhead, and on it it says "The Bomb", and then underneath "The universe began with an explosion". Good, huh? D'ya wanna come along? I'll pick you up if you like?'

'Yeh, mebbe. I'll call you.'

'You should come. You know those Valley girls, mon, when those bitches are on heat you'd better watch out!' Lionel always talked like this about women. He had a pet dog he'd named Beaver.

'Women aren't just for sex!' retorted Judd self-righteously.

'Totally. They're there for cleanin' and cookin' too.' Lionel thought this was hilarious and throwing his head back let out a raucous laugh.

303

'Jesus,' said Judd. 'You're a lost cause.' They finished up their coffee and Judd came out with the question that he had come to see Lionel to ask. 'Know where I can get a game of craps?'

His friend eyed him suspiciously. 'What, that you can afford to get in on?'

'Yeh. Hey, I'm serious!'

'Not this side of Vegas, my friend.'

'Come on man, you must know of something. You taught me how to play the goddamned game. I just want to keep my hand in.'

'I've heard that before.'

'C'mon! Give me a break.'

Lionel swilled the request around in his head for a moment or two, picking out a toothpick from the plastic dispenser that stood on the table between the two of them and rolling it to and fro across his bottom lip with his tongue, a thin white line against the purple. 'Come to the party, Saturday. I'll introduce you to a guy I know. But you'd better be sure. These people don't fool around.'

'Whaddaya mean, "sure"?' said Judd, delighted. 'Of course I'm sure.'

'OK then, I'll see you Saturday. I'll pick you up around ten. And don't wear that godawful brown suit of yours or they won't let you in.'

The lambda parameter

They pulled up in front of a house that flashed lights and music like a close encounter. All along the street, cars were pulled up on to the sidewalk. Lionel popped a pill into his mouth and offered one to Judd, who declined, thinking to himself that Rastas weren't supposed to do chemicals. Lionel shrugged. 'Your mistake, mon.'

They entered the house by the side gate and came out by a pool lit by underwater lights which turned the water into an undulating cube of neon jelly. Two or three figures sculled across the iridescent surface, faults in a jewel. But most of the guests stood fully clothed on the patio or kept to the inside of the house where the music was loudest. Lionel immediately started saying hello to people and forgot about Judd, who felt lost and a little overdressed. He loitered around the pool, smiling stupidly at other guests. A woman approached him holding an unlit cigarette. Judd took out his lighter, lit it for her. She struck up a conversation and he looked around nervously over the girl's shoulder throughout, trying to decide whether or not she was coming on to him.

'Say, are you waiting for someone?' she asked.

'Er, no, I was just wondering where the bar was. I need a drink.'

'Drink's all in the kitchen. Just help yourself. It's through there.' She gesticulated languorously in the direction of the open french windows. The DJs had obviously just swapped over because instead of wailing guitars something darker and more bass-driven had started to thump out into the night.

'Thanks. Do you want something?'

'No, thanks. I'm tripping. Alcohol's so last year.'

'Oh, right. Guess I'm out of touch then.'

'Guess you are. Say, you wouldn't happen to have any pot on you, would you?'

'No, sorry.'

'No, thought not. Don't worry about it.' She paused, took a long drag on her Marlboro and stared intently into Judd's eyes, which would have been unnerving but for the fact that she seemed to be looking right through him. 'Go on then! Go and get your drink. See you later maybe.'

'Yeh, see you later.' He left her by the pool and went inside. The music was extremely loud and the air, what little of it there was, reeked of dope. All the furniture had been pushed back against the walls and the space was crammed with people. Although there didn't seem to be enough room for dancing almost everybody was. Those who weren't hung out on the stairs or sat legs up on the sofas. A strobe came on and cut time up into discrete segments, each one of which looked like a scene from Picasso's *Guernica*. Judd wondered where all the horses had come from and pushed on through in what he hoped was the direction of the kitchen.

Just as he reached it, a girl with a seven-inch afro and enormous breasts that had been vacuum-packed into a striped spandex T-shirt stumbled through the doorway and grabbed his shoulder to steady herself. He gawped as her chest undulated before him; she caught him staring and slapped him sharply across the face. 'Keep your filthy eyes to yourself, nigga!' she snapped.

'You tell him, girl!' another woman screeched to her rear and both of them burst out laughing. 'That's three now,' they agreed. Then they did a high five, put their arms around each other's waists and staggered off into the main fray.

An enormous man in combat fatigues who was propping up the door jamb grinned at Judd through a haze of smoke. 'Don't mind them, man, that's just Rita and Leona. Here, have a pull on this.' He passed Judd an enormous joint rolled in a cigar leaf and Judd took a few tokes before passing it back. It tasted good; the smoke was sweet on the back of his tongue and the hit buzzed him all over. Feeling reinforced, he squeezed past the donor into the kitchen.

Inside, a couple leant up against the refrigerator, kissing ostentatiously. Their tongues lapped in and out of each other's mouths, eels mating in an urn. To one side of the sink a tall man with a goatee was cracking jokes to two girls and on the other side two teenagers were chasing the dragon using a plastic straw and some silver foil stretched taut across the top of a glass. The light was bright and clinical, and everyone in the room looked ill. Any chance of finding something to drink in the fridge looked slim – there was no way that the couple was moving. Glancing around he saw that the sink was filled with water – water that had presumably once been ice – and that floating among the bottle tops and cigarette butts were a couple of cans of beer. He took them both, dried them off, stuck one in his jacket pocket and opened the other, then cleared out of the room, leaving the rest of them to it. As he went, the guy with the goatee made some remark about college kids which had the girls doubling up with laughter.

On the far side of the lounge Judd spotted the Bomb. He was bent over a pair of decks, an enormous pair of headphones on his head, mixing two records together. With quick flicks of his wrist he scratched the right hand one to and fro, creating a melody off the cuff, while with his left hand he used the pitch control of the second deck to control the tempo of the bass. Judd watched with admiration as his friend improvised a perfect series of rhythms and effects, never once dropping a beat. The dance floor, which until now had been lazy and haphazard, quickly began to energise. The less committed dancers peeled away and filtered upstairs or outside. Someone threw the french windows right open, letting in a gust of fresh air, and a couple of breakdancers colonised the area immediately in front of them. The Bomb dialled the tempo up a notch, fully aware of what was happening. He let the bass run a little, allowing the floor to settle in, letting everybody expand into the extra space. Then as soon as he felt they were ready he snapped off the sound, gave one bar of silence, then plunged straight into a new and massive beat, pumping the volume sliders straight up as he did so. The floor underwent an immediate phase transition: its various factions and speeds coalesced like whipping cream. The dancers, previously a fairly heterogeneous group, began to move together. Even Judd was caught up in it, and he downed his beer, tucked his jacket beneath a table and began to gyrate. What had been a bizarre and unwieldy gathering came alive: it became a party. Time slowed down and began to loop as the scene created its own temporality, constructed a bubble that could bob oblivi- ously on top of the chattering surfs of the week. This is what everyone had come for, this take-off. Now nothing external existed; the outside world could be forgotten for as long as the effect could be sustained.

Judd lost track of how long he danced. Those not dancing had been supporting the dancers as if they were marathon runners, handing them drinks, passing them spliffs and cigarettes, cutting up lines of coke on mirrors which were then circulated through the fray. He partook of everything, found himself adopted by one of the groups that had formed like benzene rings, grooved down so far that he didn't realise how absolutely off his face he was. When Lionel appeared at his shoulder and yelled something incoherent in his ear all he thought it necessary to do was to nod wildly and mouth 'Great party! Great party!' and try to encourage him to dance.

'NO, MON, LISTEN! THAT GUY IS HERE, THE ONE I TOLD YOU ABOUT.'

'WHICH GUY?'

'THE CRAPS GUY – DON'T YOU WANT TO MEET HIM?'

Abruptly the rhythms of the day-to-day rushed back to Judd, as if he'd just answered the front door to the police. Suddenly he felt drunk and slightly dizzy. 'SHIT, YEAH. HANG ON, I'M COMING.' Lionel led the way across the room and up the stairs, and Judd followed him closely, trying not to get sucked back into the dance. The stairway lights were on and he blinked as the two of them picked their way up them, using the tiny gaps between the seated people like stepping stones. At length they reached one of the bedrooms and with the music below vibrating the floor beneath them they entered.

Inside, the room seemed like the calm at the eye of a storm. There were four or five people in there, in various attitudes of repose. The two on the bed were smoking a tall hookah that stood by them on the floor; the others sat around on large cushions. Raga played softly above the now distant sound of the Bomb's bass.

Lionel sat down and Judd followed suit. To begin with no one said anything, then one of the men offered Judd a beer, produced from a chipped polystyrene cooler that sat beside him. Judd took it and lit a cigarette, trying to fit in a little more with this new vibe. His friend began to skin up while talking in a low voice to the skinny Chinese man he had sat down next to, who was much older than anyone else in the room.

'Been dancing?' the girl on the bed asked Judd.

'Yeah. It was good. Hot, though.' He tugged at his shirt to illustrate: it was soaked through with sweat and clung to his body.

'Looked it,' said the girl. Lionel glanced up at her and leant over.

'Judd, this is Mr Chang. I've had a word with him and he would be pleased to let you into one of his games.' That was quick. He hadn't been expecting that.

'Thanks,' he said, too loudly, not knowing what else to say. Mr Chang bowed forward slightly and smiled Orientally. Judd beamed back, unable to control his facial muscles. His mind was racing. What had he taken on the dance floor? He had no idea, but his whole body seemed electrified. He felt supremely confident. Nothing, he knew, could go wrong. 'Yeah,' he said again, 'thanks. Hope you know what you're letting yourself in for!'

The Chinaman looked at Judd closely, his gaze undermining the young American's drug-maintained composure. Judd felt his cheeks begin to warm. The stranger immediately spotted his embarrassment and, in a voice as dry as the desert and spilling words like grains of sand, offered to save him. 'Lionel knows the address, Mr Axelrod. We look forward to seeing you. Next week-end, I hope.'

'Next weekend,' said Judd, committing himself at that moment. 'For sure.'

Suddenly there was a commotion in the hallway and a few seconds later a tall white hippy burst in through the door. 'The cops are here,' he gasped. 'They're breaking up the party.' Everyone jumped to their feet in a frenzy of tidying and stashing and emptying of pockets. The music had stopped and Judd headed for the door to see what was going on. A strange mixture of apathy and panic welled up the stairs. Judd looked round for Lionel and Mr Chang, wondering what they were going to do. Lionel was there, calmly emptying the ashtray out of the window and sipping from a bottle of Scotch, but Mr Chang, rather mysteriously, had already disappeared.

Under observation

They kept her under observation, put her in capsules, covered her in electrodes (just like poor Laika, though they didn't launch Emma into space), put capsules in her, gave her tests, taught her to speak, took blood samples, tissue samples (in a room with no windows), made her say 'ahhhh', taught her to read, to write, sometimes (irresponsibly) gave her a hug, got her to run, to walk, to drool, to scream, got her to tell them, to stand in X-ray machines, to submit to their CAT scan, their PET scan, their MRI, to let them shave her head and insert needles and probes, to simulate thought with machines (move her arm, move her leg, this is red, I'm afraid, this is pain), moved around her, all white coats and eyes, gave her drugs for an illness, kept her well-balanced (diazepam, nitrazepam, flurazepam, Largactil, Thorazine, LSD, mescaline, phencyclidine, amphetamine, chlorpromazine, lithium, ibuprofen, aspirin), took her for walks, left her alone, filmed her, recorded her, submitted her to scrutiny, performed exploratory surgery upon her, fed her, watered her, let her watch TV, let her watch TV, let her watch TV, restrained her, worried over her, obtained funding for her, compared her, contrasted her, ignored her, forgot about her, remembered her, discussed her, trusted her, disgusted her, frightened her, feared her, fitted her into projections and theories and statistics and charts, traced her, retraced her, raced her, put her in mazes and labyrinths, told her to find her way out, told her to find her way out, told her to find her way. So she started to, she started to, she started to look for it.

The gambler

Once he had become an initiate of the Chinaman's gambling dens, Judd never held down a proper job again. The other players, the men and women he encountered in the secret basements, in the back rooms of clubs, in the refitted apartments, were always on the look-out for a body to run the odd errand – make a couple of deliveries, stand in a phone box for a couple of hours waiting for a call, mind a warehouse for a week or two – and they generally paid handsomely for the favour. There were offers of heavier things but Judd always turned them down; he didn't want trouble, just some easy cash to help him make a stake. And most of the time he did all right. He was a cautious player, at least in the beginning, and he neither won nor lost large amounts. After the question of keeping Schemata at bay, his real interest was not the money but the shapes and patterns of the various games on offer. The 'open' games were best: craps, roulette, blackjack, Hold 'Em, games where you could see how things progressed from one stage to another. On occasion he went down to the track and played the horses but he never got into it – you had to know too much about the turf, the conditions and the animals themselves, as well as all the double play that went on behind the scenes. It was too much. With cards or craps, as long as you knew that the pack wasn't stacked nor the dice loaded you could get by, and Judd quickly developed a feel for these things. Because he always looked for patterns he could spot the lopsided rhythms introduced into the flow of play by a bent deck or a weighted wheel a mile off. Other players would notice it too, though not always consciously. They would become uneasy and bet out of character unless they were fresh to the scene, in which case they would just lose. But soon Judd could play a straight or bent game with equal aplomb and after he'd been at it six months most nights he was coming out evens at worst.

When Moses and Melinda called to check up on him he told them he had gone into partnership with a friend and they were running a night-club together. The lie had a kind of twisted truth to it for the Bomb was a rising star on the club scene and the nights when he wasn't gambling Judd would act as sidekick, organising taxis, carrying records, doing sound checks and so on – all the things that Lionel could no longer do because of his full-on day job. The Bomb used to tease him about it whenever they saw each other, *Hey Lionel! When you gettin' married? How's the mortgage? You still screwin' the bank manager's daughter?* But Lionel didn't take it to heart; he'd kind of got into his work and had some people under him now and was earning a reasonable whack. Was even talking about flying his family over to LA. And anyway, where was the fun in lugging the Bomb's record cases around? After all, he still got into the clubs for free whenever he wanted, which had been the main aim in the first place.

But Judd was happy to do the legwork. It gave him a chance to get into a scene which otherwise would have passed him by. He didn't often dance like he had at the party in the Valley but he loved to stand by the decks for a night, sucking on a bottle of beer and watching the bodies gyring and sweating before him get sliced into segments and stretched across space and time by the music and the lights. Watching the floors like he did, he began to learn how the Bomb played them, how he'd probe the mood with a couple of preliminary tracks, how he'd coax the crowd into a state where he could do something with them. On the best nights he'd pick up the groove straight away and rush with it, it would almost be like he was dancing himself; he'd reel off records in a sequence that you couldn't imagine could be any different, it would be as if he'd worked it all out beforehand, and of course some of it he had.

Judd couldn't gamble on those nights, didn't have the energy, though sometimes after the club had closed he'd turn up at a game and just sit in and watch. It seemed to him that there were parallels between a game and a club. The cards or the dice were, in a way, the DJ: they created intensities and potentials and so manipulated the moods of the participants, just as the Bomb did. The gamblers were like dancers out there to capture and surf, hoping they could fit their moves to the rhythms of the night, sniff out a winning streak and play into it, sit on it. Judd felt this was more than a metaphor. Gambling was the lizard's dance, the dance of the desert. He swore he could feel its rhythms pulsing away there deep in his limbic system whenever he played, a dim and distant song the words of which had long been forgotten, but whose tune was still hummed by the neural circuits that were part of the biological stratum deposited countless millennia previously by his reptilian ancestors. At this point the idea became nebulous and obscure, but what was certain was that there was more to gambling than chance and will, the techniques that Lionel and the Bomb had always used. Chance and will, Judd thought. Chance and will, the deuce, the loser's pair. There were patterns here, and patterns could be studied, manipulated, choreographed.

In the clubs, then, boys and girls spun and weaved in front of him. Their pink-copper-orange-brown bodies were young and unblemished, and they ignored him. But in the gambling dens middle-aged women whose bodies had spread like bursting sacks of wheat eyed him between hands, while they lit their cigarettes and placed them between their wet lips, red and pinched like vulvas. And the men, too, long since freed by the night and the cards and the booze of any moral façade, would watch his pecs and biceps flex against his shirt as he threw his dice or stretched to reach a deck of cards and suck absently at the flaps of their cheeks.

This was the life in which the offers were made and he sank deeper into it. The dice, the cards, they became his machines for mapping the contours of coincidence, and of his mind. They became the tools of his philosophy, helping him both to understand the world and what Schemata had done to him. Those limbic rhythms seemed to be deeper, more important, more powerful psychological structures than those the analyst had imposed. And those rhythms were part of a terrain across which each game would crawl, a desert creature in search of warmth, of shelter, of something to quell the naggings of its stomach.

The lizard, 'find the lizard', his own secret code for spotting the patterns in a game. It became his little mantra, something he would whisper to himself in the lost hours past midnight, those hours for which there were no maps, only insinuations. Once, the day after a particularly successful night, he drove down to Rodeo Drive himself and picked out a gold ring in the shape of a gecko. It had emeralds for eyes and he never took it off. A mineral deposit laid down around his finger, it became part of him and helped to remind him how he was remaking himself. It wasn't a charm and it wasn't a token, it was just something that was his and his alone, his own private symbol, his own private joke, something that he had built which had nothing to do with his parents, with Schemata, or with Jennifer. He'd had it with all of that, he didn't want anything to do with any of it. When he thought of Jennifer now it was not with longing but with anger. She was just the same as all the rest and they had all taken from him, all of them, they had just ripped bits off him and passed him down the line. It was a country of greed he had come from and it was a country of greed he would enter. He didn't need a passport, he had citizenship. He would pass through the iterated nights, the numberless rooms, the nameless games and the faceless players, and it would not matter to him whether he made money, it would not make any difference. Because he knew, *he knew*, about the way things came out of nothing to coalesce and exist, and then just as quickly disappear to leave one man with empty pockets and another with a head full of corrosive joy. That's what he, Judd Axelrod, had got out of all of this. That's what he had *learnt*. The numbers, the colours thrown up by the dice, the cards, they could be a zephyr or a sandstorm, could lull all the players to sleep or rip the roofs right off their huts and none of it made any difference, this was just the way it was. Forget life in the jungle, this was life in the desert, where you had to fuel yourself every day on the heat of the sun – the rush of the game – if you wanted to make it through the cold of the night. The desert, where you had to fight every minute to survive. Judd had discovered a different logic from that imposed upon him by Schemata and his father, one far more subtle and complex, that grew out of the world rather than imprinting its tenets upon it. And he would use it to cut himself free from his past, to take proper control of his life for the very first time.

Green regression

But unfortunately for Judd, his life didn't want to play ball. The first unusual event occurred in the basement of the M Club, on Twenty-fifth and W. He'd played here before, but not often. The front was a lame piano bar full of hookers; you sat at the bar and asked for Leon and were shown through a padded leather door into an office, where you were frisked and led through another door marked EXIT. It was mainly roulette and blackjack, though he knew they hosted the occasional poker game for big money, way out of his league. Tonight it was the usual clientele – small-time crooks, pimps, businessmen, professional gamblers keeping their hand in. Judd played a few rounds of cards but it didn't feel right, so he moved to one of the two roulette tables. He spotted the lizard almost immediately and it scuttled obediently across the board and wrapped itself around his constellation of bets. But then – and this was the weird thing, the state change – it stayed with him all night. Instead of him trying to follow it, to anticipate and second guess it, it was following him. He'd place his bets, the croupier would spin the wheel and it would be there, waiting for him. He couldn't believe it at first, but then he began to feel the rhythms that he had sensed before and almost to hear the song of the sand, alien sounds from the deep past that rose up out of his blood. He started to shake and stared unblinkingly at the baize, overwhelmed by its colour, until his eyes began to bulge. When he finally looked up everything in the room was tinged with green – people's skin, their drinks, the lights and the smoke that hung in the air – as if he had just taken a huge hit of amyl. The other players glanced at him uncomfortably and the man who oversaw the game whispered something to one of his men.

That night he went home with his pockets full and his head spinning, to dream of a paradise of hot rocks, cool fissures and plentiful flies. The next night, at a different venue, he played craps, but it was the same story. And the next night, and the night after that. But then, as abruptly as it began, his winning streak was brought to an end.

At first light the morning after his fourth successful night a storm blew up. It whipped through the city, turning the underside of all the leaves upwards and baring them to what little sky managed to creep down through the eddying banks of smog. It was as if the branches themselves called out to the foliage being torn from them, so windswept were they by the unrelenting gusts; like the old women of a pillaged town they raged along the streets, screaming at their oppressors who gleefully fled to the hills, having killed all the menfolk, raped all the girls and stolen or spoilt all the food.

Judd had planned to sleep late but was woken when one of his shutters worked loose from its hinges and whipped around, smashing the window it was supposed to protect. Trying to secure it he cut his hand; thick blood eased its way out of the sharp, deep split the glass had made in the web of skin stretched between his thumb and index finger. He left a small trail of splayed crimson droplets on the floor-boards as he ran across the room to grab a towel with which to staunch the flow.

All day he couldn't settle, the wind disturbed him. He watched TV and played some records but it didn't work and eventually he gave up on the apartment and went outside for a walk, deciding to brave the weather. He caught a bus downtown to where the office blocks trapped the currents of air. The wind flicked rubbish down the chasms that served as streets, nomad articles that plagued pedestrians and hunted for homes in the bushes and gutters, in the dead zones created by cars and the corners of buildings. Clumps of detritus lifted and spun as draughts clipped the local geometries and fell into secret patterns. Everywhere these vortices lay in wait, invisible, cunning, virtual. Judd strode along, blasts of air drying his eyes in their sockets. He sought refuge in a record store, flipping through the racks without buying anything. Selecting one or two things he knew from the Bomb's collection he went to a booth and gave them a listen, but they didn't sound the same without the mixing and the scratching and the dance floor full of people.

He bought a newspaper, nearly lost it to the wind, then sat in a diner trying to read it over coffee and suffering from the slight light-headedness that comes with killing time. Everyone around him was at work, their eyes on the clock all day long, their pulses beating fast and irregularly, shackled to the strange biomechanical rhythms that between them they'd created. Judd wasn't a part of it and it gave him a headache, watching them dart up and down the sidewalk outside. He felt like a rogue corpuscle that had got stranded in the most minute capillary of some far-flung and forgotten tissue of the body, his very chemical processes inhibited by his distance from the heart, the flesh around him greying, mutated by cancers. When he returned to his apartment, wired from the coffee he had drunk but still sleepy, he thought of calling up Lionel at work. But it was too much effort. And what would he say? He'd have to think of something and he was too tired. He drew the bedroom blinds, curled up on his bed and fell asleep.

Outside, the wind was still whipped up like crazy and it brought on precarious dreams of ancient landscapes and saurian economies. But when Judd awoke he remembered nothing. Instead he felt suddenly and totally alert, completely clarified, as if the nap had rinsed out his mind. His hand had scabbed and the throbbing had subsided. It was dark outside and when he checked his watch it was ten o'clock. The storm seemed to have blown itself out. He had a raging thirst and drank down a root beer that he found in the fridge and took a shower, but still his throat felt parched. There was a game that night at Geraldo's and he figured he'd go, he was in the mood for it.

Geraldo's was a den above a travel agents just off Santa Monica Boulevard and the game there had been a regular fixture for months. With customary caution, Judd parked a couple of blocks away and walked the final stretch. But when he reached the door and rang there was no answer. Bemused, he stood and pressed the buzzer repeatedly, listening to it bleating away deep inside the building. He was sure he'd got the right day. Eventually he gave up and drove to a couple more places, but it was the same story all over: games which had been going on for ever had vanished. He tried the hotel where Harvey had been running a craps shoot in a second-floor room three nights a week for five years now, but all he got was a confused Swedish couple suffering from jet lag.

The big operation in the warehouse on the outskirts of Watts, where you could get craps, roulette, poker, the works, was still going on, but Peri, the Mexican bouncer, would not let him in. 'Sorry, man, but you can' go in there.'

'What's the problem, Peri?'

317

'There's nuthin' in there for you, my fren'.'

'Peri! It's me! It's Judd for chrissake. C'mon, quit foolin' around.'

Judd pushed up the bouncer's arm and tried to walk past him, but the Mexican grabbed him by the collar and twisted, pulling Judd back around to face him. 'No entry,' he hissed. 'Unnerstan'?'

The stitches on the collar of Judd's shirt began to pop as Peri increased the pressure. 'Yeh, sure, sure,' he gasped, turning a deep shade of purple. 'Hey, you're choking me, you're choking me!' Peri let him go and his hands went to his neck. 'Christ almighty. What the fuck is this all about?'

'Sorry, man. You're not welcome any more. I'm doin' you a favour by tellin' you now. Don' come back.'

Judd had never thought about the various games he was involved in as particularly interconnected. He'd started off at Mr Chang's place, someone he'd met there had introduced him to somewhere else and it had gone on from there. Each venue seemed to have its own isolated scene, his own movements one of the few links between them. But the unanswered doors and vacated rooms could only make sense if the games he'd known were all part of something much larger, all of which was perhaps controlled by the Chinaman. Judd began to imagine the games as nodes on a thin and fragile web suspended beneath the structures of society and the law. By winning he constituted a threat and as such his access to this carefully maintained network had now been denied. The structure which had seemed so open, which had welcomed him day and night while he had observed its codes he now saw from a different perspective, one which made it appear rigorous, tight-knit, more like a cocoon, each of its earlier functions inverted to repel outsiders. Each group of regulars was suddenly a platoon, every clandestine door a battlement, every grapevine a two-way conduit for information.

Over the ensuing nights he tried various other venues but the results were no better and often far worse. On the last occasion he got a black eye and a split lip for his pains and was told he was lucky still to be solvent – and alive. Most people weren't allowed to win. It was only because Mr Chang liked him that his winnings had not been repossessed, but that would change fast if he didn't stop causing trouble.

He finally took the hint and decided to give it up. Walking back through town that night, totting up the rejections in his mind, he stopped at a bar and got himself properly drunk. It wasn't fair! It just wasn't fucking fair! What had he done to deserve this? He felt like he'd been given a chance, just one, to pull himself out the mire of shit in which, through little fault of his own, he'd been dumped and now it had been taken away. Already Schemata bubbled in the back of his mind.

After his eighth or ninth whisky he started to talk with the barman, who listened out of a sense of professional duty. Around 2 a.m., morose and depressed, he tried to call up Lionel from the phone in the corridor where the yellow boxes of beer were stacked up to the ceiling, seeping a smell of hops and damp cardboard, but he got the Ansaphone and didn't leave a message. Back at the bar someone bought him drinks and laid a hand on his arm. The hand bothered him but he couldn't see a way to do anything about it; interestingly, he could no longer tell exactly what it was he was drinking. There seemed to be lots of people around that he vaguely knew. He liked this bar; it was friendly. He'd come back (though he still wasn't sure about this hand). He was thinking of saying something to its owner when someone called him nigger, they definitely called him nigger, and why would they do that in the middle of such a friendly bar? He'd have to do something about that.

And then there was a fight and when he came to he was in the back of a prowl car and being driven downtown. He thought he was dreaming and tried to get out which gave the cop riding shotgun the opportunity he'd been looking for to rod him in the stomach with his night-stick, which only prompted him to vomit through the grille and all down the back of the driver's seat. That got him beaten up properly, by the side of the road.

By the next morning Melinda had got wind of the affair (a mother's intuition?) and sent Michael – no longer her official PA but still a trusted friend – down to the station to handle the situation and to make sure that it stayed out of the press. Judd had never liked Michael, who was practically albino and always looked as if someone had just rammed a battery up his arse which, knowing Michael, thought Judd evilly, they probably had. Michael, however, had always been good at his job. He managed to persuade the police to drop the resisting-arrest jacket, got Judd released on a drunk and disorderly, and drove the prodigal son back home. During the journey his self-satisfaction oozed through the car like an enormous cowpat, impinging on Judd far more than the awful hangover or the flesh-memories of baton and fist.

Judd tried his best to ignore Michael's chatter. All he wanted to do was wallow in thoughts of anger and remorse. He looked down at the lizard ring. It had been damaged in one of the previous night's struggles and the gecko's expression was bent into a mocking smirk. Fate was heaping insult upon injury. Judd pulled the ring from his finger, depressed the button to lower the automatic window and threw the offending object from the car.

'What was that?' asked Michael, ever watchful.

'I thought I was going to be sick.'

'Oh, whatever you do don't be sick in the car. Melinda will kill you. She's going to have your balls as it is, you lucky boy.'

'She's my mother, you arsehole.'

'Um, maybe, but we all know what Freud had to say about that now, don't we?' Judd picked a pair of sunglasses off the dashboard and put them on. He couldn't remember what month it was, but as far as he could tell it was summer all over again.

Order out of chaos

Michael pulled in at Judd's parents' driveway and leant out the window to operate the carport door with his ultrasound remote. 'Batteries are low,' he remarked, somehow managing to make even that comment sound facetious. Judd limped in through the side door and slipped up the stairs without going through the main body of the house. He headed straight for his mother's bathroom, locked the door, turned on both the taps, and raided the medicine cabinet for drugs.

Melinda, who had been notified of her son's arrival by Michael, came up the stairs and rapped on the door. 'Judd! Are you in there?'

'No.'

'Come on out.'

'I'm in the bath.'

'What in hell's name do you think you were up to?'

'Mom, I just got drunk.'

'How on earth did you manage . . .'

'I don't remember.'

'You're a disgrace. Wait till your father gets home. And I want you looking respectable. We have a party this afternoon and for once I expect you to be there. It's about time you paid some attention to family events. Dr Schemata will be coming and I don't want him to think that you've let him down. I've asked Michael to go out and buy you a set of clean clothes. He'll leave them outside the door. And you'll wear them, please.'

Judd groaned loudly, which seemed to satisfy his mother. He heard her heels clicking away along the parquet landing, brisk and efficient, possibly even sexy (he felt a fresh wave of nausea at the thought) then got into the bath and slid down beneath the surface of the water, his nostrils a dark island in a sea of white suds, an ailing crocodile nestled in slack water by rapids.

By the time he emerged the guests were already arriving. The tension between mother and son eased, now that there was no chance of a confrontation and besides, once Melinda saw the state of her son's face – its bruises nicely set off by the deep reds and purples of the Hawaiian shirt that Michael had thoughtfully provided – her anger dissipated and the mild annoyance she exhibited for the rest of the day was kept up mainly for the sake of appearances. Judd put on the sunglasses he'd stolen from Michael's car to hide his swollen eye, munched another Valium and wandered out by the pool.

He was picking at the trays of hors d'oeuvres and trying to

avoid conversation when the ex-PA sidled over and pressed a large cocktail into his hand. 'Hair of the dog,' he whispered loudly. 'Patent hangover cure. Drink up!' He patted Judd on the shoulder and moved away. Judd sipped at the dark liquid suspiciously, but it was good and he drank it down. Whatever it was, it seemed to help and he later remembered it as possibly the first really pleasant thing that Michael had done for him since he'd been a child. It seemed to be a day for firsts.

The flow of guests increased. At first they simmered incoherently around the pool and patio, trying to choose between bar, buffet and view, but gradually they settled down into clusters and rings, stabilising to form an atmosphere. Newcomers bounced between the groups like lethargic pinballs until they found one whose structure was open to their particular chemistry. Occasionally a guest came into a group and broke its harmony, causing the whole to fragment and its members to wander off, free to be sucked into another attractor. Yet others were catalysts or viruses, moving nomadically, inciting and restructuring, leaving traces of their conversation to ferment in their wake.

Then Moses appeared looking, it has to be said, really fantastic. He was wearing a beautiful pair of hand-tooled brown leather square-toed slippers with cream tongues, a magnificently tailored pair of mildly flared peach pants that hugged his thighs and arse like an attentive dancing partner and a short-sleeved silk shirt, cream with maroon stitching. His hair was immaculate and around his neck was a single, unobtrusive gold chain which offset the gold Rolex on his wrist. He had returned to IBM in 1978 (not long after the missing-computer incident at DEC, though nothing was ever proved) to work on the launch of the PC. The party was one of a series he was holding, still flushed with the product's immense success (and the immense salary he now enjoyed as a result – it had been his idea to use the Chaplin movie *Modern Times* as the advertising hook, presenting the computer not as just another tool but as something which freed the worker from the industrial metre that had come to dominate so many lives. And Moses believed in this image – the computer had freed him, hadn't it? Why shouldn't it free others too?).

He shook hands with everybody, grinning from ear to ear until he got to Judd, to whom he said in passing through the mask of a frown: 'I'll deal with you later. Until then just make sure you're polite to our guests.'

But instead of putting the fear into Judd, as his father's admonishments usually did, the comment made his blood run hot. If there was one thing he was sick of it was Moses's automatic assumption that he was in the wrong. From his mother he could take it; she always forgave him as soon as she'd ticked him off, but the old man couldn't do that, no, for him it was all bound up with this fucking black thing, about how Judd had to prove himself not just for himself – which would at least have been understandable – but so that Moses could stand alongside white people and think: my son is better than yours. Judd had plenty of time for black solidarity, that was all fine, but this wasn't that, this was bullshit. His father didn't give a shit about Africa as far as he was aware, or about the problems in the ghettos. His father only gave a shit about himself, that's right, and he wasn't going to put up with being used for Moses's ends any more. No one had even thought to ask him why what had happened had happened; there was no one around to whom it seemed to have occurred that he might have been provoked, that he might just have been defending himself, that most of the damage had been done by the cops. And although he had no intention of letting anyone know anything about the situation which had precipitated his drunkenness, the fact that the violence itself had been sparked by a racist remark was enough to make the riptide of self-righteousness drag him right along with it.

He was busy with these thoughts when from behind him a sinewy voice spoke his name. It was a voice so familiar and so internalised that he almost didn't recognise it, coming as it seemed to from his dreams rather than from the external world. But as he turned and saw to whom it belonged, a laugh bubbled up from his throat. The last time they had met it had been the psychoanalyst who had been the taller. 'Why do you laugh?' Schemata said immediately. 'Have I said something amusing?'

The doctor had spoken in his far-away tone, the one he used to suggest that his mind was not only dealing with the present

323

situation but was contemplating several other problems at the same time, the consideration of any one of which was far beyond the capability of the average human being.

'No, I er . . .' Judd paused right there. Schemata was standing with the sun behind him and its light shone hard into his eyes. Even with the sunglasses he was wearing it was difficult to see the psychoanalyst's face. Memories of that darkened room washed over him in waves. He almost began to speak, to tell the doctor everything. The grid left by this man across his being made him want to talk, to disclose. The light bathed the two of them, he was bathed in Schemata's light, Schemata shone up at him. He was ready to say the words that would let this man in again, let him flush the lattice clean and take away the agony of the previous night, the loneliness of the life he had led for the last two years. But as he opened his mouth to speak the pain in his face surged up through the layer of Valium and a giddiness swamped his body and the sun was no longer pure but was instead the anus of the solar system, spraying its light like diarrhoea all over Schemata, all over the guests, all over the city which lay beyond the railing beyond the pool. The pain in his face, the bruises on his ribs, these felt like the only things he had ever known. Where was he? What was he doing? To Schemata, to his father, to his mother, to Michael and to all of these people he was a person defined by an event that had taken place over a decade previously, one that he could barely remember, a mere conjunction of skin and skin and this . . . paltry thing somehow justified his life being placed in the hands of this maniac? This monster whose minted voice had whispered into his ear a false tale of identity for year upon year upon year?

But there was something else, too, the rank violence of the sun spoke of something else, and it had more to do with the loud nights handing records to the Bomb, with the hours spent chasing the lizard in dark, smoke-filled rooms, with all the things he had fallen into out of pure boredom than with his mother, his father, Schemata or even, yes even with Jennifer, that hollow name from all those years ago. 'I got drunk and fell over,' he said, making it sound like a lie. 'I got drunk and fell over. You'll have to excuse me Dr Schemata. I promised my mother I would help the caterers

find everything they needed, and I believe they have just arrived.'
And he turned away, although not before noticing with enormous
satisfaction the tic of surprise which leapt to life across Schemata's
face and which was just as quickly plastered over with an expression
of effusive calm as the doctor assimilated the blip into that Great
Order of Things which over the years he had painstakingly carved
and which he carried in his mind like a talisman, like a lens.

Back inside the house Judd went straight to one of the toilets
and threw up. As he vomited he thought of Jennifer and his spasms
seemed to him the ejection of the last vestige of her from his body,
the final traces of her from his self, the last memories of her from
his flesh. As he spattered the porcelain with his bile it came to him
like a foul bubble of ancient gas glubbing up from a deep sea
trench that he had kept the kernel of a wish folded away in some
forgotten spangle of his cortex, a wish that one day she would
contact him, just find a way to speak to him, to tell him anything
at all. He thought of the time he had spent watching television in
the hope that impossibly, on the far side of the world, she was
watching the same thing, and he realised how this had affected so
much of what he did, how it had helped reconfigure every thought
he'd had about himself, how it had influenced his shape in the
world as though he were an object on a lathe. But now the
spasming of his stomach seemed to eradicate her from him, and
with his belly emptied and endorphins flooding through his system
his mind began to clear a little. He stood up, and it was as if he'd
been walking with a limp for years and years, only finally to look
down and discover a pebble lodged in the sole of his shoe.

He cleaned his teeth and wandered back outside in search of
Michael and another cocktail. He found both, but no sooner had
he taken a couple of sips of the latter than he was accosted by a
figure from the more recent past: Irving Scofield. Judd hadn't seen
him since that afternoon in the repair lot – when Route 66 Autos
had been closed down, Scofield had dealt with the matter by
telephone. But he had always liked the man and he was the first
person Judd had been pleased to see all day.

'Nice sunglasses, son,' Scofield said sarcastically.

'Yeh, well, I borrowed them. Sun's pretty bright, you know,' he replied pointlessly. They were standing in the shade of an awning that had been unfurled at the house end of the terrace. Most of the guests were at the far end, on the other side of the pool, on the section of patio that was cantilevered out over the hillside. A grey haze of smog hung low over the city and spoilt the view.

'Miasma of Babylon,' said Scofield to himself.

'What?' asked Judd, not sure if he'd heard correctly.

'This city. Even the air is predicated on corruption.' The businessman rolled the words off his tongue with a thick back spin that made them weighty, lazy and hard to get the measure of. Judd was surprised to hear him speak in this way, saying things that might have come out of Lionel's mouth.

There was a bowl of cherries on the table beside them; Scofield selected one and picked it up by its stalk. It was fat and pink, and he held it in front of his face the better to examine it. Satisfied with his choice, he gently gripped it between his teeth, pulled the stalk free with a sharp little tug and bit into the fruit until it popped, only then enveloping it with his lips. Judd listened to him chew and watched as he looked around for somewhere to spit the pit. His eyes settled upon a pot in which a small orange tree was growing, and he propelled the seed into it at high speed and with a practised accuracy. 'Nice cherry,' he said. 'Your folks sure know how to throw a party.'

'Mr Scofield . . .' Judd began, but Scofield cut him off.

'Now Judd,' he said, 'I hope you weren't too upset at me closing down the business and cutting you out of a job like that?'

'No, no.' Judd shrugged. 'These things happen.'

'You're getting by OK, I hope. Found anything else yet?'

'Not yet, but I've got a few ideas.'

Scofield suddenly leant in close and began scrutinising the younger man's face. 'Police do that to you?'

'Uh huh.' He didn't ask Scofield how he knew. It seemed natural that Scofield would know. He had a knowledgeable air about him.

'I hear you've got the touch with the dice,' Scofield said quietly.

Now Judd really was surprised. 'Where d'you hear that?' he asked, trying to keep his voice firm but its modulation still betraying him.

'Same place I heard that the cops treated you worse than the boys who laid you out in that bar.' Judd's heart began to beat faster, and his limbs felt hollow. 'I hear other things, too.'

'Such as?' asked Judd, his hostility beginning to break out again, like hives.

'Like some of what happened to your face happened before you even got to the bar. Like you can't get a game any more.'

'So you're in with the Chinaman, are you?'

'I'm nothing to do with any of it,' Scofield insisted, turning towards the view again. 'Everything I do is completely legitimate. I want you to know that. I wouldn't want you to think your father associates with hoodlums. I simply make it my business to know, that's all. Moses has asked me to look out for you and I owe him a favour, and that's all I've been doing. But I've got some advice for you. You've done well. Not many people your age can get involved in that . . . in that . . . milieu, and do so well. Not many at all. People tell me you're a natural, that you've got the potential of a great player. People who know. But the scene you've been in, it's small time, it's for losers, it can't support people like you. You want my advice, take a holiday. Get out of the state for a while. See what the big wide world is like. I've got friends in Vegas and Reno. Go there, look them up.' He paused to light a cigarette. 'What do you say?'

'I say get off my back. I don't need anyone to keep an eye on me. I've had enough of that shit.'

'There's keeping an eye and keeping an eye, my boy,' huffed Scofield, unimpressed. 'You know where to find me if you change your mind.'

'Fuck you, daddy-o.'

'I understand how you feel . . .'

'No you *don't*, no you fucking don't, you haven't had your life sold down the river by your fucked-up parents, you haven't had your mind fucked up by some jive-arse shrink, you, you, all of you haven't got the faintest fucking idea about how I feel!'

'No, you're right, we don't.' It was an aikido throw: it deflected Judd's energy and left him flailing inconsequentially.

With nothing to strike against, he could think of nothing more to say. 'Yeah, right,' was the best he could manage. 'I'm off for another drink.' And he slapped off across the patio in his thongs, leaving Scofield to contemplate the bowl of cherries and the view.

Moses insisted that his son spend the night in Beverly Hills, so that he could 'see something of him, for a change' and so it wasn't until the following day that Judd returned to his apartment. When he did, he found a fat envelope waiting for him in the mailbox. It had been hand delivered – nothing was written on it except the one word, *Judd*. He had his hands full of keys, newspaper and groceries, and tore the package open awkwardly with his two free fingers. Predictably, the paper gave way suddenly and the parcel's contents spilled out across the cracked marble slabs of the hallway floor. Judd dropped to his knees and quickly shovelled everything up into the grocery bag, terrified lest somebody should happen by. There was close to ten thousand dollars there, he guessed. As well as a set of ivory dice and a bent golden ring in the shape of a laughing lizard.

Flatlands: flying in (2)

Judd called his parents, said that Scofield had fixed him up with a job in Reno and that he was leaving on the next plane. He flew into the city at dawn – by first light he saw it from the airplane window, a great calcification rising up from the desert, the husk of an all too familiar humanity. Fresh and bright as the sun soon was, the lights of the hotels and casinos were more powerful still. They glared down the daylight like the eyes of a party of rebellious angels, determined to make all of creation pay for their sufferings. Perhaps, thought Judd, we are God's horde, flying in like seraphim and ready to sacrifice ourselves happily to the cause. He tried to imagine all the people on the planet who would never take a flight, that dismal substratum condemned forever to walk the earth while above them the blessed traversed the skies in glinting silver tubes that hovered between the clouds like mirages, just as distant, just as out of reach.

The small, grizzled man who was occupying the seat next to him suddenly croaked awake. He had fallen asleep before take-off but now he stretched and yawned, rolling back the bristles of his beard as a hedgehog rolls back its coat once the danger has passed. Having roused himself he leant over Judd without asking and peered out of the window. His breath was coarse and sour with sleep. 'This town, ya see all that? Ya see all that? This town lives on nothing but that,' he cackled.

'On nothing but what?' asked Judd, confused. He thought the man meant the desert.

'Casinos and hotels. There's nothing out here but casinos and hotels. Everybody, every goddamn soul in this place lives offa that.' He pronounced 'goddamn' with a glottal stop between the two syllables. 'There's nothing else. Amazing. See those lights? Those lights burn like that twenty-four hours a day, three hunnerd and sixty-five days a year. At night they light up the goddamn rocks for miles around. Lot o' good it does the coyotes. I love it. Looks like goddamn God Almighty hissel' bent right down outta the sky and spat here in the sand, turnin' it all into jewels. Fool's jewels.' He stretched 'jewels', rhymed it with 'fool's'. 'It's a goddamn marvel, that's what it is. The town here eats up more electricity than some entire states, you know that? There's four power stations up roun' Tahoe that don' do nuthin' but power this here town. Ain't that a fact?' The stranger finished and Judd watched his mouth fold away invisibly beneath the copper-grey hairs of his thick beard. For a moment he sat quietly, then stood up and with a stubby index finger punched the yellow button that summoned the stewardess. Presently she arrived. He asked her for a cup of coffee and she explained to him that the plane had already begun its descent and he said to her he didn't see why that meant he couldn't have a cup of coffee and she said she wasn't going to argue with him it's the rules and he could take it up with the company once they were on the ground if he wished. The fasten seat-belts sign came on and twenty minutes later they had landed.

Judd escaped the hot metal cylinder as quickly as he could. The tarmac was already baking hot, although the sun had only been up a couple of hours, and he crossed it at the head of a phalanx of slightly rumpled passengers. His skin glistened faintly with the shock of leaving the air-conditioning and to the staff that met him at the terminal door it seemed almost as if he had been formed right out of the heat hazes and the black matter of the runway, a spirit summoned into the strange pentangles and runes carved by the paths of the jetliners. He located his suitcases; on one of them the strap had been broken by the baggage handlers and the contents looked as though they had been rifled, but nothing appeared to be missing.

Despite the heat the desert seemed clean and fresh after the smog of the city he had left behind. He hailed a cab and asked the driver to take him to a cheap hotel but the man replied, 'They're all the same in this town, brutha,' so Judd said, 'OK, so I trust you, so take me to one you like.' The money, the investment that Scofield had made in him had boosted his confidence enormously. Though he was still paranoid about the extent of the businessman's information network he had decided to take it on trust that the man – who obviously had a fair deal of power of some nature – was trying to help him and not to fuck him up.

They drove out towards the sick lotus of the city, Judd looking out of the windows and fingering the lizard ring he once again wore on his wedding finger. On either side of the road there was nothing but the strange desert landscape which moved in ripples and waves. Now and then a little twister would pick up, whipped into life by the heat differentials at the edge of the metalling, and a small front of red dust would spray over the lane in front of them, its particles stinging the windows like tiny pellets of hail.

'First time in Reno?' asked the driver.

'Er, no,' lied Judd, not wanting to sound like a tourist. The driver laughed.

Compared with Las Vegas, which Judd knew from TV, Reno

seemed quite restrained. They came into town and drove through streets lined with casinos and hotels and pool halls and car show-rooms and arcades, and while it was opulent and tacky it was that much smaller in scale than he imagined it would be. The larger of the gambling complexes still dominated the skyline but the streets themselves seemed relatively quiet and restrained – there wasn't the bustle of tourists and street trash that he had expected. In a curious way he felt as though he was still in the desert proper. The mauves and lilacs of the rocks had been replaced by the bright blues and greens of the lights but the sense of being in a non-place where the landscape had no form – was no longer, indeed, a landscape – was the same: both elicited the feeling that any journey he undertook might easily continue on in the same vein for ever.

The driver drew up outside a hotel-casino name of the Golden Gecko. Judd thought it a good omen, paid the man and went inside. As he opened the lobby doors a wet surge of noise flopped out into the street. The clatter of the slot machines, the screech of the compères, the chink of glasses, of chips, the rattles and pops of funfair attractions, the regurgitative rhythms of a band, the white noise of ten thousand meaningless conversations.

There was no one on the front desk so Judd took a quick look around the lobby. It was very large and all the sound was coming from one end. Judd walked down to investigate and found that the room let on to a balcony which overlooked a vast hall, mocked up to resemble the inside of a circus. No . . . this *was* the inside of a circus. Two acrobats were swinging from high wires, one of them suddenly performing a triple somersault level with Judd's nose. Down below, next to the safety net, a ringmaster led a small brass band around in a circle while Joseph Grimaldi clowns dressed in white romper suits threw buckets of fake water over one another and pretended to cause mayhem. At the other end of the platform (for it was a platform rather than a ring) a lion tamer cracked his whip at a fairly docile-looking lion, while a girl wearing nothing but suspenders, underwear, high heels, a gag and several coils of rope squirmed provocatively and tried to look frightened.

This was the children's area and sure enough there were dozens of them, charging around dressed in dungarees or summer dresses or shorts and wearing cardboard ten-gallon hats or deely-boppers or beanies on their heads and more interested, it seemed, in each other than in the amusements on offer. Occasional adults chanced their arms on the shooting galleries and hoopla stalls that ringed the hall, cheered on by enthusiastic offspring but nervous at the idea of games of skill after too many hours of playing games of chance. Everything was pink or gold or red or white or blue. One child was urinating on a heap of soft-toy bunny rabbits when he thought no one was looking. Judd watched him from his vantage point on the balcony. The child finished, put his little pecker away, then felt the eyes upon him and looked up. When he saw Judd his hand came up to his mouth in shock, then realising that the adult couldn't reach him he grinned and ran off to join a gaggle of his peers busy farting and burping round the back of the lion cage.

Judd went back to the reception desk and checked in. He liked it here.

1 0

Sea dog

Laika watched the world. She did this when she got bored with her screens, which wasn't often. But over the years she had looked at the world a lot none the less. Sometimes it was easy to forget that there was any land at all. With the sea already taking up two thirds of the planet's surface and the continents often largely obscured by clouds, the earth really did seem to be a sphere of water hanging in the void, a vast water droplet leaked from some interstellar pipe. It was a problem, actually, watching the zorby blue atmosphere forever curling away below you, inviting, delightful, forever out of reach. If Pavlov had wanted to create the ideal stimulus for drinking, Laika often wondered idly, he could have done worse than photograph this.

For it was a water world. Learning as much as she could about the sea from films and documentaries, our little Russian dog never ceased to be amazed by it. She had never seen it while still on earth and now it seemed to her to be the most important thing of all, far more vital than the constant ploughings and ragings of humankind. There it was, vast, complex, interconnected, saturated with life and death to such an extent that the dissolved bodies of its innumerable inhabitants salted and re-salted it, became part of its very fibre. In tune with the moon, unperturbed unperturbable, it sucked at the rocks that had dared to rise out of it, determined to conquer these highlands, grinding them down, returning them to sediment, packing them back on its floor where it felt they belonged. To help in the task it siphoned off energy from volcanic vents in the sea bed and created bacteria, which gathered in great floating spirillae mats that soaked up the heat of the sun and pumped oxygen out into the atmosphere. This done, the bacteria helped the sea to throw up part of itself and clip a mantle of weather around the globe, the sea which was sky. Rain and storms then littered the earth and rivers carved their way through the land-scapes, carrying more of the recalcitrant rock to the sea and allowing the waters' autonomous pods – the cells – to creep over the ground, forming slimes mosses lichens which mined minerals from the rocks, now deeply regretting their rebellion, and broke them down further into gases and screes and soils which were easily washed away by the same water that made underground caves of all faults.

This is what Laika saw when she gazed from her craft: a sea reclaiming the land as its own, twisting, extending, contorting, unfolding itself in the attempt, taking the vast processes of its currents and chemicals and waves and tides and condensing them down to form life, a handy tool in the struggle, teeming unicell agents that could be relied upon to fan out and infiltrate, multiply and report, chuckle and swarm. And even, unexpectedly, band together, form groups, *organisms*: plankton and algae, anenome and arthropod, lobopod and snail. Then, later, fungus and plant, grass and gymnosperm, lizard and fly, flower and wasp, mammal and tree: multicellular creatures that carried the offensive further and further inland – *interzone, I think I've found you* – across mountains and deserts, tundra and bog, until they were able to dance rituals in border towns, able to order themselves, to calm themselves, able to prepare for the conquest of space.

Mandelbrot memories

When the newly sensitive Joel began to wonder, about a month after he'd said goodbye to Jennifer in the summer of 1973, whether the rush he'd got from sex in any way compared with how a computer felt when being flooded with data, foremost in his mind was the network he looked after at CERN. The scratch of the modems as they switched packets of information to and fro between the workstations seemed to him as subtle as the soft rasp of groin upon groin. The flicker of LEDs on display panels were as vital as the random firings of the optic nerve triggered by the intensity of tongue upon tongue, lips upon lips, flesh upon flesh. The glow of the screens was as subtle as the half-light created in his room by the drawing of the blinds against the prying midday sun. The whirr of the tapes and hard drives was as bewitching as the music of sighs, gasps and breaths.

But already his interest in learning to gamble eclipsed even the experience of sex. Here was a whole new side to his explorations in probability. He forsook the dice and became obsessed by roulette, going so far as to buy a second-hand wheel and install it in his already cramped room. He worked out that by building a machine to predict the results of the wheel he could begin to show that chance itself had a structure, a structure that was extended in time. Roulette was a physical system in which the crucial factors should be the rate of spin (including deceleration due to friction and inertia), the speed and angle of delivery of the ball, any slight angle of tilt of the wheel itself and the exact point at which the ball entered the system. But if his hunch was right, any technique that was solely a function of these properties would not be able to predict the wheel with one hundred per cent accuracy. Any large enough sample of results should show a random distribution, but his theory – which stated that pure randomness didn't exist, at least not yet – suggested that wouldn't in fact be the case. But what it might be that linked the results together and frustrated the workings of chance he didn't yet know.

One possibility he pondered (drawing on his newly – sexually – acquired knowledge about the ability of the body to absorb and transmit information) was that if enough attention was focused on the game by its players they might themselves become part of the system and affect the fall of the ball. Since Henry had first taken him to the casino he had been back many times, both to that one and to others. He had already got to know many habitués of Geneva's gambling fraternity by face and they had got to know him – with his unkempt looks, intense air and notepad and pen, he was an easily recognisable figure. Most of the doormen knew him by sight and joked about him, tagging him – correctly – as a student from one of the universities on some research project, and many of the players knew the feel of his eyes on their backs as they played on into the night. On several occasions he had sat and watched while one or other of them had beaten the bank. It was not something that happened very often, nor was it particularly spectacular when it did. The shouts and whoops, the sudden wins and the quick catastrophes tended to come from the more casual players, those who threw down their money on a series of blind intersections with the wheel. But the regulars were an altogether different affair. They accumulated wins slowly, over time, crabbing their chips around the table in a manner that was neither plan nor chance, but which seemed to Joel more like the map of some strange country of the mind. On the most intense evenings – the nights when Joel found a player on a winning streak and stuck to him, a psychic limpet – the gambler's strategy actively enfolded its surroundings until it contained within it the behaviour of the croupier, the bounce of the ball, the flow of people to and from the table, the tides of comment and conversation. A successful player, Joel noted, made everything subsidiary to him or herself. It seemed that at such times these people could not only predict the outcomes, but influence them too. Was that possible? That was something he must endeavour to find out.

The skills he had enjoyed as a child, of being able to visualise algorithms and solve them almost instantly, had been in sharp decline over the previous couple of years. Joel had put this down to the fact that he was getting older, but the upshot was that he had begun to depend on computers more and more in his day-to-day work. For a while he'd felt bitter regret at this but now he was happy, because it had seemed after all that this transition was part of some grander design. The prediction problem he confronted as the next hurdle in his project was far too complex for him to have processed in his mind alone, even at the height of his skills, and the only reason he had managed to see a way past it at all was thanks to what he knew about these machines. So as soon as he had formulated his plan he set about building a computer that would help him to carry it out.

Although his hobby placed burgeoning demands on his time and he was kept constantly busy with his official research, Joel felt increasingly unmotivated and listless. The sight of Jennifer and Henry together, different as their habits were from those of his own family, had made him think of the life he had abandoned when he had run away from Brooklyn. A few months after Jennifer's departure he began to have doubts as to whether he should ever have left. Perhaps the intimacy that he'd discovered with her had opened him to the fact that other people really existed; perhaps his unravelling of the events of the Holocaust had unearthed in him compassion; perhaps the waning of his precocious mathematical abilities was making him pine for his disappearing youth. Whatever the reasons, over the ensuing year the doubts grew into anguish. If he had stayed he would be married by now, with a family of his own. He wouldn't be eating every meal in silence, spending every night alone, wouldn't be terrified of company and lost in a conversation. Millstein would have continued to teach him well and would no doubt eventually have persuaded Moshe to let him study at one of the universities in New York. He need never have come to Cambridge, to have begged Metric for help. That whole episode made him tingle with embarrassment whenever he thought of it – in retrospect he considered those years a dreadful mistake and although Amanda Metric occasionally wrote to him at CERN he could never quite bring himself to reply. Sometimes it seemed that numbers, which had promised him so much, had in fact served him about as well as a bout of polio. His blessings had become curses and neither his attempts to build a roulette computer nor the long hikes he still took through the peaks and forests of the local mountains managed to dispel what he came to recognise as chronic loneliness.

One evening towards the end of the second summer since Jennifer's visit, he was mooning around the Common Room when Subhash Sidwa, a lanky programmer from Lahore and a member of a fashionable 'set' of young researchers who didn't wear suits, had eclectic ideas, and raised eyebrows by hanging out with bikers in the locally notorious Boot Bar (and who – it was rumoured – took drugs), wandered in and dumped a huge pile of A4 flyers on one of the already overflowing tables, knocking over a cold cup of coffee full of floating cigarette butts in the process. Apparently oblivious to the mess he'd created the Pakistani began cheerily plastering the notice-boards with his hand-outs, stealing pins from notices that were already up and ignoring them when they fell to the floor. Joel found all this good humour and irresponsibility irritating and was making ready to leave when Subhash approached him and shoved a flyer into his hand. 'Lecture course. Starts next week. Check out the speakers, man. This is going to shake up this place like you would not believe.'

Joel said thanks and was about to drop the sheet into the nearest wastebin when one of the names on the list caught his eye.

DOUBLE BILL

24 and 25 August: Benoit Mandelbrot (IBM) presents:
'How Long is the Coast of Britain' & 'Fractal Cotton Prices since 1900'

At the mention of Mandelbrot, the bread he'd most loved as a boy, a mist came over Joel's mind and dewy tears formed at the corners of his eyes. Nostalgia rose up in him like nausea, as deep in his cortex, neurons began to chant. He remembered his father telling him the recipe in the bakery, years and years before. *Heat up the oven until it's nice and hot. Measure out a few grabs of flour and just so much baking powder and sift them together with a few pinches of salt. Then beat up three eggs, gradually adding in a cupful of sugar. That's*

how you make a batter, see, and you must beat it till it's good and thick.
Stir in some corn oil, a splash of vanilla juice and a dribble of nut oil and
then add the flour and a cup of chopped almonds. Mix it all together well,
because this is your dough. Now separate the dough into three and knead
the pieces on a board like this, folding and flattening, folding and flattening,
until everything is mixed and no longer sticky but smooth. Shape each
piece into a flat loaf so long and so thick and then in the oven with them
for a half hour. When they're done we cut them into strips, like so, like
so, like so. Then back in the oven to brown.

Folding and flattening, folding and flattening, the baker's transformation which takes distant particles and brings them closer
together. This was the process that went on in Joel's mind. Images,
smells and sounds folded and flattened and folded themselves over
and over until he was back in the bakery, tugging at his father's
apron, wiping the caramelised sugar off the baking trays with his
finger, rubbing the steam from his glasses and leaving a crust of
flour in its place. *Home.* Suddenly he longed for it more acutely
than ever. What use had it been coming here to Europe, to end
up not in some halcyon mathematical community as he had imagined but locked in the dull round of tedious research? The future
yawned before him like a giant and multiple maw, each way forward a different throat leading straight down into the same acid
belly of loneliness. He thought of the soft knishes of Jennifer's
body; he felt filthy and pathetic. He could hear his mother's voice:
Who do you think you are? A common goy? You don't even wear your
yarmulke any more!

Poor Joel! He had kept his mind so rigorously compartmentalised
that it had taken an entire decade for the feelings he had for his
family, for Brooklyn, to well up through its crystal structure. Tears
balled on his eyelashes and fumbled their way down his cheeks.
He thrust his hand into his pocket and pulled out some odd coins
and notes which he crushed into Subhash's palm. 'I must come, I
must come,' he blubbered, stabbing his finger on Mandelbrot's
name. 'Reserve me a ticket for this won't you, please?'

'Well, I'll save you a seat,' said Subhash, somewhat taken aback,
'but you count as staff, so you don't have to pay.'

'I want to, I want to,' continued Joel regardless.

339

'No, really, you don't have to, it's all right,' Subhash insisted, worried that Joel would drip tears all over his new velveteen loons.

'But I want to,' wailed Joel, 'I want to do something! I owe it to my father! Because I'm never going to see him again!' With both men trying to reject it the money fell to the floor; Joel quickly followed, his collapsing body buffeted by the most terrific sobs. Still worrying about his trousers, Subhash helped him up and led him over to the line of modular grey chairs that ran along one wall of the Common Room.

Joel cried for several minutes, blubbing big tears which despite Subhash's best efforts left salty snail trails across his precious pants. Soon, though, the flashback began to fizzle out and Joel's sobs subsided. Feeling concerned – he was a nice guy, for a programmer – Subhash offered to buy Joel a cup of coffee and silently the Jew nodded consent and allowed his good Samaritan to lead him in the direction of the cafeteria. Once there they got talking, and that was how Joel made a friend.

The triptych of time

They spoke often after that, though it was a very academic friendship and when they talked it was mainly in abstractions – partly because Joel had few other modes of conversation and also because Subhash found what he had to say interesting. That first time over coffee Joel did tell the slightly astonished Pakistani something of his family and his childhood, and his running away, but after that he never spoke of the past again. The programmer immediately recognised the intelligence of his new acquaintance, but what made Joel so refreshing was the way he would link mathematical or computing concepts with ideas from the worlds of religion, gambling, philosophy, biology, psychology. Although he didn't yet tell him about the computer he was building, little by little Joel expounded to Subhash all his theories of the links between

Kabbalistic philosophy, time, mathematics and chance. It was good to talk – for too long he'd been developing his ideas in isolation and to try to communicate them was to force himself to structure them, to make them coherent.

Once, they got on to the topic of neural nets, a new kind of computer architecture that Subhash was working on in one of the labs. 'These networks can be realised in hardware or software,' he explained to Joel. 'In essence the idea is to mimic how the brain works. Like, computers at the moment process information in a serial way, one instruction after the other, but what we want is to try and do what we think the brain does – have a load of simple processing units, or neurons, link them all together with multiple connections and get results out of the different patterns of activation levels across the entire network. It's called parallel distributed processing, as opposed to serial processing, you see? Of course, our version's still not as complex as the brain, which isn't binary – our neurons are simplified models: they have various input channels, a processing unit and a single output channel which can produce a one or a zero. But the cool thing is that by altering the relative weights of the channels you can get the network to home in on a result and you don't even need that big a network to do it. With certain architectures which feed outputs back in and readjust their own channel weights accordingly, the thing can actually be said

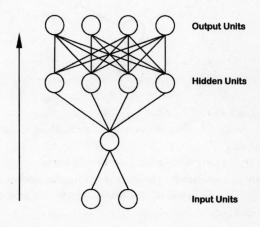

341

to learn. It's pretty cool stuff. Here.' And he flipped open a text-book and showed Joel a schematic of a multi-layer network architecture.

'But this is amazing,' Joel exclaimed. 'It's so similar to the traditional way the Sefirot are drawn.'

'I, er, I'm not familiar with that I'm afraid . . .'

'The Sefirot! According to Kabbalic doctrine, the ten vessels from the material of which the world was constructed. Look.' Joel grabbed a napkin from the chrome dispenser and, pulling out a felt-tip pen, scribbled a quick diagram on it. 'Here,' he said, and shoved it across the table at Subhash.

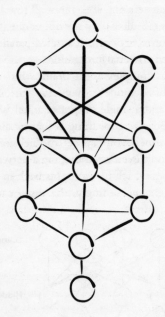

'See what I mean?'

'Yeah, yeah, I do, I suppose, though it's kind of a simplification . . .'

'But it fits exactly with what I've already been saying. Wait, let me show you something.' He leant down to the satchel at his feet and pulled out a battered library book. 'Have you read this?'

'What is it?'

'Scholem's book on the Kabbalah. Came out last year I think –' he checked the title pages ' – yes, that's right, copyright 1974. You should read it. It's already a classic. Now, listen to this.' He thumbed through the book, jumping from place to place by locating the various pieces of roughly torn paper that served him as bookmarks until he found the passage he wanted. 'OK, here: "Even man's physical structure corresponds to that of the Sefirot, so that we find Ezra of Gerona's description of the last Sefirah as 'the form [temunah] that includes all forms' applied in the Zohar to man himself, who is called 'the likeness [deyokna] that includes all likenesses.' "

'There. There's so much there, you see? We have on the one hand this thing about the correspondence of the physical structure – neural net, or brainwork as it were, and the interrelations of the Sefirot, and just remember, if you wanted to back this up you could refer to the fact, surely not coincidence, that von Neumann himself designed and *named* the architecture of the computer after the structure of the body. He was the one who first said the fact that the thing was instantiated in electronic circuits was irrelevant, that we should think of the logical units as neurons, he *said* that. And not only that but his design was broken down into organs: the central control, the central arithmetic processor – cortical functions, if you like – the *memory*, very important, I mean, why call it memory and not storage as had hitherto been the case if you weren't alert to the biological possibilities? And then the input and output *organs*. See?

'Then, on the other hand, you have this idea of "the form that includes all forms", and exactly there you have the Universal Turing Machine, yes? Turing's idea being that if you could break the operations of any physical machine – and he included in that category biological machines, animals – down into a series of logical operations, by encoding these operations in say, binary instruction sets, on a theoretically infinite magnetic tape, you could create a machine which, again in theory, of course, should be able to simulate the processes of any other. A universal machine. A computer, in other words.'

Subhash smiled – now he was being patronised. He fought back with the little bit of Kabbalic doctrine he knew: 'So I suppose this parallels the way that the Torah, with all its hypertexts, is supposed to be a living organism, right?'

'Yes, yes! I hadn't thought of that. You're getting the idea.' Triumphantly Joel slammed shut his book and plonked it down on the table before Subhash had a chance to ask him about the heavily scored passage at the foot of the page he had quoted from. It was a passage that touched closely on Joel's ideas as he'd outlined them to Professor Metric long before: it concerned the emanation of Ein-Sof and the separation of the world from God which coincided with the breaking of the vessels and the committing of the first sin. It read:

This uninterrupted communion, which is the goal of creation, was broken off at the time of Adam's sin when his lower will was parted from the divine will by his own free volition. It was then that his individuality, whose origin lay in his separation from God with its attendant proliferation of multiplicity, was born. What had been intended to be nothing more than a series of periodic fluctuations within a system now turned into an opposition of extremes that found their expression in the fierce polarisation of good and evil. It is the concrete destiny of the human race, and of the Jew as the principal bearer of this mission and the recipient of God's revelation through the Torah, to overcome this polarisation from within the human condition created by the first sin.

This was a passage Joel knew by heart.

The more his friendship with Subhash developed, the less seriously Joel took his official research work. His life was full now: he had a companion and he had his Project, and he no longer saw any need for the stability that CERN had provided. As far as his Project went, for the moment he had learnt all he could from the casinos so he stopped paying visits to the city and started instead to spend his evenings calibrating the roulette wheel he had installed in his room. Once that was done he sat up nights feverishly coding simulations of the apparatus and during the days – when he was meant to be analysing CERN data – he ran his programs on the machines, experimenting with networking the lab computers together via the Centre's LAN so that he could steal extra processing time by sucking up any surplus cycles. It was a clever piece of programming and it often struck even Joel as bizarre that the twists of logical instruction he put together should be able to travel around the Centre apparently independent of their author, searching for space in which they could run and thrive.

Conceptually, the problem was simple. The ball's behaviour, once inside the wheel, was governed by Newtonian mechanics. By calibrating the starting point of the wheel, the speed of its spin and the speed and trajectory of the ball, and by allowing for gravity and wind resistance, it shouldn't be difficult to predict the outcome to at least within the nearest octant (the eight wedges into which a roulette wheel can be divided are not even – each octant has either four or five slots). But it was a complex coding challenge, made more difficult by the fact that in order to test every one of his simulations Joel had to carry out a series of runs on the wheel in his room, measure the physical variables for all of them and then take the results over to the labs, repeat them on his virtual wheel and compare the answers.

Once he had developed a satisfactory program, further testing could only properly be accomplished by running it on a computer that he could use in his room, and since he was going to have to build a machine especially for the task Joel decided that he might as well do it properly and construct one that he could conceal on his person and smuggle into a real casino.

He began to assemble the components, asking Subhash's advice on chips and architecture (though without revealing the true nature of his Project). He scrounged and filched components from the labs, and tripped into Geneva to hunt for suitable materials for the housings and interfaces, but most of the circuitry and chips that he needed he had to order from American mail order companies, the kind that advertised in the back of magazines like *Byte*, *Popular Computing* and *Dr Dobb's Journal of Computer Calisthenics and Orthodontics*. By the mid-1970s the computer hobbyist scene in the US was massive, much bigger than in Europe, and Joel had long followed its meanderings through the pages of these publications.

Through them he heard about the Altair 8800, the first home computer, featured on the cover of *Popular Electronics* in January 1975; he read features dealing with new languages like BASIC and on the peculiar 'Homebrew Computer Club' in Menlo Park on the edge of what was already called Silicon Valley. He read about the computer evangelist Ted Nelson and his vision of something called Hypertext, a kind of interlinked computer-based publishing system, which would 'liberate' computers from the 'high-priests' that supposedly had control over them now (like himself, presumably, thought Joel) and allow laymen to get access to all sorts of data. (Again, Joel considered it odd that this Hypertext was thought of as an inherently liberating phenomenon – as far as he was aware the Hypertext of the Torah, a complex series of amendments, commentaries, exegeses, tractates and parables that grew up around the words of the Bible and which in its various stages encoded rabbinical law, was developed by priests to ensure they maintained their power base in the face of various reforms. And yet, as Subhash had pointed out, there was something about this net-like structure of the Torah which seemed organic, which appeared to operate beyond the possibility of centralised control.)

But then lots of this stuff seemed very political. He thought in particular of a vitriolic piece he'd read in *Dr Dobb's* attacking one of the Altair BASIC designers, a guy called Bill Gates, for a speech he'd given at a Homebrew conference criticising computer hobbyists for developing a culture of what he called 'software piracy'. The idea seemed weird to Joel, he had to admit. Everyone he knew at CERN who worked with the computers – Subhash for example – gave away their code for free as a matter of course. It was just what you did.

Designing a circuit diagram was what occupied most of his time now, etching out the most efficient infrastructure for a tiny computer that would only ever run the one program he burnt into its EPROM. It was a journey into a new space and it alerted Joel to something of the terrible beauty of these machines, one that had only ever been matched by the mathematical landscapes he had traversed in his mind as a child. But it was also a frustrating task, because many of the solutions which looked good on paper could not physically be built or would have bugs which he had not yet detected. He went through about a dozen prototypes before he found one that worked and he had just begun training himself to calibrate the movements of the ball and the wheel by eye – and then input the data using a somewhat awkward toe-activated interface – when Mandelbrot came to town and everything went haywire.

Basket case

So much time spent on her own meant she that thirsted for companionship and, just as the silt of a dry lake bed cracks into islands as the last moisture leaves it, so her personality shrank back into sections. These sections formed cliques and alliances, had friendships and fallings out, developed languages and systems of belief not all of which were known to any single one of them. Yet she could be coherent when she wished; when she was with a group the lake would fill and the cracked bed form a substratum for what she called her 'My', an idea she intuited from the attitudes of the adults with whom she came into contact. But when she was with just one of the nurses she didn't need to bring the My into play; one of the Other could deal with them.

The members of her populace had names: there was Echo, and Table, and No! (No! was very stubborn). Hippocrates was something of a figure of fun; his best friend Exray was always seeing through his rather pompous pronouncements. Pill was impish and dangerous and to be feared, and had a sworn enemy called Squeak who always tried to warn the others when the mischievous Pill was around (although often they paid him no heed). One of the strangest of all was Comagirl, who didn't mix much with the Others but towards whom they all showed great respect, even Pill, who never played tricks on her (Squeak was secretly very jealous of Comagirl because of this). Firealarm was something of a mystery to most of them (and some of them had never heard of him at all) and his best friend was Smoke, who was neither a he nor a she. Smoke was very receptive to the

347

Hospital Nights, as they all called the people outside the My with whom the My came into contact. Lonely Dear? thought Smoke was the strongest and strangest of them all, despite Exray's exhortations to the contrary. Learning was Lonely Dear?'s best friend and when the child attended her lessons it was always Learning and Lonely Dear? who sat at the front. (Hippocrates sat in the desk behind them, but he was a real know-it-all and always contradicted the Teacher so the Teacher couldn't Teach him a thing.) The My didn't bother too much with the Teacher; it couldn't understand the point of the things the Teacher said. All the stories the Teacher told seemed very simple: someone did this, and then this, and then this, and it was not at all what they could have done or would have done. Learning and Lonely Dear? tried to make the My come to the lessons but they weren't strong enough on their own to summon it. The best they could do was to get Smoke to come, because Smoke was good at listening and asking questions. Once Teacher brought Mouse to class (the child had never seen an animal before) and Smoke made good friends with the creature. It spent ages with Mouse and eventually Mouse left its greybody and came to live in the My with the others. Squeak put herself in charge of looking after Mouse, who couldn't talk, and said it was good that she did because it was a sign of Social Responsibility, but Pill kept hiding Mouse from Squeak which made Squeak very upset. We have to take good care of Mouse, *she'd say, in a voice not unlike Mouse's own,* or one day we might lose him! *But for all that Mouse seemed happy enough.*

Then there was Veronica, and Filthychild (the My had met them in the nursery – Horrible Things had been done to them by The Parents and they had preferred to come and live in the My). There was Chicken, and Top, and Dinnertime who was always hungry. There were others also, too many to mention. Some of them came and went regularly, like Gardener, and some would only show up occasionally, like Birthday. Some were more popular than others (everybody liked Sky and Sunshine for instance, except for Sick, but everybody hated Sick).

But the members of the populace did more than argue among themselves. They spent lots of their time in search of ways out, like they'd been told. When Emma was dreaming they probed far and wide, and the My couldn't keep track of them all, all of the time. They spread out through a world of psychic intensity rather than physical space, where human flow and endeavour were etched out against an undulating background of bacterial and geological activity. Traffic and trauma of any kind left traces and towns were like vast balls of tubes and wires, planetary radicles in the cosmic fields of the child's dreams. The populace could dart inside them and explore, chasing the morphing pulses of light that were the signatures of other minds. Comagirl would float slowly through the throbbing globules, her sleep-walking in stark contrast to the row Pill and Squeak caused as they chased each other round and round, screaming like gremlins. Veronica and Top and Table tended to explore as a threesome. Learning went through methodically but terribly slowly and the Others were always having to wait for him to catch up.

Theft as therapy

On Friday night Jennifer came back home from work to the house in Hunt's Crescent to be greeted by the sound of feedback coming from the dining-room. Out front, the garden was overgrown and tatty, full of beer cans and binliners stuffed with pizza boxes and half-eaten microwave meals. For long periods she was never quite sure who was living there; at the moment Stim and Skag were in residence, with various other members of the band they had started, Desiring Machine, randomly coming and going. The dining-room was now a studio, full of cheap guitars and salvaged amplifiers and the pieces of a drum kit that was forever being taken apart and reassembled.

As usual, the place was trashed. The bedrooms weren't so bad but downstairs the carpets were covered with stains and cigarette burns, the furniture was broken, ashtrays overflowed, windows were cracked. Curtains hung off their rails, remembering drunken teenagers clutching for them in moments of panic. The stair carpet was a dirty silver grey, the result of an Etch-a-Sketch being broken over somebody's head at a party. Every surface in the kitchen was covered with empty tins, dirty plates, pans encrusted with the remains of curries and chillis concocted under the influence. The fridge seeped CFCs and stank of sour milk, the linoleum hadn't been washed for months. Spider plants thrived on the window-sills, their runners dripping down into the sink. Flies droned happily from feast to feast and next door's cat raked carefully through the trash piled in one corner.

Jennifer slouched in, yelling a hello to the band as she passed. She threw down her bag and started a search for the kettle, which she eventually found behind the TV in the living-room. She filled it and plugged it in, then went upstairs to run a bath.

A hour and a half later she reappeared, no longer dressed in her shapeless Woolworth's smock and skirt, but wearing instead a different uniform of black stretch jeans, painted Doctor Marten boots, torn Joy Division T-shirt and a capacious woollen cardigan that had once upon a time belonged to Henry. The Desiring Machine rehearsal had deteriorated into a hash-smoking session and the band had decamped from dining-room to living-room, where they all sat slumped in front of the seven o'clock news. Jenn walked in and swiped a spliff from between the drummer's fingers.

'Wha—? Oh, hi Jenn. Awright?'

'Better now. Anyone going out to get some food? I'm starving.' The band members looked at each other, then at Jennifer, then at the TV, and burst out laughing.

'What's so fucking funny?'

But that just made everybody giggle some more, until Stim, the bass player, managed to steady himself enough to speak. 'Oh, it's nothing. We've been rehearsing all day and haven't got it together to get anything to eat, and everyone's been saying that all day. Private joke.' He wiped a tear from his eye. 'We were gonna go into town any rate.'

'Where?'

'Dunno. Probably the Dragon.'

'I thought we were gonna get some grub.' More giggles, though this time they were quickly suppressed.

'Yeah, well, better have a couple of bevs first tho'.' Endless hilarity.

It was to be a usual Friday night then: a slow crawl across town towards the Green Dragon, no doubt via the Cross Keys, the Shakespeare and the chippy. Cider and black all the way, Benson and Hedges or Embassy, punctuated with the odd spliff outside in the car-park, long and hot and wet with all the lips so keen for it. Around ten someone would chuck up, pebble-dash the toilets; around eleven-thirty, just after they'd all been kicked out into the street, the one who'd laughed the hardest would spill a mulch of beer and undigested saveloy half-way across the pavement.

There'd be talk of a curry, but no one would have any money.

For a while they'd mill around the clocktower opposite the Swan, yelling at the drunks and the delicately dressed, pulling from a bottle of something that someone with foresight had lifted from an offie earlier on. When the last of the pub-goers had gone and there was no more entertainment it would be time to shufty on down to the Bancroft – the river gardens by the theatre, empty long since. More spliffs, then, some snogs, maybe someone had some acid or some glue. Virtual cricket in the half-light of street lights reflected off the fuscous water, no bat or ball but full field action none the less. Bored with that, it would be a charge around the graveyard by Holy Trinity Church, in which Shakespeare was buried. Pissing in a dark corner, giggling, sprawling on the grave-stones, 'stoned on the stones', telling bad ghost stories that no one believed.

There'd be talk of heading out of town to the Last Resort or the Wildmoor, the town's two night-clubs, of trying to cause some trouble. But again, no money, so in the end it would be back to Jenn's for those who could be bothered, to do hot knives in the kitchen or try to build yet another bucket bong, maybe have a shot at making some music until the neighbours called the police.

Eventually what stimulants there were would all be gone and people would drift away or just fall asleep where they sat. At some point Jennifer would lever herself up and stumble upstairs to the bathroom. Locking herself in, she'd use the toilet and clean her teeth, then take out the special glass she kept in the cabinet and drink four or five pints of water from the tap. As she drank, she felt with relief the liquid run down her oesophagus and into her stomach, washing her system clean of the poisons she'd been pummelling it with and also filling her up, swelling her abdomen slightly. For, since the baby had gone, she found she slept better this way.

Saturday. Jennifer awoke alone, despite the best efforts of one of the guitarists to inveigle his way into her bed at one point during the night. Notwithstanding the water, her head felt heavy from the dope and booze, and her nose was blocked. But her first priority, as usual, was a piss.

Her bladder empty, she noted that it was already midday and she still hadn't eaten properly. Downstairs, most of the posse from the previous night seemed to have gone, except for Mike who was still passed out on the sofa. Someone had tied his trainers together and written PRAT in reversed lipstick lettering across his forehead. Jenn left him to it, took the door off the latch and went out.

It was an overcast and muggy day, as if the climate had binged the night before as well and couldn't summon the energy to put together any proper weather, so was just letting the elements seep haphazardly down out of the sky instead. Sucking at the heavy air, Jenn made her way into town across the Clopton bridge, her spirits not lifting one bit.

However, as she came in sight of the High Street her heart started to pump and adrenalin began to tingle away at her nerves. Her skin tightened, pulling at the scars across her chest, and she felt well enough to risk a cigarette. The nicotine made her head swim and she bumped into a couple of shoppers as she walked up the crowded street towards her target.

The key thing, she'd come to realise, was to be quick and authoritative. She'd spent a lot of time behind the check-out watching the store detectives, seeing whom they looked at, whom they picked up on. It was amazing how many shoplifters they missed. And it was also amazing how brazen these people could be. She'd watched them lift sweets and chocolate off the racks on the counter while she'd been handing them their change; she'd watched them walk out with records, toasters, barbecue sets in their hands, then bring them back the next week, complaining that they were faulty and asking for their money back. The trick was to look as if you were just going about your business, that's all, and not to take stupid risks.

She chose Boots because she liked their sandwiches and despite the rush – much better than she got from hash or booze – she was still hungry. As she walked into the shop she checked her purse for change, then looked up to get her bearings, noting the position of Pete, the plain-clothes security man who'd asked her out once when he used to work with her at Woolies. This is gonna be easy, she smiled to herself. An inside job. She walked over to the fridges and picked out a couple of sandwiches and a drink, which she cradled awkwardly in her left arm. Then she went to the cosmetics counter, put down the food, and tried a couple of lipsticks and mascaras under the watchful eye of the make-up-plastered assistant, a walking ad for how not to do it.

Choosing two or three things, she put them with her food then, when it was time to move on, she cradled everything in her arm like before, with the lipstick on top and closest to her body. She turned and headed for the toiletries section and as she went, well, what do you know? The cosmetics somehow slipped down inside her cardigan and got caught up where it was tucked into the front of her trousers.

The same process was repeated with some shower gel and soap, and with an extra sandwich and a carton of drink when she decided that she'd changed her mind about the ones she'd originally chosen, though she left a packet of towels in plain view. Then it was time to pay.

Feeling much better now, she went down to the Bancroft to eat her lunch and feed her crusts to the ducks.

Head games (2)

Now that she was older they called her Emma (although that wasn't the name her mother would have chosen) and took her to the nursery sometimes. The dossiers describing the dangers associated with her were largely ignored by the nurses who looked after her. There were other children here, and she mixed with them and played with them. There was a sandpit, a waterlab, building blocks, cars and dolls, books with bright pictures. The colours of it all blinded her at first. She had grown so used to her isolation that visual flux proved difficult to cope with. As she strengthened old neural connections and made new ones, the axons groping through her cortex like brambles through the forest brush, the other kids were gradually steadied and addressed. Each child, she discovered, carried with it the thrusting genes of its parents, spliced and coiled into a twisted weave of psychotic algorithms that operated more or less as a unit. They charged around the nursery, probing and pushing and inventing lines of demarcation. The clothes they wore, the accents they carried, the attitudes they harboured told her of the interleaved zones of the wider world beyond; through them, the child learnt of the neighbourhoods of money and status in the surrounding town, and back in her cell at nights she pondered their permutations.

She honed her senses to the patterns inherent in the riots of sound colour taste touch in the playgroups, all of which shaped her, all of which she shaped. The plasticity of the world fascinated her. The nurses were amazed by the complex cantilevered structures she built out of blocks and left lodged – supported by their own gravitational dynamics – on the edges of tables, on the lip of electrical sockets, on the shoulder and crown of a sleeping child. (The other children thought they were fun and destroyed them accordingly.) The cars: she rolled them across the floor by themselves. She couldn't help it, they itched at her to do it, the wheels and axles wanted to turn. All she had to do was stretch and buzz the air behind them and they would go. It was not difficult; it involved little more than directing the reflex shiver excited by the coldness of their desire. A toddler – its mouth open in a puckered ellipse, an expression of benign confusion in its eyes – might pursue the apparently autonomous toy, which Emma would move on every time the young creature grew close. If the paradox of the

354

situation became too much for it, like a sinner crying for God it would
start to wail, setting off the other children in a quick domino effect. Then
Emma would be scooped up by a nurse and promptly returned to her cell.
So she learnt to be careful, she learnt what the others could not do, she
learnt to be sly and she learnt to play games.

The art of sedimentation

Everyone gambles in Reno. People move out here and live for
years in trailer homes just to play the slots. Retired policemen
come to gamble away their memories, young couples to risk all
or nothing for a wedding licence and a down payment on a tract
home. Old spinsters come, destined to lose their pensions and end
up on a train to New York, bag ladies from the moment they hit
Grand Central. Evangelists who sailed too close to the wind are
here, betting on God in another way, as are lesbian housewives
from Milwaukee on the run from their pasts and the daily temptation of braining their deadbeat spouses with a heavy household
implement; they stand next to pimps and prostitutes, who figured
they'd do better working Reno's hotels than flushed down the
sewers that are the downtown streets of the cities of America's
Pacific Rim. Entire families, hooked as a unit on the gambling tip,
lurch between the tables and the restaurants, already booked in for
a slot on Oprah ten years down the line. And then there are the
bookies and the travelling salesmen and the frat-boys on jaunts and
the businessmen pretending they're powerful and the thirty-
somethings looking for a thrill and the rubbernecks and the pro-
fessionals and the schoolteachers and the bus drivers and the suckers,
yes, the suckers – there are plenty of those. Or maybe, just maybe,
there aren't. Maybe everyone here knows what they're in for.
Maybe everyone here's getting just what they want.

   This one is always rolling. It's five in the morning and the
cleaners are vacuuming round your feet as you stand to lose another

five hundred at blackjack. It's 10 a.m. and you've barely finished
your three-dollar breakfast of steak eggs coffee fries onion rings
coffee tomato grits pancakes coffee syrup ketchup fresh orange
juice coffee bacon muffin teacake Cheerios yoghurt eggs and coffee
all topped off with a sprinkling of bran, and they're bringing you
a complimentary cocktail or a bottle of cheap champagne because
you've passed some arbitrary win line at one of the tables and the
pit boss wants you to get drunk before you can win any more.
But the drink sits uneasily on top of all that food so you stroll
around for a while, not wanting to leave and jinx your luck, glad
to take a look at the other players, happy to watch someone else
throw away their money for a change – though it's not too long
before once again you're wishing it were you.

Although the Golden Gecko proved to be a good place to stay,
Judd rarely chose to play there, preferring the quieter, more dedicated clubs on the surrounding blocks where the gaming rooms
were isolated from the ranks of slot machines and the dreadful
cabarets, and left to generate that bustling hush that is the mark of
a serious casino. He played quietly and sensibly, more aware than
most of the shapes and the dangers. He followed the lizard through
the carpeted halls of the town, past the plastic dioramas of mythical
Wild West scenes that decorated the bars and lottery rooms, up
and down stairs whose treads were inlaid with pulsating tubes of
light, through crepuscular rooms lit only by the glare from the
myriad glitterballs that hung like the cocoons of magical insects
from the one-way-mirrored ceilings. He ate mainly in the great
subsidised self-service cafeterias with their enormous salad bars
shaped like boats or Hawaiian huts and brimming like monstrous
horns of plenty with Boston lettuce and limestone lettuce and
escarole and chicory and endive and watercress and fennel and
rocket and avocado and tomato and scallions and artichokes and
kohlrabi and jicama and beetroot and coleslaw and wheat berries
and capers and baby corn and dwarf zucchini and giant radish and
string beans and olive oil and blue cheese dressing and thousand
island and croutons and walnuts and anchovies.
Sometimes he would become so involved that he would forget

to eat at all and just drink, discovering that the soft sweet options – Bacardi and coke, vodka and orange, whiskey and ginger – would lift him and keep him going right on through the night. But after several weeks of these he dropped the mixers, their high sugar content having brought on too many headaches, and began to eat again for energy, washing down the food with beer or neat spirits. One thing he didn't do was smoke: he'd quit on leaving LA, having decided to clean up his act a bit with the change in his luck, and he became known in several of the casinos as much for his complaints about the air quality as for the quality of his play.

The lizard taught him the patience of the desert, its ways and moods, how to survive. It taught him how to reconnect, how to move in sympathy with the forces around him. It taught him how to play amid the dry breezes of chance which blew across the tables, breezes which could drown a man in money as easily as a samoom drowns a village in red dust, which could snap the phase, become sand devil, twister, trash him and flip over to the far side of the rainbow. He spotted them now, always, when he walked down the street, caught them stapled to the sides of buildings, motionless, or darting from plant to plant. He found himself defining the city in saurian terms, always on the look-out for good places to catch the sun, favourable hunting grounds for flies, possible escape routes from small children with stones. A gecko took up residence on the balcony of his room, twenty-five storeys up. He studied it in the afternoons while he sat and dozed in his deck-chair, matching the rate of his eye blinks to that of the creature. Sometimes they'd look out over the desert together, scrutinising.

Judd had moved into a smooth space structured by a more prosaic set of desires and needs than the ones that had been set up for him during the course of his analysis. It was the space of a broken, imperfect universe, a cosmos of chance, where God did play dice, where God *was* dice, but where dice always acted in concert and never alone. And it was a slower space, too; time was reframed here, in a way that he found reminiscent of the picnoleptic playground of his childhood. When he slept his dreams were green, dark green, and full of scales. Nothing coherent, just a boiling mass of tails legs backs eyes, himself looking down on it, unmoved, feeling nothing but the throb-throb of life. Awake, he settled and spread, his perceptions altering as if under the influence of a drug, until the people around him became speeding, scurrying forms, their movements hasty, repetitive and predictably instinctual, the jitterings of gerbils nervous in their cages. He watched them buzz around the craps tables and the roulette wheels, circulating in tune with the tidal jabber of molecules on distant stars, like the people Joel had once seen from the top of the Empire State. As sand blows in and out of the boles and cracks and hollows of gaunt trees and crags the chips blew in and out of their palms.

Something began to take shape in the mess of his dreams. Less angular than the reptilian limbs, less jagged and harsh. It tantalised him. What was it? He began to sleep more in order to try and coax it out. Meanwhile, in the afternoons, he looked less at the lizard and more at the desert, at the rock. The lizard had reminded him of what he'd known as a child: that time was plastic. Now he wanted to stretch it out further. He would go beyond the reptilian. He would learn to think like a rock, yes, gamble like a rock, the slowest flow, becoming stone, Zen and the art of sedimentation. He was still obsessed by Schemata, and his success in Reno had made him determined to rid himself of the doctor's influence for once and for all. If the analysis had set up a kind of psychic irrigation system inside him, one which channelled his thoughts and controlled the way he cultivated his mind, then one way out was to clog it, to let the particles of dust in its waters settle and sediment, gather and obstruct. With the system unable to flow, pressure would build until eventually the pipes would break at their joints. He would be free.

So he let the weather of chance foul up the schemas around him, within him. He watched the whips and tails of matter whirl and catch at his feet and slowly, slowly cover his shoes, ankles, knees. He rolled the dice and shuffled the cards again and again, until eventually his fingertips began to blister, harden and crack. It felt good, it was part of his power. All was going according to plan, things were ossifying, it seemed he always knew now when to play, when to leave. Layer upon layer of magic dust accumulated around him. He became impervious to loss, unaffected by bounty. All that mattered was this calcification, this turning to stone. Outcrops could be lost and strata stripped away as long as this tendency remained. He would become a sentinel of this land in which the edifice of finance forever crumbled into sand seas of cash. Perversely, he would fossilise, transmute into living rock or, more fabulously, into a gemstone constructed from wind, earth and sky. The imposed, the hated mental economy would be ended and he would enter a new crystal life of the mind.

Judd didn't see it yet but in this last he had gone too far, become in the end just like all the others who came here to gamble. Despite all his talents and skills, like the rest of them he still nurtured a hope of perfection. Something always within him? Or a Parthian arrow from Schemata? Who knows, but thus tempted he couldn't resist. He had followed the lizard too far, gone beyond what it had to teach and, blinded by jewels, he dug deep down in his dreams. He could tell what it was now, bubbling up from that tangle of saurian flesh, night after night. It was a child, a tiny child, carved out of stone and emerald-eyed, viridescent.

11

Grundrisse

Joel emerged from both of the Mandelbrot lectures with his muscles in knots, talking like a maniac. Subhash, who throughout the sessions had been surreptitiously dabbing speed from a wrap he kept hidden beneath the table, said he felt the same way. But even in his artificially accelerated state he couldn't keep up with Joel's diatribe.

For two days Joel didn't sleep. After the first lecture he pursued Mandelbrot through the corridors of the Centre, pestering him with his questions, and would have spent the night at his bedside if he could have done. The next day it was all Subhash could do to drag him away into the Common Room and leave the French mathematician in peace, but although he managed that much it was beyond his abilities to calm Joel down once he had got him there. He began to worry that Axel or Gabriel, two friends who often teased him about his friendship with Joel, had spiked Joel's coffee with an hallucinogenic; it was the kind of practical joke that would appeal to them. Indeed, it was the sort of thing he himself had been involved in in the past.

'It's astonishing,' Joel kept insisting, 'don't you realise the implications of what he's saying? God, and to think I was suckered even for a minute by the juvenile Platonism of that idiot Metric.' Subhash had never heard him be so forthright before. 'Don't you see how it mocks the very notion of dimensionality? Mandelbrot's shown that form is not static and eternal, but is an expression of content over time! That a shape of infinite perimeter can exist within a circle of measurable

360

circumference. Mathematics itself becomes a matter of perspective. Everything becomes a matter of perspective.'

Subhash couldn't follow him. He couldn't see how the conclusions followed from the premise. 'Come on,' he said, trying to dilute his friend's excitement, 'everybody knows that anyway. We don't need mathematics to persuade us of it. Of course, it's exciting that the field is opening up, but . . .'

But Joel's energy was not to be earthed. 'Einstein is only the starting point,' he went on, connecting madly and – as far as Subhash could see – meaninglessly. 'And even he tried to confine the ramifications of his theories. This shows that the actual processes infiltrate existence to a degree beyond his most fervent nightmares. It is so ridiculous, it was right in front of me all the time, all those trays and trays of bread coming out of my father's ovens. In the folding, in the leavening, where volume is created by patterns of bubbles repeated again and again on every scale, making empty space is as important as matter. It's the Julia set, don't you see? Remember, one of the fractal images that Mandelbrot showed us? It was like looking at the creation itself. Like seeing the precise construction of space! And the self-similarity across scales, it means you can leap from one thing to the other and yet retain the same relationship. It's . . . I don't know, I don't know, there's no metaphysical division.' As he spoke he rushed around the room, crouched on chairs, flailed his arms, his body stuttering on the boundary between walking and running. 'And of course what's most marvellous of all is that it fits perfectly with the idea that each of the Sefirot contains within itself an infinite reflection of all of the others. There are possibilities here, there are possibilities. If the universe is fractal, infinitely regressive, as quantum mechanics might seem to suggest, then it might help to make sense of the duality between particle and wave, and it might also help us to understand ideas of perfection! Einstein and Mandelbrot, both Jewish, you see?'

Subhash tried to field an objection: 'But wait a minute, Joel, you're not making any kind of sense, you're fudging you must see that.'

Joel turned on him: 'You don't believe me, do you? You don't believe me. Didn't you hear him? I thought you heard him. But you see what a nonsense it makes of metaphysics? If you don't believe me I'll show you,' and he headed out of the room at speed.

'Joel, Joel, where in hell are you going?' Subhash yelled as he got up to follow.

It was gone midnight and the lab was empty. All the mini-computers were on, running their interminable calculations like so many cattle munching grass. Joel went straight to the nearest machine – it was busy analysing a portion of the data from one of the accelerator experiments that had been run the previous week – and terminated the programme.

'What the fuck are you doing?' panted Subhash, running into the room. 'That's seventy-two hours of processing time you've just flushed away!'

'It's not important right now.'

'You've flipped, man, you've lost it completely. I should never have let you go to that lecture, you're not safe to be let loose on anything except that damned space invaders console you spend so much time playing.'

'Is there a colour printer around here anywhere?'

'I have no fucking idea.'

'Find me a colour printer! Come on, do you want to see this or not?'

Subhash sighed. 'I think there's a four-colour on the third floor.'

'Can you bring it down here?'

'It weighs a ton. And it's probably locked up anyway.'

'Well, find the keys and get a trolley. There must be one around somewhere.' It was pointless to argue; Joel was already entering lines of Unix code into the machine. Deciding he might as well humour him, Subhash went off to get the printer.

It turned out not to be on the third floor at all, but on the fourth, in one of the classrooms. Although he could see it through the glass the door was locked so, wondering again why he was bothering and feeling that the sensible course of action would be to telephone the local asylum, Subhash went off in search of the night porter. He found him quickly enough, watching television in the coffee area on the second floor, and persuaded him to come and unlock the door.

Fortunately there was a trolley in the classroom but even so, by the time he got the printer back down to the lab Joel had produced several screens' worth of code and was more involved than ever. Annoyed that Joel could only muster a single grunt of approval by way of thanks, Subhash trailed off back to the Common Room to get himself a cup of coffee. He ended up going to sleep across a row of chairs, the latest edition of *Scientific American* lying open across his face.

When he awoke it seemed to him that the room was full of light. His first thought was that he had slept for hours, that it was morning. But as his eyes adjusted themselves to his surroundings he saw that rudely papered across the walls, tacked up on the ceiling, strewn across the floor were huge and vivid posters of fractal scenes, shimmering with iridescent colour like slices of giant precious stones. Some of them were full sets, glaring like the giant eyes of fantastic crustaceans, others were zoomed explorations, aerial views of the idyllic reefs and beaches of some fabulous travel destination, glimpses of the tangled boughs and jungle clumps of an undiscovered Rousseau.

'Oh, God,' he murmured, 'what has he done?' Rubbing his eyes, he got up and went to look for Joel. He wasn't difficult to find. The corridors that led to the computer lab were plastered with further pixellated pictures of sets with names like Newton, Plasma, Sierpinski, Popcorn, Mandelbrot, Spider, Tetrate, Lambda, Julia, Gingerbread, Kamtorus, Manowar, Manzpower. He felt as if he were walking down the fallopian tubes of some monstrous digital womb, from whose coruscated sides silicon life forms might at any moment begin to sprout like robot maggots. When he was near enough to the lab to hear the hum of the printer and the whirr of the fans he felt afraid. It was as if the whole building was alive. Frantic light played in a rectangle on the wall opposite the open lab door, the spilled photons scheming furiously like the molecules in some protoplasmic soup.

Peering round the door frame into the room, it looked to Subhash as if the treasure chambers of the world had been rudely melted down and converted into a series of epileptic pools, each of which was the baroque tracing of an obsessed and psychotic mind. Joel had got all of the computers generating fractal sets on their screens and flashing them in black and green, green and black. In addition to the colour printer, which was still chugging out the pictures that already covered every available surface, he had found a second machine, a dot matrix, which was spewing forth an endless roll of fascinating pattern into a susurrating pile that filled a corner of the room. All the lights in the lab had been switched off: the extraordinary brightness came only from the screens and the play of their contorted graphics across the myriad printouts. Compared with this grotto, the corridor and Common Room had been mere harbingers.

From beneath the pile of snaking paper a leg protruded. Subhash picked it up and pulled, and a body appeared. He checked his friend's breathing and felt his pulse, but he seemed right enough. Half dragging, half carrying, he got Joel to the Common Room where he laid him on the same bank of chairs on which he himself had slept. Then he hurried back to the lab to try and clear up some of the mess.

The killer app

In the years since Sputnik II was launched had war, terrorism, disaster become spectator sports? For Laika they had, for certain. Trapped in her capsule, totally integrated with all modern conveniences but with nothing to do, little excited her as much as the footage of real-life events. And of those, events where real life was in danger were best.

The Six Day War had been a glimmer, a taster, there'd been a few good pictures there, but Vietnam was a treat. How she'd adored being torn between her desire for the war to be brought to an end and her love of the constant stream of explicit on-the-ground news. Munich in 1972 had been fun, when the Israeli Olympic team had been taken hostage in front of the cameras with a third of the world's population tuned in. How exciting that was, such drama! It was a shame it was too dark to see the details of the bungled rescue attempt (a few flashes of rifle fire were all you could make out as seventeen people were killed). But it was exciting none the less, watching the palpitating viscera of the world breaking through the social veneer of the Games.

Laika liked all that. Which is why the 1982 Falklands War was such a disappointment. The British, so uptight! Hardly any TV. Where were the cruisers the jump jets the Exocets the infantry pinned down on the beach? The newscasters tried to keep everyone happy with models and maps, but it wasn't the same. No spice! No pizzazz! No *action*! Action's what you need. The rhythms of TV *demand* it. If Laika knew one thing she knew that. She had, after all, watched enough of the stuff. Vietnam had been a close war, immediate enough for you to forget that the images were manipulated. But the British had closed everything down so much you could see who was calling the shots. And who wanted to be reminded of that? 'Let it be free,' she yowled, 'let the media be free.' Or at least let it look like it was.

When Nathan of Gaza sits up and smiles

Joel's room was in an even greater state of disarray than the computer lab had been on the evening after the second Mandelbrot lecture. Although the space wasn't bathed in the same fantastic light, all the furniture had been pushed back against the walls and there were papers everywhere. To Subhash they appeared to be strewn completely haphazardly, but when he attempted to free a chair from under a stack of photocopies of articles discussing the invention and use of the number zero in various different cultures Joel turned on him almost savagely.

'No! No, don't touch those. Here. Sit here.' He cleared a space on the bed and motioned Subhash towards it. Raising his eyebrows slightly, the Pakistani gingerly picked his way between the stacks of material that encrusted the floor like intellectual moraine. Holocaust paraphernalia was spliced with salvaged fractal printouts, scientific abstracts with gutted books on gambling technique, circuit boards and wiring with electronics magazines. Alerted to the fact that a Byzantine system underpinned the mess, it now looked to Subhash as if Joel was indeed using the material in an attempt to define the axes of some bizarre personal geometry, creating a construct which through hitherto impossible juxtapositions would delineate a perspective that would somehow make coherent sense of it all.

Among the papers were phase space diagrams of the cycles of strange attractors that Joel had presumably downloaded from a bulletin board somewhere. Subhash had seen a few of them in the more adventurous periodicals; there was a vogue for this kind of mathematics in a number of American universities and some of it was beginning to become pertinent to his work on neural nets. Yet even to his unpractised eye some of the eerie images, simultaneously wholly new and totally familiar, were instantly recognisable: the Brusselator, the great wings of Lorenz's simple weather model, the folded ellipses discovered by Henon among the movements of the stars.

'Help me clear a space in the centre of the room,' insisted Joel. He indicated to Subhash which piles could be moved and where they should go (mostly into the bathroom, as it turned out, as this was the only spot which remained free of clutter). When the space was clear he pulled his friend into the hallway where, around the corner by the fire exit, stood the roulette table: a squat piece of furniture like an ornate kitchen unit with a wheel built into its top. 'I had to get Clive to help me move it out a couple of weeks ago,' Joel explained. 'That was after I'd finished all the testing. I've been needing to get the background right since then.'

'The background?' huffed Subhash, struggling a little beneath the table's weight.

'You know, the background! The surroundings. The milieu. These things don't work in a vacuum. That's the whole point.' They dragged the table into Joel's room and set it down in the space they had cleared. Subhash sat down on the bed to catch his breath and light a cigarette. Joel retrieved a spirit level from beneath a pile of shoes and dirty socks and fiddled with the table's adjustable legs, trying to get the thing level. After a while he broke off and, as if trying to remember which tool he needed, gazed into space for a moment or two, apparently distracted by the patterns the cigarette smoke was making in the air as it rose towards the ceiling on the tiny thermals of the room.

Subhash brought his reverie to an end. 'Look, Joel, are you sure you're all right?'

'What? Of course I'm all right.'

'But just look at all this! What the fuck is going on?'

'I told you. It's research. Isn't it obvious?'

'Sure, sure.' Subhash paused and drew on his fag, deliberately exhaling through the curlicues of smoke when he noticed that Joel had once again become fascinated by them. 'It's so obvious that I'm afraid you'll have to tell me what the connections are between the Mandelbrot set, the Holocaust and roulette, because I'm fucked if I know.'

Blind to the sarcasm (he took everything at face value now as a matter of course), Joel was excited by Subhash's apparent interest in his work. 'I don't know . . . I don't know how to put it into words, it's the movement, do you see? Here!' He pulled a shoe box full of postcards and photographs from beneath the bed and began to rummage through it. When he found the image he was looking for he brandished it at Subhash. It was the map of Europe that Jennifer had been so taken by over two years previously, which his father had once come across in the Brooklyn library, the one where places were only identified by the number of people who had been exterminated there. 'See this? It's Europe as a field, a quantum field, with death the spectral calibration for all and any eigenvalues. That's what I mean by background. And that ties in with this –' he flapped through the mess to the picture of the Lorenz attractor '– right? Which is obvious, because it's like the weather, I mean, look at it. You don't need a computer to work it out. Which is another thing, because all these networks, in the universities and here too, you link them all together, and the Internet, you've got the Internet, you know about that, you use electronic mail, right? Same thing! And if you read this book –'

367

he picked up one of the roulette manuals in the air '– of course, you only need the first paragraph and the last line of it, and this book –' he scrabbled for another text, the title of which Subhash did not catch '– though there's more reading involved with this one, I think, then it goes right through. I mean, it all connects. From the simplicity of this –' he indicated the roulette wheel '– to the madness of this.' He touched a photograph of Goebbels with his foot. 'It's a question of reconciling the two lights of Ein-Sof, "the light which contains thought" – and which contracted to make room for the creation, according to Nathan of Gaza – and "the light which does not contain thought" – which did not. These two form a dialectic, they're the active and the passive, and evil is the outcome. The problem of evil can only be solved at the time of final redemption, and I quote, "when the light which contains thought will penetrate through and through the light without thought and delineate therein its holy forms." Scholem, page one two six. Again, it's a question of the movement towards perfection and in order to prove the existence of that we need to track the movements of chance. And what do we use to do that? The computer, right? Which, funnily enough, could be described as the worldly embodiment of the light that contains thought. Think about it.' He looked at Subhash, hoping for confirmation, a gleam in his eye that scared his friend. Subhash shifted uncomfortably on the bed and looked for somewhere to put down the cup he had been using as an ashtray so he could light another cigarette.

'Let me demonstrate,' Joel continued imperiously. 'Watch.' He went across to the roulette wheel, spun it and at the appropriate moment sent the ball hurtling round contrary to the direction of spin with a flick of his spindly wrist. As it bounced and rattled off the revolving cups he sat down and took off his right shoe and handed it to Subhash. 'What do you think of that?' he asked.

'It's your shoe, Joel,' Subhash replied caustically.

'No! Look inside! Look inside!' Timidly, as if expecting a mouse-trap to snap closed on them at any moment, Subhash inched his fingers down inside the leather upper. At the bottom, right where the toes should be, there were four small pads and a few twists of wiring. He turned the shoe over and examined it, noticing that the sole was somewhat thicker and stiffer than he would have expected. The heel was particularly large; it had obviously been hollowed out at some point and subsequently rebuilt. Subhash looked up, his eyes full of questions.

With the pride of a father, Joel explained: 'Computers. One built into each shoe. 4K of RAM apiece. They communicate by wires that run up and down inside my trousers.' Before Subhash could protest Joel had unbuckled his belt and lowered his slacks. Snaking through the exceptionally thick hair that covered his skinny white legs were a few strands of plastic-coated wire.

'OK,' said Subhash with a slight feeling of revulsion, 'I've seen them. You can put them away now.' Joel rearranged his dress. 'But what are they for, anyway?'

'For that,' said Joel, pointing to the roulette wheel. 'For beating the system. For trapping chance, if you like. Chance has its habits as well, or didn't you know?' He was crowing now, his pride having got the better of him.

'But you can't predict roulette!' exclaimed Subhash, delighted at last to have understood something of what his friend was saying. 'It's totally random!'

'Nothing's random, least of all this, at least not now. Predicting a single result has nothing to do with chance anyway. It's a simple question of physics. The shoe computers are set up to simulate the spin of the wheel. Every wheel is slightly different, of course, so I've written an algorithm which can be tuned to individual set-ups. Obviously, this one here is programmed in at the moment. That's what the right shoe is for: by using the pads I can calibrate the speed of the wheel, the speed of the ball, the angle of tilt and so on. With the speed of the wheel it's easy; you just tap a particular button every time the zero cup goes past a particular point. Same kind of procedure for the speed of the ball. It takes a bit of practice, mind.' Joel had picked up this last turn of phrase, this Midlands expression, from Jennifer. For a split second he thought of her now. 'It's a closed system, and while the ball is bouncing around it the computer calculates its full run and transmits the answer to the machine in my left foot via the wire. In that shoe the pads are solenoids which vibrate a sequence according to where the ball will end up. In a casino I should just have time to place my bets before the ball stops.'

Subhash wasn't at all sure whether or not to believe him. 'All right, then. Let's see it work.'

Joel didn't need much prompting. He pulled on the shoes and handed a ball to Subhash. 'Right,' he said, 'you be the croupier.' Subhash looked at the hard white ball between his thumb and forefinger; with its perfect, Euclidean dimensions it seemed an anomaly in the scheme of things.

'Obviously, the system isn't capable of predicting an exact number . . .'

'Obviously.'

'. . . although with a powerful enough machine and accurate measuring equipment, lasers say, I've no doubt you could do it. Although I know the angle of tilt I have to guesstimate the speed, so we have to limit ourselves to betting on octaves. OK, I'm ready. Spin the wheel.' Subhash did as he was told and set the thing in motion. Joel pursed his lips and the movement of his toes beat tiny mounds in the soft leather of his shoes. Then Subhash introduced the ball and watched it bounce and chirrup around the basin like a hummingbird in flight. There was such a look of expectancy in his eyes that Joel himself resembled a bird about to take to the air, though with his long neck, large nose and puckered flesh he was more ostrich than anything else. He'll have a shock when he finds out he can't fly, thought Subhash meanly.

'4, 21, 2, 25, 17,' blurted Joel. Subhash shifted his attention to the wheel. The ball bounced for a few more seconds, then made up its mind and fell into the basin. It was a moment or two before the wheel slowed sufficiently to let them see the result.

Subhash announced it: 'Red thirty-six.'

Joel's cheeks flushed the same colour as the cup. 'It'll take me a while to get used to your delivery,' he stammered. 'Try it again, try it again.' Obediently, but with a disrespectful smirk upon his face, Subhash retrieved the ball and spun the wheel again. Once more, pursed mouth and puckered brow for Joel, the eyes slick with expectation, the toes bubbling away inside the shoe. 'OK: 28, 12, 35, 3, 36.' The wheel slowed and the ball came to rest.

'Red twelve!'

'There! You see?'

'It'll take more than that to convince me. Again.' Subhash flicked the wheel a third time and dropped in the ball; it bounced merrily and tick-tacked away the silence of the room. Again Joel called the numbers of the highest octave.

'Three!'

'You see? You see?'

'Again!' Wheel, spin, ball, eyes, toes, 34, 6, 27, 13.

'Thirteen. Again, again.' Field, energy, element, algorithm, system. 0, 35, 15, 19.

'Zero.' A whisper. 'My god.' Subhash was sweating: his armpits and groin bled moisture. On the next round Joel missed. Then he got three in a row, two missed, two more.

'Enough. I believe you.'

'Impressed?'

'Of course I'm impressed. I can also see why you're not worried about them threatening to suspend your grant after what you did to the computer room.' Joel nodded, a smile stretched so wide across his face that he looked as if his head might split. Subhash had never seen him so happy. 'You want to be careful, you know. If they catch you with that in any of the casinos they won't mess around.'

'Oh, they won't catch me. How would they catch me? They're hardly going to look in my shoes, are they?'

'It's brilliant! You're brilliant, quite brilliant. I want to be the first to say it. But don't let it go to your head. Be careful, that's all.'

'Sure.'

'Have you told anyone else about it?'

'No, only you.' The words dropped like a pebble into the pond of Joel's mind, sending out concentric ripples of paranoia. Maybe it hadn't been such a good idea telling Subhash after all. But the fear dissipated as quickly as it had come.

'So, are you going to show me the program?' the programmer asked with a smile, hoping to change the subject. 'I want to see how you've done all that in 4K.'

'I'm not the first person to try it,' insisted Joel, his modesty returning. 'Lots of people have had a go before. In America you can buy all sorts of systems by mail order, although none as advanced as mine of course. About ten years ago Thorpe and Shannon, a couple of gambling experts, built a roulette system you could wear. They used strobes and a film camera and a clock to calibrate the wheels, and built two little analogue computers complete with radio transmitters to do the calculations. Different variables were represented by different voltage levels. Amazing, really. The machines sent the answers as musical notes to tiny hearing aids they wore in their ear canals.'

'Did it work?'

'No, not really. All the wiring had to be so small that it kept breaking. I seem to remember that the system was over-sensitive to interference, too. But I don't know if anyone's come close since. Except for me, that is.'

'But isn't it enormously complicated to calculate? What about entropic degradation? Wind resistance? The rims of the cups upsetting the bounce? What if the croupier's got a sprained wrist?'

'We-ll, those things aren't so much of a problem really. As I said, you're inputting speed anyway, and if you take enough data it's fairly straightforward to allow for friction and random bounces. They don't upset the system that much. As far as the gambling goes you're only looking for a good edge over the game anyway, though ultimately I'll need more accuracy for the Project. It's the variables you can't predict which mess it all up. Like different balls. They can be made of ivory, nylon, acetate, Teflon and so on. Even human bone. During the war the Nazis made them out of the bones of Jews. There – there's another connection between those pictures and roulette for you.'

'Wow.' Joel had taken off the shoes and Subhash picked one of them up and turned it over in his hands, feeling down inside it, inspecting it – with reverence this time. 'How long have you been working on this?'

'Oh, long enough. It's not that big a deal, really.'

To his surprise, when Subhash looked up at Joel's face he detected there a genuine nonchalance. It came as a marked contrast to the pride he'd seen earlier. Such a disjunction was unsettling. It was too reminiscent of the mood swings Joel had exhibited at the time of the Mandelbrot lectures. 'Oh, come on . . .' he said.

'No, really, it is. The only difficult bit was building a small enough device. But even the memory restriction doesn't present too much of a problem. You could do it better than me. Predicting the system itself is easy. When I found out I could do it I was a bit disappointed.'

'But you've achieved so much!'

'Oh, this is only the first step. The idea is to get the system really accurate, so that I can predict the octant that's going to come up say ninety-five per cent of the time and to use that as an index against which I can judge when chance is not operating as it should.'

'I don't understand.'

Joel's eyes began to glisten and he became animated again. 'Look, I already explained to you that the universe is heading towards perfection, right? Well, if it's not perfect now, then it shouldn't exhibit perfect randomness. If the roulette wheel is a closed Newtonian system, then every spin should be a totally discrete event and I should be able to predict every one just on the physical data available. But what I'm finding is that I can't do that – you saw that already, I didn't get all of them right just now. This means that every event is not wholly discrete, that something is linking them together. If I can show that they're somehow linked, I can show that there's no true randomness in the universe.'

'But Joel, with the greatest respect, that's crap. What about if there's a tilt on the wheel? Or your timing is off. That would alter the outcomes.'

'I already told you I compensate for all that at the beginning. Listen, if I can show there are links between the spins, that's when the really exciting work can begin. What about the way people behave around a roulette table, for example? Huh? Huh? What about the way a crowd moves through a space, or a swarm of bees? Could you use some kind of fractal resonance to work out the movements of those in advance? What about the weather, or the development of grammar, or the way that roulette itself spread through Europe, from Paris to Britain with the Royalist émigrés in 1789, then to the health spas, Baden-Baden, Saxon-les-Bains, Wiesbaden and on from there? Could that have been predicted?

Lorenz found an attractor for the weather, didn't he? Then shouldn't there be one for the Holocaust? Why not? It makes sense. It's the only thing about it that does.'

Now Subhash was really confused. 'I don't think so. I mean, at the end of the day roulette's a closed system. You're right, it's Newtonian and therefore predictable. But these things, they're so nebulous. If even the world is deterministic, which I doubt – I mean, Heisenberg has taught us that – there are surely too many factors at work to predict anything in these other cases.'

'Heisenberg? Hah! That theorem's just a mathematical device, like Gödel's theorem. It means relatively little, in real terms.' Subhash looked shocked. 'You think I'm crazy, but it's not just me, you know! Other people have noticed it too. Haven't you read *The Gambler*, you know, by Dostoevsky? No? Here, I'll lend you my copy –' Joel dived under the bed for a moment and rummaged around; Subhash sat there feeling bewildered and sparked up another cigarette ' – here it is, borrow it, read it. He came to this through roulette too, but he knew there were patterns bigger than the game, surrounding the game, waves and eddies and whirlpools. It's all in there. Read it!'

'OK, OK, I will.'

'Remember what Mandelbrot said. All these things have patterns. The financial markets he showed us, cotton prices, self-similarity over time. If the financial markets have patterns then why not everything else? Time's internal to the system. Einstein told us that! I don't know why we've taken so long to apply it. "God doesn't play dice." No, *he's learning to play* and that's how the universe manages to exist in its current form.' Joel paused for a moment. 'Does genocide have a phase space?' he demanded.

'Joel, I . . .'

'How many degrees of freedom do you think an act of genocide has? Hundreds? Thousands? Millions? Or maybe just a handful, when you really look at it. A couple of dozen. Think of the liberties we take in mapping the sub-atomic world. Yet we can't take those liberties with history, oh no. It might give us a hope of understanding it and that would never do. We can't bear the fact that we needed machines to figure all this out for us. We can't bear it! I tell you there'll be an outcry against this stuff, because it has taken our own precious logic and subverted it. All those trees and hierarchies and classifications have revolted. The machines won't put up with it. You must know how complex the networks are, even here on site. There's a guy over on the French side who's writing some protocols that will allow any computer to talk to any other. You'll be able to access information from anywhere almost instantly. He's calling it CERNET. The way he's doing it, the data will break itself down into discrete packets, each of which will find its own way through the system, then reassemble itself at the end, like teleporting or something. You'll be able to leap from databank to databank, even if the data you want are on different machines. You'll be able to search for documents across entire systems, maybe even across countries or continents if you connect networks together via telephone. It'll be like swimming, or something, except it won't be like anything physical that we've known because every point in the datasphere will be effectively next to every other. I tell you what it will be like, it will be like thinking. We're finally building machines that emulate thought, even if they don't yet think for themselves. You should know all about that! It's a new kind of logic. It's "the light which contains thought". We're going to be able to use them to understand everything. They're going to change everything, you'll see.'

'But I'm not sure if . . .'

'Oh, come on! You work with these things. You know I'm right, you must do. And what if it's time that makes all problems unintegrable, but at the same time makes patterns? Patterns are the way to understand the unintegrable. The question then becomes, you know, how to look for the patterns, how to collect the data. There's so much data out there, but how to know what's significant and what's irrelevant, that's the problem. You have to have some way of narrowing it down, some kind of system that can consolidate all these influences for you. Let me ask you, how are you supposed to make sense of the Holocaust? Do you perform numeromancies on the numbers of people who died, on their vital statistics? Their ages, weights, sizes and so on? Do you plot the co-ordinates of all the death camps and see if they make some kind of recognisable constellation? Do you measure the levels of background radiation at these sites? Perhaps, perhaps. But if it's time that makes patterns of things, if it's time that keeps them in motion, then maybe it's still happening now. Maybe the figures aren't what's important. Perhaps. I don't know.

'My father always used to tell me there were three types of time, zimzum, shevirah and tikkun. He'd been told about them by some rabbi, but he'd never found out what the teacher had meant. But I have, I have found out. According to Kabbalah zimzum is the movement in which Ein-Sof withdrew into itself and created the ten Sefirot. When something exists within this kind of time it draws into itself and perfects itself. But after the vessels of the Sefirot have been broken and the world is created out of the chaos there's a new time, shevirah, the time of the world. This is negentropic time, in which out of the energy of that catastrophe links are created between things and enough organisation occurs for this universe to come into being, imperfect though it is. It is this time which leaves its traces in the patterns of chance, in attractors and so on. And lastly there is tikkun, the time which returns, what we call entropy, the flipside of shevirah that returns everything to perfect continuum, to perfect randomness.'

'You've lost me, I'm afraid. I didn't understand a word of that.'

Joel didn't seem to care. 'It's not all worked out yet. I'm still only at the beginning of it. There's so much to do now.'

'Yes, but Joel, man, you've got to get back to your research work. They're going to kick you out if you don't. You're on a knife edge as it is after what you did to the computer room.'

'What do I care if they kick me out? It's not as if the work going on here is important.' He gestured at the roulette table and chuckled. 'And as you said already, I hardly need their grant.'

That was enough. Joel had gone somewhere and it didn't look like he was coming back. Maybe he'd been there all the time, Subhash didn't know. But he didn't see what he could do to help him. 'I'm sorry, Joel, but it's late and I'm tired. I need to get back and get some sleep. Where's that Dostoevsky?' Joel passed it to him enthusiastically. 'Right, look I'll read this and tell you what I think. Maybe it'll help me understand what it is you're on about,

I don't know.' Subhash got to his feet and picked his way through the debris towards the door. But when he got there he hesitated, suddenly afraid to leave. 'See you tomorrow.'

'Yeh, perhaps.'

'Thanks for showing me your computer. It's damn cool, you know.'

'Yeh, sure, any time. Keep it to yourself, though. I don't want word about it getting round. I intend to use this thing for real.' For some reason this reassured Subhash and he smiled a final good-bye before exiting, his last glimpse into the room as the door closed revealing Joel hunched over one of the shoes with a screwdriver, making some minor adjustment that would further improve the performance of his machine.

Just friends

The child got most fun out of playing with other children. But it wasn't until she'd met Veronica that she'd realised quite how different she was. Veronica had been hurt by the Daddy (who was one of The Parents). She had friends of her own, too, but there were only three of them: Good Veronica, Sore Veronica and Veronica-come-here-and-be-punished. But unlike the friends of the My, the Veronicas were all very frightened and there didn't seem to be a Veronica-My at all. Emma helped the Veronica friends talk to each other and it wasn't long before they were unscared and a Veronica-My came out. Then Veronica was more like the other children, most of whom (except for Filthychild, but he was a special case) seemed to have only Mys, although some Mys were stronger than others.

The other Mys didn't know like the Emma-My did what the Hospital Nights were going to do, for example. The other children were simple compared with the Emma-My. The Emma-My liked to play games with them because she could see from their trembles what they were going to do and it made it easy for her to win. Sometimes the games would be nasty, like when the child felt the others from another room and the others felt her eyes on their skin, or when she got them to give her things (buttons, crayons, coins, bracelets, sweets, shoelaces, underwear). (When she was caught by the nurses getting presents they would punish her Severely.)

What was strangest about Emma was that she wouldn't talk. She *could* talk; she would try words for size, as if they were rings, or shoes, but most of them she seemed to reject as soon as their novelty wore off. Whereas other children raced at language as soon as they discovered it was the best way to get what they wanted, Emma seemed not to be interested. The population in her head chattered enough among themselves and it was generally obvious what those without wanted from her. But since there was nothing she wanted from them there was no point in talking so far as she could see.

The nurses regarded her as backward and a little tinged with evil. There was much gossip about who she was and why she was surrounded with such secrecy. The most popular theory was that she was the bastard child of one of the two princesses currently nubile and much hounded by the popular press. A politician's daughter was a theory in vogue for a while – everybody knew that the local MP had the morals of a billy-goat (he had seduced two of the nurses during a stay in the hospital ten years previously). But the nurse whose attempt to take a blood sample had led to all the windows in the nursery being blown out had no doubts. She had seen the child move things from a distance, she knew what it felt like to be near her and have her finger the fraying edge of your thoughts, she was not prepared to laugh off the teetering structures she built as one of the peculiar skills of the young. She knew that the child was possessed.

By what or whom she yet didn't know, but she became determined to find out. She consulted a medium and through her was introduced to the local coven, a group of women from the area with whom she found that she had a great deal in common. When she felt she could trust them she told them about the child. That was when she discovered that Emma was already known to them, that they'd sensed her and tracked her for some considerable time now. But as to what or who she was – none of them knew.

★

378

It had taken a while for the My to work out just what a Mummy was (for a long time the populace had thought it was simply another kind of Hospital Night) but when it did, Emma quickly realised that she should have one too. Rather than ask the nurses she decided she would search for her herself. After all, she would surely know the Mummy if she found her.

Whenever she was taken from her room her mental tendrils came out, just in case, just in case. Over the years she had found the vestiges of many people among the geometries of the wards and corridors, mainly geriatrics who had died and carelessly left themselves lodged in the angle of a cornice or clinging to a few cracks in the plaster, spots they'd been gazing at as the tremors of life had left them, the last gasp of their consciousnesses tracing out the angles and lines, and finding there the expression of their impoverished selves. Younger patients who had died in surgery or of cancer sometimes took up residence in the tubular frame of a trolley and the squeak of its wheels, or in the layout of the lights on a ceiling and the phase of their flicker. Of course these people didn't last for long – Emma was often lucky to find them and quite frequently when she returned to the place again they were gone. Neither could they communicate – they were, after all, no longer alive. But they were there none the less, like the pattern of static left on the screen of a television that has just been switched off, a dim and simple memory of the pictures that had once played across it.

So there was a chance she'd discover her mother to be one of these frozen sprites, slowly fading from the world like a melting snowflake, but she didn't and so she turned instead to her dreams.

The hard cell

She stole because she could, because it gave her a kick. It was a hobby, in a way. But in Stratford it was too easy, having worked in several of the shops herself. To give herself a challenge she had to take the bus to Leamington or Coventry, or even to

Birmingham, where she didn't know the territory so well and closed-circuit cameras were beginning to appear, giving it all an extra edge. But even then she'd invariably come back with a bag stuffed with toiletries and knick-knacks, books or clothes, make-up and CDs and stuff. Things which she didn't need and would never use. At Christmas she made up elaborate parcels for friends and gave most of it away, just to get rid of it.

She got good at it too, good enough to forget about taking precautions. It became so easy that it seemed like a joke, so that she got angry with herself if she paid for something when she could have nicked it instead. Her friends loved her for it, of course, it made her a bit of a star in the same way that sex had once done. She got quite political about it too, never stealing from shops that were independently run, only from those which were part of the 'capitalist machine'. She began to dream of bigger things, of robbing banks, emptying their vaults and giving all the money away, just to fuck the system. It would be like her shoplifting: she stole what she didn't want deliberately, to annoy them, to show them she was better, that she didn't need their consumerist society. It was a gas. Stim, who was the political consciousness of Desiring Machine, used to quote from anarchist tracts and communist leaflets. Mao Tse-tung, he observed, had said that the true guerrilla had to move among the population like a fish through water. This is how Jennifer felt and it made her high. Until the day that the fish met a fisherman.

It happened in Leamington one Saturday. There was a Joy Division gig at Warwick Students Union and she was going with Stim, Mike and Shelley. It was a nice day and they'd decided to meet up in Leamington first, go to the park. On her way from the bus-stop to the rendezvous, Jenn walked down the Parade, checking out the shops. It would be fun to have something to give the others.

She chose Woolworth's; it would serve them right for not paying her enough. The sun was shining, she felt on form. She walked in through the front doors. The shop took up the whole block. She could make it look like she was just cutting through. She cruised between the aisles, not looking around, confident and calm.

380

Back to school, the signs bright in yellow on blue. A kid's geometry set, that would do. She palmed one as she passed, working it up her sleeve as she headed out the back of the shop. Easy.

After twenty yards she slowed her pace and checked behind her. No one there except an ugly little guy with longish hair, a drab moustache and a Sainsbury's bag. Flushed with success, she remembered a book she wanted – while she was on a roll she might as well get something out of it for herself.

Making her way back to the Parade, she headed for the science-fiction section of Dillon's. Once in the shop she picked volumes off the shelves at random, pretended to look at them, then replaced them as she worked her way towards the book she was looking for, Robert Heinlein's *Stranger in a Stranger Land*. When she found it she took two copies from the shelf at the same time, opened the top one, read a little of the first page just as she'd done with the other books, then closed it and put the bottom copy back up on the shelf, slipping the top copy inside her jacket as her arm went up. That was the key moment, that was the needle in the vein. Now for the rush.

Gently does it . . . she looked at one or two more books, peering around out of the corner of her eye just to be sure, then walked out of the shop, waves of noradrenalin breaking across her brain. She'd done it.

Only she hadn't. A hand grabbed her arm, a voice said, 'Excuse me.' It was the man with the Sainsbury's bag and the moustache. She didn't at all comprehend the fact that she'd been caught. She tried to twist free but he tightened his grip and pulled her wrist sharply up. The book fell out. She began to cry out, sure that her assailant was a sex attacker.

Another man, dressed in a suit and tie and wearing a Dillon's name badge, bent down and picked up the Heinlein, held it out to her. 'This anything to do with you?' he sneered.

They took her into the office. Once it had filtered through to her that the game was up she hadn't resisted, had admitted it, had put on her best voice and said she was sorry, that she'd never done it before, she was just so embarrassed. She was only seventeen and since her dad had died she'd got no money for things for school.

They half believed her and gave her a cup of tea. Couldn't they let her go? She'd learnt her lesson now, she'd never do it again. No, they couldn't do that. They were sorry, but it was store policy. Shit.

The police turned up and took her to the station at the bottom of the Parade in a panda car. She walked out into the street with them, her head held high, vaguely hoping that someone she knew would see her. But from then on it got slightly more scary. They wouldn't let her smoke and took her into a room where they photographed her and made records of her fingerprints. Then they shut her in a cell on her own. There was nowhere to sit. Where was the bed? You were supposed to get a bed, weren't you? One part of the floor was slightly raised and painted with thick paint. She sat on that.

She began to realise that they were serious. They were going to prosecute her. She couldn't believe it. Most of all she couldn't credit how stupid she'd been, letting the guy follow her like that. What had she been thinking? She was such a fucking freak. She'd always told herself that if someone – anyone – followed her out of a shop the first thing to do was ditch the goods and then scarper. But it had never happened, until now, and what had she done? She'd gone off to steal something else. Fuck fuck fuck! What a fucking idiot!

She thought of the others, probably still waiting for her, and wished there were at least a proper window. The only light came in through a bunch of thick cubes of frosted glass, unbreakable and opaque. Why couldn't she have bars? She wanted bars. At least then she could see out, let her mind slip free between them.

She went to the cell door and banged on it. 'I want a cigarette! Let me have a cigarette!'

She heard footsteps coming down the corridor and she shut up. Someone's chest appeared at the access slot. 'Stop your bloody yelling, will ya? You'll wake all the other idiots up, then there'll be hell to pay. 'Ere,' and there was a short pause while the man fumbled in his pockets. A moment later there was the grate of a lighter and a lighted fag appeared through the slot.

Jennifer took it. A Benson! All right! 'Ta.'

'Don't mention it. Now they'll be with ya in a minute, so just calm down.'

Jenn retreated to the back of her cell, feeling like a real jailbird now. But the cigarette didn't really help: it made her shake a little, and made her paranoid too, and she started to think about what would happen if the shop pressed charges. There'd be an investigation. They'd come to her house, maybe they'd even take her into care. Shit shit shit shit shit! What would she do then? She wanted to cry but she wouldn't let herself. She needed to conserve energy, muster her forces, man the defences. She was stronger than them.

She stubbed out the fag on the wall and listened to the drumming of her heartbeat. The cell was brightly lit and the jagged, flickering light was giving her a headache. She closed her eyes, but when she did her heart seemed to beat louder than ever, *baboom baboom baboom*, until its rhythm filled the cell. She felt queasy and stretched out full length on the floor, the pumping blood hot in her ears. *Baboom baboom baboom.* Why hadn't they come to get her yet? Wasn't she supposed to be allowed to make a phone call? *Baboomba boombaboomba boombaboomba.* Yeah, right, like who would she call? *Boombababoombaboom boombababoombaboom.* That rhythm wasn't right. That was an old rhythm, a rhythm from before, the rhythm she'd fallen asleep to every night for the best part of two years. *But she wasn't pregnant any more!* Her imagination was playing tricks on her so she opened her eyes and stood up, banged her forehead with the heels of her hands.

Boombababoombaboom.

'Get out!' she began, 'get out! Get out getout getout gerrout gerrout geough!' Before long she was hammering again on the door.

This time the duty sergeant opened it. 'I thought I told ya . . .'

'It's all right, we're ready for her now. Ms Several, would you come with me, please?' Jennifer went, trying to hide her tears.

It was her first offence and they let her off with a caution.

Some kind of home

It was Smoke that found her first. She was a screech of light and easy to spot: Smoke recognised her as readily as it would a distorted reflection of Emma's own face. But the Mummy was not out of herself like Emma was and the populace were all a little disappointed, though none of them liked to admit it. They wanted to communicate, but it was a little like trying to tease an octopus from a hole in a rock. Despite all its friends, the My wasn't powerful enough. Something else would have to be done.

The master of the name

When Subhash got back to his room he flung the book on to a shelf, where it was to lie undisturbed for several weeks. He was confused and frustrated and felt guilty too, as if it were his fault that things had gone this far. No wonder Joel had never been particularly sociable, if that was what he had been working on in his spare time. It was astonishing – he'd had no idea the guy was that clever. Maybe a little too clever: one of the truisms that got passed around CERN was that there was a fine line between very intelligent and very stupid, and Subhash had seen more than one brilliant scientist behave like a retarded child.

He avoided Joel until the worry of *how* he should help became sublimated into the worry of *whether* he should help. What right did he have to interfere, after all? Joel was a free agent, and apart from spouting a lot of nonsense and getting over-excited one night in the computer room he didn't seem to be doing anything actually harmful. In any case wasn't his sanity proven by the fact that he'd single-handedly put together that amazing roulette predictor?

The weeks passed and Subhash saw very little of his friend. They ran into each other on the campus every now and again but Joel always seemed preoccupied and Subhash was too embarrassed that he hadn't made more of an effort to keep an eye on him to make conversation. As time went by and one by one opportunities were lost, that embarrassment grew (and, correspondingly, the number of opportunities to overcome it diminished).

One night Subhash lay in bed turning some of these things over in his mind. It was very late; he had spent all evening in the labs trying to refine a piece of software which dealt directly with the detectors in one of the collider experiments. The program kept reiterating when it wasn't supposed to and what had seemed in the beginning a simple coding conundrum had turned, as he had traced out the logical threads of the problem, into a veritable Gordian knot. Finally he had come to the decision that it was the entire architecture of the program that was at fault – apart from a few key subroutines the whole thing was going to have to be rewritten and that was a couple of weeks' work at least. He had traipsed off to bed, but once there he couldn't sleep, the lines of code still racing through his mind as if he was coming down from a trip. Outside, the advancing front of a storm hummed and yawed, the fluctuations in the air pressure affecting his mood. Summer was long gone and the storm was a harbinger of the cold weather to come, weather which would bring snow to the hillsides and a frozen crust to the edges of the lakes. It was odd, but Subhash always preferred the research centre in winter: to be surrounded by the Alps at their harshest made it seem as if the work going on there was nothing less than an attempt to face down the terrifying uncertainties of nature. Like so many scientists, Subhash was a tuppenny Romantic at heart.

As the first drops of rain crackled on the window he remembered the Dostoevsky Joel had lent him. He'd look at it for a while; that would send him to sleep. He fetched it down from the shelf where he had tossed it a month or two before and, propping himself up on his pillows, began to read. It was an old paperback. The spine cracked as he opened it and the paper felt uncomfortably dry against his fingers. 'I am back at last after my absence of two weeks,' he read.

Our party has been in Roulettenburg since the day before yesterday. I thought they would have been expecting me with inexpressible impatience, but I was mistaken. The General looked at me with the coolest detachment, uttered a few condescending words, and sent me to his sister. It was evident they had borrowed some money somewhere. I even thought that the General was a little ashamed to see me. Maria Philippovna was extremely busy, and held only a short conversation with me; she took the money, however, counted it, and listened to everything I had to report. Mezentsov, the little Frenchman, and some Englishman or other were expected to dinner; as usual, as soon as there is some money there is a dinner party; the same as in Moscow. Polina Alexandrovna, when she saw me, asked me why I had taken so long, and then walked away without waiting for an answer. Of course she did it on purpose. All the same, we shall have a talk. A lot of things have accumulated.

Already the lines of code had stopped zipping through his mind and he was feeling tired. He knew it was too late to get into the book from the beginning, so he opened it to a bookmark Joel had left in the middle.

Meanwhile I watched and took note; it appeared to me that pure calculation means fairly little and has none of the importance many gamblers attach to it. They sit over bits of paper ruled into columns, note down the coups, count up, compute probabilities, do sums, finally put down their stakes and – lose exactly the same as we poor mortals playing without calculation. But on the other hand I drew one conclusion, which I think is correct: in a series of pure chances there really does exist, if not a system, at any rate a sort of sequence – which is, of course, very odd. For example it may happen that after the twelve middle numbers, the last twelve turn up; the ball lodges in the last twelve numbers, say, and then passes to the first twelve. Having fallen into the first twelve it passes again to the middle twelve, falls there three or four times running, and again passes to the last twelve, and from there, again after two coups, falls once more into the first twelve, lodges there once and then again falls three times on the middle numbers, and this goes on for an hour and a half or two hours: one, three, two, one, three, two. This is very entertaining. One day, or one morning, it will happen, for example, that red and black alternate, changing every minute almost without any order, so that neither red nor black ever turns up more than two or three times in succession. The next day, or the next evening, red only will come up many times running, twenty or more, for example, and go on doing so unfailingly for a certain time, perhaps during a whole day. A great deal of all this was explained to me by Mr Astley, who remained standing by the tables all morning but did not once play himself. As for me, I was cleaned right out, and very speedily. I staked twenty friedrichs d'or on pair straight away, and won, staked again and again won, and so on two or three more times. I think about four hundred friedrichs d'or came into my possession in some five minutes. I ought to have left at that point, but a strange feeling came over me, a kind of desire to challenge fate, a longing to give it a fillip on the nose or stick out my tongue at it. I staked the permitted maximum – 4000 gulden – and lost. Then, getting excited, I pulled out all I had left, staked it in the same way, lost again, and after that left the table as if I had been stunned. I could not even grasp what had happened to me, and I did not tell Polina Alexandrovna about losing until just before dinner. I had spent all the time until then wandering unsteadily about in the park.

By now Subhash's mind was beginning to flip-flop in and out of sleep and he was having difficulty following the text. He folded the book closed on his index finger and laid it on the bed for just a moment . . . just a moment. Code flashed up again on the inside of his eyelids and he mentally flicked it away, trying to imagine that the letters and numbers were luminous cobwebs which could be dusted out of his consciousness. Thus, brushed to the margins of his vision, the lines of text became bright strips: the flickering light when the film runs out of the projector, the fractal posters with which Joel had once covered the walls of a corridor. Then they were snow banks at the side of a rushing river and he was in the mountains and it was already winter. He thought he was alone, but no, he was with Joel, and someone else who could be Axel but he couldn't be sure, and yes, his father, too. His father was complaining that it was far too cold, that they should all go back to Pakistan where the weather at least was decent. He was trying to tell the three younger men something about a plane, waiting for them in the valley, they should go now, they should hurry.

But his words kept getting drowned out by the sound of rushing water and they were not that interested in what he had to say anyway. Joel remonstrated with him, shouted at him to speak up. Subhash argued back, standing up for his father although he didn't want to. The man who was and wasn't Gabriel was eating something and he tried to hand a piece of whatever it was to Subhash. Subhash took it, but it was terribly sticky and he couldn't scrape it from his hands. He was suddenly frightened; the argument between Joel and his father was intensifying and he was now preoccupied with trying to rid his skin of this gunk. He wanted to ignore it and stop the argument but somehow he couldn't – he had to be clean before he could proceed, it was very important. He took a few steps towards Joel. The ground gave way. He was sliding towards the river, down a gully that was opening up below him at the boundary between the mud and the snow. The gunk was all over his feet, preventing him from kicking them out and slowing his fall. Looking up, he could see his father staring down, right arm around Joel's shoulders, shouting *It doesn't matter, it doesn't matter*.

The water roared away below him, its surface seething like the leaves in a hurricane. He hit it and he woke up in the communal kitchen at the end of his corridor, of all places. It was obviously late: nobody else was about and after the mountain dream the silence was disconcerting. He looked at his watch, but he couldn't quite decipher the time. Shit. He would have to get a new one. He thought to make himself a cup of tea to take back to bed. He opened the fridge and a rat darted out. It raced through his legs and out of the kitchen door. He shrieked, but his fear sounded pathetic in the silence. The animal had eaten all of the food and had gnawed out the bottoms of the two or three cartons of milk that had been in there. The white liquid had flooded the shelves and now spilled out across the floor. Gingerly, Subhash picked up the empty cartons, afraid that they might be filled with insects or some such horror, and dropped them in the bin. He tried to mop the floor but the milk turned to putty so he gave up. Let somebody else deal with it. He went back to his room, undressed and got into bed.

He had been programming all day and the lines of code still raced through his mind as if he was coming down from a trip.

Outside the advancing front of a storm hummed and yawed, the fluctuations in the air pressure affecting his mood. Summer was long gone and the storm was the harbinger of weather which would soon bring snow and a frozen crust to all the lakes. It was odd, but Subhash always preferred the research centre in winter: to be surrounded by the Alps at their harshest made it seem as if the work going on there was nothing less than an attempt to face down the terrifying uncertainties of nature.

As the first drops of rain crackled on the window panes he remembered the Dostoevsky Joel had lent him. He'd look at it for a while; that would send him to sleep. He fetched it down from the shelf where he had tossed it and propped his head up with some pillows so that he might read it more easily. It was an old paperback. The spine cracked as he opened it and the paper felt uncomfortably dry against his fingers. There was a knock at the door. Subhash thought it must be his mother. He pretended not to be there but whoever it was entered anyway. It wasn't his mother, it was Joel. He stood at the side of the bed, his head too big for his shoulders. Subhash tried to get up but his limbs were incredibly heavy, far too heavy to move.

Joel's face floated down until it was level with his own. *What becomes of any holocaust?* he asked in an even, rhetorical tone. *The flat light of the sun and the grind of the tide levels all bones into beaches, where children build castles whose moats murmur with the rhythm of the shallows.*

Something moved on Joel's shoulder. Subhash just had time to identify it as the rat from the fridge before it leapt at his face and sunk its teeth into his nose. He screamed and woke up.

Subhash knew. He didn't know what he knew, but he knew none the less. He pulled on some clothes and went down the main stairwell and out into the night. The worst of the storm must have passed while he slept, but it was still raining heavily and as it was a good twenty minutes' walk to the accommodation block in which Joel lived he took his car. The tarmac was slick and black, the street lights twice as bright for being reflected in the giant mirrors that the rainwater made of the road. Subhash drove as quickly as he dared.

He pulled up at the end of a row of vehicles and ran from the car to the glass entrance doors, his jacket pulled up over his head to keep off the worst of the rain. The doors were unlocked and once inside he made his way up the stairs, taking two or three steps at a time, his short, plump legs working like pistons. He reached the fourth floor, half jogged half walked along the corridor to Joel's room and knocked on the door, leaning heavily against it to catch his breath. There was no reply so he knocked again, then tried the handle and found the door unlocked. The room inside was completely bare of everything except the roulette table and the furniture. There were a few coffee cups in the sink and a couple of dustbin bags full of rubbish in the corner. Joel was gone.

Subhash checked the cupboards but they were bare save for a few empty boxes and an odd shoe. In the bedside cabinet he found a plain white envelope with his name scrawled across it in biro. He tore it open; inside there was a single sheet of paper. On it were printed the words:

Joel Balaam Kluge

Subhash ripped the envelope apart in the hope of finding a more substantial message, an address, anything; he ransacked the room once more, but there was nothing. He knocked on neighbouring doors; at all save one he was met by silence or a mumbled 'Fuck off'. The exception was opened by a man whom Subhash didn't recognise, who came to the door smelling of amyl nitrate and drawled that no, he didn't know Joel and no, he hadn't seen him leave, while his lover stood in the background watching Subhash with dilated eyes and provocatively scratching at his pubic hair.

Giving up on the bedrooms, Subhash searched the communal areas, but with no more success. Then he drove around the campus for three quarters of an hour, craning his neck to try and see through the driving rain. He had the radio on low and occasionally he thought he heard his mother's voice in the music and wondered if he might still be dreaming. Eventually he gave up and went back to bed where this time, doubly exhausted, he quickly fell asleep.

Flip-side

Smoke was the most adventurous of them all and sometimes it would be gone for days at a time. Once, though, it was gone for a whole month, which worried the populace sick. When it came back, for the entire next week it slept during the day instead of at night. Lonely Dear? said this was because Smoke had been away on the other side of the world in search of a father. Exray told her not to be stupid. No one could get on the other side of the world. The world was flat, like people. Exray could prove it.

The song of the sands

Back in Reno, months and months went by that seemed to Judd like days, like hours even. He became ever more still, ever more composed. The people who milled around him gasped at his magnificence, at his profile – so strong, so self-assured for someone barely twenty-one. Women wilted as he passed, or swarmed around him suppurating as he sat steady at the bar. Judd remained aloof and uninterested, his sexual rhythm having settled into a new and longer cycle. He had sublimated his desires and channelled them into his gambling; they were now a part of the geography of chance like everything else. It was a terrain which was as familiar as the back of his hand; he could find his way across it almost without thinking.

Meanwhile, in his dreams, the child had fully emerged, a silent statue encrusted with moss, and the lizards had receded into the background. If Emma could indeed probe the world's collective psyche as though it were some kind of networked data space, then perhaps this image was some kind of residue she had left in passing – a vapour trail, a wake. One night she must have found her father and by touching him unsettled the settling sediments of his brain

391

enough to suggest not only an image of herself but one of his future, assembled from the various tendencies of his personality that she'd probed. But Judd, who had no idea that this child had ever been born, let alone that she'd fingered his brain from a distance of five thousand miles, was not likely to interpret his dream in this way. For him, the statue nightly carved from the effluent of his subconscious represented the collected deposits of Jennifer and Schemata that he was managing to mine from himself. To him, the dream was a sign that he was finally ridding himself from their influence.

So he was taken completely by surprise when tectonic activity set in, when the contours and features which he had triangulated for months with the throw of the dice, the fall of the cards, began to stray and shift. At first the movement was imperceptibly gradual: a couple of losing streaks, a series of unanticipated hands. He thought perhaps that he was tired and, when it persisted, took a couple of days off. He lay by the pool, didn't drink so much, ate in restaurants at several removes from the casinos. But on his return to the tables he continued to lose.

It wasn't simply bad luck. Judd had built bad luck into his habitat. He knew its courses and haunts, its manifestations and its omens. No, this wasn't simply bad luck. His game was slipping away. The ramparts of his edifice, carved like the earth itself from the attractors and permutations embedded in the random fields of the cosmos, were slowly crumbling, deformed by awakening internal processes. Great blocks of his gambling environment had suddenly shifted along fault lines he'd not known were there. Craters were opened and volcanoes thrown up. Rivers disappeared into the ground, only to burst out the walls of previously featureless cliffs. Lakes drained and hot springs appeared. Valleys were filled with torrents of lava. Judd didn't know what to do. Everything kept changing, nothing stayed still. He became frightened and lost among the mesas, scarps and hanging valleys of what was already an alien landscape.

In an attempt to salvage the situation Judd left The Golden Gecko and moved into a quieter hotel, favoured by professional gamblers, and from this new base he set about regrouping. He consulted the tally he kept of his winnings: four months of steady gaming had seen the ten thousand Scofield had given him turned into eighty-three – and that was after he'd deducted his expenses. But that had been two weeks ago; in the past thirteen days he had lost steadily, to the tune of almost thirty thousand bucks. This still left him forty grand up, a tidy sum by any account, but that lost thirty thou nagged away at him. He could feel it like an ecthyma on his palms, an ulcerating itch that only the dice could balm.

He moved to yet another hotel, hoping that would change things, but he continued to lose. Every morning he sat in his room trying to make the decision to leave Reno, rolling the ivory dice Scofield had given him out across the glass top of the coffee table, a hundred times, a thousand times, until he drove himself mad with the noise they made and ran downstairs to play. One morning he managed to pack his bags, left everything out but a bottle of bourbon and the dice, sat there throwing them in the hope they would tell him to go, but all the time changing the rules of the game so that he could make sure he'd stay. The suite was expensive, much larger than the others he'd taken, and plush – if he stood barefoot on the deep-pile carpet he couldn't see the tips of his toes. The double bed was a waterbed, with a switch at the side which set the whole thing vibrating.

The bourbon made him dizzy. He looked at the dice on the table top, the two objects complicated by their reflections. There seemed many more possibilities here than he had previously accounted for. It suddenly occurred to him that he had become very proud. He was in trouble.

Three times he picked up the telephone and began to call Scofield. Three times he put it back. He didn't want to do this. He wanted a cigarette. His palms itched and sweated, and he wiped them on his pants. Shit! The fourth time he finished dialling and let it ring.

A woman answered: 'Hello?'

'Yes. Get me Irving Scofield.' He would be curt. He was not in the mood to be fucked around.

'You would like to talk to Mr Scofield?'

'That's what I said.'

'Mr Scofield is busy right now. Can you call back?'

'Tell him it's Judd.'

'Judd. Judd who?'

'Just tell him Judd. It's urgent.' The woman said nothing and the line went quiet for a while, and Judd wondered if he'd overdone it, but then Scofield came on the line. Judd explained the situation as best he could, which was not particularly coherently.

'So you've got trouble with your game?' said Scofield, trying to sum it all up.

'I guess so.'

'Well, I do know a man. You'll have to go to him, though. He doesn't travel. And he may not help you. I'm not sure he takes students.'

'That's fine. I'll try it. Where is he?'

'London, last I heard.'

Judd hesitated for a moment. The prospect of returning to England was not immediately attractive.

'No problem.'

'Give me the fax number of your hotel. I'll send you a letter of introduction. He's an interesting guy – I think you'll like him. But go easy. He's not the kind of person you meet every day.'

'Who – what's he like?'

'He's an old friend of mine. I never told you, did I, that I used to gamble a bit myself? Back in Atlantic City, just after the war. Anatole was kind of my partner. We worked the seafront together. He had your talent, Judd, and he really knew how to use it. Me, I couldn't take it.'

'What happened?'

'Well, it's a long story, but back then Anatole had a mouth on him; still has, for all I know. When he won big, which he began to do most of the time, he couldn't shut up about it. Doesn't take a man too long to make enemies that way. Guess you know all about that, huh? Anyway, things got a bit out of hand and we had to skip town. We were lucky – back then we were always lucky. But it put the shits up me and I decided to leave Anatole to it. I'm kind of attached to my balls.'

'So what happened to him?'

'He moved around the States for a while, made himself a small fortune, then went to Europe. Set himself up in this big villa in Monte Carlo, filled it with beautiful women, designer furniture. I went to visit him once, 'bout ten years back.'

'But I thought he was in London.'

'Yeah, he is now. Or so I was told. Tell you the truth, I haven't heard from him pretty much since I saw him in France. But a mutual friend told me he'd moved to London, so I guess that's where you'll find him. I'll fax the address along with the letter.'

'Thanks, Mr Scofield.'

'Don't mention it, Judd. You go see Anatole. He was always the best. If he can't help you, nobody can.'

Judd put the phone down and lay back on the bed. Using the remote control he flicked through the cable channels, stopping when he reached some porn. For a moment the blood rushed to his penis and there was a glimmer of hope, but then just as suddenly the writhing bodies disgusted him. He switched off the set and went to the balcony door. The hotel was on the edge of downtown and his room was on the twenty-fifth floor, so he could see the desert beyond the low buildings which stretched away into the middle distance, the homes of the service workers who vacuumed and cleaned and polished after people like him all day long, all night long, all year round. The empty land hissed and curled its way to the horizon, where giant facets of the heat haze reared up, great flat silver glints which spanned the burning air like electrons leaping orbits, a new realm between earth and sky. In the silence, the no-sound vanished by the steady hum of the air-conditioning unit, Judd fancied that he could determine the vast roar of it all. It was out there, coming for him, for all of them. All maps, not just his own, would be melted down by the blast. There would be some great reconfiguration, perhaps so great that no one would even notice it.

He opened the door, the seal cracking with the hiss of an airlock, and stepped out on to the tiny balcony that jutted like an eyrie from the face of the building. Far below, the traffic squelched and shrieked along its net of melting tarmac. He looked at the street directly beneath – on which the entrance to the hotel was situated

– and, as he watched, a taxicab swerved to avoid another car coming blithely down the middle of the road and hit a woman who had just stepped down off the sidewalk. She was knocked back and lay splayed out in her short yellow dress and blue jacket like some fabulous seabird washed up on to a beach slick with oil. The traffic backed up and other people gathered around, creating a scene. A dissonant chorus of horns began to chime upwards from the traffic stuck at the neighbouring intersections. Someone was attending to the woman; from his height Judd couldn't be sure, but it seemed from the newcomer's behaviour that the victim was still alive, if only barely.

Now that his eyes had grown used to the distance, Judd began to make out minute objects that were scattered across the street. They splayed out from the woman's prone form in a fan; she must have been carrying them when she fell. But he couldn't tell what they were, these small items that lay in such profusion on the roadway. He looked on for several minutes more, until the suck of sirens indicated that an ambulance was threading its way through the stationary traffic. The blare of horns had grown even louder; it seemed as if the whole city was in gridlock. On the horizon the silver hazes still flickered, but without their previous urgency: the threat, whatever it had been, had apparently evaporated. Perhaps, he reflected, it had been neutralised by the sacrifice below. Judd thought of the fax that would be arriving and turned back inside, letting the building swallow him up, not realising that of all the rooms he'd stayed in Reno, this was the first not to have a gecko in residence on its balcony.

Twenty-five floors down the paramedics loaded the stuttering body of the croupier into the ambulance, while onlookers surreptitiously squabbled over the casino chips which speckled the road like some strange and magic dust.

0 1 1

'Woof, woof!'

Laika, first dog in space

12

The sorcerer's apprentice

His ideas had progressed. He'd milked the Geneva casinos for money and in the process had become more and more aware of the nature of his own role in his Project, in the great scheme he was trying to uncover. He could feel the pull of tikkun in his gut. He meditated on his middle name, Balaam. He knew that names were important, magical even. He'd been given this name by a mohel, a ba'al shem, so his father had told him. In the Bible, he knew, Balaam was the sorcerer, the one who could draw forth the spirit of impurity from the kelippot – the dark forces of the universe which took on substance from the shards of the broken vessels – and mix together the clean and the unclean, using the power that emerged to fight the demonic. According to the Zohar, to complete his skills the sorcerer must journey to the 'mountains of darkness' and find Aza and Azael, the rebel angels who lived there. He, Joel, was the sorcerer. And he knew well enough about the mountains of darkness. He knew about Hitler's obsession with the Spear of Longinus, Himmler's design for Wewelsburg castle and the street plan of the city that was to be built there; he had read of the Thulegesellschaft and a thousand other conspiratorial organisations. And he'd developed his own theories about magic too – that magic was a language, a way of understanding and manipulating power, and that as techniques, physics or political rhetorics were no more or less magical than the occult simply because they were couched in rational terms.

He travelled by train, trying to keep to the old lines, the ones that pre-existed the war. He went to Lyon and from there up to Dijon, then on to Vittel and finally to Munich, where he stayed for several weeks while he applied for the appropriate visas for East Germany, Poland and the USSR.

By day he wandered the streets, entering the well-appointed stores and Bierkeller at whim, touching and drinking, asking shop-keepers and barmen blunt questions about the war, about the Jews, about their families, demanding to know the extent of their involvement. More than once he was attacked, but he was angry now and no longer concerned for himself – and besides, his thin, hard body made a poor target and an effective, if flailing, weapon.

Four or five times a week he took the train to Dachau, quietly horrified by the way the metropolitan service took him through neat suburbias to the site of the old camp. He sat among school-children, unemployed youths, tourists encumbered with their day sacks and cameras. The old gates were still there, *Arbeit Macht Frei*, a couple of the dormitories (now museums), the gas chambers and ovens (which had never been used), the walls against which people had been lined up for the firing squads (their brickwork pitted and pocked). Neatly raked gravel covered the site like a living-room carpet. The positions of the original dormitories were marked out by two courses of bricks, mathematical figures under a pallid sky. He could have been looking at Aztec markings in the desert.

Had the birds stopped singing here, was that true? He wasn't sure, he couldn't tell.

It was so abstract. It was a geometric fancy, a blueprint, a foun-dation for something rather than something's remains. But somewhere among these angles and their relationships were the equations he was seeking. He had read about a spherical temple being constructed in the international city of Auroville in the south-east of India which was to house the world's largest crystal – Zeiss were growing it now in their laboratories not far from Dachau itself. The design had come to the architect, a woman, a disciple, the Mother she called herself, in a dream. The proportions of the temple accorded to certain physical constants. Something like that was happening here. He thought about Nazi psychology, that bizarre blend of Madame Blavatsky's theosophy, Gurdjieff's mysticism and the archetypes of Nordic mythology.

He had purchased various measuring devices in Munich: a retractable tape measure, a small Geiger counter, several pairs of dividers, a compass, a kelvin thermometer and even a small theodolite. Thus equipped he took measurements of the distances between the bullet holes, of the radii of the iron letters above the gates, of the width of doorways and height of windows and thickness of the walls, of the angles between buildings, of the levels of background radiation. He noted everything down, kept it with him, transformed and plotted it, turned it into equations and matrices, used these to perform translations. The numbers of spectacles left, the numbers of gold fillings melted down, the weight of hair shorn, the numbers dead from shooting, starvation, cholera, shock, spotted fever, torture, suicide, gassing, incineration. There was a huge board, white words on black, the towns of Europe and the numbers killed there, hundreds of places, millions of people. It was the original of the photograph he had, the one that he'd shown to Jennifer and Subhash. No borders, no coastlines. Names and numbers. White on black. Names. Numbers. Indices. Vectors. A zone. *A quantum field, with death the spectral calibration for any and all eigenvalues.* And every time he took a measurement or wrote down a figure he rolled a pair of dice and scribbled the total alongside.

In the beginning he couldn't see his way. He felt overwhelmed. He couldn't see how it would work. By day he wrote measurements and dice throws in notebooks, by night with the machine in his shoe he visited the casinos in town. He needed the routine. The desire to give in and search for patterns already was terribly strong. But he wouldn't do it, he wouldn't take short-cuts. Everything had to be done in an orderly fashion. Only that way would he be able to factor it out. He threw the dice for hours, made notes.

He read books, made lists. Chelmno, Belzec, Sobibor, Treblinka, Buchenwald, Majdanek, Auschwitz-Birkenau, Bergen-Belsen, Mauthausen. He noted down latitudes and longitudes, added them to his databanks. He watched the news, read anti-Zionist pamphlets about Israeli attacks on Palestinian Arabs, mass expulsions, massacres. This was all part of the equation. He found out about the Gypsies, plotted their movements across the continent, before and after the war, guesstimated the population densities at various times in various nations.

He took day trips to old offices and the sites of factories that had once belonged, or still did, to I. G. Farben, Krone-Presswerk, Graetz and Krupp (in their various modern incarnations). He purchased a camera, took photographs. What was it that Mengele had said to Dr Ella Lingens? That was it, that there were only two gifted nations in the world, the Germans and the Jews, and that the only question was which one would dominate. Could it be that simple?

He thought about Nazi physics: of the cosmic force, vril; of the hollow-earth theory; of Hans Horbiger's Welteislehre, the doctrine of eternal ice. Twisted, perverse sciences that mocked centuries of patient work in mathematics, physics and logic. It disgusted him that the Germans could have been so sure of themselves, so certain that their theories were anything but filth. Yet he had to admit that at the time the evidence had seemed in their favour. How could anyone look at the Holocaust and think that the dice weren't loaded against the Jews, the Gypsies and the rest? It seemed so obvious to him, as obvious as it must have seemed to Hitler himself. Yet Hitler had been wrong and hadn't known why. But Joel knew. He knew that this colossal destabilisation of luck, of chance, was a sign that fortune's wheel itself was out of kilter that the events of the world weren't running true. Just look at the statistics! Six million! What more proof was needed? The detours from perfect randomness that he'd found in roulette and the dice were part of the same phenomenon. He would scientifically prove that the Nazis had been wrong to imagine that their sick success had anything to do with validating the destiny of the thousand-year Reich. The truth was that the Jews had been caught up in a great vacillation as the merry-go-round of chance had tottered and reeled, and then the Germans themselves had been affected as the system wobbled back the other way, cybernetically correcting itself and causing them defeat after defeat. There was no authenticity here.

Thus, by comparing the wartime fluctuations operations with those he was uncovering in the casinos he visited, Joel hoped to be able to calculate some kind of constant for the time of tikkun itself, that gradual progression of the universe towards perfection which would eventually pull chance back into line. From that, he reasoned, he'd be able to deduce how much longer there was before perfection was finally achieved and the creation could begin over again. It would be a breakthrough as important as that made by Hubble when he discovered, by statistically linking the red shift of a galaxy with its distance from the earth, that the universe was actually expanding.

He was going insane.

By 30 April 1943 (7):

   94,000 men's watches (8)
   33,000 women's watches (3)
   25,000 fountain pens (7)
   14,000 propelling pencils (6)
   14,000 pairs of scissors (12)

had been taken from the Jews and delivered to the Germans. Every statistic matched up with a dice roll. Notebook after notebook was filled.

As soon as the last of the visas came through he left Munich. He travelled north to Hanover and from there took a sealed train through East Germany to West Berlin. He looked into a hotel near Bahnhof Zoo and early the next day went out to Spandau to visit the fortress where they still held Rudolf Hess. He bought a small pair of binoculars and sat in the bus shelter opposite the prison, watching the windows and throwing his dice. They said you could sometimes catch a glimpse of him. What did he look like? Joel measured the walls, the dimensions of the buildings, the number of windows. Estimated the number of bricks – red bricks, many of them. He noted the number of guards, the changes of watch. He wasn't alone; others watched too, stooped figures in overcoats and Homburgs with expressionless faces and hollows for eyes. Joel felt like an impostor: this was their vigil, not his. But they welcomed him quietly, shared their flasks of coffee with him, their sandwiches. He asked them about Aza and Azael, what did they know of them? They nodded and listed names from the past, told him anecdotes, smiled and patted him on the shoulder. Whispered to him portentously: *We should have let him go. It would have been a greater punishment.* He didn't tell them he was Balaam.

The following morning they boarded the Warsaw express. The carriages were very different from those he'd become used to. They were uncomfortable and cold, and there was a stench of stale cigarettes about them. There was less plastic, more wood; wood which was worn and old and pitted with scars. He risked a Geiger counter reading. It was unusually high.

The train drew out into November. Outside, there was a biting cold and the rain came down, nearly sleet; no different to many days he had known at CERN. The weather made him think of Subhash and of the note he had left him. Joel Balaam Kluge. Master of the name.

The guards came by, young men in angular reds and greens, checked his passport and his luggage. They made him think of Gobineau's essay and of old beer mats he had seen which bore the legend: *Wer beim Juden kauft ist ein Volksverräter.*

The train yawed through the town, east of the Wall. Joel looked smugly out at the decay, the blankness, the dereliction, the pathetic attempts at modernisation. The sleet turned to snow which gyred and flurried, and quickly laid an ash-like scum across the roofs of the buildings and the empty lots between them.

The city sprawled on for miles, then they were out in the fields and there was nothing to see. The snow stopped and there was no more precipitation, not even rain to batter the windows and make you feel thankful for being inside. The farmland looked desolate, forlorn, the site of years of unremarkable struggle on every level of the food chain. Joel tried to do some paperwork but the vibrations of the train made it impossible. He rolled the dice idly on the miniature table underneath the window, enjoying the sound they made, the way they felt in his hands. People continually wandered up and down the corridor outside his compartment, talking, smoking, ferrying cups of tea backwards and forwards, all of them bracing themselves against the movement of the carriage.

Warsaw. Half a million people – a third of the city's population – crammed into 1.3 square miles. Joel did the calculations. That would have meant about seven to a room. He walked the streets behind the railway station, tracing the 1941 borders of the ghetto: down Okopowa and past the Jewish cemetery, left along Jerusalem Avenue and left again at Marszalkowska Street. Around Tiomackie Square and then a complicated dog-leg back around to the station. At each corner he took a dice roll. Half a million.

He took a train to Lublin and from there a bus to Majdanek, where a vast concrete dome covers the ashes of the 360,000 people who were destroyed there. Flowers died there too, wound into bouquets by those who came by. Joel thought about calculating the number of flakes of ash under that dome.

There were shoes, of course. Rooms full of shoes.

The barracks, crematoria, watch towers, barbed wire – all still there, folding into themselves with the passing years. He threw for them all, then surveyed them with his theodolite.

From Lublin to Lvov, where he had to pay a man to drive him in a Lada out to 'the sands', a nexus of low, sandy hills and deep pits. This was where the occupants of the Janówska camp had been stripped naked and put to death, their bodies burnt on huge pyres. Children who were too frightened to undress were swung by their feet against a tree until their skulls caved in, while their mothers were forced to look on, then flung on to the burning mounds. In each case the officer watched the mother for any sign of protest. At the slightest reaction she would be beaten half senseless, then hung from a branch by her feet until dead.

The car stopped at the base of a footpath and Joel and the driver climbed out.

'Is this it?' Joel asked, in pointless English. 'Are we here? Janówska?'

The driver nodded absently and waved in the direction of what Joel presumed was the camp, then pulled a packet of cigarettes from the breast pocket of his jacket, took one out and tried to light it. A stiff wind was blowing: even under several layers of clothes, Joel still felt cold. The driver bent over his cupped hands, apparently immune to the chill, wisps of grey hair detaching themselves from his scalp. A small flame flared up between his palms and he bent lower still and sucked hard, the sound of his rasp a part of the weather itself. Joel watched, convinced the match had gone out, but a moment later the driver's fingers swelled with smoke and he stood up, pulling hard to coax the ember into life. Success. He leant against the bonnet, smiled at Joel as if to say *are you still here then?* and picked a strand of tobacco from his tongue.

Joel smiled back, remembered himself, and started on up the first hillock.

He worked his way across the dunes, trying to gauge his direction by the position of the weak winter sun. He touched the trunks of trees with his fingertips whenever he passed them. His shoes filled with sand and he would have taken them off but it was too cold and this made him feel ashamed. Eventually he came to one of the pits. Around its perimeter was a rude fence of posts and barbed wire. Rusted signs hung from it, their words and designs weathered into oblivion. In several places the fencing had begun to collapse, affording points of access. Joel stepped over the wire at one of these and gingerly made his way towards the edge. Reaching it, he peered in. The sides of the pit sloped steeply down. Landslide upon landslide. The caked slopes were riven with branching rivulets and wadis. At the bottom was a slick mirror of dark water. What had he expected to see?

It was hard to roll the dice here, on the sand. He found a metal sign half buried in the ground. Pulled it out. Used that.

He walked on for a while, but the sun was going down and he decided he had better make his way back. It was on his return journey that he realised that nothing distinguished this place. Why had he come here? What was it that he'd expected to find? He checked his thermometer, made a note of the temperature. Yes, it was cold.

★

The taxi took him back into the town and he left Lvov that day on a train bound for Minsk. By the time they crossed from the Ukraine into Belarus the snow lay across the countryside in an unbroken swathe. They crossed the Pripet just to the south of Luninets: it was frozen over and a layer of white made the river resemble a glacier, a sluggard worm of ice that rent the land in two.

The locomotive broke down as they pulled out of Baranovichi and he spent a night there, in a hotel not far from the station. He trudged from the train, his baggage slung uncomfortably about his shoulders, the suitcase containing his many notebooks now too heavy to carry with ease. He could barely bring himself to speak to anyone. He didn't want any help. He could think of nothing but suffering; it was the least he could do to carry his own bags. Again, the gesture was such a pathetic one that made him feel utterly wretched. He didn't unpack. The maid warmed his bed with an iron bedpan full of hot coals.

All night there was traffic up and down the stairs outside his door and he could hear creakings and manoeuvrings from the adjacent rooms. Unable to sleep, he read by gaslamp. He read about the station at Treblinka, how during Christmas 1943 the Germans had put signposts on the buildings: *Telegraph, Telephone, Restaurant, Ticket Office*. They put timetables up too, a station clock, enormous signposts: *Change for Eastbound trains; To Bialystok and Baranovichi*. Tempted the people from the trains. Hid the clothing stripped from the endless line of victims. The prostitutes and their customers kept him awake. He thought of the conditions in the cattle trucks. Of deception. He couldn't comprehend the cruelty involved. He thought of his family. Deception. He couldn't sleep. Absolute cruelty. Everywhere. Normality. Signs to Baranovichi. Everywhere. It was happening everywhere. He had to be everywhere. He couldn't move.

Next day, the train was five hours late. He slept on the platform, wearing most of his clothes. He had a strange dream. He dreamt that he spoke magic names and created a golem from copper. He awoke with a rime on his face. He hadn't eaten yesterday, he remembered. He put his hand into his luggage and touched his notebooks, his numbers, just to make sure they were there. Computers in his shoes, somewhere. The train had heating that worked and he scalded his hands on the grille. A man with a huge moustache who looked like Josef Stalin came into the carriage with a samovar of tea. Joel bought several glasses' worth and Stalin gave him some black bread and pickles. He had chilblains on his toes, he realised.

He reached Minsk and stayed there for several days. It was December now and winter was beginning to bite. He made a day trip to Sobibor. It was less well tended than Dachau or Majdanek and somehow more real. He was told there was a field of burnt and crushed bones here that looked like a coral beach, but everything was covered in snow. It snowed the whole day he was there and he could only think of the ashes raining down from the chimneys. He went to the field anyhow and dug down through the frozen crust with his hands. Others followed him – despite the weather several dozen people had come out to the camp that day. They all started to dig. One woman – about Joel's age, attractive – wasn't wearing suitable shoes, so she took them off and walked across the snowfield in stockinged feet, a painful reminder of his failure to do the same on his visit to Janówska. They dug, all of them, like Inuit digging for fish. Most of them found fragments of some description and buried them back where they'd found them. Joel buried his dice in his hole. Walking back, he counted the footprints the small search party had made. Several of the men spoke to the woman in Russian. Joel didn't understand, but he thought they were offering to carry her. Whatever it was, she refused.

In one of the few remaining buildings was posted – in five languages – an excerpt from the speech Himmler gave at Poznan on 4 October 1943.

We have taken from them what wealth they had. I have issued a strict order, which SS Lieutenant-General Pohl has carried out, that this wealth should, as a matter of course, be handed over to the Reich without reserve.

We have taken none of it for ourselves. Individual men who have lapsed will be punished in accordance with an order I issued at the beginning which gave this warning: whoever takes so much as a mark of it is a dead man. A number of SS men – there are not many of them – have fallen short, and they will die without mercy.

We had the moral right, we had the duty to our people, to destroy this people which wanted to destroy us. But we have not the right to enrich ourselves with so much as a fur, a watch, a mark or a cigarette, or anything else.

Because we have exterminated a germ, we do not want in the end to be infected by the germ and die of it. I will not see so much as a small area of sepsis appear here or gain a hold. Wherever it may form, we will cauterise it. Altogether, however, we can say that we have fulfilled this most difficult duty for the love of our people. And our spirit, our soul, our character has not suffered injury from it.

Joel ran into the toilets and vomited. The toilets were tended by volunteers. Their bowls were scrubbed clean and white. The perversion was absolute. The Nazis had declared themselves agents of tikkun, they had claimed themselves as the light which issued forth from the forehead of primordial man to reorganise the confusion brought on by shevirah. But they were the kelippot, the shards the husks the shells, they were of the sitra ahra, the realm of demons. It was he who was the agent of tikkun. *It was he, Joel, he, Balaam*. Tikkun brought about a catharsis of waste matter in the divine system and so now he vomited, it was his prayer, he emptied his stomach for all who had died, his eructation a magical act, his discharge a balm.

Enter the dermatophyte

She needed allies if she was to contact the Mummy, send her a message, and she found them underneath the linoleum and along the base of the wall where they corrugated the institutional plaster and messed up the skirting board. There were thousands of them, woven into mats, peppered with spores. They were fungi, basidiomycetes. They were her friends.

She encouraged them, farmed them, stripped wood from the back of her bedside table, soaked it with her urine and transplanted them to it, hid the little cultures in the bottom of the wardrobe. Later, when her plantation was going strong, she took the mattress from her bed and encouraged the hyphae to take root in its foam. The process took months, despite Emma moving it along with her mind, coaxing and stroking the organisms, chiding and training them. All this time she studied the fungi, examining the spore-bearing basidia which resembled tiny tuning forks, the mycelia, thick and tangled, the septa partitions with their dolipore septum pores and pore caps. Too small for her fingers to touch and her eyes to see, she rubbed away the epidermis from the pad of her middle finger with an emery board kept back from the nurses and settled her new friends in the shallow wound, capturing them with her skin cells, encouraging fluid exchange, becoming symbiotic.

When the mattress was ready she turned it over and stripped the sheet from it at nights, lay there sleeping on a bed of mildew, truffles, fairy rings, encouraging the mycobiont into her flesh, where it extended haustoria and itched its way between sebaceous gland and nerve, follicle and fat like some cryptoendolithic lichen in the rocks of a dry Antarctic valley.

Eventually she no longer needed the mattress and allowed its farm to wither and die. Her skin was supple and soft and showed no sign of the parasite within, which drew water and gases from the air through her pores and which was sensitive to all sorts of things she had not registered before: nitrogen levels, the salts and sugars on the skin of her nurses, barometric pressure. It also helped her to understand what the bacteria were up to.

The day after Sobibor

The day after Sobibor Joel took to the woods, memories of hiking round Lake Geneva. Five thousand Jews had fled to the forests from the Minsk ghettos between July 1941 and October 1943; half of them had died, one way or another. The other half had survived to form partisan groups and hidden enclaves. He had new dice with him. He threw them.

He didn't know which way to go: his map didn't show land use beyond the city limits. He identified six roads that led radially out of the city and threw a die to determine which one he would take. Then he started walking. He set off early, at six-thirty, when despite it still being dark and well below freezing people were already beginning to move around the city. Not all the street lights worked and the glow from those which did was so flat that it emphasised the impression he already had that there were no colours here, that he was moving through a world of black and white. He walked for an hour, following the paths that pedestrians had made through the rotting snow, stopping every fifteen minutes or thereabouts to fumble with his map which, though crude and inaccurate, was the best he'd been able to find. The heavens had begun to lighten, but it did not look as if there'd be a spectacular dawn – clouds covered the sky in one placid and unbroken bank.

The roads had started to fill with cars. They passed him in little convoys, their wheels hissing in the two inches of slush that lay across the carriageways. People teetered along on bicycles and buses throbbed by, their engines hot and exposed like the naked arses of baboons.

He realised that it was going to take him for ever to walk and so when a bus stopped near him he climbed aboard. The driver asked him (he presumed) for his destination. Joel said 'American', made a gesture which he hoped meant 'straight ahead', and handed over some money. The driver shrugged and muttered something, half to himself, half to the passengers in the nearby front seats.

They all laughed. Joel took his ticket. The other passengers nodded at him and smiled.

He was in luck. The bus made a long sequence of stops but stayed on the main road and followed it out into the countryside. It was daylight by now and the clouds had begun to clear and as they travelled through a snowy landscape of pine- and fir-covered hills there was an occasional flash of low sun. When they drew up outside a lumber yard to pick up a lone man Joel got off. The bus drove away, its passengers watching him from the windows, a few of the older ones still smiling as if they were relieved to have something new to do with the pallid features that most of the time just lurked motionless beneath their enormous fur hats.

With a crunch of icy gravel beneath his feet Joel shouldered the small bag he had with him and walked away from the road and up the hill behind the yard. The trees had been stripped from it long since and he picked his way between old stumps and saplings. There was about a foot of snow, more in places, and his ankles were soon soaked, but by the time he had crested the summit and descended into the next valley the sky was nearly clear and the sun bright. He was in the trees by now, following tracks made by deer and fox. In some places the branches had grown so entwined that the snow could not penetrate, and he walked on a soft rug of dead needles and moss. But mostly the ground was thick with the white crystals and each tree trunk had one white side and one dark and so that he didn't get lost he kept the snow-covered sides to his left, a trick he'd learnt from his hikes in the Alps. All around him water dripped down from the higher branches.

By noon he'd covered a lot of ground. Ahead was a steep-sided spur of land which he worked his way around all the while looking for a possible ascent. It took him about an hour to clamber up to the top of the ridge and hike along it to the point. When he got there his reward was a magnificent view northwards over the city and its environs. To his left he could see the road he'd come down snaking between the hills, which in turn were enveloped by the forest that curled towards him before unfurling itself in a great dark sheet to his right, the tracts of trees beginning to alternate with white slabs of farmland as his eyes swept north. On the central horizon, a giant splash of concrete, was Minsk.

The tip of the point had collapsed over the years and a tree which had once stood upright there now grew outwards at an angle of forty-five degrees, its trunk stripped bare by the elements and only a small fuzz of green left at its tip. The roots had exploded out of the ground and become hypertrophic; they merged and knotted like the tangles in the brain of an Alzheimer's victim. Joel brushed the snow from their smooth surfaces and sat down to eat his lunch.

While he ate he rolled his dice, noted down the figures and asked himself if he could have done it, whether he could have eked out a secret life here among the hills trees rocks, unable to light a fire during the day, continually threatened by hunting parties of Nazi officers and their dogs. And operating as resistance too – felling trees across roads, disabling telegraph wires and bridges, removing railway tracks and jamming points. He shivered to think of it, of how pathetic those actions must have seemed in the face of the genocide. How to keep on going, how ceaselessly to knit and re-knit the slightest threads to keep a coat of hope across your back, a coat without which you were nothing.

The sun reached its low zenith and the windows of Minsk flashed, and across the snowfields and forests a trillion ice crystals twinkled with the rhythm of fireflies pulsing in concert in the boughs of a tree. From up here, nothing seemed to divide the city from the countryside around it. It was only another outgrowth, its concrete merely another kind of bark. Parasitic upon the land just as the trees were, as the land itself was parasitic upon the molten centre of the planet, itself a parasite bleeding off the energies of the sun. Joel looked out over the land, over the city, thought of the people teeming like bugs within its nooks, crannies, causeways, walkways. Thought of the people hiding in the forests, fleeing from the Nazis with their guns, dogs, gas. Thought of the death camps he had visited, of the pits and the pyres, of the machinery of death, that most peculiar parasite which derived its energy from millions of tiny and personal wills to power, millions of little prejudices, millions of blind eyes, millions of people trying something out or jumping through hoops, millions of sexual fantasies, millions of rapes, each one unique and yet totally predictable, human pistons and cylinders, an integrated powerhouse for biological destruction. All these little decisions, these tiny chances, they formed a pattern, told a story. In his notebooks, gathering like a stalagmite, was the shape of it. He could feel it.

He started as a bird took to the air behind him, his mind suddenly focused. The blood raced beneath his skin and he began to sweat. He got up from his seat and walked around, trying to remain calm. He bent down, took a handful of snow from the ground, patted it on to his overheating face. He thought of the accelerator ring at CERN, tended by thousands, of the data back in his hotel room that even he, with his prodigious though waning mathematical talents, couldn't hope to make sense of without a mental prosthesis. Where was the boundary between concrete and flesh, tarmac and flesh, metal and flesh, copper and nerve? He thought of the axe and the shoe and the car and the gun, each blooming out of the human condition, defining, inseparable. How could you tease them apart? He thought of the telephone, the TV, the satellite, the radio, of the protocols being developed at CERN, of databases, data transfer, data and death, statistics and sex. He grew hard. The computer network would encircle the planet. He thought of the traces he'd left in the systems thanks to his grant cheques, his credit cards, his junk mail, his telephone calls, his passport, his medical records, the closed-circuit cameras at the research centre. We all leave traces, he reflected, all of us, and our technology takes up this slack. Axe marks in fossilised trees, pottery shards and burial mounds, bones and trinkets deep in the mud, piles of stones, plastic bags, nuclear waste. The ice crystals blinked all across the horizon. They were a trace: of his angle of view, of the height of the sun, of the composition of the atmosphere. The mountains of darkness were so bright they were dazzling. He leapt up and down, his circuits on overload, heat pumping from the top of his head. He screamed the names of the rebel angels – 'Aza! Azael!' – at the horizon. He thought of his notebooks, could sense the networks of power, of time itself, that bubbled between their covers. Before him the city lay like a circuit board, tricking quantum events into logic, trapping chance in the plan of the cosmos. He screamed a scream of this, cast it to the skies, burst the eardrums of squirrels and brought birds to the ground. Thus opened to the world, he cast his spell.

An online edit

Perhaps Laika will turn out to be another missing link. Travelling for the sake of it in circles around the globe, scooping up the dross of the media as a blue whale filters plankton (more scurfing than surfing), Laika is a mill, forever grinding sounds and images into different forms. She's a kind of motor now, a habitus in the manner of the eye, the next stage in the meander of violence and vision that began with that engine of death the Gatling gun – all barrel revolutions and straight line projections, creating no man's lands out of lines of sight – and progressed to the film camera. This replaced bullets with photons and hurled them, a trillion rounds a second, at the screen, at the eye, at the brain, marking out a different kind of forbidden zone, one that was hostile to straightfor-ward truth. Then after the camera the car, the motor now a petrol engine with spoilers and fins bolted on, the screen the scene outside the window, a plotless ever scrolling plane grounded by the infinite perspectives of crash barriers, chevrons, traffic lights and busy city streets. Now, via the circumfluous aircraft journeys of the jet set and Howard Hughes, the motor migrates from the roadway to outer space, where in a cybernetic frenzy it points its cameras up and down, staring at the earth, staring at the sun, losing itself in vision.

With her body uncritically interfaced with her capsule and her mind processing images at a tremendous rate, Laika's old concep-tion of objects had long disappeared: everything had now been dissolved in the rush of the world. Her preliminary mode of self-consciousness had been superseded by something rather closer to the awareness she'd had as an everyday pup back in Baikonur. Cause and effect had vanished for her and in their place was a maelstrom, a concoction of high winds and difference. Forms were no longer abstract and eternal, but bloomed up from the rush of footage that bled through her porthole and screen, contingent and incredible. The sun was no disc but an enfolded and pulsating explosion; the earth was round only by dint of its billennial rollings through space. Time was process, space was intensity.

The dog's earlier paranoias had disappeared and she'd begun to feel totally at home in orbit. Thoughts of astronauts discovering her or of the shuttle retrieving her or even of collision with other satellites didn't frighten her now – death, when it came, if it came, would be merely a technical hitch. She was no longer an individual, lost in space, but an agent of change traversing the datasphere.

My Berlin PET

In Berlin it was autumn 1977, and Joel took a cheap room and for the next few weeks consolidated and prepared his data. It was a mammoth task – thousands and thousands of measurements, from distances, dates and degrees to dimensions, inventories, dice throws. Somehow to make sense of all this, somehow to analyse it, to boil it down, find its flavours and odours, find its shape. To begin with he sketched out two landscapes – the patterns of death during the Holocaust and the behaviour of chance in modern Europe. He bought a Commodore PET, one of three makes of personal computer that had been launched that year.

But he found he needed still more data. He visited the casinos, his little computers hot in his soles, and took notes and made money. During the days he noted the dimensions of the Brandenburg Gate, Checkpoint Charlie, Unter den Linden, the Reichstag, Hitler's bunker.

In West Berlin he drank Evian water, thought of the Evian

agreement. At Evian in 1938 the other European countries, faced with the option of opening their borders and admitting the many Jews trying to flee Germany, hesitated and did not liberalise their immigration policies. David Ben-Gurion, who a decade later would become Israel's first prime minister, felt it was better that the decision went this way – if Jews managed to find refuge in countries other than Palestine it might damage the cause of Zionism.

Sometimes he drank Vittel and was forced to think of the camps that had been set up in the town as way-stations for Auschwitz. He copied down the mineral composition data from the labels on the bottles, compared it with the inventories of goods taken from the death camp victims.

He stayed in Berlin for over a year. He grew tired of hotels, got himself a small apartment, filled it with more books, papers, continued his research. He taught himself to cook and learned some German too. He made friends with one or two of the croupiers in the casinos he frequented and even had them over to dinner, though his intensity scared them and they never came back, judging him a crank. But for the most part he worked away at his analyses, collecting and collating, a rock climber scaling a sheer rock face, inch by merciless inch.

By the beginning of his second winter in the old capital he felt he'd lost sight of the Project. He was so far into it that going back was out of the question, but neither could he see any end. And he'd lost any sense of up or down, too – all directions on his wall of information seemed to be much the same. It was only his lizard brain which kept him clinging on; his cortex had forgotten about the dangers of gravity long before and, indeed, was suffering from vertigo.

So he left Berlin. He put his possessions into storage and travelled down to Monte Carlo, where he spent the summer exploring the casinos and swimming in the sea. After that he worked his way back up through France, starting with the sites of the internment camps in the Pyrenees – Rivesaltes, Noé, Récébédou, Portet St Simon and Gurs – and moving north through the countryside. Once again he stuck to the old routes of deportation when he could, followed the logic of the railway lines, a logic that had subjugated and delineated the fields of pain and madness which were the camps and termini and their corresponding catchment areas. It took him a year to cover France and as he went he adhered to far more stringent practices of data gathering than he had employed in the East. He visited Evian and Vittel, of course, and stopped in Paris for two months to have another stint at the casinos. From there he went to Brussels for more roulette and then on into the Netherlands. In Amsterdam he visited Anne Frank's house and was going to stay longer, but his shoe computer was in a bad way – it had been broken and botched back together one time too many – and he needed to return to Berlin where he had the tools to fix it.

But fixing it took longer than he thought. Most of the wiring was shot and there seemed to be problems with the motherboards too. Getting the components apart in order to test them meant causing a lot of damage (he had sealed them inside a special resin in order to protect them from sweat and the rigours of being walked on) and once he had broken the machine down it seemed simpler just to rebuild the whole thing from scratch. This he did, but he couldn't resist trying to improve on the original model and he allowed himself to be led off down this side-track for another year. Computer components had vastly improved and were much more widely available than when he'd originally built the machine – the microprocessor was now ubiquitous and had sold seventy-five million units world-wide in that year alone. Working with the new, smaller and more powerful devices was a positive joy.

When it had been finished and tested he set off for Italy, the data from France still untouched. More notebooks were filled, though now he mailed each one as he completed it back to a postal box he'd rented in the old German capital. He travelled as far as Greece and the Mediterranean islands occupied by the Axis powers during the war.

Eventually he headed back to Berlin, rented a new apartment and got down to work. What had seemed impossible before now appeared, with all this extra data on board, completely ludicrous. It took him six months just to go through what he had and put it in some kind of order.

For most of this time he was profoundly depressed. Going over his old notes and conclusions again, they seemed immature and he became embarrassed that he'd ever identified himself with the figure of the sorcerer or imagined his trip around Europe as some- how being equivalent to a sojourn in the fabled mountains of darkness. All the travelling had changed him, had given him a new set of routines and different things to think about. Sometimes he found it hard to remember why he'd ever started the Project in the first place. But the thing had its own irresistible momentum now and he found himself plunging into his task regardless, wrap- ping it around himself like a blanket, forcing himself to forget about reasons. He read about an international satellite telephone system, Inmarsat, that had been launched a couple of years before, and this cheered him, coinciding as it seemed to with the visions he'd experienced on the hill outside Minsk.

Once he'd catalogued the notebooks the next stage was to trans- fer their contents to the PET. More months of toil. He dumped them in a pile on the floor of the room where he worked. There were dozens and dozens, all shapes and sizes: hardback, softback, ring-bound, spiral-bound, stapled, flip, loose-leaf, spined, red, white, yellow, black, green, blue, khaki, ruled, graphed, plain, perforated, non-perforated, parchment, wood pulp, hemp. The pile reminded him of the piles of shoes in the concentration camp museums and he got into a groove in which he imagined that every time he finished entering a notebook into the machine he had somehow atoned for one of those pairs of shoes. He typed for hours at a time, for days at a stretch. He typed till his eyes hurt and the tendons in his arms throbbed and ached, until the muscles in his neck and shoulders were knotted hard. About half-way through the pile he came across an IBM PC in a shop, a new machine much more powerful than his PET, and agonised about whether or not he should upgrade. In the end he decided against it, though never again could he think of his PET with the same measure of affection. Six months later he had two data sets: all the Holocaust measurements, and all the gambling results and dice scores. Every data point was attributed both a date and an approxi- mate geographical position. Then came the intellectual challenge

– to bring out the mathematical characteristics of both sets and map one on to the other.

It was a massive relief to be manipulating numbers again instead of merely compiling them. He tried many approaches and wasted many months, but even his failures felt sweet because with each one he felt he knew the data better. It was like an animal, this information, and he was the hunter tracking it, observing its behaviour patterns, carefully noting the manner in which it moved about, chose its lairs, marked its territory. For sure, he was always one step behind, but he felt confident that the gap was narrowing all the time.

For over a year he worked like this, his life emptied of everything but modes and means, medians and matrices, distribution functions and probability densities, Fourier transforms and take-away food. And yet little by little the feeling he'd had that he was closing in on the beast, on the rebel angel, began to evaporate. He couldn't find any shapes, any correlations that made sense. He'd discover a relationship in one location but it would hold there and there alone. He couldn't find any patterns, or anything that would tell him how things might have changed in the four decades since the war. The information was outwitting him. He pulled at his hair, gnashed his teeth, butted the walls of his room with his head. He wandered the streets in a daze, shouted at strangers, rode the subway for hours drinking rum. It was 1983, seven years since he'd left CERN, and in that time he had covered thousands of kilometres and compiled mountains of data. It struck him – a terrible thought – that perhaps it was these which were the mountains of darkness, mountains of his own creation which now threatened to engulf him, and that the archeology of Nazism he'd been exploring was nothing but the fossil remains of a world which was dead.

Desperately he explored one avenue of approach after another, continually tracing and retracing his steps like a child lost in the snow. He even re-plotted all the geographical data, not just in terms of the position on the earth's surface where it had been taken, but in respect of the planet's changing position in space over time. But none of it did any good.

His hair had grown long and he now had a full beard, having

given up shaving soon after he'd left CERN. When he stalked out for victuals dressed in a dark overcoat and hat he looked almost Hasidic again, except for the fact that he was so thoroughly unkempt. He worked and worried almost incessantly, slept intermittently, ate hardly at all. Pizza boxes and cans of soft drinks carpeted his apartment. Cockroaches moved in. He didn't notice – most of his brain was in the machine.

Eventually he thumped the PET in frustration one time too many and the computer broke down. He tried to fix it himself but didn't know enough about the architecture so he took it to be mended and this forced him to take a break, to step back a little. Of course, it wasn't that straightforward. First he had to rage around Berlin for a couple of days, furious at his machine, terrified the thing would never get working again. But after he'd calmed down and the man in the shop had repeated to him several times during as many phone calls that the problem was not serious and that he could have the PET back in a week, ten days at the most, he managed to get some sleep and some distance. It was then he began to realise that he needed help.

Unfortunately, the kind of help Joel decided to seek was not the kind that a good friend might have recommended. He had decided that his problems were being caused not by a mistake in his theory but by an error in his data gathering. He simply hadn't enough of it. It had been wrong to concentrate on the Holocaust in the way he had – he should have thrown the net wider. But he wasn't so unhinged that he thought he could expand the Project alone. No, he needed an assistant. He was a sorcerer, wasn't he? He would summon a golem, as in the dream he'd had on the railway station, long before.

He went to the Jewish library in Berlin and pored over mystical books. He ordered pamphlets from Israel, America. But he could find little in the way of specifics about the creation procedure itself. That the golem was a soulless artificial creature created by the performance of a magical dance and the uttering or writing of holy names was plain enough; that such a creature had a hidden power to see, which was associated with the element of earth from which it was taken, was obvious also. But apart from the fact that the creation process was similar to that with which God brought the world out of Ein-Sof (the primordial man Adam Kadmon, Joel discovered, is himself often identified with the figure of the golem – his third eye, the light from which helps remake the world, his special power of sight) nothing was clear.

The night before he was due to collect his computer from the repair shop Joel had a peculiar dream. He dreamt he was in a restaurant – it seemed familiar, but he couldn't place it – and was eating, then visiting the toilet to shit, then eating again. He was dressed in his overcoat and his hat was on the table beside him, and a waiter stood attentively by. All the other tables were empty save one. At that a woman sat alone, drinking wine and watching him as he devoured course after course. Every time he went to the Gents he had to pass her and on each occasion she smiled at him. She had long, dark hair and a pale face.

He was half-way through an enormous bowl of moules marinière when she walked over and sat down at his table, facing him. He carried on eating but underneath the table he began to develop an enormous erection. She reached out a hand and laid it on his arm, halting the rhythm of void and consume, void and consume. Joel looked at her. Everything in the room stopped except for the tick of the clock and a small dribble of marinière sauce that ran down through the hairs of his beard and splashed on to the white linen table-cloth. The waiter stood motionless, perfectly still. Joel's erection throbbed in the silence. He was furious and his anger was being channelled into his dick. In bed, his body moaned and sweated, wound the sheets around itself. In the restaurant he pushed the table aside and shoved the woman to the floor, then leapt on her and tore at her clothes. She scrabbled back, but meekly, twisting her head this way and that, like in films that he'd seen. He tore at her skirt and her underwear, and the fabric came away easily and twirled itself round his hands. And then he forced himself into her, felt the heat of her dry insides, the clutch of her frightened membranes.

Immediately she started to shrink. She shrank away from him, smaller and smaller, her genitals – her whole body – retreating from his, leaving his penis naked and wilting, dripping with cum. As she shrank, the tones of her skin began to change and become less vibrant, more regular. Soon she was only two feet long and had become plastic, a doll, staring up at him with lifeless eyes that lay passive beneath bobbing artificial lashes. The waiter still stood there, unperturbed. Gingerly, Joel reached out a hand and put his fingers to the doll's naked chest. At his touch it split open. Inside the hollow interior were two synthetic hearts, one to the left and one to the right. Each was made of some sparkling red material encased in a clear plastic shell, the kind of thing a novelty pen or key-ring might be made of. Each throbbed with pulses of inner light.

Smoke had found him as well.

Joel burst awake and kicked himself free from the soaking sheets. That day he didn't go to pick up his machine as planned. Instead, he was at the library as soon as it opened, scouring the shelves for books on sex magic. He knew how to make his golem. He would make it of copper and silicon – naturally, as it was in the realm of information that he needed its help. The ritual dance he'd read about would be a dance of electrons and to bring it to life he would conduct a sex rite. For this he would need a partner, and who could that be but the one person with whom he'd had sex? For he'd finally recognised the restaurant in his dream. It was the one in Geneva, the Café Alsace, where he'd first had lunch with Henry and Jennifer.

Local space

The Alcester road leads northwards out of Stratford-upon-Avon; it runs past the livestock market and humps across the railway line. The next mile is crammed with houses advertising 'Bed & Breakfast'. These were here when Stratford first began – some say remains of Roman versions have been found, complete with chintz sofa covers, fake fireplaces and thimble racks – and they'll presumably be here at its end. If you take the turning to the left you'll quickly find yourself in the old town of Shottery, now a kind of dry and hollow bole on Stratford's trunk, but keep straight on in the direction of Alcester and you'll pass the Three Witches pub, the petrol station and the remains of the Last Resort night-club – in its prime little more than a collection of Portakabins sunk into a concrete car-park. The Last Resort marks Stratford's northernmost boundary, or at least it did in Jennifer's time (it is no more, that strange disco in the transitional zone between country and town, where real men drove Ford Capris and real women drank Malibu and coke) and beyond it lie the mythical fields of the Midlands, where cows graze on sheep offal and giant blocks of yellow rape stain the rolling hills in summer.

Back in town where the road begins you would once have found Stratford Hospital. In the eighties, the hospital was discovered to be incubating super-germs resistant to all known forms of antibiotic, so they knocked it down and doused the ruins with fire, leaving the little medical centre that had been built in the hospital grounds around the time that Emma was born to grow and grow – much like one of those super-germs – and strive to fill the vacuum left by the demise of its parent body.

Debate over whether or not this would be possible flourished for a while in the town community, itself a collection of viruses (mostly dominated by stubborn Tory strains). Some complained that the health service cuts were an outrage, that a medical centre was not sufficient to cope with the town's already large and rapidly expanding population. Others maintained that the hospital had never been much good anyway, and pointed to cases like that of the young singer electrocuted on stage in the Green Dragon (now a theme pub, in the old days the building was directly opposite the hospital), who had died because it had taken fifteen minutes for any ambulance men to make it across the road. The first group then responded with cries that such situations only arose in the first place because of financial cuts and that to deny funds to a place and then close it because of falling standards was typical of government hypocrisy. Then a third faction tried to convince everyone that they were all basing their arguments on rumour and conjecture, and that nothing would ever improve if people didn't look at the facts. At which point a small but well-organised fourth group tactfully remembered the super-germ. And then . . . and so it went on.

But in the early 1980s Stratford has all this yet to come. Bands play at the Green Dragon, sublimely unaware of the corporate future in which the old wooden bar, scored with the memory of bottlings and knife fights, will be replaced with a clean one of treated blond oak, the hospital razed to the ground, the cattle pens overshadowed by a superstore. On this particular Friday night Jennifer is in the toilets doing speed with Stim, still bass player of Desiring Machine which, against all the odds, has got it together enough to be tonight's main attraction. Stim is bent over the top of a ceramic cistern in one of the cubicles in the Gents, chopping at the powder with a razor-blade and continually flicking back fronds of hair from his long and wilting mohican to prevent them from disturbing the thin grey lines he's measuring out. Satisfied they're equal, he takes out a length of plastic straw and snurfs up the largest, and – coughing as he does so and rolling his eyes around in their sockets – hands the straw to Jennifer so that she can do the other. She bends over daintily and presses one carefully painted purple fingernail to her nose to close off her left nostril. Stim has already left the cubicle, the door swinging free behind him (the lock has been kicked off long before) and is at the handba-sin dabbing his fingers with water and sniffing the liquid up his nose (he's been suffering from nosebleeds and this is his solution). The nasal douche complete, he hawks a plug of mucus round into his mouth and spits it into the basin, immediately wasting most of the drug. Jennifer comes out of the cubicle rubbing her nose and hands the straw back to Stim with a sniff.

From inside the toilets the support band had been just a deep bass tremble, but as Stim opened the door and the two of them stepped out of the damp pools of piss and on to the worn carpet of the rear bar the music slapped into them like a dirty wet blanket. They moved out into the fray and stood together for a while, eyes glazed, until Stim – pretty sure that Jennifer wouldn't notice – wandered off on his own. But she knew the very moment that he slipped away; in fact, she'd been waiting for it. She swayed a little as she watched him work his way around the edge of the crowd to where the rest of the band stood huddled in a gaggle at one end of the tiny stage, fiddling with their equipment and looking cool. Already that evening she had drunk three pints of cider, two rum and cokes, a vodka and black and a bottle of Newcastle Brown that someone had asked her to hold while they went off to mosh in front of the speakers. Not to mention absorbing several lines of speed and the THC from a spliff out back in the car-park. For a while it had all mixed together well, but now she was beginning to feel a little out of control. She got out a cigarette and lit it, teetering dangerously as she did so. It was difficult to focus. She looked for a seat but there were none; the bar was rammed. She dragged on her fag but the nicotine rush made her feel even worse, so she squeezed backwards through a couple of rows of people to the wall and propped herself up against it. The rail of the old wooden dado was hard against her shoulder-blades but it was somehow a comfort to have discovered something which was solid enough to be uncomfortable. The sound of the band ripped past her ears. A tall skinhead stumbled into her, catching her in the ribs with his scrawny elbow and spilling beer all down her jeans. She cried out and shoved him away, but the sudden movement made her head spin and she immediately felt the bile begin to rise in her throat. The skin mumbled something which may or may not have been an apology and veered off into the crowd, but not fast enough for Jennifer who needed out, now, and shoved past him in the direction of the exit. She squeezed through the press of bodies at the door but it was no good; she couldn't get by. It was now or never.

'I'm going to throw up!' she screamed. Instantly two waves rippled through the group in front of her: the first a wave of expression as horror struck every face, and the second a wave of movement as everyone dived out of the way. It was a miracle; it was a Red Sea all her very own. She felt like Moses – and it was time to talk to God. She hurtled down the path that had been made available and out into the street, making it outside just in time to vomit all over the base of a traffic light.

She leant against the cold metal pole for a while, retching plaintively. A police car drew up alongside. The copper wound down his window and asked if she was OK and she hid behind the puke-spattered tangle of black hair that hung down from her crown and waved them away. They drove off, and laughter rose up from the car like the bile in her throat and she heaved again.

Another car drew up, but this time its occupants had no interest in her. One of them got out and went up to the pub, started trying to argue his way in. The other kept the engine running and its low throb was comforting in the same way that the wooden rail had been earlier. But the sounds of the car interfered with the music that pulsed out of the open pub door and in the space in which Jennifer stood a quite different sound envelope was suddenly and bizarrely produced. She wasn't hearing the noises that she should hear at all, but rather the silence of an almost empty room, footsteps in a corridor somewhere beyond, the echo of a cough and a sob that seemed to come almost from herself – and something else, something that she couldn't recognise at first but which she suddenly realised was a heartbeat, no, two heartbeats, very loud, as if two people were standing either side of her with stethoscopes on their chests and the ends jammed in her ears.

A long time had passed since her experience in the police cell and she was too drunk to remember it; in any case there wasn't time, because just then there was a tap on her shoulder and the peculiar haecceity was gone, the experience fading slowly into the background roar of alcohol like a retinal after-image. It was Stim and he was holding a glass out to her. 'You OK? You want something to drink?'

She waved the glass away. 'You fucking idyut,' she slurred, 'can't you shee I'm fucking shick. I don't want another fucking drink.'

'It's water, brighteyes. Here, have some. What did you think it was? Half a pint of vodka?' Jennifer pushed back her hair and took the glass, saying nothing. She drank a little and swayed a lot, clutching at the lamp-post to steady herself. Again Stim asked her how she was, unable to think of anything much else to say.

'All right, I think.' She stood up a little straighter and tried letting go of the traffic light. 'Better for puking.'

'Yeah. Nothing like a tactical puke. Always sorts you out. You coming back inside to see the set then? We're on in five minutes.'

Jennifer tried to think, but all her energy was focused on focusing. Images that didn't belong in the street kept flickering across her field of view. 'Um. Yeah, in a minute maybe.' But at the idea of going back inside she was struck with another blast of nausea. 'Uh, on second thoughts maybe not. I think I'd better go. Shorry. I don't feel too good. Ta for the whizz though. Nice of you.'

'No problem. Wish I hadn't given it to you now.'

'No, no. I drank too much.'

'Yeah, but it's a waste though, innit?'

'What? Oh, fuck you.'

'You going to be OK?'

'Yeah, yeah, really, I'll be fine.' She turned away from him and stabbed at the button on the pedestrian crossing. There was no traffic but she waited for the light regardless, too far gone to do anything but let the machine take her decisions for her. Stim stood behind her, holding the half-empty glass of water. He watched her, thinking how forlorn she looked in her red crushed-velvet bodice and ripped jeans. He hadn't really known her before her father died, but he'd known about the scandal, that she'd shagged that American boy, years ago, when she was just a kid. Everybody knew about it; it had been the choicest bit of local gossip for years. Amazing that they'd kept it out the papers, him being the son of an actress and all. Wouldn't be able to keep it quiet now – times had changed. Funny thing was, nobody he knew held it against her. It was like it made her cool. Anyway, she *was* cool. She'd let him and his mates squat in her house for about two bloody years, hadn't she? Never asked for any rent, never hassled them to clear up, let them do what they wanted. And it could hardly be said that they'd treated the place with respect – though they had lent a hand redecorating when she'd wanted to sell it. But it was strange, though, 'cause through all the time he'd lived with Jenn he hadn't really got to know her any better than he did after the first week.

Sure, he became more familiar with her moods, with what she liked or didn't like, with things like her shoplifting (and she was fucking good at that, he'd never seen anybody so good), but as to what she thought about things, why she did things, what she felt – he hadn't a clue. She never talked about the American kid, nor about her dad (most of his other friends, even the most relcalcitrant punks, would bang on about their old men on occasion – what they'd have to say might not be complimentary, but at least it was something). A lot of the time she seemed unaware that he and the band were living in her house; she came and went as if they were just there for a day or two, something weird that had fetched up in the dining-room and would be on its way soon enough. The other thing was that she'd never had a boyfriend, not while he'd known her, though lots of blokes had tried. And that was weird too. He guessed that the scandal had put her off men for good, but if that was the case then it was a shame.

The lights changed and began their blind man's bleep. Jennifer didn't move.

'It's green,' Stim yelled. She raised a drunken hand in recognition and began to cross the road, turned her heel as she stepped up on to the opposite kerb but managed to keep her balance. Stim resisted the temptation to run after her, take advantage of her drunken state.

'Where the fuck have you been? Come on, wanka! We're on!' It was Skag. The bass player took a last look at the dwindling figure stumbling off in the direction of Old Town and then stepped back inside the pub.

With Michael Hedges's help, Jennifer had sold Henry's house some years previously and had bought herself a small flat on the Evesham Road with the proceeds. She lived with two stray cats that she had rescued from the streets. The first – which she called Judd – she had saved from being pelted with stones by some neighbourhood boys; the second – Joel – had just turned up on her doorstep one evening and demanded to be let in. Both cats were toms and carried on a continual semi-playful tussle for food, territory and attention. This would occasionally erupt into real violence, usually

429

when Jennifer was asleep, and more generally seemed to involve a lot of noise, a lot of posturing, a lot of trashing of the furniture, a lot of vying for her attention and a lot of cat piss. Her friends kept telling her to have them neutered but she couldn't bring herself to do it.

When she came in drunk that night the cats were fast asleep and barely looked up from the chairs in which they had ensconced themselves. Her ears were still ringing from the noise of the support band and she switched on the fire and lay down on the couch wondering if she was going to be sick again. After a while she worked out that she wasn't and got up to put the kettle on and also the television. The set was the same one Henry had bought her, still going after all these years; most of her furniture had come from the old house too. She had taken what she'd thought she'd need and sold the rest with the property but for some time now she'd been wondering whether to get rid of it all and start afresh. She had the money – there'd been quite a lot of cash left over from buying the flat and it was hers now, having been released to her on her twenty-first birthday. A lot of stuff she'd kept for sentimental reasons including, for a while, all of Henry's clothes. But she didn't have that much room and they'd just been sitting there in cardboard boxes, so eventually she'd donated them to one of the charity shops on the High Street. She'd kept her mother's outfits, though. Henry had preserved Nadine's wardrobe through all those years; after his death Jennifer had found suitcases full of her clothes in the loft, all meticulously folded up in tissue paper and smelling faintly of naphthalene. It was the single most tidy, most organised thing she had ever known him do, and she finally realised as she carefully removed the clothes and tried on each garment how much he had worshipped her.

She'd adapted much of the clothing – although she'd never be as skinny as Nadine she'd lost most of the fat she'd put on in her mid-teens – and wore it without compunction; never having known her mother no deep thread of nostalgia could be triggered by the odours or the cut of the cloth. There was a certain symbolic value and that was all.

In the living-room the television babbled away to itself. An old

430

episode of *The Twilight Zone* was showing and Jennifer remembered something she'd read about Rod Serling being involved with that writer, L. Ron Hubbard, the one who invented the Scientology thing that some people she knew had been into a couple of years ago. One of her hobbies – one of the things she did to fill her time and offset the boredom of her job – was keeping track of various conspiracy theories, and to this end she stole all the latest books and clipped articles from magazines.

She wanted to sleep but the speed was well into her and she had to watch most of the way through the plot of the show before her mind began to shut down. As her waking state steamed off the sound of the television, the hiss and flutter of the gas fire and the drone of cars on the street outside meshed into an odd configuration, just as the noises outside the Green Dragon had done. But this time the hallucination was not only aural: through her half-closed eyes the play of chiaroscuro from the TV, the flames of the gas fire and the headlamps of the passing cars which moved in planes across the room together conjured images. She was in a larger space this time, although it was screened off in such a way that the portion she occupied was quite small. She was sitting down, too, but when she tried to get up she found she couldn't move her arms or legs. Figures drifted past her, dressed in white. Everything was very white. Sometimes dark eyes swooped down to inspect her, but they didn't settle for long and no attempt at rapport was made by any of them. Then they went and for what seemed like a very long time she was left alone. The screens were hospital screens, white polythene curtains hung from wheeled frames. There were hints of some activity from behind the one directly in front of her and the sound of the double pulse, just like before. Sitting there for such a long time, she had a chance to study it – and to remember the police cell, though this time she felt calm enough not to be scared. Listening carefully, she noted that one of the beats was dominant and led the other in a complex rhythm. There was a pain in her chest, as if from a giant bruise.

Finally someone emerged from behind the screen. It was a stout woman, dressed in sky blue, who came up and leaned over her and smiled. She walked around behind her, too far for Jennifer to follow with her eyes. Then the screen was being moved. No, no it was her that was moving. She heard voices to her rear. She must be in a wheelchair. She was being manoeuvred out of the room and into a corridor. People stepped out of doorways, then moved back against the walls to let her pass. They passed through several sets of swinging doors, each of them made of a transparent polythene a hundred times thicker than the screen curtains; it was like being pushed through great labial flaps of flesh. Then they were outside in the open air, in a small garden. There were rose beds and other buildings, and a bright sky dappled with cumulus, but everything was shades of grey, no colour. She looked around, bemused. A mile away a town rose up, blanketing a hillside. She could just see a church steeple and a great concrete building, a car-park or something, jutting above the low weathered buildings that smothered the hill. Then she was turned round and her view was restricted to the single-storey buildings whose external walls formed three sides of the garden. The sharp pain in her chest grew and the two heartbeats were now accompanied by a violent vibration. Across from her two geriatrics sat dribbling on a bench, their jaws working noiselessly at the sun. A few feet from them a patient plastered from head to toe in bandages sat motionless in a wheelchair. A bearded nurse stood in an open doorway, smoking a cigarette. The woman who had wheeled her through the corridors was chatting to two doctors. The pain in her chest became unbearable and she tried to scream.

She woke up and threw her hands to where the pain had been, but they never reached her flesh because Joel was in the way. He shrieked and shot from the sofa, doubly upset at being dislodged so unceremoniously from the warmth of Jennifer's chest – for not only had she made a comfortable bed, but her left breast had jutted out at just the right angle to make a good flex pad for his claws. On the TV *The Twilight Zone* episode was burbling to a close. Rod Serling came on to deliver his homily and Jennifer crawled across the floor on hands and knees to switch him off. She turned off the fire, too, and went to bed, but the short sleep had refreshed her and she lay awake for a while wondering (as she often did) about her child and what she'd have been like if she'd have lived. In her mind she'd christened her Rachel, her own mother's middle name.

Becoming lichen

Emma liked to get outside. She liked to get outside and eat the grass. She asked for outside a lot and since she never caused any trouble outside the nurses were generally happy to take her there. Down the corridors she'd go, pushed along in her chair, giggling with glee as the plastic doors flapped past her, pointing out the windows at the sunlight.

Out in one of the gardens she liked to run around, kick at a football or play catch with a hoop, lie on the lawn. Usually the nurse would bring a book or a magazine — or a friend and some fags — and let Emma get on with it for an hour. This was best for Emma, because then she could do what she really came for without being noticed. She could eat grass.

She would grab surreptitious handfuls and work them into balls, then pop them in her mouth when the nurse wasn't looking. Before swallowing she'd mulch and suck at the vegetable fibres like gum, breaking the leaves down into juice. Later, free-floating chloroplasts extracted from the plant by bacterial action were captured by fungal filaments that had extended from her skin to her stomach. Channelled back up to the dermis they were put into service by the mycobiont, which could now photosynthesise. As the months went by and Emma's skin took on the faintest tinge of green, the fungal parasite was able to give back energy in exchange for the nutrients it took from the child. The symbiosis was complete. Now Emma could eat less, and she was far more sensitive than before to the experience of light and the economies and networks that underpinned life. This would help a great deal in her wanderings around people's dreams.

She'd been consulting Veronica, too, because she'd found out from Smoke about her two fathers. Veronica said it was very unusual, to have three parents like that. Most people only had two and some had only one, or even none at all! Emma decided she liked having three. It made her *feel special. Especially since everything seemed to suggest that she'd see them all soon.*

Making faces

The child was so frequently in her mind that it often seemed to Jennifer as if she'd never died. Sometimes, as she did some housework, or fed the cats, or made alterations to yet another piece of Nadine's clothing, she talked to her out loud in a kind of absent-minded, one-sided banter as she'd seen other mums do with their kids. It was similar to the way she talked with the cats; maybe she was just talking to the cats all along. When she'd been about nineteen she'd gone through a period of stealing baby clothes, toys, child-care books, even nappies, and hiding them in her room in the house. She would go into shops and look at cots, and chat to the sales assistant about the child that didn't exist. One awful night when the others were asleep she discovered herself making up a bottle: she couldn't get the sachets of powdered milk to open properly, she'd spilt boiling water all over her hands, all the time she was crying, not for the fact that she was doing this but because it was too late, too late – if Rachel had lived she'd be too old for bottles by now. The realisation broke the spell for her and she gathered all the baby things up, dumped them in binliners and took them to an unsuspecting charity store.

A pharmaceutically raddled tortoise of an old woman was behind the counter that day and she eyed Jennifer eagerly as the girl approached, clutching the two black plastic bags. Like heads of Grandfather's Beard the first tangles of Alzheimer's were beginning to bud in her brain. As soon as she saw the bags' contents she assumed that Jennifer had miscarried her first child. 'Are you sure you don't want to keep these, luvvie?' she jabbered, taking Jennifer's wrist in a vicelike grip and fondling the soft, pastel-coloured garments with her free hand. 'Not sure whether to buy for a boy or a girl, eh? I was just the same at your age. I'm sure you'll get another chance, dearie. Your husband's a strapping lad, I'll be bound, and you're such a pretty thing I'm sure he won't take too much persuading to give you another.' Jennifer's feelings twisted between horror and prudishness: horror at the suggestion that she might ever get pregnant again and prudishness because she could not help but think that sex was not an appropriate subject for this dried-up old shroud of a woman to discuss. 'Why don't you hang on to them, eh?' the shroud continued. 'They're so expensive these days. Time's past when you could rely on hand-me-downs from the family. Everyone wants everything new these days, don't they? I don't know. Seems such a waste to me.' And so on and so forth.

The experience cured Jennifer of going to such extremes again but she couldn't stop the little obsessions, even when she moved out of the house and into the flat. Keeping constant track of Rachel's age, for instance, and paying extra special attention to children who would have been her contemporaries. She kept a mental image of how Rachel might have looked which she constantly updated, although it was hard because she was never really sure which was the father, Judd or Joel. So she incorporated aspects of both.

In the beginning she looked for physical echoes in the children that she encountered. The curve of Joel's ears here, the angle of Judd's nose there; elsewhere her own eyebrows, there Judd's laugh. But the picture she built this way soon began to seem too artificial, too contrived, and it was then that she began to recognise aspects of her daughter which suggested themselves not because of their self-similarity to a memory but thanks to a more subtle resonance of their parts. Thus she discovered Rachel's torso in the way a young boy in a striped top held his arms above his head to frame the sky. She found her daughter's eyes in a girl who stood with her mother in the Post Office queue – it wasn't the eyes themselves that Jennifer recognised, but the way the girl turned her ankle this way and that out of boredom. The hair she knew from a giant advertising hoarding from which an old poster was being stripped. There was something about the jagged pattern that the torn strips made against the wood beneath . . . One Saturday afternoon Judd walked past the curved metal surface of the gas-fire surround; Jennifer happened to glimpse his reflection and it gave her the general shape of the face. And the skin, when it finally came, was not from another child at all but from the tawny sandstone of a building in Sheep Street. It was the texture of the stone which gave it away, the way it had been worn into long, deep folds and peppered by a subcutaneous growth of lichen. The smile was that of the girl downstairs, who never said a word to anyone but grinned the biggest grin. The nipples she found in a field one damp October day when she and Stim and Skag drove to Wales in Stim's Mini to search for magic mushrooms.

As the pieces of the puzzle began to come together they lived inside her not like a photograph which had been carefully memorised and filed away, but as an active site of recognition, a vague recipe for assembly that updated itself as time went by. With the passing years she found herself recognising new hair, new hands, new shapes, new colours in the skin, as if her idea of Rachel was growing up of its own accord.

The night of the Desiring Machine gig Jennifer finally fell asleep while contemplating the shape of Rachel's legs in the patterns made on the ceiling by the light from the street lamps and the cars, and as she slept she dreamt her daughter was nothing more than a collection of crazily circulating parts which, even if you brought them all together, would never form a quite coherent whole.

1 3

He-ere's Denzel!

The first available flight to London included a one-night stopover in New York. Judd took it anyway. After he landed he got in a cab, but when the driver asked him where he wanted to go he didn't know. 'The Plaza,' he said off the top of his head – it was the only New York hotel he could think of. But staying there turned out to be a mistake: because he was young and black and well-heeled everyone assumed he was either a drug dealer or an actor. He could see them trying to make up their minds as he sat at the Oak Bar on the first evening, sipping a whiskey and water.

A coked-up student from one of the art schools in SoHo walked in and stared straight at him. He returned her stare and could see her eyes fogging over. She let out a high-pitched yelp and moved towards him quickly, as if pulled by some kind of tractor beam. 'Oh my gard!' she began in a whisper – a whisper which quickly developed into a shriek. 'Oh my *gard*! Oh, my! *Oh*, my! You are, aren't you? You really are? I can't be-*lieve* it! It's Denzel, look it's *Denzel*!! It's really you, isn't it?' She arrived at his chair and started foaming slightly at the mouth, telling him how much she worshipped him, how she had seen all his films.

Judd kept trying to tell her that he wasn't Denzel Washington, but she wouldn't listen. Everyone in the bar was staring. It didn't take him long to lose his temper. 'Look, I know it's hard for you, baby, with us being black and all, for you to tell us apart. But I'm not Denzel Washington and I'm not anybody else you know either, *so just get the fuck outta my face before I smack you!*' The girl stood there stunned and Judd turned back to the bar, and a security guard arrived and led her away. She went willingly, sobbing that she couldn't believe how Denzel had said that to her, and that she would never, never go and see one of his movies again. As if he cared, thought the guard.

Judd had forgotten how much he'd hated New York. Or maybe it was that he'd never hated it, had never had an opinion, and just hated it now. When he ventured out of the hotel after dinner he was shocked by the speed of the place, the dark scenes of the future playing across the terrible technologies of its buildings.

Although it was ten o'clock at night he found himself caught in crushes on the sidewalk and yelled at by people for being in the way. He tried the subway, but even that was frantic, and hot too, desperately hot. He wandered in and out of one or two shops, vaguely lonely, suffering with the constant transition from air-con to air so humid it felt like a solid wall. He began to understand why for years those with the money to get out of New York in the summer months did exactly that, leaving the city to settle a little further into its degradation and decay without them.

Walking aimlessly, he ended up in the West Village, in a street full of bars which he began to trawl, a drink or two at each, thinking – contrary to his earlier mood – that he might try and pick somebody up. But he was unable to mesh with the atmosphere in any of the places, to interface with the night. Bored and drunk, he gave it up, went to get a cab uptown to the hotel, sure that it was a cliché that the taxi drivers here wouldn't stop for blacks. But no, it was true, and after a couple of yelling fits in the middle of the street he resigned himself to the subway.

Down on the platform he stares at a map, tries to make sense of the topological spaghetti rendered more complicated still by a dense scrawl of red tagging. The station is massively hot and he feels faint, so he leans against the board to steady himself. OK, try again, now what station does he want? But the graffiti seem to inch and ooze, their redness deepens and splatter patterns start to form, droplets squeeze out from minute Perspex pores. Suddenly Judd sees the city: from Van Cordlandt Park to Breezy Point the subway's trackmarked veins lift into bold relief, swollen, purple, pitted, dense, a creep of ivy upon a ruined wall, a rib-cage flayed, laid bare . . . in Clark Street, Red Hook they're shooting in the streets; in Nevins Tremont Alphabet they do it another way; in Calvary New Calvary Mount Zion Olivet they lie and bleed in lines, staining green and pleasant fields; at Times Square they cut throats, at West Fourth they cut purses; in Jamaica they burn the summer, in Crown Heights they burn each other; at King's Highway they burn a bum who's passed out on the platform, spray him with lighter fuel and toss a match; at Chambers Broadway they burn files tapes records blueprints; in Central Park they burn trees; on Ellis they burn immigrants; on Fifth they burn money on Broadway they burn reputations on Forty-second they burn the candle at both ends; at Columbia they burn books; in Harlem they burn buildings, they burn it up; at UN Plaza they burn bullshit, you can smell it over on Vernon-Jackson where they're burning pipes . . . *Interzone I think I've found you, and you're burning*, streets and rivers ablaze, bridges arching over chasms of fire, boatmen poling down steaming creeks of lava, sulphur fills the air, blinding, cauterising mucous membranes, the only rain a rain of pumice a rain of ash, the streets, the streets are full of ash, are full of dread, the people wade to and fro, they stride, they step, they turn their eyes away, they build and burrow, reach out away, try to haul themselves away, you see them drawn out down the street their minds in towers their feet in filth their midriffs a hundred feet or more of taut gut stretched over an eternal flame, the spindle never turns but seized and stuck it's frozen, the spit stuck here as if on ice, a cold wind blows in from the north and the towers quick and crust and fracture, the weather turns, faces glisten now with dewy snow, the flames slow and twist and grind, their turmoil easing, their colours go through cadmium and violent green to mauve and now to blue, blue licks of ice grip up and swan like stalactites that felt the agony of time and urged and coiled and thrust their solid bodies into telling shapes of pain; the lava, pouring down the Hudson and the East slows to a halt, its plumes becoming intermittent, its

439

surface rills of fire now shuddering into diamond studded rock, the hulls of ships caught on the cooling surface inwards crack, spilling cargo out like stomachs sliced with bayonets or heads caught in a press; the citizens find their feet stuck to the chilly streets, their hands glued to handles, railings, like fortune cookies their arms snap at the wrist; in Central Park the ducks freeze in the lakes, squawk and quack incomprehension until their bills freeze at random angles and the cries freeze in their throats; in offices the secretaries' fingers stick icy to their keys, the boyish grins of office boys freeze on their boyish faces, the buttocks of executives are welded to their padded leather swivel chairs; in the alleys the cars freeze on the roads; in the cars the drivers freeze to the wheels, their necks freeze as they crane to look at the sounds freezing on the radio; in the clubs the music freezes to the horns the sticks freeze to the drums the money freezes in the tills the liquor freezes in the glasses . . . even the cigarette smoke freezes in the air, forming crystal banyans which pirouette in ashtrays and spread throughout the room until their own weight becomes too much and they tinkle shatter tumble on the frozen hairstyles of the frozen clientele . . . outside the air is gently freezing, the last breaths of people stopped in their tracks form cotton balls which protrude from their icy lips as a woodland fungus grows from a frozen stump . . . there will be no more violence in this city, no more muggings neighbour killings rapings lootings random shootings slaughters stalkings in the park gang retributions money cleanings machine-gunnings drugs and dealing spiving pimping racial beating land dividing overcharging underpaying appropriating segregating taunting stealing Wall Streeting or world trading . . . but deep below . . . deep below the rib-cage . . . a red light flickers on, a gentle breeze of warmth is felt, a tiny movement . . . a scurry . . . a rush . . . a touch of air, a hiss, a shudder, a lurch, a bustle . . . the gentle stubborn pulse of life . . . the subway is still running . . .

. . . pulling back, Judd runs from the station. It's not so far to the hotel – maybe he'll just walk it after all.

The next day he flies into London and books himself into a small hotel off Russell Square. He is excited, expectant, the hallucination has keyed him up. For some reason he takes it as a sign that his trip to London will be a success.

Chemical generation

The dog is in the image now, reflected back upon itself, DOG:GOD, refracted through the prism of the atmosphere, wave and particle, extended in space. Underpinning space, even, dataspace at least, Laika half-way into the image now, powered by the mitochondria of the flickering screen, her existence a continual rave, a techno track, an obliteration of the dimensions learned down there, on 3D planet earth. Fully acid. Phased.

So where is she, then? Has she leapt, like a salmon up a waterfall, like an electron across two orbits, to a higher (better?) place? Does she now traverse a utopia of communication, an undulating info-sea, womb-like and salted with fragments of savoury data? Has she reached heaven at last? Or, as some would maintain, has she simply disappeared altogether, has she ceased to exist, her brain turned to mush, her concentration span attenuated, her soul shrivelled, her muscles atrophied? Is she chemical generation, drop-out, slacker, loser, junkie, thug?

Why not ask Laika herself? If you do, you'll find that she's not concerned with your theories. Her parameters have changed, she has different degrees of freedom, she's in a different phase space now. Back on earth she was mongrel dog, instantiation of age-old intersection of genotype and phenotype, fitness landscape and gene pool desire (a different kind of chemical generation, a much older kind). But now she's something else, a bacterium that was carried by accident out from beneath humanity's thumb and into its brain, forced to adapt and adjust, an irritant around which an abscess has formed.

But although she has thrown a reflection on to this new and hostile environment, to cross over and enter the image completely, to leave dog behind and become god – that is quite another matter. She doesn't have enough energy to make the transition from machine-flesh-and-blood into the virtual realm where she'd become a format for pictures, a reel in the weather, a shape for the stars. Laika long ago managed to make the most of a bad situation and her talents have brought her this far, but like Emma she can't make the final leap – can't make contact – alone. A hybrid Narcissus, she's stuck where she is on the lip of the pool, her fascination a dead end unless something extra can be found to help her over the edge. *She* wouldn't turn from her Echo.

*

Check in

While Jennifer stood outside the Green Dragon contemplating the contents of her stomach, Joel was a few hundred miles away and also being sick, hurling his guts up and over the rail of the overnight ferry that ran between Portsmouth and Caen. It was the first time he had ever been on a boat and he'd explored every inch of it while it was still in port, astonished by its size. He'd gone from floor to floor, checking out the bars, the restaurants, the cinema, the games arcades, as hyper as the children who were charging around in unruly packs ignoring their parents' frantic screams. Once the engines had started and the entire vessel had begun to vibrate, Joel rushed out on deck to watch the bilges pump and the stern swing out from the quay. He went as far forward as he could and breathed in the air and stood in the spray and watched the great swathes of foam sliced up by the prow chase themselves into an endless churn. When he tired of this he shifted his attention to the sun, which was setting off the port bow.

It was a remarkable thing, to watch the huge orb redden, set fire to the clouds, then sink below the perfectly clean line of the horizon. Joel was suddenly acutely aware of something that was so obvious he had never stopped to think about it before, namely that he lived on the surface of a planet much as a bacterium might live on the skin of an orange. How odd that the world was not flat. The thought made him feel terribly dependent on the disappearing sun and, as if to confirm his fears, no sooner had the last rind of its colour shrunk from view than the wind picked up and the sea took on a heavy swell.

The decks of the boat were fairly empty now, with most of the passengers having already gone inside to eat or retire to their cabins, and Joel decided to retreat from the bows. Watching the sunset he had started to get hungry himself, but the exaggerated motion of the vessel knocked the edge off his appetite and the moment he stepped inside a sudden claustrophobia conspired with the smell of diesel fumes, warmed-over food and clustered humanity to turn his stomach. The boat was pitching quite unpleasantly and though he made it to the nearest bar to buy a coke he couldn't seem to manage to keep his balance and count out the correct change at the same time (the fact that English currency had been decimalised since he'd been in Cambridge didn't help matters). The children who had been running around earlier were more sedentary now. Many of the younger ones were squalling and tugging at their tired British mothers, through whose bodies the soft music of holiday was still playing. The memories of beach and beer and sex were still strong in these women, insulating them from the domestic grind that waited for them at the other end of the short voyage as surely as the white chalk cliffs of England's south coast. Surrounded by duty free, they lay back in their shellsuits and sighed.

In an instant one impulse dominated Joel's thoughts: get back outside. He reached the rail just as his lunch was ejected and then hung there, the metal rod lodged under his armpits, watching the contents of his stomach get swept into the sudding turmoil that nagged away at the sides of the hull. When he could retch no more he staggered over to the benches which lined the steel cabin walls and lay down. The acrid tang of the engines, so romantic an hour before, was now a sulphurous reek that attacked his nostrils. He was weak, terribly weak, weak as a child fresh from the womb. He wanted to die.

Night fell quickly and dense clouds obscured the stars. The

443

moon could not be seen, although Joel ran his eyes across the sky from where he lay, wishing he could spot the satellite and gain some point of reference from beyond the pitching deck for at the moment there was none, not even a horizon. He laughed weakly – the Nazis had hated relativity theory for being a Jewish idea. He gave himself over to the smoothness of the space in which he found himself: he was too drained and it was too alien for him to try to impose a structure upon it. The ferry was a small speck of light in a vast cauldron of blackness – so what could he do? He stared out into the apparently featureless night. Here was the sublime, he thought, here was the unformed and primal chaos of existence. How boring, banal and unpleasant it was. He thought of *Moby Dick* which he, like Judd, had once started but never finished. He wondered what happened in the end.

It began to rain, a cold, dank drizzle that felt good against his clammy skin. He fell asleep. The winds which whipped the waves which tossed the boat which made Joel sick had started out somewhere in the Arctic and followed the line of the Labrador current down past Nantucket, from whence the *Pequod* had once set sail. Further south, off New York, they'd picked up a few of the more odorous particles on the run from Moshe Kluge's bakery (now in larger premises in front of which were parked two smart delivery vans). Then the winds turned west with the North Atlantic Drift and the particles hurtled their way across three thousand miles of ocean and by a remarkable coincidence found their way up Joel's large Jewish schnoz, where they fell upon the receptors of his olfactory organ and sent a dim signal down the olfactory nerve to the olfactory bulb, where it caused an increase in activity just sufficient to trigger the last dream of his family that Joel would ever have.

It was odd to be back in England. He realised at once that he hadn't missed it at all. He purchased a train ticket to London and got some breakfast at the station, which proved to be a mistake – he'd left for CERN in 1971 and thirteen years on the Continent had left him unprepared for the completely unpalatable nature of British Rail food. Stoically, he ate a stale doughnut that sat in his stomach like slow-setting cement and drank a cup of a thin acidic liquid which the woman behind the counter assured him was orange juice. He bought a magazine but once settled in his seat couldn't focus on the words and so he let his head loll on the headrest and closed his eyes and tried to wish away the noise of squalling children and the stench of stale cigarettes. It was like being back in East Germany. He managed to slip into a kind of fuddled slumber, the clacking pulse of the train incredibly comforting after the unpredictable motions of the ferry. He dreamt once again he was back in the restaurant eating, then visiting the toilet to shit, then eating again, and that once more Jennifer tried to seduce him away from his rhythm of void and consume, void and consume, void and consume, void and consume. Her interfering made him mad, and eventually he stood up from the table and pushed her away. Once again she shrank at his touch and became a plastic doll with unblinking blue eyes, her upturned head jutting at a peculiar angle. Where his hand had touched her chest it split open and inside were those two synthetic hearts, one on the left and one on the right, made of that strange red material and throbbing with light.

At Waterloo he was woken by the guard. He got through a pocketful of change calling round hotels from a payphone on the concourse, trying to find a room that would let him have his own telephone at a less than extortionate rate, but he eventually made a reservation at a place not far from Paddington. He took a cab.

The hotel was on Prince's Square and the taxi pulled up outside the front door. Joel got out and looked up and down the street; there were at least fourteen or fifteen other hotels packed into the short Georgian terrace. All of them looked a little battered, the paint peeling from their window frames, plastic signs poking out from their columned porticoes. Outside his own, two men were sitting on the pavement mending a bicycle, reggae chugging out from a boom box beside them. The machine was in pieces, its oily sprockets, chain, nuts and washers laid out on pages from the *Sun*. A washer ringed a pin-up's nipple, and Joel saw this and wanted to go over there and arrange the rest of the parts around her so that her flesh would have a little machinic magic all of its own.

The moment passed, and he paid the cabby and went up the steps into the hotel. The front door was blocked ajar and glass doors had been fitted just beyond it. A small air-conditioning unit had been inset above them and the usual array of credit card signs were stuck to the glass. The hallway was freshly painted and cool, and there was a floral-pattern carpet underfoot. Inside, the building seemed larger than it did from the street.

One of the men from the pavement followed Joel in and wiping the oil from his hands with a piece of rag entered Joel's name in the register and gave him his key. 'It's the receptionist's afternoon off today,' he explained. He checked Joel's passport, then showed him up to his room. He tried to take both the holdalls but Joel felt secretly embarrassed that a black man should carry his bags and insisted on taking one of them himself.

Once inside the room – which was on the front of the building, overlooking the portico – he tested the locks on the door and windows and checked that the telephone socket was suitable. Then he unpacked his rucksack and one of the holdalls and took a shower, and – for the first time in months – had a shave, using scissors and a razor he had bought on the ferry before he'd got sick. Locking the door behind him, he went downstairs and out into the sunlight. He felt supremely confident and set off in a random direction, nodding to the bicycle tinkerers as he went. The one who'd signed him in returned his nod; the other ignored him.

He found his way to Queensway and bought a stack of computer magazines which he studied in a café while he had something to eat. The next morning at nine he was on the telephone ordering kit with his credit card and by the end of the following week he had spent several thousand pounds and the hotel room was crammed with cardboard boxes, polystyrene packaging, tools, computer components, measuring and calibration devices and medical equipment, not to mention empty take-away cartons and discarded clothing. He worked away happily in the centre of the mess, a child with his toys, covering the carpet with lengths of wire and glistening drops of solder that dulled as they cooled and set into the nylon weave. The dream-figure of the double-hearted doll often seemed to hover over him while he worked, a kind of muse. He thought of the restaurant dream often and dreamt it whenever he slept; it carried an enormous sexual charge, exciting him to an extent he had never previously known. So much did it turn him on that he often had to break off from his work and masturbate, grinding himself to orgasm between the loving surfaces of two copper-dappled circuit boards in an attempt to splice his pleasure with his plan. His balls ached constantly and he had pins and needles in the balls of his feet. Preferring to work at night, he often slept in the afternoons and when it was warm he liked to walk down through Hyde Park to the Serpentine, have lunch in the café at the eastern end, then fall asleep under a tree near the edge of the water for a few hours. He enjoyed these siestas: memories of the afternoons he used to spend reading by the Cam were easily elicited from the conjunctions of water, breeze, willows and ducks that enveloped them.

He used empty boxes and a door which he unscrewed from the wardrobe to construct a desk on which gradually materialised a fantastic meshwork of circuit boards, terminals, disk drives, keyboards, modems, cables, video cameras, printers and other electronic paraphernalia. In the abstract, impersonal space of the hotel room the structure looked obscene, resembling the innards of some murdered and mutilated robot.

Totem

The growing obsession with her dead child began to worry Jennifer. Every night now she dreamt about Rachel; all through the day she would be on the look-out for any aspects of her that might be secreted in the world. Although it had started out as an hallucination brought on by extreme circumstances, the double-pulse rhythm came to her often now, triggered by the most distantly related sounds – the rhythm of the cash tills at work, a piece of music, the sound of rain on the windows of the flat. Perhaps she had read too much bad science fiction, perhaps she was too into those books on conspiracy theories and psychic phenomena, but it was becoming increasingly hard to ignore the possibility that she was being sent some kind of message. It was either that or the onset of schizophrenia, and since she knew more about the former than the latter and had been left with a fear of hospitals after the harrowing experience of her pregnancy and the subsequent birth, she far preferred it as an explanation.

So everything became important now, everything became significant. Her past was trying to tell her something and everything must be examined: changes in the weather, objects abandoned in the street, the behaviour of animals and birds, any coincidences, anything out of the ordinary, even the ordinary itself. She fingered her scars almost continuously and studied them at night before she went to sleep, in case the network of razor marks (which, in retrospect, seemed to have been part of a subconscious process culminating in her caesarean, the greatest and most traumatic of all her wounds) might in some way serve as a key to help her interpret whatever message was being transmitted, the lines drawn on her chest shoulders breasts comprising a peculiar Rosetta stone of the flesh.

But this opening of herself to the world was threatening, too. She'd been so withdrawn, so self-contained for so long that any acknowledgement that the scars she had drawn as armour might be functioning instead as interface was hugely unsettling. It suggested a return to her childhood, a prospect that made Jennifer ripple with fear. Looking back on the flow of her life, most of it seemed beyond her control, shaped by currents and tides far larger than herself, and to go back would not mean the chance to change things but merely the repetition of pain and distress she had hoped she had put behind her for ever.

In play

She was in touch with all three of them now, one way or another. Through her mutations and her close relationship with other eukaryotes, Emma has managed to amplify material affects, extend her senses, manipulate and evaluate at a distance. She has become extended in space.

Her space is a dream of protein and chromosome, photon and chemical, mineral and fluid. She is image and rock, lizard and tree, data and tool, network and sea. And now she dreams her parents, as they once dreamt her (though that was a strange kind of dreaming, phantasm of gamete and drive). They deserted her once and to make them return she plucks threads in the loom of the mind, engineers coincidences and conjunctions in matter, as if the two were the two different aspects, the woof and the warp, of one single stratum. Her child's fingers dapple the surface of being and Jennifer, Judd and Joel bounce together, like three metal balls.

Fresh in town

Back in London, Judd found himself severely depressed. England had so many associations for him, most of them unpleasant, that he couldn't seem to focus on the situation in hand. Day after day he put off contacting Scofield's friend, and he grew more nervous about it the more he realised just how crucial this meeting might be. He felt enervated the entire time, as if the downturn he'd experienced in Reno was still draining him, still drying him out. He appeared to have succeeded in breaking up the old psychoanalytic patterns, but now he felt out of control in a different way, giddy

449

and heavy, and unclear about which way to turn. To give himself direction he began grasping at straws, wandering round London and trying to reconstruct from the city and the memories hidden among it like Easter eggs some sense of the childhood he'd had before he'd met Jennifer. It worked, up to a point, but at the same time it made him feel somehow submerged, as if he were a collection of sediments and the flux that was the young Judd was above him, currents and whirlpools just below the waves. He worried that he'd been wrong to interpret his vision of a flaming then frozen New York as a positive sign and eventually pushed it to the back of his mind.

He watched the children who passed him in the street, certain that he could tell from their eyes whether they were innocents or already saddled with the structures and strictures of the adult world. From facets of their faces and expressions he constructed a mental simulacrum of how he might have been if he had never slept with Jennifer or if – and this was the version he preferred – he had slept with her without discovery or guilt. Thinking about her again made him wonder whether he should try to get back in touch, but he dismissed the notion. It was pointless, stupid. It would surely just bring back the anger, take him back down a path already well trodden. He felt cold, as though the world were closing in around him, beginning to glance his way.

Lonely, he took a card ('Inexperienced Schoolgirl, Fresh in Town') from one of the telephone boxes on Southampton Row, called up the number printed on it and went back to his hotel to wait. From his window he could just see the sunset, the neon scribbles of the clouds tacky decorations on a contaminated horizon. When the prostitute finally arrived she didn't look particularly inexperienced or too much like a schoolgirl either. She was bottle-blonde and five-two and probably around twenty-eight. If it hadn't been for the uniform she wore beneath her leather coat you'd never have known. She said her name was Sara and she was very complimentary towards Judd and he, used to callous American call-girls, was flattered to observe that she actually did want to sleep with him – although he almost sent her away again when, as they lay down together on the bed, she asked him if anyone had

450

ever told him that he looked a little bit like Denzel Washington.

'You can spank me if you like,' she said bluntly, as Judd handed over her fee, 'but hands only, no objects. And it'll be extra.' She smiled at him. 'Though I'll give *you* a discount.' Judd adjusted his previous guess to twenty-five, reflecting that girls aged fast in this profession. Then again, he thought to himself, did you ever see a check-out girl who looked good for more than a couple of months?

Sara lifted up her skirt to show her panties and the tops of her suspenders. Then she walked around behind him and began to massage his shoulders, after a while removing his shirt. As they moved in the general direction of coitus Judd found he was not becoming aroused and he finally had to admit to himself that after all what he wanted was Jennifer, Jennifer as he remembered her. He rolled over and switched off the light and tried to imagine that the hands and thighs belonged to a girl with red hair and a dark-green coat whom he had seen in the National Gallery that afternoon and who couldn't have been more than twelve. She had stood alone in one of the halls, perhaps looking for her mother, and for a moment Judd thought she had stepped right out of the picture behind her – Erich Heckel's *Two People in the Open Air* – so closely did the tones of her coat and hair resemble those of the painting. She had looked directly at Judd, then lifted up a single finger as though readying herself to say something profound. Her cheeks were sallow and pale, almost bruised, and she had about her an aura of neglect. Her forehead was very high, her hair a gingery red, her eyes were shot through with emerald. The pigmentation of her skin was curious and unfamiliar: it was dappled, with a translucent quality, and by some trick of the light was faintly glaucous, borrowing colour perhaps from the verdant collar of her coat.

For a full minute the child had stood motionless while Judd watched her, playing with the ring on his finger all the time. Then a bell went off very loudly just behind him and he turned to see a Malaysian tourist being admonished by a guard. The man had poked the lens of his camera too close to one of the paintings and had triggered the alarm, that was all. Judd turned back to the girl, but she had gone.

She was beneath him now, her frail body prone and submissive, shuddering with each one of his thrusts. His hands clutched at her prepubescent flesh and he could feel her rib-cage bowing beneath the weight exerted by the heels of his palms, the bones still green and resilient with the plasticity of youth. In a frenzy he pumped away; he was sweating hard and the hot smell of him suffused the air. As he wondered, quite irrelevantly, why it was only himself he could smell, why she didn't have an odour, he felt two different rhythms, two immense pulsations, surge up his arms from her chest. He tried to pull his hands away but he could not; the very tides of his blood were in thrall to the dark oscillators hid snug beneath her flesh. He pulled again and a giant jab of pain shot through both forearms, as if hot copper wires wound loosely around them had been suddenly wrenched tight. He dug his nails into the flesh below as hard as he could, wanting to tear, wanting to rip . . .

The woman threw him off and slapped him hard across the face in one quick movement. He immediately went limp and lay with his head over the end of the bed, panting his way back into the room.

She kneeled over him, a trickle of blood running down her left breast. 'What the fuck do you think you're doing?' she yelled. He didn't respond so she thumped him on the back. In the next room someone hammered on the thin dividing wall. She lowered her voice to a hiss. 'That may be OK where you come from but I don't put up with shit like that, understand? And don't get the idea that I'm here alone. D'you think I'm fucking stupid? People know where I am. Anything happens to me and you're history, right? Understand?' She punched him, her hand balled into an extremely hard little fist. 'DO YOU UNDERSTAND?'

The neighbours banged the wall again and Judd nodded. He was shocked by his own behaviour; he had never acted anything like this before. But it was pointless to say anything. Sara leant back against the wall and they both lay there for a while, recovering their wits. In what little light crept through the gap in the curtains she examined the scratch on her breast.

Eventually Judd turned to look at her. In the crepuscular glow the scratches showed up black. 'Hey, look, I'm really sorry. I didn't mean it. I mean I never . . .'

'Well look it's done now, OK,' she snapped, but something in his expression suggested he was being sincere so she altered her tone. 'Anyway, it's not that bad. I've had worse. I'll survive.' There was a pause, then she said, 'You were going pretty well there for a while. If you promise to stay calm I'll let you finish if you like. It'll be double, though.'

'No, thanks but no thanks, I think it's best if you go.' He got off the bed and went into the bathroom, and she dressed quickly and left without another word.

He slept poorly that night and his eyes throbbed blearily all the next day, as if his retinae had been the mixing palette for some hallucination far vaster and more intricate than the one he remembered. The incident had deeply disturbed him, he didn't understand it at all, and he realised that he had to go and visit the man whose address Scofield had given him before things got any further out of hand.

The big hack

Once his new machinery was configured Joel began to connect to as many computer networks as he could find. He hooked up with ARPANET, which had been divided into ARPANET and MILNET the previous year. He explored the BITNET via its gateway at the City University of New York and the Computer and Science Network in Wisconsin. He downloaded information from the Japan Unix Network (JUNET) and from the UK's Joint Academic Network, JANET, which was in fact his nearest major gateway and the one he used most often. When he'd left CERN the networks hadn't been integrated on anything like this scale; nobody had even heard the word 'Internet'. But Unix and TCP/

IP connection and the new transmission protocols meant that the various systems were expanding and interlinking at an extraordinary rate. Indeed, computers were big news now. A year before, in January 1983, *Time* magazine had featured a computer on its cover for the first time since the 'sailor shot' of January 1950. This time the computer was an IBM PC. And now it was 'man of the year'.

Hunting for information on the networks was an extraordinary experience. To sit in front of a terminal in a London hotel room late at night, the blinds drawn and the lights off, the only illumination coming from the zorby glow of the screen, and be able to jump from Cambridge, to New York to Tokyo to Delaware to Paris to Addis Ababa to Stockholm in seconds was something which even a few years previously could hardly have been imagined. It changed everything, this space of data which was everywhere and nowhere simultaneously, in which every point seemed connected to every other, in which whole companies, whole universities, sometimes even whole societies appeared to exist.

One of Joel's earliest hacks was the British Telecom database. It was a trial run, but one with a purpose: he wanted to search for a telephone number. He could have picked up the phone and dialled directory enquiries, but it was more fun this way. It didn't take him long; online security was still in its infancy and stories of school kids breaking into nuclear defence systems seemed to turn up in the papers every other week. Once logged on, he ran a national search and in a few seconds got the number he wanted – Jennifer's – along with her address.

But the overall aim was not to take data out but to put data in. The golem he wanted to create was to be a virtual beast, a familiar that would wander the networks and bring him back data. But it was to have a human form, too – he wanted it to act within his own parameters, to be an agent of his, to take shape in the datasphere in his form. If he was going to play god, he wanted his primordial man to be in his own image. It was a Christian idea, but it seemed somehow appropriate.

He still wasn't sure whether or not he was going to carry out his plan, or even if it would work if he did. Rather than growing in confidence, as the various aspects of it came together he was increasingly racked with self-doubt. After the initial rush his work proceeded more slowly and he found himself becoming increasingly pensive. He would often forget what he was doing and stare blankly at whatever was on the screen or in his hand at the time, or even just at the wall, suddenly struck by the lack of sense it all made. For hours he would debate with himself whether or not to call Jennifer, always deciding against it in the end, managing to come up with a different excuse every time. But at the same time the Project seemed clearer than ever. Prevaricating, he began to write out his theory on his computer, printing out completed sections and pinning them up on the walls.

The subject matter dealt with more than just physics and Kabbalah, magic and chance. Humanity was rotten, he wrote, tragically flawed, capable of feeding only off itself. The human race was a rabid animal that tore at itself in a frenzy, its very attempts to mitigate its own misery merely producing more of it. He wrote that nothing but direct and total application of technology could unfold new dimensions of human possibility and prevent self-destruction. The Internet was merely the first stage of the process: this network of networks would eventually achieve consciousness, at which point there would no longer be any way of telling the difference between human and machine. He himself would lead the way, a manifestation of tikkun, the third type of time. He would transcend the vast movements in which the world was trapped and push forward into a new space where death was forgotten and the universe became perfect. Increasingly obsessed with his dream of the restaurant and his memories of Jennifer, he fitted her into his scheme: if he was an agent of tikkun, Jennifer was an agent of shevirah; she represented the chaos of the world, its living imperfection. It was only fitting, then, that she should midwife the next stage of the Project, be the golem's surrogate mother, its incubator.

Writing all this down wasn't easy. In his head it was clear, but committed to paper it became childish and muddled. It still lacked a purity, a simple coherence, but the more logical the arguments became the more they seemed lifeless and naïve. He still wasn't sure of the precise role that Jennifer would play, nor could he identify the third term which kept re-presenting itself. Who, after all, was the agent of zimzum? Joel didn't know. Perhaps it would be his golem. Could that work? It didn't seem likely.

Frustrated into action, he stopped writing and began to make the appropriate measurements. He started with the obvious ones: height and weight, the length and girth of every limb, skin tones, size and colour of eyes and degree of myopia, rate of hair and nail growth, pulse rates corresponding to various levels of physical exertion, size of penis (flaccid and erect), calorie intake and so on. These completed, he progressed to the more complex internal statistics, some of which required repeated visits to the nearby hospital of St Mary's: size and length of throat, skeletal dimensions, deduced weight of individual bones, blood type and red and white cell counts, sperm count, lung capacity, bladder capacity, stomach capacity, intestinal length, skull thickness, brain size and weight, sinus diameters, hearing thresholds, metabolic rates and bio-rhythms, genetic fingerprint.

The double-hearted doll haunted him more and more intensely and he often thought he could hear its double pulse beating away inside the walls of his room, as if their thick plaster were flesh skinned with paint. For a period he only slept when sleep overtook him and this meant no more afternoons dozing beneath trees in Hyde Park; now he simply lay down like a dog among the mess which cluttered the floor, the bed and every available surface. But then the site of his dreams changed from the restaurant to the room itself, and he began to lose track of the difference between sleeping and waking.

Within the first fortnight of his moving in, the chambermaid had kicked up a fuss about the state of the room and he had given her two crisp fifty-pound notes in exchange for a promise that she would leave him alone and not let on to the management. But now she was gently extorting money from him, letting herself in with her pass key when he least expected it and complaining about how difficult it was to keep the truth from the boss. She was a petite American girl with very blonde hair and metallic eyes and although she had no idea what on earth it was he was up to she had quickly figured out that whatever it was, it had required a significant investment of both time and money to set up. She concluded, correctly, that this put her in a position of some power and Joel had little choice but to meet her demands. His funds, already greatly reduced by the hotel bill and the computer equipment, had dwindled almost to the point of invisibility, and he realised that some time soon he would have to break off from his work and pay a few visits to the city's casinos, or he would not have enough money left to make a decent stake.

What cash he had he counted out on the bed; it came to a little under £500. The chambermaid had just demanded another fifty and at the end of the week he would have to settle his bill as usual. There was nothing else for it but to polish his computer shoes and brush off his suit. He asked the hotel receptionist to recommend a casino and she suggested the Victoria, on the Edgware Road. He had to join first – a legal formality, but waiting for the membership to be processed delayed everything by a couple of days. He put the time to good use: trouble-shooting the gambling machine, replacing old cables and solenoids, re-soldering connections, but the wait still made him nervous. It had been a while since he had done this, even thought about it. Could he still do it? What if he blew his stake? What if he couldn't calibrate the wheel correctly? What if, what if, what if? But as soon as his membership cleared and he walked through the doors of the Victoria all his doubts were dispelled. He was suffused with a feeling he had never had before, that of coming home. It simply meant that he knew: what to do, what was expected of him, what the looks and actions of other people meant, the parameters of the system.

But something *had* changed. That night he felt so confident that he never got around to switching on the machine but played much as Judd had done in the early days when he'd first discovered the lizard and followed it through the back rooms and dens of LA. But while for Judd the impression had been that chance was alive, that its patterns and poems were something dynamic, for Joel it couldn't have been more different. He felt as if he were absorbing the imperfect universe into himself, overcoming it, processing it, finally performing the task he'd been working at since his first years at Cambridge. It seemed that he'd got back some of the mathematical talents he'd had as a boy, except that now it wasn't his imagination which did the work of manipulating shapes, planes and figures, but his entire body. Predicting the results of the wheel that night was an unmistakably physical sensation: he could feel data being churned in the muscles of his neck back arms, could feel sensors in his thighs groin belly crunching numbers. He watched himself in the mirror, saw his time move quite differently from that of all the others around him. While they faltered and hesitated, grew old before him, he moved more and more smoothly. Even as he looked, his features became more honed, his aspect more measured. For the first time in his life he felt at one with his flesh. He was getting there, he'd made the right decision to come, he was becoming machine.

He left the table and cashed in his chips. He'd cleaned up, won over seven thousand pounds. With the cheque safely in his pocket he wandered down towards Marble Arch and into Hyde Park, elated with his success. It was a clear summer night and he took off his jacket and unbuttoned his shirt, wanting to feel the air on his new and confident skin. He sat in his favourite spot on the bank of the Serpentine and gazed up at the fathomless ink of the sky, identifying constellations and tagging each star with its distance from earth. His mind was electric, totally clear.

Back at the hotel he threw open the windows and tidied his room, filling empty boxes with rubbish and throwing them out into a skip that was conveniently parked outside. Then he did something he had not done for weeks: he slept in a bed unencumbered with junk and with no fear of his dreams. Tomorrow he would call Jennifer.

The telephone call

The telephone rang and rang, and eventually Jennifer could stand it no more. She pulled herself up out of her bath with a great sucking noise, frightening Judd and Joel, who had been dozing underneath the sink where the hot-water pipes warmed the floor. Swearing loudly, she wrapped a striped towel around herself and padded down the hallway, leaving a trail of wet foot-prints for the cats to sniff in her wake. She grabbed the phone. 'Who is it?'

'Er, hello, is that Jennifer Several?' said a shy voice from a hundred and one miles away, and an inch away too.

'Yeah, what of it? Hope you're not going to try and sell me something.'

'Um, no, I don't think so. Jennifer, is that you?'

'I'm sorry, but who is this?'

'Oh, well, you probably don't remember me, I mean it was a long time ago. It's Joel. Joel Kluge.'

'Oh!' Jennifer sat down suddenly on the chair into which Joel had climbed unnoticed just a moment or two before. He shot out from beneath her descending buttocks with a shriek and nearly landed on Judd, who was sitting washing himself on the floor. Judd took this as an insult, flattened his ears and launched a counter-attack. 'Joel, my god, Joel. What a surprise . . . Er, where are you? How did you get my number?'

'Oh, I got it from the telephone company,' he said, accidentally artless. 'I hope you don't mind me calling you out of the blue like this . . .'

'Oh. Not at all, no. It's, er, great to hear from you. It's just a bit of a shock, that's all.'

'. . . but I'm in England and you're the only person I really know here any more, and I thought, well, I . . .' He tailed off. A hint of static crackled down the line while both of them desperately tried to think of something to say.

Jennifer got there first. 'No, god no, that's absolutely fine.' I

459

sound like a right stuck-up cow, she thought. 'So how are you? What have you been up to?'

'Oh, you know. I left CERN, by the way. Been doing some travelling.'

'Travelling? Where?'

'Just around Europe. Nowhere exotic. What about you? I, er, I expect you're married by now.' Feeling his way.

'Me? Married? You must be joking.'

'How's your father?'

'Oh . . . he died. I should have written I suppose, but I . . . it was a while ago now anyway.'

'That's terrible. I'm sorry.'

'Well, it wasn't your fault, was it? He always drank and smoked too much. It was inevitable, really.'

'You sound very upset.'

'No, I'm fine. Christ, it was years ago now. Just a couple of years after we last saw each other. How long ago was that? Ten years? Fuck, is it really ten years?'

'About that, yes.' The static got louder, the copper wires responding to the tension between them. 'It's a terrible line.'

'What are you doing in England?'

'I'm working on some things and I needed somewhere to stop for a while so I thought why not London? I've been living in Berlin.'

'Berlin! Right. Wow. I've never been to Berlin. So, er, what are you working on?'

'Some computer things. I don't know if you'd find it interesting.'

'In London?'

'Yes, in London.'

'Are you with a university or something?'

'Sure, I mean no, I mean, it's just me really, I work from my room. I have a room, in a hotel. I have my own computer equipment. And with a modem, it's OK.'

'What's a modem?'

'It's a device which converts digital bits into analogue electrical impulses so that they can be transmitted as a frequency-modulated tone, which can then be demodulated by another, similar device.'

460

'What?'

'Oh, sorry. It allows two computers to communicate down a phone line.'

'Right.'

'Are you still working at your maths?'

'No, I'm sorry, Joel, I gave it up years ago,' she faltered. 'I had to give up school, it's complicated, because when Henry died . . .'

'Yes, of course, I understand . . .' said Joel, a little crestfallen.

'No, no, Joel, you don't, it was more difficult than you can imagine, you see there was, I don't know how to say this, but, well, oh god . . .'

'Yes?'

'. . . well, there was . . . *something else.*' Jennifer flushed hot all over, although she was still wet from her shower and wearing only a towel. Her face prickled. Water ran from her wet hair and dripped on to the telephone book (stolen from W. H. Smith) which lay on the table next to the phone. The globules plashed on to the heavy manilla paper and curdled it into a series of discrete wavy patches. She sniffed and found that her nose had started to run. What was all this, then? From down the line she could hear Joel's silence expressed in the static. 'Joel,' she said in a voice so fluid it threatened to melt the lines which carried it away, 'Joel, could I, do you think I could, I mean could I see you?'

'Yes, of course, please . . . when . . . ?'

'I could come to London. I work during the week, but I could come down on Saturday, and we could meet in the afternoon and spend the evening together.' She had a half-day on Friday and some money in the bank that needed spending. She could get the coach from Stratford to Victoria and she'd be there by nightfall, and she could stay with Shelley, who'd moved to London three years earlier and lived in Finsbury Park. And on Saturday morning she could go shopping, proper shopping, for some new things to wear.

'Yes, perfect.' Saturday, thought Joel, that's three days. Would he have time? Would he be ready? Yes, maybe, yes, he could probably just do it. 'Yes, yes, Saturday is good, there's a place where I sometimes eat. We could meet there, it's open all day.

We could meet there at four o'clock. Do you know the Notting Hill Gate? It's there on the corner, it's a modern-looking place, an Italian café, by a pub called the Prince of Wales, we could meet there at four. You can't miss it, it's right on the sharp corner . . .' Jennifer, infected by Joel's excitement, scribbled down directions. She couldn't tell now if she was laughing or crying. So the arrangements were made and they both said goodbye, and it wasn't until she'd put down the phone that she realised Joel hadn't given her either his phone number or the name of his hotel. Down in London Joel lay back on his bed, feeling elated, and it didn't occur to him either.

Oh, well, thought Jennifer, as she ran some more hot water into her bath, sure there wouldn't be a problem. Joel was here. Fuck. Joel was here! She was so happy. The omens and hallucinations hadn't been signifying a message from the past at all. They'd been auguring a message from the future!

Tea with Yosemite Sam

The man's name was Anatole Crimp and he lived in Glengall Road which according to the *A to Z* was in Kilburn. Judd boarded the tube in Russell Square and rode it south, the hot compartments filling with passengers as they were moved from station to station. Soon they passed beneath the West End, and dozens and dozens of people tried to get on and off at every stop. It was total chaos, and while the driver kept telling passengers to please move down inside the carriages, her words blurred almost to incomprehensibility by the static of the Tannoy, Judd couldn't see that there was any place left for them to go. There were people everywhere. A dark-haired young woman stood jammed against his legs, chatting with her friend. The doors were trying to close but somewhere along the train someone was blocking them. They shuddered to and fro like the giant eyelids of a malfunctioning android. Through a gap in the scrum, Judd spotted a station nameplate. Green Park. Wasn't he meant to change here? He struggled to his feet and, muttering 'Excuse me, excuse me', elbowed his way through the crowd, slipping through the doors just before they closed for the final time. Behind him the brunette swung deftly into the vacant seat. On the platform Judd readjusted his clothes and followed the signs for the Jubilee Line. Negotiating the packed tunnels, he began to wish he had taken a cab, but soon enough he was on a train heading north, this time making sure he checked off every station on the way.

Back up at ground level a stiff breeze was blowing, taking with it all the heat from the weak sun. Judd walked against the wind up the High Road to Glengall Road, which turned out to be an unremarkable street opposite a branch of Safeway's. A betting shop, a launderette, an off-licence clustered around its mouth; all three seemed to be constructed entirely out of ageing Formica. The street sign was darkened with streaks of traffic grime and a couple of bicycle tyres had been hooped over one end of it. Broken Lucozade bottles encrusted the cracked paving slabs below. Judd strolled down the road until he reached number 32, then taking a deep breath, he knocked on the door.

There was no reply so he knocked again. The breeze was quickly filling the sky with clouds from the east, which were beginning to form a pall across the afternoon. It looked like rain. Up the street a couple of thick, angular women emerged from the launderette and started down the hill towards him. He could hear their gossiping above the squeak of their shopping trolleys, their Irish accents making him feel for a moment that he was back in New York. He looked up as they passed so as not to stare and in the clouds he saw the face of the girl from the National Gallery. Freaked, he knocked again and when there was still no reply, decided to see if he could work his way around the back of the house.

Further along the street was an entrance to an alleyway that let on to the back gardens. Counting houses as he went, Judd made his way down it, carefully stepping between small piles of broken masonry and discarded pieces of household junk: washing-up bowls with the bottoms kicked out, rusted mangles and top-loading wash-ing-machines, amputated bicycles.

The gate to Crimp's garden was rotten and its hinges gave as he tried it. Lifting it away from the entrance, he slipped past and into the middle of an unbelievable mess. The tumble of oddments that littered the alleyway would have seemed to have had its origin here, except that out there everything had been junk – old or broken items that were out of date and had no obvious further use – whereas in here most of the rubbish looked modern and perfectly serviceable. Caught in the weeds like the stiff carcasses of long-snared animals were a sleek television set, two CD players, a rowing machine, a personal computer, a glass-and-chrome coffee table, a Sinclair C5 electric car, a series of injection-moulded toys, a door from a 1982 Lotus Esprit, a carphone, a video recorder and a microwave oven. All the items were trashed beyond repair; they had obviously just been tossed out (or rolled out, in the case of the C5) and left to the mercy of the elements. But beneath the scratches and dents they looked new. One or two of them still had their price stickers on. They had probably never been used.

Judd picked his way through the junk. He stood on the Lotus door, intending to hop over the TV, but an invisible layer of mildew covered the metal and as soon as he placed his weight on it he slipped. He went arse over tit; as he fell his elbow made contact with the television screen and the vacuum tube instantly imploded with a *whump*. He grabbed at various parts of his body to check that they weren't damaged, and when he looked up he saw the net curtains in one of the downstairs windows twitch and a shadow flit across behind them. Encouraged, he got to his feet and brushed himself down, rubbing with annoyance at a heavy streak of grease marking the thigh of his Kappas. He was just raising his hand to knock on the back door, thinking at the same time that it was a good thing he hadn't worn his ochre jacket, when it snapped open a fraction and something long, hard and black was thrust out towards him, nearly striking him in the face.

It was a shotgun, a side-by-side Spanish sporting model, and a brace of monstrous glints flickered up out of its twin barrels and into Judd's eyes. He began to back off but the gun pursued him, quickly followed by its owner. Judd tried to get a look at whoever it was but his attention had been completely commandeered by the gleaming length of metal.

'Get back further,' the man said. Judd did so, instinctively holding his empty hands out at his sides. 'What do you want?' Judd wanted to tell him, he really did, but in his panic the appropriate network in his brain was refusing to anneal. He ventured a look over the barrels: the man at the other end of them was much shorter than himself and the young American found himself looking down upon a thick domed knead of pink skin settled into a tangle of wiry grey. For his aggressor was completely bald, although this baldness was more than compensated for by the enormous beard that sprouted from his jaw and which hung down to well below his navel. He was stocky, with broad shoulders and large, slightly splayed feet, and was dressed in two pieces of a three-piece pinstripe suit, a collarless white shirt complete with cufflinks and elasticated metal armbands, and lace-up black leather ankleboots which were cracked across the toes. His eyes were quiet and thoughtless. Judd had seen those eyes before across many a craps table (and even, from time to time, in the mirror). They were the self-obsessed eyes of someone who has consciously placed his life in the hands of chance and not looked back; they were the eyes of a narcissistic bore.

Just as Judd realised that the man was capable of killing him without a second thought, he found himself able to speak: 'Scofield sent me out here!'

'Never heard of him.'

'You sure? Scofield. Irving Scofield. South Central LA. You sure?'

'Hell, I know lots of Scofields. Could be any one of them. Could be none of them. Who knows. What's your point?'

But Judd sensed something positive in the man's voice, a hesitancy in his phrasing that had not been there before. 'Scofield! Irving Scofield sent me. I've got a fax for you from him. You must be Anatole Crimp.'

Crimp allowed Judd to take out the paper, then snatched it from him and unfolded it dextrously with one hand, all the time drawing a careful bead on him with the gun. He read it quickly, nodding and muttering to himself as he did so. Once or twice the mutterings liquefied into a brief spurt of laughter. When he turned the fax over to see if anything was written on the back, the little man twisted his wrist and elbow around into a flat 'S' so extreme that Judd could only assume he was double-jointed. Satisfied he had read all there was to read, he lowered the gun and turned back into the house. 'Aha. Hum. Come in then, come,' he said as he disappeared inside. 'You might as well, you're here now. Next time, use the front door like a sane person. Creeping around in the back garden like that! Could get yourself shot!'

Judd followed him in without arguing the toss and found himself in a depressingly sordid room. Not much light made its way through the grime-encrusted windows, but in the fuscous gloom he could make out the essential elements of a kitchen. There was a sink, a huge cube of a thing supported on twin brick pillars, old taps on exposed pipework wobbling above it; there was a cooker, old and yellow, with blackened saucepans piled up high upon its overhead grill; and there was a free-standing dresser, the top of which – along with every other available surface in the room, from the window-sill to the draining board – was cluttered with paint cans, mugs filled with mould, tins of food with faded labels, kitchen forks green with oxidisation, matchboxes, corks, drawing-pins, flowerpots, fungus and dead plants that had long ago given up the struggle. No attempt had been made to integrate the various items of culinary furniture into some kind of harmonious whole. There were some wall cabinets, but they stood on their ends on the floor and the markings and gouges in the plaster above them testified to the fact that they had been ripped rather hastily from their moorings. Most bizarrely of all, a brand-new dishwasher stood in the centre of the room, the tangle of umbilical tubes behind it tied into a giant knot, the water pipes to which it had once been connected crudely clinched off and bunged with plumber's putty.

Crimp's mood had undergone something of a transformation and he was now charging around the room enthusiastically, his beard tucked under one arm. 'You'll want some tea, I expect,' he kept repeating, mostly to himself, 'I'd better make some tea. Do

466

you want some tea? I'll make you some tea.' From the murky water that filled the sink – 'damn thing's blocked, can't seem to fix it' – he fished another blackened saucepan which he ran beneath the tap briefly by way of rinsing, then filled with water and plonked down upon the stove. 'So how's old Scofield, then, eh, eh? How is he? Haven't seen him for years. Those were the days, ha ha, Atlantic City, goodness me, I'd all but forgotten, ha ha.' His manic chuckle bubbled up out of him like the gases from a pool of hot mud, closer to a belch than a laugh. His voice sounded like a child swinging on a creaking door. Judd tried to reply, not that he had much to offer in the way of information, but every time he opened his mouth he barely got more than a couple of words out before Crimp was off again: 'Ah, I'll make you some tea, ha ha, and then we can talk.' The old man's cold eyes shone like spheres of ice in the twilight of the kitchen and lent a distinctly demonic edge to his already weird chuckle.

Try as he might, Judd couldn't reconcile the strange figure before him with Scofield's description of a debonair gambler who'd once lived in the south of France in a richly furnished villa. He'd obviously got the wrong end of the stick. Scofield did say he hadn't seen Crimp for ten years . . . Judd began to feel claustrophobic and more than a little fearful that he'd been sent on a wild-goose chase. The prospect of a cup of tea was doing little to comfort him: Crimp had dropped several cobwebby teabags into his pan, followed by several spoonfuls of coagulated demerara sugar from a great jar which also contained two dead wasps, and now he added the contents of a small tin of condensed milk he had punctured open with a chisel retrieved from among the debris on the window-sill. As the evil-looking brew came to the boil he opened the dishwasher and removed two mugs. To Judd's surprise they were of a delicate, fine china decorated with an elongated checkerboard of hatched burgundy glaze, and clean to boot.

'Kodziez,' said Crimp, seeing Judd peering. 'Very fine, don't you think? Shame you can't say the same about this heap of junk,' he continued, indicating the dishwasher. 'Maybe you could help me get it out into the garden or something. Cluttering up the kitchen like this, useless thing. It upsets everything.' And he kicked it, before taking the pretty mugs across to the antediluvian stove. Judd remembered that Scofield had mentioned something about designer furniture – were those mugs all that was left?

They were not, as he was to discover when his host ushered him into the adjoining room which, though not large, seemed like a great and glorious atrium after the dungeon of the kitchen. 'We have to go in here,' he crackled mysteriously, 'I can't get on with anything in there, not till that dishwasher's gone.' The room was filled with the kind of chic sixties items that reminded Judd of shows like *The Prisoner*. Along two of the walls stood matching walnut side cabinets, angular, modernist pieces each over six feet long and perched on tubular metal supports, and in one corner of the room was a white fibreglass sphere with a television screen in it. Seating consisted of an egg chair, with brown leather upholstery and aluminium pedestal, and three pieces of a modular sofa each in a different tone of green with a matching occasional table in olive plastic. It would have been cool if the place weren't so trashed – books, papers, magazines and shoe boxes overflowing with all sorts of junk covered the floor and were stacked up in precarious piles that ran up the walls like stalagmites; the furniture was tattered and worn, and a thick layer of London grime lay over everything; ashtrays and plates full of half-eaten meals were dotted around like traps. Even the television housing had turned a nicotine yellow. Trying to ignore the mess and the unpleasant smell, Judd picked up a wooden object that looked like a three-dimensional puzzle game.

'That's a Brian Wilshire original,' said Crimp proudly.

'Uh, yeah, of course,' said Judd, facetiously concealing his ignorance. He pointed to a painting that hung on the wall, at the centre of a display of black-and-white framed photographs. 'And I suppose that's a Dali.'

'Yes, ha ha, an original, absolutely. I met him in Monaco at an exhibition opening. Fantastic, isn't it?' Crimp cleared some books from the seat of the egg chair and motioned to Judd to sit down, which he did, his feet jammed between a magazine rack stuffed full of mouldering copies of *Picture Post* and an elephant's foot umbrella rack filled with Real Tennis balls, then unfolded a collapsible card table, placed the cups of 'tea' on it and drew up a chair for himself. The two men now faced each other, Judd wondering how he could remove the teabag floating forlornly in his drink without appearing rude.

Crimp looked serious again and Judd felt intimidated. He kept thinking that he had another appointment, that he would have to make his excuses and leave. Why had he come? Who was this man? What was he expecting to find?

'So, er, how do you know Irving Scofield?' Judd said eventually.

'Tell me about yourself,' came the reply.

Judd was understandably fazed. 'Oh, er, well what's to tell, ha ha?' Crimp's chuckle seemed to be infectious.

'Well, how about your name.'

'Haven't I told you already? I'm sorry. I'm Judd, Judd Axelrod. What else do you want to know?'

'What do I *want* to know? What, my boy, do I *need* to know. You tell me.'

'I came here because I thought you could help me.'

'With what?'

'With my game.'

'Ah *ha*! So you are having problems with your game. Ha ha. And what is your game?'

'I play everything, but mainly craps.' Crimp said nothing so Judd decided to go ahead and elaborate. 'I know the game, I know the dice. I . . . I don't know how to explain it, but I know their shape somehow. I can see which way they're going to move. I'm not talking about runs of luck. That's part of it. But it's more than that. I can predict them most of the time. And then a month ago it started slipping away, like I couldn't see it any more. Something was different, I don't know. It was like I knew it all too well and so it all changed, became something else.' He was searching for the words but none of the ones he could find seemed equal to what he was trying to say. 'You don't think I'm making any sense,' he said, instantly regretting it for no particular reason.

'I see. So you used this, ha ha, technique and you were winning?'

'Oh, yeah. I was way up. I haven't worked for a few years now. I've done all right. I had to leave LA because I got too good. I was playing in the illegal clubs, and word got around and they all barred me. Lost a couple of teeth over that one. So I went to Reno. I'd been there a while, was doing OK, but then it all got weird. See, I'd been slowing everything down, I don't know if that makes any kind of sense, but when I was winning it was like I was real cool, real slow, and because everything around me was faster I could see what it was going to do, like I was in a separate stream of time. But then, then the ground started to shift under me, I didn't know what was happening, everything seized up or changed around, and I couldn't . . . couldn't get a handle on it any more.'

'And that's when you went to see Irving.'

'Well, I called him, yeah.'

'And he told you to come and see me.'

'Yeah.'

'That's very trusting of you.'

'I've known him for years. And what else could I do?'

'You could have tried leaving Reno and playing somewhere else.'

'I guess, but . . .'

'Don't you think it was rather cowardly not to do that?' Judd was instantly defensive. Crimp clearly didn't get it. He wasn't into gambling for money or power. It had only ever been a way to reclaim his own character. But how was he to explain that to the old man? And anyway, he hadn't come here for more psychoanalysis. The most important thing was to find out what had gone wrong, get practical solutions.

He made up an answer. 'Look, I knew, OK. I knew it was fucking up. I was losing money fast. Maybe I couldn't afford to risk a stake in another town. It takes a while you know, you can't just bust in there.'

'Ha ha ha! It takes a while. Yes, it takes a while. That's right. Exactly.'

'Yeah. Yeah, it takes a while.' Judd was getting angry – he was being mocked. But he couldn't admit how frightened he was, how desperate he was for guidance, not even to himself. A single hoverfly flew silently above their heads, its trajectory a succession

470

of straight lines and acutely angled corners. It changed direction as effortlessly and abruptly as a sprite on a computer screen, its path apparently both predetermined and perfectly random. Crimp wrinkled his nose and sneezed loudly into his tea, splashing it up over the edge of the cup and on to the table. The fly cornered three or four times in quick succession, went into a quick corkscrew dive, recovered and continued much as before.

From somewhere beneath his beard the old man had produced two dice and was rolling them over and over. 'Well, then. What does that tell you?'

'I don't know. What does it tell me?'

'I can't help you if you won't think for yourself.'

Judd felt like he was back at school. Or – which was worse – back with Schemata. 'I'm not so sure you can help me anyway.' He pouted.

'Ha ha. Give me two numbers.'

'What?'

'Come on, come on, I haven't got all day. I've got better things to do, you know. Two numbers.'

'Twenty-four and thirty-seven.'

'Oh, god help us.' He held up the dice. 'Each between one and six if you please.'

'Double six.' Crimp looked tired. He cupped his little hands together and shook the dice inside them, then dropped them on to the table. Judd noticed for the first time what extraordinarily long fingers the man had. The dice came to rest and each showed a six.

'Gee, loaded dice,' Judd said sarcastically. 'I haven't seen them before.'

'Two more numbers then.'

'Two and four.' Crimp rolled the dice and a two and a four came up.

'Two and five.' Again, Crimp rolled them to order.

'Double three.' And again.

'Use mine.' Judd took out the bone dice which Scofield had given him and passed them across the table, their bright shapes stark against the light tan surfaces and deep purple lines of his palm.

Crimp threw a couple of sequences to order and then, to show off, produced a shaker and did the same again. Then he passed them back to Judd. 'Now you roll. Go on. Roll them. Roll me a three and a two.' Judd tried to fix Crimp in the eye, something that he was suddenly finding rather difficult. He took the dice and rolled. A two and a three. 'As you see, the question is not whether I can teach you anything, but whether I should bother.'

Judd felt cold, as if his spinal fluid had been turned to Freon. It looked like Scofield had been right – this guy was the real thing. 'But I need your help,' he protested, his flippancy gone. 'You must help me. I'm stuck.'

'Do you think I had any help? Old Irving certainly wasn't much use, pissing off at the first sign of trouble. I've already given you more than anybody gave me by letting you come in here. There's nothing more I can give you.'

'But you've just shown me . . .'

'You want me to teach you tricks? I'm disappointed. You come all this way and then you want tricks. The fact that you are here should be enough. Look around. Why do you think I choose to live like this, instead of in some palace? Why do you think I stay in this place, so wrapped up in myself that I can't get a single machine to work? No mod cons – nothing after 1967, at least. The boiler's twenty years old, thank Christ, but when that packs up, god knows what I'll do. One or two nights a week in a casino is all I'd need to escape, ha ha, followed by a short stint on the stock exchange. I used to have a beautiful home in Monte Carlo, you know, cliff-top, secluded. Beautiful. But then it all stopped. Just like you, I couldn't do it any more. I'd become too full of myself, too self-assured. I'd let my desires run away from me. I wanted to make it my servant. "I can really use this," I thought, "I can really do something here."

'It took a month. That's all. One month to lose the villa, have my bank account closed, work up debts that I couldn't repay. I had to ship out, come here, bring what I could with me, so that I could try and recapture something of what I had before it went wrong. And that's when I started to learn, to fathom really how special it was. That's when I discovered how fascinating it was,

472

too, how wonderful, just for its own sake. For me, now, it is everything. And I had it all.' Crimp gave Judd his iciest stare and Judd glanced away.

'Yes, but . . .' he began, but the man was into his stride and was not to be stopped.

'You have to understand that there are two types of control. You've got this far because you were prepared to start off from within the system itself. Don't ask me why, because I don't know. There's not many who can do it, but there's a few. But you haven't perceived what that means, have you now? Which is that to succeed you must relinquish all hope of ever having the other type of control, control from the outside, that kind of control which is achieved by trying to define the system instead of letting it define you. Now it seems to me that you, my boy, have tried to cross over and look where it's got you. You wanted something from it, like I did once. You tried to fuck with it and now it's fucking with you.'

'But I didn't have any choice!' Judd blurted, able to speak at last. 'It might have been about money for you, old man, but in my case it was just about me! You can't understand! You haven't been through what I've been through! You're not listening to me. You're just telling me about your own experiences!'

But with Crimp this was the wrong tack to take. 'Don't yell at me, you little bastard,' he hissed, his avuncular mood immediately swamped by anger. 'I'm trying to help. I'm telling you, if you want it back then look around you, see how it works. You saw what I did with the dice, but I can only manage that by understanding limits and enforcing limits. Simply by being here you're upsetting the balance already. Can't you feel it? It's a trade-off.'

'I told you I don't care about any of that. All I want is to be free from all the shit that's been piled on me. To be my own person.' Even as he said the words, Judd knew they were wrong, that they'd be misunderstood, that Crimp would take them for weakness.

'Ha! Free? Free? You've got this far and you still think freedom's an option? How dumb can you get? I told you already, you try get outside the system and the system will fuck with you. You've got to make do with what you've got. And quite frankly, young man, what you've got is quite a lot.'

'How the fuck would you know what I've got?' Judd almost screamed. 'Why are you judging me? I came here for help!'

'And I have given it to you. Maybe what you experienced in Reno is the end, my friend, not the beginning. Everything I have to teach you is in front of you. Wrap yourself in surfaces, wear nothing but a cloak. You are like the bull, fascinated by the play of the cape but only because you are convinced there is something behind it. But you have to love it for its own sake. Cut it to fit where you can and where you can't ignore it. There is nothing behind it but the unnameable air! It is the surface which is intense, which provides all the meaning. Look beyond it, think of it as infinite, you lose it all. You are American, you should understand that! Why do you keep asking for something more?' But the old man's words fell on deaf ears.

'Look, you, you . . . I found something! *I* found it. I found an alternative, I found something that let me know who I was! And I want it back, that's all. Why can't I have that? Aren't I entitled to my own self, for chrissake?' Judd was beside himself, nearly in tears, the years of frustration vibrating the membrane of his cortex like the cardboard of a speaker cone. 'Maybe you can't grasp that, maybe you can't, but I found it and it's gone, and I need your help to get it back!'

Crimp let out a huge, scornful squawk of a laugh. 'What did they do to you to make you so stupid? You've got to give it up, my boy. You've got to forget about it before it's too late. Go on, get out. I won't be insulted in my own home. Go back to America! Take your little problems back there, where they belong!' And he leapt up, pulled Judd from his chair and started to shove him towards the kitchen door, knocking the card table flying in the process. Tea shot across one wall and ran in muddy rivulets down the Salvador Dali. The old man was strong and Judd was in the kitchen before he knew it. Then Crimp rushed back into the living-room, grabbed his gun and returned immediately shouting, 'Get out of my house, get out, get out!' and looking for all the world like Yosemite Sam. Judd scrambled for the back door and wrenched it open, but as he ran out the pocket of his Kappas caught on the handle. Seeing him stop the old man let off a shot at the kitchen ceiling. Enveloped in a cloud of plaster dust Judd ripped his pants free, staggered backwards into the garden, tripped over the dead television, put a foot down on the slippery car door, skidded, fell and cracked his head on the computer terminal. The next thing he knew was nothing: he was out cold.

1 4

Conspicuous consumption

That Saturday morning the coach had brought Jennifer into London, dropped her at Victoria. She took the tube up to Finsbury Park, to Shelley's house, then the two women headed into town. They trawled the boutiques in Covent Garden, Shelley warning Jennifer not to steal anything and Jenn laughing and flapping her cheque-book, saying that she'd given up all of that. Anyway, today was special and she didn't want to spoil it.

Shelley found a jacket she liked and bought it, and Jenn bought some trousers and a skirt. Still, she really wanted some shoes, you couldn't get decent shoes anywhere in the Midlands, and Shelley suggested Harvey Nichols – if they couldn't find anything there, they could always go down the King's Road.

So they got on the tube, which was rammed, went the few stops to Knightsbridge, Jenn swinging into a seat vacated by some black geezer who got off at Green Park. The shoes at Harvey Nichols were too expensive but Jenn picked up some new stockings to match her skirt and got changed in one of the fitting rooms. They had lunch in the coffee shop and walked down to Sloane Square, chatting all the way. Somewhere along the King's Road Jenn found the shoes she wanted, and a blouse, too, and a new belt. Then it was time to go and meet Joel. She gave her shopping bags to Shelley, kissed her on the cheek and rushed off back to the tube, trembling a little with anticipation.

Electric café (001)

In the days leading up to the rendezvous Joel hurried to complete his preparations. He finished measuring his body and fed the results into his machine, constructing special databases that could be accessed by the golem as it took shape. So that the thing would have maximum freedom to roam he wanted to make sure it could route itself through as many networks as possible. He hacked into JANET and the telecom computers and satellite base stations and gave himself priority clearance.

He was rushing the whole time, his nerves shot to pieces. He wanted Saturday to come at once, just to lie on his bed and wallow in the fact that he was nearing his goal. The work was simultaneously a pressure and a release, and he kept at it as an addict keeps at his drug. On the Friday he paid a quick visit to the Victoria without the shoe computer, just to see if he could still predict the bets. He could, it was fine, though before he left he had a somewhat freaky experience. As he was cashing in his chips he caught sight of someone he thought he recognised sitting at one of the blackjack tables. Cautiously, in order to see better, he moved across to the bar and ordered a drink, carefully watching the man all the time. He was in a terrible state – his eyes were wild, his grey hair a mess, his suit crumpled – and it was clear that he was losing hand over fist. Joel asked the barman if he'd seen the gambler before. Yes, indeed, he came down at least two or three times a week, though probably not for much longer – lately he'd been on a losing streak that didn't look like it was going to let up. Joel smiled quietly to himself and finished his tomato juice. As he left he strode past the blackjack table and stole a closer look. There could be no doubt about it: it was most definitely Professor Metric.

So that's what had become of him, the old fool! He'd always been sure his philosophy had been superior to that of his mentor and now here was the proof! His ego thus reinforced, Joel left his old tutor to his moral decline, hurried back to his hotel and worked on his machine through the night. By lunch-time the following day he was finished. He looked round the room with a sense of pride, glorying in his accomplishment. Everything was ready. The walls were covered with his writings rather as photographs had once covered the walls of his room at CERN and he'd placed candles everywhere, and even, on the mantelpiece, some incense. The glyphs and magic words that he needed for the spell were printed out and placed ready on a chair. He tested the manacles he'd attached to each of the bed posts in case Jennifer didn't agree to go along with the plan and as an afterthought he made the bed and slipped a gag underneath the pillow. He ran a last check on the two video cameras he'd placed on tripods on either side of the room, making doubly sure that they could operate satisfactorily in the half-light and that the image-processing software was working correctly. But the focus of it all were his computers, which slumbered across the makeshift table, pregnant with data. As a final touch he took a sheet from the wardrobe and threw it over the humming machines. Yes, he was ready.

Naturally, he arrived at the café early. He sat there trying to read a book on advanced networking but was unable to keep his eyes on the page for more than a couple of minutes at a stretch. By the time four o'clock came round he knew every inch of the street outside. But four became four-thirty became five and his euphoria receded, leaving a mudflat of doubt and paranoia in its wake. He felt as if someone were jabbing hot needles, the long beaks of wader birds, into every pore of his body. The black man sitting facing him at the next table unnerved him. The stranger had been here almost as long as he had and, apart from taking occasional sips of his beer or moving his eyes, had remained almost totally motionless throughout. He found the man frightening, mysterious. As the racist circuits implanted in his brain as a child began sparking with life he became convinced that the stranger was watching him.

But watched or not, he couldn't sit here waiting for much longer. It was making him crazy. How many times he checked his watch or ran out into the street or read and reread the menu or played with the sugar he didn't know, but eventually he could stand it no longer and, convinced that Jennifer had either lied to him or forgotten about him, he gave up. Livid, he headed back to his hotel, coursing between the summer drinkers who had spilled out of their pubs and on to the pavements, his tall form slicing along like the prow of some sleek yacht. As he went he shot his gaze to starboard and port like cannon, still searching for Jennifer, still sure she'd look just like the woman in his dream.

Electric café (010)

Jennifer had taken a clockwise Circle Line train from Sloane Square, but just beyond Gloucester Road it came to a halt. Immediately she began to worry and when a fractured voice came over the Tannoy announcing a security alert she began to worry even more. She was already running late and she sat in the carriage silently urging the train northwards. Five minutes went by, then ten, and she became so racked with tension that every limb felt spavined. But still the train did not move. Ever since Joel had phoned their meeting had obsessed her and now, telling him about the child which had almost certainly been his seemed the most important thing in the world. The promise of this imminent event had brought a new light to bear upon her life and thrown her loneliness and aimlessness into sharp relief. For the first time in over a decade she really felt that focus and meaning – absent from her life since Henry had died and she'd discovered her pregnancy – were about to return. In her mind she glamorised Joel, imagining him older and wiser, and using the fact of his 'travels' to extrapolate from the nerdy, depressive loner she had known in Geneva a much sexier figure. On one particularly excessive and recurrent flight of fancy – which she repeatedly tried to excise from her thoughts – she envisioned him arriving in a limousine, sweeping her off her feet and showering her with luxuries. But whichever simulation of events she ran through in her head they all shared a common theme – that one way or another Joel would cushion her against the pain and loss she felt more keenly now than she could ever remember.

A hundred and one miles away, in a Warwickshire hospital, Emma rolled around on her bed in torment. She had this thought, it was so nearly there . . . on the tip of her tongue as it were . . . but it would not quite coalesce. And until it did, she didn't know what it would be. It was like having an itch in an amputated limb. She was playing this game, a strange game, which brought on a strange feeling, like trying to force the southern poles of three magnets together. She'd had them all in her mind for months now, had been loitering in their dreams like a concupiscent ghoul. The My had grown powerful, it had kept them in its sights, wanting them for itself. But now, when everything was ready, one of them wouldn't flow down its channel. There was a blockage somewhere. Smoke and Squeak probed and explored, but neither could find what was wrong.

As the minutes ticked away even the most prosaic of Jennifer's fantasies slipped gradually beyond her grasp. Why hadn't she taken the bus, as Shelley had suggested? She sat and shivered with apprehension in the company of the other passengers, all of whom were beginning to oscillate with their own particular frustrations until, like the molecules in a melting crystal, they began to break free of the structures which bound them to the events of the everyday and to communicate with one another.

That said, it was hardly a social revolution. Most of the words exchanged expressed anger and annoyance, although two members of a circus troupe who happened to be aboard did start doing the splits along the ceiling, to the great delight of several children who had been complaining loudly up until that point. The overheated adults all clapped until their kids, encouraged by the display, became over-excited and started to run riot inside the carriage. Then someone tried to smoke a cigarette and was nearly lynched; would have been, if there'd been anything high enough to string him up from.

Meanwhile, above ground in Notting Hill Gate, Joel sat in the window of his café looking forlornly out at the slowly lengthening afternoon shadows, reading the menu over and over, beginning to jitter from all the coffee he'd drunk.

It was an hour and a half before the train began to move, by which time Jennifer was in tears. When it finally drew in to Notting Hill Gate she charged up the stairs as fast as she could, shoved her way through the ticket barrier and skirted around the shoppers congealed on the street corner outside, wiping her face as she ran. But when she reached the café it was empty except for a very un-Jewish looking yuppie who was munching on a ham and cheese croissant, a black guy sitting staring out of the window and four old women at a table drinking tea.

She went up to the barman. 'I was looking for a friend of mine. He's meeting me here.'

'We have many men in here,' said the barman, who wasn't impressed by her question. 'What does he look like?'

Jennifer opened her mouth to describe Joel, but realised that she couldn't really remember. 'Oh, I don't know. He's tall, I suppose, and he wears glasses. And has a big nose . . .'

'I don' know. There were some men here before, maybe one of them is your friend. But I don' know. Why don' you have a cup of coffee and see if he come back?'

Electric café (011)

Judd had lain there for hours, his consciousness whipping to and fro like a curl of spume on the unfolding surge of that fungal bloom called space-time, a light summer rain tapping with the sweetness of foreign fingers on the tarpaulin that Crimp, in a brief fit of sympathy, had thrown across his prone form. But now the sky was clear and the sun was getting lower – England was revolving away from the day. He rolled his eyelids back and looked around. The garden with its heaps of consumer items was like a vast cladogenic graveyard that seemed to stretch into the distance for ever. Sliding out from beneath the waxed canvas, he had to battle for a minute in order to try and restore harmony in the face of constant shifts of perspective. Getting upright was difficult; he felt sluggish, his joints ached and his feet were painfully heavy, so he inched his way forward through the viable junk on his knees, only getting to his feet when he reached the broken door at the end of the garden. But his mind was reeling and when he finally made it out of the alleyway and on to Glengall Road he turned left by mistake.

The summer moon was in the sky, ball of rock, dove grey against the blue. He looked up at it and far below the threshold of his vision Sputnik II drifted across the pale disc. Inside, Laika was busy tuning her equipment to the BBC and trying to work out why she had such a sudden interest in London. Judd felt like a planet, trapped for aeons in the interlocking self-organisations of gravity. Fear, fear of forever, rippled through him. He wandered south down Tennyson Road, past two kids playing on their bikes.

He passed the entrance to a cemetery and got freaked when, looking in through the gate, he saw the stones shiver and turn. He shuddered and rubbed his eyes, and tried to increase his pace, but his legs had found their rhythm and were adamant. Continuing south, he crossed the railway lines via the bridge at Queen's Park with the inevitability of a grain of sand finding its way through the narrow neck of an hourglass, then tumbled down through the residential back streets of West Kilburn and rolled out on the Great Western Road, passing underneath the Westway as the traffic thundered high above him, the cars tracing out a million paths from east to west, from west to east, the roar of their engines exploding off the tops of the buildings that peeked above the parapets like so many broken spires.

He trudged through the council estates, turned into Chepstow Road and followed it down through Pembridge Villas, hardly noticing as the houses became progressively grander and set further back from the road, and the black folk transmuted into white. He became aware of the slap slap of his shoes against the speckled paving slabs. His mouth was parched. He looked at his watch but it had stopped at half past eleven, which was when he'd arrived at Crimp's. He must have broken it when he'd fallen that first time. He took it off and slung it into a skip.

The road curved round and he passed clothing stores and a second-hand record shop, then came out on a staggered junction that let on to the lights and litter of Notting Hill Gate. There was a small crowd of people waiting for a bus; he asked two girls if there was an Underground station nearby. They giggled at his accent and gave him directions, and he thanked them and walked away. Behind him the bus pulled up, a green CitySlicker, and beneath the moaning of the brakes he thought he heard the name 'Denzel Washington'. He glanced back and sure enough the two girls blushed and lowered their eyes, before quickly climbing on board. Judd bit his lip in exasperation and studied his reflection in the dark window of a café. It was true, he did resemble the film star. Even his looks weren't his own any longer.

The café took up the whole of the acutely angled street corner in a way that reminded him of San Francisco. He needed to drink and he needed to think, so he went inside and sat in the window across from a tall man with lank, unkempt hair, thick spectacles and an enormous nose, which he kept tugging at nervously. Judd ordered a beer and watched the coloured reflections from the traffic and pedestrians play across the curved glass, though from time to time he shifted his gaze to the stranger who, although nominally reading the enormous textbook that lay open on the table in front of him, was clearly having difficulty concentrating. He kept scanning the tables as if looking for someone, and on several occasions got up and rushed out into the street, only to return a few seconds later and sit down again. Eventually he paid his bill and left the café for good.

Judd felt trapped, lost, stuck. All the time he had thought the gambling would be a way out, but in the end it had led him to Crimp, and Crimp had turned out to be just like all of the others: Jennifer, his parents, Schemata – they'd none of them been interested in him, only in imposing themselves upon him. The weight of them on his back was already immense, but now Crimp had been added to the pile and with him came all of those sediments that Judd had let build up inside him in his attempt to block the channels that Schemata had cut. He felt as if he was being buried alive. He was suffocating. He was barely able to breathe. The pressure upon him was so great that he could feel it compressing the blood in his veins, squeezing out the water and leaving the task of delivering oxygen throughout his body to cascades of dusty minerals. What was he to do? He wanted to be angry but he didn't have the energy.

His lungs felt flat and leaden, and his heart laboured. His vision seemed to stretch out a little and all the objects around him seemed further away than they were. His limbs felt elongated, too, and numb and unwieldly, and there was a metallic taste in his mouth. It took him a moment or two to place the sensation and then he remembered – it was one he'd often had as a boy, lying in bed and waiting to fall asleep. For a moment he felt that the child that he'd been and that he'd lost was calling to him, trying to tell him something, and he chased the sensation down. But it dissipated as soon as he focused his consciousness on it, slipping away between the fissures of his mind like a family of geckos, a puddle of mercury.

He wanted to cry but his eyes were dry as dust. What could he do now? There seemed only two possibilities: return to the States and ask Scofield for help one more time; or try to go all the way back to the beginning by finding Jennifer and confronting her. But the first was unbearable and the second insane. And both involved him throwing himself on another person's mercy. Why? Why was this the only way he seemed able to do things? Couldn't he manage to do anything for himself? What was wrong with him?

While he fulminated, someone else entered the café – the young woman with dark-brown hair who had taken his seat in the tube train earlier that day. Judd didn't see her sit down, didn't even hear her question the waiter. She took the seat right behind him and she'd been there about ten minutes when another green bus flashed past the window and caught his attention – something had seemed to run by, a dart of beryl, jasper . . . it was her, it was the

484

stony-faced girl in the green overcoat. He had forgotten all about her. She stopped and stood there right in front of him, her finger in her mouth, and his arms remembered the pain of the night before last. Suddenly he made the connection between her and his dreams of the statue. He had to talk to her! Instantly energised, he leapt up, ready to run outside, but at that moment the waiter arrived with the dark-haired woman's coffee and Judd caught the tray with his shoulder and the cup was knocked to the floor. A detonation, shockwave of black liquid and shrapnel, impact zone the legs of the waiter and woman. Everyone looks round.

'Oh, Christ, excuse me, I'm sorry, I didn't see, excuse me . . .' Judd panics, half his mind on the minor disaster in hand, the other half on the figure outside and the idea that she might be the key to it all. Waiter puts down his tray and goes to bar for a rag, throws it down on the floor, picks up ceramic shards with his fingers. Judd grabs napkins, dabs at sodden legs of woman. Woman pleads: 'No, it's OK, really, thank you,' takes the napkins from him. Four eyes meet for a moment full of clouds, there's something here, there's a mystery here, Judd can't clear his mind, the eyes, the young woman, the girl in the street. He breaks the gaze, sprints outside – but she is gone. Barman comes with mop and broom, debris swept away. Judd returns and sits back down, apologising one last time. Young woman says it's nothing, turns away, dabs at her new stockings with a cloth.

The waiter brings her another coffee which she quickly drinks. Judd can't think – this girl, what where why which? The dark-haired young woman pays and leaves. Judd sits and ponders, sipping at his beer. Through the window he watches her walk down the road. And then, aha! He has it now. Yesterday, the tube, Green Park, that's where he saw her. Coincidence. Dismissed.

He has to make a decision, he has to *think*. Without thinking, he picks up the dispenser of table salt and pours some into his beer, stirs it with his knife, starts to drink. Minutes, hours, pass while he sips at it. The logic he'd used to battle Schemata has a hold of him now. His brain starts to desiccate. He begins to dry out.

He is still there at closing time.

The world has ideas of its own

Emma had failed. The world had ideas of its own and they were bigger than her, stronger. The surface had been too complex, the forces at play too intricate. She would revert to the original plan and try for the Mummy alone.

Red Adam

By the time he reached his room all the undischarged energy Joel had built up during three days of cathexis had curdled into anger. He fell to his knees and began to pummel at the floor with his fists, bruising and grazing his knuckles against the hard artificial fibres of the carpet. Then he started to cry, to kick the bed, to cry again, to attack a stack of cardboard boxes he had piled in the corner of the room. He collapsed among their broken forms and lay there, sobbing. But once he had dissipated some of the tension his composure returned and it occurred to him that, during their telephone call, he hadn't told Jennifer where he was staying. If there was a problem she'd have no way of contacting him. What a fool he was! Any number of things could have gone wrong! Sniffing his sinuses free of mucus and controlling his breathing he picked up the phone and called her. At the sound of her voice he began to speak, blurting out a few words of apology, until he noticed that he was talking to her answerphone. He left his address and number, smashed the handset against the bed post until he realised that he really didn't want to break it. Then he lay down on the bed. He was hungry but could not stomach the idea of food. Jennifer's failure to appear gnawed away at him. He drew the curtains, hoping that he would be able to apply the darkness to his mind like a salve. But it didn't work and doubt continued to erode away all the confidence he had built up over the previous few days, leaving him in torment, his soul a wind-ripped valley of sands and toothy ruins.

He closed his eyes and on the inside of his eyelids began to see rushing tunnels and spirals as the random firing in his visual cortex self-organised into Turing patterns. After a while the images slowed and morphed into a cloudy landscape in which everything was tinged with the same orange glow. Then maybe he was asleep and maybe he wasn't, but more colours seeped in, shapes became more defined and he was in an empty railway carriage, that of his journey up from Portsmouth, sitting opposite the double-hearted doll.

The doll was no longer passive and inert as she had been before. She stood on the seat on tiptoe, looking out of the window, the line of her legs and buttocks simultaneously childlike and imbued with a powerful sexuality. Joel sat in his seat sweating, as she turned towards him and dropped her pink hand to the smooth plastic of her crotch and began to simulate masturbation. Through the transparent casing of her chest he could see her hearts beating faster and faster as she rubbed her crabbed fingers back and forth. Then she stopped and hopped up on the table and began to dance a slow and erotic cachucha. Joel became aroused and his engorged penis rose up above the edge of the melamine table and bobbed with pulsing blood as if it wanted to partner the doll, make the cachucha a fandango. Then she stopped, tottered forward on her hard plastic feet (her womanly grace all disappeared), bent over at the waist and with her tiny painted lips planted a kiss on the very tip of Joel's exaggerated prick.

Joel opened his eyes and looked around, dizzy and disoriented. He felt a vague panic, as if he had slept for hours, but when he checked his watch he discovered he'd only dozed off for about five minutes. Inside his trousers his penis throbbed painfully. He looked across the room at the computer equipment under its sheet and noticed for the first time that the shape made by the various components resembled that of a female cadaver stretched out on a mortuary slab, legs spread conveniently wide. The hardware was all still switched on and beneath the sheet fans whirred and LEDs blinked their silent codes, these pinprick signatures diffused by the cloth into eerie patches of electronic blood. The robot corpse had the afterglow of life about it, as if it had been freshly killed and its vital systems were only now shutting down and beginning the short, quick road to decay.

He found himself drawn to the uncanny form. Still lying on the bed he undid his belt and flies and slipped off his trousers. Then he rolled on to the floor and crept across the carpet on all fours, moving towards the table like some lathered beast in rut, his penis hanging stiff and low. Carefully, not sure that it would support his weight, he slid up on to the table and arranged his limbs around the appropriate affordances. With his body correctly distributed he clasped the bony form and began to move slowly in and out of the rough cleft created by the genital locus of processor, port and bus. The structure cradled him lovingly and creaked and whirred beneath him, and as he moved faster, broke into a sweat, the collection of objects seemed no longer a corpse but a coherent, living being. His neck began to ache and he dipped his forehead to the corner of the terminal which from beneath the folds of the sheet mimicked the shape of a head. He suckled at the eject buttons of a twin floppy drive as if they were nipples. The whole table began to shudder as his rhythms became more frenetic and the equipment rattled away beneath him, its agitated components emitting a grinding collective moan. Finally he came and in the spasm of ejaculation damaged a chip with the heel of his right hand. Suffusing through the sheet, his jissom dripped through on to the circuit board that had been serving as part of the vaginal wall. On the moment of contact electrons danced and leapt across it, gleefully inventing new connections through the cum. Somewhere in the system a modem silently began dialling numbers. It wasn't too long before it made a successful connection and started to upload the files full of Joel's personal statistics from the various disk drives linked into the system.

Joel's elation quickly soured to self-disgust and he disentangled himself from the equipment. His flesh felt hot and he buzzed all over. He cleaned himself and dressed, and as he did the imprints that the hard edges of the machinery had made upon his palms, chest, genitals and thighs began to fade. The room felt tight and claustrophobic and he went out into the street, intending to head towards the Edgware Road and the Victoria, perhaps to gamble, perhaps to think.

Contact

Since Laika had been launched into space the infosphere had expanded to such an extent that she was almost continually busy with something to watch, something to absorb. There did not seem to be a single patch of the upper atmosphere left undisturbed by a radio transmission, television broadcast, or mobile phone call. She passed another satellite at least every couple of hours, could see them glinting from her porthole, great blue and silver mobiles turning slowly in the void like prehistoric insects suspended in some great amber cosmos.

As a result of nearly three decades spent surfing this material, she was familiar with dozens of languages and almost every facet of human life. From Latin-American soap operas to Scandinavian cartoons, from American political propaganda to documentaries on the plight of steelworkers in Siberia, from news reports on famines and air crashes to rock concerts, murders, chat shows, she'd seen them all. She had cooed at male seahorses giving birth, panted at women with surgically enhanced bodies having sex, gasped at men landing on the moon, cried at television personalities dying in helicopter crashes. She had listened to the musics of the world: Tatar folk, European classical, Southern Gospel, Andean pipe, Chechnian balalaika, British electro-pop, Northern Soul, English Punk, American Funk, Welsh choral, Indian raga, Cuban rumba, French Pop, international Rock. She'd heard the sounds of the Aurora Borealis and the sounds of the sun. She had seen a hundred thousand movies and heard a million DJ links. And she'd watched it all without any sense of what was better and what was worse, what was global and what was local. It was all flat to her. Throughout it all she'd conceived of herself as traversing an ambient plane of sounds and images on which one point was as good as any other. If you had put booster rockets on Sputnik II and given Laika the controls it would not have made a great deal of difference to her life. This was a space to be spectated, not traversed. If there had been other dogs out there it would have made all the difference, because then an element of desire would have disrupted the situation. But there weren't, at least not permanently. So she continued to weave her wall of sounds and pictures and watch the world, undisturbed except for the occasional rocket launch, shuttle mission, shooting star or burst of paranoia, happily dissolving the boundaries between her body and her capsule, between her mind and the ocean of information in which she swam.

But space wasn't as safe as it might have been. Apart from all the data clutter, by the 1980s it was also littered with physical detritus: malfunctioning probes, discarded launch stages, frozen astronaut piss (pretty deadly if you hit it at a few thousand kilometres per hour), camera lens caps, fragments of solar panel, wing nuts, paint flecks, chunks of heat shield and lumps of Laika's own faeces. It was a veritable minefield up there. The cosmodog often thanked her lucky stars that she'd never actually been hit by anything more dangerous than the odd particle of intersellar dust.

But her luck ran out when Joel hacked into a satellite base station and accidentally pinged her with a message. Laika had been wedged in front of a news programme on which scientists and politicians were discussing or denying the epidemic proportions of a new strain of influenza virus, when the dimensions of Joel's skull flashed up on her screen. Deftly spinning a couple of dials with her mouth and prodding a few buttons with her nose she checked the provenance of the transmission and discovered to her surprise that it had been aimed directly at her. How odd, she thought to herself. No one had actually tried to contact her since she had been given up for dead by Renko and the rest of the Soviet team. She found the experience most disconcerting. She started to shiver slightly and in what little room they had left the hackles on the back of her neck began to rise, an experience she hadn't had since she'd seen the space shuttle capturing a satellite with its articulated arm and taking it out of the sky. But now, as before, the only thing she could do was sit back, try to relax and wait to see what would happen.

A kick up the arse

Judd wanted to go when they came to kick him out, but he couldn't seem to move. The waiter – the one who had spoken to Jennifer and Joel earlier on – approached, told him it was time to pay up and leave. He wished to comply, but he could barely feel his arms and legs. How much had he drunk? He couldn't remember, but surely it wasn't that much?

After the third warning the waiter lost his temper, grabbed Judd under the arms and lifted him from his chair. With some difficulty he propelled the unwelcome customer towards the door and out into the street, aiming a farewell kick at the American's arse as he stumbled out on to the pavement. The kick was a mistake – Judd's arse was unnaturally hard and the Italian yelped in pain as his toes crushed up against an unyielding buttock.

But Judd didn't seem to notice. Under the impetus of the kick he began to stagger – very slowly – across the junction and down towards the traffic lights on Notting Hill Gate. Although barely fifty yards away, it took him quarter of an hour to reach them. His feet were like lumps of concrete and he had to strain to lift them. When he let them drop they banged down on the pavement with a thump that drew strange looks from the other pedestrians.

His head felt heavy, too, his mind fugged and gritty. He wasn't quite sure what was happening. At the corner he followed the pavement round, encouraged by the railings and the kerbstones, and began to make his way eastwards along the Bayswater Road.

An hour later he'd made it the half-mile to Hyde Park, and the slip road that leads into Lancaster Terrace and from there into

Sussex Gardens. He followed this route and the first light of dawn found him hovering motionless beneath the Marylebone flyover, trapped there by his fascination with the giant presence of the concrete buttresses until a patrol car on its way to Paddington Green police station pulled up and moved him on.

Mother and child

Jennifer was very upset. After she'd failed to meet Joel she'd gone back to Shelley's and had spent the evening with her and Terry, her boyfriend, sinking a bottle and a half of tequila and berating herself for having been such an idiot and not getting the address of his hotel when she'd spoken to him on the phone. The next day she and her hangover took the coach home. Joel had her number; if she was back in Stratford then at least he could contact her there. She had to get back for work on Monday in any case.

On Sundays the coach takes a roundabout route, calling in not just at Banbury and Leamington Spa as it always does but also at the old town of Warwick. These days Warwick is to all intents and purposes conurbated with Leamington. Its famous castle and churches now occupy the higher ground in a sea of predominantly middle-class suburbia that has congealed around four or five focal points (the castle itself, the spa baths, two High Streets, the race-track) like fat in an oven dish. Having entered Warwick–Leamington, the coach threads through the narrow streets around the castle, eventually stopping in the old square, where a handful of passengers will disembark. Leaving the centre via the 'back way', as it's called by local shoppers and the mothers who daily deliver their brood to one of Warwick–Leamington's many schools, the coach then continues out of town, past the Porsche garage, the hospital and the IBM facility. When it reaches the bypass it will travel south to the Fiveways roundabout and pick up the road to Stratford.

If, as the coach passes the hospital, a passenger should happen to glance out of the back window, he or she would see the Warwick end of Warwick–Leamington arrayed across the slope of the hill with the concrete bunker of a police station and the grim spire of St Mary's clearly standing out above the grey-brown buildings huddled all around. Jennifer had not been this way before, but she did look out of the back window as the coach passed the hospital, and she did see this view.

This was more than déjà vu – this was the very view she'd seen in the dream of wheelchair and garden, and witnessing it now brought on a seizure. She froze where she was and let out a small cry, which was killed in her throat as her tongue swelled and her mouth dried up. Her eyelids trembled but lost the ability to blink and her arms began to twitch. Across her cortex the neurons fired in great synchronised groups, their collective electrical output peaking around three times each second. Her retinae, flooded with light, screamed and contracted, warping the image of the hillside. This continued until her head nodded forward, both her arms jerked upwards together and she folded over at the waist. Then she rolled off the seat and down on to the floor, where she lay twitching.

Of the three other passengers on the coach one was asleep, one was listening to a personal stereo and one saw Jennifer collapse, but thought he had better not get involved. Fortunately the driver had spotted her in his rear-view mirror and quickly pulled the vehicle into a lay-by. His sister had suffered petit-mal seizures as a child and he recognised the symptoms immediately. He ran up the aisle and put Jennifer into the recovery position, working his fingers down inside her mouth so that she wouldn't swallow her tongue.

Fortunately, the fit quickly subsided and Jennifer soon came round, although she was confused and her gestures remained quite automatic for some time. The driver gave her some hot tea from the flask he kept beneath his seat. She drank and the liquid burnt trails through her body, gullies through the dust. Moist now, she could blink and swallow.

An ambulance passed them and turned into the hospital entrance.

The driver asked her if she was OK, they were right by the hospital, he could take her in if she wished. She shook her head, but it was a reflex more than an action, an attempt to clear her thoughts. As he helped her back up on to her seat she could see the other passengers gazing down the aisle at her with eyes of dim concern. 'Where do you live, love? Stratford?' the driver asked. Jennifer managed a nod. 'All right then, we'll take you home.' He flipped over the label on the overnight bag she had on the seat beside her. 'This your address? Evesham Road? No problem. I can drop you right there. How does that sound. OK?' He rubbed her on the shoulder, then went back to his seat and started the engine, adjusting his mirror a little so that he could keep an eye on her as he drove.

She was still quite bewildered. Everything was concatenating and connecting all around her, everything was in disarray: the striped design of the seat covers, the woven hinges of the ashtray in front of her, the bromide taste left in her mouth by the tea – these things made no kind of sense. Images and memories clattered incoherently through her brain. It took about half an hour for them to reach Stratford and true to his word the driver took a detour and dropped her off outside the flat. She teetered down from the coach and up the stairs, still dazed from the tempest that had blown up in her mind. But worse was yet to come.

As soon as she opened her front door, Rachel was everywhere: in the design of the wallpaper, the details of a rug, the patterns of afternoon sunlight across the furniture, the texture of a table top. Reeling, feeling hot and faint, she made for the kitchen, where she perched on a stool and leant her head into the sink, not so much because she thought she was going to be sick – though the tequila was still floating around in there somewhere – but because it was cooler. Judd and Joel jumped up and sat contemplating her from the draining board, wondering what all of this meant.

The fit had left her too exhausted to cry, to think, to understand what was going on. She stayed bent over the sink for a while, until the sun had gone and the room was dark and the cats were clamouring for their meal. She got up to feed them but was overcome with dizziness as she took the food down from the cupboard.

The room charged at her; she dropped the bag and grabbed at the corner of the fridge for support. Biscuits spilled everywhere, the tiny brown shapes exciting patterns of interference across her field of vision. She dropped to her knees and crawled into the living-room, her daughter in every movement, every sound, every smell. She was being bombarded by this other personality, the petals of its psyche hard as hail upon her body. The view of Warwick from the bus window came to her again and again – she kept thinking of *Close Encounters of the Third Kind* and felt she should be building a model or making a sketch or something. But this storm that raged around her, within her, this force that tapped her senses, bled them off; it left her all but helpless.

Although her toes and ankles had gone numb the soles of her feet prickled with heat. There was a coldness in her knees that prevented her from standing up (her kneecaps felt disconnected, as if they might slip down inside her legs at any moment). The bottom had dropped out of her stomach and her bowels felt loose – not as if she was going to shit but as if she already had done so and her sphincter was now an empty tube open to the air. There was a sensible void in her womb. The lips of her vagina were curling and uncurling in the strangest way, though when she shoved her hand between her legs to calm them nothing was actually happening. Her breasts felt large, as they had done when she was pregnant and swollen with milk, though now the nipples were as red and sore as if they'd been recently suckled. Her arms were long and insubstantial, and cut off at the wrist; it was strange to move her hands, which felt cramped and useless. Her mouth and throat felt perfect, her saliva tasted so good, she wanted to drink but she didn't want to spoil it. For a while she sucked on her thumb and that felt wonderful, comforting. Her vision had become blurred and her hearing hypersensitive.

This initial rush lasted several hours. Throughout it, Jennifer lay sprawled on the floor, incapable of even climbing into a chair, continuous with the room as if both it and she had been trans-formed into shapes of just-set gelatine. As that sensation began to level off she started to experience a purity and clarity that surpassed anything she'd ever felt before. Her body began to reintegrate itself and it was just so . . . perfect and beautiful. Having recovered some of her physical co-ordination she undressed herself and examined it. Her scars, her dominant feature as far as she was concerned, seemed to dissolve, to be absorbed as she ran her fingertips across them. They were . . . they seemed unimportant, invisible . . . neither the restraining net nor the interface that she'd previously imagined . . . so many times she had hated them, despised herself for them, but now she knew they were part of her and that she loved them too. Quickly, she ran her hands all over her body, up and down her legs, across her stomach and breasts, around her shoulders . . . there was a peculiar feeling of spatial displacement . . . it was like feeling two bodies, her own and the body of her child. The cats crept in, confused by her behaviour, and she grabbed them both and held them to her. Their fur felt so good against her skin. She fetched a comb from the bathroom and groomed them carefully one by one.

The child came in waves now. Jennifer would be stable for a while, stroking her body, combing the cat, contemplating something simple and beautiful like a mark on the wall, then Rachel would buzz through her once more, switch her on like an electrical element. She'd slip back into the room again as the feeling assembled itself and when it passed she'd be left beneath a blanket of joy. That first enormous breaker had told her that her child was alive and each spray of surf after that was just confirmation, an echo in flesh in this body of hers which was now a cave by the sea.

The next day she welcomed the sun with her skin and all day she let it touch her through windows. She was free from hunger and from pain. By the time evening arrived the rushing had subsided almost completely and she slept, her brain gently fizzing like a bottle of tonic, her dreams gentle dreams of her child.

When she came to the next morning she felt like her favourite clothes, washed, dried and warmed, and knew that she wasn't going to go to work that week. She got up but didn't dress, felt too complete already, put the kettle on to boil and cleaned up what was left of the spilled cat food. Cup of tea in hand she wandered around the flat, taking it in. It was all so unquestionably clear.

★

Joel's message was on the answering machine and Jennifer called the hotel, but every time the receptionist tried to put her through the line was engaged. She was no longer worrying about having missed him; she knew now that she would see him again. The certainty with which she felt that Rachel was alive and in Warwick Hospital had already infected every aspect of her life and the future pattern of all kinds of events was fast becoming obvious to her. She floated through the next few days high as a kite, screening her calls, meditating a lot, talking with the cats, rejigging her flat, making arrangements. No longer, she realised, did she need the paraphernalia of the past. It was time to jettison things. She hired a van for the week and began filling boxes and binliners with stuff she no longer needed. Her mother's clothes were among the first to go. Then Henry's old letters, pieces of furniture, knick-knacks she'd saved, her parents' death certificates, the old TV. Yes, the time of the television was past, out with it. No more TV afternoons, no more *Twilight Zones*. After all, that's where all the trouble had started.

Once she'd started getting rid of stuff she found it hard to stop; the next thing she knew she was clearing out everything she couldn't think of a direct use for: books, papers, all the junk she'd shoplifted over the years, pictures, records, the contents of the kitchen cupboards, old sheets and towels, shoes, hats, the bedroom carpet, curtains . . . she ripped it all out, crushed it into the dustbins or piled it into the van. She was happy and with each item gone she felt happier. The last thing to go was the sofa, the one on which Henry had died, on which she'd had her first visions of Rachel. Waiting till the neighbours had left for work she shoved and pulled until she'd got it out of the door, down the stairs and into the street, where she left it propped up on one end hoping that the council would take it away. Piling everything else into the van, she drove to the landfill site just out of town and dumped her old life in a hole in the earth.

Now, now she was ready, now she was free. She packed two bags, withdrew all her savings from the bank, collected together everything she might need in the coming days. The only thing that did not fall into place was Joel: his phone was engaged every

497

time she rang. But it was a simple matter to stifle the glimmer of doubt raised by this niggling fact – she asked the receptionist to leave him a note.

'His line's engaged,' the woman had said for the umpteenth time that week.

'I've been trying to reach him since Sunday. Are you sure you haven't seen him? Maybe his phone's off the hook.'

'Mr Kluge has given express instructions that he is not to be disturbed. He has pressing business in London and uses the telephone a great deal.'

'Well, could I leave a message for him, then?'

'Yes, you could,' the receptionist said coldly. 'Mr Kluge is one of our most valued guests. I'm afraid it wouldn't do to upset him.' She didn't mention that the only reason Joel was still resident in the Albion was that he was now paying a double rate to placate the management for his overuse of the telephone and electricity (and that was on top of the money being extorted from him by the maid).

'Well, you might tell him that I shall be visiting at the weekend,' said Jennifer in her haughtiest tone. 'And while you're on the phone, I'd like to reserve a twin room for Saturday night.'

'Of course. I'm sorry, I didn't catch your name,' said the receptionist, who was now rather more eager to oblige.

'Several, Jennifer Several. The room will be for my daughter and for myself.'

The reservation is made and the message written down on the uppermost sheet of a yellow telephone pad. Someone rings the bell in the bar and the receptionist leaves her desk. The clock on the wall reads six-thirty; it is Wednesday evening. The small lobby is now deserted, the Georgian plasterwork groans and worries itself with dust. The deep reds and golds of the worn bramble-patterned carpet tumble and compete for attention. The floor is a complex tangle, the walls and ceiling a blank zenith. The hotel manager strolls into this space, tuts when he sees no one on the desk. The phone rings and he leans across to answer it. 'Yes, ah ha, um, yes of course, no problem at all. Goodbye.' He puts down the phone, turns the yellow pad around and tears off the top sheet, which he then places on the receptionist's typewriter. He takes a pen, scribbles a note to himself, tears off that sheet, folds it, puts it in his pocket, walks away. The lobby is silent again, but loud with potential. Outside in the street the air pressure changes slightly as a bank of cloud moves across the city. Air sluices out through the open windows and the gaps underneath the doors, and an invisible eddy kicks up in the vicinity of the front desk. There's just enough movement to lift the sheet of yellow paper from its resting place and with the softest scrape it slides off the grey metal and down the side of the desk. Whipping back on itself in the air, it changes direction and floats beneath the drawers and down out of sight. This has nothing at all to do with Emma. This is something else she has overlooked. A hundred and one miles away she sleeps, oblivious and exhausted.

15

The last picture show

Warmed by the morning sun, Judd began to move a little faster, matching the speed of the pensioners with their sticks and zimmer frames by the time he passed through the estates on Lisson Grove, though the concrete towers and moulded walls and partitions kept on distracting him, begging him to stay, tempting him with the resonance their modernist geometries struck up with the graphs drawn by the vapour trails of jets across the blank blue slate of the sky. With the movement came some feeling, though it was mostly one of despair, of being cheated. If this was the world then he despised it.

At the junction a man in a Stüssy shirt asked him for directions and he couldn't answer but veered away from him, down the channel formed by the synagogue and Lord's cricket ground, two places of worship one opposite the other.

Mid-afternoon saw him moving among the palm courts of art deco blocks in St John's Wood, lumbering slow as a B-movie dinosaur, and that evening he traversed the wide suburban expanse of the Finchley Road, the exposed balconies of the apartment blocks like TV screens, small domestic dramas flickering intermittently across them.

The jumble of buildings around Swiss Cottage offered some kind of refuge for the night (he felt increasingly safe among buildings; their solidity swaddled him). At one point the pavement was caged in scaffolding and the skeleton of a high-rise soared up on

Judd's right, its stone and metal entrails exposed. Arteries and veins fanned out along every girder and joist. Judd realised he was witnessing the birth of a great machine, a robot which would be as oblivious to its tenants as people are to the bacteria which thrive inside their stomachs and make digestion possible.

Night fell. In a parking lot a group of people sat on rows of folding chairs and watched a film being projected on to a blind wall. Two loudspeakers thundered white noise and in the front row members of the audience sat with their fingers in their ears. One man wore sunglasses and headphones, and held a silver microphone in the direction of the screen. Another sat with his shoes off massaging his feet. The screen was a scintillating chaos in which human figures continually threatened to appear but never quite did. The sequence of images kept stopping and starting, and when the film finally came to an end nobody realised and the projectionist had to prompt the applause.

Judd leant up against the chain link fence and looked on as the reels were changed. After a couple of minutes of darkness a square of light flicked on, followed by a raggedy visual countdown and a shot of an open doorway. The camera went through into the room beyond, which had two windows looking out on to a skyline. It was late afternoon; shadows lounged down from the potted plants on the window-sill and across the table below them. Quickly, the shadows deepened and extended, turned into darkness, swallowed the room. Outside the twilight gave way to the deep hue of a lightly starred night. From the right-hand window's lower right-hand corner the moon, round and bright, swiftly arced across the glass and sank away. Moments later, the sky lightened. The mourning of the room, before so freely draped, rolled itself back into lengthy strips of sable. Within seconds noon struck hard, but just as quickly the sun began to fail and shadows stretched and shrugged their way across the floor, taping out the scene again for night.

Next were views of clouds streaming through the heavens like boiling vats of Indian rice full of bubbles strung with scurfy foam; then vehicles weaving threads of light across the Golden Gate; then other processes, all cycling past in inhuman modes of time. A naked tree, starkly standing in a field of snow while winter

501

mornings hastened by, suddenly bulged and sapped and creaked forth shoots which greenly multiplied and fanned out leaves and buds. Buds blossomed, blossom blew away, spiky fruits weighed down the boughs, cracked off, fell upon the earth and sprouted. Birds and squirrels gorged themselves, fought and squabbled, nested in nooks among the branches. Leaves turned golden brown, grew brittle, whirled away. Rain and hail beat back the summer's show of health, frost clipped off the last few leaves, the smaller twigs.

On an ancient bed a baby with bright bright eyes began to scream, still smarting from the midwife's slap, then screamed some more with teething. Its eyes grew wide, then calm, and on its scalp a fuzz of hair grew long and lank, its limbs straightened and grew more firm. A tall and slender pre-pubescent looked around. The circle of the face drew in and pudgy contours sculpted themselves into individual features. Hair darkened . . . in turns the face cracked into smiles and ran with tears. Fingernails extended into long gnarled spirals, toenails grew back beneath themselves. Under the arms and around the genitals wiry tufts began to sprout. Fluff napped the jaw and the skin of the face developed lines as it grew tighter. The torso broadened and the chest expanded. The leg muscles grew strong and well-defined. The bedclothes rumpled as the body extended to a full six foot. A lambent shock of hair fell down around the shoulders. Features compacted, grew still finer. Sinews and veins pulled taut and ribbed the flesh. Pores dilated. The skin darkened, then paled and relaxed. Wrinkles seeped across the face, converging on the eyes and the corners of the mouth. The eyes turned watery and bloodshot. The pupils dimmed. Flesh dehydrated and sagged loose from thinning bones. The skin fell down in folds, too much of it to wrap its dwindling contents. Cheeks and belly sank, hair greyed and fell and matted the soiled sheets. Hollows developed at the wrists, between the ribs, around the eyes and neck. Short gasps of breath rattled in and out of the throat and mucus gathered around the colourless lips. The eyes stared wildly, then dumbly, then ceased to focus altogether. The breathing popped and ceased. The skin wrinkled tight once again and the limbs stiffened. Around the raw bedsores the flesh turned grey and started to decay.

The camera drew back, revealed the room as sparse and dusty, illuminated by a single flickering flame that cast living shadows upon the walls around the corpse. Back the camera drew, back, through a doorway and out into the sunlight. It rose up above the shoddy dwelling and looked down upon the tree-tops all around. Figures buzzed into the frame. Moving as a blur, they stripped the house, rebuilt it, chopped down trees, cleared back the forest, threw up houses barns fences churches, marked divisions, built walls, wore muddy tracks, dug them out, laid roads, knocked down cabins built brick houses dammed streams built waterwheels and windmills. They held meetings demonstrations celebrations, covered the land to both horizons with buildings of all kinds, filled the streets with more people, horses, carts, then with cars, buses, trucks, trains, trams, knocked down buildings, widened roads, filled the air with fumes. The skyline dipped and soared, the streets and sky shifted with activity. To the east the horizon flamed with sudden flashes. Then the sky was filled with smoke lights balloons and then with waves and waves of aeroplanes. The city was a place of fire and smoke and then a place of calm and crumbling ruins, the only movement falling buildings and lonely dots picking through the rubble. Dots which found each other and began to clear and build again.

The camera grew back still further and the film went on. Judd turned his attention to the flautist who'd been playing a musical accompaniment. The notes were soft and round and ran in chains like bubbles from a bubble pipe, and Judd watched them ripple skywards between the overbearing buildings while on the screen below a white and turquoise planet grew old and diseased and died.

Artificial life

Joel was far too preoccupied to try to call Jennifer again and besides, he was half convinced that she had stood him up deliberately and he had his pride. He drove her from his thoughts, worked furiously at his machine – he'd continue anyway, without her. He'd just be more exact, that's all, to compensate for the fact that he'd have to find a different sexual partner. So he reread his manifestos, made annotations, taped the sheets of paper back up on the walls. He purchased a scanner and stripped himself naked and laid the surfaces of his body against the flat illumination of the glass until every inch of skin had been digitised and entered into his machine. He had another set of X-rays done, just to be sure. He cruised telephone boxes collecting the prostitutes' cards, figuring they'd be a good place to start looking for a replacement for Jennifer.

He went almost entirely without sleep now; when he did nod off it was after long sessions of repetitive data entry during which he behaved like an automaton, his fingers working away at the keyboards on their own, the nerves and nets of his digits clack clack clacking with the shadow dream of insect legs, each one subtly independent of the whole. He inputted and cross-referenced everything that he could remember of his life, trying to reconstruct himself within the limitations of the machine. He outlined his personality, summarised his personal history, wrote character sketches of the members of his family and the other people who'd had a major impact on him – Millstein, Jennifer and Henry, Subhash, the Metrics. Over the six days of continuous work the already substantial mass of data grew into a giant snarl of ones and zeros that heaved away in packets around the machines in the small network he had built. And all this time the malfunctioning modem dialled away, dispatching his various parts to the databases of banks, telcos, advertising agencies, government departments, law firms, tourist information offices, census co-ordinators, motor manufacturers, television companies, scientific laboratories, Antarctic base stations, religious institutions, libraries, personal computers, industrial robots, magazines and newspapers, millenarian cults, traffic-light controllers, police stations, security firms, space stations, air-traffic control towers, software companies, nuclear bunkers. Joel's vital statistics, his rants, his skin tones, his skeleton found their way across every national boundary. They became seamlessly woven into the very fabrics of a hundred societies. Image samples from his buttocks were used to smooth the face of an ageing American model in a skin-cream advertisement. His waist and inside leg measurements formed a ratio that became the recommended dosage for a new heart drug and dozens of middle-aged businessmen died as a result (which in turn caused a series of upsets on NASDAQ and wiped out several personal fortunes, made various others and bankrupted a small African country). The insertion of the radius of his jaw into previously uncertain data allowed the reconstruction of a somewhat bewildering fossilised remain: hitherto guessed to be some kind of anthropod, it was now reclassified as belonging to a member of a completely new Cambrian phylum. His genetic fingerprint, spliced into a crucial systems code, triggered an accident in a Russian nuclear reactor which led to meltdown, the contamination of vast swathes of territory, decades of insect and animal mutation, and thousands and thousands of cases of cancer, leukaemia and other, more subtle, illnesses. His initials were worked into an anthemic song by a Dutch pop band which topped their national charts for weeks, and in the stacks of a giant museum near Los Angeles his blood type became mixed up with the catalogue data and the oldest extant copy of Virgil's *Aeneid*, on loan from the Vatican library, got classified as rubbish and incinerated. The date of his circumcision replaced the firing sequence for the boosters aboard Voyager II, as the probe headed with great speed towards Jupiter. The upshot was a marginally different heading which would, some eight hundred years hence, bring the little spacecraft into contact with an alien civilisation.

All week Joel worked on, oblivious to the fact that his plan was being overtaken by events. On the sixth day he felt that the construct was finally complete and on the seventh he rested, passing out, totally exhausted, just before dawn. But as soon as he slept the doll with two hearts appeared in his dreams, her servomechanisms whirring and clicking as she walked. She came towards him, less lithe than before and more mechanical, and he could not tell what size she was – she seemed simultaneously to tower above him and to hardly reach his knee. She took his bony hand in hers and led him through the neuronal tangle of some forest of the night until they reached a clearing where the trees gave way to a rock face that rose clear and monumental out of the ground. A waterfall cascaded down from a plateau high above and all about them rainbows bobbed like arcs of electricity on the clouds of mist and spray. The doll dropped Joel's hand and moved away, making her way around the edge of the pool at the base of the falls. Joel stood and listened to the roar of the water. Little by little he began to distinguish blips of sound within it. He closed his eyes so as to listen more intently and the blips became more intense until he could ascertain discrete burbles of noise. The burbles became screeches, which seemed familiar but most unwaterlike, and Joel suddenly realised that he was no longer listening to the sound of a waterfall at all but to something quite different. He looked up at the cliff but it was a cliff no longer. The craggy slope had become a sheer black face, the waterfall a giant strip of copper. It took him a moment or two to realise what it was he was looking at. It was one section of a colossal silicon chip and the tumult he could hear was not of water but of bits. He began to laugh at the absurdity of it; he laughed and laughed, harder than he could ever remember laughing before. In fact, he couldn't remember ever having laughed at all. He'd smiled a few times, perhaps once or twice he had grinned. But had he laughed? He couldn't be sure.

He laughed until he remembered the doll. Where had she got to? He set off around the pool in search of her and as he moved the silicon chip morphed back into waterfall and cliff, the black plastic crackling and melting into rock as if it were being heated from behind, the copper sparkling and dancing until it was all light and motion. The ground was treacherous with moisture and Joel lost his footing several times as he hunted through the mists. Eventually he spotted the doll and when he did she was still neither short nor tall, neither distant nor near. She was standing beside a glass elevator that ran all the way up the side of the cliff. She smiled and beckoned him inside. Her chest was exposed and he could see her silver-red hearts blinking away in unison through the artificial membrane that served as her chest. He glanced upwards to the top of the cliff, to where the lift would take him. High above, the edge of the plateau was stiff and pure against the softness and indeterminacy of the saturated sky. Should he go with her? He put his hands to his face and entered.

The lift started slowly but then went faster and faster, the rock and the pool disappearing quickly from view as they shot above the top of the cliff, into the air and through the first clouds. Joel's stomach hit the floor and he grabbed for a handrail (there wasn't one). The doll stood behind him, looking out through the glass, her face a blank slate. Had she done this before? To his amazement he realised that far away to the right he could see the curve of the earth.

The glass elevator hung still in the night. Joel's feet no longer came into contact with the floor. The doll was floating too, her legs folded into what might have been a lotus position had they not been fat and made of plastic. She looked up (what he assumed was up). He followed her gaze through the roof of the capsule and out into a space bright with stars, much brighter than he'd ever imagined they could be. Everything was there and nothing; he didn't understand what she was looking at. He glanced back at her but she was still staring, so he looked up again, harder this time, and as he watched he noticed that far above their heads was a large black patch of space from the edges of which the stars were beginning to vanish. His first thought was of some kind of cloud, but then he realised that it wasn't that at all, all the clouds were below. Something else was approaching.

There was a click and he looked down just in time to see the doll releasing the door. He tried to scream but it was too late: she opened it a crack and the air immediately exploded out from the elevator, hurling the doors wide and blowing Joel and the doll into the void. As his lungs pleaded for breath he felt himself expand and at the moment he was going to explode he woke up.

He came to, fighting with the sheets that had somehow got wrapped round his head and stuffed inside his mouth. He cleared them away and hyperventilated, recalling the dream. Something was wrong. He switched on the bedside lamp but in spite of the light everything was hazy. He felt around for his glasses but couldn't find them. Where had he put them? He searched the bed and the floor beside it, but they weren't there. Eventually he went into the bathroom to look for them. He fumbled for the light but the wall seemed flat and textureless, and it took him a few moments to locate the cord. Even with the light on his eyesight was so poor that he could hardly see, but he continued to explore around the sink and along the shelves with his hands. The glasses weren't there. Exasperated, he went across to the mirror to rub his eyes, only to find that the elusive spectacles were perched on the end of his nose, where they'd been all the time. How odd. He took them off, examined them, rinsed them under the tap, dried them with a piece of tissue, replaced them on his nose, but there was little improvement. He flushed with a minor panic as he wondered if he hadn't damaged his vision from sitting in front of a screen for too many hours at a stretch. He drank a glass of water, then wet a flannel, went back to bed, and laid it across his face. Across from him, on their table, the machines were talking to one another. The malfunctioning modem had managed to dial the number that would connect Joel's computer to the satellite base station he had hacked into the previous week and was now merrily dumping all the data it could find down this channel. Along the phone line it went, through the silicon circuitry of several computers and up in a narrow beam to Sputnik II, where it blurted into Laika's little world.

The poor dog never knew what had hit her. These data of Joel's broke the glass of her screen and grabbed at her. They came on like a rape, a barrage of sounds pictures codes that in the confines of the capsule took on a tangible quality. Laika's twenty-seven years of solitude were over and something terrifying had broken the silence. She didn't even have time to bark as multimedia dissolved her, and her body and her craft were outlined with pulses of blue electronic light.

Lax RV

The next day, Judd tackled Hampstead, now sure of where he was going. He meandered up Fitzjohn's Avenue, surrounded by rich young mothers herding their kids into school, passing the heavy red houses. He rumbled unnoticed through the centre of the village, oblivious to the international pact made by the bourgeoisie through their purchase of reliable cars, his movements too slow to be registered by the security cameras.

He spent the afternoon lost in the small maze of streets around New End but by evening had found his way out on to the Heath, which he inched his way across, navigating by the moon and frightening couples and cottagers. Dogs ran up to him and barked; one even pissed up his leg, marking him out, a node in some esoteric canine topology that would, by continuing its slow traverse, upset the power balance in the neighbourhood and lead to internecine border disputes. Judd felt that he was fixed in one place, that all he was doing was lifting his feet one by one as the earth moved beneath him like an enormous conveyor belt. Infinitesimally, inexorably, high above his head the sweep of stars rotated.

He came out by Highgate ponds and dawn saw him shuffling his way up Fitzroy Park, a private road lined with the highly styled abodes of millionaires. Pretty soon a police car drew up beside him. Its occupants, having discovered that he seemed incapable of even registering their presence, sat there and watched him for a couple of hours until he was up the hill and out of the area.

His excitement grew as he passed close by Highgate cemetery, where many others who had already turned to stone now resided, and it peaked soon after that, when he came down the High Street and saw London below him for the first time, the buildings of the City misty in the morning smog, the various environs locked into the twists of the Thames in bricks of leaden, patchy grey. The view reminded him of that of Los Angeles from Beverly Hills, the one he'd scampered up hillsides as a child to discover, and for the first time since he had returned to London he felt a brief moment of peace, as if this place had finally abandoned an ancient dispute with his home. But the moment passed and feeling angry with himself for being so seduced he continued eastwards across the hillside, skirting the view, until he came to the Archway bridge on Hornsey Lane. Here, hundreds of feet below, the expressway sped away to either side, carmine and amber and beryl and turquoise and all hues of pinprick lights tacking down its undulations all the way. Kept from the abyss by a cast-iron rail, Judd watched the lanes of cars roll beneath him, the thousand thousand shifting suns of a spiral arm combusting through the twilight. A milky way. And in each car the planets of personality spun: the drivers, the passengers, the women, men and children, the burnt the raw the old, the travellers salesmen doctors thieves and lawyers, the grocers masseurs surfers judges guards, the chefs singers smokers drinkers hikers drummers palmists prophets racers chasers consumers cripples comedians Catholics capitalists Muslims communists Baptists Jews Hindus heteros homos lilos, every one a freak punk poet mystic pool-player pervert redneck syphilitic necrophiliac nymphomaniac terminally ill terminally insane terminally terminal sociopath psychotic. God, how tired he was of them all.

Jennifer to the rescue

The Saturday following her abortive journey to London, Jennifer packed a couple of bags, put them in the van, and made a bed in the back with a mattress and some blankets. Before she set off she put down fresh food for Judd and Joel and secured the house, leaving the back window ajar so that they could come and go as they pleased. She locked the front door and pushed her spare set of keys through the letter-box of the couple who lived in the flat below, along with a note asking if they'd look after the cats while she was away.

She drove straight from Stratford to Warwick, taking the most direct route to the hospital that she knew. It was August Bank Holiday weekend and the roads were congested, which she hoped wouldn't be a problem later on. But the thought didn't bother her for long. She was still happy. Everything would be fine.

It surprised her now how little thought she had put into the rescue itself, especially considering how much time she had spent dreaming about all the things she would do with her daughter once they had been reunited. But she wasn't scared at all. Events would take their own course.

It took her about half an hour to reach the hospital. She turned into the entrance and drove slowly through the complex until one of the car parks felt right. Then she came to a halt and sat behind the wheel smoking a cigarette, each drag bringing back a tinge of the ecstasy she'd experienced the weekend before, not sure what to do next. The buildings were meaningless to her, so much so that if it weren't for the signs everywhere ('Radiology', 'Out-Patients', 'Maternity', 'Emergency', 'Princess Anne Ward') the collection of long, low, prefabricated buildings littered around this nexus of car parks could just as easily have been a university faculty or a school as a medical facility.

She finished the cigarette and stepped out of the van, leaving it unlocked. The mid-morning sun blazed down across the open concrete, emphasising the cracks and folds in the surface where frost and tree roots had taken their toll. She walked in the direction of her shadow, thinking how thin this concrete surface was and how just beneath it worms and moles and roots and beetles fought, thrived and combined. A door presented itself to her and she opened it. She went inside. The corridor ahead was long, dark, soft, empty, quiet. It smelt of Germolene and disinfectant. The linoleum tiles, alternately red and brown, stretched before her like the squares of a checkerboard. She made her way across them, her trainers squeaking at every step. She had gone about ten yards when there was a loud buzzing sound, very close, as if an insect had flown into her ear. She leant against the yellow wall and shook her head, wanting to sneeze, not sure if it was pain that she felt. Everything around her was laid bare. The walls churned through

the leviathan patterns of measureless aeons of geological mor-
phology. The floor hissed of open fields of flax; the wooden skirting
whispered of a million generations of trees. She inched forward,
using the wall as a support. A nurse came round the corner. Jennifer
wanted to run but she couldn't and the inability to obey this direct
impulse made her realise for the first time how little control she
had over whatever was going on. Her coming here had nothing
to do with her. She was being manipulated. Just what, exactly,
was happening?

The nurse came over. 'Are you all right, dear? You look very
pale.' She gave a lot of weight to the 'very'.

The words came to Jennifer. 'Yes, I'm fine, really. It's my
mother, taken ill, just been visiting, bit of a shock . . .'

'Oh, yes, well you take care. There's a community room around
the corner, you can sit in there if you want, get a cup of tea from
the machine. Want me to show you where it is?' These words:
the interactions of prokaryotes and eukaryotes dribbled through
time's vegetal mass.

'Oh, no, thank you, it's all right, I can manage, I think.' The
nurse nodded and went on her way along the corridor, the heavy
soles of her shoes slapping loudly against the hard floor.

Alone again, Jennifer could feel her daughter near now, as close
as she had felt during the final moments before her collapse, before
they tore her out from the womb. She placed her hand underneath
her sweater and ran her fingers along the line of the old caesarean
scar, caressing its puckers. The rhythms of the child's twin pulses
came down the corridor towards her like streamers of blood flowing from a suicide's wrists into a bath of warm water. She began
to move faster and started to cry, and her tears made trellised
patterns down her cheeks. There she was running through the
corridors, turning left and right on impulse, as if chasing through
the ventricles of her daughter's very mind.

Finally there was a door, bolted on the outside. She slid back
the bolt and pushed it open. The room had a window of reinforced
glass, a hospital bed covered with a thin, flowery spread, a cabinet
or two, a trolley. Standing at the end of the bed with her back to
Jennifer was an eight-year-old girl with deep red hair, dressed in

a dark-green overcoat, a grey school dress, white stockings and grey leather shoes. Beside her on the bed was a small bag, already packed.

'Rachel?' said the mother. 'Rachel?' The girl turned towards her and for a second Jennifer was shocked by the face. She had never known it, except in fragments, and here it was complete and flooded with light. It was a face of exquisite ugliness, a face which broke every rule of proportion but so subtly that the effect was quite disarming. It lacked symmetry: the high forehead overshadowed a weak chin, the mouth was the merest line and the lips non-existent, the nose was pert but squat and broad. And the eyes were old, too old for the skin which, though mottled, was still flushed and fresh, old with the aura of that flotsam that gathers on the back of the ever breaking wave upon which we live and which gets cycled and recycled as a signpost for a future we can never know, an impossible marker which tells us only that we are the rising and rotting yeasts of unaccountable eternal returns.

Then the child put her finger to her mouth and she was just a little girl.

'Rachel?' asked Jennifer. There was a pause, in which she felt her daughter die again.

But the child opened her mouth and began to speak, in a voice wracked with catarrh and difficult and deep. 'Emma. I'm Emma.'

'Emma,' repeated Jennifer, choking with joy. 'Of course, Emma. Emma, Emma, Emma. Emma, do you know who I am?' Emma nodded and went over to her mother. Jennifer bent down and they embraced.

Mother and daughter hurried through the maze of identical corridors, Emma leading so that they wouldn't run into anyone on the way. They reached the van without a problem and the child wanted to look (she had never been out here before) but Jennifer made her lie down on the mattress in the back and covered her with a blanket. Her hands were trembling as she tried to insert the key into the ignition and she dropped the bunch twice before she managed to start the engine. She drove as sedately as she could through the car-parks and back towards the main road. As they passed through the exit a deafening high-pitched whine vibrated the air behind them. Jennifer thought it was a helicopter and nervously searched the skies, even as the whine became more intense, every molecule in the vicinity now excited. She clasped her hands over her ears but as she did so the sound passed beyond the upper limits of her hearing. For a moment there was silence, nothing but the noise of the engine. Then every window in the hospital exploded outwards in one great throb of energy, a thousand flowers of glass blossoming into the air, each one a bloom of a billion shining shards. For a moment the explosion was contained by a vast and delicate tinkling, a bubble of silence on an expanding front of vibration. Then the fragments hit the concrete and glass skidded on stone and all the terrible beauty was lost as the sonic boom broke. Emma lay in the back calmly and smiled; Jennifer slammed the van back into gear and drove.

She made her way out to the bypass and followed it round to the south-east corner of the town, then cut back through Warwick–Leamington along the Myton Road, heading in the direction of Daventry. It took her about half an hour to reach Northampton and the M1, and by this time she was calm enough to break the chain of cigarettes she'd been smoking. Just before she turned on to the motorway she pulled into a lay-by and told Emma to come and sit up beside her. She settled her in the front seat, clipped the seat-belt around her and gave her one of the cartons of drink she'd brought along. She hugged her and felt her hair and cried for a while, attentions which the child accepted impassively, and then she drove on, keeping to the slow lane and continually stealing glances at her daughter. She touched her whenever she could and she started to talk, then talked without stopping. Throughout the journey Emma sat looking slightly bemused, absorbing as much as she could, as if she'd been presented with a banquet having been brought up on gruel.

The cinema of city lights

Along Crouch End High Street it was the same story, bums and drunks harrying him away from their patch, shoppers streaming about him like the customers in Reno's casinos. But the shadow of the hill was ahead of him, the highest point, and it gave him heart. Judd smiled, an effort that split his lips and brought forth springs of blood. Soon it would be over. It was nearly time to prove that he could take control, that he was capable of making at least one decision, even if it would be his last.

He waited at the foot of the town centre clock for what seemed an age, girding himself for the final ascent. He looked terrible: his hair was patchy and worn, the roots dying as his scalp began to harden and rift. His face was emaciated and the bones of his skull jutted out, drawing dark escarpments out of his face. His eyes were glazed with a crystal film and stared without blinking at everything; his hands were chipped and cracked. His clothes hung from him loosely, worn thin by the ramparts of his frame. His feet were naked, smooth, his shoes long knocked from them like corn husks from grains pounded by millstones. Yet from beneath the crust of the city, London's chalk and clay encouraged and supported him; he was part of their realm now, moving at speeds which they could comprehend.

The next morning he tackled Park Road. It took him all day to cover its length, this chunk of strange suburbia with its petrol stations and semis. But at the top there it was, the gate to Alexandra Palace, like an enormous welcome sign. He made straight for it and was half-way across the junction when a car sped down the hill towards him in an attempt to catch the lights. The driver didn't see Judd until it was too late. Whining and protesting, suspension axles rubbed and juddered, locked. Oil pumped in massive pressure and the brake discs clamped and swore. Metal of the body all in forward motion slowed and gripped and lurched, forward over tyres, chassis straining bending, rubber left in lines upon the road.

Impact.

Driver through the windscreen (no seat-belt, you see), through the air past Judd who turned his head, surprised. He felt the heat all down his side – the car was there, bunched up around him like a lover, touching all his curves and spaces, panting burning breaths in short hot gasps upon his cheek. Hot lungs. Broken, dying. But unperturbed and with a creak, a sound of stone on metal, Judd pulled away, his imprint there inside the beast, leaving a mould, a negative. Slowly, he carried on towards the gate.

The road wound up through trees and parkland to the Victorian palace which formed London's vertex. Porticoes and balustrades, patterned brickwork, great rose windows: like an Indian fortress the building aped the sky. It was the biggest sky Judd had ever seen in England, the biggest one of all; as if the transmitter on the palace roof, that iron pylon, that talking Blackpool tower, were an anti-magnet that had repelled the troposphere itself.

Judd stood at the foot of the brick turret which supported the tower. There being no one about he began to climb, desiring the sky, needing it to bear witness for him. Like the chalk and the clay, the brickwork sympathised with Judd's fingers and toes, afforded them purchase, loved them as he inched up the building storey by storey. Above the climbing man the sky dulled, as if a great dragon were breathing on its sheen, and the sun began to dip towards the night. It fell and fell, and at the end tipped off the earth and dragged its cape down with it. To the east it was already dark. A few light cumuli floated overhead, showing their bloodied bellies like culled seals. Within minutes the crimson bled out across the ocean of the sky and the clouds grew grey, as atrophying corpses do, to hang stiff and cankered in the air while the livid sunset blind was rolled away above them. What could be more lovely than decay? Birds flew across the sky to roost and in the valleys' slits the halogens which mark the streets became denser, more intense. In windows, lights came on and claimed the outside spaces, the city's bulwarks against the night. Judd had reached the top and stood beneath the mast. He could see it all now. He looked.

Cupped inside its crooks the city blazed, the spangle of a zillion uncharted constellations. In groves and hollows on rises over water electricity splayed forth into the atmosphere: the static lights of towers and vapour lamps, the ons and offs of domestic windows framed yellow or electric blue, the flowing, halting whites and reds and blinking ambers of the cars, the traffic signals' crimson amber green, the pulsing pods of buoys upon the water, the bridges stretched taut across the Thames like gleaming cords, the waters themselves, polluted and amniotic, soiled by toxic effluents and riddled with machines, the blank white light of offices like surgeries, the port and starboard signals of slowly roving ships easing in and out of dock, the beacons of tugs and yachts and fishing boats, the flashing disembodied wink of scrolling aircraft, the diaphanous cones of helicopter spotlights steadily patrolling, the twin whirl of police lamps, the grim glare of the floodlights gripping the great dome of St Paul's, the cobalt sprays of sparks from welders working on the bridges, the rays firing out in all directions from the tips of chaos and tall buildings. Half closing his eyes, Judd gazed at the patches of darkness where small parks or trees soaked up the photons, looked at the juddering flames of fires on the mudbanks to the east, at the rows of arc lamps making miniature days inside the football stadiums, the halogens and kliegs and cressets and strip lights and lanterns, the laser light taut from Canary Wharf, the mounted searchlights boring tubes through the smoggy haze. He saw all these fizzing lights throw cadmium phosphorescence across the underbelly of what clouds there were, and watched it rain back like fall-out.

Down there, where it fell, people danced ate wooed sang rushed sat trembled, precariously alive. Down there they grew morose, withdrawn, wombed in electricity. Like individual souls the lights, some burning bright, some dim, some snapping on or off, were all involved. Judd wished them all away and he wished them all together, wished them into one single brilliant filament blazing out in all directions. He felt his anger ignite within him, fuelled by the oxygen of pain. He wanted people punished for what they had done to him, for what they had done to the world; he wanted them flogged for scarring and scabbing this virginal basin, for soiling its immaculate waters, for bringing time here. He wanted them to feel the thrust of the death they denied and yet carried within them. He wanted the carpet of European Man rolled back. He wanted this place smashed like his face had once been, back in LA, ground against the rock; he wanted this TV mast torn apart in revenge for those TV afternoons which had brought him no good. He wanted the buildings to crumble, the streets to crack and rift, the earth to vent up and spout first fire and ash and later orange poppies and long-husked grasses. He wanted this concrete Reich brought to an end. He wanted the seals to return in their droves to the rocks, the bats to appropriate the palaces, the wood-worm and the death-watch the bee and the ant to hollow out the foundations of the banks and the buildings. In the parks he wanted teepees, buffalo; in the streets he wanted prairies. He wanted steppes and forests from the shoreline to the hilltops; in the waters he wanted silver fish teeming to and fro across the sunken girders of Blackfriars Bridge, of Tower. He wanted octopi and sharks, eels and dolphins. On the land he wanted wolves and deer and snakes and bears and muskrats. In the skies he wanted eagles, vultures, hummingbirds. On the wind the sound of howl and song and cry. In the soil, worm and beetle, mole and root. Streams would roll and tumble where once goods trains had rattled. Trees would quiver tall where telephone poles had stood. In place of apartment blocks there would be camp fires. In place of garages, caves. No automobiles, but wild horses would gallop and graze. Excited into swift action for the first time in days, he whirled his hands to kindle the spell, to foam and ferment the firmament. He gesticulated at the ground and commanded it to heave and spume, to make an alembic of the city and so distil the god that would strike at this aberration playing across the surface of the earth.

But nothing at all occurred, nothing at all, except that a breeze blew up and melted through the air. It unfurled itself through the stanchions of the television mast and gently goaded Judd for his concern. He knew it was useless. In all the days in all the years in all the centuries to come these buildings would always stand here, they would never be repelled, earthquakes eruptions famines plagues and floodings would prove nothing but minor setbacks. And what was worse, the malaise would creep forth to feed on other planets, it would seep across the solar system and thence out through the galaxy, engulfing all the stars just as a dewy mould on a rotting fruit sends out its spores to set at all the other apples in the rack. He felt helpless before this steady march, this trickling divagation, this murmuring stream, this chatter. Above him, satellites softly slipped between the stars. Cars passed far below and he watched their headlights run along the wires red and white in pulses. Dark buildings loomed on corners. Night was coming to an end. Slowly, the nerve impulses lumbering awkwardly through his sluggish body, Judd shuffled across towards the building's eastern edge. He was moving slower than ever now, no more than an inch a minute. Before long the sun would be up; then he'd warm, gain heart, the moment would be lost. It was now, now or never. The thought echoed through the desiccating caverns of his cortex, reverberating like a mantra, helping him up on to the parapet. As the street lights in the city below began to blink off his toes creaked over the lip and, as the first atomic wisp crept into view above this fawning earth, he toppled.

The wind held its breath as night flipped into day. For an instant everything seemed to halt as millennia were compressed into microseconds. Judd stopped in mid-air, half-way between parapet and concrete. There was a fracture in the world, an irreducible lacuna. The last things he saw as his eyes turned to crystal were the markings on the road, white against the oily blackness of the tarmac, their frozen motions now pinned for ever to his glassy retinae. The minerals in his bloodstream multiplied like cancers and hardened into feldspars, transmuting his muscles into bands of pink granite. His brain petrified into spongy dolerite. His fingernails became moonstones and his testicles mica swirls. His kidneys and liver metamorphosed into basalt and his bones became chalk. His heart ossified and was changed into a pyroxene-rich lump of andesite. He had rubies in his arteries, jade in his veins, pearls in his glands. His tendons and nerves formed seams of copper, silver, gold. With the heat of the transformation he curled into a ball and when it was over his skin cooled and vitrified, becoming obsidian.

Then the wind breathed out, the air was rent by explosion, and the surface of the sky began to flicker and dance as the force unleashed vaporised tower and mast. Judd thudded down on the boiling ground, black, solid, round and encrusted with rings of quartz where his mouth, ears and anus had been. Far below, in the city, the whine of fire engines could already be heard.

Beneath the glowing sky the firemen would find the new rock, cooling fast, at the centre of the crater it had formed. They would remove their shiny helmets, scratch their heads with blackened fingers. Later that day the scientists would come and take Judd away. They'd shave him into sections with lasers and examine him carefully under microscopes. To their astonishment they would find within him what seemed to be the fossilised remnants of cells. They would speak to the press and the story would sweep round the world:

MARTIANS INVADE EARTH!!!

METEORITE CONTAINING EVIDENCE OF
EXTRA-TERRESTRIAL LIFE DESTROYS
WORLD'S FIRST TELEVISION TRANSMITTER!

Full English breakfast

The next time Joel awoke he could focus. His limbs still felt numb but everything else was all right. He hadn't eaten for seventy-two hours and was ravenously hungry. He called room service and ordered some breakfast, and when the chambermaid arrived he took the tray from her at the door. He devoured everything on it – two dry and peeling croissants, a large fry-up, three rounds of thin toast, a glass of orange juice and several cups of tea – but the food did nothing to displace the strange feeling of emptiness he felt.

He had eaten his breakfast lying on the bed, but now he went over to the computer table and sat down at it. As always, the machines were humming with activity, and he tapped in a series of brief instructions and ordered up his construct, the raw material ready for the spell.

But something had gone wrong. The computer could not find the construct. He ran a check on his hard disk and discovered that great chunks of his data had been corrupted or were missing altogether. He started to panic. This couldn't be right. Where was his work? Where was his golem, his perfect creation? He ran the search again but still there was nothing, so with trembling fingers he did a systems check and discovered the modem malfunction. How had that happened? How had it been running continually and unnoticed all week? Incredibly, his machine had made a remote connection with another computer and was uploading his data to it, then overwriting the dispatched files with garbage. He tried to shut the modem off from within the operating system but it would not recognise the command. He reached around the back of one of the housings to unclip the serial cable from its port, but the metal was red hot and he whipped back his burnt finger in pain.

There was nothing for it but to shut off the power and reboot, but before he did that Joel quickly scrolled through the various directories to see just what he had lost. Parts of the retinae and the visual cortex had been corrupted earlier in the day but they were still largely intact. One of his kidneys had gone completely, as had a large section of one thigh. With a sudden flash of horror he remembered the strange loss of vision he had experienced when he had woken in the middle of the night. He moved his hand down to his groin and inched it out across his leg. There was a strange void into which his trousers sagged. He croaked in disbelief as the machine began to send out chunks of his lower intestine and then wipe them from the disk. As the data unwound like a skein of wool from a spindle, Joel felt his breakfast drop inside him. There was no mistaking the soft flop of pieces of undigested tomato on to his prostate gland or the hideous glissando of albumen sliding down the inside of his spine.

He burst into action and started to tear at the cables on his desk, but he had screwed all of them down and now he couldn't pull them free. The power points were located around by the side of the bed and he dived across the floor, his legs too weak to stand, retching as the contents of his belly slapped around like baby squids in a bucketful of glue. Grabbing at the nearest bed leg he hauled himself forwards, then scrabbled at the carpet in order to travel the remaining distance to the socket. But as he stretched out his hands across those last few inches they began to fade. The nails and cuticles went quite suddenly and then, millimetre by millimetre, his flesh was stripped away. Knuckle by knuckle the bone began to go too, until all he had left were two stumps of wrist that trailed off into the air.

The shock was so great that his terror turned to fascination. He gave up and rolled on to his back, clutching at the air with his rapidly dwindling lungs. Above him on the table the machine chattered away to itself, mindlessly busy with its task of deleting the rest of him.

Time for tubby bye-bye

Jennifer followed the M1 until it terminated in Neasden, then took the A5 through London, watching it cycle through its incarnations as the Edgware Road, Cricklewood Broadway, Shoot Up Hill, Kilburn High Road, Maida Vale, then back into the Edgware Road once more. Emma gazed out of the window, drinking in the houses and the people and the cars, amazed by the solidity of these things she'd only ever seen in her dreams. The fact of the world was so blatant, such a barrage, and she kept blinking at its complexity as if taking mental photographs to study later at her leisure.

The sun was high in the sky as Jennifer rounded Marble Arch. Trying to drive and follow the map at the same time, she almost ran into the side of a cab. The driver swore at her and blew his horn, and Jennifer screamed back, glad to be able to release some of the tension gathered by her body during the journey. The taxi drew up alongside her at the lights and the cabbie wound down his window the better to shout abuse. Emma looked across at him and thought about the tyres on his vehicle. The compressed air inside them began to heat up and within seconds the rubber was smoking. The chassis rose imperceptibly up into the air, there was a short series of explosions, and the vehicle dropped the few inches to the road. The driver leapt out and examined the shreds of his tyres in disbelief.

The lights changed and Jennifer drove on. At the next set of lights she stopped, turned to Emma and stroked the girl's hair. 'You don't need to do that,' she said calmly. 'You don't. You're with me now. You don't have to be angry.' The child looked at her mother, then took her hand in her own and laid it against her faintly glaucous cheek. It was an awkward display of affection, as though she had intuited an expectation and tried to fulfil it. The lights changed again and Jennifer had to remove her hand and apply it to the gearstick, and Emma turned away again, unsure. They continued down the Bayswater Road towards Queensway, Jennifer nervous, searching for the turn. The traffic slowed and stopped.

Leaning out of the window, Jennifer looked up ahead: the road was blocked off by a police van and a row of orange cones. Suddenly she felt dazed, the euphoria that had been with her all week swept away. Christ, oh, Christ, what was she doing? What the fuck was going on? She grabbed Emma and bundled her over the seats and into the back of the van, told her to get under the blanket and stay down. Then she reached for her cigarettes and lit one.

A policeman strolled up to the car and stuck his head through the window. 'Road's closed. Right or left only from here.' He didn't offer an explanation and Jennifer didn't ask for one. She wound up her window and when her turn came swung right into Westbourne Terrace. She was planning to take the next left and go on into Prince's Square but the road was barred with metal railings, so she turned right again instead and parked on a single yellow line.

They left the van and continued to Prince's Square on foot.

The streets were clotted with people heading west and in the distance Jennifer could hear a low, ambient throb. She was shaking now and unsure. Even though the police hadn't been interested in her she still hadn't recovered her composure. As they walked she tried to get straight in her head just what the last week had all been about. Was this girl really her child? She must be insane, she'd just kidnapped this kid for no reason. Oh, god, and she'd thrown most of what she owned away! What had she been thinking? She glanced down at Emma, expecting to see an eight-year-old with confusion stamped across her face, but Emma seemed fine.

Indeed, the child could sense the massive concentration of energy up ahead and was becoming more and more excited. She skipped along beside Jennifer as her mother hurried along. They passed a couple sitting on a low wall drinking beer. The man had his shirt off; a whistle dangled from the red, gold and green ribbon that was tied around his neck. Jennifer asked him what was going on.

He laughed. 'You not from round here, then? It's the Carnival, lady. August Bank Holiday, innit?'

Jennifer thanked him, greatly relieved. Now someone had said it, now she knew the words, now everything was OK. Emma slipped back into place and Jennifer's high partly returned. She was here. She had done it. 'Come on, darling,' she said to Emma. 'It's just a big, big party. They'll never find us now. Let's go and find your Uncle Joel, then we can go somewhere and have a nice lunch, just the three of us.' More words. With these she invented a family ex nihilo. She thought of her fears during the previous half-hour and giggled. The sunlight poured down through the green leaves of the cherry trees which lined the road and she wanted to dance she was so happy. Emma had started to skip again and Jennifer skipped with her. The child giggled too, a new sound to her, and Jennifer picked her up and held her to her and kissed her over and over.

She carried her around the corner and into Prince's Square, then put her down as they arrived outside the Albion. But as they climbed the steps the smile disappeared from Emma's face. Jennifer caught her eye and was surprised at the bleakness in her expression.

She squatted down and tweaked the child's nose. 'It's all right, angel. We're just going to see a friend. Everything's going to be fine. You'll see.'

Inside and upstairs, Joel was still shrinking. His eyes had gone long before, as had his arms and most of his legs. When his genitals had begun to vanish he had wanted to scream, just like in his dream, but then his mouth had disappeared too and he was left unable to do anything but listen for his fate and sniff at it.

Jennifer tickled Emma under the chin until she laughed, then took out a tissue and wiped the girl's face clean. They went up the steps and through the glass entrance door and then they were out of the heat and the noise, and into the calm of the reception area.

They approached the reception desk. Emma watched the brambles on the carpet swirl around their feet. 'We're here to see Mr Kluge.'

'Of course. Just a minute, please.' The receptionist had the day off again and the manager was minding the desk. He dialled the number of Joel's room. 'I'm afraid his line is engaged. Would you mind waiting while I go up and call him?'

'Oh, he's expecting us. Which room is he in?'

'Three ten, but I don't know if I can let you . . .'

'You don't understand. This is his daughter. He's expecting us.'

'Well, I suppose . . .' But Jennifer wasn't listening. She led Emma past the desk and the two of them began to mount the stairs. As they ascended the first flight the child looked back at the man and stuck out her tongue. They quickly climbed the narrow staircase to the third floor, then hurried along to Joel's room, their nostrils heavy with the dusky anonymity of hallways. They reached three ten and Jennifer knocked.

There was no reply. She knocked again, a little harder this time. She felt faint; her skin seemed to tremble, to become excited by the mere fact of contact with the material of her clothes, with the molecules of the air. Her scars vibrated, felt like bands of light. For a moment, as goose-pimples washed across her body and the hairs on the back of her neck stood up on end, she thought she was

525

going to trip out again. She looked down at Emma, who was still staring at the patterns on the carpet, and the child again seemed different, nothing to do with her, something very far away. There was still no reply from inside and she could hear somebody beginning to climb the stairs behind them. She turned the handle and entered.

The room was sweltering. The curtains were drawn but the light was on so she could see the piles of boxes, the unmade bed, the clothes strewn everywhere, the dirty plates and take-away cartons, the papers pinned to the walls and the computer equipment clustered on the makeshift table. 'Hello?' she called. 'Hello? Joel, are you there?' She took a couple of paces and stepped on to a discarded chopstick, which snapped and made her jump. Emma wandered on in front and began to inspect the blinking, whirring hardware which was pumping out heat like a stove. Following closely behind, her mother put out her hand to touch one of the boxes, yelping when she received a jolt of electricity. 'Don't touch it, it's dangerous,' she warned the girl, hoping that by identifying this concrete hazard she would calm her own fears.

She turned round to search in the bathroom and that was when she saw down the side of the bed. She screamed and clutched Emma to her, automatically turning her daughter's head from the sight. There wasn't much left of Joel — just a pile of undigested food where his torso had been, a set of disembodied shoulders and a head with no features other than a nose and empty holes where there should have been eyes, ears and a mouth. Jennifer knew immediately that it was him; Joel's nose was one you couldn't easily forget. But what was left of the poor man was quickly vanishing, atom by atom, sinew by sinew, line by line. As she watched, the shoulders dwindled and disappeared and the head was eaten away upwards from the back of the skull, so that it seemed to be sinking into the floor. The whole process lasted no more than a minute and then there was no more head. Just the nose, sitting on the carpet among a pile of dirty clothes, Joel's glasses still perched upon it. Jennifer had presumed that was going to vanish too, but it didn't. Despite all his careful measurements and calculations, Joel had forgotten to quantify the one thing which he saw in the mirror every day of his life, his single most salient feature, that which preceded him everywhere, the part of him upon which those most ancient of prosthetics – his spectacles – depended. He hadn't fed his schnoz into the computer.

'Get out in the corridor,' Jennifer whispered at Emma. 'Get out.' She propelled the child with her hand and reluctantly the girl went. Alone and trembling, Jennifer knelt down by what was left of Joel's body and started to cry. She remained there for several minutes until a fizzle, a crackle and a bang came from behind and she turned to see bolts of electricity arc between the bastardised electronic components on the table. Quickly now she fetched out another tissue and, holding it between her shaking fingers, gingerly reached over and picked up the nose. She wrapped the tissue around it and placed it carefully in the bottom of her bag.

Over on the table the computer equipment had finally reached the limit of what it could take. Flames leapt out of the casings and licked at the curtains, which immediately began to smoulder. Within seconds they were sending plumes of black smoke up and across the ceiling. Taking one last look at where Joel had been Jennifer backed around the end of the bed and out into the corridor, where Emma was waiting. Consumed by panic she grabbed the girl by the arm and pulled her towards the stairs, stopping only to smash the alarm on the wall with her elbow. Throughout the building, bells jangled.

Half-way down the stairs they passed the manager. 'Fire, fire in three ten,' Jennifer gasped. The manager nodded and charged past her. Jennifer and Emma continued down into the lobby and out into the street, the sounds of danger clanging in their ears.

Something old . . .

By the time the computers in the Albion caught fire, it was already too late for Laika. The Joel construct had slipped inside her capsule like a digital sperm burrowing its way into a cosmic egg and the

527

elements of man, data, dog and machine immediately started to blend. The physical sensation the dog experienced was not dissimilar to that which had so affected Jennifer on her return home from London. But while Jennifer had been suffused with euphoria, Laika got the bum's rush, the bad trip. Self-consciousness was useless to her now. The myriad media memories she'd amassed over the years were woken from their slumbers in the hammocks of her ventricles by the shock of Joel's invasion; like schizo armies they now skirmished through her mind, combining and recombining, engaging each other in combat, making a battle zone of her brain. Laika tried to tune her instruments to different channels, to bring in information that would dilute the power of the invader and dampen down the rebels in her psyche, but to no avail: images, sounds, smells, thoughts and impressions curdled over the sides of their proper categories and gelled into new and horrifying forms, dragons of the datasphere. Through the capsule which had become her skin, through her copper-nerves titanium-flesh, through her Russian engineering, she could feel the information surrounding her, the excitement in the fragile fabric all around her, gamma wave to long wave, concentric wrinkles in the infinite bed sheet of space.

Her consciousness turned outwards, only to discover that it could no longer turn back in. Joel had flowed into her systems and fountained up into her brain, a whale spout of virulent variation and malignant meme, a lost spirit desperate for a home, a nematode of Boolean logic. Dog capsule construct circled around the pucker of the planet, buzzing off the mediascape and bombarded by the stars. The capsule became a tiny Io, a volcano moon with whirlwind skies, its inner turmoil so intense that it generated tectonic movements in the outer shell and meltdown at the core. Something was happening here, something very old.

Carnival

Back on earth in the Albion, the manager reached the top of the stairs, grabbed a fire extinguisher from the wall and ran down the corridor towards Joel's room. Inside, most combustibles – the curtains, the bed, the easy chair, patches of the carpet – were already alight, and a boiling mass of dense black smoke was collecting across the ceiling and threatening to ignite. Flash-over. The manager pulled the pin from the extinguisher, smashed the knob with the heel of his hand and played the thin jet of liquid into the room. But it was clearly a hopeless effort. Even standing at the door the smoke was choking him and the wall of heat, so intense it gave the doorway the aura of a portal to another world, was threatening to melt the very threads of his viscose suit. He threw the extinguisher into the room; it rolled across the carpet and lay on its side, its hose flicking spastically back and forth under the power of the jet.

He reached in to grab the door handle and pull it closed, hoping to contain the blaze. As he went for it – one hand reaching, the other on the door-sill, one foot on the threshold, the other as a counterbalance extended out behind – the smoke cleared for a second and he got a proper glimpse of the humanoid shape of the computer equipment on the table by the window, the source of the fire. 'Christ!' he said, a Christian man. 'They've got a fucking corpse in there!' He slammed the door closed and raced downstairs. Taking the steps three or four at a time he reached the lobby in about three seconds flat. 'Fire!' he yelled at whoever it was that was standing at the reception desk. 'Call the fire brigade and the police and the ambulance. Call everybody! I think there's some-body still in there. HURRY! Where's that woman and her kid? *Which way did they go?*'

The figure opened its mouth and tried to point, then closed its mouth and managed to point. 'Street,' it said, that being the fastest way to get the information across. 'They went out into the . . .'

But the manager had already gone, carried through the glass

doors on the vector of that initial word. He blinked in the daylight, dull though it was, got his bearings. The street was busy with people heading west towards Carnival. He couldn't see the woman or the child. The flow of pedestrians made up his mind for him and he headed with it, using it for momentum, charging ahead and dodging the people in front of him. He reached the first corner and jumped up on the low wall which protected the basement area of the houses in that row. Craning his neck, he spotted them, a dash of green, a dark head of hair, turning left two streets up. Then he was off again, dodging and weaving, the smooth resin soles of his shoes barely gripping the pavement.

When he reached the next corner he jumped and saw them again, turning right this time. He shoved on through the crowd. The exertion was already getting to him. At the top of his field of vision a silvery border was strobing at an incredible rate and whenever he blinked he could see the whole of his optic nerve, silver on black, a wild bloom with a stem that tunnelled away into darkness. He ran straight into a white cop, who was busy gazing at the crowds and secretly wishing he were a homeboy.

'Oi, where the 'ell d'you think yore going, then?'

'Oh, officer, thank God. I'm chasing a woman, woman and kid, set fire to my hotel, I . . . gasp . . . I think they might have . . . gasp . . . might have killed somebody.'

'And which 'otel would this be, sir?'

'The Albion, Prince's Square. Hurry, they're getting away!' And with the energy of the valued employee the manager somehow sucked more air into his bleeding lungs and darted off after Jennifer and Emma.

Fun at last! 'Attention all units, this is PC 668, am in pursuit of three suspects, woman, child and man, heading west in the direction of Chepstow–Pembridge intersection, possible arson, murder, request assistance . . .'

Mother and child hurried through the streets hand in hand, aware that they were being followed and conscious of the Carnival up ahead, a healthy throb of energy that felt dark, obscure, that would afford them cover. They avoided an intersection marked out by the tensions of converging police and ran straight up Hereford Road instead. Then west towards Powis Square and one of the hearts of the festival, steering clear of anything that smacked of the vertical lines of authority or organisation: pubs, floats, sponsored sound systems. Cut across the channels. Avoid switches and sphincters, dissectors of flow. It's guerrilla tactics, fish-in-the-water stuff – remember what Stim used to say about Mao Tse-tung. Blend in. Be aware of the structures of power and side-step them. Be quick, be rude, be quiet.

The streets were rammed. Thousands of people had made the road into a river, one current forward, one current back, a hundred little eddies along the way and a riverbed of cartons, corncobs, cans, roach ends, empty bottles of Dragon Stout underfoot. On every corner the sound systems slammed out hip hop, rap or dub and the noise was immense, not one kind of music but an absurd and outrageous mélange. Islands in the stream, men stood selling enormous bunches of the steel whistles with the red gold green straps. Everyone seemed to have one and to be blowing it; the whole day was borne on shrill metal screams.

Emma was terrifically excited. Now that they were among the crowds she'd forgotten about the danger and was drinking from the vast fonts all around: the sounds, the smells, the sights. It was a world at play, a thousand dances all at once, and her over-connected mind fizzled and sparked with the thought of it. She couldn't get over the colours of the people, dozens of shades and hues in minute variation. And there were dancers everywhere, not just at street level but on balconies, up in trees, atop lamp-posts and speaker stacks. They got propelled past a system pumping ska; on the stage a white hippy wearing African costume swayed to and fro, an enormous joint in his hand. (There was tension here.) The smell of marijuana was everywhere, mixed in with the odorous fronts of saltfish fritters, goat curries, Thai noodles, ackee and candy floss that were filtering through the crowds from the stalls which lined the pavements.

Jennifer, however, was more frightened than ever. She had no time for any of this. Her head turned this way and that, at odds with the rhythms around her. There were so many police! Male and female, some in shirt-sleeves, some like wasps in bright-yellow jackets striped with reflectors in warning. They wore caps, hats, helmets. Some were on horseback. So many! It was enough to incite a riot. When Emma started to pull at her again she held the child back. They had to stay with the crowd. If they broke out into space they were lost. With all the whistling she couldn't tell what was police and what wasn't. Right now, that was probably good.

The child was busy working on the bigger picture. She'd begun to get a sense of how the whole thing moved, of the hydrodynamics of half a million people in this small maze of streets. In terms of size and population the area wasn't all that far off the Warsaw ghetto, the boundaries of which Joel had walked five or six years earlier. Except that these people were in motion, being channelled rather than contained. Emma concentrated on the shapes the mass made as it moved, on the hidden dragons in the crowds, the attractors and the slow tides. They crossed Westbourne Park Road and worked their way up All Saints. Jennifer had never seen anything like it. The street was a sea of black faces, wall to wall, everybody leaping up and down to three separate sound systems, the tops of their heads undulating in waves from one end of the road to the other. They hooked on to the end of one of the trains of people that was threading its way, impossibly, through the crowd, and followed it. Every time they passed one of the sound systems – each one had curved banks of speakers on both sides of the street which created a chaotic zone of vibration and sound in between – their viscera juddered in sympathy with the bass, a noise so low that it came up through the soles of their feet, grabbed their heart liver lungs and dragged them down into their groins.

It took them about twenty-five minutes to get that eighty yards and when they emerged on Tavistock Street there was a wall of police to their left. Jennifer dragged Emma round and they headed east as fast as they could. And at that point the day turned darker still and it started to rain.

. . . *something new*

The blend of Joel and Laika bounced around the globe, from satellite to satellite, from cable to fibre-optic, from microwave to radio. They were the mail daemon, the packet, the gopher, the virus. They were neither nothing nor everything. She was code, he dogmeat. He charged around, electrons up his arse. She took notes and puzzled at probability. He turned her inside out; she gave him fleas. They bled and bred, turned out something new.

Evolution? Not in the sense that you mean.

This body I wear too well

Clouds of asphalt and khaki had woven a carpet over the sky. The rain, once it came, came quickly. The dancing crowds didn't seem to mind – people held up their hands and let the rain fall on their faces, on their hands, on their naked arms and shoulders. The rain poured down harder, blue-black streaks of data streaming from the heavens, and they danced all the more. Women bared their breasts to the water, men opened their mouths and tried to drink. Babies began to cry and screech, and children chased each other around in circles, throwing sticks of sugar cane and grooving in the quickly forming puddles.

The rain stung Jennifer's skin. It had begun as a prickling sensation, an uncomfortable feeling, as if her hands were beginning to freeze. The day was warm and the rain was warm, yet her hands and face were agony. She glared at two heavily built black women, dancing opposite each other, gyrating and wobbling and whooping, and delighted to have the water soak them through. How could they bear it?

It ran in channels now, along the filthy roads and concrete

pavements, worked its way around islands of discarded corncobs and cans, half-eaten plantains and patties. Emma was fascinated by it. She'd only ever seen the rain from inside before; being in it was a strange experience. She liked the feel of it thrumming on her scalp and she sucked on the wet ends of hair that hung down her face. She watched the other kids playing, thought it looked fun.

They passed two policemen on the corner; Jennifer glanced down a moment too late. One of them had caught her eye and a glimmer of something passed between them before she actively cut it off. Still watching her, the cop radioed base, asked for a description. Jennifer began to run, hauling Emma along with her, and the cop tagged his colleague and they both sped off in pursuit. Mother and daughter headed into the crowd, forcing their way through groups of people. *Excuse me, sorry, excuse me, excuse me, let me through.* Glancing back, she could see that more police had joined the chase. The hotel manager was among them, baying for her blood. 'Come on, darling, come on,' she said to Emma, and slipping her arms around the child's waist she swung her up on to her hip. The crowd was getting scary now, it was so closely packed. The press of people was moving as one; there was no way back and the roads to either side were blocked off, though there was no hope of getting to them anyway. Jennifer forced herself on ahead, screaming, 'I have to get my child to a hospital,' clearing people out of the way with her voice.

She was approaching Westbourne Park tube. Perhaps she could reach it, get away on a train? But as she rounded the corner it became obvious that no way was this an option. Police ringed the entrance and already there was a violent ebb of people trying to gain access. A PA boomed out across the crowd: *Do not attempt to travel without a ticket . . . do not attempt to travel without a ticket . . .* again and again, the same thing: *. . . do not attempt to travel without a ticket . . . do not attempt to travel . . .* It made the crowd angry, which was a bad thing, because the crowd had stopped moving. Jennifer had thought when they'd got to the intersection that the throngs would disperse but she couldn't have been more wrong. All three feed roads were feeding only one way – inwards. In each direction – north, over the bridge and under the Westway, south down through the council estates and west from whence she had come – every inch of space was jammed with flesh and every face was looking to the centre, which is where she now found herself. Her skin was alive again, on fire with feeling, and she felt quite delirious. Over the heads of the people she could see yellow police clawing their way through towards her like beetles, trying to save their hats from being knocked off by the homeboys in the crowd. The rain was coming down harder then ever and it felt to Jennifer as though it was tearing into her face and hands. Emma reached up and tried to cling to her neck, finally frightened, nearly pulling her down. To fall would be fatal; there were so many feet that they'd never get up again; they'd be trampled to death. (Beneath those feet, where Jennifer could not see them, lay hundreds and hundreds of flyers. They must have been printed up only hours earlier, because each one bore the image of Joel's face, sans nose, and advertised a post-Carnival party at a club called Balaam.) She began to call for a miracle, to scream at the sky, 'Save me, save me, I can't go back there!'

Mounted police arrived and panic quickly percolated through the crowd. The attempts of those nearest the horses to get away from the violence merely communicated it. Any movement was immediately amplified and transmitted: the resultant surges carried people bodily before them. More than once the press was so strong that Jennifer and Emma were lifted off their feet like dolls and moved four or five metres before being set down. There was nowhere at all to go. Desperate, Jennifer continued to scream and yell at the elements, demanding action, as Judd and Joel had done before her. Fights started to break out in the vicinity of the police and also at the intersection where men whose tempers had already been frayed by their fear got shoved one time too many.

Then Emma looked at her mother and screamed, and Jennifer looked down at her daughter, took her face in her hands and saw then that these same hands were losing definition. At first she didn't understand what it was and she stared for a moment, confused. And then . . . it was the rain – each drop of rain was eating into her, carrying a little trace of her away. Nobody else seemed affected, it was just her. She started to shake and brought her hands up in front of her own face. She was experiencing the rushing sensation again, a high bandwidth tingle that shivered up her arms and arced across her mind. It was the feeling she'd had that night on the floor of her living-room, of becoming continuous with her surroundings. She didn't know whether it was joy or pain. Perhaps it was release. She felt her network of scars beginning to glow and this gave her heart. She started to cry and the tears cut furrows into her cheeks.

The rain sliced into her skin. She began to reel and spasm, and a space formed around her as people found gaps where previously they would have sworn there had been only flesh. She dropped her bag and reached for Emma, then drew back and fell to her knees on a thin bed of pictures of Joel. Gently, she touched her face. It gave beneath her fingers like mush. Water ran down her forehead and on to her hands and continued to wash them away. The ring of people around her looked on in horror but Emma stood there and gazed, irises of steel, emerald and dew. Mother and daughter, eyes met for one final time.

How much is conveyed by a look? Enough, in this case, for Jennifer to realise what was at stake, for her to know that Emma was the whole of life, from the chemical dance to the soft touch of breath, just as any daughter was to her mother. She knew then that all was material, that this was the world's wonder and that the thought of rocks in the earth, bones on a beach, sparks in the sun, clouds out of reach was her own thought, too – and that her own thought was in her fingers in her toes in the scars on her skin and in the sound of her name, in her sex in her grip in her womb. Thumb to mouth, cock to cunt, hand to breast, lip to lip, flower to wasp, man to dog, club to skull, cunt to eye, eye to brain, voice to tree, voice to plain, word to deed, wreath to grave, leaf to groin, cell to stave, stone to sea, sea to salt, salt to charge, charge to pain, sea to breeze, breeze to rain, rain to hill, hill to face, face to place, place to space, space to frame, frame to gain . . . with these the world remade itself at every turn, made its time and space too, because these grew as well, these were alive, these were the yeasts of it all, these were its joy. Emma's eye danced and whirled, clicked and weighed, sifting input through the meshworks and filters of . . . Jennifer knew by now that there was no word here, only a plane, a zone across which words could stray, could dream, could compute, could connect. She let herself go, becoming the liquid she always was, ready at last to conquer the land. Her dark hair disappeared and the water carrying it away ran an inky black. She looked at Emma with the last of her eyes, but the girl's green coat quickly faded to grey and then she was gone.

Jennifer slumped over and rolled flat out on the ground. The sky belched and retched, and the rain came down more heavily than ever. Back in All Saints the revellers had lost their enthusiasm. This wasn't dancing weather any more, it was dangerous weather. People started to flood out of Notting Hill, although it was rapidly becoming increasingly hard to leave: the surrounding areas were already saturated and were having difficulty blotting all these extra people up. Emma crouched by her mother, holding on to her skirt, her flesh vanishing too fast now to afford a grip. Her clothes sagged as the water ran through them and carried away her blood: from out of her sleeves and hems the scarlet fluid poured.

As her skull began to go the fear surrounding the two of them reached its apogee and someone vomited, then a huge and hyper-trophic man in trackies, a leather T-shirt and an Adidas cagoule bent down by Emma, touched her shoulders, took off his jacket and used it gently to cover what was left of Jennifer's head. 'You better come with me, chicken,' he said softly, and took the child's tiny hand in his own. 'Bad things are happenin' to your mom, we wanna make sure you're safe.' Emma didn't look at him, still looked down at Jennifer though there was nothing left to see, just a discarded set of clothes lying there in the street, nameless clothes, belonging to nobody, filthied by the rain.

Then a shout went up and the horses broke through, and the ring that had remained stable around Jennifer's disintegration finally gave way. The stranger held Emma to him, kept her close against his body so she shouldn't be seen, started to pull her away. People were sucked into the now empty space and the pile of soaking clothes was on the verge of being engulfed when Emma broke free from the man and rushed back towards it. Time itself seemed to eddy and curve for her; there's a hydrodynamics in there some-where, too. Darting between the forest of legs, she shot out a hand and grabbed her mother's bag – or did it fly up towards her? – then turned and ran back to the stranger. No sooner had she gone than time reasserted itself and the tangle of horses' legs and humans came trampling in and Jennifer's clothes were instantly torn to shreds.

The stranger held her again and manoeuvred her south. Behind them a full-scale battle had broken out between the revellers and the police. Hands sprang up from the mass and tugged at the nearest policemen, trying to unseat them from their steeds. Terrified, the coppers lashed out left and right with their truncheons, telescopic devices that extended to a full three feet, catching people indis-criminately across their shoulders and heads. Off to the left someone dressed in a kilt was yelling, 'They tried to wipe out the bagpipes three hundred years ago, but they're two thousand, three thousand, four thousand years old.' Whoever it was had a set of pipes with him and now he swung them into position, put the mouthpiece to his lips and began to heave out a Scottish battle tune at breakneck speed. A roar went up from the crowd and it pitched into the police with renewed vigour. On top of the tube station, officers stood with a compound-lens camera taking head shots of those in the crowd, ten thousand every ten seconds. The pictures were captured in digital format and fed down a cable to the portable up-link which sat on the rooftop next to the camera. This beamed them up into the sky, up and up, until they reached a satellite high above the earth and were bounced back down to Scotland Yard. Once there, each face was separated out by computers which then churned through vast databanks searching for matches. As she was led away, Emma reached her hand down inside Jennifer's bag and felt for Joel's nose. When she found it, she held on to it tightly. It was warm.

To the sea

Jennifer ran and ran, laughing as she went. She flowed away from the intersection, beneath and around the frightened feet of the crowd. She disappeared down gutters gratings storm drains, splashed over parapets and down the brick sides of bridges, dripped off overhangs and arches, slid into gardens and filtered her way through the earth. She spread out across the city, eased into sewers and basements, sped along underground railways, made her way down to the Thames. She was lapped up by dogs, sprayed out by cars, sneezed in by rats. She crept her way through pores into bloodstreams. She seeped into cisterns and osmosed into plants. When the storm was over and the sun came out she disappeared into the air and was breathed into lungs, sucked into engines, swollen as clouds and blown this way and that by the buffeting winds. She sat in toilets, played from fountains. Pigeons pecked at her and ducks paddled on her. Birds flew through her, crops drank from her. She was everywhere and nowhere, a sprite of the city, a queen of the land. She did nothing, thought nothing; did everything, thought everything. She matched herself with the great movements of liquid, with the strata of weather and groundwater, pipelines and plumbing, flora and fauna, mist and sea. She aligned herself with the circuits of evaporation and precipitation which power these planes and enable movement between them. She slept in lakes and danced down rivers. Replete with chemicals and minerals she energised soil and plant, plant and animal, animal and air, linking the cells of the biosphere. Fish spawned in her, dew formed from her. Snow snowed by her. People washed in her, swam in her, lived through her. She was everywhere now and this was her solution.

AFTERWORD

A dog called Om

Some time later, Emma stepped off a train and on to the light gravel of the station platform at Stratford-upon-Avon. She no longer wore her green coat; it had been replaced with blue dungarees and a black Puffa jacket. Her hair had been cropped short and the new haircut made her look a little less ugly. It was a bright day, crisp, autumnal, a Saturday. She watched the train draw out then went up the stairs and over the tracks, down again and out into the weak winter sun. The trees were bare, the last remnants of the leaves a dark sludge beneath her trainers.

She left the station and began to walk north, back over the tracks via the road bridge and past all those Bed & Breakfasts that had bordered that roadside for ever. The air was sharp after London, clean and brisk. The houses were detached, screened by low walls and privet. She seemed to know where she was going.

She passed a school and its playing fields where other children were hot–cold with their games. Their yells knocked back and forth between the buildings, counterpointed by the peep of the schoolteachers' whistles. Although it was late morning a mist hung above the grass. Dried pats of mud with neat holes bored through them, the negatives of football boots, were strewn across the pavement in front of her.

She walked for about half an hour before she reached what was left of the Last Resort, but she passed it, as most did, without so much as a thought. It took her another thirty minutes to walk eastwards along the roads skirting Stratford and reach the entrance to the civic tip. The gates were open and she walked through them and beneath the wooden cross-beam that prevented lorries from entering. The track was paved and well-kempt but at either side steep banks reared up behind the pale-grey edging stones. Brambles nettles hawthorn crowded down them, tussling for space. Unripe blackberries hung thin and raw from studded boughs, and sparrows and blackbirds chuckled among the dark tangles.

She reached the metal viaduct and passed underneath, ignoring the traffic light, knowing that there was nothing approaching. Round the corner there was bustle and noise: several cars were parked there and their occupants were throwing boxes of junk into massive green skips or feeding empty bottles into colour-coded metal containers. To the north, men unloaded refrigerators into a hole in the ground. Emma ignored them all, walked past them to the edge of the tarmac and followed a trail laid by caterpillar tracks. Some hundred yards further on she came to the landfill, the midden, dead now, the same one Jennifer had used. The junk had been levelled and a meniscus of rubbish lapped up the earthy walls to within a metre or two of her feet. At one end about a third of the pit was already filled in with topsoil and clay, but the diggers stood idle now, their drivers busy downing Saturday pints at the pub.

She stood at the edge of the pit, breathed it in, steadied herself under the assault. This was shattered relationship, densely packed, dynamic upon dynamic laid down like sandstone sediments. Potentials buzzed from item to item, from one discarded object to another, as if each broken thing were a Tesla coil of emotion. Rotting sofas with entire families encrusted upon them, infested mattresses with twenty years of marriage in their springs, broken vases, standard lamps, bicycles that knew so many miles. Plates with a thousand meals ingrained on their faces, cane chairs with quivering buttocks lost among their splits, typewriters with love letters hidden in their ribbons, telephones strangled by long strings of sound. Record players silenced by too much vibration, books whose pages held the memories of thumbs, baths ringed with layers of limestone and skin, mirrors filled with rooms in reverse.

Crows wheeled above it all, points on the vortex that spun out of this dying technology. Emma watched them for a while, wondering, probing, then turned and inched her way into the pit. Once safely down she started out across the surface of rubber wood plastic and steel, going slowly and testing each step before trusting it. She let herself be guided across, the cracked clocks and broken shelves signposting the way for her, until somewhere out in the middle she found what she'd been looking for.

It was the television, Donald's old box and the centrepiece of Jennifer's movie matinée parties. There was not much left of it now. The screen was cracked and the control panel caved in, and the thing looked to the sky, forlorn, as if waiting for one last viewer to come from the heavens and scry it. It had been cursed while alive to form a link in the world, to fold space into colours and flickers. But nothing could do that for long.

Emma looked at it: it would do. Picking up a rusty golf club she swung it at the TV and smashed in the screen, hitting the tube again and again, splintering the glass into fragments. Struggling now, she heaved the set up by a corner and rolled it over, emptying out the shards before rolling it back. She wrapped her hand in an old piece of fertiliser bag and picked out the last of them then set the thing upright, directing it up at the sun. And then she crawled inside.

Folding herself up like one of its pictures she worked her way in and made a nest of the hulk, fitting herself to its shape. Here she was, an everyday girl in an everyday place. From the dump all around her, the motion of the crows, the events of the sky, she drew strength. She had lost her parents so, like them, she had to grow up, shoulder her responsibilities, take the world into herself. She'd been there an hour when her skin began to blister and breathe, forming thousands of stomate-like openings through which pale filaments began to protrude. Her clothing started to rustle and bulge as these hyphae sought a way out, eventually exiting through her collar and waistband and cuffs, as her mother had done when trapped in her clothes a few weeks before. Once free, they quickly filled the space of the old television, then ate into its housing, stripping molecular compounds from the wood and the metals, and using them to build novel types of lignin and bark.

A core thus established, they plunged down into the tip, infiltrating the products that had been dumped there, drawing on the minerals and the memories and the festering emotions stored up within. In this way a wider root system was formed, an enormous rhizome that broke down the old technology, sucked it dry. At the base of the pit Emma found clay, pierced it with radicles, increasing proportions of smectite and kaolinite as she did so, changing the geological balance beneath; nearer the ground she penetrated the topsoil and sought partners symbionts parasites and hosts. Everything she found was drawn in, made use of: ascomycetes and zygomycetes helped her to integrate with the nature around her, basidiomycetes donated psilocybin that helped her to think, roots of oak and ash linked her with the wind and sky, angiosperms taught her the circling ways of the insects, rubber and concrete lent her resilience and strength, plastics and chemicals helped her adapt and taught her more of the ways of the human.

Within days, she started to put forth new shoots and by the time a week had gone by the tip was verdant, a bower of lianas made strong with metals from motors and fibres from linen, lianas which fluttered like bunting with rich green leaves whose impossible sheen was achieved by the leaching of fluids from discarded cans of furniture polish and industrial cleaner. More crows began to circle around, drawn by the tempting secretions Emma leaked from her limbs. Their droppings enriched the tips with the ammonium and calcium phosphates she hungered for, and before long she would puff spores on to their wings so that they could carry her progeny forth.

She was a lake now, a tiny ocean whose vascular currents were home to microbes and viruses, viroids and pentastomes and other organisms too varied to count, an ecology complete in itself, a replay of the birth of the biosphere. At the centre her old body lay curled, its limbs and the television around them no longer distinguishable from the creak and vegetable spurl, her mind distributed among the autotrophic cells that made up the thicket she'd become. But the TV set still worked as a focus. With her shiny

543

leaves all angled towards it Emma channelled photons into the old wooden box, made it her eye. Through it, silently and in her own time, she watched the skies, scanned the stratosphere, reached out into space for the message she guessed would come soon, a new type of chloroplast that with a biological gamble, a spin of the wheel, a roll of the dice, urged itself on to a strange photosynthetic reaction, the like of which had never before been seen.

For she wasn't alone. High above, skidding round the dip of the planet and sending out signals, a motor-cycle rider on gravity's grim wall of death, is a dark moon of flesh and technology. No one can tell where it starts, where it ends, no one can decipher the orders it gives. It's a point of view, a remote camera, it's something that cares that the planets align in a series of curves. It's a metal egg, a cosmic egg, it's oeuf and oeuvre. Inside its cells things burble and spoil. It's a series of loops and dead-ends and exertions with no sense of itself. It has drives and dynamics, but can't scent or see them. It's not a sphere, more a plane, a wafer of lattice and flux that, like Emma below, creates its own space, its own time. It expands, but not outwards – outwards and inwards mean nothing to it. It envelops and probes, but never equally, never with measure. It heads off in countless directions from multiple centres and goes nowhere. It's frogspawn, bacteria. It's a hopeless god, a lost cause, a blind harbour-master, a crazed midwife, a corrupted disk, a mongrel pup. It is a node, an eddy, a storm, a singularity. It is only something, not one thing. It's a man called machine. It's a dynamic called data. It's a dog they call Om. The only word, perhaps, that is not an instruction.

If such a thing is possible, that is.

ACKNOWLEDGEMENTS

I am indebted to Hillel Schwartz's essay 'Torque: The New Kinaesthetic of the Twentieth Century' (published in *Incorporations*, Zone,
1992) for the identification of the links between Wilbur Wright,
Isadora Duncan and comptometer operators, and to Paul Virilio's
The Aesthetics of Disappearance (trans. Philip Beitchman, Semio-
text(e), 1991) for isolating the phenomenon of picnolepsy and
uncovering the disappearance fantasies of Howard Hughes.

The description of Nadine's pre-frontal leucotomy owes a great
deal to Geoffrey Knight's 'The Orbital Cortex as an Objective in
the Surgical Treatment of Mental Illness' (*British Journal of Surgery*,
1964, Vol. 51, no. 2, February). The translation of Himmler's
speech at Poznan is taken from Martin Gilbert's *The Holocaust –
the Jewish tragedy* (Fontana, 1987). The launch vehicle characteristics
of Sputnik I, diagram and text, are copyright Mark Wade and
taken from his website (solar.rtd.utk.edu/~mwade/spaceflt.htm)
and the Dostoevsky excerpt is taken from Fyodor Dostoevksy, *The
Gambler* (trans. Jessie Coulson, Penguin, 1966). I am grateful to
the Athlone Press for permission to quote from *Difference and Repetition* by Deleuze, translated by Paul Patton, 1994; to Flammarion
for permission to quote from *Angels* by Michel Serres, translated
by Francis Cowper, 1995; and to Gollancz for permission to quote
from *Invisible Man* by Ralph Ellison, 1953.

Details of Joel's shoe computer are largely taken from *The Newtonian Casino* by Thomas A. Bass (Penguin, 1991) and of SABRE
and SAGE (and a few other technological snippets) from *Computer*
by Martin Campbell-Kelly and William Asprey (Basic Books,
1996). I am beholden to Sadie Plant for ideas about Ada Lovelace,

to Nick Land for setting me straight, and to Mark and Dianna McMenamin's *Hypersea* (Columbia University Press, 1994) for the concept of, well, hypersea.

Finally, immense thanks to Pauline, Hari, Hannah, Jonny, Katie, Josh, Charles and the Pig – couldn't have done it without you.